W9-AOE-650

STAR WARS

THRAWN
ASCENDANCY
LESSER EVIL

THRAWN
A S C E N D A N C Y
BOOK III:
LESSER EVIL

TIMOTHY ZAHN

NEW YORK

Star Wars: Thrawn Ascendancy: Lesser Evil is a work of fiction.
Names, places, and incidents either are products of the author's
imagination or are used fictitiously. Any resemblance to actual events,
locales, or persons, living or dead, is entirely coincidental.

Published in the United States by Del Rey,
an imprint of Random House, a division of
Penguin Random House LLC, New York.

DEL REY is a registered trademark and the
CIRCLE colophon is a trademark of Penguin Random House LLC.

LIBRARY OF CONGRESS CATALOGING-IN-PUBLICATION DATA
Names: Zahn, Timothy, author.
Title: Lesser evil / Timothy Zahn.
Other titles: Star Wars. Thrawn ascendancy. book 3, Lesser evil
Description: New York: Del Rey, [2021] | Series: Star Wars: Thrawn ascendancy; book 3
Identifiers: LCCN 2021039710 (print) | LCCN 2021039711 (ebook) |
ISBN 9780593158326 (hardcover) | ISBN 9780593158333 (ebook) |
ISBN 9780593496985 (international edition)
Subjects: LCGFT: Novels.
Classification: LCC PS3576.A33 L47 2021 (print) | LCC PS3576.A33 (ebook) |
DDC 813/.54—dc23
LC record available at https://lccn.loc.gov/2021039710
LC ebook record available at https://lccn.loc.gov/2021039711

Printed in the United States of America on acid-free paper

randomhousebooks.com

2 4 6 8 9 7 5 3 1

First Edition

Book design by Elizabeth A. D. Eno

For all those who've had to choose between two evils and wished there was a better choice . . . and for all those who have worked to make that happen

THE ⋆STAR WARS⋆ NOVELS TIMELINE

THE HIGH REPUBLIC

Light of the Jedi
The Rising Storm
Tempest Runner
The Fallen Star

Dooku: Jedi Lost
Master and Apprentice

I — THE PHANTOM MENACE

II — ATTACK OF THE CLONES

Thrawn Ascendancy: Chaos Rising
Thrawn Ascendancy: Greater Good
Thrawn Ascendancy: Lesser Evil
Dark Disciple: A Clone Wars Novel

III — REVENGE OF THE SITH

Catalyst: A Rogue One Novel
Lords of the Sith
Tarkin

SOLO

Thrawn
A New Dawn: A Rebels Novel
Thrawn: Alliances
Thrawn: Treason

ROGUE ONE

IV — A NEW HOPE

Battlefront II: Inferno Squad
Heir to the Jedi
Doctor Aphra
Battlefront: Twilight Company

V — THE EMPIRE STRIKES BACK

VI — RETURN OF THE JEDI

The Alphabet Squadron Trilogy
The Aftermath Trilogy
Last Shot

Bloodline
Phasma
Canto Bight

VII — THE FORCE AWAKENS

VIII — THE LAST JEDI

Resistance Reborn
Galaxy's Edge: Black Spire

IX — THE RISE OF SKYWALKER

DRAMATIS PERSONAE

SENIOR CAPTAIN THRAWN | Mitth'raw'nuruodo—Trial-born
ADMIRAL AR'ALANI
THALIAS | Mitth'ali'astov—Trial-born
PATRIARCH THURFIAN | Mitth'urf'ianico—blood
MID CAPTAIN SAMAKRO | Ufsa'mak'ro—merit adoptive
SENIOR CAPTAIN ZIINDA | Irizi'in'daro—Trial-born
SUPREME GENERAL BA'KIF
CHE'RI–SKY-WALKER
THE MAGYS

SYNDIC THRASS | Mitth'ras'safis—cousin
CAPTAIN ROSCU | Clarr'os'culry—blood
PATRIACH LAMIOV | Stybla'mi'ovodo—blood

QILORI OF UANDUALON—Pathfinder navigator (non-Chiss)
GENERALIRIUS NAKIRRE—ruler of the Kilji Illumine
JIXTUS—Grysk

CHISS ASCENDANCY

Nine Ruling Families

UFSA

IRIZI

DASKLO

CLARR

CHAF

PLIKH

BOADIL

MITTH

OBBIC

Chiss Family Ranks

BLOOD

COUSIN

RANKING DISTANT

TRIAL-BORN

MERIT ADOPTIVE

Political Hierarchy

PATRIARCH—head of the family

SPEAKER—head of the family's delegation to the Syndicure

SYNDIC PRIME—head syndic

SYNDIC—member of the Syndicure, the main governmental body

PATRIEL—handles family affairs on a planetary scale

COUNCILOR—handles family affairs at the local level

ARISTOCRA—mid-level member of one of the Nine Ruling Families

Military Ranks

SUPREME ADMIRAL

SUPREME GENERAL

FLEET ADMIRAL

SENIOR GENERAL

ADMIRAL

GENERAL

MID ADMIRAL

MID GENERAL

COMMODORE

SENIOR CAPTAIN

MID CAPTAIN

JUNIOR CAPTAIN

SENIOR COMMANDER

MID COMMANDER

JUNIOR COMMANDER

LIEUTENANT COMMANDER

LIEUTENANT

SENIOR WARRIOR

MID WARRIOR

JUNIOR WARRIOR

A long time ago, *beyond* a galaxy far, far away. . . .

For thousands of years, it has been an island of calm within the Chaos. It is a center of power, a model of stability, and a beacon of integrity. The Nine Ruling Families guard it from within; the Expansionary Defense Fleet guards it from without. Its neighbors are left in peace, its enemies are left in ruin. It is light and culture and glory.

It is the Chiss Ascendancy.

STAR WARS™

THRAWN
ASCENDANCY
LESSER EVIL

PROLOGUE

"Prepare for breakout." Senior Captain Mitth'raw'nuruodo's voice echoed across the *Springhawk*'s bridge. "All officers and warriors stand prepared. We're not here to start trouble, but I intend to be ready for it."

First Officer Mid Captain Ufsa'mak'ro scowled to himself. Of course Senior Captain Thrawn didn't plan to start trouble. He never did. Yet somehow trouble always seemed to happen.

If that pattern was determined to continue, it couldn't have picked a better spot for it.

Bad enough that Zyzek was an alien system. Worse that Chiss records had nothing about it beyond its location and that it was a trading center for several of the small nations to the east and southeast of the Chiss Ascendancy. Even worse that Thrawn believed this to be the system where Captain Fsir and his fellow Watith had been recruited to launch their ambush attack on his ship.

Worst of all that no one else knew the *Springhawk* was here.

They should have gone straight back to the Ascendancy. They should have left the planet Hoxim and the skirmish Samakro had privately dubbed the Battle of the Three Families and headed back to Csilla for repairs, debriefing, and what was likely to be a memorable job of sweeping the whole mess out the door. All the other Chiss warships, the ones crewed exclusively by members of the Xodlak, Erighal, and Pommrio families, had done exactly that, making the slow jump-by-jump back home while their commanders no doubt struggled to write all this up in their logs.

But not the *Springhawk*. The hours Thrawn had spent studying the Watith freighter before its destruction had somehow convinced him that Zyzek was where Fsir had come from. From there, it was only a small leap of tactical logic to swinging by that system on their way home and taking a look.

Samakro understood the strategy. On one level, he even agreed with it. The *Springhawk* had Sky-walker Che'ri to speed it on its way through the twisting hyperspace pathways of the Chaos, while any observer who'd been lurking around to report on the battle would have some lesser navigator or none at all. The fact that Thrawn could get to Zyzek ahead of that news could be a major advantage in information gathering.

But that was one small plus, and it was piled on top of a whole stack of minuses.

"Breakout: Three, two, *one*."

The star-flares collapsed into stars, and the *Springhawk* had arrived.

"Full scan," Thrawn ordered. "Pay special attention to the ships in the various orbits. I'll want as complete a catalog of ship types as possible, along with where in the orbital stack they are."

"Yes, Senior Captain," Mid Commander Elod'al'vumic acknowledged from the sensor station.

"Kharill, assist her with the cataloging," Thrawn added.

"Yes, sir." The voice of Senior Commander Plikh'ar'illmorf came over the speaker from secondary command. "Dalvu, mark which sectors you want us to handle from here."

"Yes, Senior Commander," Dalvu said. "Marking them now."

"Watch for movement, either inward as an attempt to hide from us or outward in an attempt to flee," Thrawn said. "We're here to see if we can create a reaction." He nodded toward the helm. "Azmordi, start moving us inward. Sky-walker Che'ri, stand ready in case we need to leave quickly."

"Yes, sir," Lieutenant Commander Tumaz'mor'diamir said from the helm.

"Yes, Senior Captain," Sky-walker Che'ri's caregiver Mitth'ali'astov echoed.

Samakro let his eyes sweep slowly across the bridge. Dalvu, Kharill, Azmordi. Officers he'd served with a long time, dating back to when he'd commanded the *Springhawk* and continuing through Thrawn's current tenure as captain. He knew them and their abilities and trusted them with his life.

Thalias, on the other hand . . .

He focused on the caregiver as she turned back to the viewport, her hand resting reassuringly on Che'ri's shoulder. Thalias was still far too much of a mystery to him, with uncertainties and doubts swirling around her.

Worse, from Samakro's point of view, she carried the stench of family politics. Syndic Mitth'urf'ianico had done some fancy maneuvering in order to get her aboard the *Springhawk,* and Samakro still didn't know what Thurfian's game was.

But he would find out. He'd already planted the seeds, feeding Thalias a story and conspiracy theory that painted Thrawn in a bad light, a story he knew she would eventually spill to Thurfian or possibly to someone else. When she did—when she betrayed that confidence—he would finally have proof that she was a spy sent to destroy or at least damage the *Springhawk*'s commander. Then, maybe, he'd be able to convince Thrawn to get her off his ship.

Until then, all Samakro could do was watch her and guard as best he could against any mischief she might make.

We're here to create a reaction. Unfortunately, Samakro had seen the kind of reaction Thrawn's unexpected appearances tended to spark. Especially in potentially hostile territory and moving among large numbers of probably unfriendly ships.

But Thrawn was the *Springhawk*'s commander, and he'd given an order. Samakro's job was to do everything in his power to carry it out.

And if part of his duty was to defend his ship to the death . . . well, he was prepared to do that, too.

"Conquest."

Generalirius Nakirre gazed out the viewport of the Kilji war cruiser *Whetstone* at the dozens of trading ships orbiting the planet Zyzek. "*Conquest.*"

"An interesting concept, is it not?" the being known as Jixtus suggested.

Nakirre eyed his guest. It was unsettling having to deal with a being whose garments of robe, hood, gloves, and veil wrapped him in total concealment.

Especially given that such complete anonymity gave him a serious negotiating advantage over Nakirre and his Kilji vassals. Once Jixtus learned how to read the emotional responses reflected in the patterns of ripples and stretches that moved through the dark-orange Kilji skin, he would gain insight that went far deeper than Nakirre's words.

But Nakirre had agreed to travel here with the alien, and the Kilji Overlords had affirmed his decision, and so here they were.

And truth be told, Jixtus *did* have some intriguing ideas on how the future of the Kilji Illumine could be shaped.

"People who would otherwise ignore the wisdom and guidance of the Kiljis would be encouraged to listen," Jixtus continued. "People who would otherwise scorn and scoff at your philosophy could be silenced or sent where their rantings would not disturb or disrupt."

"It would allow us to bring order," Nakirre agreed, images of unprecedented stability running through his mind. *Conquest.*

"Exactly," Jixtus said. "Order and enlightenment to billions who currently struggle and flail helplessly in darkness. As you well know, encouragement and persuasion—even passionate persuasion—can move a culture only so far. Conquest is the only way to bring Kilji insight to the whole of a region."

"And you believe these beings are prepared to receive such insight?" Nakirre asked, sweeping his hand across the viewport at the merchant ships floating placidly in their orbits.

"Is there ever a time when enlightenment would *not* be beneficial?" Jixtus countered. "Whether they realize it or not, whether they accept it or not, the Kilji path is what will ultimately bring them prosperity and contentment. What purpose delay?"

"What purpose, indeed," Nakirre agreed, gazing at the ships. So many merchants, so many nations, all standing helpless before the might of the Kilji Illumine. Which should he choose first?

"As I promised, we will guide you as to the nations most quickly and easily conquered," Jixtus continued. "There are representative traders here from each of the four the Grysks feel are the most promising. We'll speak with them in turn, perhaps sample the goods they've brought for sale. You will then—"

"Generalirius?" Vassal Two called from the sensor station. "A new ship has arrived. Unknown configuration."

Nakirre looked at the visual display. The newcomer was indeed unlike any of the other ships already in orbit. Representatives of some new nation, no doubt, here to join in barter and trade.

Or perhaps not. The design of the craft was not that of a merchant. Its shape, the systematic groupings of bulges along its sides and shoulders, the distinctive sheen of a nyix-alloy hull . . .

"These are not traders," he said. "That is a warship. Is it not?" he added, turning to look at Jixtus.

Only to find the Grysk silent and unmoving. The veiled face was turned toward the visual display, the robed figure as still as if the being hidden beneath the robe had turned to stone.

Usually Jixtus had a comment for everything. For once, he didn't.

"If you're concerned, you need not be," Nakirre reassured him. The newcomer was about two-thirds the size of the *Whetstone*, probably no more than the equivalent of a Kilji picket cruiser, with a comparable ratio of weaponry. Should they choose to initiate combat, he had no doubt the Kiljis would win.

He could only hope they wouldn't be so foolish. The destruction of their ship would mean those aboard would never hear the Kilji philosophy and thus could never achieve true enlightenment.

"Generalirius, the warship is broadcasting a message," Vassal Four said. He touched a switch—

"—to all assembled merchants and traders," a smooth, melodious voice came over the *Whetstone*'s bridge speaker, the Minnisiat trade language words articulated with clipped precision. "I am Senior Captain Thrawn of the Chiss Expansionary Defense Fleet warship *Springhawk*. I have news for any Watith who may be present. Are there any of that species to whom I may speak?"

"Are there?" Nakirre asked, looking back at Jixtus.

Jixtus stirred, breaking whatever paralysis had overtaken him. "Are there what?" he asked, his voice odd.

"Are there any Watith?"

Jixtus seemed to gather himself together. "I don't know. I didn't notice any of their ships when we arrived, but I also wasn't looking for them. I suggest we hold here and see if anyone answers him."

"If no one else stands forth, I will speak with him," Nakirre declared. "I would learn what news he bears."

"I would advise against that," Jixtus warned. "The Chiss are a devious species. He is likely asking that question in the hope of drawing you out into the open."

"Drawing *me* out?" Nakirre asked. "How would he even know I'm here?"

"I didn't mean you specifically, Generalirius," Jixtus said. "But be assured he's hunting for information. That's what this particular Chiss does."

"If no one wishes news," Thrawn continued, "perhaps someone will give us the location of their world, so that we may return our prisoners to their people."

Nakirre looked at Jixtus with surprise. "He has *prisoners*?"

"No," Jixtus bit out. "He doesn't."

"He says he does."

"He lies," Jixtus said. "As I told you already, he's hunting for information. This is a trick."

"How do you know?" Nakirre persisted.

Again Jixtus fell silent. "Tell me how you know, Jixtus of the Grysks," Nakirre repeated, making it an order this time. "If the Chiss mounted a raid, there would of course be prisoners. If there was a battle, even the most fearsome often leaves survivors. Tell me now, or I shall ask *him*."

"There was a battle," Jixtus said reluctantly. "But there were no survivors."

"How can you be certain?"

"Because I was the one who sent the Watith against the Chiss," Jixtus said. "Twenty-three Watith went into that battle. Twenty-three Watith died."

"I ask again: How do you know that?"

"There was an observer at the battle," Jixtus said. He sounded more on balance now. "One who was concealed from the combatants' view. He brought me that news."

"I see," Nakirre said, pretending he was satisfied.

Only he wasn't.

Because an observer who had spoken of Watith deaths would also have warned that the *Springhawk* had survived that battle. Yet Jixtus had clearly been surprised by the Chiss warship's arrival. Was it merely the *Springhawk*'s appearance here at Zyzek, and not the simple fact of its survival, that had startled him?

And how did he know that this Chiss was seeking information? Did Jixtus know him personally?

For a moment Nakirre considered asking those questions. But there would be no gain. Jixtus was withholding information, and would undoubtedly continue to do so. That was the way of those who lacked enlightenment.

No matter. There was after all another source of information close at hand. "Vassal One: Yaw rotation to face the Chiss ship," he ordered. He waited until the *Whetstone* was lined up precisely on the incoming warship, then keyed his mike. "Senior Captain Thrawn, this is Generalirius Nakirre of the Kilji Illumine warship *Whetstone*," he called. "Tell me how you come to have Watith prisoners."

"I greet you, Generalirius Nakirre," Thrawn said. "Are you an ally or trading associate of the Watith?"

"Sadly, I am not yet either," Nakirre said. "But perhaps soon."

"Ah," Thrawn said. "You have come here to initiate new trade relationships, then?"

Nakirre's skin stretched in a wry smile. Jixtus had been right: This Chiss *was* on the hunt for information. "Not specifically," he said. "We of the Illumine travel the Chaos teaching others the Kilji way of order and enlightenment."

"A noble undertaking," Thrawn said. "Have the Watith been among your students?"

"Again, not yet," Nakirre said. "We are newly arrived in this part of space. But such things are for the future. Tell me how you come to have Watith prisoners."

"For the moment, those details must remain confidential."

"No matter," Nakirre said. "I will accept your prisoners and return them to their home."

"Do you know where that home is?"

Nakirre hesitated. If he said yes, Thrawn would likely ask for the coordinates and take the prisoners there himself. If he said no, Thrawn would probably refuse to hand them over. "I have already made many contacts among the traders here," he said, choosing a third option. "One of them can surely provide that information."

"I appreciate your offer," Thrawn said. "But I cannot in good conscience accept it. If there are no Watith here to receive the prisoners, we will take our search elsewhere."

"I would not have you go to such trouble."

"That is my choice to make, not yours."

"Enlightenment requires that I serve others."

"You serve here best by permitting me to go my way," Thrawn said. "Or does your enlightenment require you to take away my freedom of choice?"

"Let him go," Jixtus murmured. "Just let him go."

Nakirre felt a ripple of anger. Anger at Jixtus; anger at Thrawn.

There were important details here that neither of them was willing to give him.

He needed Jixtus and the Grysks to show him which nations were most open to conquest and thus enlightenment. He didn't need Thrawn. "You should learn of what you speak before offering judgment," he said, keying his board to begin the *Whetstone*'s ramp-up to combat status. "Someday soon I shall bring the Kilji philosophy to the Chiss."

"I fear you will find little interest," Thrawn said. "We have our own ancient paths."

"The Kilji path will prove superior."

"No," Thrawn said, his voice flat. "It will not."

"Again, you dismiss our wisdom without even hearing it."

"In my experience, superior wisdom can stand on its own merits," Thrawn said. "It does not require a warship to force acceptance."

"You also bring a warship to this place."

"But I do not claim to offer others superior wisdom," Thrawn said. "Nor do I intend to impose my wisdom upon others."

"He's trying to goad you into attacking him," Jixtus warned quietly, his voice sounding strained. "Don't let him."

Nakirre felt a stretch of contempt. Why *shouldn't* he let the Chiss build his own destruction? The *Whetstone* was far mightier than Thrawn's *Springhawk*. It would be the work of a few minutes to destroy him.

"He's trying to obtain data on the *Whetstone*'s capabilities," Jixtus went on. "*And* on your abilities as its commander."

And why *shouldn't* he demonstrate the might of a Kilji war cruiser? Whatever knowledge Thrawn might gain would be lost in the abyss of his death.

Still, there were others here who would witness that battle. Perhaps it would be unwise to show them the full might of the Kiljis before the Kilhorde visited their worlds to show them the path of enlightenment.

But to even *look* as if he was allowing the Chiss to dictate his course of action . . .

"Warships, this is Zyzek System Defense." A new voice came over the bridge speaker. "You are both requested to stand down."

Nakirre felt a ripple of cold amusement. The four patrol craft that had risen from the mass of merchant ships and split into pairs to confront the *Whetstone* and *Springhawk* were smaller and even more pathetic than the Chiss warship. Should they demand battle, it would take only a single laser volley to send them beyond all chance of enlightenment.

"The Kiljis cannot enlighten them if they are dead," Jixtus reminded him.

He was right, of course. More important, perhaps, it gave him a legitimate excuse to refuse combat with the Chiss.

"Zyzek System Defense, I comply with your request," he said. "Senior Captain Thrawn, you may keep your prisoners. I will see you again when I arrive among your people to change the ancient paths of the Chiss to the fuller enlightenment of the Kiljis."

"I will look forward to our next encounter," Thrawn said. "Farewell."

"Until the meeting," Nakirre said.

He keyed off and turned yet again to Jixtus. "You spoke of four nations that the Kiljis should first seek to enlighten," he said. "I choose instead the Chiss."

"Not yet," Jixtus said. "You must start with other beings."

"Why?"

Jixtus shook his head, the motion rippling the hood and veil. "Because I know these Chiss, Generalirius. They are resilient and powerful. I've seen them resist attack from without and manipulation from within. Only a combination of the two will succeed in bringing about their destruction."

"Enlightenment is incompatible with delay," Nakirre warned. "And you spoke of conquest, not destruction. If all are destroyed, who then shall we guide to peace and order?"

"A remnant shall certainly survive," Jixtus promised. "The common folk, those who will accept Kilji rule without question or resistance, will be yours to enlighten. But to achieve that, the leaders and commanders must fall."

"I agree," Nakirre said. "So let us proceed to their world and begin that process."

"They must fall on the schedule the Grysks have constructed," Jixtus said. "If we deviate from that time line, all will be lost. *But.*" He lifted a finger. "That doesn't mean you have to wait to meet them. In fact, I've always intended that you and the *Whetstone* would carry me on my first visit to their worlds and their leaders."

"Very well," Nakirre said, gazing at the display. The *Springhawk* had turned away from the planet now and was heading back out of the gravity well toward deep space. "I will follow your guidelines. For now. But be warned: If I feel you're proceeding too slowly, I'll take that time line into my own hands."

"Understood," Jixtus said. "Hold fast to my guidance, and the Chiss will be yours. In good time."

"In *swift* time," Nakirre corrected. "And when you destroy their leaders, you will leave me this one, this Thrawn." His skin stretched in a grim smile. "I am anxious for him to face true enlightenment."

The *Springhawk* was back in hyperspace, and the tension of that brief encounter was finally starting to leave Thalias's shoulders when Samakro finished his search of the ship's archives. "There's nothing here about a species or government called the Kiljis, Senior Captain," he reported. "Also no references to a Generalirius Nakirre."

"Understandable," Thrawn said. "But we *have* heard that title before."

Thalias stole a look over her shoulder. Samakro's face, she noted, had that telltale hint of someone chewing on something sour. "Yes, sir," he confirmed. "The Battle Dreadnought that attacked the *Vigilant* and *Grayshrike* at Sunrise mentioned it."

"Suggesting they and Generalirius Nakirre may be in some way connected," Thrawn said.

"Yes, sir," Samakro said again, a hint of reluctance joining the hint of sourness.

Small wonder. The first officer had argued with Thrawn—

respectfully and quietly, of course, but still argued—about Thrawn's plan to swing by Zyzek before returning to the Ascendancy. Samakro had suggested it would be both dangerous and pointless, while Thrawn had been convinced the side trip would be worthwhile. Once again, Thrawn had been proven right.

Though whether anything he'd learned would ultimately prove useful, Thalias couldn't guess.

"We also know that the generalirius wasn't alone just now," Samakro continued. "There were four instances when we could hear a second voice behind the first—very faint, but definitely not the same person. Probably not even the same species."

"I agree," Thrawn said. "Have the analysts been able to draw anything from those interruptions?"

"Not yet," Samakro said. "The voice was quiet, and Nakirre's transmission wasn't as clear as we might have hoped. We've been able to identify a few of the words, but a full analysis may have to wait until we can hand it over to the experts on Naporar."

"Have the analysts continue their work," Thrawn said. "Not just the words, but also as much of the vocal profile as they can obtain."

"Yes, sir," Samakro said.

Thalias glanced back again. Samakro had moved off and was logging the order into his questis. Thrawn, for his part, was gazing thoughtfully across the bridge, his eyes slightly unfocused, a sign Thalias had learned to recognize as deep thought.

She turned back forward, looking down at Che'ri. The girl's eyes were likewise unfocused, though in her case it was because she was totally immersed in Third Sight as she guided the *Springhawk* toward home.

"Caregiver."

Thalias twitched and spun around, to find Thrawn standing right behind her. "You shouldn't sneak up on people that way, Senior Captain," she said reproachfully.

"My apologies," Thrawn said, sounding more amused than actually sorry. "You need to learn how to think and ponder without sacrificing the awareness of your surroundings." He nodded toward Che'ri. "How is she?"

"She's fine," Thalias said, looking down at the girl. "She'll need a rest break in about forty minutes, but she got plenty of sleep last night and seems to be doing fine."

"That's not what I meant," Thrawn said, lowering his voice. "I'm talking about her and the Magys."

Thalias felt her throat tighten. She'd hoped she'd been the only one who'd seen that. "It may have just been coincidence."

"Do you believe that?"

Thalias sighed. The Magys, the leader of a group of alien refugees, had been woken from her forced hibernation in order to look at a sample of jewelry that was being used by a group called the Agbui against a Xodlak family Councilor on Celwis. Once the Magys had identified the brooch, Thrawn had asked for her to go back into hibernation until she could be returned to her people, currently waiting for her on the Paccian homeworld of Rapacc.

Not surprisingly, knowing now that her world was under outside threat, the Magys had resisted the idea of going back to sleep. Thrawn's warning—that she needed to be kept hidden lest she be spotted by an officer who came to the sky-walker suite on other business—had made no impact on her whatsoever. She'd been so adamant, in fact, that Thalias had thought for a minute that Thrawn and Samakro would have to physically force her back into the hibernation chamber.

And then, all at once, she'd abandoned the fight and meekly accepted Thrawn's order.

But before she settled back into the chamber, her eyes had flicked in the direction of Che'ri's sleeping room.

Back on Rapacc, at the first meeting between Thrawn and the refugees, the Magys had somehow recognized that Thalias had once been a sky-walker, able to use Third Sight to navigate through hyperspace. Had she also sensed Che'ri's presence and her much more powerful connection with whatever it was that Third Sight allowed her to access?

"No, I don't really believe it," she conceded. "But I still hope it was. I mean, there were two bulkheads and the whole dayroom between her and Che'ri. How could she have known through all of that?"

"The Magys claims her people join with the Beyond after death," Thrawn reminded her. "The fact that she recognized you'd once been a sky-walker suggests there's something of that connection present during life, as well."

"But on Rapacc she was at least *looking* at me," Thalias said. "If she'd seen Che'ri, I might understand it. But she never did."

Thrawn shifted his gaze to the viewport and the hyperspace swirl outside. "If the Beyond is the same Force that General Skywalker told me about, it appears to have many aspects and manifestations. It's possible this is a new facet that the Magys hadn't yet experienced."

"I thought all her people were connected to the Beyond."

"If all your species hummed a particular note, you'd become used to hearing it," Thrawn said. "If you then met a species who didn't hum at all, but then also found an individual who hummed a different note, that would be something both new and notable."

"Ah," Thalias said, nodding. "Yes, I see. Anything new, either presence *or* absence, can be informative."

"Yes," Thrawn said. "As you undoubtedly noted with Generalirius Nakirre."

Thalias's lips puckered. She'd thought she was the only one who'd spotted *that*, too, and had planned to keep it to herself until she could mention it privately to Thrawn. "You mean the fact that he never asked how many Watith prisoners we had?"

"Very good," Thrawn said approvingly. "Your analytical skill has grown considerably since you first came aboard the *Springhawk*."

"Thank you," Thalias said, feeling her cheeks warm with the compliment. "Though if it has, it's due to your skill as a teacher."

"I disagree," Thrawn said. "I don't teach, but merely guide. Each person approaches problems differently. All I do is ask the questions that set that person on their best path to the solution."

"I see," Thalias murmured. But only if that person was willing to put forth the effort to learn that path to logic and reason, she suspected. Too many people, possibly even the majority of them, were all too content to let others do that thinking and analysis for them.

"So what do we conclude from Nakirre's lack of curiosity?" Thrawn prompted.

"That he already knew how many people Captain Fsir had in his freighter." Thalias frowned. "Or possibly that they were all already dead?"

"The latter is the explanation I'm leaning toward," Thrawn said. "Which would in turn suggest that the other person speaking in the background was connected with whoever hired Fsir."

"Yes, that makes sense," Thalias agreed, thinking it through. "A trading center like Zyzek draws a lot of different nations and species. If our mystery alien had success hiring Fsir, he might well go back there for his next hire."

"I agree," Thrawn said. "Which brings up yet another question."

Thalias winced. "What exactly has he hired Nakirre to do?"

"Yes," Thrawn said. "I was hoping that these attacks on the Ascendancy had come to an end. I fear they haven't."

"Doesn't look like it," Thalias said, a hollow feeling in the pit of her stomach. Because even if and when the threats to the Ascendancy ended, the threats to Thrawn himself were likely to continue.

Fleetingly, she thought back to her brief conversation with Patriarch Thooraki at the Mitth family homestead. There he'd encouraged her to help protect Thrawn from the political pressures that, despite his military genius, he seemed unable to recognize and counter.

Thalias certainly had the will to do so. The crucial question was whether a lowly sky-walker caregiver had any of the necessary power.

"But if the attacks continue," she said, wondering if Thrawn even realized she was giving a two-fold answer, "we'll just have to beat them again."

The summons to Sposia had been quick and abrupt, and had given Supreme General Ba'kif barely enough time to close down his office in an orderly way and get across Csaplar to the landing field just outside the city. The scout ship he'd requisitioned was ready, one of the five that were always kept on fifteen-minute readiness for senior Defense Hierarchy Council officers, and twenty minutes later he was out of Csilla's gravity well and into the mesmerizing swirl of hyperspace.

It wasn't the way Ba'kif liked doing business. Many of his colleagues, in fact, would never move this quickly for anything short of all-out war.

But the summons had come directly from Stybla Patriarch Stybla'mi'ovodo's office, and the Patriarch had said it concerned Senior Captain Thrawn, and that was all Ba'kif needed to know.

Lamiov was waiting outside the massive door of Vault Four when Ba'kif finally finished with the rigorous Universal Analysis Group security protocols. "Supreme General," the Patriarch called in greeting as Ba'kif walked across the entry chamber, doing his best to ignore the silent guards standing their impassive watch over the Ascendancy's most secret base. "Thank you for coming."

"It's always a pleasure to visit the UAG, Your Venerante," Ba'kif said as he reached the other. "Mind you, a bit more warning would have been appreciated."

"Trust me, you had only about ten minutes less than I got," Lamiov said. "Senior Captain Thrawn was playing this one even closer than usual."

"Does it have anything to do with why he's so late back from whatever the Xodlak, Erighal, and Pommrio were involved in?"

"Is he *that* late?" Lamiov asked, frowning. "I was under the impression that those family ships only arrived a day ago."

"True enough," Ba'kif said. "But the *Springhawk* had a sky-walker, and the family ships didn't. By all rights, Thrawn should have been here at least a day or two ahead of them."

"Interesting," Lamiov murmured. "Maybe he stayed at Hoxim to take a closer look at the freighter crash site."

Ba'kif gave a little snort. "You *do* realize you're rattling off details that only the Council is supposed to have, right?"

"Really, Supreme General," Lamiov said drily. "If you haven't figured out by now that the Stybla have our own special information sources, you really have no business in your current seat of power. Seriously, though, you're going to love this one. Shall we go take a look?"

"After you," Ba'kif said, falling into step beside Lamiov, peripherally noting that the nearest guards stirred slightly as the two men walked the rest of the way to the vault door. Early in the UAG's existence, Ba'kif had been told, there'd been some thought in the Syndicure of removing family ties from all of its personnel, as was routinely done with senior military officers, and for the same reason of hopefully eliminating family politics.

Ultimately, it was decided that such an action would draw too much unwanted attention to the facility, and the idea was dropped. As a compromise, though, UAG uniforms didn't include any family identification, neither the family crests of the Nine and the Forty nor the stylized names used by the Ascendancy's other, lesser families. Here at UAG, in theory, all were equal.

Still, Ba'kif suspected that most if not all of the guards on Vault Four were Stybla. Lamiov would have seen to that.

Given that a new alien artifact had just arrived, Ba'kif had fully expected the large receiving area at the front part of the vault to be crowded. He wasn't prepared, though, for just how crowded it actually was.

Part of that was the sheer size of the artifact: a four-meter-long lattice of white metal ribs that looked like a section of some giant sea monster's torso skeleton. A dozen techs were hovering around it, taking readings and measurements or attaching leads to other analysis devices. Two senior UAG staff were also in the mix, one of them overseeing the work, the other working busily with his questis.

Standing off to one side, silently watching all the activity, were Senior Captain Thrawn and Mid Captain Samakro.

Both men looked over as Ba'kif and Lamiov walked up to them. "Patriarch Lamiov; Supreme General Ba'kif," Thrawn said in greeting. "You honor us with your presence."

"You honor *us* with yet another intriguing device for our collection," Lamiov said. "Go ahead and tell Supreme General Ba'kif what you've brought."

"Yes, Your Venerante." Thrawn shifted his attention to Ba'kif. "During our search for remnants of the Vagaari pirates, we encountered an alien freighter that was supposedly being attacked by three gunships. We subsequently determined that the battle had been staged for our benefit, and that the scenario was merely the first step in a trap."

"Obviously, the aliens didn't know much about you," Ba'kif commented.

"No, their knowledge of the Chiss was quite limited," Thrawn said, apparently missing the subtle compliment completely. "What intrigued me was the fact that the feigned attack was already in progress when we emerged from hyperspace. That suggested to me that the aliens had a way of predicting when and where a ship would arrive."

Ba'kif looked over at the skeletal artifact, an odd tightness settling into the pit of his stomach. "And this is what allowed them to do that?"

"We believe so, yes," Thrawn said. "The lattice was built into the space between the freighter's inner and outer hulls and was attached to the equipment boxes via those cables."

Ba'kif nodded as he belatedly spotted the rolling tables off to the side with oddly shaped boxes and neatly coiled wires resting on them. "Was the entire lattice like this?" he asked.

"The parts we were able to investigate were," Thrawn said. "Unfortunately, the time we had to devote to our analysis was severely limited."

"Any idea how much warning the device gives before the incoming ship arrives?" Ba'kif asked.

"Based on the state of the false attack as it appeared to us, I estimate they had at least ninety seconds to prepare," Thrawn said. "Possibly more."

"Ninety seconds," Ba'kif murmured, his mind spinning with the possibilities. Put a couple of picket ships equipped with such early-warning devices in orbit at the combat edge of each Chiss world, and sneak attacks would be all but impossible.

Even better, if the lattice could detect all ships moving through hyperspace even if those vessels weren't preparing to return to space-normal, the Defense Force could monitor the most common lanes through the Ascendancy. And if the device could not only detect passing vessels but also give an estimate of how many were involved . . .

"Easy, Supreme General," Lamiov warned.

Ba'kif blinked away the string of thought. "What?"

"I know that look," Lamiov said. "I'm bound to caution you that just because we have one of these devices doesn't mean we'll be able to reverse-engineer it."

"I know," Ba'kif said, his excitement fading somewhat. So far both of Thrawn's major contributions to Vault Four—the Vagaari gravity-well generator and the Republic advanced shield technology—had resisted the UAG's best efforts to tease out their secrets. Ba'kif had no doubt that, sooner or later, the Ascendancy's techs would succeed, but it was clearly going to continue to be an uphill climb.

Unfortunately, there was no reason to believe this advance-warning detector would deviate from that pattern.

"I just wish I knew why every item the Defense Force could find an immediate use for takes forever to crack," Ba'kif added.

"That does seem to be the way of the universe, doesn't it?" Lamiov conceded. "That high-density electronics memory unit that was brought to us a hundred years ago was being utilized in questis storage bars within twelve months. The specialized cooking system someone found thirty years ago was on the market in five months."

"But something that could upgrade a warship's electrostatic barrier defenses by a thousand percent or more . . ." Ba'kif shook his head.

"Perhaps we'll have better luck with this one," Lamiov said, nodding to the lattice. "It's a shame you couldn't bring back the entire freighter." He raised his eyebrows slightly in silent question.

"Yes," Thrawn said simply. Either he'd missed the invitation in the Patriarch's tone and expression, or he'd already decided not to provide any further details about what had happened to the freighter.

"We removed what appeared to be all of the equipment, plus as much of the lattice as we could," Samakro added, also ignoring the unstated request. "Hopefully, it will be enough for you to work with."

"We'll do our best," Lamiov assured him. "Is there anything more the techs should know?"

"I don't believe so," Thrawn said. "Mid Captain?"

"Nothing major that I can think of," Samakro said. "I'll note in passing that even though the freighter was part of an ambush, and therefore might be considered a type of warship, its hull was standard civilian design. No nyix, not even a nyix-alloy inner shell."

"That could be significant," Lamiov said.

"It could," Samakro said. "My inclination is to put it down to the designers preferring to maintain the freighter illusion, and that it has nothing to do with the detector itself."

"Probably," Ba'kif agreed, his thoughts heading off in a new direction. Still, nyix had some unique characteristics, which was one reason it worked so well for warship hulls. If one or more of those features interfered with the advance-warning detector, that might provide some clues as to how the device worked.

"Regardless, I'll make the techs aware of that," Lamiov said. "And now, I believe the Council is expecting you on Csilla."

"Yes," Thrawn said. "But before we leave, Supreme General, I request your presence aboard the *Springhawk*. There's another situation we need to discuss."

"Can it wait?" Ba'kif asked.

Thrawn and Samakro exchanged looks. "Yes, sir, I suppose it can," Thrawn said reluctantly. "For a time."

"Then it waits," Ba'kif said firmly. "I have only a few hours to discuss some pressing matters with Patriarch Lamiov before I also have to return. And as the Patriarch said, the *Springhawk* is already overdue back at Csilla for examination and whatever refitting and rearming are necessary."

He raised his eyebrows toward Samakro. "At which point you, Mid Captain, are on my list of officers to speak with about the Hoxim incident. You'll have until then to prepare your statement and organize any documents you might wish entered into the record."

"Understood, Supreme General," Samakro said. "Though if I may—" He glanced at Thrawn. "—I would urge you not to delay your trip to the *Springhawk* any longer than necessary."

"I'll take your suggestion under advisement," Ba'kif said, frowning. Samakro's expression was the standard neutral of an officer addressing a superior.

But there was also an unusually strong layer of tension beneath it. Whatever Thrawn wanted to discuss with Ba'kif, Samakro wasn't looking forward to the conversation.

Even with that added level of intrigue, though, it would have to wait. Right now, Hoxim and its fallout were Ba'kif's priority.

"I'll see you back at Csilla, then," he said, gesturing the two officers back toward the vault door. "Get started on the refit, and I'll call when I'm ready for your interviews."

CHAPTER ONE

The *Vigilant* was three minutes from its destination, and Admiral Ar'alani was starting to wonder if her ship would be ready when they arrived when Senior Captain Kiwu'tro'owmis finally returned to the bridge. "Sorry about the delay, Admiral," Wutroow said as she crossed to Ar'alani's command chair. "Breacher One *really* didn't want to be fixed. But we persuaded it."

Ar'alani looked over at the weapons status board. The number one breacher missile launcher still showed red . . . flicked to green. "Excellent," she told Wutroow. "Be sure to log a commendation to the repair team. It's never a good idea to head into a situation with one hand stuck in your pocket."

"Yes, ma'am," Wutroow said. "Though if I may, I'm still not entirely clear as to what you're expecting the situation to be."

"Because I'm not entirely clear about it myself," Ar'alani confessed. "It's just something about that last Nikardun base that still bothers me."

"Which part?" Wutroow asked. "The lead time the attackers needed to set up that slow-approach asteroid attack? Or the fact that the base was too big to have been a listening post or anything else on Yiv's lists?"

"Both, plus something else I can't put my finger on," Ar'alani said. "I'm hoping I'll recognize it when I see it."

"Let's also hope the Council won't be annoyed with us for taking this little side trip," Wutroow warned. "We're already way beyond the time limit Ba'kif gave us for checking out Sunrise. Even Thrawn's already made it back from his pirate search, and you know how long *he* takes when he's on the hunt. *And* we still don't know why our friends with the Battle Dreadnought are so interested in this place."

"It has to have something to do with the mining operation Senior Warrior Yopring spotted," Ar'alani said. "The amount of activity down there already tells us something big is happening. Add in the fighters who chased him away, and I'd say we've got it pinpointed."

"Unless we've got two different groups in play," Wutroow pointed out. "The miners and the Battle Dreadnought could be fighting each other. But I suppose that's unlikely. My main concern is that even if we agree that the mines are the focal point, we don't know what's down there."

"Mines usually mean metal ore of some sort."

"Right, but digging doesn't always mean mining," Wutroow said. "It could also be something the inhabitants deliberately buried that someone else wants to dig up."

Ar'alani frowned. That possibility hadn't occurred to her. "You mean like some weapon or artifact?"

"That's what I was wondering," Wutroow said. "It's not like we haven't run into things like that before. Senior Captain Thrawn, for one, has almost made a second career of digging them up."

"Though not literally *digging* them up," Ar'alani pointed out. "Usually they've been sitting out in the open ready to be walked off with."

"Maybe *we'll* get to pick up this one," Wutroow said with a wry smile. "Maybe you can work a deal with Thrawn. He gets the stuff that's aboveground, you get the stuff you have to dig for."

"I'll be sure to bring that up next time I see him," Ar'alani promised, looking at the chrono. Almost there. "Prepare for breakout," she called, raising her voice so that the entire bridge could hear her. "And be ready." She gestured an invitation to Wutroow. "Senior Captain?"

"Yes, ma'am." Wutroow paused, watching the timer. "Breakout," she called. "Three, two, *one*."

The star-flares collapsed to stars; and as it had once before, the

Vigilant found itself floating among the scattered debris of the demolished Nikardun base.

"Biclian?" Wutroow prompted.

"Yes, ma'am," Senior Commander Obbic'lia'nuf called from the sensor station. "Combat range clear. Mid-range clear. Far range . . . Admiral, we have movement: three ships close-in to the central base structure."

"Any identification?" Ar'alani asked, frowning at the tactical. Two of the ships were relatively small, while the third was much larger with the typical shape of a freighter.

"No beacons," Junior Captain Evroes'ky'mormi reported from the weapons station. "The large ship shows no weapons emplacements. Probably a freighter; possibly a mobile repair dock."

"I'd say the latter, Admiral," Biclian said. "There are some spots along the ventral plane that look like mounting nodes. The two smaller ships . . . definitely warships. Patrol ships at least; possibly destroyers."

Ar'alani scowled. Under normal circumstances, a Nightdragon man-of-war like the *Vigilant* could defeat a pair of patrol ships practically in its sleep.

Unfortunately, the situation here wasn't normal. The *Vigilant* and Senior Captain Lakinda's *Grayshrike* had taken on that unidentified Battle Dreadnought over Sunrise, and even with Lakinda handing over all her remaining breacher missiles and plasma sphere fluid before she headed back to the Ascendancy, Ar'alani was still severely underarmed.

Up to now the *Vigilant* had been lucky. Ar'alani's investigation of the devastated planet had reached her chosen end point without drawing enemy attention or interference. But that luck might be about to run out. "Any idea if they've spotted us?" she asked.

"No indication of it," Biclian said. "They seem to be concentrating on whatever they're doing at the base."

"Admiral, we have activity," Junior Commander Stybla'rsi'omli spoke up urgently from the comm station. "Tight-beam laser transmission; we're just catching the edge of it."

"Uh-oh," Wutroow muttered.

Ar'alani nodded, wincing. For Larsiom to be picking up the edge of a laser transmission, the intended recipient must be almost directly behind them. "Full barriers," she ordered. "Octrimo, yaw ninety degrees starboard."

"Yes, ma'am," Mid Commander Droc'tri'morhs confirmed from the helm. The electrostatic barriers came up, and the collection of debris outside the viewport spun sideways as the *Vigilant* rotated—

"Incoming!" Oeskym snapped, his warning punctuated by a blaze of light as the *Vigilant*'s spectrum lasers flashed out at the pair of missiles streaking toward them. "Patrol cruiser—mark it as Bogey One—coming in fast from behind us."

"Defensive fire; lasers only," Ar'alani ordered, looking at the tactical. The *Vigilant* could run its lasers indefinitely, but had only six breacher missiles and enough fluid for twenty plasma spheres. That wasn't nearly enough to go toe-to-toe with a patrol cruiser and a pair of patrol ships.

Which just meant she would have to get creative.

"Oeskym, have the thrusters in Breachers One and Two disabled," she told the weapons officer. "As quickly as possible. Let me know when they're ready."

"Yes, ma'am," Oeskym said, frowning at his board but knowing better than to question his commander in the middle of a battle. "Techs are on it."

"Remind them that neatness doesn't count," Ar'alani said. "Octrimo, some mild evasive maneuvers—keep us clear of their missiles, but don't move us out of this general area. Biclian?"

"Patrol ships have been alerted, Admiral," the sensor officer reported. "Designating as Bogeys Two and Three. Still hugging the base, but they're turning weapons toward us."

"Let me know if they start moving." On the tactical, Bogey One was accelerating toward them and had now launched another pair of missiles. At this range the *Vigilant*'s lasers had enough time to take them out, but if the attacker got close enough that window would close and Ar'alani would be forced to use her limited supply of breachers or plasma spheres to protect her ship. "Oeskym?"

"Almost there," Oeskym said. "Techs report . . . yes. Thrusters disabled, Admiral."

Finally. "Drop them out of their tubes," she told him, giving the tactical another look. "Octrimo, as soon as they're clear of the hull, get us moving toward the base and Bogeys Two and Three. Again, minor evasive, but don't stray far from the direct vector."

"And stand by aft lasers," Wutroow added as the *Vigilant* turned away from the incoming patrol cruiser and started accelerating toward the wrecked base.

"Understood," Oeskym said. "Timing, Admiral?"

"Use your best judgment," Ar'alani told him. "Octrimo, keep an eye on Bogey One. Make sure we're leading it in the right direction."

"Yes, ma'am."

"Bogeys Two and Three are on the move," Biclian warned. "Leaving the repair dock now and heading toward us."

"Probably trying to box us in," Wutroow said.

"Probably," Ar'alani agreed. "Oeskym?"

"Thirty seconds to optimal positioning," the weapons officer said. "Octrimo, tweak us about five degrees starboard."

"Five degrees starboard, acknowledged," Octrimo said, and once again the outside view shifted.

"Bogeys Two and Three opening fire," Biclian announced. "Don't know why—they're way out of range."

"Probably trying to distract us or slow us down," Octrimo said. "We're starting to pull a little ahead of Bogey One."

"Slow down to match," Ar'alani ordered. "We don't want to lose him—"

"Bogey One pitching negative," Oeskym snapped. "It's angling out of line with the breachers."

"They must have spotted them," Wutroow bit out. "Get a tractor on it—bring it back up onto vector."

"Belay that," Ar'alani said, keying the tactical to her chair's repeater display. Oeskym and Wutroow would be running the numbers, but it was already clear to her that at the patrol cruiser's current distance it was too massive for the *Vigilant*'s tractor beams to have any effect.

But a little farther away and just past the cruiser was a small meteoroid . . .

"Tractor on this instead," she said, marking the chunk of rock and sending the target data to the weapons station. "Full power—try to draw it up into the cruiser's ventral bow area."

"Got it," Oeskym said, busying himself with his board.

Ar'alani turned to the tactical. The tractor beam caught the meteoroid, yanking it out of its lazy tumble and sending it arrowing toward the patrol cruiser. If they spotted the sudden new threat, and if they responded as reflexively as Ar'alani hoped—

"Bogey One pitching back positive," Biclian reported. "Dodging the meteoroid; heading back toward the breachers."

Not exactly toward them, Ar'alani saw. But close enough. "Fire at the breachers," she ordered.

Once again, there was a stuttering of light as the aft lasers blazed, this time targeting not the attacking ship but the breachers. The missiles disintegrated, sending their payloads bursting out into an expanding cloud of acid.

The patrol cruiser had almost instantly recognized its mistake and was again pitching to try to evade the attack. But its momentum was working against it, the acid was spreading outward too rapidly, and before the warship could get clear the edge of the cloud swept over its portside flank.

And as the acid burned into the hull, destroying sensor nodes and missile targeting systems and digging blackened pits into the metal, the *Vigilant*'s lasers once again opened fire, blazing into the ragged surface and digging even deeper through the hull.

Fifteen seconds into the barrage, the *Vigilant*'s laserfire burned away enough of the hull to reach the patrol cruiser's remaining missiles, and the warship disintegrated in a violent explosion.

"Full acceleration," Ar'alani ordered. "And keep scanning. If there's anything else out there, I want to know before it starts shooting at us."

Wutroow stepped closer to the command chair as the *Vigilant* leapt forward toward the wrecked base and the remaining three ships. "Nicely done, Admiral," she said quietly. "I'll just point out what the number-squinters on Csilla will probably say: that we could have cut and run and saved the Ascendancy a couple of breachers."

"What, run away from a patrol cruiser and a couple of patrol ships?" Ar'alani scoffed. "We'd never have heard the end of it."

Wutroow shrugged. "There's that, of course."

"More important, we'd have lost the chance to see what they're doing over there," Ar'alani continued, nodding toward the distant station.

"Unless . . . no," Wutroow said. "I was thinking an in-system jump, but it would have been dangerous with all the wreckage floating around. So what *are* they doing?"

"That's what I want to find out," Ar'alani said, studying the tactical. Bogeys Two and Three were still coming toward the *Vigilant,* still firing useless laser blasts. But they were moving almost leisurely, as if not wanting to bring things to a head any sooner than they had to. Meanwhile, the repair dock was still floating close beside the wrecked station.

Were they getting their people out? Or were they—?

And suddenly Ar'alani understood.

They weren't getting anything *out.* They were putting something *in.*

"Spheres—target the station," she snapped. "Saturation volley, and keep going until we're dry."

"Yes, ma'am," Oeskym said.

"Admiral?" Wutroow asked quietly as the launchers began spitting plasma spheres toward the distant station. "The station, not the patrol ships?"

"Yes," Ar'alani said. "All that laserfire is their way of hiding what the people from the repair dock are doing at the station."

"Which is?"

"I think they're planning to destroy it," Ar'alani said grimly. "Not just wreck it, like the original attack did, but completely disintegrate it."

"Interesting," Wutroow muttered. "Must be something in there they *really* don't want us to see. Though I'd have sworn we checked out the place pretty thoroughly our last time through."

"Maybe something new has been added," Ar'alani said. "I'm hoping we can hit and scramble whatever self-destruct devices they've put in before they detonate."

"Well, if we can't, it won't be through lack of effort," Wutroow said, nodding at the stream of plasma spheres still racing away from the *Vigilant*. "You sure you don't want to keep a few back in case they decide to make a real fight of it?"

"They won't," Ar'alani said. "As soon as the sabotage is finished, they'll all be out of—and there they go," she interrupted herself as the two patrol ships veered off in opposite directions, angling away from the *Vigilant*. Behind them, the repair dock was now turning and driving away from the station.

"Orders, Admiral?" Oeskym asked from the weapons station.

Ar'alani checked the displays. The *Vigilant* had covered a lot of distance toward the station in the past few minutes, but they were still too far for a decent shot. But it wouldn't hurt to try. "See what you can do with the repair dock," she said. "Lasers only—keep the spheres saturating the station."

"Yes, ma'am," Oeskym said, and a triple blast of concentrated laserfire joined the stream of plasma spheres.

Ar'alani considered Oeskym one of the best weapons officers in the Expansionary Defense Fleet, and he did his best. Even at their marginal range, he managed to get three clean hits on the repair dock as it moved clear of the station.

But they were too far out for any significant damage. A minute later, the dock and both patrol ships escaped into hyperspace.

"Sorry, Admiral," Oeskym apologized as the laserfire ceased.

"Not your fault," Ar'alani assured him as the plasma sphere launchers also went silent. "The priority now is to get to the station and dismantle or destroy whatever bomb or bombs they put aboard before they can wake up. Wutroow, get two shuttles prepped and loaded."

"On it, Admiral," Wutroow said, punching orders into her questis. "Don't worry, we'll get there in time."

Ar'alani looked out the viewport. And if they didn't, she reminded herself soberly, everyone aboard those shuttles would probably die.

She could only hope that whatever secret was lurking inside that battered hull was worth the risk.

Ar'alani had been concerned that their attackers might have had time to set several bombs aboard the wrecked Nikardun base before fleeing. Fortunately, there was only one very large one. Even more fortunately, it remained dormant, frozen by the massive ion storm the *Vigilant* had hit it with, until the Chiss techs were able to get aboard and disarm it.

It was as the survey teams worked their way through the station that Ar'alani finally realized what had been nagging at her.

"There," she said, pointing to one of the images being sent back to the ship by the survey teams. "That blast point. A single close-range shot, just enough to break through the hull and depressurize the compartment."

"But *not* so much as to make the damage a lengthy pain in the neck to repair," Wutroow said thoughtfully. "So after their sneak-attack asteroid missile blew in the front door, and a few follow-up missiles popped open the command and control areas, they charged in and just poked holes in the walls until everyone inside was dead."

"And then continued the same pattern in the interior," Ar'alani said, pointing to another set of images. "Their plan all along was to kill the Nikardun who were running the base, make enough of a mess to convince any passersby that they had gone away, then slink back after everyone left and put the station back together."

"Because why would anyone ever come back for a second look at a place that was obviously useless?" Wutroow agreed. "So most of the debris out there was just for show?"

"I doubt that," Ar'alani said. "The Nikardun probably had a fair number of ships here, both visiting and standing guard. *That's* where all the wreckage came from."

"Right," Wutroow said. "Which makes this . . . what? Some kind of fueling stop that Yiv wanted to downplay?"

"No, I think it was more than that," Ar'alani said, a shiver running through her. "I think this base was set up as a rendezvous and coordination point for Yiv's people and their allies."

"I don't remember any allies showing up at the Primea battle," Wutroow said. "You think we and the Vaks just wiped out the Nikardun before Yiv had time to bring any new forces into play?"

"Or they were never intended to be brought in," Ar'alani said. "Note the base's location: hidden and out of the way, but relatively close to Sunrise."

"*And* between Sunrise and the Ascendancy," Wutroow pointed out.

"That, too," Ar'alani agreed. "An ideal spot for someone who wanted to keep an eye on either us or the Magys's people."

"Or both," Wutroow said. "At least that explains why we kept seeing the same Battle Dreadnought at Sunrise. This was also probably going to be their repair and refurbishing center, only they don't yet have it up and running."

"That was my thought, too," Ar'alani said, nodding. "I'm guessing they didn't expect us to find Sunrise as quickly as we did."

"Which only happened because Thrawn met the Magys and her refugees and decided to play a hunch," Wutroow murmured. "*That's* going to frost some people."

"Thrawn's ability to frost the Aristocra is hardly new," Ar'alani pointed out. "Regardless, the fact that the same asteroid missile launcher trick was used in both places adds additional confirmation that the people we tangled with over Sunrise are the same ones who hit this base."

"Plus the other Nikardun base we checked out before this one," Wutroow reminded her. "Can't be a coincidence that both were hit." She lifted a finger for emphasis. "Something else occurs to me. You called them allies a minute ago; but for them to come in and wipe out two different Nikardun bases . . . ?"

"You're right," Ar'alani said, feeling her lip twitch. "The Nikardun weren't the attackers' allies. They were just their tools. And you don't destroy a good tool unless you have something better at hand."

"Or unless you think that particular tool is about to break," Wutroow said. "I wonder if they know Thrawn took General Yiv alive."

"Interesting question," Ar'alani said. "We might want to suggest a couple of new topics for the Council's interrogators."

"Assuming we make it back to Csilla in one piece," Wutroow warned. "Even if this base isn't open for business, those patrol ships may have friends in the area."

"Excellent point," Ar'alani said, touching her command chair's comm key. "Survey leader?"

"I'm here, Admiral," Biclian's voice came back. "We just found another equipment dump. That makes at least four of them, and we're not even quite done yet."

"Actually, you are," Ar'alani said. "I have the sense we're close to overstaying our welcome. How long will it take to make recordings of this latest dump?"

"If you don't want any additions to the physical evidence we already sent to the *Vigilant,* we can have it done in fifteen minutes," Biclian said. "If you want a sampling, it'll take another hour."

"Just make the recordings," Ar'alani said. "I think we have enough crates to keep the Naporar techs happy. Pass the word to the other teams that they're to finish up and get back to their shuttles. I want to be back in hyperspace in forty minutes."

"Yes, ma'am," Biclian said. "We'll be there."

Ar'alani keyed off the comm. "You all heard," she added, raising her voice to include the rest of the bridge. "Hyperspace in forty minutes."

"Hyperspace in forty minutes," Wutroow acknowledged, keying the order into her questis. "Do you want me to go get Ab'begh? I assume you'll want her to handle the first leg of the trip home."

"Definitely," Ar'alani said. "But there's no rush on that. You can leave her in her suite for another half hour."

"Right," Wutroow said drily. "We wouldn't want her to get bored."

"I'm not worried about boredom," Ar'alani said grimly, looking across the bridge at the tactical display. "As you said, those patrol ships may have friends."

Many years ago, when Senior Captain Xodlak'in'daro first joined the Expansionary Defense Fleet, there had been an elaborate ceremony to celebrate her rematching from her birth family to the Xodlak family. Lakinda didn't remember much about the ritual except that it was big and flashy and completely overwhelmed her simple commoner tastes.

Today's rematching, she suspected, would be far less extravagant. Not because being rematched from one of the Forty Great Families to one of the Nine Ruling Families wasn't a big deal—because it most certainly was—but because all the flurry of activity in the wake of the fiasco out in the Hoxim system was taking up the majority of everyone's focus today.

Which was fine with her. Most people who were offered such a social step up, she knew, would grab at it with both hands, moving into their new position without so much as a glance backward. But while Lakinda recognized the honor that was being given to her by the Irizi family, she couldn't help feeling a certain guilt over her abandonment of the Xodlak. They'd taken her out of obscurity, after all, and she'd always believed that such a gesture should be repaid with loyalty.

Of course, she'd never expected any other family to want her enough to try to rematch her, so she'd never taken the time to really think it through. But now that had happened. Moreover, the Irizi offer had been extremely generous, raising her as it did from merit adoptive of the Xodlak to Trial-born of the Irizi, and the friends she'd consulted with had unanimously recommended she take it.

So here she was in Csaplar, capital city of the Ascendancy, walking through the Convocate Hall toward the central Syndicure offices of the Irizi family. It was the best move for her, she told herself firmly. Whatever guilt she might feel was an artifice of her own mind, to be ignored until it eventually faded away.

Or so she hoped.

The ceremony, as expected, was short and slightly distracted. Speaker Irizi'emo'lacfo took her to his office where the witnesses were waiting, declared her rematched from the Xodlak to the Irizi, ran her through an oath where she and the family declared their mutual loyalty, then congratulated her on her new position. The single pang of guilt she felt during the oath was quickly brushed aside by the flurry of datawork that the Speaker then proceeded to hand her.

Thirty minutes after her arrival, she left. No longer Senior Captain Xodlak'in'daro, but now Senior Captain Irizi'in'daro.

Ziinda. She repeated her new core name over and over in her mind as she strode back down the corridor toward the shuttle landing area. It sounded pleasantly exotic, but it was definitely going to take some getting used to. *Ziinda. Ziinda.*

"Senior Captain Ziinda?" a voice called from behind her.

Even with all her preparation, it took a good second and a half before her brain caught up with the fact that she was the person being called to. "Yes?" she replied, stopping and turning around.

The woman striding toward her wasn't anyone she recognized. But the blue-red thinstripe outerwrap robe with its dark-red sleeves and black filigree was a combination she knew all too well. Adding in the distinctive Speaker shoulder band—

"Senior Captain Ziinda?" the woman repeated.

"I am she," Ziinda said, her heart sinking as her dormant guilt surged back to the surface.

"I am Speaker Xodlak'brov'omtivti," the woman said stiffly as she strode up to Ziinda, stopping barely half a meter away. "I'd hoped to catch you before you met with Speaker Ziemol. I see I'm too late."

"Yes," Ziinda said. "Can I help you?"

For a moment Lakbrovom just stared at her. Ziinda forced herself to meet the other's gaze, silently ordering herself not to be intimidated. Speaker Lakbrovom might be the Syndicure's highest-ranking Xodlak, but Ziinda was Irizi now, and the Xodlak hierarchy no longer meant anything to her. "I hoped I could offer incentives for you to stay with our family," Lakbrovom said at last. "I understand the Patriarch was somewhat offended that you didn't tell anyone of the Irizi offer before accepting it."

"I'm sorry if I broke protocol," Ziinda said, knowing full well that she'd done nothing of the sort. A person who'd been offered rematching *could* speak to their current family if they chose to do so, but it was certainly not required. "But I felt it was time to move on."

"Why?" Lakbrovom asked bluntly. "Did the Irizi offer a higher status? We could have matched it. Did they offer money or land or position?"

"None of those was the deciding factor," Ziinda said. So Lakbrovom wanted to be blunt? Fine. Ziinda could be blunt, too. "I knew my time with the Xodlak was nearing an end when my first officer aboard the family frigate *Midsummer* relieved me of command. *And* got away with that act of mutiny because he was blood."

"Family rank isn't supposed to be a factor on naval ships," Lakbrovom said.

"You weren't listening," Ziinda said. "This wasn't an Expansionary Defense Fleet ship. This was a *family* ship."

Lakbrovom's glare slipped a little. Maybe she'd skimmed the Hoxim report a little too quickly. "That's no excuse," she said. "No one of Xodlak blood should use his or her position that way. *I* certainly wouldn't have."

"I'm glad to hear it," Ziinda said. "The fact remains that this one did. If you'll excuse me, I'm expected back on my ship."

"I apologize on behalf of the family," Lakbrovom said as Ziinda started to turn away. "I'll see to it that he is properly reprimanded."

"As you wish," Ziinda said, turning back to her. "But *only* as you yourself wish. The internal workings of the Xodlak family no longer concern me."

This time, when Ziinda turned away, Lakbrovom remained silent.

Perhaps that last jab had been unnecessary, Ziinda thought as she continued down the corridor. Perhaps it had even been a bit childish. But she had to admit that it had felt good.

But really, wasn't that what family politics and relationships were all about? Give or take; win or lose; deliver the jab or receive it. That was how it had always been. That was how it always would be. No matter the family, certainly no matter the individual people.

It was the Chiss way. And it would never change.

MEMORIES I

Of all the duties foisted on low-ranking family members, Aristocra Mitth'ras'safis had often heard, the task of welcoming new merit adoptives to their formal rematching dinner was one of the worst. The newcomers were either highly skilled additions to the Mitth, in which case they tended to have an overblown opinion of themselves and their value; or they were freshly initiated into the Ascendancy military, in which case they were self-conscious and, well, extremely military. Nearly all of the blood, cousins, and ranking distants opted out of reception duty, leaving most of the burden to fall on Trial-borns and other merit adoptives, none of whom had enough pull to avoid it.

Which made Thrass a definite anomaly . . . because unlike practically everyone else in his circle of friends, he genuinely enjoyed the service.

Of course, he'd only been doing it for the past three years, and in that time he'd only welcomed eleven merit adoptives. Maybe after a couple more years the excitement of meeting and evaluating new people would fade and he would become as cynical and world-weary as everyone else.

But he doubted it. Every one of these people had been approved by the Patriarch's Office, a fair percentage of them by the Patriarch himself, and Thrass liked to see if he could figure out what made each of them special in the family's eyes.

This one, for example. The young man freshly renamed Mitth'raw'nuru was standing inside the reception room, looking around the walls at the Avidich landscape paintings and the corner statuettes representing or created by some of the ancient Mitth Patriarchs. To Thrass's eye he looked just a bit lost, a fairly common reaction from someone who'd been rematched from a nondescript family on a minor world into one of the greatest of the Ascendancy's Nine Ruling Families. Thrawn was wearing the uniform of a Taharim Academy cadet, which meant he'd been taken from his home directly to Naporar and then been brought here to Avidich for his welcome and orientation.

Thrass frowned. For new warriors it usually went the other way around, first to Avidich and then to Naporor. Apparently, someone in the family had wanted him signed into the Expansionary Defense Fleet as quickly as possible, before even his formal welcoming.

Hopefully, he wouldn't look as intimidated in the heat of battle as he did in a grand Ruling Family reception room. The one common attribute of Ascendancy military types was their outward confidence.

The younger man turned as Thrass walked in through the archway. "Cadet Mitth'raw'nuru?" Thrass asked formally.

"I am he," Thrawn said.

"Welcome to Avidich," Thrass said. "I'm Aristocra Mitth'ras'safis. I'll be guiding you through the various protocols that will fully and officially rematch you to the Mitth family." He waved a hand to encompass the room. "And try not to be overwhelmed by all the fancy flourishes and curlicues. This reception room is also where dignitaries and emissaries from other families are brought in, and we like to make sure right from the start that they know who they're dealing with."

"I wasn't intimidated," Thrawn said mildly. "I was merely noting the unusual fact that the same artist who did three of the landscapes also created two of the statuettes. It's uncommon for a single artist to excel at both artistic forms."

Thrass looked around. He'd been in this room dozens of times, and had twice visited the Csilla homestead's collection of official family art, and as far as he could remember none of them had visible signatures or other identifiers.

In fact, that was the whole point of these displays. These were *Mitth* artworks, to be seen as coming not from individuals but from the family as a whole.

So how did Thrawn know which pieces had been done by which artist? "Which ones?" Thrass asked. "Show me."

"Those three landscapes," Thrawn said, pointing. "And those statuettes." He indicated a pair in one of the corners.

Thrass stepped over for a closer look. Just as he'd remembered, there was nothing to indicate the artist on any of them. "What makes you think they're by the same person?"

Thrawn's forehead furrowed in a frown. "They just *are*," he said, sounding a little confused. "The lines, the color, the material mix. It's . . ." His lips compressed briefly.

"Obvious?" Thrass suggested.

Thrawn looked like he was going to agree, then seemed to think better of it. "It's difficult to explain," he said instead.

"Well, let's find out," Thrass said, pulling out his questis. The artwork here might not be labeled, but the specific artists were surely listed in the archives. "Anything else you can tell me about them?" he added as he started the search. "The artist's height or favorite foods, maybe?"

"No, neither," Thrawn admitted. If he'd noticed Thrass's little joke, he didn't show it. "But I believe a personal or family tragedy may have occurred between the creation of these two." He pointed to two of the landscapes, one showing a churning ocean tidepool, the other with a snowcapped mountain jutting into the sky. "Actually, the tragedy may predate all of the pieces except the one with the tidepool. I also have the sense that the artist was a woman, but that's just an impression, not a solid conclusion."

"Why that impression?" Thrass asked, peering at his questis. There was the listing. Now to sort through and tag the five pieces Thrawn had specified.

"It's something about the line and edging," Thrawn said. "But as I say, I don't claim that's necessarily accurate."

"I understand," Thrass said, suppressing a smile. Though of course an assertion like that *did* give him a fifty-fifty chance.

His hidden smile became a hidden grimace. Earlier, he'd told himself he would never get cynical about meeting newcomers to the family. Was he breaking that promise already? The listing came up . . .

He stared at the questis. No. It wasn't possible.

"Is there trouble?" Thrawn asked.

Thrass threw a hooded look at him. No—there was no way the cadet could have simply looked at the works and come to those conclusions. He must have dug into the archives himself in advance.

Except that there were hundreds of thousands of Mitth family artworks, and they were rotated frequently among the various family holdings and official offices. The odds that these particular ones would be on display in this particular reception room at this particular time were practically nonexistent.

He took a careful breath. "You're right," he said, forcing his voice to stay calm. A Mitth cousin had no business reacting in even moderate awe to a freshly chosen merit adoptive. "All five were created by the legendary Twelfth Patriarch, Mitth'omo'rossodo, sometimes called the Tragic. All four of her sons died in battle—" He pulled up her bio and did a quick comparison of the dates. "—three months after the tidepool piece."

"All four," Thrawn murmured, looking again at the landscape. "A terrible loss indeed."

"According to the archives, she was determined not to let it influence her rule," Thrass continued. "But that mountain landscape was the last piece she ever did. Or at least, the last surviving one."

"I can understand that," Thrawn said. "An artist of such skill and self-awareness might well have seen how the scars of memory had affected her inspiration and resolved to put her artwork aside until she could regain her former tranquility."

Thrass winced. "Only she never did," he murmured.

"No," Thrawn said softly. "Some losses run too deep to ever fully heal."

Thrass studied his face, noting the fresh tension lines in his cheeks and throat. "You sound like you've had experience."

Thrawn shrugged slightly. "No more than many others in the Ascendancy have suffered," he said, the tension lines smoothing out.

Though it took a conscious effort, Thrass saw. Whatever pain was lurking behind those eyes, it wasn't going away anytime soon.

But that sort of ache wasn't for public display. It certainly wasn't for a new acquaintance to casually poke at. If life had taught Thrass anything, it was to respect others' privacy. "I'm sorry to hear that," he said, gesturing toward the door. "Perhaps a discussion for another day. Let me show you to your room. Dinner's in three hours, and you may want to practice your part of the ceremony."

The rematching dinner was, as always, a grand and—in Thrass's private opinion—slightly overpompous ceremony. Still, it was traditional, and the guests and attending dignitaries alike all seemed suitably impressed and happy.

Thrawn possibly being the one exception. He was seated on the other side of the long table and several people down, and Thrass couldn't hear any of what he was saying. He seemed to be holding his own, fielding questions put to him by his neighbors, and those conversational partners all seemed satisfied with his answers. At least none of them rolled their eyes or turned away from the young man in revulsion.

But Thrawn also never seemed to initiate any conversations on his own. Mostly he sat and ate in silence, watching and listening to everything going on around him. Once, Thrass caught him looking at the row of tapestries lining the grand banquet hall, his eyes moving slowly from one to another.

The welcoming ceremony also went well. Thrawn held his own there, too, speaking his lines correctly and with the proper solemnity. But to Thrass's eye he still seemed uncomfortable.

Perhaps not surprisingly. Thrawn was by far the youngest of tonight's thirty rematches, and in his simple cadet's uniform he looked rather out of place beside the junior commander and mid captain who were also being welcomed into the family.

The ceremony had been over for half an hour and the open conversation time well under way before Thrass was finally able to catch up to the younger man. "Though you've now heard this at least a dozen times, welcome to the Mitth," he said in greeting. "May I offer a drink of family kinship?"

"Thank you," Thrawn said. "I have to say, this isn't like anything I've ever experienced."

"I'm not surprised," Thrass said, steering them toward the nearest drink station. "The Mitth are famous for our ceremonies. How long are you staying on Avidich?"

"Just the one night," Thrawn said. "I was given special dispensation to come here, and I can't afford to be away any longer than necessary."

"Sounds rather petty to me," Thrass said with a sniff, snagging two of the drinks and handing one to Thrawn. "Coming all the way here only to turn around and hurry back. What would extending your leave an extra day really cost? Two downmarks? Three? We could probably even get them canceled."

"I appreciate the offer," Thrawn said. "But since I'm already working off fifty, I don't think—"

"*Fifty?*" Thrass felt his eyes widen. "What in the world did you do?"

"I was caught where I wasn't supposed to be during the voyage from Rentor," Thrawn said, a little ruefully. "I'm not even sure why I'm here tonight. Surely my rematching ceremony could have waited another few weeks."

"On that one, at least, I can enlighten you," Thrass said, feeling rather proud of himself for having figured it out during dinner. "See that woman over there wearing the violet outerwrap robe with the pale-blue trim? That's the Irizi Patriel for Avidich. The local Patriels are always invited to these ceremonies, though usually they're too busy to attend. But the Irizi generally at least send a representative."

"Interesting," Thrawn said, as he sipped at his drink. "I was told the Mitth and Irizi were rivals."

"That's rather like saying Csilla is cold," Thrass said drily. "No, their attendance is less courtesy and more wanting to keep tabs on what we're up to. At any rate, one of their big goals in life is to get as many of their people into the Defense Force and General Ba'kif's new Expansionary Defense Fleet as they can, and our Patriarch decided he'd rather have three military rematches to unveil than two. A quick word to Colonel Wevary, a one-day travel pass, and here you are."

"I see," Thrawn said, the frown on his face suggesting that he didn't see at all.

"But that's politics," Thrass continued. "I'm just sorry you can't stay longer. The Patriel's art collection is hardly to the standard of the Csilla homestead, but it's excellent in its own right. I'd hoped to give you the grand tour and see what other details you could glean from the pieces."

"I—that would be most enjoyable," Thrawn said, an odd hesitation in his tone.

"It wasn't a demand," Thrass assured him. "Only if you'd like to."

"Oh, I would," Thrawn said. "It's simply . . . you're blood, are you not?"

"I'm a cousin," Thrass corrected. The first few times he'd made that assertion, he remembered distantly, he'd felt a certain level of guilt. Now it didn't bother him at all.

Though it was clearly bothering Thrawn. Not a surprise, really, given the cadet's current low ranking and how seriously newcomers to the family took the unspoken rules regarding proper etiquette. "But a difference in our status doesn't mean we can't talk or look at artwork together," he added.

"I understand," Thrawn said. Again, Thrass sensed that he really didn't. "Someday, perhaps, you can give me that tour. But for now, I really should retire for the night. My flight leaves early."

"Of course," Thrass said. "Sleep well, Cadet Thrawn, and safe travels. I trust we'll meet again."

"I hope so, Aristocra Thrass." Thrawn's lip twitched in a

rather self-conscious smile. "For the next two years, at least, you'll know exactly where to find me."

"I don't get to Naporar very often," Thrass said. "But if I'm ever there, I'll be certain to look you up."

"Thank you," Thrawn said. "Good night."

"Good night."

For a minute Thrass watched as Thrawn made his way across the reception room floor, weaving past the conversational groups with a grace that contrasted starkly with his less nimble conversational and social skills. The man was definitely an odd doklet.

But at least he was an *interesting* odd doklet. So few odd doklets were. It might be worth a few minutes every now and again to pull up the cadet's Taharim records and see how he was doing.

In the meantime, there were other people here that a Mitth cousin ought to at least say hello to. Starting, unfortunately, with that haughty Irizi Patriel over there. Picking up another drink for fortification, he headed through the crowd.

And as he did so, he found himself looking at the tapestries and paintings adorning the room. Wondering what exactly Thrawn had seen in them.

CHAPTER TWO

A week ago, Mitth'urf'ianico mused, when he'd been merely Syndic Prime Thurfian, he'd been accustomed to rising every morning at six. Now, as Patriarch Thurfian, the most powerful person in the Mitth family, his workday was beginning a full two hours earlier.

"It will get easier, Your Venerante," Senior Aide Mitth'iv'iklo assured him as he sent yet another stack of files to Thurfian's questis. "I remember Patriarch Thooraki getting up every day at four o'clock when he first became head of the family. But after a couple of years he was able to sleep in until five-thirty."

"Really," Thurfian said, eyeing him. Thivik had been with the Patriarch's Office a long time, but he didn't look *that* old. "I didn't know you were with him that early in his administration."

"Oh, I wasn't with the Patriarch directly," Thivik said. "I was merely an aide to one of his officials. But we all talked together."

"Of course," Thurfian said, briefly wondering what the officials, aides, and assistants were saying about their newest superior.

Nothing very complimentary, he suspected. Patriarch Thooraki had been a strong and effective leader, well liked by his staff and most of the senior Mitth officials. He'd cast a long, wide shadow across both the family and the Ascendancy, and it would be a long time before Thurfian or anyone else would even come close to filling that shadow.

Maybe that was one reason why the Speaker and Patriels had all turned down the position and instead nominated Thurfian for it. He could only hope it wasn't their *only* reason.

"Your nine o'clock appointment has also arrived," Thivik continued. "He's waiting in the main anteroom."

"Thank you," Thurfian said, frowning at him. The words had been perfectly proper, but there'd been just a hint of a disapproving tone beneath them. "Is there a problem?"

"Of course not, Your Venerante," Thivik assured him. "You're the Patriarch. You may meet with whomever you wish."

"Only why am I meeting with an Irizi syndic?" Thurfian prompted.

Thivik hesitated. "You may meet with whomever you wish," he repeated, this time with clear reluctance. "It merely seems to me that you send a strange message by seeing one of our adversaries before you've even met with all of our own Patriels and Councilors."

"An interesting point," Thurfian agreed. "Did it occur to you that I might *want* to send a strange message? That I might want to signal to the Irizi and the Ascendancy in general that we may be entering a new era of cooperation between families?"

"Your Venerante, that's—" Thivik broke off, his throat working as he seemed to search for words. "Our rivalry with the Irizi extends far into the past, on both sides."

"Perhaps it's time we revisited that rivalry," Thurfian said.

"Your Venerante—"

"Which isn't to say that I'm going to be handing over the keys to the homestead," Thurfian continued. "I intend to make it clear that if we're to reconcile with the Irizi, it will be on *our* terms, not theirs."

"I see," Thivik said, his earlier composure starting to creep back into place. "Yes. I . . . naturally, you're the one who makes such decisions."

"Yes, I am," Thurfian said softly. "Please show Syndic Irizi'stal-'mustro in."

"Yes, Your Venerante." Bowing, Thivik turned and hurried from the office, his posture somehow conveying relief, subservience, and a hint of lingering concern.

It was a lot to pack into such a compact package, Thurfian noted as the senior aide closed the door behind him: surface obedience with underlying disapproval. Briefly, he wondered how long it had taken Thivik to master that particular combination.

He was sifting through the second of Thivik's new set of files when the door opened again and Thivik silently ushered Syndic Zistalmu into the office.

"Ah—Syndic Zistalmu," Thurfian greeted him, motioning him forward toward the guest chair at the corner of the desk. "Thank you for coming. Please, sit down."

"Thank you, Patriarch Thurfian," Zistalmu said, his tone and expression cautious as he crossed to the chair and eased himself into it. "May I begin by congratulating you on your new position as head of the Mitth family. Your Patriels have shown great wisdom and foresight in choosing Patriarch Thooraki's successor."

"Thank you," Thurfian said, inclining his head and looking past Zistalmu at Thivik, still standing by the open door. "That will be all, Senior Aide."

"Yes, Your Venerante," Thivik said. Bowing again, he backed out of the room, once again closing the door behind him.

Thurfian looked back at Zistalmu. "What you mean, I presume," he suggested with a wry smile, "is, *How in the Ascendancy did the Patriels accidentally trip over you on their way to choosing a real Patriarch?*"

"I wouldn't put it in *exactly* those terms," Zistalmu said, some of the tension leaving his face. "I *did* mean the congratulations part, though."

"Thank you," Thurfian said. Technically, of course, Zistalmu should be addressing him as *Your Venerante* now that he was a Patriarch. But given their history together, Thurfian was willing to let it slide. "And you are now . . . ?"

Zistalmu gave a small shrug. "Syndic Prime," he said.

"I thought so," Thurfian said. "The dynamics I was seeing at the last full Syndicure assembly . . . but that's neither here nor there. Congratulations in turn."

"Thank you," Zistalmu said. "I presume you invited me here to tell me that our plan to bring down Thrawn has ended?"

"On the contrary," Thurfian said grimly. "I called you here to see if you knew what in blazes went down two weeks ago among the Xodlak, Pommrio, and Erighal families out at that useless planet."

"Hoxim," Zistalmu supplied the name. "At least, that's what Councilor Lakuviv called it at his interrogation. All we know is that there was supposedly a rich nyix mine there and that he sent Xodlak family ships to go seize it. All for the greater good of the Ascendancy, of course. I'm told he repeated that defense at least four times."

"Of course."

"What happened after they arrived there is . . . let's just say it's muddled."

"But we know that Thrawn was somehow involved."

"Isn't he always?" Zistalmu asked sourly. "We also know that the mine was obliterated, apparently having been landed on by a crashing freighter."

"Convenient," Thurfian muttered.

"Very," Zistalmu agreed. "I presume Thrawn isn't talking?"

"Not to anyone we have connections with," Thurfian said. "And that includes Supreme General Ba'kif's office."

"Ditto for us," Zistalmu said. "I take it you hadn't heard any of the details?"

Thurfian shook his head. "None of our allies was involved, and everyone's being very quiet."

"Yes, you'd think they all had something to hide," Zistalmu said. "I'd hoped we might be able to pry some more information from Senior Captain Ziinda, but she's been as closemouthed as everyone else."

"Ziinda?"

"Senior Captain Irizi'in'daro," Zistalmu said. "Formerly Xodlak-'in'daro. Her rematching to the Irizi was formalized three days ago."

"Ah," Thurfian said, nodding. He remembered reading that a Senior Captain Lakinda had been in command of the Xodlak force at

Hoxim, but hadn't realized the Irizi had snatched her away from that family. "You have an interesting approach to intel gathering."

"Thank you," Zistalmu said. "Freshly minted member of one of the Nine, a very family-oriented woman, proud and exhilarated and anxious to please. It was worth a shot."

"But didn't work?"

"As I said, closemouthed." Zistalmu shrugged again. "Still, even without that she's an excellent officer. Well worth taking into the family."

"So her record would indicate," Thurfian agreed. Though taking someone from one of your allies, he knew, could sometimes be tricky. If the Xodlak Patriarch decided he was insulted by Ziinda's rematching, it could cool relations between them and the Irizi.

On the other hand, given the undefined but clearly unpleasant aftermath the Xodlak currently found themselves in, he doubted that complaints about losing even a senior Expansionary Defense Fleet officer would be high on the Xodlak priority list.

"So mostly all I know is the official story," Zistalmu continued. "Three of the Forty sent family ships out to this Hoxim system and ended up fighting a group of alien gunboats that had somehow caught the *Springhawk* in an ambush."

"Plus the fact that a nyix mine was involved."

"That part, I think, everyone knows," Zistalmu said sourly. "It's about the only excuse for their behavior that all three families can point to."

"For whatever it's worth," Thurfian said. "You believe that bit about an ambush?"

Zistalmu snorted. "Of course not. Thrawn caught in a trap? Not a chance."

"So in other words, Thrawn has again skated to the edge and managed to hold his balance," Thurfian said. "Only this time, it wasn't just military targets that were involved. This time, he dragged in the Forty, with every bit of the messiness you'd expect. *And* for once came out of it with nothing to show."

"Maybe, maybe not," Zistalmu said darkly. "There are rumors that the *Springhawk* stopped by Sposia on its way to Csilla."

Thurfian felt his eyes narrow. "The UAG?"

"So says the rumor," Zistalmu said. "Whether or not it's true . . ." He shrugged again.

Thurfian scowled down at his questis. The Universal Analysis Group on Sposia was the clearinghouse where all alien artifacts and technology collected by the Ascendancy were taken to be studied. Most of the historical pieces eventually went to museums or art collections, while most of the technological items proved too damaged or fragmentary to be of any use and were either cataloged into storage chambers or simply destroyed.

But every so often a piece of technology was found that was complete enough to be studied. Those rare items were taken to a special underground complex where teams of scientists and techs worked painstakingly to coax out their secrets.

And occasionally—*very* occasionally—one of those was deemed of military value and moved to Vault Four.

The gravity-well generator Thrawn had stolen from the Vaagari pirates was somewhere in that work complex. So was the immensely powerful Republic shield generator he'd taken from the Separatist base at the edge of Lesser Space and used against General Yiv.

So, once, had been the device called Starflash.

"I keep having this disturbing image," Zistalmu continued. "An entire UAG wing dedicated solely to Thrawn's findings."

"I wouldn't doubt it," Thurfian said. "You'll recall we've speculated once or twice that someone high in either the Syndicure or the Defense Hierarchy Council has been protecting Thrawn from the repercussions of his political blunders. Maybe that artifact wing is the reason."

"I don't know," Zistalmu said doubtfully. "The UAG is mostly the province of the Stybla family, and they don't have anywhere near enough pull with either the Syndicure *or* the Council. If I had to guess, I'd say it was Patriarch Thooraki who was Thrawn's primary defender."

"Perhaps," Thurfian murmured.

"In which case, you may now have the power to finally get rid of him." Zistalmu tilted his head slightly. "*If* you still want to."

"If I hadn't already been convinced that was necessary, the fiasco at Hoxim would have done it," Thurfian said heavily. "The question is still *how.*"

"Yes," Zistalmu said, nodding. "Good."

Thurfian frowned. "What do you mean, *good*?"

"I mean," Zistalmu said, "from your new position the solution to the Thrawn problem is obvious. You simply petition the Defense Hierarchy Council to promote Thrawn to commodore—"

"And put him in a position where he can cause even more damage?" Thurfian cut in. "Are you serious?"

"—thereby removing him from the Mitth," Zistalmu continued calmly, "and guaranteeing the family name won't be tarnished when he finally falls from grace."

"I hardly think I would find solace in Mitth family honor remaining intact if the Ascendancy itself had fallen," Thurfian said stiffly.

"I agree," Zistalmu said. "I just wasn't sure you did. As I said: Good."

For a long moment the two men locked eyes. Then Thurfian took a deep breath. "So you trust me now?"

Zistalmu shrugged. "More than I did when I walked in here today. So. We take him down?"

"Yes," Thurfian said. "I don't know how yet, but we do."

"Well, we can start by figuring out what happened at Hoxim," Zistalmu said, standing up. "I'll get back to the Syndicure and start digging. I assume you still have a lot of pomp and ceremony to go through?"

"More than I like, yes," Thurfian conceded. "But as soon as all of that is over, I'll start looking at what options I have as Patriarch."

"All right." Zistalmu smiled slightly. "I suppose we won't be meeting anymore in the March of Silence."

"What we give up in secrecy and convenience, we make up in comfort," Thurfian said, giving him a same-sized smile in return.

"The food is better, too, if and when we have enough time to sample it. Let me know when you have something, and we'll set up another meeting."

"I will," Zistalmu said. "And once again, congratulations."

Thurfian gazed at the door a moment after he left, sifting through the bits of data Zistalmu had given him, then turned back to his questis.

He was in the middle of Thivik's third file when the senior aide returned. "Has he gone?" Thurfian asked.

Thivik nodded. "He and his escort are on their way back to Csaplar," he said. "I must also soon head in that direction."

"Your trip to Naporar?"

"Yes, Your Venerante," Thivik said. "Your credentials must be officially presented to the Expansionary Defense Fleet."

"Understood," Thurfian said. Thivik had already made a similar trip to the Defense Force. But their headquarters were only a couple of thousand kilometers away, outside the capital, an easy trip by tube car. Traveling to the Expansionary Defense Fleet headquarters, in contrast, required a family spaceship and a couple of days for the round trip.

But it could be worse. A hundred years ago, the new Patriarch had been required to present all those credentials in person. Five hundred years before that, a grand tour of all the Ascendancy's worlds and meetings with all the Mitth Patriels had also been required.

The Patriels now had to do all that traveling on their own. But the military still wanted at least a senior aide to make the journey to them.

Maybe in another hundred years, the traditions would bend enough to allow all of it to be done via comm.

"Before you leave, check and see if there are any documents that need to be taken to Naporar," he instructed Thivik. "If so, you can save some courier a trip."

"I'll do so, Your Venerante," Thivik said. "I'll be back as quickly as I can. In the meantime, do spend some time with the new files I sent you. There are a great many subtleties involved with your new position."

"I'm sure there are," Thurfian said. "I'll do my best to master them as quickly as possible."

"I know you will," Thivik said, bowing again. "Good day, Your Venerante."

He left the office, and with a tired sigh Thurfian turned again to his questis and the stack of files.

Besides, even if he tried to push the Expansionary Defense Fleet into promoting Thrawn, they probably wouldn't do it.

CHAPTER THREE

It took Ba'kif three days to finish interviewing the captains of the three groups of family warships that had been at Hoxim. He saved the *Springhawk* for last, partly because the ship was still being examined for damage and he wanted both Thrawn and Samakro on hand at the bluedock to oversee the work, partly because he expected Samakro to finally offer him information he wasn't getting from anyone else.

On that latter, at least, he was disappointed. It was clear that Samakro held crucial facts about the *Springhawk* and its participation that none of the family ship officers was aware of. It was equally clear that the *Springhawk*'s first officer wasn't going to divulge those details without more pressure than Ba'kif was prepared to bring. It was also unfortunately clear that asking Thrawn those same questions would be a waste of time.

Which didn't mean that Ba'kif wouldn't eventually get the whole story. *That* much he could promise himself. But right now, with the Syndicure buzzing like stingflies whose nest had been kicked, discretion was the better option.

And so he contented himself with finishing his interviews, writing and filing his reports, and otherwise making the military side of the Hoxim issue as quiet and straightforward as possible. It was only when that was finished that he requisitioned a shuttle to Bluedock One, where the *Springhawk* was currently housed, to finally find out what Thrawn had wanted to tell him back at Sposia.

It was quickly clear why Samakro hadn't been looking forward to the conversation.

"What in the depths of the Chaos were you *thinking?*" Ba'kif demanded as he stared in disbelief at the alien figure lying motionless inside the hibernation chamber. Not just in hibernation, but in hibernation in Caregiver Thalias's sleeping room in the sky-walker suite, supposedly one of the most secure places aboard the *Springhawk*.

"It was a humanitarian gesture toward the Magys's people—" Thrawn began.

"I don't want to hear any excuses," Ba'kif cut him off.

"She was the cause of a death aboard the *Springhawk*—" Samakro offered.

"I don't want to hear you quote protocols, either," Ba'kif snarled.

For a long moment no one spoke. Ba'kif glared at Samakro, standing stiffly beside his commander, feeling a small pang of guilt at his outburst. From Samakro's expression it was clear that he didn't approve of Thrawn's actions in keeping the alien aboard any more than Ba'kif did. And given Thrawn's past record on such things, Ba'kif was pretty sure Samakro hadn't been consulted about this decision before it was made.

None of which altered the fact that he, Supreme General Ba'kif, was now sitting beside the two of them on the hot seat. Just the fact that the alien was here—in a close-orbit space dock, with workers roaming the compartments and passageways—was enough to trigger alarm bells in the back of Ba'kif's brain. An accidental glimpse, a thoughtless word, and the cascade of repercussions would be felt all the way to the top of the Syndicure.

What in blazes was Ba'kif supposed to do?

He took a careful breath, forcing away the simmering anger and dismay. The problem was obvious. Time to find a solution. "First things first," he said. "Who else knows about this?"

"Caregiver Thalias, of course," Thrawn said. If he was concerned about the political ramifications they were all facing, he wasn't show-ing it. "And Senior Captain Lakinda of the *Grayshrike*. No one else."

"You mean Senior Captain *Ziinda*," Ba'kif growled. "She's been rematched to the Irizi."

"Really," Thrawn said, a flicker of surprise crossing his face. "I hadn't heard."

Ba'kif looked at Samakro. *He'd* heard, Ba'kif saw, and from the other's expression it was clear Thrawn's first officer had been work-ing through the possible implications of Ziinda now belonging to the Mitth family's most implacable rival.

He was worried, and rightfully so. With a secret like this hovering over them like an unstable breacher missile, they could only hope Ziinda's loyalty to the Expansionary Defense Fleet surpassed what-ever loyalty she felt for her new family.

But there was nothing any of them could do about it. Again, time to find a solution. "All right," he said. "So you think the Magys's planet, this *Sunrise*, is the key to all that's happened to the Ascen-dancy over the past year or so?"

"Perhaps not *everything* that's happened," Thrawn hedged. "But certainly Sunrise and its resources were involved in the Agbui at-tempt to precipitate a civil war within the Ascendancy."

"Yes," Ba'kif murmured, suppressing a wince. *Civil war.* He still had only pieces of the Hoxim story, but the fact that three members of the Forty had simultaneously invoked family emergency protocols carried ominous overtones. It might be that Thrawn was overstating the case; it might equally well be that the Ascendancy had narrowly escaped the kind of heightened internecine rivalry that in the past had sometimes led to armed conflict.

Unfortunately, serious though that was, it wasn't as serious as Ba'kif might have hoped. He needed a case strong enough to stand against the Syndicure, which meant being able to tie Sunrise and the sleeping Magys to not only the Agbui but also General Yiv, the Paa-taatus, and maybe even the Vagaari pirates.

Because once the Syndicure was on board, the rest would be easy. A set of connections that strong would give the Council sufficient justification to authorize a mission to Sunrise. Not just a quiet intelligence-gathering probe like the one he'd sent Admiral Ar'alani and the *Vigilant* on, but a full-fledged military strike on whoever was parking Battle Dreadnoughts over the planet and taking potshots at every Ascendancy warship that happened by.

But it didn't sound like Thrawn could make that case. And without it, there was little chance the Council would risk leaning over their legal limits any farther than they had already. In fact, if the Syndicure hadn't been distracted by this whole Hoxim fiasco, they might well have already come down hard on Ba'kif and Supreme Admiral Ja'fosk for Ar'alani's quiet mission.

And that grace period wouldn't last forever. For now, the Nine Ruling Families were exerting quiet pressure on their wayward allies in the Forty Great Families, working to resolve the conflicts and bury the messes that Hoxim had created. Whatever Ba'kif decided to do, he had a limited window of opportunity before someone noticed and started screaming about it.

"All right," he said. "We all agree you need to get her back to her people. That much is unarguable. The question is whether you take the *Springhawk* to Rapacc or whether I dig up a scout ship that's not being used and put you and the Magys aboard."

"Either would work," Thrawn said. "In the latter case, would I also be allowed to take Sky-walker Che'ri?"

"Absolutely not," Ba'kif growled. Thrawn had gotten away once with taking the girl off on an adventure, but both the Council and the Syndicure had been furious about that and neither body was likely to let him skate on it a second time. "You'd have to go jump-by-jump. Granted it would take longer, but I think I could get the Council to allow you a leave of absence."

Beside Thrawn, Samakro stirred. "With all respect, sir, I don't think a scout ship would be a good idea," he said. "The enemy we faced over Sunrise could have traced the Magys's refugees back to Rapacc by now. I don't think the Paccosh are ready to deal with them, and a scout ship certainly won't be."

"You're recommending he take the *Springhawk*, then?"

"I don't think it works any other way, sir," Samakro said.

"No matter what the repercussions?" Ba'kif pressed. "And not just those that rain down on Senior Captain Thrawn?"

Samakro's lip twitched, but his nod was firm. "Whatever the repercussions, sir, I'm prepared to accept my share of them."

On one level, Ba'kif knew, a casual acceptance of as-yet-undefined penalties was dangerously brash. On another level, it was exactly what he'd expected from an officer like Samakro. "Unfortunately, I have to agree with your assessment," he said. "Very well. Senior Captain Thrawn, you and the *Springhawk* are hereby authorized to return the Magys to her people on Rapacc. *But.*" He let the word hang in the air a moment. "You will then immediately return to Naporar for further consultation and orders. *Immediately.*"

"I *had* promised to return her and her people to Sunrise," Thrawn pointed out.

"That's a promise you'll have to break," Ba'kif said bluntly. "I need you back as quickly as possible, before the Syndicure notices the *Springhawk* is gone and starts wondering loudly about it. That means no additional side trips."

"Sir—"

"You did the Paccosh a favor by taking her to check out the condition of her world," Ba'kif interrupted. "It's their turn to do one for us."

Thrawn and Samakro exchanged looks, and it wasn't hard to read their thoughts. The alien Battle Dreadnought the *Springhawk* had encountered had pushed even a pair of Chiss warships to the limit. Unless the Paccosh were a far more aggressive species than had yet been demonstrated, they wouldn't have a chance against an enemy like that.

But they knew an order when they heard it, and both were familiar enough with Ba'kif to recognize that the time for discussion and bargaining was past. "Yes, sir," Thrawn said. "The *Springhawk*'s resupply is nearly complete, and the last of the on-leave officers and warriors are due back in three hours. We'll leave as soon as they're aboard."

"Good," Ba'kif said. "Just get there and back as quickly as you can."

"Understood, sir," Thrawn said. "I'll escort you back to your shuttle, then begin preparations for departure."

"Mid Captain Samakro can see me to the shuttle," Ba'kif said. "I'd prefer you get started immediately on departure prep."

A hint of a frown flickered across Thrawn's face. But he merely nodded. "As you wish, Supreme General. Don't worry, the *Springhawk* will be back before anyone misses it." He straightened briefly and nodded, then strode from the sleeping room.

"At your convenience, Supreme General," Samakro said, gesturing toward the hatch.

"In a moment, Mid Captain," Ba'kif said. "I have a question for you first. Aside from Senior Captain Thrawn, can you find out how many Mitth are aboard the *Springhawk*?"

"Five, sir," Samakro said. "One junior officer, three warriors, and our sky-walker's caregiver."

Ba'kif frowned. He'd expected Samakro to have to look up that information. "An odd fact to keep at your fingertips, Mid Captain."

"Not really, sir," Samakro said. "I've long had the sense that the Mitth Patriarch was working in the background to smooth Senior Captain Thrawn's path through the political brambles he so often gets tangled in. Now that Patriarch Thooraki has been replaced by Patriarch Thurfian . . ." He left the sentence unfinished.

"An interesting conjecture," Ba'kif said. "The questionable aspect being the implication that a Mitth Patriarch might stand against a respected naval officer of his own family."

"Perhaps, sir," Samakro said. "Questionable or not, though, I've been at enough Syndicure hearings to know how the Aristocra behave in public. The one time I was called in front of Syndic Thurfian, it was pretty clear he didn't like Thrawn very much."

"I see," Ba'kif said. Personally, he would have put it a lot more strongly. "But Thurfian is Patriarch now. His attitude and vision for his family may have changed."

"Maybe," Samakro said. "But he also now has the ability to give direct orders to each and every Mitth family member."

"Yes, he does," Ba'kif murmured. "Unlikely he would do anything blatant, of course. Certainly not aboard an Expansionary Defense Fleet warship."

"I agree, sir," Samakro said. "But it never hurts to be prudent."

"Indeed," Ba'kif said. "And now, Mid Captain, I believe my shuttle is waiting."

"Yes, sir," Samakro said. "At your convenience, Supreme General."

"That one?" Thalias asked, pointing at the festive red-and-blue wrap-around dress hanging on the rack. "You're sure?"

Che'ri's face screwed up in indecision, her eyes darting to the other three dresses hanging beside it. She'd tried on all four, and she clearly wanted all of them.

But even ten-year-olds had to learn that life was limited and decisions had to be made.

"Che'ri?" Thalias prompted.

The girl's expression cleared, and she nodded. "Yes."

"You're *absolutely* sure?" Thalias pressed again, smiling to herself. As the *Springhawk*'s only two civilians, she and Che'ri were supposedly allowed to wear whatever clothing they liked on duty. If Che'ri had set out to deliberately test that freedom, it was hard to imagine that she could have found a better way to do it.

Which was a pretty big leap all by itself. Up to now, Che'ri hadn't shown much interest in clothing style, mostly dressing in functional slacks and shirts in the muted color palette that better fit in with the black uniforms worn by the *Springhawk*'s officers and warriors.

But now, suddenly, the girl had caught the fashion bug with a vengeance. Thalias had a fairly unlimited budget with which to buy Che'ri toys and art supplies, and in the past the girl had taken full advantage of that largesse. But while such things could be crammed into drawers and under-seat storage, there was only a limited amount of space for clothing in her sleeping room's closet.

Plus, of course, the whole life lessons thing.

Thalias's internal smile saddened a little. Che'ri's awakened interest in her appearance was a sign of growing up . . . and for a sky-walker, growing up meant that the end of her Third Sight now loomed on the horizon. Another three to five years, and she would lose the ability to navigate ships through hyperspace. At that point, she'd leave the fleet and be rematched to one of the Nine Ruling Families.

Thalias could remember vividly her own fear and uncertainty at that life change. Fortunately, she'd had a chance encounter with a young Cadet Thrawn at the beginning of that time, and he'd given her words of comfort and encouragement that had helped her get through it.

She could only hope that when Che'ri's time came, she would be there to offer the girl similar support.

"Yes, absolutely sure," Che'ri said firmly. Nevertheless, she threw a last lingering look at the green-and-gray high-collar tunic she'd also tried on. "That's the one."

"Okay, great," Thalias said, indicating to the shopkeeper that they were finally finished.

And with money, closet space, and time now effectively used up, they needed to get moving. "We need to go straight back to the shuttle," she told Che'ri as she paid for the dress.

"But you said we could get ice cream," the girl protested.

"That was about two dress fittings ago," Thalias reminded her. She took another look at Che'ri's face—"All right, but at one of the kiosks, not a walk-in," she amended. "And you eat it on the way, and you *don't* spill any on yourself."

"Oh, please," Che'ri said, a look of mock reproof briefly interrupting her relieved smile. "I *do* know how to handle a spoon, you know."

"*Or* spill any of it on me," Thalias added as she took the bagged dress and prodded Che'ri toward the door. Excitement over a new dress; excitement over ice cream. Straddling that line between child and midager.

When, she wondered, did children begin growing up so quickly?

They were within sight of the *Springhawk* shuttle, and Che'ri was cleaning the last of the ice cream from the inside of her cup, when an elderly man waiting on a nearby bench stood up. "Mitth'ali'astov?" he called.

"I am she," Thalias said, slowing and frowning as he strode toward them. She'd never seen him before, but he was wearing the Mitth family crest on his jacket. Some local Naporar official?

"I am Mitth'iv'iklo," he introduced himself, giving her a small bow. "Senior aide to Patriarch Mitth'urf'ianico. May I have a word with you?"

"Yes, if you're quick," Thalias said, frowning a little harder. What would someone from the Patriarch's Office want with her?

And then, like a punch in the stomach, the name clicked. Patriarch Mitth'urf'ianico—*Thurfian*. Back when he was a Syndic, he'd pulled strings with an Expansionary Defense Fleet personnel officer to cut through the bureaucratic obstacles and get her assigned as Che'ri's caregiver aboard the *Springhawk*.

But the price of that favor had been her reluctant agreement to spy on Thrawn for him.

Now Thurfian was no longer just a Syndic, but the head of the entire Mitth family. Was he finally calling in that promise?

If so, she needed to get out of here, and fast. "I'm sorry, but we really have to go," she said, taking Che'ri's arm and pulling her toward the shuttle.

"This won't take long," Thivik assured her, changing direction to intercept their new path. With his longer legs, it took only four steps for him to catch up. "I have something I was asked to deliver to you."

"From Patriarch Thurfian?" Thalias asked. She desperately wanted to pick up her pace, to try to get away from him, even breaking into a full run if she had to.

But if she did that, she would leave Che'ri behind. There was no way she was going to do that.

"No, this is from the late Patriarch Thooraki," Thivik said, producing a data cylinder from his pocket. "He left this with me before his death with instructions to give it to you."

Thalias slowed to a stop, frowning at the cylinder in his hand. If this was some kind of trick . . . "Patriarch *Thooraki*, you said?"

"You and he had a short conversation when you were last at the homestead," Thivik said, as if Thalias would ever forget that unexpected meeting. "He told me afterward he was most impressed by you."

"I was very impressed by him, too," Thalias said, eyeing him closely.

"Thus, he decided you would be the best person to have this," Thivik said.

He stretched out his hand and the data cylinder toward her. Slowly, Thalias reached out and took it. "And it's from Patriarch Thooraki?" she asked again, just to make sure.

"To be specific, the files were gathered and compiled by the late Syndic Mitth'ras'safis," Thivik said. "He delivered the package to the Patriarch shortly before his death, where it has remained until now. One of the Patriarch's last instructions, as I said, was for me to privately deliver it to you at my earliest convenience."

The skin on the back of Thalias's neck tingled. *Privately?* "Did he say what I was supposed to do with it?"

"He said you would know when the time was right," Thivik said. "And now, I believe you're due to return to your ship. Good day." He smiled at Che'ri. "To you both."

Thalias watched as he walked away, the data cylinder feeling hard and cold and mysterious in her hand.

"Thalias?" Che'ri murmured anxiously at her side.

"It's all right," Thalias soothed her, belatedly noticing that she was still gripping the girl's arm. "It's all right," she repeated, letting go.

She waited until Thivik had disappeared into the stream of other pedestrians. Then, putting a gentle hand on Che'ri's shoulder, she turned and steered them toward the shuttle. "Come on," she said, trying to sound cheerful and unconcerned. "We don't want to be late."

"What did he give you?" Che'ri asked.

"Whatever's on this," Thalias said, showing her the data cylinder. "Right now, I don't know any more than you do."

"But we're going to find out, right?"

"*I'm* going to find out," Thalias corrected. "It might not be something you're allowed to see."

"If I can see it, you'll tell me, right?"

"We'll see."

"Does that mean yes?"

"It means we'll see," Thalias said firmly.

"Okay." Che'ri was silent another few steps. "Who is Syndic Thrass?"

"He was one of the top Mitth in the Syndicure," Thalias said. "He died a couple of years ago."

"What does he have to do with you?"

"I don't know," Thalias said, slipping the cylinder into a pocket.

But she was absolutely, positively going to find out.

MEMORIES II

Thrass had seen Patriarch Mitth'oor'akiord exactly three times in his life. The first two had been while visiting the homestead as a child, the third when he was a midager learning the protocols for transporting documents from Avidich to Csilla. All three sightings had been from a distance, but just the same Thrass felt honored to have even glimpsed the man who'd guided the Mitth for the past thirty years. Even the majority of family blood never got such an opportunity.

It was therefore a slightly unnerving surprise when a casual visit with his mother was abruptly interrupted by a summons to Thooraki's office.

The Patriarch was sitting behind his desk when Thrass arrived, talking with Senior Aide Mitth'iv'iklo. Thooraki looked up as Thrass was ushered in, gave a short nod in silent welcome, and returned to his conversation. Thrass took the cue and stayed where he was, standing at the door well out of earshot. Wondering whether he was here for some special honor, an assignment, or a particularly stinging reprimand.

Two years ago, while admiring Avidich artwork with Cadet Thrawn, Thrass had used the word *legendary* to describe the Twelfth Patriarch. In his opinion, Patriarch Thooraki had already exceeded even the Twelfth's record of accomplishments. His skillful diplomacy through the ever-shifting alliances among the Ruling Families had raised the Mitth from a relatively weak stance vis-à-vis the Irizi to full parity with their longtime rivals. Equally important, his work in building relationships within the Forty Great Families had further brought the Mitth out of the political stagnation they'd languished in as recently as a few decades ago.

If this was an assignment, Thrass would do his very best to accomplish it. If it was a reprimand, he would strive to face it with the proper humility, and to learn from it.

At the desk, the two men finished their conversation. "Thrass?" Thooraki called, beckoning.

"Yes, Your Venerante," Thrass said, hurrying forward. "How may I serve?"

"I'm told you know a Taharim cadet—actually, he'll have just graduated—a lieutenant in the Expansionary Defense Fleet named Mitth'raw'nuru. Is that correct?"

"I know him slightly, sir, yes," Thrass said. If it was a reprimand, this was an odd way to begin. "We met at his welcoming dinner, and since then I've kept tabs on his time at the academy."

"Your opinion of him?"

"He has great potential, Your Venerante," Thrass said, thinking quickly. His interest in Thrawn's progress had been fairly casual, and it had been several weeks since he'd looked at the Taharim records. Still, apart from that near fiasco with the training simulation, he couldn't remember hearing that Thrawn was having any problems. As to the simulation question, the fact that he'd not only gotten out from under the cloud but emerged looking better than before spoke volumes about his talents. "I think he'll be a fine officer."

"Good," Thooraki said. "All the more urgency to your assignment, then. I'm told that the Stybla family is hoping to steal him away from us. I want you to go to Naporar, reestablish your old contact with him, and make sure that doesn't happen."

"Yes, sir," Thrass said, a little uncertainly. The lack of a reprimand was reassuring; but *this* was the task he'd been brought into the Patriarch's Office to receive? To keep a single merit adoptive from being grabbed by another family? And particularly by the *Stybla*?

Certainly that family had some impressive history. Millennia ago, when the Chiss were first reaching outward to the stars, the Stybla had been *the* Ruling Family guiding everything and everyone. But as time passed and the Ascendancy grew from one world to many, the Stybla Patriarch had decided the task of governance had become too overwhelming for a single family to handle. His solution had been to step aside and appoint three other families to rule in the Stybla's place.

Thrass could appreciate the family's contributions to the Ascendancy. But their time had long since passed, and they had to be delusional to think they could offer Thrawn anything better than what he currently had with the Mitth.

But if Patriarch Thooraki was concerned about even such a minuscule chance of losing Thrawn to some smooth-talking Stybla, Thrass should take it equally seriously. "I'll leave at once, Your Venerante," he said. "Am I authorized to offer him any additional incentives?"

"Not at this time," Thooraki said. "But you might want to remind him that the friendship of the Mitth family is worth having."

Thrawn had estimated it would take him ten minutes to arrive at the bistro Thrass had specified. Just out of curiosity, Thrass set a timer; and exactly eight minutes after his call there was movement at the corner of his eye as someone pulled out one of the small table's three other chairs. "Hello, Thrawn," Thrass said, looking up.

The rest of the greeting froze in his throat. The middle-aged man sitting down beside him was a complete stranger. "Excuse me, but this table is taken," he said.

"My apologies for the intrusion," the stranger said calmly. "I thought it would save time if I joined you, given that we're both here to meet the same person. You're Aristocra Mitth'ras'safis, I presume?"

Thrass felt his eyes narrow. As a fairly low-level functionary in the Syndicure, his name and face were not exactly at the front edge of public knowledge. "I am he," he said cautiously. "And you?"

"Stybla'ppin'cykok," the other said. "Senior aide to Patriarch Stybla'mi'ovodo. Congratulations on finalizing that Tumaz shipping contract, by the way. And right out from under the Irizi, too. Whoever the Mitth principal was on that negotiation, she's quite skillful."

"I'm sure she is," Thrass murmured. Not only did this man know about the deal the Mitth had just worked out with the Tumaz family, but he apparently even knew that the head of the Mitth negotiating team was a woman. "You're very well informed."

Lappincyk shrugged. "The Stybla don't exactly dominate the list of the Forty," he said, as if that fact had somehow escaped Thrass's notice. "We have to compensate for our lack of influence and successes by keeping track of everyone else's."

"How the mighty have fallen," Thrass said under his breath.

"We prefer to think of it as how the mighty have graciously stepped down," Lappincyk said. "Speaking of Mitth successes, your Lieutenant Mitth'raw'nuru seems well on his way to becoming one of them."

"I agree," Thrass said. "The key word being *your*. Thrawn is a Mitth, and we have every intention of keeping him."

"A reasonable goal," Lappincyk said. "Though I would remind you that *intent* and *result* don't necessarily coincide. I imagine the Stybla could offer him more incentives than the Mitth have, at least thus far."

Thrass gave him a knowing smile even as his stomach knotted up. Now, when it was too late, he wished he'd pressed Patriarch Thooraki harder on the whole incentives question. With Thrawn currently at the very lowest Mitth rank, anything higher that was offered would be a strong inducement to be rematched. Even to a family like the Stybla. "Perhaps," he said, trying to sound casual. "Of course, he would have to assess the relative advantages of being a Mitth versus being a Stybla."

"Lieutenant Thrawn is intelligent enough to make that calculation," Lappincyk said, giving Thrass a knowing smile of his own. "Or will it soon be Lieutenant Larawn? The name has a nice ring to it, don't you think?"

A figure among the stream of pedestrians a block away caught Thrass's eye: Thrawn had rounded the corner and was striding toward them.

"So tell me, Aristocra Thrass," Lappincyk said, his smile fading. "What can you offer Thrawn that I can't?"

"Is that a question or a challenge?"

"Take it however you wish." Lappincyk nodded down the street. "But take it quickly. Once he sits down, he *will* hear my proposal."

Thrass looked at Thrawn, his mind racing. What *could* he offer? Higher status? He wasn't authorized to do that. Advancement in military rank? That was completely in the hands of the Defense Hierarchy Council. Money? Ridiculous.

There was nothing. Nothing except maybe . . .

"You see in him a shiny new piece the Stybla can add to

the political board," he said, looking back at Lappincyk. "But that's *all* you see."

"And you think the Mitth see more?"

"I don't know what the Mitth see," Thrass said. "All I know is what *I* see."

"Which is?"

Thrass took a deep breath. The young, socially awkward cadet fascinated by artwork. The unique ability to understand that artwork, while beneath the intellect was the quiet pain of a hidden loss. The newly commissioned officer who had already shown such a depth of tactical ability that he'd attracted allies like Junior Commander Ziara and General Ba'kif to his side.

What exactly *did* he see in Thrawn?

And then, Patriarch Thooraki's last admonition to him drifted up from his memory. Now he finally understood what the Patriarch had really been saying.

"What I see," he said, "is a friend. *My* friend."

For a long moment the two of them locked eyes. Then a small smile tweaked at Lappincyk's lips. "Really," he said. "Interesting."

There was a motion across the table. Thrass turned, slightly startled to see Thrawn sit down. Focused on Lappincyk and his own musings, he'd completely missed the other's final approach.

And it had indeed been exactly ten minutes.

"Hello, Thrawn," he greeted the other, reaching across the table for a quick formal grasp of forearms. "I'm glad you could make it."

"As am I," Thrawn said. "Thank you for working around my schedule." He looked at Lappincyk. "I don't believe we've met."

"No, we haven't," Lappincyk acknowledged. "I'm Stybla-'ppin'cykok, senior aide to Patriarch Stybla'mi'ovodo."

Thrass braced himself. This was it. Lappincyk would make his offer, and Thrass had nothing to counter it.

And then, to his surprise, Lappincyk pushed back his chair and stood up. "And I was just leaving," he added. "Enjoy your meal and your conversation." He looked at Thrass, and it seemed to him there was an odd sense of satisfaction in his nod. "Both of you."

"A friend of yours?" Thrawn asked as Lappincyk wove his way into the pedestrian flow.

"Actually, we just met," Thrass said, frowning at Lappincyk's back. What in the name of Csilla had just happened? Had the Stybla been playing him? Him *and* Patriarch Thooraki? If they had—

If they had, so what?

Really, so what? This depth of political game was far beyond Thrass's position or skill. The Patriarchs and Speakers and high-level Syndics could play if they wanted. Not Thrass. All he was here for was to have lunch.

With a friend.

"But never mind him," he continued, pulling up the bistro's menu and swiveling his questis around so that Thrawn could also see the listing. "Let's get our order in. After that, I want to hear more about this Junior Commander Ziara who single-handedly saved your career."

"It wasn't *quite* like that," Thrawn protested mildly.

"Then tell me how exactly it was," Thrass said. "Because when I tell the story later to prove to people why the Mitth are the finest of the Ruling Families, I want to get all the details right."

"What if the details don't support that slightly biased conclusion?"

"Oh, I'm sure they will," Thrass said with a smile. "Really, the only thing that will change about the story is how smug I let myself sound when I tell it."

CHAPTER FOUR

Patriarch Thurfian's childhood was far behind him, but he could still remember bits and pieces of it. One of the most vivid memories was of a stormy day when he and his three siblings had tired of other activities and started a spontaneous indoor game with rules that were mostly made up, and only when the need for one arose. Madcap running had quickly become part of it, the chase ranging through the entire house with noise and laughter and a fair amount of bumping into walls and furniture. Their mother's secretary had intervened twice, and the housekeeper and security guard once each. None of them had achieved any noticeable success.

Finally, their mother had paused the meeting she'd been moderating and taken a personal hand, corralling her rambunctious offspring and finally bringing the chaotic frenzy to a halt, or at least back down to a low simmer. One of the most striking parts of Thurfian's memory was the stressed look on her face as she herded them to the dining nook and ordered a snack that would hopefully keep them occupied long enough for her to finish her meeting.

Frenzied activity. Few if any rules. Children who didn't want to stop doing something just because someone said so. His mother's harried expression.

Now, as Patriarch all these years later, he finally knew exactly how she'd felt.

Especially right now.

"I appreciate you taking the time to talk with me, Your Venerante,"

Patriel Thistrian of Avidich said. "I know you must be extremely busy, what with settling into your new position and all."

"I'm always available for consultation with my Patriels," Thurfian said, suppressing a grimace. Thistrian had been the Mitth Speaker when Thurfian was first made an Aristocra and brought into the Syndicure, and while Thurfian had learned a lot from him he'd never forgotten how garrulous the old man could get when the mood struck him. Hopefully, today wouldn't be one of those days. "What's this *matter of possible importance* I'm told you wish to discuss?"

"I'm actually a bit unclear on that," Thistrian confessed. "I've just had a conversation with an alien who tells me there's some kind of new alliance brewing between the Dasklo, Xodlak, Erighal, and Pommrio. He included part of a vid—"

"Hold it," Thurfian interrupted. "What alien? When?"

"His name is Jixtus, and it was about an hour ago that we spoke," Thistrian said. "He's traveling with a group of aliens called the Kiljis—"

"Hold on," Thurfian said, punching up the latest Defense Force data feed. Hadn't there just been something about an alien warship showing up unannounced over Avidich?

Yes—there it was. "Are you talking about the battle cruiser that arrived two hours ago?"

"Yes, that's the one," Thistrian confirmed. "Not all that impressive, actually, as warships go. It would probably do well enough against pirates, but it would be no match for Avidich System Patrol. Actually, our family frigate and missile boats could probably take it. I had the frigate moved into combat position, but really there doesn't seem to be a need—"

"Is he still there?"

"Oh, yes," Thistrian said, as if that should be obvious. "But really, Your Venerante, you don't need to worry. Patrol Command says the missile tubes and lasers have all been peace-sealed, so there's really no danger. And as I said, the patrol ships and our frigate are in position."

"Very well," Thurfian said. The presence of an alien warship in

Chiss space, peace-sealed or not, was definitely cause for concern. But if Patrol Command said it was safe, it probably was. "So why exactly are you calling me?"

"I was getting to that," Thistrian said. "As I was saying, he showed me part of a vid that seems to show a group of Erighal and Xodlak ships play-attacking an armed freighter while a Dasklo ship looks on."

Thurfian frowned. The Erighal part he could understand—they were already longtime Dasklo allies. But the Xodlak? That was an odd combination. "For what purpose?"

"As I said, the Erighal and Xodlak seemed to be practicing an attack, with the Dasklo either supervising or just there to watch."

"Yes, I know you just said that," Thurfian said, his mother's stressed expression once again flashing to mind. "I meant what was Jixtus's reason for showing it to you?"

"I believe he wants to sell us additional information," Thistrian said. "The location of the incident, confirmation of the participants, perhaps more details on the purpose of the test. That sort of thing."

"Very helpful of him," Thurfian said. "Do you have a copy of that vid?"

"Yes, of course," Thistrian said. "Though the part he gave me is only about five seconds long. Here, I'll show it to you."

His image disappeared from the display, replaced by a group of five blurry ships set against a starry background. Three of the ships were trading low-level laser shots with a freighter-sized vessel, while the fifth ship floated a little way off. As Thistrian had said, the vid only lasted a few seconds. "And Jixtus says the attackers are Erighal and Xodlak ships?" he asked.

"Oh, no, Jixtus didn't say anything about their identities," Thistrian said, his image replacing the starscape. "I had my people run it through an enhancer, then spoke to my military advisers—"

"You have an *enhanced version?*" Thurfian demanded. "Why didn't you send that instead?"

"I assumed you'd first want to see the product Jixtus wants to sell us," Thistrian said, a little stiffly. "Here's our version."

Once again, his face was replaced by a vid. But where the ship images had previously been blurry, now they were sharp and clear. The three attackers were a cruiser and two patrol craft, the cruiser and one patrol ship bearing Xodlak insignia, the other patrol ship marked as Erighal. The freighter at the center of the exercise didn't seem to have any markings.

And the larger ship standing off the action—a frigate, Thistrian's experts identified it—did indeed carry the Dasklo family crest.

"So the Dasklo are watching some Erighal and Xodlak run a play battle," Thurfian said. "And this Jixtus wants us to *pay* him for this meager meal of information?"

"Your Venerante, I'm not sure you understand," Thistrian said. "If this is the prelude to the Dasklo adding the Xodlak and possibly the Pommrio to their list of allies, we could be facing a serious challenge."

"I suppose that's possible," Thurfian said. "I'll make some inquiries."

"He's also offering military assistance, should we desire it," Thistrian said. "He says he has other warships at his disposal that could reach the Ascendancy with just a few days' warning."

Thurfian felt his eyes narrow. Offering information was one thing. Offering one of the Nine a group of alien mercenaries was not just outrageous but could easily be construed as a deadly insult. Not to mention that even a casual reading of the Ascendancy's ancient history showed how destructive and ultimately futile foreign alliances could be. "I would strongly suggest he keep his warships out of Chiss space," he growled. "You can tell him that. You can also tell him that the Mitth are declining his offer, and that he had best be on his way."

"Your Venerante, if I may suggest—"

"Thank you for bringing this to my attention," Thurfian said, reaching for the comm control. "Farewell, Patriel." Before Thistrian could protest further, he cut the link.

For a moment he gazed at the blank screen, thinking it through. The offer of military aid he could dismiss without a second thought. But what about this supposed Dasklo-Xodlak alliance? Was such a thing even possible?

It seemed unlikely. The Xodlak were firmly in the Irizi orbit, unlikely to leave that comfortable position without a severe and visible push. As for the Dasklo, for the past thirty years their full attention had been on their private little power struggle against the Clarr. During that time they hadn't paid much attention to the rest of Syndicure politics, and Thurfian didn't expect that to change anytime soon.

And he should know. At Speaker Thyklo's request, he'd spent much of his final three months in the Syndicure running profiles and assessments of all Nine Ruling Families, watching in particular for signs of dissension, overt clashes, and possible upcoming realignments. He hadn't quite finished his analysis of the Forty Great Families when Patriarch Thooraki's death unexpectedly raised him into his new position, but he'd completed enough to conclude that the current political web was remarkably stable.

No. The Clarr might believe monster stories about the Dasklo, but the Mitth weren't going to fall for such nonsense. If the Ascendancy fell into crisis, it would be because individuals like Senior Captain Thrawn did something that pushed it over the edge.

Still, it wouldn't hurt to have the homestead techs take a look at the vid and see if any additional information could be teased out of it. He logged the order, then put the whole thing out of his mind. There were plenty of more urgent family issues to attend to.

And later, when he found himself in need of a break from Patriels, Councilors, and interfamily maneuverings, he would see if there was any news on where Thrawn and the *Springhawk* had apparently disappeared to.

Ar'alani finished reading through the report and looked up at Supreme General Ba'kif, waiting silently behind his desk. "Well, we were half right," she said.

"More than half, I'd say," Ba'kif said. "You'd tagged the station as a repair and refurbishing site. You just didn't know the kind of refurbishing work it was doing."

"And they're *sure* it's nyix hull work?" Ar'alani asked. "We looked at what the team collected on our way back, and I didn't see any nyix there."

"The analysts are sure," Ba'kif said. "Of course, they're basing much of that on the misfire burns in the decks, so they could be wrong."

"Not likely," Ar'alani conceded, looking at the relevant part of the report. "They're right—class six cutting torches *are* the tool of choice for working nyix alloy. I think we can take their word that the depth and width suggests that the plates or enhancements were relatively thin. So our friends with the Battle Dreadnought are upgrading their hull armor."

"Or else adding armor to a ship that normally doesn't have it," Ba'kif said. "A scout, perhaps, or a freighter or civilian transport."

"Hard to see what kind of advantage they think that'll give them," Ar'alani said. "A nyix-alloy hull is pretty obvious even before you get into full combat range, so it's not going to be a surprise to anyone. And something as thin as the analysts are talking about won't provide much protection."

"Perhaps the plan is to add to an existing hull," Ba'kif suggested. "Or they were armoring a freighter or transport and then adding another layer of standard hull metal on top of it as camouflage."

Ar'alani made a face. "Either way, it looks like that freighter-sized ship wasn't the mobile dock that we thought it was. The mounting nodes we spotted were for attaching new hull segments. And the analysts don't think that was the first job they'd done there?"

"That's what they conclude from the number and placement of the torch burns," Ba'kif said. "No way of knowing how many ships had already passed through, and it was obviously not yet working at full capacity. But it does indeed appear to have been up and running."

And alien freighters and other transports visited the Ascendancy all the time. "I presume we're going to make sure it's shut down permanently?"

"I've recommended that action to the Council," Ba'kif said. "Whether they and the Syndicure approve is another question." He shrugged slightly. "Though now that you've caught the Battle Dreadnought's friends in the middle of a job, I'm guessing the Council will assume they'll write it off."

"We can hope." Ar'alani shook her head. "So Yiv builds a station out in the middle of nowhere. Our mystery people let him do it, then wreck it, kill all the Nikardun there, and move in. I'm still not getting the *why* of it."

"Maybe the middle of nowhere is exactly where they wanted to be," Ba'kif pointed out. "I'll also point out that this particular patch of emptiness is conveniently positioned between Sunrise and the Ascendancy."

"Yes, we'd noticed that."

"Good." Ba'kif gestured to her. "Let's run through the time line, shall we?"

"Yes, sir." Ar'alani paused, collecting her thoughts. "General Yiv and the Nikardun move into this region, conquering small nations and threatening the Ascendancy. At roughly the same time, someone discovers that Sunrise has massive nyix deposits and starts a civil war there to give them free access to the ore."

"Two questions," Ba'kif said, lifting a finger. "First, do we *know* that an outsider started that war, as opposed to it being something homegrown? Second, has it been confirmed that Sunrise was the source of the nyix that the Agbui were waving under Councilor Lakuviv's nose on Celwis?"

"I don't think we know for sure about the war," Ar'alani said. "Though the timing is a strong indicator, especially since some of Yiv's forces were quick to chase the Sunrise refugee group to Rapacc."

"Also especially since the asteroid missile technique we've seen ties the Battle Dreadnought to the attack on the Nikardun bases," Ba'kif said. "And the nyix?"

"Thrawn's report says the Magys identified the Celwis jewelry as being made on Sunrise," Ar'alani said. "But of course her assessment is hardly proof."

"Agreed," Ba'kif said. "Now add in a few other points. The Battle Dreadnought aliens apparently persuaded Yiv to build that base, knowing full well they were going to attack it and kill all the Nikardun there. The asteroid attack alone shows that it was a long-term plan. That means that not only did Yiv trust them, but also that he was ignorant of their overall strategies."

"Yes, I see," Ar'alani said slowly. "And since the Agbui used some of that same nyix in whatever *their* plan was at Hoxim, that suggests the Agbui and Battle Dreadnought are working together."

"Which further suggests a coordinated operation," Ba'kif said grimly. "An attack from the outside by the Nikardun; an attack from the inside by the Agbui. And now—" He tapped his questis, sending her a report. "—we have *this*. I gather from your lack of any comment when you first arrived that you were unaware of it?"

Ar'alani felt her eyes narrow as she skimmed through the report. An alien ship—an alien *warship*—had entered the Ascendancy? "Yes, sir, completely," she gritted out, pulling out her comm. "When did this happen?"

"The ship arrived at Avidich four hours ago," Ba'kif told her. "You were probably testifying about Sunrise in front of the Syndicure hearing committee at the time."

"Yes, I was," Ar'alani said, swallowing a curse as she pulled up her comm's message listing. Senior flag officers were supposed to receive automatic alerts when there was any kind of threat against the Ascendancy. Most Syndicure committees, unfortunately, insisted witnesses turn off their comms during questioning.

But she'd checked her messages after leaving the chamber, and there'd been nothing there about an alien warship. As she skimmed through them now, there still wasn't.

"You won't see anything," Ba'kif said, a hint of acid in his tone. "After the initial report went out, someone in the Council apparently decided there was no reason to panic the public, so the notifications were withdrawn."

"With all respect, Supreme General, that was a stupid decision," Ar'alani said. "The whole idea of alerts is so that the military can be ready if potential trouble appears. We can't do that if we don't know about it." She held up her comm. "And the public doesn't see these anyway."

"I know," Ba'kif said. "But the warship was reported to be peace-sealed, and it left Avidich two hours after it arrived, so—"

"It *left?*" Ar'alani interrupted. "Who authorized *that?*"

"Apparently, the Mitth Patriel told them they could go, and Patrol Command didn't object," Ba'kif said. "Though they didn't have much choice, given that the alien hadn't attacked anyone or even behaved aggressively."

"They could at least have tried to keep it there until a Defense Force ship could be sent."

"Actually, the *Venturous* was already en route," Ba'kif said. "But the alien was gone when it arrived." His lip twitched. "And as I said, they hadn't been the least bit hostile."

Ar'alani unclenched her teeth. No, Patrol Command probably hadn't had any other option.

In general, she agreed with the strict Ascendancy policy of never taking the first shot, even when facing a blatant threat. But there were times when she sympathized with Thrawn's view that allowing an enemy to control the timing and location of hostilities was foolish. "So it's still wandering around?"

"Apparently," Ba'kif said. "But all Patrol Commands are on the alert, and the Defense Force has ships ready to move if and when it shows up again."

"I hope they're faster on the uptake than they were this time," Ar'alani said. "You said the *Mitth* told them they could go?"

"Yes," Ba'kif said. "Apparently, someone aboard had a conversation with the Mitth Patriel before they left. The topic of that discussion is still unclear, but Patriarch Thurfian has been in contact with us and is putting together a full report."

And if any of that discussion put the Mitth in a bad light, Ar'alani had no doubt that those particular aspects would quietly disappear. "What do you want me to do, sir?"

"I *had* planned to ask you to put together a Sunrise task force pro-

posal we could present to the Council," Ba'kif said ruefully. "Even if
the planet itself remains off-limits, we should be able to make a case
that the Battle Dreadnought or its successors attacked you and are
therefore legitimate targets."

"But now we have an unknown alien warship poking around."

"So it would seem," Ba'kif said. "Which puts anything having to do
with Sunrise off onto a side table."

"Very convenient for someone."

"I agree," Ba'kif said. "But we're not going to convince the Syndicure to let us focus our attention anywhere except on the Ascendancy
itself."

"I assume you're pulling in all the Expansionary Defense Fleet
ships to bolster the planetary patrols?"

"Not all of them," Ba'kif said. "The Council and Syndicure are still
working out the numbers and details. But yes, most will probably be
brought back in and redeployed." He raised his eyebrows. "The *Vigilant* will definitely be one of them."

"I hope they understand that the situation at Sunrise isn't something that can simply be set aside until a less inconvenient time,"
Ar'alani warned. "Someone with serious military power is willing to
take on Chiss warships in order to keep the place to themselves. We
need answers, and delaying our investigation just gives our enemies
more time."

"I'm not the one you need to convince, Admiral," Ba'kif reminded
her. "Would you like me to set up a meeting with the Council or the
Syndicure so you can plead your case?"

"You think it would do any good?"

"Not really, no," Ba'kif said. "But you're welcome to try."

"Probably not worth the effort," Ar'alani conceded. "So the *Vigilant* is going on defense duty?"

"Yes, at least for the time being," Ba'kif said, picking up his questis
and touching a key. "Ah—they've worked out the preliminaries. The
Grayshrike ... *Venturous* ... there we go. The *Vigilant*'s been assigned to Sposia."

Ar'alani wrinkled her nose. But at least Sposia was one of the Ascendancy's more vital worlds. Better than being sent out to Kinoss or Rhigar or somewhere else on the physical or cultural fringes. "Understood, sir. With your permission, I'll alert my officers and return to my ship."

"Very good, Admiral," Ba'kif said. "And I *will* keep up the pressure on the Council regarding Sunrise."

"Thank you, sir." Ar'alani stood up, straightened a moment in respect, then started to turn to the door.

And paused. "A moment, sir," she said, turning back. "You said you'd be willing to set me up with a meeting?"

"Of course," Ba'kif said. "Who do you want to talk to?"

Ar'alani braced herself. The supreme general, she was pretty sure, wasn't going to like this.

The supreme general didn't.

Enlightenment, according to an ancient Kilji dictum, was seldom an individual's first choice. But that choice could be changed, the dictum continued, and it was the duty of each and every enlightened to facilitate each and every such change.

There was another dictum, one that spoke of those who foolishly and defiantly stood against that goal. Their fate, unlike the choice of enlightenment, could not be changed.

"You lied to me," Nakirre said.

Jixtus's hooded head lifted, the veiled face rising from the reading device he'd been studying. "Excuse me?"

"You lied to me," Nakirre repeated. "Tell me now why I should not have you removed from my ship."

For a moment Jixtus remained motionless. Then, moving slowly and deliberately, he turned off his reader and set it on the table beside him. "You make a serious charge," he said. "Would you care to explain it?"

"You told me you would bring enlightenment to these Chiss," Nakirre said. "Yet you permitted the Mitth Chiss to order us away without even allowing me to speak of the path to him."

"I never said *all* Chiss would be enlightened," Jixtus said. "Indeed, I expect most of them will resist to the point of leaving their dead bodies in our wake."

"You said the defiance would come only from the leaders and commanders," Nakirre countered. "You said those leaders would die, but that a remnant of the common people would eagerly accept enlightenment."

"So I did," Jixtus acknowledged. "And so they shall."

"Yet you allowed this Mitth Chiss leader to go his way."

"Would you have preferred I ordered the *Whetstone* to bombard the planet from space?" Jixtus asked.

"Why not?" Nakirre demanded. "They have nothing that holds terror for us. We've seen the insignificant defenders that guard their worlds. We've seen the larger but still pitiful warship they use to travel outside their nest of ignorance and darkness. Why not bring them enlightenment right here and now?"

For a moment Jixtus was silent. "There is a star system to the side of our current path," he said. He picked up his reader, tapped a control, and handed the device to Nakirre. "It lies at the end of this vector. Order your vassals to take us there, and I shall answer your questions."

Nakirre looked at the numbers, his skin stretching in contempt. Jixtus was stalling for time, of course. The tricks of the unenlightened were both obvious and pathetic. "Why do you wish to go there?"

"Order your vassals to take us there, and I shall answer your questions."

Nakirre could ignore the request, of course. He could force Jixtus to answer, or begin the Grysk's first steps on the path to enlightenment.

But both could be interpreted as fear. Fear of Jixtus, or fear of the unknown. And the enlightened were never to show fear. "Vassal One: Alter course to this vector and system," he commanded, handing Jixtus's reader to the pilot.

"I obey," Vassal One said. He peered at the numbers a moment, then keyed the new course into the helm.

"How far?" Nakirre asked.

"It is close, Generalirius," Vassal One said. "Approximately thirty-five minutes."

"Increase speed," Nakirre ordered. "Make it ten."

Vassal One rippled with surprise and some concern. "I obey." The sound of the *Whetstone*'s engines rose in pitch as Vassal One ran them to full power.

Nakirre turned back to Jixtus in malicious amusement. If the Grysk had counted on having a full thirty-five minutes with which to prepare an explanation or craft an apology, he would now have to work more quickly. Was he even now feeling the fear of the unknown that so often enmeshed the unenlightened?

But as always, there was nothing to be seen, either of fear or anything else. Jixtus remained silent and motionless, his robe, hood, and veil fully concealing whatever stress or concern or arrogance might be lurking within. For a moment Nakirre considered walking over to him and tearing away the coverings so as to finally see this unenlightened alien he'd allowed to travel aboard his ship.

He resisted the urge. He was generalirius of the Kilji Illumine. Such actions, like fear itself, were beneath his dignity.

Besides, unless Jixtus could make an acceptable apology for his lack of action at the Chiss world, the alien's enlightenment would soon begin, and all his secrets would be revealed. Until then, he could keep his face hidden and those secrets buried.

Cultivating his patience, Nakirre turned away from the unenlightened and gazed out the *Whetstone*'s canopy at the swirling disorder that was hyperspace.

The minutes passed in silence. Then Vassal One called a warning, and the disorder gave way once again to the proper harmony of the universe's starry sky. In the near distance, Nakirre could see a half-darkened world; in the far distance was a dully glowing sun. "Your last request has been granted," Nakirre said, turning back to Jixtus. "I will have answers now."

"The answers will arrive momentarily," Jixtus said. "In fact they should be arriving . . . now."

From behind Nakirre came a soft gasp and the sound of skin rippling against clothing. "Generalirius!" Vassal Two called in a stran-
gled voice.

Nakirre turned. Floating in front of the *Whetstone*, drifting into
view from around the war cruiser's starboard side, was another warship.

But not just any warship. This craft was *huge:* three, possibly even
four times bigger than the *Whetstone*. The bow bristled with clusters
of spectrum lasers, with more lasers and missile tubes pointed toward
the Kiljis from the massive weapons shoulders. Lines of running
lights marked the flanks and dorsal spine, accenting the warship's
length and sheer presence.

"Do you see that warship?" Jixtus asked quietly from behind him,
the words seeming to float in front of Nakirre's stunned disbelief in
much the same way that the warship facing him floated in front of
the stars. "That is the *FateSpinner*, a Grysk *Shatter*-class WarMaster.
It could destroy the *Whetstone* in ten minutes. It could turn your
entire Kilhorde battle fleet to scrap in two hours. Do you hear and
understand, Generalirius Nakirre?"

Nakirre felt his skin rippling, his eyes and thoughts still frozen.
That *ship* . . .

"Do you hear me, Generalirius?"

Nakirre found his voice. "Yes," he said.

"Then hear and understand," Jixtus said. His voice was still quiet,
but now there was an edge of dark threat beneath it. "You serve the
Grysks. The Illumine serves the Grysks. You and your people live or
die at the pleasure of the Grysks. I do not travel aboard the *Whetstone*
at your pleasure; rather, you and the *Whetstone* survive at mine. I will
travel aboard this ship wherever I wish, for as long as I wish, and you
will obey every command I choose to give. Do you understand?"

Nakirre forced himself back to a semblance of calm. *The enlightened are never to show fear.* "And what of our agreement?" he asked.

"It still stands," Jixtus assured him. "We'll assist you in bringing
enlightenment to the peoples of this region. But it will be the peoples
of *our* choice, and on *our* schedule."

Nakirre's mind was still struggling. If Jixtus had access to such ships, why did he need the Kilji Illumine? Certainly the Grysks could conquer the peoples of the Chaos all by themselves. Was their talk of enlightenment and conquest merely a way to keep the Kiljis busy and out of their way while they strode unseen along their own path? Why had Jixtus even requested transport aboard the *Whetstone*?

He felt a stretching of shame. That last question, at least, he could now answer. No Chiss would stop to listen to Jixtus's message of warning if he arrived in a warship like that. They would open fire, and the war would be on.

Nakirre couldn't imagine what kind of warships the Chiss must have if Jixtus wanted them weakened before that happened. But those warships must be awesome indeed if the Grysks hesitated to launch a direct assault with ships like the *FateSpinner*.

In the end, though, those details didn't matter. What mattered was that Jixtus still needed Nakirre's assistance, and in return would help the Kiljis spread enlightenment. Whatever was about to happen between the Grysks and the Chiss was none of the Illumine's concern.

"Understood," he said. Tearing his gaze from the warship, he turned back to Jixtus. "What now?"

"I'll go aboard the *FateSpinner* for consultation and any updates the captain has for me," Jixtus said. "Then you and I will continue on." He paused, the hooded head inclining slightly to the side. "And have no fears about my abilities or plans. Approaching the Mitth first wasn't a mistake. I knew their Patriarch would turn us down."

Nakirre drew himself up. Just because the Grysks had overwhelming force didn't mean he should humble himself before this alien. The Illumine had enlightenment, and with enlightenment came wisdom. The Grysks had neither the one nor the other. "Then why waste our time with him?"

"My time is never wasted," Jixtus said. "Do you give up hopes of enlightening someone merely because your first attempt was rebuffed? Of course not. That's why the Kiljis need to add conquest to their tools, so as to have more time to enlighten those other beings."

"Then you expect the Mitth to eventually listen to you?" Nakirre asked, thoroughly confused now.

"Not at all," Jixtus said. "My time with the Mitth was to provide a baseline, a plumb against which all our future interactions with the Chiss will be measured."

"I see," Nakirre said. He didn't, but he had no intention of admitting that to this alien.

"Good." Jixtus stood up. "The shuttle from the *FateSpinner* will be here shortly to take me aboard. While I'm gone, you will prepare a course for the Chiss planet Rhigar." He paused, and Nakirre had the eerie sense that the unseen face behind the veil was smiling. "There we will find the Patriarch of the Clarr family, and our first *true* target."

CHAPTER FIVE

Clarr family captain Clarr'os'culry was in her office, working on her second cup of hot caccoleaf, when she got the alert that an alien ship had arrived over Rhigar.

She was at the Clarr homestead defense center in thirty seconds flat. "Duty officer?" she invited briskly as she strode to the command chair in the middle of the ring of displays and sat down.

"Single alien warship moving into high orbit," Lieutenant Clarr'upi'ovmos replied, just as briskly. "Configuration and size match the battle cruiser that was reported over Avidich two days ago. The three Clarr destroyers that were in that sector are moving to intercept, and the two frigates have taken up equatorial guard positions in case this is a feint or first of a two-prong. System Patrol's ships are moving into backup positions."

Roscu nodded, running her eyes over the displays. *Battle cruiser* wasn't so much a specific class as it was a convenient label for mid-sized alien ships until their capabilities could be better defined. In this particular case, factoring in the earlier reports from the Mitth Patriel on Avidich, she would tentatively place it between a Chiss frigate and a heavy cruiser, probably at the smaller end of that range. If it decided to be a problem, the patrol ships plus the Clarr destroyers orbiting Rhigar ought to be able to handle it. "No indication of hostile intent, I presume?"

"No, ma'am," Rupiov said. "And the destroyers report the alien weapons are peace-sealed. They've hailed us in Meese Caulf, Taarja, and Minnisiat, but I assumed you'd want to respond to them in person."

"Yes, I would," Roscu confirmed with a flicker of satisfaction. It had taken a while to whip the homestead defense forces into shape when she'd first taken this job, but they were finally starting to act like proper military professionals. Rupiov in particular was rapidly becoming an excellent second-in-command. "Did they sound particularly fluent in any of the languages?"

"Their Taarja was probably the clearest," Rupiov said. "Unfortunately, that's the hardest for most of us."

"We didn't do things in the Expansionary Defense Fleet because they were *easy*, Lieutenant," Roscu said tartly. "We did things because they needed to be done. Give me comm."

"You have comm, Captain."

Roscu cleared her throat. "This is Captain Roscu, commander of the Clarr family homestead defense force," she said in Taarja, trying not to wince. It really *was* an unpleasant language for the Chiss vocal apparatus. "Identify yourself, and state the purpose of your visit to the Chiss Ascendancy."

"I am called Jixtus," an alien voice came back, raspy yet strangely melodious. The Taarja words were clear and precise, but there was a hint of a strange accent beneath them. "I travel with Generalirius Nakirre aboard the Kilji warship *Whetstone*. I've come to your world to deliver your Patriarch a warning."

Roscu felt her eyes narrow. Mitth Patriarch Thurfian's report had been suspiciously sketchy on what this Jixtus and the Mitth Patriel on Avidich had talked about. "Explain," she said, turning her attention to the tactical display. The three Clarr destroyers were already in attack positions, and the planet's general patrol ships were closing in at backup positions. "What sort of warning?"

"I believe your family to be in danger," Jixtus said. "I ask permission to speak about the threat directly with your Patriarch."

"The Clarr family is flattered by your solicitude," Roscu said. "May I ask why you're being so helpful?"

Jixtus chuckled, a dry, raspy sound. "For payment, of course," he said. "I am a broker of information. I learn from those who have secrets, then sell to those who would best profit from those secrets."

"I see," Roscu said. At least he wasn't pitching a tale of selfless altruism or something equally ridiculous. She didn't have much respect for mercenaries, but she *did* understand them. "I'm sure you'll understand that I can't disturb Patriarch Rivlex without something more on this threat than merely your word as to its supposed existence. If you'll provide me with the details, I can decide whether or not to bring it to his attention."

"Will you also then be judge on whether payment is justified?" Jixtus asked pointedly. "Your offer carries the risk of enriching you while impoverishing me."

"You're a stranger to the Chiss Ascendancy," Roscu said. "You may therefore be forgiven your suggestion that the Clarr family would cheat you. I assure you that your information will receive full payment for its value."

"That value to be judged by you, of course." Jixtus gave a sort of whistling sigh. "I suppose I have no other choice. Very well. If you will give landing instructions to my shuttle pilot, I shall come down and deliver to you the details of this threat."

"There's no need for that," Roscu told him. Out of the corner of her eye she saw one of the status displays change, and she looked over to see a new message: *Defense Force ship* Venturous *en route; ETA three hours.*

She made a face. Three *hours.* So much for the Defense Force's highly touted ability to protect the Ascendancy. Fortunately for the people of Rhigal, the Clarr were ready. "This communication is secure," she said. "You can give me the details right here and now."

"*Is* it secure?" Jixtus countered. "Are the Clarr then alone on your world?"

Roscu frowned. "What do you mean by that?"

"I mean this threat is not coming from outside," Jixtus said, lowering his voice as if afraid others were listening in. "The danger is, in fact, coming from others of your kind."

Roscu sent another look at the tactical. After the Ascendancy's tangle with General Yiv, she'd assumed Jixtus's alleged threat would come from the remnant of the Nikardun forces, or possibly from someone new arriving in Yiv's wake. For that matter, the threat might even be Jixtus and these Kiljis he was riding with.

But from the Chiss themselves? Ridiculous. None of the other Nine would be foolish enough to take on the Clarr.

Unless, of course, by *threat* he meant some political machinations were in the works. *That* sort of thing happened all the time, and the Clarr and their allies could deal with that without paying some meddlesome alien for information they probably already had.

Still, that *was* an alien warship up there. Even if Jixtus's information was a waste of time, there might be other ways Roscu could gain from this encounter. "Understood," she said. "Unfortunately, the Patriarch's standing policy is to refuse landing permission to non-Chiss vessels."

"I understand," Jixtus said. "With danger pressing so closely all around you, you would be unwise indeed to allow an unknown into your midst. A shuttle's worth of soldiers within your very gates could inflict unspeakable damage."

Roscu felt her eyes narrow. Threats of danger she could hear and dismiss. But insults against her and the Clarr family were another matter. "You don't know much about Chiss if you think even one shuttle would be any threat to us," she said. "Your entire warship would represent little more than an exercise for our defending forces."

"What did you say?" Jixtus said, sounding almost flustered. "How did you know?"

Roscu looked at Rupiov, got a puzzled shrug in reply. "How did I know what?" she asked.

"That the threat is indeed represented by a war exercise," Jixtus said. "How did you know of your enemies' ships' practice attack?"

"Wait a minute," Roscu said. "What practice attack? What are you talking about?"

"You have a depth of knowledge and wisdom we did not expect to find among the Chiss," Jixtus said. "But I cannot say more when others may hear. If I may not visit your world and your Patriarch, perhaps you can send a representative aboard the *Whetstone* for a more secure conversation."

Roscu chewed at the inside of her cheek. But really, why not? There wasn't anything to lose—surely Jixtus wouldn't try to harm her or hold her hostage, not with a group of Chiss warships holding the *Whetstone* in their targeting sights.

On the contrary, there was a lot to be gained by accepting such an offer. The Mitth Patriarch had sent Jixtus away without trying to get a closer look at the *Whetstone* or even to learn more about Jixtus and the Kiljis. Now the Clarr family was being offered the chance to do both.

"Very well, I accept," she said. "I'm sending you orbit information. Reposition yourself as instructed, and I'll be there shortly."

"We shall eagerly await your arrival."

Roscu keyed off the comm. "Feed him a mid-altitude orbit," she told Rupiov. "Make it a polar loop."

"A bit tricky to get to one of those from their current vector," Rupiov pointed out.

"That's the point," Roscu told him. "Let's see how much trouble they're willing to go through to talk to us. And make sure the orbit never puts them directly over the homestead."

"Yes, ma'am," Rupiov said hesitantly. "You're really going up there?"

"Why not?" Roscu asked, watching the orbital data flow across the comm display as it was transmitted to the *Whetstone*. She couldn't decipher the numbers as quickly as a trained nav officer could, but it all seemed correct.

"Alone?" Rupiov pressed. "They're *aliens*, you know. We don't know what they're capable of."

"That's all right," Roscu assured him. "They don't know what *I'm* capable of, either. More to the point, this is my chance to get a close look at that ship, inside *and* out, and to actually meet these people. Neither of which the Mitth bothered to do."

Rupiov's lips puckered in a smile. "No, they didn't," he said. "That should make for some interesting conversations in the Syndicure."

"And possibly some good leverage points," Roscu agreed. "Get me a shuttle and pilot. I want them ready to fly as soon as possible."

"Yes, ma'am," Rupiov said. "They'll be outside the main entrance in fifteen minutes."

Fifteen minutes. Just enough time for Roscu to tie back her hair, change into her dress uniform, and get to the main entrance to meet the shuttle. Whatever these aliens were really here for, she wanted to make her best impression on them.

Especially since the Clarr family dress uniform went so well with a holstered charric. *And* since it also had a nice little concealed pocket that was perfect for a two-shot backup weapon.

If Jixtus was planning trouble, he would indeed not know what she was capable of. Not until it was far too late.

From the outside, the *Whetstone* looked like any other mid-class warship, with heavy nyix-alloy hull plating, weapons blisters scattered around its hull that housed lasers and missile launchers, and an ordered array of nodes marking the presence of an electrostatic barrier system.

The peace-sealing that Rupiov and the Mitth report had both mentioned consisted of heavy metal plates bolted over the missile tubes and spectrum laser openings. They looked sturdy enough, but Roscu suspected that they could be removed quickly if Jixtus decided he needed to fight. Still, whether the release mechanism consisted of explosive bolts or fracture metal, opening the weapons to combat status would still give the planetary defenders a few seconds' warning.

For the Clarr family warships, at least, that would be more than enough. She couldn't speak for Patrol Command's competence.

Two bipedal aliens were waiting for her inside the docking vestibule when the shuttle door opened. One was tall with dark-brown hair and wrinkled, rubbery-looking orange skin, wearing an outfit made up of half a dozen different shades of blue. The other was much shorter, a bit shorter than Roscu herself, dressed in a black robe, hood, gloves, and face veil that completely obscured everything except his basic body shape.

"I am Jixtus," the shorter alien identified himself. Here, in person, his voice sounded slightly less melodious and slightly more raspy than it had from the defense center speaker. "I greet you, Captain Roscu, and welcome you aboard the *Whetstone*. This is Generalirius Nakirre, ruler of the Kilji Illumine and master of this vessel. We appreciate your promptness. Allow us to show you to a place of comfort and refreshment where we may speak together at ease."

"Never mind the refreshment," Roscu said. The *Venturous* was blasting its way toward them in hyperspace, and she wanted the aliens gone before Admiral Dy'lothe got here and tried to take over. "You spoke of a threat and a practice attack. I'd like to hear the details."

"A being of direction and focus," Nakirre said. His voice was far less melodious than Jixtus's, the Taarja words delivered in a grating monotone. But there was an intensity beneath the voice that sent a chill up Roscu's back. "I approve."

"I'm so glad," Roscu said, regretfully aware that the sarcasm was probably wasted. "If one of you will lead the way . . . ?"

"Of course," Jixtus said. "Follow." Turning, he walked through a hatchway at the side of the vestibule, Nakirre striding along close behind. Brushing her forearm against the charric belted at her right side, feeling the additional reassuring pressure of the hidden backup weapon, Roscu followed.

The corridor was as utilitarian as the *Whetstone*'s exterior. Thirty meters ahead was an open hatchway with soft light spilling out onto the gray metal passageway deck and wall. Jixtus and Nakirre turned and disappeared through the opening; again touching her forearm to her holstered charric, Roscu followed.

She'd assumed the compartment would be more of the same cold metal and ceramic as the corridor and the *Whetstone*'s exterior. To her surprise, she found herself in something that looked more like a child's playhouse. The walls were patterned with the pinpricks of colored chase-pattern lights, while floating light globes hovered in each of the compartment's upper corners. The carpet was thick and brush-topped, and the round table and six chairs that dominated the room were made of contrast-carved wood.

But at least the multiscreen set into the center of the desk was modern and efficient. The image on the displays showed five ships of various sizes and configurations set against a starry background.

"Please; be seated," Jixtus said, gesturing to the table as he and Nakirre headed for the two chairs closest to the hatch.

"Thank you," Roscu said. She circled Nakirre as he settled into his chosen seat, picking the chair to the tall alien's right where she would have clear views of both the hatch and the display on that side. As an extra bonus, sitting there also put her charric and gun hand out of Nakirre's reach. *Even paranoids,* the old saying whispered through her mind, *have enemies.*

"This recording was made in an unidentified star system seven days ago," Jixtus said, pulling the multiscreen's control toward him. "I believe you will recognize the ships, as well as the activity." He keyed a switch, and the image unfroze into a vid.

Roscu leaned closer, studying the ships. There was some distortion and fuzziness in the images, indicating that the scene had been recorded from some distance, but the view was clear enough for her to easily make out the larger details. Two of the ships were system patrol craft of the sort that guarded Rhigal and every other inhabited world in the Ascendancy. Together with what appeared to be a light cruiser, they were circling one of the two larger ships—by its size and configuration probably a freighter—firing barely visible laser shots at it and receiving fire in return. "Is this vid enhanced?" she asked.

"An insightful question," Jixtus said, a note of approval in his tone. "Yes, the laser intensities have been enhanced for clarity. Otherwise, they wouldn't be visible to the unaided eye."

Roscu nodded. So: a practice battle, all right.

Moreover, one that the participants wanted to keep secret. There were no planetary bodies visible, and from the lighting patterns on the ships she guessed that there weren't any just off-vid, either. Official Defense Force training exercises were never held very far from a planet, since that was where most real-life combat took place.

But Jixtus might not know that. It might be interesting to see what his response would be to that suggestion. "Probably just a training exercise," she said offhandedly. "The Chiss Defense Force does a lot of those."

"I beg to disagree," Jixtus said. "This record was taken at a great distance from any habitation, and only a single recording vessel is present. No, I believe it to be a war game. Or," he added thoughtfully, "a rehearsal."

"I don't know why anyone would rehearse an attack on a freighter," Roscu said. So her tentative conclusion had been right, and Jixtus had just handed off a valuable bit of information for free.

"Perhaps the target was the only ship they could find to use," Jixtus offered.

"Perhaps," Roscu said. So now he'd also confirmed that the target ship was a freighter. Two bits of information for free. This Jixtus really was terrible at negotiation.

"Have you yet examined the observers' craft?" he asked.

Roscu focused on the other large ship. Now that she was looking more closely, she could see that it did indeed seem to be standing back and observing the exercise without taking part. It was larger than the three attackers, possibly a light cruiser or frigate, though with only its stern and part of its starboard flank visible it was hard to tell for sure. As she watched, the ship shifted position, pitching its bow upward slightly and yawing a few degrees to starboard.

And Roscu felt her breath catch in her throat. It was a frigate, all right, the fifth largest Chiss warship behind heavy cruiser and the three man-of-war classifications. The markings on the hull were still blurry . . . but for a Clarr family military officer there was no mistaking the crest that marked it as a Dasklo family frigate.

She looked back at the patrol craft and cruiser. They also had family markings, she could see now. But those ships were smaller and farther away, and the resolution of the vid wasn't quite good enough for her to make them out. "Can you give me more magnification?" she asked.

"Sadly, no," Jixtus said. "This is the full stretch of Kilji capabilities."

Roscu pursed her lips. So tantalizingly close.

But just because the Kiljis couldn't enhance the vid didn't mean that was the end of the road. The equipment back at the homestead might be able to coax a little more out of the images. "I'd like to take this recording back to my people," she said. "Maybe we can do more with it."

"Of course," Jixtus said. He keyed another switch and the displays went blank. Another tap on the panel, and a cover flipped up and a small rectangle popped out. "I trust you can read this?" he added, offering it to her.

"Of course," Roscu said, taking the card and sliding it into a pocket. All the computers she was familiar with used data cylinders, but the Clarr family traded with several alien species and *someone* on Rhigar ought to have equipment that could translate Jixtus's card into a more usable format. "I'll return it as soon as we've made a copy."

"And at that time you'll also bring my payment?" Jixtus asked pointedly.

"As I told you before, we'll pay what we decide the information is worth," Roscu said, standing up. "But I think I can assure you the Patriarch will authorize a reasonable amount." She turned and started toward the door. "And you said the star system where this took place is unknown?"

"Not unknown," Jixtus said. "Merely unidentified."

Roscu paused, frowning back over her shoulder at him. "What's the difference?"

"The difference," Jixtus said, "is that I simply haven't identified it to *you*. Withholding that information is why I know you will return with my fee."

Roscu's first impulse was to be furious. How *dare* an alien play with her that way? Her second was to recognize that there wasn't a single thing she could do about it. She had no choice but to give in to the extortion.

Her third was to realize that maybe Jixtus wasn't as careless at negotiations as she'd thought.

"Very well," she said. "When I return with your recording and your payment, I'll bring enough extra to buy the location of the system."

"Excellent," Jixtus said. "I shall eagerly look forward to our next meeting." He lifted a gloved finger. "One other thing." He paused.

"Yes?" Roscu prompted, clamping down on a fresh ripple of annoyance. She'd never appreciated dramatics, visual *or* verbal, and she especially didn't like them in combination.

"If it should turn out that your Patriarch and his family are indeed in danger," Jixtus said, "Generalirius Nakirre and the Kiljis stand ready to assist in your defense."

"Do they, now," Roscu said, eyeing the taller alien. "What would this assistance consist of?"

"We have many mighty ships of war," Nakirre said. "Some could be put at your disposal if you felt the need."

"I appreciate the offer," Roscu said. "But I think the Clarr family can handle this on our own."

"Of course," Jixtus said. "I simply wanted you aware of all the alternatives."

"Trust me," Roscu assured him darkly. "I'm aware of them." She looked at Nakirre, visually running his *Whetstone* battle cruiser against the Clarr defense profile. Maybe these ships would be powerful against pirates or raiders. Not so much against a family of the Nine. "I'm aware of *all* of them."

Roscu was right on two counts. The Clarr techs were indeed able to read and copy Jixtus's unconventional data card. They were also able to dig more information out of the recording.

"The frigate is definitely Dasklo, Your Venerante," Roscu confirmed, touching the distinctive family crest on the image frozen on Patriarch Clarr'ivl'exow's desk display. "But here's the interesting part. One of the patrol ships is Erighal; the other patrol ship and the cruiser are Xodlak."

"Xodlak," Rivlex echoed, stroking his lower lip thoughtfully as he peered at the display. "Not a family I'd expect to be working with the Dasklo."

"I agree," Roscu said. "Given the Xodlak closeness with the Irizi, my concern is that this may signal a new alliance between them and the Dasklo. That could pose a serious threat to us."

"I think that unlikely," Rivlex said. "The Irizi are quite heavy-handed with regard to their allies, and the Dasklo are hardly noted for their ability to work smoothly with others."

"Maybe they've learned," Roscu said. "Or maybe the impetus isn't coming from either family."

"Meaning?"

"Meaning the suggestion may have come from the Xodlak."

Rivlex's eyebrows went up with polite skepticism. "One of the Forty pushing one of the Nine? That's even less likely than the Dasklo learning some manners."

"One of the Forty who used to be a Ruling Family," Roscu reminded him. "And what if it wasn't *just* the Xodlak? What if it was a newly formed alliance among the Xodlak, Erighal, and Pommrio?"

"Why would they—?" Rivlex broke off, his eyebrows abruptly lowering into a thoughtful frown.

"Exactly," Roscu said. "Everyone's been assuming the recent military action at Hoxim was either some absurd treasure hunt or else a huge mistake. But ask yourself this: How could three members of the Forty make the same mistake?"

"You think their meeting was a cover for something else?"

"Possibly," Roscu said. "Or else they really were all lured out there somehow, but in successfully defeating the alien gunship attack they realized they worked well together."

"Interesting theory," Rivlex murmured. "But that's not what I'm reading in the reports."

"Reports made out by the participants themselves," Roscu said. "Reports that could easily have been edited by the three families to say only what they wanted the rest of the Ascendancy to read. In that case, what Jixtus's source may have recorded was a combat demonstration, the Xodlak coordinating with the Erighal to show the Dasklo what they can do."

"It doesn't make sense," Rivlex said firmly. "Patriarch Kloirvursi would never accept overtures from one of the Forty. Alliances with the Dasklo invariably travel the other direction, from him outward."

"Unless, as I said, we're starting from an alliance among three of the Forty," Roscu said. "I'll also note that Sarvchi, where the Pomm-rio family ships and crews assembled for their trip to Hoxim, is home to a Dasklo stronghold."

"One of their smaller strongholds."

"But with an important manufacturing facility," Roscu persisted. "For that matter, who says this dance among Xodlak, Irizi, and Dasklo is all that's going on? If the Pommrio are part of it, what if they're also trying to talk the Plikh into this new alliance? *Or* have already done so?"

"That makes even less sense," Rivlex said. "The Plikh wouldn't make any such deal without consulting with us first."

"Wouldn't they?" Roscu countered. "Just because our families have been allies for a couple of generations doesn't mean they wouldn't turn on us if something more advantageous came along."

"It would have to be *significantly* more advantageous."

"I submit that a solid alliance among them, the Irizi, the Dasklo, *and* three of the Forty would qualify."

"The key word being *solid*." Rivlex pondered a moment. "No. No, I don't find your reasoning compelling. However," he added, lifting a hand as Roscu opened her mouth for a protest, "stranger things have certainly happened throughout the course of Clarr family history. Just because I don't believe this alliance is likely doesn't mean we should ignore the possibility. Especially given that the Xodlak seem to feel the need to demonstrate military prowess to the Dasklo."

Roscu felt her throat tighten. Family rivalries and challenges nor-mally played out in the political and economic arenas. In this case, a combined Dasklo-Irizi group could bring the kind of pressure that might result in significant concessions from the Clarr. Some of the Clarr farming and processing facilities on Ornfra might change hands, or possibly the big electronics manufactory on Jamiron, both of which the Dasklo had been salivating over for years. It would all be neat, quiet, and civilized, and was the sort of thing that happened all the time in the Ascendancy.

But if the Dasklo and Xodlak were out in the middle of nowhere playing war games . . . "You have a plan, Your Venerante?" she asked.

"I do," Rivlex said. "First, you'll go back to Jixtus with enough to pay for this sample and the location where this event took place. If there's more of this vid, you'll purchase that, as well."

"Yes, sir," Roscu said. Both were points she'd been planning to suggest if he didn't. "I didn't ask him about the cost."

"Whatever it is, pay it," Rivlex said. "If this is all a fraud, we'll find a way to deal with him later. After that, we'll send one of our ships to check out the location and see if we can glean any more information."

"Yes, Your Venerante," Roscu said. "May I also suggest a quiet tour of some of our major holdings throughout the Ascendancy? If someone is plotting against us, there may be signs of that elsewhere."

"A reasonable idea," Rivlex agreed. "Do you have a suggestion as to ship and captain?"

"Yes, sir, I do," Roscu said. "I suggest the *Orisson,* commanded by me."

"Really," Rivlex said, cocking his head slightly. "Forgive me if I'm mistaken, but I believe you already have an important position."

"Lieutenant Rupiov is more than capable of handling homestead security in my absence," Roscu said evenly. "More important, if the Dasklo and Xodlak are preparing something that involves their militaries you'll want the *Orisson* commanded by the Clarr officer with the widest combat experience. That person is me."

"*Is* it," Rivlex said, a small smile twitching at the corners of his mouth. "You have a high opinion of yourself, Captain."

"I'm merely stating facts, Your Venerante," Roscu said. "And the most critical of those facts is that *something* happened at Hoxim, and something happened out there with Dasklo and Xodlak warships. We don't have nearly enough information on either incident, and we need to."

"I'm afraid I have to agree," Rivlex conceded, his smile fading. "Very well, Captain. I'll order the *Orisson* prepped, and inform Commander Raamas you'll be taking over. Go pack whatever you need for the voyage—your shuttle might as well take you directly across to the *Orisson* after you've dealt with Jixtus. And make it quick; I want both you and the *Whetstone* gone before the *Venturous* arrives."

"Understood, Your Venerante," Roscu said, standing up. "Thank you."

"Yes," Rivlex said, his voice going a little odd. "One final question."

"Sir?"

The Patriarch's eyes bored into hers. "I trust this doesn't have anything to do with the fact that Jixtus apparently approached the Mitth first. *Or* the fact that Senior Captain Thrawn was also present at the Hoxim incident."

"Not at all, Your Venerante," Roscu said, forcing herself to meet his gaze. "Not on either count."

"Because I know how you feel about him," Rivlex pressed. "Whatever's happening here, it's too important to be compromised by other considerations."

"Trust me, Your Venerante," Roscu said. "The fact that Thrawn's involved won't affect my investigation, my judgment, or my conclusions."

"Good," Rivlex said. "Go get packed. I'll speak with you again before you leave."

"You are disturbed," Nakirre said.

"You are mistaken," Jixtus said. "The Clarr Patriarch behaved exactly as I wished."

"I wasn't speaking of the Clarr," Nakirre said. "I was speaking of the news from your warship."

The veiled face turned slightly toward him. "What news would that be?"

But there was a tang of irritation mixed into the Grysk's tone. "I don't know," Nakirre said. "I know merely that you haven't spoken to me as frequently since your return, and that your manner has become colder and less haughty. Has your lack of enlightenment finally made you recognize the value of the Kilji Illumine?"

Jixtus was silent a moment, the unseen face still pointed at Nakirre. Nakirre remained silent as well, waiting for the Grysk to reveal whatever secret he was concealing.

The alien stirred, one gloved hand twitching in a sort of abbreviated gesture. "It's of no importance," he said. "The facility where we hoped to manufacture more of our small warships has been discovered and attacked."

"By the Chiss?"

"Who else would attempt such a thing and still survive?" Jixtus growled. "*Yes,* by the Chiss."

"Ah," Nakirre said, stretching with cautious enjoyment. Jixtus was always so confident in his plans. Seeing him humbled by circumstances was a new experience. "And the facility?"

"Undamaged, but no longer useful," Jixtus said. "Now that its location is known, we would need to intensify its security, and I don't wish to tie up the necessary warships." The hand twitched again, this time making a more complete gesture of dismissal. "No matter. The ships that were to be assembled there would have permitted us to bring the crisis to a boil more slowly and more deeply. Now we'll simply have to move up the timetable."

"Or you could make up the loss with warships of the Illumine," Nakirre offered. "We stand ready to assist."

Jixtus gave a sort of bark. "Don't make me laugh, Generalirius. The only part you can play is the one we've already given you: to conquer key border nations and close them off as havens to which Chiss forces or refugees might attempt to retreat."

"We can do far more than that," Nakirre insisted. "You underestimate the power of the Kilji Illumine."

"No, I don't think so," Jixtus said, his old edge of superiority now returned. "Be content and play your part and the Kiljis will have millions of new prospects to bring enlightenment to."

"And if we desire more?"

"There will be no more," Jixtus said quietly. "But there can certainly be less." He seemed to stir. "You have our next destination?"

Nakirre forced calm upon himself. The enlightened never let threats overwhelm their thoughts or wisdom. "I do."

"Then let us be off," Jixtus said. "Time is passing, Generalirius. We cannot afford to let it leave us behind."

"Understood," Nakirre said, gesturing to the helm. "Vassal One: You have your course."

"I obey," Vassal One said. He keyed the helm, and a moment later the *Whetstone* was once again in hyperspace.

Nakirre watched the flowing pattern, stretching in quiet resolve. No, the enlightened didn't let threats overwhelm them.

But they also didn't forget those threats. Not ever.

MEMORIES III

Thrass was seated at his new desk in the Syndicure office complex, skimming a report on crop projections for Sharb's northern hemisphere, when a data cylinder came sailing over the privacy divider on his left and landed on the desk. It bounced twice, then rolled to a halt beside his computer display.

"Did I make it?" one of the other syndics asked, popping her head into view over the divider. "Where did it land?"

"There," Thrass said, pointing to the cylinder and frowning at her. "If you were trying for my desk, yes, you made it. And?"

"And what?"

"And what is it?" Thrass asked, picking up the cylinder and peering at the side. The only labeling was a Defense Hierarchy Council sequencing number.

"Part of the autolog record from the Expansionary Defense Fleet patrol cruiser *Parala*," she said. "Syndic Thurfian wants it analyzed."

"Don't we have techs for that sort of thing?" Thrass asked, holding the cylinder out to her.

"Yes and no," she said, making no move to take it. "Thurfian doesn't want anyone below syndic rank even knowing he has it, let alone that we're digging into it. And you know the saying: *Last hired, first mired.*"

"Right," Thrass said, suppressing a grimace. And since he was the latest addition to the elite group of Aristocra who made up the Syndicure, he was the one who caught all the mud-slog work. Whether that work fit into his official responsibility sphere or not.

In this case, decidedly not. His current job was overseeing Mitth agricultural interests and coordinating with other families' farming and crop distribution systems. The Defense Force and Expansionary Defense Fleet were watched by Thurfian and one or two others, who oversaw military activities and could, in extreme cases, offer support from the Mitth family's own modest fleet of warships. "Anything in particular he's looking for?" Thrass asked, sliding the cylinder into his computer's reader.

"He thinks someone aboard the ship pulled some kind of scam," she said. "Illegally fed assistance and information to a merchant-hub station at some alien planet."

"Wait a minute," Thrass said, frowning. "Illegally fed—?"

And then, abruptly, it clicked.

The Expansionary Defense Fleet warship *Parala*, stumbling into a pirate attack against a Garwian merchant-hub station at Stivic four months ago. The pirates, who'd been steadily beating down the Garwian defenses, suddenly getting caught by an unexpected Garwian tactic and subsequently being destroyed or driven off. First Officer Mid Captain Roscu, insisting to the Council and the Clarr Speaker that someone aboard the *Parala* had violated standing orders against Chiss intervention in the affairs of other nations. The ship's commander, Senior Captain Ziara, insisting in turn that no one aboard her ship had done anything wrong, and that they'd merely observed the battle from a distance.

And standing squarely in the center of the controversy, Fourth Officer Senior Commander Thrawn.

"Yes, that's the one," the other syndic confirmed, correctly interpreting Thrass's reaction. "Have fun, but be quick. Thurfian wants a report before lunchtime."

"Understood," Thrass said, wincing as he opened the datafiles. The only reason he'd noticed this event in the first place was that Thrawn and Ziara were both mentioned in the report. Now, it appeared, they weren't just mentioned but were up to their necks in it.

Or, more likely, it was Thrawn who was up to his neck, and Ziara was once again trying to pull him out.

Ideally, this should have been a purely military matter. But just because the Syndicure wasn't supposed to meddle in fleet business didn't mean they didn't occasionally invite themselves in. In this case, Roscu's complaint had gotten the Clarr involved, and now Thurfian had responded by hauling in the Mitth. If the questions dragged on long enough for the Irizi to notice that one of their own—Ziara—was also involved, they could soon have a full three-family growzer jump-pile on their hands.

In this case, though, it wasn't clear as to how those piles would line up.

Family sides with family. That had been the number one unspoken rule of life for millennia, since well before the earliest days of star flight and the establishment of the Chiss Ascendancy. But it didn't take much scratching beneath the surface of such platitudes to realize things were rarely that simple.

And when a Mitth syndic's dislike for an individual was greater than his loyalty to his family, things could get complicated very quickly.

Thurfian no doubt thought he was being subtle about his opposition toward Thrawn. But Thrass had seen the signs in Thurfian's face and voice, and if he'd seen them it was likely others had, as well. Thrass didn't know the source of the animosity, but in such things the usual culprit was simple personality differences.

The more immediate problem, at least from Thrass's perspective, was that in this case he didn't know whether Thurfian was hoping to vindicate Thrawn or indict him.

It was an important question, but largely irrelevant to the task that had been literally dropped on Thrass's desk. He'd been charged with analyzing the data and finding the truth, and that was what he was going to do.

And if the truth showed Thrawn had violated his oath, then that was what Thrass's report would say.

"What do you mean, *nothing*?" Thurfian demanded, glaring across the desk at Thrass. "There's *something* on that ranging laser profile."

"Yes, of course," Thrass said hastily. "Forgive me for misspeaking. What I meant was that there's nothing suspicious there."

"Really," Thurfian said, his tone gone icy. "You don't find all those modulations in the carrier frequency suspicious?"

"To be perfectly honest, Syndic, I find them to be largely the product of Mid Captain Roscu's fevered imagination," Thrass said. If there was one thing he'd learned growing up amid Mitth family politics, it was to point all doubts and hazy claims at one of the other families. "The rapid fluctuations along the main laser frequency are indeed there, but their pattern doesn't match up to any known encryption or open conversational pattern."

"Did you check for conversations in different trade languages?" Thurfian asked. "Or did you just look for patterns in Cheunh?"

"I tried Taarja and Sy Bisti," Thrass said, choosing his words carefully. This was the most critical part of his whole presentation. "I was about to move on to Minnisiat and

Meese Caulf when I noticed that the laser's modulator disk had been replaced shortly after the incident."

Thurfian's forehead creased slightly. "Which means . . . ?"

"The modulator controls the laser's frequency," Thrass explained. "A ranging laser has to be able to work through different levels of dust, atmosphere, or solar wind, and its frequency has to be adjusted to compensate if it's going to deliver accurate information to the ship's gunners. It's similar to how spectrum lasers work—"

"I don't need a lecture on military equipment," Thurfian interrupted brusquely. "What does replacing the modulator have to do with anything?"

"I looked it up," Thrass said. "It appears that modulators can sometimes develop a sort of flutter that manifests as small, rapid frequency shifts, not unlike those Mid Captain Roscu noted and brought to the Council's attention. The fact that the modulator was replaced after the incident strongly suggests it was suffering from this malfunction."

"Strongly *suggests*?"

"Yes, sir," Thrass said. Pointing at another family was good; pointing into the unknown was sometimes even better. "Unfortunately, there's no way to know for certain whether or not the disk was faulty. If a piece of equipment can't be fixed, it's put into the recycler for materials recovery, and that's the end of it. And while there's a log entry for every piece of equipment that's replaced or recalibrated, only the date and time are listed, not the person who did the actual work or even necessarily the reason it was replaced."

"Why not?" Thurfian demanded. "Crew members should be accountable for their actions."

"I'm sure they are," Thrass said. "But since the crew leaders are the ones responsible for keeping their areas running, and since they're supposed to confirm their crews' work before logging the details, apparently over the years the Council decided that additional details would clog up the records and make it harder to search for anything meaningful."

"Meaningful?" Thurfian all but spat out the word. "You're telling me this isn't *meaningful*?"

"I didn't mean it that way, sir," Thrass said, ducking his head in apology. "Please forgive my inexact choice of words."

"There's no excuse for verbal sloppiness, Syndic Thrass," Thurfian ground out. "If you can't learn precision, I suggest you ask to be demoted from syndic and returned to your previous position."

"Again, my apologies," Thrass said. And when the personal attacks began, he knew, the attacker had given up on the original goal.

"Don't *apologize*," Thurfian said. "*Improve*. That will be all."

"Yes, Syndic." Thrass stood up and turned toward the door—

"Could Senior Commander Thrawn have been the one who replaced the modulator?" Thurfian asked.

"I don't know how or why he would," Thrass said, putting puzzlement into his voice as he turned back to face the other. Again, a place to step carefully. "Bridge officers normally don't visit that section of a warship."

"He was down there during the incident," Thurfian reminded him, a fresh hint of suspicion rising into his voice. "When exactly was that modulator replaced?"

"Fourteen hours after the *Parala* returned to hyperspace," Thrass said. "Senior Commander Thrawn was duty officer on the bridge at the time."

"I see," Thurfian muttered, the suspicion fading into sullenness. "Very well. Dismissed."

And just like that, it was over.

Thrass headed down the corridor back toward his office, keeping his expression neutral. *Yes*, the modulator swap had been logged fourteen hours after the incident; but that didn't necessarily mean that was when the exchange had taken place. *Yes*, Thrawn was indeed on the bridge at the time; but it didn't necessarily mean someone else might not have made the replacement at someone's quiet request. *Yes*, Thrass had tried to match the laser modulation to two of the best-known trade languages; but other sections of the *Parala's* log had stated that the Garwians first hailed the Chiss in Minnisiat, one of the two languages he'd carefully put to the end of the line.

Fortunately, Thurfian hadn't thought to question any of those points, which had enabled Thrass to remain completely truthful while still blunting Thurfian's latest attack on Thrawn.

How to walk that delicate line was yet another lesson he'd learned from family politics.

He frowned, a sudden thought occurring to him. He'd noted in Thurfian that personal antagonism toward an individual could be detrimental to family loyalty. But was the opposite also true? Could Thrass's friendship with Thrawn be clouding his own loyalty to the family in exactly the same way?

He gave a little huff. No, of course not. Friendship and kinship were the whole basis of family, after all. Without those connections the structure would collapse into a mass of individuals striving against one another for personal gain. For that matter, hadn't Patriarch Thooraki all but told him that on the day when he'd sent Thrass to beat back the Stybla's attempt to rematch Thrawn?

Besides, loyalty to Thrawn *was* loyalty to the family. There were great things ahead of Thrawn, a future that would raise the Mitth to even greater heights than they enjoyed now. The Patriarch clearly saw it; and if a visionary like Thooraki recognized Thrawn's potential, who was Thrass to say otherwise?

And speaking of opportunities . . .

He checked his chrono. If the debriefing of the *Parala* officers was still on schedule, Thrawn should have finished up his testimony half an hour ago. If he was still on the ground, maybe Thrass could grab his friend for a quick lunch before they both had to return to their respective duties.

Mentally working out a short list of cafés near the Defense Force HQ he could offer, he pulled out his comm.

CHAPTER SIX

The *Springhawk* was still eleven hours out from Rapacc, and Thalias was reading in the sky-walker suite's dayroom, when she heard whimpering coming from Che'ri's sleeping room.

She frowned, setting down her questis and crossing to the hatch. Che'ri had always been something of a noisy sleeper, making odd sounds and slurred words as she hit the dreaming part of her sleep cycle. It had taken Thalias a couple of months of waking up to the noises before her brain learned to recognize them as normal and allow her to sleep through the bouts.

But there was noise, and there was *noise,* and frightened-sounding whimpers were something new.

"Che'ri?" Thalias called softly through the hatch. "Are you all right?"

The whimpering stopped abruptly. "Che'ri?" Thalias called again, wondering if her call had woken up the girl. But if so, why hadn't she answered? "Che'ri?"

Again, there was no answer. Then, the whimpering started up again.

Thalias had always tried not to intrude on Che'ri's privacy, especially now that the girl was edging toward her midage years. But enough was enough. "Che'ri, I'm coming in," she announced and keyed open the hatch.

She'd expected to find Che'ri tossing and turning like someone in a fever, her sheets and blankets twisted around her or falling off the bed. Instead, the girl was lying rigidly on her back, her eyes squeezed shut, her face twitching. "Che'ri?" Thalias called, hurrying to her side. "*Che'ri!*"

Che'ri's eyes snapped open, wide and frightened. "Thalias?" she gasped.

"I'm here, Che'ri," Thalias said, sitting down on the bed beside her and taking the girl's hand. "Are you okay?"

"I—I don't know," Che'ri said, the fear in her eyes slowly fading. "I saw it, Thalias. I saw all of it. The death and destruction . . . I *saw* it."

"It was just a dream, Che'ri," Thalias soothed. "Just a horrible dream."

Che'ri squeezed her eyes shut. "No, it wasn't a dream. It was . . . it was Sunrise."

"Sunrise?" Thalias echoed, frowning. "You mean the planet?"

"Yes," Che'ri murmured.

"That's not possible," Thalias said firmly. "You never saw any of that—"

She broke off, a sudden knot twisting into her stomach. No, Che'ri had never seen Sunrise's destruction.

But the Magys had.

"It's all right," she said, forcing down the impulse to look over her shoulder in the direction of her own sleeping room and the hibernation chamber set against the wall. Were these images coming from the Magys? Was she invading or influencing Che'ri's thoughts or dreams? Was she somehow implanting her own memories into the girl? "You can go back to sleep. I'll stay with you awhile if you'd like."

"No," Che'ri said, the fading fear surging back again. "I mean, no, I don't want to go to sleep. I'll just . . . I'll see Sunrise again. Can't we just—can't we keep going? To Rapacc, I mean? Can't we just go?"

"It's your sleep time, Che'ri," Thalias reminded her. "You need to rest."

"But I can't sleep," Che'ri said, some pleading in her voice. "I don't *want* to sleep. Can't we just *go*?"

"I don't know," Thalias said. "Let's find out. Come on, get dressed— we're going to the bridge."

Mid Captain Samakro was on duty when Thalias and Che'ri arrived. "Caregiver; Sky-walker," he said in greeting, frowning in turn at each of them. "What are you doing here?"

"Che'ri can't sleep," Thalias explained. "She was hoping she could go back on duty."

"Sorry, but this is her sleep period," Samakro said, looking closely at the girl. "We can't do that."

"I thought there were emergencies where the captain can run the ship's sky-walker past the usual time limits," Thalias said.

"Where the *captain* can decide that," Samakro said. "There's no provision for the sky-walker herself to do so."

"Well, there should be," Thalias said. "Can you call Senior Captain Thrawn and ask him?"

Samakro shook his head. "Senior Captain Thrawn's off duty, the same as you are."

"We need to talk to him." Thalias glanced around, confirmed that no one else was close enough to overhear. "Tell him," she added, lowering her voice to a whisper, "it concerns the Magys."

Samakro's eyes narrowed. He looked at Che'ri, back at Thalias. "Go back to your suite," he said. "I'll ask him to meet you there."

Thalias and Che'ri were sitting on the couch together, the girl sipping at a box of warmed grillig juice, when Thrawn and Samakro arrived. "Caregiver," the senior captain greeted Thalias gravely. "Skywalker. Mid Captain Samakro tells me there's a problem."

"Yes," Thalias said. She'd spent the last few minutes trying to organize her explanation into the most compact form possible. "Che'ri's having nightmares of Sunrise, a place she's never visited, remembering events she's never seen."

"I see," Thrawn said. "What do you propose?"

Thalias drew back a little. She'd expected to have to go into a lot more detail before he even believed her, let alone started looking for a solution. "Che'ri doesn't think she can sleep anymore, at least for now," she said. "She'd like to go back to the bridge and continue our journey to Rapacc."

"I see." Thrawn turned his eyes onto Che'ri. "Do you concur, Sky-walker Che'ri?"

"Yes, sir," Che'ri said in a small voice. "Every time I try to sleep—"

"It's all right," Thrawn said, holding out a calming hand. "You don't have to explain further. Mid Captain, what's the hyperdrive's status?"

"The new coils have been installed and the diagnostics are nearly complete," Samakro said. "Four more minutes, five at the most, and we'll be able to leave."

"Thank you," Thrawn said. "Che'ri, one final time: Do you wish to return to duty?"

"Yes, Senior Captain," Che'ri said.

"Caregiver?"

"I think it would be best, sir," Thalias confirmed. "I'll stay with her and keep watch as long as she's there. If she seems to be tiring or losing concentration, I'll bring her out."

"Very well." Thrawn turned to Samakro. "Alert the bridge, Mid Captain. We return to hyperspace in ten minutes."

Thalias was gazing out the bridge viewport at the hyperspace swirl, feeling dullness and fatigue pulling at her eyelids, when the aroma of hot caccoleaf snapped her back to full alertness.

She turned. Thrawn was coming up behind her with a steaming non-spill mug. "Senior Captain," she said, nodding wearily at him. "I thought you were off duty."

"I am," Thrawn said, handing her the mug. "As are you and Sky-walker Che'ri. How is she doing?"

"As far as I can tell, she's fine," Thalias said, savoring the aroma before taking a sip. Not too hot, and extra strong. Exactly what she needed right now. "She doesn't seem to be affected by the images while in Third Sight. Or when she's awake, either."

"So just in her dream state," Thrawn said thoughtfully. "Was this the first time she's had these dreams?"

"It's the first time I heard her in the middle of one," Thalias said. "But I asked her about it while we were waiting for you, and it turns out she's had two or three others over the past two weeks. Not nearly as vivid or terrifying, though, she said. Just odd."

"And all of them occurring after we brought the Magys out of hibernation to look at the nyix brooch."

Thalias nodded. So he was thinking the same thing she was. "Yes."

For a moment Thrawn was silent. "I checked the hibernation chamber," he said. "There's no indication of any malfunction."

"So how is she doing it?"

"I don't know," Thrawn conceded. "Perhaps her dreams are somehow intersecting with Che'ri's."

"I thought people in hibernation didn't dream."

"*Chiss* in hibernation don't," Thrawn said. "But the Magys is an alien. Her mental and physiological responses may be different." He nodded toward Che'ri. "There is, of course, one other obvious possibility."

Thalias winced. "You think she's connecting somehow with Che'ri's Third Sight?"

"It's a possibility," Thrawn said. "Especially given the Magys's still-undefined connection to the Beyond."

"That seems so strange," Thalias said, shaking her head. "To connect with something you can't see or touch."

"Very strange, indeed," Thrawn said.

Thalias looked at him, feeling her eyes narrow. There'd been a hint of dry humor in his tone. "It's nothing like Third Sight," she insisted. "We just see dangers that are in front of the ship and maneuver to get around them. We're not connecting with anything."

"Perhaps," Thrawn said. "The question has been debated for centuries without a resolution. Again, I find myself thinking about my conversations with General Skywalker concerning the Force. There was a certain vagueness in his descriptions, too, but he seemed quite capable of tapping it for both power and insight."

"Well, it's creepy," Thalias declared darkly. "Especially when she's picking on someone like Che'ri. Do you think we should . . . I don't know. Wake her up and tell her to stop?"

"I think not," Thrawn said. "If it's not deliberate, the effect on Che'ri would likely distress her. If it *is* deliberate, we would be confirming for her that her scheme is working." He hesitated. "More concerning to me is that if she's affecting Che'ri this strongly while asleep, the danger may be much greater once she's conscious."

"Yes, that would be bad," Thalias agreed. Though if the connection was there *only* when Che'ri was asleep . . . but they really didn't have enough data one way or another on that. "So what do we do?"

"We continue on this path," Thrawn said. "We're currently seven hours from Rapacc by sky-walker, forty-nine by jump-by-jump. We'll keep going as long as Che'ri can stay awake, then continue jump-by-jump while she sleeps. If she's again woken early by more nightmares, and if she's alert enough, she can again take over navigation."

"You're talking a *lot* of awake time, Senior Captain," Thalias warned, looking down at Che'ri. The girl still looked all right, but Che'ri knew the toll this was taking on her mind and body. "More than is legally allowed."

"I know," Thrawn said. "But a ship's captain has leeway in extraordinary circumstances. At any rate, a rest period hardly seems useful if she's unable to rest."

"That may be," Thalias said. "But I don't know how much she can take before she risks serious damage."

"I did look into that possibility," Thrawn said. "The medical data suggests that in the case of prolonged wakefulness, her body will force her to sleep before any damage occurs. It also suggests that a sleep cycle continually interrupted by nightmares isn't much better for her, either. Still, even if she only gets two or three hours' sleep at a time before we reach Rapacc, we'll arrive in less than two days. At this point, I think the best thing we can do for her is get her there as quickly as possible and get the Magys off the *Springhawk*."

Thalias breathed out a sigh. She still didn't like it, but couldn't think of anything better to offer. "All right," she said. "I'll stay here and watch her until she needs to sleep."

"Or until *you* need to sleep," Thrawn said. "I can have someone else watch her."

Thalias squared her shoulders. "I'll stay here," she repeated firmly, "until she needs to sleep."

"Understood," Thrawn said, and Thalias could hear the quiet approval in his tone. "Carry on, Caregiver."

The trance ended, the Great Presence faded back into the mists of thought and waking dream, and with a final twitch of his fingers Qilori of Uandualon brought the Kilji war cruiser *Anvil* out of hyperspace. With a tired sigh, he pulled off his sensory-deprivation headset—

"Why do we stop here, Pathfinder?" a gruff voice came from behind him, chewing the Taarja words like they were sour fruit.

Qilori's cheek winglets twitched in disgust and annoyance. General Crofyp, commander of the *Anvil*, was short, loud, impatient, and his wrinkled, rubbery skin was utterly repulsive. All other things being equal, Qilori would probably have refused the job of guiding Crofyp and his ship to Rapacc.

But this trip had been undertaken under Jixtus's orders. And with Jixtus, nothing else was quite equal.

"The *Hammer* has lagged a bit, General, and is a few minutes behind us," Qilori explained, half turning to face him. "You said earlier that you wanted both ships to arrive at the same time, so I thought we'd stop an easy jump outside the Rapacc system and wait for them to catch up."

"Foolish unenlightened," Crofyp said, his voice fairly dripping with disdain. "We are here, and Colonel Tildnis is in hyperspace. He will not know we've stopped, but merely pass us by unnoticed."

"I don't think so," Qilori said. "I expect the *Hammer* to appear nearby in approximately four minutes."

Crofyp made some rude-sounding noises in his own language and shifted his attention to the status displays. Qilori turned back to his nav board, his winglets twitching with some scorn of his own. He wasn't surprised at the Kilji's skepticism; the fact that Pathfinders could sense, locate, and follow each other in hyperspace was a closely held secret.

Still, Jixtus probably knew, and General Yiv had certainly known, and anyone who had dreams of conquest really should have done some basic research into the people who made long-distance travel feasible.

Besides, anyone who talked about *enlightenment* as much as Cro-fyp should have learned a little more understanding and humility regarding the limits of his knowledge.

Qilori reached down to the warmer beside his knee and pulled out his flask of galara tealeaf. This whole mission was something of a mystery to him; not the kind that was pleasantly intriguing, but the kind that made him nervous. From what little Jixtus had told him, it sounded like the Grysks had sent at least a couple of quiet probes into the Rapacc system, all of them having apparently been chased away. Whatever Jixtus's goal was, sending in a pair of Kilji warships sounded like a serious escalation.

The big question was: Why *Rapacc,* of all places? Qilori had been there once before, hired by the dangerous Chiss military leader Thrawn, during the period when one of General Yiv's commanders had been occupying and blockading the system. Rapacc was an off-the-path place, not allied or even trading partners with anyone Qilori knew of, with nothing special in the way of resources or inhabitants. Qilori hadn't known at the time why the Nikardun were even interested in the place, and he still didn't know.

But Yiv and the Nikardun were the past. This was the present; and now it was Jixtus and these Kiljis who had set their sights on Rapacc.

Unfortunately, Jixtus had also set his sights on Qilori himself.

He scowled out the viewport at the starry sky. He'd told Qilori about Thrawn hiring him to fly him to Rapacc . . . and yet, as Jixtus had pointed out, for the most part Chiss warships seemed perfectly capable of traveling the Chaos without Pathfinders or any other of the region's navigators. It was a mystery that had caught Jixtus's attention, a puzzle he'd now handed over to Qilori to solve.

The problem was, Qilori couldn't.

He'd looked into the matter, quietly and unobtrusively, sifting through the records at his home base of Navigator Concourse 447 and talking to other Pathfinders. The obvious answer was that the Chiss had discovered some hitherto unknown group with the gift of navigation and had kept their services completely to themselves.

But the more Qilori studied the problem, the less likely that seemed. The gift was exceedingly rare, and sifting those individuals out of a species no one had ever heard of would be nearly impossible.

Which led to the more intriguing possibility that Jixtus had raised. Millennia ago, the Chiss had traveled extensively in Lesser Space, where legends said the inhabitants used computerized machines to chart their way between the stars. If the Chiss had brought such machines back with them, and if one of those machines could be captured and studied—

"Your stated time is up, Pathfinder," Crofyp growled.

Qilori's wandering thoughts snapped back to the present. "There are yet twenty seconds left," he pointed out.

Crofyp growled something else, probably another reference to Qilori's sadly unenlightened status.

Which was fine. Qilori didn't really care what the bombastic Kilji thought about him. What he *did* care about was the fact that no one had let him in on the master plan. A pair of warships obviously implied expectation of combat, but whether the Kiljis were here to study, to conquer—Crofyp used that word a lot, too—or to destroy was unclear.

Maybe things like that didn't make a difference to Jixtus or the Kiljis. But they made a huge difference to Qilori. He had no stake in what was about to happen, and he'd long ago decided he had no interest in leaving his bones floating among the debris of someone else's war.

Fortunately, most of a Pathfinder's time aboard ship was spent on the bridge, and most ship bridges were well equipped with escape pods. On the *Anvil*, the two closest were directly to either side of him, the portside one slightly closer to his station than the starboard one. But either would do in a pinch.

The sensor operator spoke up in the Kilji language. Crofyp answered in kind, and to Qilori's ears he sounded even more annoyed than he had earlier.

Small wonder. In the distance off to the *Anvil*'s side, close enough to be visible through the viewport, was the picket cruiser *Hammer*, having arrived right on Qilori's projected schedule.

The unintelligible conversation continued, and Qilori felt his cheek winglets twitch in cynical amusement. Crofyp was clearly trying to put off the moment when he'd have to admit to Qilori that the Pathfinder had been right. As if Qilori couldn't see that for himself.

But it was Crofyp's schedule, and his time to waste if he chose to do so. Qilori, for his part, was perfectly happy to extend his unplanned break.

Finally, the Kilji couldn't put it off any longer. "The *Hammer* has arrived," he growled, switching back to Taarja. "Why do we still stop here?"

"I'm merely awaiting your instructions, General," Qilori said, choosing the Taarja word that could mean either *orders* or *suggestions*. Not in any way insubordinate, but guaranteed to rankle if Crofyp was skilled enough with the language to catch the nuance.

"Then go," Crofyp bit out, sounding even more annoyed. Apparently, he was skilled enough.

"I obey," Qilori said, keying the comm signal that would alert the *Hammer*'s Pathfinder that they were ready to go. "We'll be there in fifteen minutes." Slipping on his headset, he reached out to the Great Presence and took the *Anvil* back into hyperspace.

Rapacc was what the Pathfinders called a box system, surrounded by variable electromagnetic fluxes and with the entire inner system littered with so many asteroids and other shifting masses that entry from hyperspace was limited to only a handful of vectors. Adding in the necessity for the two ships of Crofyp's small task force to stay together, that dropped the entry points to really only one. Qilori moved the *Anvil* into position along that vector, feeling the Great

Presence guide him through the twists and past the obstacles, sensing the other Pathfinder matching the *Hammer*'s path at his side. They reached the indicated end point—

Once again, the Great Presence faded from Qilori's consciousness as Qilori pulled the ship out of hyperspace. He pulled off his headset, taking a deep breath as he looked out the viewport. There was the *Hammer*, right where it was supposed to be on the *Anvil*'s starboard flank. In the distance ahead he could see Rapacc's sun, though the planet itself was too far away for the unaided eye to see.

Directly ahead of them, floating in place like a silent messenger of death, its weapons trained on the Kilji cruisers, was a Nikardun blockade frigate.

Qilori's winglets flattened with shock. By all accounts the remnants of General Yiv's battle forces had been obliterated, some of the troops and warships taken out by Yiv's victims, others destroyed by the Chiss Ascendancy itself.

How in the Depths had this warship survived?

"Intruders into the Rapacc system, you face the Nikardun warship *Aelos*." The Taarja words came over the *Anvil*'s speakers. "Identify yourselves."

"I am General Crofyp of the Kilji Illumine," Crofyp said. If he was surprised or worried by the unexpected presence of a Nikardun warship, it didn't show in his voice. "Move aside or be destroyed."

"Identify your purpose here," the voice said, ignoring the threat.

"I say again, move aside," Crofyp repeated.

"Identify your purpose here."

"I said—"

"General?" Qilori spoke up, turning and lifting a hand for attention. "With your permission?"

"You will not interrupt one of the enlightened," Crofyp snarled, shifting his glare from the frigate to Qilori.

"My apologies," Qilori said. "But with your permission, I believe I can end this confrontation without violence. I know these people."

Crofyp's skin rippled repulsively, and it was all Qilori could do to keep his winglets still. The general's pride, battling with his burning desire for all people to live until they could be forced into Kilji enlightenment. "You have one minute," he said.

"Thank you." Qilori turned back to the viewport. "*Aelos*, I am Qilori of Uandualon," he said into the nav station's mike. "Former associate of General Yiv the Benevolent, who was himself an associate of the one named Jixtus, agent and coordinator of the Grysks. General Crofyp and the Kiljis are also associates of Jixtus, which makes us all allies. There is therefore no reason for conflict."

"We know of no one called Jixtus," the Nikardun said.

"Perhaps not," Qilori said. "He and his people are content to keep to the shadows. But I can affirm that he was the one who guided General Yiv's conquests, here at Rapacc as well as elsewhere across the region."

There was a short pause. "Was this Jixtus also the one who brought General Yiv to his doom?"

"No, of course not," Qilori said. "General Yiv was overwhelmed by massive forces beyond even his ability to withstand."

Which wasn't at all what had happened, of course. But it would sit better with a group of Nikardun survivors than the true story of how Yiv was defeated. "But with the arrival of the Kiljis, the Nikardun now have the chance to rise again."

"How would this be?"

"Under the guidance of Jixtus, they will—"

"Enough," Crofyp growled. "The Nikardun are defeated, Pathfinder, and will never again arise. Speak lies and soothings when it is only *your* time that you waste. We are the Kiljis, and we will take what we want. Move from our path, Nikardun, or die."

"Then you do not in fact serve with Jixtus, as the Pathfinder said?" the Nikardun asked, his voice still calm.

"The Pathfinder told you what you wanted to hear," Crofyp said contemptuously. "Here is the enlightened truth. Yiv did not serve *with* Jixtus, but *under* Jixtus, as a slave serves under a master. Nor are the Kiljis *associates* of Jixtus, but his masters. We use him as a guide and adviser to our voyages, nothing more."

"On what subjects does he advise you?"

"He identifies which of the ignorant peoples of this region require enlightenment," Crofyp said, his voice going icy. "Your Nikardun remnant will be one of those, have no fear. But that task will be for later. For now, we merely require that the refugees who fled from their world and now hide here among the Paccosh be handed over to us."

Qilori's winglets twitched. *Refugees?* This was the first time Crofyp had mentioned refugees.

"What do you want with the refugees?" the Nikardun asked. His voice had changed subtly, Qilori noticed, as if he'd boosted the clarity, focus, or overall power of his transmission.

"Are you deaf as well as unenlightened?" Crofyp demanded. "Like all others, they walk in darkness. We are here to take them to a place where they can be enlightened."

"Can you not enlighten them here?" the Nikardun asked. "They are useful servants to us. We don't wish to lose them."

"The wishes of the unenlightened are of no importance," Crofyp said. "Do you move aside, or do you die?"

"You who claim to offer enlightenment seem all too willing to extinguish the lives of those who need your guidance," the Nikardun said pointedly. "But no matter. I accede to your demands. The Nikardun warship *Aelos* will lead the way. Prepare to follow as I guide you through our orbital defenses."

"I need no guide," Crofyp said. "I need you merely to stand aside."

"The defenses are subtle and mighty," the Nikardun insisted. "Without a guide, you will quickly be overcome."

Crofyp growled deeply in the back of his throat. "Move aside," he ordered. "I will not tell you again."

"I have my orders," the Nikardun said. "I must stand firm until assistance arrives."

"Then you will die where you stand."

With a flick of his finger he cut off the *Anvil*'s transmission. "Vassal Four, signal Colonel Tildnis that upon my signal *Hammer* is to move past the *Aelos* along its portside and continue on to the planet," he ordered. "Vassal One: Prepare to likewise move us past the *Aelos* along its starboard side. If the Nikardun moves into our path, Vassal Three, you are to destroy him."

"I obey," Vassal One acknowledged.

"I obey," Vassal Three added.

Qilori's winglets twitched. Crofyp was in an arrogant mood, with his maneuver clearly calculated to show both dominance and contempt for the *Aelos*. Certainly there was reason for both—the blockade frigate was smaller and less well armed than either of the two Kilji cruisers. No match for either, let alone both.

But at the same time, passing on its flanks was practically an invitation for the Nikardun to open fire on both ships, with the Kiljis forced to restrict their own counterfire lest they overshoot and hit each other. If the Nikardun was willing to sacrifice himself and his ship, he could do significant damage to the Kilji force. "General, if I may suggest—"

"You may not," Crofyp cut him off. "Never forget, Pathfinder, that you and your kind are also in need of enlightenment. The more you demonstrate the darkness of your current path, the more tempted I become to move you to the top of the Illumine's list. Is that how you desire this day to end?"

"No, General," Qilori said, fighting to keep his winglets from spasming. He still had no idea what Kilji enlightenment consisted of, but anything decided on by generals and administered beneath the weapons of warships was unlikely to be pleasant.

"I didn't think so," Crofyp said. "Vassal One: As soon as the Nikardun moves to attack, execute my order."

"I obey."

"Why isn't he moving?" Crofyp demanded.

Qilori's winglets settled into a frown. Crofyp was right—the Nikardun was just sitting there. What was he waiting for?

"General, a new ship has appeared to starboard," Vassal Two put in suddenly from the sensor station. "Unknown configuration."

"The ship is hailing us," Vassal Four added. He touched a switch—

"Unidentified ships, this is Senior Captain Thrawn of the Chiss Expansionary Defense Fleet warship *Springhawk*," an all-too-familiar voice said from the *Anvil*'s bridge speaker. "You stand near our prey. Move clear of the Nikardun blockade frigate *Aelos* or suffer the humiliation of becoming collateral damage."

MEMORIES IV

"I'd like to say you're in trouble," Thrass commented. "But in all honesty, I can't."

Thrawn shrugged as he moved one of his firewolves across the Tactica playing board laid out on the game café table between them. "I appreciate the vote of confidence in my game," he said. "I'd like to say in turn that you're playing far better than you did at our last session. Unlike you, however, I *can* honestly do so."

"And I appreciate that, as well," Thrass said, looking pointedly at the two holding zones along the sides of the board. "Though all the compliments in the universe can't hide the fact I'm still down a firewolf and a whisperbird."

"But you're up three stingflies," Thrawn reminded him. "Not a bad showing for someone who only learned the game eight weeks ago."

"And I'll never know how I ever let you talk me into this," Thrass said, mock-crossly. "A game that plays to all of your strengths and against all of mine? Foolish syndic that I am."

"Really," Thrawn said, mock-chiding. "I thought tactics and strategy were basic tools of the trade in the Syndicure."

"Oh, they're important enough," Thrass agreed. He

moved his groundlion, tapped one of Thrawn's stingflies, and took it off the board. "But not as important as verbal skills and basic theatrics."

"Yes, I've seen the Syndicure in action," Thrawn said drily. "Perhaps *in full voice* would be a more accurate description." He moved his nightdragon, tapped the groundlion, and handed it to Thrass. "You'll want to put this beside the whisperbird," he added, pointing to Thrass's holding zone. "They'll be better able to support each other if you decide on a sortie."

"Right. Thanks." Thrass set the groundlion where Thrawn had suggested. He was getting better at the main game, but still had a bad tendency to lose track of the sortie option. "I always forget about that."

"It's easy to do," Thrawn agreed. "But you need to keep it in the back of your mind as a fallback option if and when your main strategy fails."

"I know the theory," Thrass said ruefully. "I just usually don't have it in my head where I can get at it." He cocked an eyebrow at Thrawn. "By the way, joking aside, I really *do* enjoy the game, and I appreciate you teaching it to me."

"Oh, I know," Thrawn assured him.

"Good," Thrass said. "I'm never quite sure if you're picking up the subtexts and nuances beneath what I'm actually saying."

"Sadly, I *do* sometimes have problems in that area," Thrawn admitted. He picked up a cheese triangle from their snack platter and popped it into his mouth, then moved his nightdragon to an attack position against Thrass's remaining whisperbird. "I suppose that's why you're in the Syndicure and I'm in the Expansionary Defense Fleet. We don't have much need of subtext and theatrics in my profession."

"Oh, I don't know," Thrass said, pondering how he could get his whisperbird out of harm's way. Invoking the onetime transference rule would do nicely, but if he did that he would lose the use of one of his firewolves if and when he tried for a sortie down the line. "Theatrics have their uses in any profession. In moderation, of course."

"Jaraki?" an anxious voice came from the left, rising above the background murmur of conversation. *"Jaraki?"*

Thrass turned to look. At one of the tables across the café, a man was slumped over in his chair, his hands clutching at his throat and chest. His two companions had shoved back their own chairs and scrambled to their feet, the man hovering uncertainly over his companion as he punched at the emergency key on his comm, the woman clutching the sick man's shoulder. "He's having an attack," she gasped, her voice rising in volume and pitch, her face contorting with anguish and fear. "He's having an attack! Someone help! Someone, *please*!"

"Hang on," the cashier at the charge register called back. She was already on her way toward them, the café's emergency kit in hand, dodging through the array of tables and past the other patrons staring at the stricken man.

"I wonder where the other man is," Thrawn murmured.

Thrass shot him a look. "What?"

"There were four people at that table," Thrawn said, his forehead creased in thought. "One of the men is missing."

"Really," Thrass said, frowning as he looked around the room. There were a few people who were away from their tables, but all of them looked like they'd been on their way for food or bathroom breaks before the sudden drama froze them to their sections of floor. "What did he look–?"

He broke off. There, crouching behind the counter with the top of his head just barely visible, someone was tapping into the charge register.

"It's a robbery," Thrass said quietly. "Remember what I just said about theatrics being useful in any profession?"

"A diversion," Thrawn said, nodding grimly. "And the

patrollers aren't likely to get here in time. I suppose it's up to us to stop it." He started to get up.

"No, no," Thrass said, waving him back down. "I've got this. Watch and learn."

He stood up and headed quietly toward the charge register, angling across the open space as he walked to put himself between the thief and the main exit. He had no idea how long it would take to crack the safety locks on the café's register and download the payments, but the plan was probably timed to get the group safely out before the emergency medical personnel arrived.

Assuming, of course, that the accomplice who'd *looked* like he was summoning help had actually done so. If he'd just gone through the motions for show, and to prevent any of the onlookers from doing likewise, the thief would have a lot more time to work with.

The cashier had reached the table now, and she and the other woman were pawing through the contents of the emergency kit. The accomplice, Thrass noted, was deftly refusing all the cashier's suggestions of inhalants and broad-spectrum med-relief jectors, probably spinning a story of some rare disease and warning against counterproductive medicines. Thrass reached his chosen starting position and took a deep breath.

Then, abandoning his inconspicuous walk, he broke into an all-out run toward the counter. "Pontriss!" he shouted. "Come on, buddy—Jaraki's in trouble!"

Like magic, every eye in the café turned toward him. "Come on, buddy," he repeated. "You've got the spare jector, right?"

Behind the counter, the thief raised his head a few centimeters, his eyes wide with confusion and growing alarm as he saw Thrass rushing toward him. He opened his mouth as if about to protest, maybe to claim he wasn't Pontriss and didn't have any jector.

But it was too late. Everyone was looking at him now, crouched behind the counter where he wasn't supposed to be. From Thrass's new vantage point as he ran toward the man, he could see the data siphon plugged into the register. There was a sudden scrambling sound from Thrass's left.

And as if that was a signal, the thief leapt to his feet and charged toward Thrass, clearly intent on getting past or through him and escaping out the door. Thrass braked to a stop, shifting to a poised stance that would let him move in any direction if the thief tried to dodge around him.

The thief snarled something and snatched out a knife. Thrass took a reflexive step backward, then grabbed a nearby chair and held it in front of him like a shield. Too late, he realized he should have signaled for the patrollers as soon as he and Thrawn realized a robbery was in progress. Too late now.

From behind him came a pair of dull thumps followed by a much louder one. Thrass kept his eyes focused on the man still running toward him—

And then, abruptly, the man faltered and came to a stumbling halt. His eyes flicked over Thrass's shoulder, then came back to Thrass, a frustrated weariness settling onto his face. With a sigh, he tossed the knife onto a nearby table where another group of wide-eyed gamers was sitting.

"Are you all right?" Thrawn's voice came.

Thrass risked a look over his shoulder. Thrawn was standing near the exit, his hands raised in combat stance, the man who'd been faking the illness stretched out unconscious on the floor at his feet. The woman and the other man were standing like stunned statues a couple of meters farther back, Thrawn's quick and efficient neutralization of their friend having apparently convinced them to abandon their own bids for freedom. "I'm fine," Thrass said, turning back and motioning the fourth member of the gang to move away from his discarded knife. Even with a weapon in hand, he'd apparently decided not to risk it.

But then, like his friends, he'd had a full view of the brief fight. Thrass was starting to regret having missed the show.

He shifted his gaze to the other patrons, most of them just starting to recover from their bewilderment. "Everyone relax—it's all over," he called. "Oh, and if one of you fine people would like to call the patrollers?"

The patrollers arrived, the thieves' data siphon was marked and inventoried and the contents returned to the café's charge register, and Thrass and Thrawn were finally able to return to their table.

Where a fresh platter of snacks had already been delivered by the café's grateful manager.

"Now," Thrass said briskly as he sampled one of the fruit sticks. "Where were we?"

"I believe you were expounding on the use of dramatics in diversionary tactics," Thrawn said. "I was about to ask if you could offer me a good example."

"Consider it offered," Thrass said. "You'll note the technique can also be used to draw attention away from one place and point it to another."

"Yes," Thrawn said, looking thoughtfully at the board. "Very well done, too, I might add. Unfortunately, the tactic appears to require skills that I don't possess."

"Don't worry, you have plenty of other skills to fall back on," Thrass assured him. "Did the fleet train you to introduce people to the floor like that? Or did you pick up that trick on your own?"

"The fleet gave me the basics," Thrawn said. "But yes, I moved on from there. Aside from the valuable exercise involved, simulated combat also helps train the eye to notice small errors, and the mind to learn how to take advantage of them."

"Which occasionally results in free food," Thrass said drily, waving at the platter. "So where were we really?"

"I believe my nightdragon was threatening your whisperbird."

"Right." Thrass shifted his attention back to the game. "So should I let you take it?"

"If you think you're ready to try a sortie," Thrawn said. "If so, you'll need to bring in either the whisperbird or one of your firewolves to have any reasonable chance of success."

"Right," Thrass said, studying the board. "I think letting you take the whisperbird puts me in a better strategic position."

"It does indeed," Thrawn said approvingly. "Excellent. At this rate, I'll soon have to rescind the spotting advantage I've been giving you."

Thrass frowned at him. *What* spotting advantage?"

"Haven't you noticed?" Thrawn said innocently. "I've been playing you left-handed."

"Ah," Thrass said drily. Right. Playing a board game left-handed. Huge tactical sacrifice. "Now you're just making fun of me."

"Not at all," Thrawn said. "Merely employing controlled confusion as a diversion."

"I knew that," Thrass assured him. "Okay, let's give it a shot. Will you help walk me through this?"

"Certainly." Thrawn moved his nightdragon, tapped the whisperbird, and handed it to Thrass. "You'll probably want to put him first in line. So set him there, in front of that groundlion . . ."

CHAPTER SEVEN

The last hour was the hardest. The last half hour was almost literally painful to watch.

Samakro spent that time standing beside Thalias, watching as she swayed visibly despite her grip on the back of Che'ri's chair, waiting for her to either call an end to the session or else collapse onto the deck from sheer exhaustion. If it came to the latter, hopefully he would be quick enough to catch her.

More worrisome, though far less visible, was the physical and mental state of the sky-walker herself.

Sitting in her chair, gazing at nothing as she manipulated the controls, she looked mostly the way she always did. But Samakro could see the fresh creases around her eyes, the unnatural paleness of her skin, the slightly jerky movements of her fingers. She was as fatigued as Thalias, probably more so, with her smaller child's body less able to handle the accumulating stress. The longer she kept this up, the more likely she would miss something in the Chaos they were driving through and either damage the ship or send it skating completely off course.

Thrawn surely knew that as well as Samakro did. And yet he continued to sit quietly in his command chair, his eyes moving systematically among the status displays, keeping an occasional eye on Thalias but making no attempt to intervene. Samakro had done a search earlier on his questis, and Che'ri was already long past the record for a sky-walker navigational session. Was Thrawn so obsessed with Rapacc and getting the Magys off the *Springhawk* that he was willing to risk everything to do so?

Possibly. Or possibly it was simply that Thrawn knew Che'ri better than Samakro did. The senior captain and sky-walker had spent several weeks together out at the edge of Lesser Space, after all. Perhaps during that time Thrawn had gained insight into Che'ri's stamina and ability to spend extended periods in Third Sight.

But everyone had their limits, and with the *Springhawk* one easy jump away from Rapacc, Che'ri and Thalias finally reached theirs.

The bridge viewport was glowing with the swirl of hyperspace when Samakro returned from escorting Thalias and Che'ri back to the sky-walker suite. "How are they?" Thrawn asked as Samakro came up beside the command chair.

"About as close to being literally asleep on their feet as I've ever seen," Samakro said. He lowered his voice. "In my opinion, Senior Captain, and off the record, that was an unnecessarily dangerous thing to put the *Springhawk* through."

"I agree, Mid Captain," Thrawn said evenly. "Except for the *unnecessarily* part."

Samakro frowned. "I don't understand."

"I don't entirely understand myself," Thrawn conceded. "I simply note that the sudden intensity of Che'ri's nightmares may point to something significant."

"You think that the Magys was pushing her extra hard for reasons of her own?"

"Or else that the Magys's pressure on Che'ri has reached a breaking point," Thrawn said. "Either way, it suggests that we should take whatever actions and risks are necessary to get her to Rapacc as quickly as we can."

Samakro looked at the hyperspace swirl. "I hope you're right, sir."

"As do I," Thrawn said, looking over at the nav display. "Lieutenant Commander Azmordi, stand by. Bring us to space-normal a bit farther out from the inner system than you did our last trip here."

"Yes, Senior Captain," Azmordi said from the helm. "Breakout position marked."

"Thank you," Thrawn said. "Prepare for breakout. Three, two, *one*."

The star-flares burst out of the swirl and contracted into stars, and the *Springhawk* was back in space-normal. "Full scan," Thrawn ordered.

"You think Uingali foar Marocsaa will still be on station in their captured Nikardun blockade frigate?" Samakro asked.

"That's one of the things I hoped to see," Thrawn said. "If he's not, that may tell us something about the situation here."

Samakro nodded silently. The last time the *Springhawk* had paid a visit, Uingali had mentioned other ships having tried to enter the Rapacc system. If one of them had decided not to take no for an answer . . .

"Combat range clear," Dalvu called from the sensor station. "Midrange . . . three warships, Senior Captain."

Samakro looked at the sensor display as Dalvu keyed in full magnification. There were three ships out there, all right, though the distance made positive identification impossible. Two of them, battle cruiser size, were facing away from the *Springhawk*, while the third ship, smaller and somewhat more distant—Uingali's blockade frigate?—was facing off against them. All three were holding position, and something about their bearing and positioning gave Samakro the impression that he was seeing the last stages of a confrontation.

"Acknowledged," Thrawn said. "Battle stations."

The warning lights came on, and the quiet calm of the bridge became an equally quiet flurry of activity as weapons and defense systems were activated and weapons crews summoned to their posts. "Can you identify the two larger ships?" Samakro called.

"No need," Thrawn said. "They're sister ships to the Kilji warship *Whetstone*."

Samakro peered at the display. "Are you sure, sir?"

"Quite sure," Thrawn said. "Even from here I can see the similarities between them and the ship we saw at Zyzek."

"Senior Captain, we're getting a transmission," Lieutenant Commander Brisch called from the comm station.

"What do you want with the refugees?" a voice came from the bridge speaker.

Samakro felt his stomach tighten. It was Uingali's voice, all right, and the comm display marked the signal as coming from the smallest ship of the distant trio.

"Are you deaf as well as unenlightened?" a new voice cut in, rich with anger and arrogance, with the slight echo that indicated the signal was being received by Uingali and then transmitted back out to the *Springhawk*. "Like all others, they walk in darkness. We are here to take them to a place where they can be enlightened."

Samakro nodded to himself. *Enlightened.* Generalirius Nakirre had talked about enlightenment, too. Thrawn was right: These were more of Nakirre's Kiljis.

"Can you not enlighten them here?" Uingali asked. "They are useful servants to us. We don't wish to lose them."

Samakro looked at Thrawn, saw his commander's eyes narrow. Unless things had changed drastically on Rapacc, the refugees from Sunrise weren't being worked by the Paccosh. So why would Uingali say such a thing?

Because he was mainly talking to the Kilji warships, of course. They were here to gather up the Sunrise refugees, for some reason, and Uingali was trying to stall them.

An effort that was, unfortunately, doomed to failure. The blockade frigate was vastly overmatched by the two battle cruisers. If and when the Kiljis decided the conversation was over they would move on, and Uingali could either let them go or die in a futile attempt to stop them.

Unless Uingali knew something the Kiljis didn't.

Samakro looked at the sensor display. The Kilji warships were still facing the blockade frigate without making any attempt to come around to face the far larger Chiss heavy cruiser that had now appeared in the Rapacc system behind them.

Which strongly suggested that, with their attention focused on Uingali and their drive emissions interfering with their aft sensors, they'd completely missed the *Springhawk*'s arrival.

He felt his lips crease in a tight smile. That was the kind of mistake Thrawn was *very* good at taking advantage of.

"The wishes of the unenlightened are of no importance," the Kilji said. "Do you move aside, or do you die?"

"You who claim to offer enlightenment seem all too willing to extinguish the lives of those who need your guidance," Uingali replied. "But no matter. I accede to your demands. The Nikardun warship *Aelos* will lead the way. Prepare to follow as I guide you through our orbital defenses."

Samakro looked at Thrawn. The senior captain had his questis out and was punching in a series of orders and targeting vectors. He finished and keyed them to their respective stations.

"I need no guide," the Kilji said. "I need you merely to stand aside."

"The defenses are subtle and mighty," Uingali said, trying one more time. "Without a guide, you will quickly be overcome."

There was a brief, guttural sound. "Move aside," the Kilji ordered. "I will not tell you again."

"I have my orders. I must stand firm until assistance arrives."

"Then you will die where you stand."

"Senior Captain, we can't interfere," Samakro warned quietly.

"I think we can," Thrawn said. "Azmordi? Can you make the necessary in-system jump?"

"Yes, sir," the pilot confirmed, leaning over his displays as he keyed in the location Thrawn had sent him. "I can't guarantee closer than a hundred meters, though."

Samakro felt his stomach tighten. In-system jumps were notoriously tricky, and Thrawn's plans unfortunately usually required laser-point accuracy. If a hundred meters was too far off the mark, there could be trouble.

But for once, apparently, Thrawn's strategy had a bit more margin for error. "That will be acceptable," Thrawn said. "Afpriuh, I trust you can be more accurate?"

"Yes, sir," Senior Commander Chaf'pri'uhme said confidently from the weapons station. "Spheres armed and locked on targets."

"Azmordi?"

"Ready, Senior Captain."

"Afpriuh, fire on my signal," Thrawn said. "Three, two, *one*."

The *Springhawk* gave a small twitch as the double salvo of plasma spheres blasted from their launchers and disappeared ahead into the darkness. "Azmordi, stand ready," Thrawn continued. "In-system jump, then yaw portside ninety degrees. Three, two, *one*."

The starscape shifted subtly, sparking an equally small flicker of disorientation in Samakro's brain. It was followed immediately by a much more obvious shift as Azmordi rotated the ship ninety degrees to portside.

Bringing the *Springhawk*, no doubt exactly as Thrawn had intended, to face the starboard flanks of the two Kilji cruisers.

They were Kiljis, all right, Samakro noted as he looked them over. From the *Springhawk*'s new vantage point, even he could see the design similarities Thrawn had already noted. One of the warships was also noticeably shorter than the other, with smaller weapons shoulders and fewer electrostatic barrier nodes. Possibly the Kilji equivalent of Chiss heavy and light cruisers.

"Unidentified ships, this is Senior Captain Thrawn of the Chiss Expansionary Defense Fleet warship *Springhawk*," Thrawn called in Taarja. "You stand near our prey. Move clear of the Nikardun blockade frigate *Aelos* or suffer the humiliation of becoming collateral damage."

Samakro felt his eyes narrow. If the Kilji ships did anything other than simply turn in place . . . "Sir?" he asked urgently.

"Generalirius Nakirre showed us that same maneuver at Zyzek," Thrawn reminded him. "It's a very deliberate, very confident move, and one I expect he taught his chief commanders." He smiled faintly. "Plus, I ordered him to move away from the *Aelos*. He doesn't strike me as the sort to readily obey an adversary's commands."

Sure enough, even before Thrawn finished speaking, the two Kiljis began to move. Rotating sideways toward the *Springhawk*, exactly as the senior captain had anticipated.

"Who are you to speak of prey?" the Kilji's voice rang out over the bridge speaker. "And who are you to give orders to warships of the Illumine?"

"I already gave you my name," Thrawn said. "Do you need me to repeat it?"

There was a vicious-sounding snarl from the speaker. "Your name will die with you, unenlightened fool," the Kilji bit out.

An instant later a volley of laserfire lanced out from both cruisers' shoulders and bow emplacements.

"Apparently, he means for us to die *right now*," Samakro commented.

"Apparently so," Thrawn agreed, keying the mute switch. "Afpriuh?"

"Barriers holding," the weapons officer confirmed. "Eighty-nine percent dissipated. I don't think they've found the frequency for our hull yet."

"Let's make certain they don't." Thrawn keyed the comm back on. "You make an extravagant promise," he said as the Kilji ships sent out their second salvo. "Does he who makes that promise fear to identify himself to the one he intends to kill?"

"I fear nothing," the Kilji said. "I am General Crofyp of the Kilji—"

And as the third laserfire barrage blazed across the vacuum, the plasma spheres Thrawn had launched from the *Springhawk*'s original position completed their journey and slammed into the Kilji cruisers' starboard flanks.

"Return fire," Thrawn ordered as the ion burst scattered across the cruisers' hulls, instantly silencing the weapons they impacted. "Lasers on the portside; breachers on starboard. And one sphere on the *Aelos*."

Samakro shifted his attention to the blockade frigate. Uingali was pulling back from the Kilji warships, apparently trying to get clear of the line of fire.

He frowned. Why would Thrawn order a plasma sphere that would thwart that effort?

"He's moving into position for a cross-fire attack," Thrawn said, answering Samakro's unspoken question as a single plasma sphere shot out amid the flurry of breacher missiles and laserfire. "The Kiljis seem to think he's an ally or at least a neutral. I'd like to preserve that misunderstanding for the moment if I can."

"Yes, sir," Samakro said. That made sense, he supposed, though what use Thrawn might have for such a misconception he couldn't guess.

"Never throw away a possible weapon when it's unnecessary to do so." Thrawn nodded toward the viewport. "Especially when the enemy is making a move like that."

Samakro followed his gaze. The larger Kilji cruiser had moved a short distance toward the *Springhawk,* driving straight into the storm of laserfire. But as it edged forward, it was also turning its paralyzed starboard flank into the *Springhawk*'s attack.

Samakro frowned. Were they *trying* to get themselves destroyed?

And then he understood.

So did the *Springhawk*'s weapons officer. "Captain, Cruiser One is moving to shield Cruiser Two," Afpriuh warned.

"Recommend we move dorsal or ventral to compensate," Azmordi added from the helm.

"Hold position," Thrawn said. "I think Cruiser One is hoping to give Cruiser Two a chance to escape."

He smiled grimly at Samakro. "We're going to let them."

No! The word bounced screaming through Qilori's head, spinning fear and sheer disbelief like a giant spider's web through his mind. No. Not Thrawn. Not here. Not again.

The Kilji lasers lanced out, burning at the Chiss warship with little or no effect. The Chiss remained silent, taking the fire without responding. The silent shout of denial continued its crazed path through Qilori's mind.

Then, even as the Kilji lasers continued to wash across the *Springhawk*'s hull, the *Anvil* shuddered as multiple objects slammed into its starboard side.

And as Qilori stared in horror, the complete right-hand side of the weapons, sensors, and defenses displays went solid red.

"Plasma spheres!" he gasped. "General, the Chiss have hit us with—"

He broke off as he belatedly recognized the terrible truth. The *Springhawk* was right *there*, directly in front of them. But the plasma sphere attack had come at them from the side. That could only mean— "They're not alone," he shouted. "General, they're not alone. There's another Chiss warship out there!"

"Where?" Crofyp demanded. "I see nothing."

"Fool," Qilori spat. "Of *course* you don't see anything. They've disabled all the sensors on that side. We have to get out of here." He grabbed for his restraints, popped the catch.

"Step out of that seat and die," Crofyp said, his voice suddenly gone the temperature of liquid nitrogen. "The enlightened do not run. We stand, we fight, and we prevail." Turning away from Qilori, he began jabbering away in the Kilji language.

"So you think," Qilori muttered, his winglets beating desperately against his cheeks. Thrawn in front of them; another Chiss warship to starboard. Whether the Kilji recognized it or not, they were all dead.

Unless . . .

He looked at the sensor display. If the Nikardun had evaded the plasma sphere attack and was in position to help, they might still have a chance. Three ships against two . . .

But no. Even as Qilori's searching eyes located the blockade cruiser, he saw a plasma sphere arrow across from the *Springhawk* to explode into a brief light show across the Nikardun's bow. There would be no help coming from that quarter. The stars shifted as the *Anvil* began to move.

Qilori's winglets paused briefly in their rhythm to give a surprised twitch. Was the *Anvil* turning away, giving up its attack on the *Springhawk*?

It was. More than that—*worse* than that—it was turning its paralyzed starboard flank into the Chiss barrage.

What in the Depths was Crofyp *doing*?

And then he understood. Crofyp was maneuvering the *Anvil* to shield the *Hammer* from the *Springhawk*'s laserfire. Giving the smaller picket cruiser time to recover from the plasma sphere attack. So that it could join in the battle?

No. So that it could run.

His winglets' twitch of surprise turned into a ripple of contempt. So much for *stand, fight, and prevail.* He could appreciate Crofyp's willingness to sacrifice himself and his ship to get word of the ambush back to Jixtus, but it was still a far cry from taking the Chiss head-on with the usual Kilji bluster and arrogance. Even if there was no chance of success.

And speaking of chances and success . . .

Furtively, Qilori looked around the bridge. Crofyp's vassals were working frantically at their boards, trying to bring plasma-frozen weapons back to life even as the Chiss laserfire systematically blasted those same weapons into scrap. The general himself was having a loud and animated discussion with someone, probably the *Hammer*'s captain, and was paying little attention to anyone or anything else. If Qilori was going to make a run for it, this was his chance.

Carefully, making sure to keep his movements small, he finished disentangling himself from his restraints. If Thrawn would be kind enough to accommodate him just this once . . .

And there it was, exactly as he'd hoped: a sudden double jolt as a pair of breacher missiles slammed into the *Anvil*'s numbed side, the impact jerking everyone on the bridge against their restraints.

Qilori was ready. He jumped from his seat, hit the deck running, and wove his way desperately between the control stations toward the orange-rimmed door of the portside escape pod.

He was nearly there before Crofyp spotted him. "Pathfinder!" the Kilji bellowed. "*Stop!*"

Qilori kept going, his back tensing in anticipation of the shot that was surely about to shatter his spine or blow out the center of his chest. But the shot didn't come. He reached the escape pod, one hand thrust out toward the wall to slow his momentum, the other reaching out to slap the hatch release. Both hands connected, and as the hatch rolled open he tumbled inside the pod. He slapped the sealing control as he fell past it, managing to turn halfway over for one final look over his shoulder as he slammed onto the deck. Crofyp was standing at his station, swinging up a large black weapon toward him.

Too late. The hatch rolled shut, cutting off Qilori's view and Cro-fyp's last chance to punish his Pathfinder for his cowardice.

But just as the hatch closed, Qilori got a single glimpse of the starboard bridge wall exploding in a burst of fire and vaporized metal as the Chiss lasers punched through.

An instant later Qilori was thrown up and back against the hatch as the thrusters ignited, blasting the pod out of its tube. He bounced off the unyielding metal, then spun helplessly through the center of the pod as the *Anvil*'s artificial gravity vanished and was replaced by the free fall of deep space. Grabbing a handhold, he shoved himself into one of the seats and strapped in.

Only then, with the stars and black of space filling the pod's small viewport and the mad desperation of his near death fading, did he have a chance to fully assess his situation.

The *Anvil* was destroyed. The *Hammer* either was destroyed or had made its escape. And Qilori was arrowing through the void in a small metal cylinder, surrounded by enemies who would probably assume he was an escaped Kilji and react accordingly.

There was only one chance. Thrawn was one of those enemies, and he seemed to enjoy gathering information. If he spotted the escape pod and thought it might contain someone or something useful, he might go to the effort of chasing it down and retrieving it intact instead of offering it to his laser crews for target practice.

Might.

It was a small chance. Infinitesimally small, probably. But right now, it was all he had.

Closing his eyes, feeling his winglets slow to a tired stop, he settled back to wait.

With a violent multiple blast that seemed to shiver from the breachers' impact point all the way aft to the stern, the larger of the two Kilji cruisers disintegrated.

Samakro took a careful breath. It hadn't been easy, but it hadn't been nearly as hard as he'd expected it to be. That was good.

Or else it was very, very suspicious.

"Damage report?" Thrawn called.

"Minor damage to Breacher Two, port-ventral sensors, and barrier nodes four through eight," Brisch said from the comm station. "Repairs under way."

"Very good," Thrawn said. "A question, Mid Captain?"

"Sir?" Samakro asked, frowning.

"You seem concerned," Thrawn said. "Is it the unexpectedly quick victory, or the fact that we fired first?"

"Not so much the latter, sir," Samakro said, a small part of him noting how proficient he was becoming at rationalizing away the Council's standing non-aggression order. "We may technically have fired first, but they fired on us *before* our spheres hit them. I assume you somehow knew they wouldn't engage in a lengthy conversation?"

"I thought it likely," Thrawn said. "These Kiljis seem impatient, even short-tempered. I also note that their ships are designed around a first-strike strategy. Was it the quick victory, then?"

"Not the victory itself," Samakro said, "but the fact that the commander gave up so easily on his attack. I realize his maneuvers were designed to allow the other cruiser to escape unscathed, or at least relatively so, but that behavior doesn't mesh with their vocal arrogance. I'd have thought sheer stubbornness would keep them fighting longer."

"Agreed," Thrawn said. "And when a person or species acts contrary to what seems to be their nature, one must look to see if there's a higher factor or directive involved."

"Senior Captain, the *Aelos* is hailing us," Brisch put in.

Thrawn touched the comm key. "This is Senior Captain Thrawn," he called, switching back to Taarja. "My apologies for the attack, Uingali foar Marocsaa. It appeared you were preparing to fire on the Kiljis, and I didn't want you revealing your true identity."

"So I gathered," Uingali said calmly. "My compliments on the quick and efficient way you delivered that message, given that any comm signal would have been intercepted by our common enemy. They *are* our common enemy, are they not?"

"They are certainly a common opponent," Thrawn said. "Whether we and the Kiljis are truly enemies still remains to be seen. I trust your systems have recovered from our attack?"

Uingali made an odd sound. "In fact, Senior Captain, they were never affected. You didn't see—and neither, I presume, did our enemies—that I had moved a shuttle into position just off my bow where it was likely to escape notice. It was that shuttle that took the brunt of your plasma sphere."

"Indeed," Thrawn said, and Samakro could hear both admiration and amusement in his voice. "Well done. You and your people continue to surprise and impress me."

"We'll take that as a compliment," Uingali said. "I presume you're here to return the Magys and her companion to her people?"

"Just the Magys," Thrawn said, the amusement fading from his voice. "But we'll speak of that later. Before we continue inward, I'd like to take a few hours and collect some of the debris for analysis."

"We shall leave you to that," Uingali said. "In the meantime, would you like us to retrieve the escape pod?"

Thrawn sat up straighter in his command chair. "I was unaware a pod had been jettisoned."

"It was near the end of the battle," Uingali said. "After the smaller ship escaped to hyperspace, just prior to the larger ship's destruction. From your position, it wouldn't have been visible."

"You're tracking it?"

"Yes," Uingali said. "Would you like its position and vector?"

"Yes, thank you," Thrawn said. "With your permission, I'd like to take the *Springhawk* to retrieve it."

"I have no objections," Uingali said. "I presume you'll share its contents with the Paccosh?"

"Certainly," Thrawn said. "Azmordi?"

"I have the pod's location, sir," the pilot confirmed.

"Take us to it," Thrawn said. "Best possible speed."

"Yes, sir."

"We'll speak again soon, Uingali foar Marocsaa," Thrawn said, and keyed off the comm.

"You think the ship's commander might have been less willing to sacrifice himself than he was his ship and crew?" Samakro asked as the *Springhawk* leapt forward, driving through the debris cloud and toward the distant mark Azmordi had added to the tactical display.

"Unlikely," Thrawn said, an intense expression on his face. "I expect that aliens who call themselves enlightened will follow their leaders unquestioningly. But there *was* likely someone aboard who might have felt differently."

Samakro looked out the viewport with sudden understanding. "They had a navigator."

"I would say almost certainly," Thrawn said. "And whether General Crofyp released him or he made the decision to leave the ship himself, I think we'll find him in that pod."

Samakro smiled tightly. "And where you find a ship's navigator, you find where that ship has been."

"And perhaps who that ship has been associating with," Thrawn said. "Senior Commander Afpriuh, prepare a tractor beam."

He looked up at Samakro. "And you, Mid Captain Samakro, please prepare a proper welcome for our guest."

MEMORIES V

It was pure luck that the courier ship scheduled to return Thrass to Csilla was delayed an hour. That was the only reason the ship was still rising through Naporar's atmosphere when the emergency message came through ordering him to head immediately to the Stybla stronghold a quarter of the planet away from his original meeting in the Expansionary Defense Fleet headquarters.

The message carried no additional details. But the courier's pilot clearly knew what *immediately* meant, and he had Thrass on the landing area outside the Stybla mansion in record time.

Senior Aide Lappincyk was waiting inside the ornate outer doors. "Welcome, Aristocra Thrass, and thank you for coming," the other greeted him, his expression grim. "The Patriarch will see you in his office." Without waiting for a reply, he turned and strode off down the wide hallway.

"I look forward to seeing him," Thrass said, hurrying to catch up and wondering what was going on. There were no smiles or sly comments from Lappincyk this time, as there'd been when he invited himself to Thrass's bistro table a handful of years ago. There was no posturing, either, nor had there been any of the reflexive tonal sparring that occurred whenever officials from one family met those from another.

This was a man who was worried. Desperately worried.

Bypassing the larger doors, which Thrass knew from other stronghold mansions led to more formal audience and meeting chambers, Lappincyk led the way to a more unobtrusive door, plain wood with no markings or decoration. He opened it, moving to the side and gesturing Thrass to enter. Thrass gave him a nod of thanks, then stepped into the room.

There were two others already there, Thrass noted as Lappincyk followed him in and closed the door behind them. In the center of the room, seated behind a carved desk, was Patriarch Lamiov, dressed in a formal dark-green outerwrap robe with gold filigree on the collar and down both arms. He was old, his skin paled with age, his close-cut hair displaying a scattered starfield of white. But his eyes were clear and his face was sharp and intelligent.

Standing at the front corner of the desk, half turned toward the door, was Thrawn.

"Welcome, Syndic Thrass," Lamiov said, his voice grave. "The Stybla are facing a potential disaster of the highest order, and Patriarch Thooraki has graciously offered your assistance in resolving it."

"We stand by our Patriarch in all things, Your Venerante," Thrass assured him, picking his words with practiced ease. There was no harm, after all, in reminding Lamiov that he and Thrawn were here at *Thooraki's* request, not his.

"Twelve hours ago a Stybla cargo ship left Csilla bound for Sposia and Naporar," Lamiov said. If he'd noticed the subtle underscoring in Thrass's comment, he gave no indication. "Seven hours later, it was on its approach to the Desum Industrial Field on Sposia when it was attacked by a pirate ship disguised as an Obbic transport. Before anyone could intervene, the pirates overpowered the crew, took possession of the ship, and escaped into hyperspace."

Thrass felt his throat tighten. So that was why he and Thrawn were here. The Obbic, the Seventh Ruling Family, were recent and slightly wobbly allies of the Mitth. If someone was hoping to use this incident to tarnish their name and standing, it would make sense for Lamiov to want one of their allies as part of the investigation. "Do we know if any Obbic were actually involved?" he asked.

Lamiov gave a small snort. "I hardly think an Obbic pirate squad would use one of their own ships."

"Unless they assumed everyone would think that way," Thrass pointed out.

"Are there recordings of the incident?" Thrawn spoke up, pulling out his questis.

"Yes, three of them," Lamiov said, picking up his own questis and tapping to send across the data. "I'm afraid none of them are very clear."

"Understandable," Thrawn said. "If no one was close enough to intervene, no one would be close enough to make good recordings, either."

"Who's in charge of orbital security at Sposia?" Thrass asked, pulling out his questis and keying for his own copy of the recordings.

"Excellent question," Lamiov said. "Lappincyk?"

"It's a combined force including elements of the Kynkru, Obbic, Clarr, and Csap," Lappincyk said. "All four families have strongholds here, which is why the security duties are shared."

Thrass nodded, gazing at his questis with a sinking heart as the hijacking unfolded. The pirates' plan was straightforward enough: Their Obbic transport eased up toward the Stybla cargo ship, feigning maneuvering thruster problems, then suddenly slammed alongside and locked the two ships together. For three and a half minutes they remained that way, their mutual orbit continuing to sink them slowly toward the planet below, before the Stybla's drive suddenly came to full power and drove the still-linked ships toward deep space. Two minutes after that, as the planet's patrol ships scrambled in a vain attempt to intervene, the hijackers and the hijacked vanished together into hyperspace.

He went through the attack three times, once from each of the recordings' viewpoints and angles. The multiple viewings didn't make the mess any easier to watch.

"These patrol ships are designed for two crew members," Thrawn said. "Yet I see only a single pilot listed on each."

"That's correct," Lappincyk said. "They've ordered an upgrade to all their ships, and System Patrol decided the most efficient course of action would be to pull half the pilots off active duty and begin their retraining."

"Which family arranges the patrol schedule?"

"Again, a joint command group including each of the four families."

"We already looked at that, Mid Commander," Lamiov added. "We can find no evidence that the schedulers conspired to maneuver the security forces far enough away that they couldn't assist the cargo ship in time."

"I see," Thrawn said. "In that case, I believe the pirates were of the Clarr."

Thrass looked up at him in amazement. "The *Clarr*? Why would they want a Stybla cargo ship?"

"I didn't suggest it was an upper-level Clarr operation," Thrawn said. "I merely suggested the pirates were from that family."

"Why do you think so?" Lamiov asked.

Thrawn gestured to his questis. "Look at the recordings again. The indicators are there."

"There's no time for a game of Riddle Me," Lappincyk said, an edge of impatience in his voice. "Just tell us."

Thrass looked at Thrawn, and it seemed to him that a flicker of resignation crossed his face. "There are three families represented in these recordings," he said. He tapped the one made by the Clarr pilot. "But only this pilot is already recording before the attack begins."

Thrass frowned at his questis. Thrawn was right. "Because she knew it was about to happen."

"Yes, I see," Lamiov commented, his voice cold. "Sloppy."

"Pirates and hijackers are not known for their overall cleverness," Thrass pointed out, sifting through the possibilities. Criminal gangs typically were organized within a single family, with very few of them crossing family lines. If a Clarr pilot was in on it, as Thrawn had already deduced, presumably the rest of the hijackers were Clarr as well. "You need to detain that pilot immediately, Your Venerante," he said. "You should also contact someone on Rhigar. Patriarch Clarr'ivl'exow needs to know what's happened."

"The pilot is already isolated in a debriefing room," Lappincyk said, working his questis. "We'll make sure she doesn't leave." He frowned thoughtfully. "As to Patriarch Rivlex, he may already know. We're getting reports that a number of high-level communications have gone back and forth from his office in the five hours since this happened."

"He knows about the theft and is trying to track down the hijackers," Lamiov said grimly. "So he knows."

Thrass shot a look at Thrawn, saw his same surprise reflected in the other's face. Had Lamiov just repeated himself?

"So it would seem, Your Venerante," Lappincyk said. "But Syndic Thrass is correct. You need to discuss this matter with him at once."

"Agreed." Lamiov looked at Thrawn and Thrass. "With your permission, I'd like to keep you here for the next short time. We may need more of your assistance to resolve this situation."

"As I said, we're here at the behest of our Patriarch," Thrass said. "Until he says otherwise, we're yours to command."

"Though—" Thrawn shot a look at Thrass. "I'm scheduled to take up my new post aboard the *Springhawk* in three hours. I'm not certain how this delay would be perceived by my superiors."

Thrass winced. And after the politics-edged debacle with the Lioaoi and Garwians that Thrawn had just suffered through, he could imagine the Hierarchy Defense Council being eager to get him and his picket group out of the Ascendancy and off onto their distant pirate hunt.

"I'll speak with General Ba'kif," Lamiov said. "There will be no adverse repercussions, I assure you."

"Then I also am at your service," Thrawn said.

"Thank you both," Lamiov said. "If you'll follow Senior Aide Lappincyk, he'll take you to a place where you may rest until I've finished my conversations."

A minute later, the two Mitth found themselves in a small but well-furnished lounge. "What was the problem back there?" Thrass asked as he chose one of the lounge chairs and sat down.

"The problem?"

"You looked somewhat put out when Lamiov and Lappincyk wouldn't play Riddle Me with you," Thrass said.

Thrawn looked away, an echo of that same expression again crossing his face. "I wasn't put out, Thrass," he said quietly. "I was disappointed. People who can't see things that are right in front of them . . ." He shook his head.

"This may come as a shock to you," Thrass warned, "but

most people don't see things nearly as quickly or as clearly as you do."

"I know," Thrawn said. "I just wish . . . it's not important." He lowered himself into the chair beside Thrass's and pulled out his questis. "We need to focus our attention on the hijacking."

"Right," Thrass agreed, pulling out his own questis. "Can't let Lamiov and the Stybla have *all* the fun. You have a plan for tracking down the criminals?"

"No, we'll leave that to the two Patriarchs," Thrawn said. "It's clear that something aboard that ship is vital to Lamiov. Let's focus on that."

Thrass frowned. "I assumed he cared about the whole cargo."

"No," Thrawn said. "At least not primarily. There's one particular item that he's predominantly interested in."

"If you say so," Thrass said. "How do we start?"

"We find the cargo listings and the locations where each of the items was taken aboard," Thrawn said. "We try to ascertain the pirates' specific target, then try to figure out where they might have taken it."

"Sounds good." Thrass said. "And Thrawn?"

Thrawn looked up. "Yes?"

"Remember what I just said about people not seeing things as quickly as you do?" Thrass asked. "That thing about the Patriarch mostly caring about one item. That was one of them."

CHAPTER EIGHT

Qilori had expected to spend at least a couple of hours floating through the vast emptiness while Thrawn decided whether or not the pod was worth picking up. Discovering that the pod's automatic beacon wasn't functional raised that estimate to somewhere between several hours and the remainder of his short, oxygen-starved life.

It was therefore a surprise, though a welcome one, when he'd been traveling for barely twenty minutes when a section of the starscape was blotted out and he felt the tug of a tractor beam as it locked onto the pod. Ten minutes after that, the hatch opened into the warmth and security and artificial gravity of the Chiss warship.

Five minutes and a *very* thorough security frisking after that, he was standing in a small ready room facing Thrawn.

"Senior Captain," Qilori said, bowing his head. "I thank you for the rescue—"

"Does the other Kilji ship also employ a Pathfinder?" Thrawn interrupted.

Qilori felt his cheek winglets twitch. What kind of question was that? "Ah . . . yes. They do."

"Good," Thrawn said, standing up and gesturing to Qilori's guards. "Take him to the bridge. You're going to chase down that other Pathfinder for us."

"*What?*" Qilori managed as the two blueskins took his upper arms and turned him back toward the hatch. "No—I can't. That's not possible."

"You forget, Qilori of Uandualon, that I know your secret," Thrawn said, falling into step beside him as the guards marched him down the corridor. "I know how Pathfinders in hyperspace are able to sense one another." He turned those disturbing glowing red eyes on him. "You've used that ability to aid pirates, military attack forces, and General Yiv himself. Do I need to remind you what the other nations of the region would do if they also knew that?"

"No," Qilori said between clenched teeth. "But I didn't say I was unwilling. I said it wasn't possible. I left my sensory-deprivation headset on the *Anvil,* and without it I can't join with the Great Presence."

"You also forget that I've seen the headset you use," Thrawn said. "Something similar will be waiting for you."

The bridge was a flurry of activity when they arrived. Qilori was escorted to the navigator's chair—a very nice, very well-padded chair, he noted as he sat down—and was handed a cobbled-together monstrosity of a headset. "Will this suffice?" Thrawn asked.

Qilori pretended to study the headset, his eyes flicking over the board in front of him as he did so. He could read the Cheunh labeling reasonably well; unfortunately, there was nothing there that might indicate the presence of a mechanical navigator. But then, those controls would probably be disguised, lest some casual alien visitor notice them.

He slipped on the headset for a quick test. The thing was clumsy and inelegant, but it should do the job. "Yes, it will work," he said. He took it off, set it on the edge of the board, and began strapping in.

"Good," Thrawn said. "You will locate the other Pathfinder and follow him. I'll let you know when you're to stop." The Chiss put a restraining hand on the headset as Qilori picked it up again. "And I'm fairly certain I know where that ship is going," he warned. "Don't try to mislead me."

Qilori's winglets twitched. "I won't."

Thrawn lifted his hand away and Qilori again settled the headset in place, blocking out the bridge, the Chiss, and the rest of the universe. Slipping into his trance, he let the Great Presence surround and fill him. The *Hammer*'s Pathfinder . . . there he was.

Qilori felt his winglets tense. He'd expected the picket cruiser to return to the system where the two Pathfinders had been brought after being hired. But that wasn't the case. Instead the *Hammer* was headed in a completely different direction. If Thrawn thought he knew where they'd come from, and expected them to go back . . .

But there was nothing Qilori could do about that. He'd been ordered to follow the *Hammer,* and trying to anticipate or second-guess what Thrawn wanted or didn't want would be a dangerous and probably futile game. Bracing himself, he reached for the controls.

He frowned inside the headset. The chair itself, as he'd already noted, had been set at the proper height and width. But the control board itself was noticeably too close. Had they somehow missed the length of his arms when they preadjusted it for him?

No matter; he could make do. Getting a grip on the controls, he launched the ship into hyperspace.

It seemed that he was nestled within the Great Presence for a long time, the glow permeating his mind, the other Pathfinder an extra-bright spark in the distance. But it was probably only a few minutes before he felt the distant touch of a hand on his shoulder, a touch that gradually grew stronger and more insistent. Reluctantly, he let go of the glow, and the Great Presence faded, and he was once again blind and deaf in the midst of people who probably distrusted him and certainly resented him.

He pulled off the headset. Thrawn was standing beside him, gazing out at the pulsating hyperspace sky. "Is there a problem, Senior Captain?" he asked carefully.

"No," Thrawn said.

Qilori felt his winglets stiffen. From Thrawn's expression and voice it was clear there was definitely something wrong. Fortunately, the problem didn't seem to be with Qilori himself. "What happens now?"

"You'll be taken to your quarters," Thrawn said, motioning him out of the chair. "And then we'll return to Rapacc."

Your quarters. Apparently, Qilori was to be a guest aboard the blueskin warship for awhile.

Still, it could have been worse. Thrawn *could* have had him taken to the brig.

"Thank you again for the rescue," he said as he stood up. "Please let me know if there's anything more I can do for you."

"I will," Thrawn said softly, those glowing eyes once again digging deep into Qilori's soul. "Indeed I will."

Thalias's intent, to the extent that she had enough mental ability left to form any goals at all as she stumbled to her bed, was to sleep as long as she could. Eight hours at least, possibly ten or even twelve, and she would wake up bright, alert, and refreshed.

She was therefore somewhat surprised to find herself still bleary-eyed when the insistent yapping of the intercom dragged her out of a deep and dreamless sleep.

A surprise that turned to groggy disbelief when she checked the chrono and found she'd been asleep barely three hours.

She propped herself up on one elbow, too tired even to be annoyed, and tapped the key. "Yes?"

"Bridge." The voice of Senior Commander Kharill came from the speaker. "Senior Captain Thrawn needs to see you right away."

Thalias frowned, some of the sleep cobwebs dissipating. Last she'd heard, the *Springhawk* had been within a quick jump-by-jump of Rapacc, where Thrawn was supposed to wake the Magys from her hibernation and turn her over to the Paccosh. The whole process should have taken several hours at least.

Had something gone wrong?

"Understood," she told Kharill, pushing herself the rest of the way into a seated position and looking across the room at the hibernation chamber.

Or rather, at the empty section of bulkhead where the hibernation chamber used to be. Sometime in the past three hours, while Thalias had been asleep, someone had come in and taken it out.

"Just make sure you're ready," Kharill warned. "He's in a hurry."

"Understood," Thalias said again.

She keyed off the intercom and ran her fingers through her hair, flinching at the itchiness of her scalp. She hadn't bothered to change into her nightshirt before collapsing onto the bed, so at least she didn't have to worry about getting dressed. Unfortunately, that had also left her skin with the unpleasant sticky feeling that always happened when she slept in her clothes.

From outside her sleeping room came the hatch chime. Thalias got to her feet, weaving slightly for the first couple of steps as she fought to get her balance. She crossed her room and the dayroom and opened the hatch.

Thrawn was standing there, his face grim, his eyes looking distracted. "Caregiver," he greeted her tersely, stepping past her into the dayroom before she could even invite him in. "I need to speak with you."

"Of course," Thalias said, closing the hatch behind him. "Would you like to sit down?"

"There's no time," Thrawn said, stopping three steps into the room and turning to face her. "I'll be leaving the *Springhawk* in half an hour, and I need you to—"

"You're *what*?" Thalias interrupted, the last remnants of sleep flash-burning from her mind.

"Please just listen," Thrawn said. "I don't have much time. We reached the Rapacc system to find two Kilji ships threatening the Paccosh. There was a battle—a brief battle—and one of the ships escaped and appears to be headed toward Sunrise. I need to get there as quickly as possible to see who they're meeting with, try to learn their plans, and determine how they can be stopped before they inflict more damage."

"All right," Thalias said, her head spinning worse than it had been when she first woke up. She'd slept through a *battle*? "Do you need Che'ri on the bridge?"

"No, she needs sleep," Thrawn said. "I'll be leaving Mid Captain Samakro in command here while Uingali and I head out in the *Aelos*. We're taking the Magys with us—"

"No, no, wait," Thalias protested. "You're going too fast. Why are you going with Uingali instead of taking the *Springhawk*?"

"Because the *Springhawk* is under orders from Supreme General Ba'kif to return to the Ascendancy immediately after we deliver the Magys to Rapacc," Thrawn said. "Disobeying that order would bring serious consequences, not just for me but also for all my senior officers. Samakro and the ship *have* to go back."

"But why can't you stay with us?" Thalias pressed. "Can't Uingali and the Paccosh go without you?"

"Of course they can." Thrawn's lip twitched. "But they won't. Uingali will only put his people into a mission of such danger if I agree to command it."

Thalias stared at him. "Oh," she said, wincing at the sheer emptiness of the word. "I . . . well, can we come along? Che'ri and me? I know she'd be willing."

"Thank you, but no," Thrawn said. "I need you and Che'ri to take the *Springhawk* home."

"What about just me, then?" Thalias pressed. "I mean . . . I was with you at the start of this whole Paccian thing. I should be allowed to see the end of it."

"This is hardly the end," Thrawn said. "No matter what happens at Sunrise, the Paccosh will endure. Besides, you need to be here to take care of Che'ri."

"Not really," Thalias said. "She can navigate the *Springhawk* just fine on her own."

"Thalias, this is becoming silly," Thrawn chided gently. "I know you feel the late Patriarch Thooraki told you to watch over me, but risking your career and reputation isn't the way to do that."

Thalias set her jaw. "I don't have much career, I don't have *any* reputation, and I don't care about either of them. Lives are on the line here. And not just yours. The Paccosh and the Magys's people are also at risk."

"I commend your priorities and your sense of justice," Thrawn said. "But this is a path I must take on my own." He gestured toward her sleeping room. "Now you need to get back to sleep. Samakro will begin the journey home via jump-by-jump, but he'll need you and Che'ri as soon as you're able to take over navigation. Take care of her, and please give her my farewells."

Thalias swallowed against the sudden lump in her throat. "I will. Please be careful, sir."

"I will." Thrawn smiled at her. "Farewell, Thalias."

For a long moment after he left she just stared at the closed hatch, a cold sense of dread fighting against her exhaustion. Never mind what Thalias might do to her career—what was Thrawn about to do to *his*?

She took a deep breath. Samakro. She needed to talk to Mid Captain Samakro.

But not now. Not yet. She needed to carefully time that confrontation, to make sure it fell between the moment Thrawn left the *Springhawk* and the moment when he and Uingali planned to depart for Sunrise. The *Springhawk* had captured and carried a Nikardun blockade frigate once before—surely Samakro could do the same thing again. And once the smaller craft was secured, Thrawn would either listen to reason or be bodily hauled back to the Ascendancy.

Uingali wouldn't like it. The Syndicure would be furious. But at least Thrawn would still be alive.

Turning, Thalias headed toward the food-prep area. Half an hour, Thrawn had said, before he left. Not enough time for a shower, but more than enough to brew herself a cup of strong caccoleaf. She would sit on the couch, get some stimulant into her, and be ready the moment Thrawn left the ship.

Only that wasn't what happened.

Five hours later, she woke with a start from a horrible nightmare, her neck cricked from the odd angle her head had settled into against the back of the couch, the mug of cold caccoleaf sitting barely touched on the side table.

And the repeater displays below the snack bar showing that the *Springhawk* was already in hyperspace.

Cursing viciously, uselessly under her breath, she got her shoes on and raced to the bridge.

Samakro was seated in the command chair, gazing moodily at the hyperspace swirl rushing past outside the viewport. "Mid Captain," Thalias breathed as she hurried to his side.

"*There* you are," Samakro said, his voice as dour as his expression. "I expected you five hours ago."

"We're on our way back to the Ascendancy?" Thalias asked, just to be sure.

"Where else would we be going?" Samakro countered. "We're under orders. As I'm sure Senior Captain Thrawn told you."

Thalias swallowed back another useless curse. "So you just let him go?" she accused. "I thought you weren't big on Expansionary Defense Fleet officers abandoning their posts."

He looked sideways at her. "What makes you say that?"

"You weren't happy with Senior Captain Lakinda leaving the *Grayshrike* for the Xodlak family emergency call."

"No one who was at that meeting would have told you that."

"I'm getting good at reading faces." Thalias raised her eyebrows. "I also note you're not denying it."

With a snort, Samakro turned back to the viewport. "My commander gave me an order," he said. "My duty is to obey that order."

"Even if it costs that commander his career?" Thalias shot back. "Even if it costs him his *life*?"

"He'll be all right," Samakro said.

"You can't possibly believe that," Thalias bit out. "You're the one who told *me* that the rest of the Nikardun were gathering their forces at Sunrise where they could launch new attacks."

"I never said we knew that for a fact," Samakro said, his voice sounding a little odd. "It was only a theory."

"But Senior Captain Thrawn's theories are usually right."

"Usually, but not always," Samakro said. "In this case . . . look. Uingali has a full commando squad aboard the *Aelos*. They wanted to be ready for an enemy ship that was careless enough to get within boarding range. Trust me, he knows what he's doing."

Thalias frowned. "I thought he needed Senior Captain Thrawn to lead the attack."

"Is that what the senior captain told you?" Samakro gave a little snort. "Hardly. Uingali wants him aboard because if it goes badly a Chiss senior officer will have been captured or killed."

Thalias stared at him, her stomach wrenching with sudden understanding. "They're trying to force the Ascendancy to take military action."

"Of course they are," Samakro said, his lip twisting. "Don't sound so outraged—it's the exact same trick you and Senior Captain Thrawn used against General Yiv. I'm just a little surprised Uingali knew about it."

"I figured that by now *everybody* knew we don't attack unless attacked first," Thalias said between clenched teeth. "So how do we get him out?"

Samakro grimaced. "We go back to the Ascendancy and report. If we're lucky, this and the attacks over Sunrise will be enough to get the Syndicure off their collective rear end."

"That'll be way too late."

"Maybe." Samakro huffed out a sigh. "Probably," he conceded. "But it's all we've got."

For a moment neither of them spoke. Thalias gazed out the viewport, watching as the *Springhawk* flew farther and farther from its captain. "Thank you for your honesty, Mid Captain," she said.

"You're welcome," Samakro said. "I suggest you go back and get some more sleep. We'll want you and Che'ri back on duty as soon as she's ready. The faster we get to Csilla, the faster we can get something put together to go help Senior Captain Thrawn."

"Yes," Thalias murmured.

Samakro was right, of course, she knew as she returned to the skywalker suite. Speed was going to be called for, and the faster the better. A crisis was upon them, and Thalias knew what she had to do.

She could only hope Che'ri would be willing to do the same.

CHAPTER NINE

Thurfian delivered his report to the Defense Hierarchy Council three hours after the Kilji warship left Avidich orbit and disappeared back into the vast reaches of interstellar space between the worlds of the Ascendancy. Within six hours the Dasklo, Xodlak, Erighal, and Pommrio families had all lodged protests with the Syndicure, accusing the Mitth of engaging in innuendo tactics, denouncing Thurfian's report, and demanding he withdraw his accusations or else offer proof of his claims. The fact that Thurfian had made no claims of his own but had merely reported on someone else's either passed them by or were deliberately ignored.

Usually, such political outrages quickly faded into the background as the various families sorted out their alliances and rivalries, strengthening, re-forming, or redefining as needed, until a new dispute arose to replace it. But in this case, the outrage melded with a rising level of dark anticipation. This latest scandal had come on the heels of the Hoxim incident, which was itself far from resolved. Moreover, it had originated from an alien warship, and as the Defense Force scrambled to provide additional protection for the major Chiss worlds the various families began making quiet preparations of their own.

Three days after making his report, Thurfian finally received the expected call from Syndic Prime Zistalmu.

"I don't know what to say," Zistalmu growled, his expression showing a mix of disbelief and suspicion. "An alien warship pops in over

Avidich, talks to your Patriel, spins some wild claims about the Dasklo being up to no good, and then pops out again?"

"I know it sounds fantastic," Thurfian conceded. "But that's what happened."

"He talked to *your* Patriel about a threat to the Clarr," Zistalmu said. "Not the *Clarr* Patriel. Yours."

"Maybe Jixtus wasn't sure who he should talk to," Thurfian said. "The Mitth have the largest presence of all the Nine and Forty on Avidich. Maybe he wanted to talk to the family more or less in charge of the planet."

"He knew the names of the four families he says are involved," Zistalmu countered. "Why not one of them? Why *you*?"

"I already said I don't know," Thurfian said patiently. "I presume you have a theory?"

For a moment Zistalmu seemed to study his face. "The Erighal, Xodlak, and Pommrio were at Hoxim," he said. "Jixtus could have learned those names there."

"Or from the Agbui who apparently goaded them into going to Hoxim in the first place."

"I suppose that's possible," Zistalmu said. "But there was one other family present at Hoxim. Senior Captain Thrawn and the *Springhawk*."

"Which according to all reports was being pummeled by alien gunships when the three family forces arrived," Thurfian reminded him.

"So they say," Zistalmu said, his eyes narrowing slightly. "We've already dismissed the idea that he was caught in an ambush. So tell me, Thurfian: When was the last time you heard about him being pummeled?"

Thurfian felt his throat tighten. He'd wondered that same thing since the first bits of information about Hoxim began trickling out. He'd wondered about it a lot. "I thought the whole premise of our private conversations was that he was eventually going to mess up. Maybe this was it."

"No," Zistalmu said firmly. "We expect him to fail on a massive, disastrous level. Not in something as mundane as simple combat. No, something happened at Hoxim, something that involved Thrawn. Apparently, this Jixtus knows all about it." He cocked his head slightly to the side. "My question is, do *you*?"

"I know nothing beyond what was in the Hoxim reports, and what I reported to the Syndicure about Jixtus," Thurfian said. "I presume you noticed that when he showed up again at Rhigal, he *did* talk to the Clarr?"

"Whose report on the incident, I also note, was remarkably similar to yours," Zistalmu said. "Including how Patriarch Rivlex virtuously sent the aliens on their way without making any deals."

"You think he did?" Thurfian asked.

Zistalmu snorted. "The way the Clarr and Dasklo have been at each other's throats forever? I think that if you dangled something in front of Rivlex that he thought he could stab them with, he'd buy it like a shot."

"That vid Jixtus showed us certainly isn't that magic spear," Thurfian warned. "All it's good for is to light unverifiable fires under the Dasklo, the other three families—"

"Hold it," Zistalmu cut in, his eyes shifting away from the cam. "There's an emergency alert coming in."

Thurfian looked over at his own data feed monitor. Nothing was showing the double-red border that would indicate an alert. It must be something on the private Irizi channel, a situation pertaining only to the Irizi or one of their allies.

Zistalmu muttered a curse. "What was that you said about lighting fires?" he asked, his voice suddenly grim.

"What is it?" Thurfian asked.

"Jamiron," Zistalmu told him. "A Clarr convoy there is being attacked."

"That's impossible," Thurfian insisted, keying the monitor into the Defense Force feed. "Jixtus and the Kiljis can't be stupid enough to think they can get away with an overt attack—"

"It's not the Kiljis," Zistalmu cut him off. "It's—" His lips compressed. "It's the Erighal and Xodlak."

Thurfian felt his mouth drop open. "*What?*"

"Four Clarr freighters from the family's electronics manufactory complex have been intercepted by two Erighal and two Xodlak patrol ships," Zistalmu said. "Their escort cruiser's fighting back . . . three Clarr system patrol ships are trying to assist . . . damn. Three more Erighals are engaging the Clarr patrol."

"You're sure about their identities?" Thurfian asked, his mind reeling. What did they think they were *doing*?

"Their family crests are covered," Zistalmu said. "But the reports say the obscuring masks fit the proper shapes for those crests. They also say the ships show their families' specific design peculiarities."

"I see," Thurfian said, keying his monitor to the Mitth family fleet status listings. This attack made no sense at all, but right now that didn't matter. There would be time enough to sort it out after the Clarr freighters were safe. "All right," he said. "We have two patrol ships at Rentor—I can send them to assist."

"They'll never get there in time."

"Depends on how well the defenders can hold up," Thurfian said. "We've also got a light cruiser traveling from Rentor to Sposia that should be passing Jamiron just about now."

"No, don't bother," Zistalmu said.

"It's a long shot," Thurfian said, "but if the captain decides to stop at Jamiron I can send a message—"

"I said *no!*"

Thurfian twitched. "What are you saying?"

"I'm saying we'll handle it, Thurfian," Zistalmu ground out. "I mean, we'll handle it, *Your Venerante*."

Thurfian stared at him. Zistalmu's expression was tight, his eyes blazing with emotion. "Zistalmu, what's going on?" he asked carefully.

Zistalmu took a long, shuddering breath. "This *could* be an attack by the Erighal and Xodlak. Or it could be something entirely different."

"Such as?"

"Such as a trick by the Mitth," Zistalmu said bluntly.

"That's absurd."

"Is it?" Zistalmu countered. "Face it, Thurfian—*Your Venerante*—our families have been locking antlers for centuries. We've both tried to create alliances with the Clarr over those years, and neither of us has ever succeeded. Now we've suddenly got aliens in the Ascendancy warning that the Xodlak—one of *our* allies—are thinking about teaming up with the Dasklo. What better chance for the Mitth to stage a false Xodlak attack against the Clarr and then swoop in to save the day? I imagine the Clarr would be very grateful for that assistance."

"You can't possibly believe we'd do something like that," Thurfian protested. "Fine, so our families are rivals. But I thought *we* had an understanding. Our common enemy, remember?"

"Thrawn?" Zistalmu snorted. "Maybe that was what he was once. I'm not so sure he is anymore."

"Nothing has changed," Thurfian insisted. No—surely Zistalmu wasn't going to fall apart on him. Not now. "He's still a threat to the Ascendancy—"

"I have to go, Your Venerante," Zistalmu said. "My Speaker and Patriarch need my attention." He paused, and his lip twitched. "And it's *Syndic Prime* Zistalmu." He reached off-cam and his face vanished from the display.

For a few seconds Thurfian stared at the blank screen, his mind still spinning. What madness could have possessed the Erighal and Xodlak families to pull something like this?

He had no idea. But right now that didn't matter. Zistalmu's wishes and suspicions be damned—if the Mitth could help in this crisis, they would.

Starting with a continuous broadcast message to the light cruiser he'd mentioned. With the relatively safe hyperspace travel within the Ascendancy, there was no particular reason for the cruiser's captain to pause in his journey for a navigation check or repositioning before continuing. But experienced and meticulous commanders sometimes did that anyway, just to be on the safe side.

Thurfian could only hope this particular captain was experienced and meticulous.

———

"Prepare for breakout," Ziinda called out to the *Grayshrike*'s bridge crew, watching as the timer counted down.

She gave a small, private sigh. Defense duty. The reason she'd joined the Expansionary Defense Fleet instead of the Defense Force in the first place was to avoid the monotony of general Ascendancy patrol work. She'd wanted to explore the Chaos and look for threats out there, not sit in orbit around a planet waiting for those threats to come to her.

But with an alien warship lurking in the darkness between star systems, and everyone from the Nine Ruling Families on down worried about it, she could understand the sudden shuffling of duties.

The Defense Force plus the Ruling Families' private fleets were perfectly capable of taking on that Kilji battle cruiser without any help, of course. But no one seriously believed that Jixtus had come alone, and with General Yiv's brief diversionary attack on Csilla the previous year still fresh in everyone's memory, the Syndicure wasn't interested in taking chances.

On the other hand, the cautious approach carried its own set of risks. If there was an enemy fleet lurking within the Ascendancy, it made sense to pull all available Chiss forces into a defensive posture. But if the enemy was still gathering strength out in the Chaos, suspending Expansionary Defense Fleet patrols that might otherwise spot supply depots, assembly points, and communications relays could give the enemy time to organize. Coupled with the strict prohibition against preemptive action, that self-imposed blindness gave the enemy the opportunity to choose both timing and location.

The last time Ziinda had ordered the *Grayshrike* to be at full alert when they arrived in a star system, she remembered, she'd gotten a few tactful questions about whether all that effort was really necessary. This time, there hadn't been a word out of anyone. Just one more small indication of how much life had changed in only a few short days.

She looked up at Mid Captain Csap'ro'strob, standing silently beside her command chair, his eyes sweeping rhythmically around the bridge as he confirmed the *Grayshrike* was ready. He hadn't said anything about their new assignment, but Ziinda could tell he wasn't any more excited about guard duty than she was.

But at least he would be spared whatever hassle Jamiron System Patrol put them through as they integrated the *Grayshrike* into their defense pattern. Apros's watch had ended half an hour ago, and the only reason he was still on the bridge was to be available if Ziinda needed him for any last-minute details. Once he confirmed that everything was in hand, he would be safely off the bridge.

Ziinda looked back at the timer. "Stand by breakout," she called. "Three, two, *one.*"

The hyperspace swirl became stars, and the *Grayshrike*'s guard duty at Jamiron had officially begun. "Full scan," she ordered, searching the starscape. The planet was home to several major manufactories, which meant a fair amount of traffic in and out, and any prudent pilot knew to bring them out of hyperspace at a cautious distance to make sure they didn't run into anyone. "Signal Patrol Command that we've arrived," she continued, searching the sky. Even at the *Grayshrike*'s current distance, they should be close enough to at least see a hint of their ultimate destination. There was a faint flicker just about where the planet should be—

"Senior Captain, I've got laserfire," Vimsk said sharply. "Mid-range, level, four degrees starboard."

"It's near the planet," Senior Commander Erighal'ok'sumf added from the weapons station. "Combatants too small to make out from here; probably patrol ships or gunboats."

"Belay that call to Patrol Command," Ziinda ordered as Apros crossed the bridge to the weapons station. "If whoever's shooting out there hasn't spotted us, let's not announce ourselves. Mid Captain Apros?"

"Weapons systems and crews are ready," Apros confirmed, leaning over Ghaloksu's shoulder as he checked the monitors.

"Acknowledged," Ziinda said, frowning at the sensor display. Vimsk was right—the ships were too small to show anything other than vague blurs from here. But none of the reports had said any-thing about the Kilji battle cruiser having any fighter escorts. Had Jixtus brought in more forces, like everyone was expecting him to? Or was this something new?

Well, whoever they were, they were going to regret starting a fight over a Chiss planet. "Wikivv, I need an in-system jump to combat range," she told the pilot. "As close as you can without sacrificing a safety margin."

"Yes, ma'am," Wikivv said, peering at her displays as she worked rapidly at her control board. "We can't get too close anyway—they're still pretty deep in the gravity well. I can't get us closer than about fifty kilometers."

"Good enough," Ziinda said. "Tell me when you're ready."

"Yes, ma'am."

The seconds ticked by. Ziinda gazed at the distant planet, forcing herself to remain calm. Sitting here watching helplessly as a battle raged was excruciating, but she knew better than to rush an in-system jump, especially one that would take them close to the critical line in Jamiron's gravity well. She ran her eyes over the status displays, just for something to do—

"Got it, ma'am," Wikivv said.

"Bridge, stand ready," Ziinda said. "Wikivv: Three, two, *one*."

The starscape twitched, the distant planet grew instantly to fill half the viewport, and the tiny flickers Ziinda had seen became the blaz-ing laserfire of a running battle directly ahead. "Shrent, warn them off," she ordered. She looked at the sensor display, noting the number of ships and their positions—

And felt her eyes widen. "Vimsk, confirm sensor readings," she said.

"Confirmed, Captain," the sensor officer said. "Targets are four Clarr freighters with one light cruiser escort. Attackers are—" Her professional tone stumbled. "—four Chiss patrol ships."

"Two Clarr patrol ships coming around from polar orbit," Gha-loksu reported. "Three more Chiss patrol ships . . . they're engaging the two Clarr."

Ziinda hissed between her teeth. Was this some family dispute that had boiled over into armed combat? In past millennia such things had been distressingly common, but that kind of violent over-reaction had supposedly ended three hundred years ago following the creation of the modern Syndicure. Was someone seriously trying to go back to the old ways?

If they were, starting a fight in the middle of an Ascendancy-wide crisis was just plain stupid. She could only hope the *Grayshrike* could stop the nonsense before it went too far. "Wikivv, get us in there," she ordered. "Ghaloksu, prepare spheres."

"Spheres ready, ma'am," Ghaloksu confirmed. "We need to be a little closer for optimal range."

"Understood," Ziinda said. "Use your best judgment on the timing. Shrent, any response?"

"No, ma'am," Shrent said. "The attackers are jamming all communications."

"You have IDs on anyone?"

"Not yet, ma'am," Shrent said. "I can see through the jamming enough to tell that the freighters and cruiser are running beacons, but they aren't clear enough to make out. There's nothing coming from the attackers."

Ziinda nodded. Hardly surprising, given the circumstances. "Vimsk, can you at least tell if they're the local Jamiron defenders or if they're outsiders?"

"Sorry, ma'am," Vimsk said. "I should be able to see ID numbers or family crests at this range, but I'm not spotting anything."

"Looks like they've been masked or obliterated," Apros said. "Maybe we'll be able to pick up some hints when we're closer."

"Or pick up some prisoners," Ziinda said. "Vimsk, what's the freighters' status?"

"The patrol ships are taking them apart," the sensor officer said grimly. "Looks like they've already disabled the freighters' hyper-drives. Clean punches in just the right places. One or two shots each—they knew what they were doing."

"Understood," Ziinda said, scowling. Family warships usually showed slight variations in weaponry and exterior decoration. Freighters were just freighters, though, and everyone used mostly the same standard models with standard internal layouts.

And that uniformity had now played into the attackers' hands. Ziinda had hoped that if they could distract the patrol ships long enough, the freighters might be able to cover the short distance to the edge of the gravity well and escape. With their hyperdrives gone, that was no longer an option.

But if the *Grayshrike* couldn't help them escape, it could at least give them some breathing space. "Spheres: Six-shot volley on the attackers. Three, two, *one.*"

The *Grayshrike* gave the usual twitch as the half dozen plasma spheres shot out from their tubes. "Spheres on target," Ghaloksu reported. "Impact in—"

"Spheres are disintegrating, ma'am," Vimsk cut in.

Ziinda looked over at the tactical display. Vimsk was right: All six plasma spheres had somehow lost their self-focusing sheaths and were boiling away their ionic energy into empty space. "Ghaloksu?"

"Confirmed, Senior Captain," Ghaloksu said tightly. "I don't know how. They shouldn't all have gone at the same time that way."

"You can sort it out later," Ziinda said. "Get me a second salvo."

"Second salvo ready, ma'am."

"Fire."

Another twitch of the *Grayshrike,* and another six plasma spheres blazed toward the battling ships. Ziinda shifted her attention to the vid display, watching closely as the cam tracked the spheres toward their targets.

Once again, the tightly packed balls of plasma abruptly shimmered and de-formed, their containment balance failing as they broke apart into multiple flashes of released energy.

But this time Ziinda spotted something. A group of somethings, actually, arrowing away from the attackers and intercepting the spheres. Were those . . . ?

They were. "*Damn,*" she bit out under her breath. "They're using *dibbers.*"

"What?" Apros asked, half turning toward her.

"Dibbers," Ziinda repeated, her mind racing. "The little anti-fighter missiles the Battle Dreadnought used against the *Vigilant*'s spheres and breachers the last time we tangled with it at Sunrise."

"That can't be," Apros objected, craning his neck to look at the sensor display. "How could Chiss patrol ships get hold of those?"

"I don't know," Ziinda said. "Vimsk?"

"The image is blurry, ma'am," Vimsk said, inclining her head slightly as she listened to the voices coming over her private speaker. "The analysts say these are smaller than the Sunrise dibbers, and are probably shorter-range."

"Different weapons, but the same tactic," Apros said.

"So it would appear, Mid Captain," Vimsk said.

"Interesting," Ziinda murmured, an icy resolve settling into her. And with *that,* she decided, it was time to stop playing nice.

This was no longer a simple family dispute. Whoever was flying those patrol ships, they were connected to or working with the Ascendancy's enemies, and it was time to take them out. With survivors if possible; with shards of scrap metal if not. "Ghaloksu, give me lasers," she ordered. "Full volley on—"

"Captain, they're changing vector," Vimsk warned. "Two bogeys breaking off freighters, moving to engage us."

"Good," Ziinda said, checking the vector marks on the tactical. The freighters were still under attack by the other two patrol ships, but the group movement was taking that battle away from the two that were now targeting the *Grayshrike*. If Ziinda held off her own counterattack a few more seconds, the freighters should be safely out of her line of fire. "Ghaloksu, target bogey lasers. Hold fire until my command."

The words were barely out of her mouth when the two patrol ships opened fire.

"Targeting Sensors Two and Three hit," Apros reported. "Near miss on Lasers One and Three, two hits on portside hull and one on starboard. Barrier nodes intact; no significant damage to the ship."

"Barrier down five percent," Ghaloksu added. "Crews are taking over fire control from the damaged sensors."

"Acknowledged," Ziinda said, feeling a frown crease her forehead. A remarkably ineffective attack, all things considered, especially given that the patrol ships had already demonstrated impressive marksmanship by wrecking the freighters' hyperdrives. "All right, Ghaloksu, show them how it's done. Three, two, *one*."

The *Grayshrike*'s lasers flashed out, burning across Jamiron's ionosphere and slashing into the patrol ships. A second laser salvo lanced out from the attackers toward the *Grayshrike,* digging into the electrostatic barrier but again causing no real damage. For a few seconds the lasers dueled, the intensity of fire from the patrol ships dropping steadily as Ghaloksu's counterattack systematically destroyed their weaponry. The final patrol ship lasers went silent—

"Bogey lasers destroyed," Ghaloksu reported.

"Bogeys changing course," Wikivv put in. "Pitching positive . . . looks like they're going to head back to the freighters."

"Like hell they are," Ziinda said. "Ghaloksu: Cripple them."

Once again the *Grayshrike*'s lasers blazed out, this time targeting first the maneuvering thrusters along the patrol ships' ventral sides, then shifting to the main thrusters as the bogeys' pitch turn presented them to view. The turn faltered as the patrol ships' drives died, their final vectors angling them away from the ongoing freighter battle and toward the edge of Jamiron's planetary rim.

"Bogeys disabled and drifting, Senior Captain," Apros reported, reaching past Ghaloksu to key a pair of controls. "Tractor beams ready, if you want to bring them in."

Ziinda checked the sensor readouts. The two patrol ships were no longer under power, but their reactors were still at normal function. If they could somehow repair their thrusters, they could conceivably get to the edge of the gravity well and escape into hyperspace. Chasing after them and reeling them in would eliminate any chance of that happening.

But the Clarr freighters were still under attack, and the light cruiser that had been escorting them had fallen silent and was drifting behind the battle. Rescuing the civilians had to be the *Gray-*

shrike's first priority. "They'll keep, Mid Captain," she told Apros. "Wikivv, get us over to the freighters. Ghaloksu, set up a full spread of spheres. If we're lucky, we can flicker everyone and sort them out at our leisure."

"And if these bogeys also have dibbers?" Apros asked as the *Grayshrike* turned toward the battle and increased its speed.

"Then Ghaloksu will just need to be very precise with his lasers," Ziinda said. "Think you can handle that, Senior Commander?"

"Yes, ma'am, I can," Ghaloksu assured her. "Spheres ready."

Ziinda nodded. "Stand by." The *Grayshrike* was nearly to firing range. A few more seconds . . .

"Senior Captain—the cruiser," Vimsk said suddenly. "I think it's—"

And without warning, the light cruiser lagging behind the freighters opened fire, its lasers blasting into the attacking patrol ships' main thrusters. The targets twitched violently, then veered out and up as they attempted to get clear of the cruiser's attack.

Unfortunately for them, that evasive maneuver also moved them away from the freighters and put them squarely on the *Grayshrike*'s targeting vector. "Ghaloksu—spheres at the bogeys," Ziinda snapped. "Three, two, *one.*"

The plasma spheres shot out toward the patrol ships, aiming for Ghaloksu's best guess as to where the bogeys would be when the spheres arrived. Ziinda's eyes darted back and forth between the viewport and the tactical, watching the spheres' progress, wondering if the patrol ships would spot the incoming attack in time to evade. The distance was closing . . . almost there . . .

Ziinda jerked in her seat as a second blast of laserfire erupted from the Clarr cruiser and blazed into the patrol ships. Once again the targets tried to get clear.

But this time they were unsuccessful. Even as the *Grayshrike*'s plasma spheres swept toward them, both patrol ships disintegrated in violent explosions.

Ziinda swallowed a curse. So much for taking prisoners.

But maybe the ones Ghaloksu had disabled could still be chased down. "Wikivv—" she began, turning to look out the viewport in that direction.

The command died in her throat as those ships, too, burst into writhing flame and disintegrated.

For a moment the *Grayshrike*'s bridge was silent. "Looks like we won't be taking prisoners," Apros commented quietly. "Awfully convenient for someone."

"It *does* look that way, doesn't it?" Ziinda said, looking back at the vid display. Earlier, Vimsk had said the attackers were taking the freighters apart. Now, as the *Grayshrike* continued toward them, she saw that they were in worse shape than she'd realized. The freighters' thrusters were silent, their power levels were barely registering, and two of the four seemed to be leaking air at a slow but steady rate. The *Grayshrike* had arrived just in time.

Especially since their escort cruiser had gone dormant again, its final bit of power apparently having been expended on those last two laser attacks.

"Senior Captain?" Vimsk spoke up. "The other battle appears to be over."

Ziinda looked at the tactical. With her full attention on the freighters and cruiser, she'd nearly forgotten about the two Clarr patrol boats rounding the planet that had been set upon by three more unidentified attackers. Now the two Clarr were alone, with dust and flickering fire where their assailants had been. "Destroyed, or self-destructed?" she asked.

"Looks like a little of both," Vimsk said, and Ziinda could see a high-speed repeat of the battle playing on one of her sensor displays. "The Clarr got in some good shots, but then the bogeys just blew up."

"Interesting timing," Apros added, watching the same repeat on one of the weapons monitor displays. "They destructed right after the freighter pair were destroyed, and just before our two bogeys did likewise."

"So; nothing intact left to be captured," Ziinda said. "As you said: convenient. Let's hope the analysts on Csilla can get something from the debris."

"Signal from the cruiser, Senior Captain," Shrent spoke up, keying his board.

"*Grayshrike,* this is Captain Roscu of the Clarr family warship *Orisson,*" a voice came from the bridge speaker. "Thank you for your timely arrival."

"Glad we could help," Ziinda said. "What happened here?"

"Just what it looks like," Roscu said, and Ziinda could hear a hint of frustration and embarrassment drift into her voice. "We were caught off guard, pure and simple. They moved on us before we realized they weren't Jamiron security, hit us before we could get our barrier up, then did a very professional job of overloading and crashing our main reactor."

"Good thing we came along when we did," Ziinda said. "What's your current status?"

"Reactor's nearly back online," Roscu said. "We were just lucky that my crew was able to pull enough power from backups and non-essentials in time to get in those final laser shots."

"Yes, we saw," Ziinda said. "Might have been nice if you'd left a few prisoners alive so we could figure out what this was all about."

"Weren't a lot of options for fine-tuning," Roscu said, a bit tartly. "What are you doing, *Grayshrike*?"

Ziinda frowned. "What do you mean?"

"You're moving on our freighters. I need you to back off."

"Excuse me, Captain, but the freighters are in bad shape," Ziinda said. "Maybe your sensors were damaged too much to—"

"My sensors are working perfectly, *Grayshrike,*" Roscu interrupted. "As I said, we appreciate your assistance with the battle. But we'll take it from here."

"With all due respect, Captain Roscu, it looks like you have enough on your platter just getting your own ship back up to speed," Ziinda said. "We're more than happy to help out the freighters."

"Maybe I need to make it clearer, *Grayshrike,*" Roscu said bluntly. "You're not needed. More than that, you're not wanted. Whatever your reason for coming to Jamiron, I suggest you get on with it and leave Clarr matters to the Clarr family."

Ziinda looked over at Apros, saw her same surprise and disbelief in his own expression. She'd seen family stubbornness before, but Roscu was pushing it way beyond the limit.

But there was nothing to be gained by going head-to-head with her. Time to try a different approach. "I understand," she said in a conciliatory tone. "But we really don't have a choice. By statute, we're not only permitted but required to aid a vessel in distress."

"Kindly do not insult my intelligence," Roscu growled. "*Or* my knowledge. That statute applies only to the Defense Force. The Expansionary Defense Fleet has an entirely different set of protocols and governing directives. I know that because I was once an officer there. I'll say it one more time: This is Clarr family business, and the Clarr family will handle it."

"Do you even hear what you're saying?" Ziinda demanded, her already strained patience finally snapping. "Are you going to risk the lives of the freighters' crews out of pride?"

"*Pride?*" Roscu shot back. "Is that what you think it is? *Pride?* Don't be ridiculous. Those freighters are carrying highly secret, highly proprietary tech, and we have no intention of letting officers or warriors from other families get their hands on it."

"Do you seriously think we're interested in industrial espionage?" Ziinda countered. This whole thing was sliding straight off the edge. "Fine. I give you my word that no one will—"

"Your *word*?" Roscu echoed. "Don't make me laugh. The word of an *Irizi*?"

Ziinda stared at the bridge speaker, a sense of unreality flooding through her. The Chiss military was supposed to be immune from family pressures and rivalries; and now a former Expansionary Defense Fleet officer was throwing those tangled webs straight into her face? "My family has nothing to do with this," she said, forcing calmness into her voice. "I'm an officer of the Expansionary Defense Fleet—"

"Really?" Roscu said scornfully. "We're attacked by Xodlak patrol ships, and you want me to believe their Irizi allies have nothing to do with it?"

"The attackers were *Xodlak*?"

"Xodlak and Erighal," Roscu said. "Don't try to deny it—we got a *very* clear look at them."

"Captain Roscu, this is Mid Captain Apros," Apros put in.

Ziinda looked sharply at him, opening her mouth to deliver a sharp reprimand for interrupting the conversation.

And closed it again. No—he was right. Roscu had already made up her mind to resist anything Ziinda said or suggested. Apros was from the Csap family, allies of the Obbic and Mitth and not at all friendly to the Irizi. Maybe he could talk some sense into her.

"Mid Captain Apros, you say?" Roscu said. "So the Irizi and Xodlak give up and turn it over to the Csap and Obbic? Hardly qualifies as a step up."

Apros's back stiffened, just noticeably. "I understand your skepticism and distrust," he said, and Ziinda could hear the effort he was putting into keeping his voice steady. He never said much about his family, but Ziinda knew he was quite proud of it. "However, whatever you may think about the Irizi, Senior Captain Ziinda is correct about our current status. The Council has assigned the *Grayshrike* to Jamiron protective duty, and as such we are temporarily under Defense Force protocols. We have no choice but to render aid."

"You're obligated to offer it," Roscu said. "I'm not obligated to accept it. And *I* have no choice but to do everything necessary to protect my family's interests. Don't worry about the crews—they'll be fine until someone can get to them. Someone who's not connected in any way to their attackers."

Apros shot Ziinda a frustrated look. "You seem very certain, Captain. I trust you have evidence to back up your allegations?"

"They're not *allegations*," Roscu said. "They're established facts."

"Then you won't mind letting us look at the data ourselves," Apros pressed. "Unless you think an impartial analysis will yield a different conclusion, of course."

"You can't bait me, Mid Captain," Roscu said with a touch of scorn. "I know what I know. But fine. I'll have the recordings and data analysis compiled and sent to you. I've also just been informed that we have thrusters again, so we should be on our way to the freighters very soon."

"Vimsk?" Ziinda asked quietly.

"Confirmed, Senior Captain," the sensor officer said, just as quietly. "*Orisson*'s thrusters are powering up . . . *Orisson* is on the move."

Ziinda nodded. "Then we'll leave you to it, Captain Roscu," she said. "Please don't hesitate to call on us if we can be of assistance. Farewell." Without waiting for any final comments Roscu might want to unload, she keyed off the comm.

"Well, *that* was interesting," Apros growled, his eyes flashing with anger and frustration. "I don't wish to speak disrespectfully of a former fellow officer—"

"Then don't," Ziinda cut him off. She could sympathize with her first officer—she was mad enough at Roscu herself to flay the other woman alive. But such emotions weren't to be vented in public, certainly not on the bridge. "And I'd ignore that *hardly qualifies as a step up* gibe. Some people just don't like anyone. Her loss, not yours."

"I suppose, Senior Captain," Apros said, still sounding irritated.

"Trust me—I've been hated by experts," Ziinda said, a small part of her noting the private irony of her long and nurtured dislike of Senior Captain Thrawn. Her loss? Maybe. "Mid Commander Wikivv: Take us to what's left of that first pair of patrol ships. Mid Captain Apros: Prepare two shuttles to sweep for debris. Mid Commander Shrent, do we have Captain Roscu's data yet?"

"It's coming through now, Senior Captain."

"Good," Ziinda said. "Make sure it's complete, then get the analysts started on it. I want to know exactly what Roscu saw that made her conclude the attackers were Erighal and Xodlak."

She looked out the viewport. The *Orisson* was moving toward the crippled freighters now, though at low speed. Hopefully, it would get there before anyone died. "Or maybe," she amended, "what Roscu *thought* she saw."

MEMORIES VI

For the next three hours, Thrass and Thrawn worked alone in the Stybla stronghold lounge where Patriarch Lamiov had left them. Thrass used the time to pull up the cargo listings as Thrawn had suggested and start sifting through them.

But those records held a *lot* of detail. If there was anything unusual, it wasn't obvious from his first pass.

Thrawn, with his talent for seeing things that other people missed, would probably have done a better job. But while Thrass had been slogging through the manifests, Thrawn had gone off on some other tangent entirely, concentrating on something that was apparently so engrossing he couldn't even spare enough mental capacity to hear Thrass's questions and subtle probings.

Thrass had just decided it was time for his questions to get less subtle when Lamiov finally returned.

Returned alone, Thrass noted with mild surprise. Up to now, Senior Aide Lappincyk had always been hovering close to the Patriarch's side, ready to offer information, advice, and support. His current absence was a bit perplexing, maybe even a little ominous.

"Good evening, Your Venerante," Thrass greeted the Patriarch as he hastily stood up. Thrawn, focused on his questis, didn't seem to notice the other's arrival. "I'm afraid we haven't made much progress."

"Understandable," Lamiov said, eyeing Thrawn still seated in his chair but apparently deciding it wasn't worth calling him on his breach of etiquette. "It's a complicated matter. Has food been brought in for you? No? I'll make sure that oversight is remedied."

"No need, Your Venerante," Thrawn said, finally looking up. "We can eat aboard the ship."

Thrass frowned at him. *Ship?* Was Thrawn planning to leave already? He opened his mouth to ask, glancing at Lamiov to see the other's reaction to Thrawn's odd comment.

The question died midway to completion. The Patriarch's face had gone rigid, his posture suddenly stiff. "How did you know?" he asked, his voice as strained as his face.

"How did he know what?" Thrass asked, thoroughly confused now.

"The good news, from your perspective," Thrawn continued, ignoring both questions, "is that I don't think the Clarr Patriarch knows about the special cargo. I believe the intensity of his search for the hijackers is motivated solely by a desire to find them before you and the Stybla do."

"Wait a minute, you've lost me," Thrass put in, looking back and forth between Thrawn and Lamiov. Whatever Thrawn was talking about, the two of them were clearly on the same page, whereas Thrass hadn't even found the right book. "What special cargo? What desire?"

"Your Venerante?" Thrawn prompted.

Lamiov waved his hand, a short, twitchy motion. "You seem to know everything," he said. Crossing to them, he sank into the chair across from Thrawn. "Please; explain it to him."

"Thank you," Thrawn said. "Let me begin by saying I was wrong about the Clarr patrol pilot being part of the plot. I believe now that she was working as an agent of the Clarr Patriarch and had been alerted that the supposed Obbic transport might be a pirate in disguise and was preparing to hijack another ship."

"If she knew, why didn't she alert Patrol Command?" Thrass asked.

"Because the Clarr Patriarch didn't know for certain the attack would take place," Thrawn said. "Alerting Command or deviating from her proper patrol path might have warned the hijackers and frightened them off."

"Which would have been a good thing, right?"

"For that particular ship, yes," Thrawn said. "But the hijackers would merely have traveled to a different system and chosen another target."

"I see," Thrass murmured. This way, at least the Sposia authorities had a record of the attack.

"It's also likely she hoped she would be able to intervene," Thrawn said. "Unfortunately, the hijackers apparently moved faster than she anticipated." He turned back to Lamiov. "I've been studying the criminal law agreements between the Clarr and the Stybla, Your Venerante. From the tiered penalty clauses involved, and given the Clarr Patriarch's determined efforts to catch the criminals without assistance, I suspect at least one of the hijackers is a Clarr cousin."

Lamiov huffed out a sigh. "Blood, Mid Commander," he corrected, his voice heavy. "He's Clarr blood. And you're right. You saw the agreements. You know the penalties if anyone of that rank commits a crime against us."

Thrass nodded, wincing as he finally understood. Families took their delicately balanced relationships with other families *very* seriously. A blood relative committing a crime like this could rock that relationship to the core, which was why there were always huge disincentives written into family accords.

But only if the perpetrator was caught by the victimized family. If the Clarr could grab him first and cover up proof of his crime, both families could officially pretend it never happened.

Unfortunately, allowing the Clarr the freedom to pursue the hijackers would leave Patriarch Lamiov and the Stybla sitting idly with some mysterious and valuable cargo hanging in the balance. "I presume you've offered help in catching him?" he asked.

"I've spent the past three hours making every possible variant on that suggestion to Patriarch Rivlex," Lamiov said. "He's rejected all my offers, including a onetime leniency for the penalty if our families jointly take him into custody."

"Worried about the aftershocks," Thrass murmured. "No one likes dealing with onetime agreements."

"Understandably," Lamiov said. "At the same time, I can't afford to just sit by and trust Patriarch Rivlex to bring this to a satisfactory end."

"What about us, then?" Thrass asked. "Thrawn and me? The hijackers haven't committed any acts against the Mitth, so we're not encumbered by those agreements or their penalty clauses. Would the Clarr work with us if the Stybla stayed out of it?"

Lamiov gave him a faint smile. "That was also one of the options I presented, Syndic Thrass. It was also rejected." He shook his head. "In a way, I can't really blame him. He has no idea of the seriousness of the situation."

"Then perhaps you should tell him," Thrawn said.

"No," Lamiov said firmly. "That information isn't mine to share."

"Can you tell *us*, then?" Thrawn persisted. "It would help if we knew exactly what we were trying to retrieve."

Lamiov gave a little snort. "What part of *not mine to share* was unclear, Mid Commander?"

"Understood," Thrawn said. "Perhaps you'll change your mind after we deliver it to you."

"After *you* deliver it?" Lamiov asked with a wan smile.

"Thrawn, the Clarr already said they won't work with us," Thrass reminded him.

"That's why we're going to find it ourselves," Thrawn said calmly. "Can you tell us, Patriarch, where the Clarr patrol ship pilot sent her report after the hijacking?"

"Excuse me?" Lamiov said, frowning at Thrawn. *"You're* going to find it?"

"Along with Senior Aide Lappincyk, of course," Thrawn said. "I assume that's your reason for sending him to prepare a patrol ship. I ask again, Patriarch: Where did the Clarr pilot send her report?"

"How do you know what Senior Aide Lappincyk is doing?" Lamiov asked, still frowning.

Thrawn glanced at Thrass, the same hint of resignation on his face that Thrass had seen earlier in Lamiov's office. "Aside from the few moments when he was greeting Syndic Thrass, Senior Aide Lappincyk has been at your side since I arrived," he said. "We've watched him anticipate your orders and information requests. Clearly, he's your closest confidant. Yet now, when you're negotiating what may be a crucial agreement between us, he's nowhere to be seen."

"Yet I didn't know myself until just now that you would offer your cooperation in this matter," Lamiov pointed out.

"Of course you did," Thrawn said. "That was your whole purpose in bringing us here in the first place."

"You planned to maneuver us into this position," Thrass said, feeling like an idiot as he finally got it. Politics was supposed to be his strong point; he really should have figured this out himself. "Can we assume Patriarch Thooraki also knows about this? No, I'm wrong," he corrected himself before Lamiov could answer. "Patriarch Thooraki *suggested* it, didn't he?"

"As a matter of fact, he did," Lamiov conceded. "With the concurrence and support of General Ba'kif." He smiled faintly. "I confess I thought both of them were inflating your investigative and deductive skills far beyond reality."

"Hopefully, your doubts have been calmed," Thrawn said. "The patrol pilot's transmissions?"

"She made two calls: the first to Cormit, the second to Rhigar."

Thrass frowned. Rhigar, location of the chief Clarr family stronghold, was an obvious choice to send an alert. But Cormit? "What's at Cormit?" he asked.

"A Clarr fleet depot," Thrawn said, frowning down at his questis. "Currently anchored by the light cruiser *Orisson*. The fact that the pilot called there first suggests the hijackers are heading southeast, and she hoped family forces could intercept them before they left the Ascendancy."

"*Could* they intercept them?" Thrass asked. "That class of transport is pretty fast."

"But they'll have to carry the Stybla freighter while they transfer the cargo, which will slow them considerably," Thrawn said. "Their other option would be to stop somewhere while the transfer takes place. Either way, there'll be a delay that the Clarr clearly hoped to take advantage of."

"You think they're heading to some alien world, then?" Lamiov asked.

"I think so, yes," Thrawn said. "There are a number of border worlds that function as rendezvous points between Chiss thieves and some of the small nations of the region. The more cautious ones use a rotating schedule, with the rendezvous point shifting each month from one planet to another. The Clarr must know or suspect that these particular hijackers favor the group to the southeast, which is why the pilot sent her first alert to Cormit."

"If you're right, the Clarr have a considerable head start," Lamiov pointed out.

"Only if they know which specific world the hijackers are heading to," Thrawn said. "I don't believe they do."

"Why do you say that?" Lamiov asked.

"Because you said you spent three hours discussing the issue," Thrawn said. "The only reason for Patriarch Rivlex to keep you busy that long was if he was trying to offer you hope of an agreement and thus delay your people from beginning their own pursuit."

"So we have a chance?" Thrass said.

"Yes," Thrawn said. "And I believe it's a good one. It all depends on whether we can reach the hijacked ship first."

"And you know where it is?" Lamiov asked.

Thrawn held up his questis. "As a matter of fact, Your Venerante," he said, "I believe I do."

CHAPTER TEN

Samakro was sound asleep in his cabin when the call came in from Senior Commander Kharill that the *Springhawk*'s first officer was wanted on the bridge.

He found Kharill standing at the helm station, conversing in a low voice to the pilot and looking out the viewport at the starscape. "All right, I'm here," Samakro said, sending a quick look around at the status displays as he started across the bridge. "You said there was a crisis?"

"I think so, yes, Mid Captain," Kharill said hesitantly.

Samakro came to a stop. "You *think* so?"

"Yes, sir," Kharill said, flinching a bit at his superior's tone. "Mid Commander Ieklior was attempting to continue our trip to the Ascendancy when he realized the stars weren't lining up properly."

"What do you mean, not lining up?" Samakro asked, starting forward again. "How far off course are we?"

"That's the problem," Kharill said. "We don't know. We're still trying to figure that out."

"That makes no sense," Samakro insisted, eyeing the starlight blazing coldly through the viewport. He reached the other two and gave the nav displays a careful look.

Kharill was right. The pattern wasn't anywhere near where it should be.

"Ieklior has checked both the known sharp-variable stars and the quasi-stellars," Kharill continued. "He's looking at the other major microwave sources." He paused, and Samakro saw his throat work. "I'm wondering, sir, if there could be something wrong with our sky-walker," he added, lowering his voice. "She's not supposed to lose Third Sight this young, but stranger things have happened."

"So they have," Samakro murmured, gazing again at the stars.

"And she just came off a full ten hours at the nav station," Kharill reminded him. "If she was accidentally going the wrong direction that whole time, it could take us a long time to sort this out."

"Maybe not." Samakro took a deep breath, then turned and headed back toward the bridge hatch. "Continue your analysis, Senior Commander," he said over his shoulder. "Find out where we are. I'll return shortly."

It was supposed to be a sleep period for both the *Grayshrike*'s sky-walker and her caregiver. To Samakro's complete lack of surprise, Thalias was still awake and dressed when he arrived at their suite.

"Good evening, Mid Captain," she greeted him gravely as she stepped out of the open hatchway to let him inside. "I've been expecting you."

"I imagine you have," Samakro said, looking across at the closed hatch of Che'ri's sleeping room. Good—this wasn't a conversation he wanted the girl listening in on. "I take it Sky-walker Che'ri won't be joining us?"

"No, she was too tired," Thalias said, gesturing Samakro toward the dayroom couch. "Won't you sit down?"

"Just as well," Samakro said, ignoring both the invitation and the couch. "I trust you realize that during wartime, disobeying a direct order is punishable by death."

A muscle in Thalias's cheek tightened. "I guess it's lucky we're not at war."

"Given everything that's happened over the past few months, I wouldn't make any blanket assumptions if I were you," Samakro ground out. "I'd also take this situation a *lot* more seriously."

"I *am* taking it seriously, Mid Captain," Thalias said, her voice going dark. "Senior Captain Thrawn is heading alone into horrible danger. I couldn't just stand idly by and let that happen."

"So you talked Che'ri into committing mutiny and hijacked the ship."

"You don't want to let him die, either, sir," she said, her voice quavering a little with emotion. "I know."

"What you know and what I want are completely irrelevant," Samakro countered. "I've been given an order, and my job is to carry it out. If you persist in standing in the way, I can have you confined."

"You think Che'ri will navigate the ship if I'm locked up?"

"I think Che'ri knows her duty," Samakro said. "Maybe better than you do. If not, we'll just head for home via jump-by-jump. That will give both of you plenty of time to regret your decision and wonder what kind of futures you have. If any."

"Is that supposed to scare me?"

"It's supposed to bring you back to your senses." Samakro said. "Right now, all we've got is a failure of the nav system to locate our position. If you and Che'ri turn us back toward the Ascendancy— right now—nothing more needs to be said about it."

"And then what happens to Senior Captain Thrawn?"

"He rises or falls by his own decisions, just like all the rest of us have to," Samakro said. "That's how the universe works, Caregiver."

"No," Thalias said flatly. "No, I don't accept that. We don't all live in our own private niches, with no one else affecting or being affected by what we do." She gestured toward Samakro. "What about you, Mid Captain? Are *you* willing to just let him go off into danger?"

"I've already said I don't have a choice."

"What if you did?"

Samakro cocked his head slightly. "I'm listening."

"I did a quick calculation of how long it'll take to get home via jump-by-jump," Thalias said. "My numbers may be off a little—" She gestured the point away. "Anyway, what I'm saying is that if Che'ri navigates we can get to Sunrise and then back to the Ascendancy faster than heading back from here via jump-by-jump."

"But slower than if she took us directly home."

"Yes," Thalias conceded.

"You also assume she'll side with you and not with her legal commander," Samakro added. "That she'll risk the dishonor and criminal charges of mutiny just because you want her to."

Thalias's eyes drifted away from Samakro's, a tumble of conflicting emotions chasing each other across her face. "You have it backward, Mid Captain," she said at last. "This isn't my idea. It's hers."

"Right," Samakro scoffed. "As if a ten-year-old girl—"

He broke off at the expression on Thalias's face. "Why would she do that?"

"She's afraid for Senior Captain Thrawn," Thalias said. "She spent a lot of time with him, you know, out at the edge of Lesser Space. I think she probably knows him better even than you do. She knows the kind of tasks he takes on, and she knows this one could get him killed." She seemed to brace herself. "And I think . . . *she* thinks . . . the Magys agrees we have to help him."

Samakro felt a chill run up his spine. Thrawn had told him about his conversation with Thalias and the idea that the Magys might be intruding into Che'ri's dreams. But he'd dismissed it as fuzzy-edged speculation at best and complete fantasy at worst. "I thought the Magys only did that when she was asleep."

"I thought so, too," Thalias said. "But the Magys was in hibernation at the time. Maybe they both had to be asleep for it to work. Maybe now it only works when they're both awake."

"And you didn't *say* anything?" Samakro demanded. "It didn't occur to you that it might be something Senior Captain Thrawn needed to know?"

"I didn't know about it until I told Che'ri you'd ordered us back home," Thalias said. "She hadn't said anything until then."

"Then it should have occurred to *her* to tell us," Samakro muttered, Thalias's revelation swirling through his mind like a whirlwind. The sky-walkers and their Third Sight were one of the Ascendancy's most closely guarded secrets. If this alien could intrude or tap into that ability, the consequences could be catastrophic.

And with that, this whole thing had suddenly taken an unexpected turn. "Why is she steering Che'ri around anyway? Just for the fun of it?"

"I don't think there's any real control involved," Thalias said. "At least, that's not what Che'ri says. The Magys is afraid for the Guardian's safety, and sees Che'ri and the *Grayshrike* as his only protection."

"She's calling him the Guardian, now?" Samakro asked sourly. "What does that mean? She's adopted him into her clan?"

"I don't know how she sees him," Thalias confessed. "I just know she thinks he's in danger, and that—"

"And that we're the only ones who can save him," Samakro said. "Yes, you already said that."

"Because if another Battle Dreadnought is waiting at Sunrise, Senior Captain Thrawn and the Paccosh will be in big trouble," Thalias said.

"Their blockade frigate plus the *Springhawk* won't do much better," Samakro pointed out. "Not in a straight toe-to-toe fight. The last time we tangled with one of them, it took the combined power of the *Vigilant* and *Grayshrike* to take it down."

"I know," Thalias said, wincing. "Senior Captain Thrawn showed me their report."

"So you realize going there would likely just mean death for all of us," Samakro concluded. "Does the Magys know that? Or does she even care?"

"I don't know," Thalias confessed. "All I know is that Che'ri cares, and she's convinced we need to be there."

Samakro looked at Che'ri's closed hatch. "What about you?" he asked. "What do you say about all this?"

"I don't think my vote really counts," Thalias said. "You're the *Springhawk*'s current commander; Che'ri is your sky-walker. All that matters is what you two decide."

"Except that if I don't side with Che'ri, we're a long time getting home," Samakro pointed out. "Doesn't sound like I get much of a vote, either."

"Your commander's in trouble." Thalias hunched her shoulders. "At the very least, we should go watch him get himself killed. It would help the Syndicure keep its files tidy."

"That it would," Samakro agreed heavily. "And we all know how much they like keeping records."

"I understand if you don't want to go along with this, Mid Captain," Thalias said. "All I can say is that Che'ri thinks it has to be done, and I trust her judgment."

"I realize that," Samakro said, eyeing her closely. "Let me make my position clear. Heading to Sunrise would be a violation of my commander's explicit order. The fact that following his order might lead to his death doesn't change my obligation to obey it."

"I know," Thalias said. "But I thought—"

"I'm not finished," Samakro interrupted. "At the same time, the sky-walker is a critical part of every Expansionary Defense Fleet voyage. Over the months that Che'ri has been aboard, I've kept a close eye on her moods and needs. I've never known her to present any outrageous or frivolous demands, and her current defiance of her orders is so unlike her that I'm inclined to take her fears seriously."

He looked again at the sky-walker's sleeping room. "Luckily for her, I'm the commander on the scene. That means I'm authorized to change or ignore orders as I deem the situation requires."

"Are you saying . . . ?" Thalias seemed to wilt. "Thank you, Mid Captain."

"Don't thank me yet," Samakro warned. "If we're going to make it in time, there are needs, and there are conditions."

He lifted a hand, started ticking off fingers. "Point one: If we're going to get to Sunrise and then back to Naporar before Supreme General Ba'kif starts worrying about us, the two of you are going to have to push yourselves right to the limit. Short breaks, short sleeps, meals on the run—basically, you're going to be living on the bridge. If you don't think you can handle that, say so now and I'll order Senior Commander Kharill to turn us back toward the Ascendancy."

"We can do it," Thalias said firmly.

"I hope so," Samakro said. "Point two: You don't talk about this thing with the Magys to anyone. Not here, not at Sunrise, not back at Naporor. Whatever needs to be said to the Council or Syndicure, I'll be the one to say it."

"Understood."

"And point three." Samakro let his eyes narrow. "Before we do any-thing more—before I let Sky-walker Che'ri back on the bridge—you make it abundantly clear to her that if this whole thing goes face-down, it could mean the end of all our careers. Not just yours and mine, but hers as well. If she had hopes of joining any of the Ruling Families, she can forget them right now. In fact, even the Forty might not want her after this. If *that's* something you don't think she can handle, say so right now."

"She can handle it," Thalias said. She took another look at his expression—"But I'll make sure," she added.

"You do that," Samakro said. "How long has she been asleep?"

Thalias looked at the chrono. "About twenty minutes."

"How long does she usually sleep?"

"About eight hours at a time."

"She's got four," Samakro said. "Four hours and fifteen minutes from now I expect to see you both on the bridge."

Thalias winced, but her nod was firm enough. "We'll be there."

"So will I," Samakro said. "Until then, I'll get us traveling jump-by-jump. I assume Che'ri was taking us straight toward Sunrise?"

"From the point where she took over, yes."

"Good," Samakro said. "Now that I know we were looking at the wrong part of the charts, we'll be able to calculate our position easily enough. Remember: four and a quarter hours. Don't be late."

"We won't," Thalias promised.

"*And* remember that the Paccosh have a Pathfinder with them," Samakro warned. "If we're going to get to Sunrise before them, or even before it's all over, we need to push it."

"Don't worry, Mid Captain," Thalias promised. "We'll make it."

"I hope so," Samakro said. "For all our sakes."

The suite hatch closed behind Samakro, and for a few seconds Thalias stood facing it. Then, with a tired sigh, she walked back to the couch and sat down. "You heard?" she called.

"Yes," Che'ri's voice came as the girl walked into the dayroom. Not from her own sleeping room, with its closed hatch, but from the open hatch into Thalias's room, which Samakro had luckily not thought to check. "Thank you."

"For what?" Thalias bit out. With the emotional turmoil of the confrontation draining away, the hard cold facts of what she'd just done, and what she'd just agreed to, were roaring back. "For letting you listen in? Or for agreeing to work with Mid Captain Samakro to destroy your future?"

"For letting me listen," Che'ri said. Her voice and face were calm, though Thalias couldn't tell if that was from some inner self-assurance or if the girl was simply too exhausted to feel anything. "No one's future has been destroyed."

"I know," Thalias said, feeling a brief rush of shame. There was no reason to dump her own doubts and guilt on Che'ri. "So. You heard his conditions. What do you think?"

"We can do it," Che'ri said. "We have to."

"I know," Thalias said. "Well. You'd better get to sleep now. Those four hours are going to go by really quickly."

"Okay," Che'ri said. She crossed to her sleeping room. "I have a question," she said, pausing with her hand over the hatch release. "Why did you say that about the Magys calling him the Guardian?"

"I thought Mid Captain Samakro needed more persuasion," Thalias admitted. "I guess it sounded good. Why do you ask?"

"I just wondered," Che'ri said. "Because I didn't think I'd told you. Anyway, good night." She keyed the hatch open and started inside.

"Wait a minute," Thalias called after her. "What do you mean, you never told me? Never told me what?"

"About the Magys talking about the Guardian of her people," Che'ri said, pausing again and half turning to give Thalias a puzzled look. "I didn't think I had, but I guess I must have."

"No, you didn't," Thalias said, a strange feeling creeping over her as she stared at the girl. "Never. I just . . . I thought I made it up."

"I don't know," Che'ri said. "Doesn't matter. Wake me up when it's time, okay?"

"Sure."

Thalias watched as the girl went inside and closed the hatch behind her. Then, her head reeling from fatigue, she headed to her own sleeping room.

Reeling from fatigue, and from dark, ominous thoughts.

She *had* just made up the Guardian bit, hadn't she? Of course she had. It was pure coincidence that it happened to match something the Magys had told Che'ri.

Because Thalias couldn't hear the Magys. Her Third Sight was long gone. She couldn't navigate ships, or see a few seconds into the future, or do anything else that sky-walkers could do. She certainly didn't hear any alien voices in her head. Absolutely not.

And yet . . .

Guardian.

Carefully, she made sure to set an alarm for the time Samakro had specified. She was exhausted; but there was something she had to do before she slept. Something she probably should have done a long time ago.

The data cylinder Senior Aide Thivik had given her on Naporar was tucked away in the bottom of one of her dresser drawers. She retrieved it and her questis, kicked off her shoes, and lay down on her bed.

And with all the fears and uncertainties still swirling around in her brain, she began to read.

Qilori didn't know the name of the system Thrawn had directed him to guide the Paccian ship to. He wasn't sure it even had one that was known to anyone outside of its inhabitants. Certainly neither General Yiv nor Jixtus had ever mentioned the place to him. And that worried him.

Though to be fair, right now *everything* about this trip worried him.

During his time of secretly serving Yiv, he'd gotten used to getting advance warning of battles or incursions or even just critical points in the Nikardun plans of conquest that the general needed a Path-finder to guide his ships to. There'd been less of that under Jixtus—the Grysk played things a lot closer to himself, and of course he had his own navigators to rely on for secret travel.

But Yiv was gone, and Jixtus was off somewhere orchestrating some scheme or other, and Qilori had been handed over to the Kiljis. They didn't like him, they considered him vastly inferior to them-selves, and they hadn't told him anything about their mission to Ra-pacc beyond the fact that he was to take them there and then guide them to a rendezvous point General Crofyp would specify.

But now even that small crumb of forewarning was gone. Qilori was with the Paccosh and Thrawn now, and in two more days he would be thrown completely unprepared into the unknown.

Two more days for him to worry about what might be awaiting them at the end of the trip.

He brooded about it as he sipped at his galara tealeaf, his cheek winglets beating out a nervous cadence. Six more minutes until his break was over, and then it would be back under his headset and back into hyperspace. At least while he was wrapped in the folds of the Great Presence he could mostly forget his current situation.

But only mostly.

Behind him came the sound of the bridge hatch opening. Qilori turned, expecting to see Uingali foar Marocsaa or his commando team lieutenant, here to confirm the ship's progress with the bridge crew.

It wasn't either of them. It was Thrawn.

"Qilori of Uandualon," the blueskin greeted him gravely as he crossed to Qilori's station. Those glowing red eyes flicked back and forth across the bridge as he walked, taking in everything. "I under-stand our journey is on schedule."

"Yes," Qilori confirmed. "I estimate two more days until we arrive."

"Excellent," Thrawn said. "How is the headset working?"

"It's not quite as isolating as a true sensory-deprivation headset would be," Qilori told him, looking at the headset resting on his con-trol board. "But it's adequate." He threw a look of his own around the bridge. "The Paccosh have also learned how to be quiet. That helps considerably."

"I'll be certain to pass on your approval to Commander Uingali," Thrawn said. "Who is Jixtus?"

Qilori forced his winglets to remain motionless. He'd known this conversation was coming. He'd known with equal certainty that there would be no way to get out of it.

And that was a huge problem. Everyone who'd ever met Jixtus, who'd seen the pains he took to conceal even his physical appearance, knew how secretive he was. He would not appreciate his name being bandied about, especially not to people he intended to destroy.

But Jixtus wasn't here. Thrawn was, and in his own way he was just as dangerous as the Grysk. All Qilori could do was try to give enough information to satisfy Thrawn without setting himself up to die a slow death when Jixtus caught up with him. "I'm not absolutely sure," he told Thrawn. "He's very secretive, but he seems to be the one directing the Kilji Illumine."

"You said earlier that Jixtus was merely their associate," Thrawn said. "Now you say he's their leader?"

Qilori felt his winglets twitch. He'd hoped Thrawn hadn't been in range when he was babbling his big mouth to what he thought were Nikardun.

But of course, Uingali would have played the recording for him afterward. "Actually, I'm not certain how it works," he said. "I have the impression that Jixtus sometimes gives directives, but sometimes also accepts them."

"Directives from Generalirius Nakirre?"

This time, even Qilori's best efforts couldn't stop his winglets from reacting. He hadn't given Uingali that name—he was certain of it. How and where could Thrawn have picked it up? "I don't know who Jixtus speaks to."

"But you know Generalirius Nakirre's name?"

"I've heard it, yes," Qilori hedged.

"You also know that Jixtus commanded General Yiv."

"They were associates—"

"You know that he commanded the Nikardun."

Qilori's winglets flattened across his cheeks. "All I know for certain is that they were associates."

"That's not what you told Uingali at Rapacc."

"I thought I was talking to a group of Nikardun," Qilori said. "I told them what I thought would soften their resistance and get them to let us pass without violence."

"A commendable goal," Thrawn said. "Your General Crofyp also said the Kilji commanded Jixtus, not the other way around."

"I don't know what General Crofyp thinks," Qilori said. "He *does* have an inflated opinion of himself and his people, though."

"*Had* an inflated opinion," Thrawn corrected. "He's dead now."

Qilori winced. "Yes. I know."

For a moment Thrawn was silent. "Something you should consider, Qilori of Uandualon," he said. "Eventually, I will know everything. Everything about Jixtus, the Kiljis, the Nikardun"—his glowing eyes seemed to glitter—"and you. If you lie to me, I will eventually know that. Do you wish me to explain what would happen then?"

A long shiver ran through Qilori's body, sending his winglets stretching rigidly outward. "No," he said. "But I really *don't* know very much. Jixtus doesn't tell me more than he thinks I need to know."

"Understandable," Thrawn said. The quiet threat in his voice was gone now, just two beings having a conversation. "Tell me about the Grysks."

"Jixtus has said that word," Qilori said. "But I don't know if they're a species, an organization, a family, or even just a philosophy."

"Like the Kilji goal of universal enlightenment?"

"It could be, yes."

"What is Jixtus's goal?"

Qilori snorted, his winglets fluttering. "The same as that of General Yiv, the Kiljis, and everyone else in this part of the Chaos," he said. "The neutralization of the Chiss Ascendancy as a threat."

There was another moment of silence. "Is that truly how we're perceived?" Thrawn asked at last.

If you lie to me, I will eventually know that. "A lot of nations and species see you that way, yes," Qilori said reluctantly.

"I see." Thrawn gestured to Qilori's headset. "Your break time is nearly over. One final question. The Pathfinder of the other Kilji ship, the one we're pursuing to Sunrise. Is he a friend of yours?"

"No," Qilori said. "Actually, I hardly know him. Why do you ask?"

"Because when our journey ends, he will most likely die," Thrawn said, his voice calm.

"I see," Qilori said. He hesitated, knowing down deep that this was probably a stupid thing to say, especially right now. But he couldn't resist. "And you wonder that the Chiss don't have any friends."

Thrawn's expression hardened, and for that single awful moment Qilori thought he'd made the final mistake of his life. "Let me explain something, Qilori of Uandualon," the Chiss said softly. "My job—the sole reason for my existence—is to defend the Chiss Ascendancy and protect my people. I will do whatever is necessary to achieve that goal, and I will allow nothing and no one to stand in my way. Do you understand?"

With a supreme effort Qilori kept his winglets motionless. "Yes," he said.

"Good." Thrawn held his gaze another moment, then inclined his head. "And now I believe it's time we both returned to our appointed tasks."

"Yes. Sir." Qilori turned back to his station and picked up his headset. Behind him, he heard the bridge hatch open again. He put on the headset and started to adjust it—

"We continue on?" an unfamiliar voice came.

"We continue on, Magys," Thrawn confirmed. "Have you news?"

"I do," the other said. "Friends will be prepared to greet us when we arrive."

"It's good to have friends," Thrawn said, his voice going oddly wistful. "I'm told that the Chiss have none."

"That would indeed be a tragedy," the Magys said. "Come. I would speak with you about how you will free our world. And what the cost of that freedom will be."

CHAPTER ELEVEN

Planetary guard duty, as Ar'alani had expected, was pretty monotonous. Even the presence of alien warships lurking in Ascendancy space couldn't change the fact that the *Vigilant* was spending all its time going around and around Sposia, staying clear of edgy patrol ships and nervous civilian transports and waiting for potential threats to show themselves.

So far they hadn't. But Ar'alani knew better than to let her officers and warriors grow complacent. That only worked to the enemy's advantage. Drills, snap alerts, and other physical and mental challenges became the order of the day.

Still, after a few such unexpected challenges even that grew to be routine.

At least the *Vigilant* wasn't getting the quiet hostility that some of the other Expansionary Defense Fleet ships were experiencing with their new duties. Most of the major Chiss worlds were dominated by families of the Nine or the Forty, and too many of those elites saw any intrusion into what they considered their territory to be an insult to their own defense capabilities. Sposia, while technically controlled by the Clarr and Obbic, also included the Kynkru and Csap families in their patrol system, and all four of them were generally willing to defer to the Stybla in matters of defense policy. The Stybla themselves, given their family's position at the lower end of the Forty, were more than happy to accept whatever help Csilla and Naporar offered in the way of warships.

Ar'alani was sitting in her command chair, trying to think up something new to throw at her crew, when Larsiom stirred in his seat at the comm station. "Admiral?" he called across the bridge. "We're receiving a transmission from Supreme General Ba'kif."

"Acknowledge and connect," Ar'alani said, keying her mike. "Supreme General Ba'kif, this is Admiral Ar'alani."

"Good day, Admiral," Ba'kif's voice came back. "I understand things are still quiet at Sposia?"

"Yes, sir, so far," Ar'alani said. "Are you expecting that to change?"

"That's a good question," Ba'kif said. "I presume you've been following the reports on our mysterious Jixtus and his travels?"

"Yes, sir, I have," Ar'alani said, scowling to herself. So far the Kilji battle cruiser had visited six planets and Jixtus had conversed with four senior officials of the Nine and thirteen of the Forty. At this rate, he'd have most of the Chiss hierarchy covered within the month. "Is Sposia next on his schedule?"

"We don't know," Ba'kif said. "So far we haven't been able to find a pattern in his travels, relating to either planetary position or rank among the Aristocra. But that brings us to another, more pressing issue. Since last night, two more of the Nine have begun moving their warships around."

"Wonderful," Ar'alani said, wincing. "That makes, what, five of them?"

"Correct," Ba'kif said. "What's ominous about these particular repositionings is that they're not focused on bolstering the family's own defenses, but seem to be aimed at adding an extra presence to Pommrio, Erighal, and Xodlak stronghold worlds."

"The ones Jixtus is pointing fingers at." Ar'alani shook her head. "This is ridiculous."

"I agree," Ba'kif said. "And under normal circumstances I'd say it was unthinkable that anyone would pay two seconds' attention to the ravings of an alien. But with all the uncertainties and suspicions still swirling around the Hoxim incident, old rivalries are bubbling closer to the surface."

"And naturally, the families' protests of innocence do nothing to change those suspicions."

"Of course not," Ba'kif said heavily. "Their Patriarchs continue to deny any involvement with aliens. They say Jixtus is lying, and that the vid he's been showing around is a complete hoax."

"*Is* it a hoax, sir?" Ar'alani asked.

"That is indeed the question," Ba'kif said. "The quality of the vid is pretty low, and I'm told the enhancement techniques everyone's been scrubbing it with are as likely to create new parts of the image as they are to provide clarity to what's already there. More concerning is information I received less than an hour ago that—"

"Just a moment, sir," Ar'alani cut in, scooping up her questis. It was bad form to interrupt a superior, but a sudden thought had occurred to her and it needed to be chased down before the conversation went elsewhere and she lost the mental thread. "You said *everyone* was using enhancements. Does that include the Clarr?"

"Their report included an enhanced version of the vid, yes," Ba'kif said. "What are you thinking?"

"The *everyone* part, sir," she said, searching rapidly through the *Vigilant*'s data records. There was the folder . . . there was the file . . . "Patriarch Thurfian's report said that Jixtus had offered the Mitth military assistance, didn't it?"

"Yes, it did," Ba'kif confirmed. "He also said he turned it down flat."

"As did all the other Patriarchs," Ar'alani said. "All of them *except* Patriarch Rivlex. His report didn't even mention such an offer being made, let alone that he'd turned it down."

"Interesting," Ba'kif said, a fresh level of attentiveness in his voice. "And Rivlex is the only one who sent someone to the *Whetstone* to talk directly to Jixtus. I believe he claimed he just wanted one of his people to get a closer look at the battle cruiser."

"Yes, that's what he *said*." There it was. "I've found what I was looking for, sir. Can you pull up the enhanced recordings from the Mitth and the Clarr reports?"

"A moment." There was a short pause. "I have them."

"Please run them together in parallel."

Another short pause. Ar'alani also ran the two five-second clips, just to double-check her memory.

"Interesting," Ba'kif said. "The Clarr version is a quarter second longer than anyone else's. I hadn't even noticed."

"It's not at all obvious," Ar'alani said. "I happened to notice, but had forgotten about it until you used the word *everyone*."

"Any thoughts as to what it means?"

"Nothing solid," Ar'alani said. "I'm assuming the Clarr got more of the recording, either as a gift or for a price, and when they needed to send a copy of the enhanced recording they missed slightly with their editing."

"Or else Jixtus gave them a longer recording to throw that precise suspicion on the family."

"Yes, sir, that's also possible," Ar'alani conceded.

"Either way, a pattern is starting to emerge with respect to the Clarr," Ba'kif said thoughtfully. "A longer recording, their visit to the *Whetstone*, and the fact that they immediately sent the *Orisson* off on a tour of major Clarr worlds and facilities. Add to that the *Orisson*'s possibly coincidental presence at Jamiron when the alleged Xodlak and Erighal patrol ships attacked four of their freighters, and the pattern starts to become a bit disturbing."

Ar'alani frowned. The first report from Senior Captain Ziinda had said the freighters' attackers were unidentified, with the follow-up from Captain Roscu stating that they were in fact Xodlak and Erighal. Now Ba'kif was adding the word *alleged* to the mix? "I take it something new has been added?" she asked.

"Indeed it has," Ba'kif said. "I was starting to tell you about it when you pointed out this other curious bit of information."

"Yes, sir," Ar'alani said, feeling her face warming. "My apologies for the interruption."

"No apology needed, Admiral," Ba'kif assured her. "The information was both useful and timely. As for this latest revelation, I'm still trying to decide whether to release it or keep it private for the moment. I've been talking with Senior Captain Ziinda, who passed it on to me, and—well, I think it might be best to let her give you the details. Give me a moment to bring her into the discussion."

"Yes, sir," Ar'alani said, frowning a little harder as she keyed Ba'kif's transmission from the bridge speaker to the more private command chair position. This whole thing was getting stranger and stranger.

"Admiral, we've got company," Wutroow called.

Ar'alani looked up. The *Vigilant*'s first officer was standing behind Oeskym and the weapons console, pointing out the viewport at a ship that had appeared in the distance. "As we speak, so we get," Wutroow continued. "It's the *Orisson*."

"Is it, now," Ar'alani said. "Interesting timing. Junior Commander Larsiom, give them a call and ask what they're doing here. Frame it as an offer to assist in whatever they've got planned."

"Yes, ma'am," the comm officer said and turned to his board.

"All right, Admiral, I have Senior Captain Ziinda tied in now," Ba'kif announced.

"Senior Captain," Ar'alani said, catching Wutroow's eye and beckoning to her. "I trust you're doing well?"

"I am, Admiral, thank you," Ziinda said. "Interesting tidbit about the Clarr version of the Kilji recording. I confess I missed that completely."

"In a situation like this, it doesn't matter who finds the pieces as long as they're found by somebody," Ar'alani said as Wutroow arrived beside her in range of the command chair's speaker. "I understand you've found an important piece of your own."

"I believe so, ma'am, yes," Ziinda said. "I had our analysts take a close look at Captain Roscu's images of the attacking patrol boats. As I presume you're aware, Erighal warships are decorated with subtle dot-and-line decoratives laid out in wavelike patterns, supposedly evoking memories of their family's prominence in the old seafaring days."

"I've heard that, yes," Ar'alani confirmed, though she would have been hard-pressed to come up with it on her own. Every family had its own quirks and traditions, and it was nearly impossible to keep track of all of them. "It was originally to help them identify a ship that had been damaged beyond other means of recognition, wasn't it?"

"Yes, ma'am," Ziinda said. "The key point is that all the patterns are similar, but since they're done by hand no two of them are exactly alike."

"And you were able to identify which patrol ships were at Jamiron?" Ar'alani asked.

"That's the problem," Ba'kif put in. "The two Erighal patterns were exactly the same."

Ar'alani frowned up at Wutroow. "And Roscu didn't notice?"

"I doubt Captain Roscu cared," Ba'kif said. "But it gets worse. Continue, Senior Captain."

"Not only are the two patterns identical," Ziinda said, "but they match that of one of the Erighal patrol ships that was at Hoxim."

"Well, isn't *that* interesting," Wutroow murmured.

"Isn't it?" Ar'alani agreed, feeling a tightness in her throat. "So someone's counterfeiting Chiss patrol ships and throwing them at Chiss freighters?"

"So it would seem," Ba'kif said. "I assume Roscu has been in contact with her Patriarch, but we have no idea what their thinking is about this situation."

"Maybe we should ask her," Wutroow suggested. "She's right outside our viewport."

"Interesting," Ba'kif said. "I knew the *Orisson* had left Jamiron, but didn't know it was headed for Sposia. I wonder what it's doing there."

"The Clarr are a major presence here," Ar'alani reminded him. "It may be that she's just checking out their defenses and preparedness."

"That's possible," Ba'kif said. "As Senior Captain Wutroow said, we could just ask her."

"Not a good idea," Ar'alani said, throwing a scowl at her first officer. The last thing she wanted was to try for a friendly conversation with the woman who'd once been her first officer on the patrol cruiser *Parala*. Especially since those weren't particularly pleasant memories for either of them. "Captain Roscu and I didn't part on the best of terms. I doubt she'd be willing to talk to me."

"Maybe she'd talk to someone else," Ziinda suggested. "I don't know what the history is here, but this seems too good an opportunity to pass up."

"I agree," Ba'kif said. "What about you, Senior Captain Wutroow? The Kiwu family has taken a pretty neutral stance in the current situation."

"More than willing, sir," Wutroow confirmed. "Admiral?"

Ar'alani glowered at the approaching ship. "Junior Commander Larsiom, did you get through to the *Orisson*?"

"Yes, Admiral," Larsiom said hesitantly. "Captain Roscu acknowledges our contact and our presence. She also . . . declines to share her mission with us."

"In other words, she said it was none of our business?" Wutroow asked.

Larsiom winced. "More or less, ma'am."

"She wasn't any friendlier to me, if that helps any," Ziinda offered.

"It doesn't; and she's wrong," Ba'kif said firmly. "With alien warships threatening the Ascendancy, the Defense Force is entitled to request any and all relevant information. Tie me in, Admiral—I want to talk to her."

"Excuse me, Supreme General," Wutroow put in. "With all respect, sir, I believe you offered me first crack at her."

"You think you can bring the necessary weight to bear, Senior Captain?"

"I don't think weight will be the factor, sir," Wutroow said. "I know her type, and I think I can get her talking."

"Very well, Senior Captain. You've got one minute."

"Thank you, sir," Wutroow said. "Junior Commander, give me comm to the *Orisson*."

"You have comm, ma'am," Larsiom confirmed.

"Captain Roscu, this is Senior Captain Wutroow, first officer of the *Vigilant*," Wutroow called.

"Senior Captain, I already told your comm officer I can't talk about my assignment," a woman's terse voice came back.

"Don't worry, I wasn't going to ask," Wutroow said. "I understand family business—it's like that with the Kiwu family, too. No, this is personal, just between you and me. I was hoping you could tell me why Admiral Ar'alani flounced off the bridge in a snit when she heard you were here."

Ar'alani twisted her head to look up at Wutroow, feeling her mouth drop open. Wutroow caught her eye, gave a quick shake of her head, and motioned for Ar'alani to remain silent.

"She did?" Roscu asked, some of the animosity fading into a sort of malicious amusement. "Really?"

"Oh, you should have seen it," Wutroow assured her, giving Ar'alani a sly smile. "It was like she didn't even want to share the same patch of space with you. I've never seen her lose it that way before. You have any idea what it was all about?"

"I know *exactly* what it was about," Roscu said, a slight hesitation impinging on the satisfaction in her voice. "This is a secure comm, I assume?"

"I sure hope so," Wutroow said, putting some caution into her voice. "Any of this gets back to the admiral and I'll be up to my neck in rabid growzers. You know the type."

"All too well," Roscu said. "So she's gotten more vindictive in her old age, has she? Good. Let her past eat her from the inside."

"Trust me, her past is having a fine meal," Wutroow assured her. "Come on, don't keep me in suspense—she could be back any minute. What's going on?"

"The short version: When she was my commander, she covered up a serious policy violation by one of her officers," Roscu said. "I called them both on it and had them brought up on charges. They both managed to skate free, but I imagine it made a nice mark on her perfect record. She's resented me ever since."

Ar'alani sighed silently. She hadn't resented Roscu then, and she didn't resent her now. But Roscu apparently saw things differently.

So which one of them, exactly, was being eaten from the inside?

"Wow," Wutroow said, sounding awed. "And she was your *superior*? That takes a lot of courage."

"It just takes conviction and integrity," Roscu said. "Something the people who covered for her and Thrawn apparently missed out on. But that's all right. Let her have her nice white uniform and her ship and no family. I hope I was at least a bump along that road."

"Given her reaction just now, I'd say you were more than just a bump," Wutroow said. "Though it doesn't much matter where you are on the command ladder right now, not with whatever the hell is going on. At least *you* just have the Clarr family to take care of and won't be getting caught in any crossfires. So what *is* going on? You have any idea?"

"Of course I do," Roscu said disdainfully. "I'm not surprised Csilla hasn't figured it out yet. But then, they're the same people who were blind to Ar'alani and Thrawn. Now they're just as blind to the Dasklo."

"Blind is blind, and a lot of people never learn," Wutroow agreed. "So what are the Dasklo up to this time?"

"Just more of their usual conniving," Roscu said. "They're letting this Jixtus alien get everyone worked up and looking at everyone else while they secretly build their family fleet up past the legal limits."

"Sounds nasty," Wutroow said. "They're figuring to take out the Clarr once and for all, I suppose?"

"Or at least knock us down," Roscu said. "Maybe even try to push us out of the Nine."

"That's crazy," Wutroow protested. "Your family fleets are the same size, aren't they? How do they think they can go up against you?"

"Weren't you listening?" Roscu growled. "I said they're going to build up their fleet. Only it's not going to *look* like they're doing it."

"Sorry, but you've lost me."

"It's very simple," Roscu said patiently. "They're going to look like they've got lots of help. They're going to come at us pretending the Erighal, Pommrio, and Xodlak are supporting them."

"That's exactly what Jixtus has been saying," Wutroow said eagerly, as if her slower brain had finally managed to latch onto something important. "He said the Dasklo are building an alliance with those three families."

"That's what he *says*," Roscu said. "Maybe even what he thinks. But he's wrong. There will be lots of ships with the Dasklo when the attack comes, but they won't be from the Erighal or anyone else. They'll all be Dasklo."

Wutroow raised her eyebrows questioningly at Ar'alani. Ar'alani shrugged back. *Ask her,* she mouthed.

Wutroow nodded acknowledgment. "Sorry, but you've lost me again," she said to Roscu.

"It's very simple," Roscu said again, her patient tone shifting into the patronizing mode that Ar'alani remembered driving all the rest of the *Parala*'s officers crazy. "The Dasklo are making fake Erighal patrol ships."

"They're *what*? How?"

"With a little sleight of hand, and a lot of sheer audacity," Roscu said, clearly enjoying Wutroow's apparent astonishment in the face of Roscu's own superior knowledge and intellect. "Patrol ships all have the same basic hull, after all. You pick up someone else's ship, copy the crest and family design ornamentation onto a freshly built ship of your own, and there's your fake."

"But if they were caught—no, that can't be," Wutroow said. "How could they get away with it? They'd never get away with it."

"They already have," Roscu said, her voice now going dark. "No one on Csilla would ever notice, but two of the alleged Erighal patrol ships that attacked our freighters at Jamiron were exact duplicates of each other. Obviously supposed to make us think the Erighal have gone rogue; just as obviously built by the Dasklo."

"Why is that obvious?" Wutroow asked. "I don't doubt you—that's the kind of thing the Dasklo would do—but how do you know it's not the Erighal themselves?"

"One: The Erighal aren't smart enough to come up with this," Roscu said. "Two: They don't have the facilities that could hide this much new construction. Three: They don't have the bloodlust and sheer unmitigated gall."

"Okay," Wutroow said slowly, as if she was still having trouble following the logic. "But we've all seen Jixtus's vid. It shows the Erighals and other ships running a combat demonstration for the Dasklo. Doesn't that mean all four families are working together?"

"That's what everyone thinks, because everyone else was too cheap to buy the entire vid," Roscu said acidly. "*We* were willing to pay, which is why we know the whole story. In fact, I don't think even Jixtus has a complete handle on it."

"Well, don't keep me in suspense," Wutroow said. "If the Dasklo frigate wasn't watching some war game, what *was* it doing?"

There was a short pause. "Sorry," Roscu said, the fire and passion suddenly gone. "I can't talk about it. In fact, I've probably already said too much."

"Oh, come on," Wutroow cajoled, making a face at Ar'alani. So close . . . "You can't cut me off *now*. What if no one else ever figures it out? I'll be stuck wondering about it forever."

"Welcome to a life of not getting everything you want," Roscu said with an edge of bitterness. "But don't worry—you won't have to wonder forever. Just another few days."

"A few days? Is that when you'll tell the rest of the Ascendancy—?"

"Nice talking to you, Senior Captain. Watch your back around your glorious admiral." There was a tone—

"Transmission ended," Larsiom confirmed.

Wutroow huffed out a breath. "Sorry, Admiral," she said.

"Not your fault," Ar'alani assured her. "I'm actually surprised she gave as much as she did."

"I meant sorry about saying you flounced off the bridge," Wutroow said. "You know, come to think of it, I'm not sure I've ever actually seen anyone *flounce*. But I've always liked the word."

"We'll try to use it more in conversation," Ar'alani said. "So she *did* notice that the attackers at Jamiron were duplicates."

"But completely missed the point of who was making them," Ba'kif said back into the conversation. "So the Battle Dreadnought aliens weren't simply armoring their own freighters or transports at that supposedly wrecked Nikardun base. They were putting shells on them and turning them into Chiss patrol ships."

"Apparently so," Ar'alani agreed. "Now that I think about it, the ships we saw at the refurbishing station were just the right size and shape for that kind of transformation."

"And the big ship we thought was a mobile repair dock would have worked as a Chiss freighter," Wutroow added.

"So what are they up to?" Ziinda asked. "And what is this Dasklo grand scheme that Roscu thinks is under way?"

"First, I think we can assume that all her suspicions about the Dasklo are wrong," Ba'kif said. "It's clear that Jixtus is controlling this whole narrative and manipulating everyone, including the Clarr. Maybe even *especially* the Clarr. You two keep talking—I'm going to drop out while I check on something."

"Yes, sir," Ar'alani said, thinking back over the conversation Wutroow and Roscu had just had. "All right. Roscu thinks the Dasklo are planning some aggressive military move against the Clarr. What could she have seen in the rest of Jixtus's vid that would convince her of that?"

"I was just reviewing the free sample," Ziinda said slowly. "Odd thought. Did you see the way the Dasklo frigate lifted its bow just a bit at the end of the vid? That looked almost like it was setting up to launch plasma spheres at the Erighal."

"Hold on, let me check," Ar'alani said, pulling up her copy and running it. Ziinda was right; the move was definitely there. "Could be," she agreed. "Pretty subtle, but it's there."

"Or it could be setting up to aim and fire a tractor beam," Wutroow added.

"Or it could be doing both," Ziinda said. "You think that's what's on the rest of the vid? The Dasklo flickering the Erighal and then pulling it in for a close look at its hull design?"

"Maybe," Ar'alani said. "Roscu *did* talk about someone picking up someone else's ship."

"Which would ensure they could get the hull decoratives correct," Ziinda said.

"Right," Ar'alani said. "She also said she didn't think Jixtus knew exactly what had happened. At the distance the vid was taken from, a sphere barrage would barely register, even with enhancement, and a tractor would be completely invisible."

"Only that scenario doesn't make any sense," Ziinda said. "The Erighal are already Dasklo allies—they wouldn't have to go to all that effort just to get a good look at an Erighal patrol ship's hull decoration."

"*And* the Dasklo would know Erighal hull decoratives are never identical," Ar'alani said. "All of which is moot, of course, since we're assuming the whole vid was faked."

"True," Ziinda said. "A fake confrontation and fake ships, courtesy of whoever was recording the Hoxim battle."

"They probably got patterns for the Xodlak and Pommrio ships that were there, too, while they were at it," Ar'alani said, scowling at the vid. "And are likely also using those same recordings to study Chiss battle tactics."

Ziinda muttered a sudden curse. "Including how to shoot at Chiss warships without doing serious damage," she said in a chagrined voice. "*That's* why those patrol ships were able to fire so uselessly at me at Jamiron. They wanted to make sure the *Grayshrike* survived so that there would be another witness to the battle."

"What do you mean, fire uselessly?" Ar'alani asked, frowning. "Where did they learn *that*?"

"From Hoxim," Ziinda said. "They saw how Thrawn's gunners—" She broke off abruptly.

But it was too late. Ar'alani looked up at Wutroow, saw her expression echoing Ar'alani's own surprise. "What did you just say?" Ar'alani asked. "Senior Captain Ziinda? What did you just say?"

"My apologies, Admiral," Ziinda said, her voice under rigid control. "I misspoke."

"Yes, that can happen, Senior Captain," Ar'alani said. "Nevertheless, I'd like you to finish your sentence."

"Admiral, I really can't—"

"All right, I'm back," Ba'kif's brisk voice came from the chair speaker. "You reach any conclusions?"

Again, Ar'alani looked at Wutroow. The first officer gave an uncertain shrug and a rather helpless gesture. "Nothing but the obvious ones," Ar'alani said, turning back to the mike. "The Battle Dreadnought aliens were apparently at Hoxim and used their recordings to create duplicates of one of the Erighal patrol ships at that battle."

"Probably duplicated some of the others, as well," Ba'kif said. "Though it was probably less duplication than camouflage. Unfortunately, the self-destructs of the Jamiron attackers left very little that could be identified. We'll continue checking for genetic material and metal profiles, but that will take time."

"Roscu said it would only be another few days," Ar'alani murmured.

"Yes, she did," Ba'kif said grimly. "At any rate, I've just taken a look at the *Orisson*'s travels since Jixtus first arrived at Avidich. Captain Roscu's journey began with her checking all the Clarr strongholds and other major manufacturing, farming, and distribution centers."

"Reasonable enough, under the circumstances," Ar'alani said.

"True," Ba'kif said. "But in the last few days her focus has widened a bit. She's now also checking systems where the Dasklo family has major shipbuilding and refurbishing centers."

"Uh-oh," Wutroow said under her breath. "She's trying to catch them in the act."

"That's my assumption," Ba'kif said. "She has just one left: Krolling Sen on Ornfra."

Ar'alani felt her throat tighten. Not just the premier Dasklo shipbuilding facility, but also the center of their space travel research and development department. They would not take kindly to someone poking around demanding answers, especially a Clarr like Roscu who so plainly suspected them of violence against her family's interests. "I don't think that's going to end well, sir," she warned.

"Agreed," Ba'kif said. "But as long as she's just flying around the Ascendancy, looking and talking, she's not violating any laws or protocols."

"Even if she starts pushing against the Dasklo?"

"As long as it remains verbal, there's nothing we can do to hinder her activities," Ba'kif said. "If someone starts shooting—on either side—then the Syndicure and Defense Force can get involved."

"Only by then it'll be too late," Wutroow muttered.

"Very possibly," Ar'alani said. "We need someone to intercept her at Ornfra before she crosses the line and talk her down."

"May not be possible, but it can't hurt to try," Ba'kif said. "Senior Captain Ziinda?"

"Sir?" Ziinda said, sounding a bit startled at being called on.

Small wonder. After that mysterious, choked-off comment about Thrawn's gunners, she'd stayed totally silent, probably hoping she would be forgotten in the crush of more important business.

Small wonder. Even smaller chance. As far as Ar'alani was concerned, any such hopes and efforts were a waste of time.

"I'm issuing you new orders," Ba'kif told her. "You'll go to Ornfra, wait there until Captain Roscu arrives, and do whatever you can to defuse the situation."

"Ah . . . yes, sir," Ziinda said. "I'll point out, Supreme General, that she doesn't trust me. As a member of the Irizi family, she considers me to be her enemy."

"Frankly, I doubt she trusts *anyone* at this point," Ba'kif said. "Regardless, you're the only one I can spare right now. If Roscu follows her usual pattern, she'll remain in Sposia orbit another few hours, consulting with the Clarr leadership, before she leaves for Ornfra. Make sure you're there ahead of her."

"Yes, sir," Ziinda said.

"As for you, Admiral Ar'alani," Ba'kif continued, "you'll turn over command of the *Vigilant* to Senior Captain Wutroow and prepare a shuttle for Csilla. Your meeting request has been approved."

Ar'alani stiffened. "Understood, sir," she said through suddenly dry lips. "I'll leave as soon as I can."

"I'll be waiting," Ba'kif said. "Senior Captain Wutroow, watch yourself and Sposia very carefully. There's no reason to believe Jixtus knows about the UAG or the items stored there. But since we don't know the full extent of his conversations with Patriarch Rivlex, I don't want to take any chances."

"Understood, sir," Wutroow said. "We'll be ready for whatever anyone throws at us."

"Good," Ba'kif said. "I'll be in contact if and when there are further updates. Until then, you all have your orders. Good luck."

Ar'alani keyed off her mike. "Junior Commander Larsiom, close comm," she ordered. "Then alert Senior Warrior Yopring to prep a shuttle for Csilla; full long-range crew; one passenger."

"Yes, Admiral."

"Well, that was an interesting way to spend an hour," Wutroow said as Ar'alani picked up her questis and stood up. "Any further orders, Admiral?"

"Just the one Ba'kif already gave you," Ar'alani said. "Stay alert and watch for trouble. Oh, and if trouble *does* arrive, squash it."

"The simple orders are always the best." Wutroow cocked her head. "Speaking of *not* simple things, any thoughts as to what Ziinda meant by that *Thrawn's gunners* comment?"

Ar'alani shook her head. "Aside from the fact that she *really* didn't want to talk about it, nothing at all."

"I presume you're going to rectify that omission?"

"You presume correctly," Ar'alani assured her. "But not right now. We've got bigger problems than whatever connivance Thrawn might have pulled off at Hoxim. More important, Ziinda and Thrawn are two of our best and most trustworthy assets, and I have no interest in losing or weakening either of them."

"Does that mean you're also not going to mention this to the supreme general?"

Ar'alani hesitated. There were still things about Hoxim that no one knew, and that everyone wanted to know.

More than that, there were things people like Ba'kif *needed* to know. Whatever scheme Thrawn had pulled off at Hoxim, it might be something that could be used in the future.

But if the plan had required Thrawn to once again skate over the line, Ba'kif would be bound by the protocols to pass it on to the

Council. And there were only so many times he could cover for Thrawn.

Besides, it wasn't like Ziinda had actually said anything critical. There was certainly nothing in the protocols that required officers to pass on rumors or half-truths to their superiors.

"Not right now," she told Wutroow. "We'll wait until we have more details. Assuming we can get Ziinda to give those to us."

"Understood," Wutroow said. "And speaking of things people don't want to talk about . . . ?"

"If you're asking about my meeting request to Supreme General Ba'kif, I didn't say anything about it to you because I assumed it would be denied," Ar'alani told her. "Now that it's been granted . . . I think it might be best to keep it quiet a little longer. At least until I get back from Csilla."

"I see," Wutroow said. "You know, there's an old saying that keeping secrets killed the whisker cub."

Ar'alani snorted. "There's no such saying. You just made that up."

"Well, if there isn't one, there ought to be," Wutroow said. "Safe flight to you, Admiral." She turned her head to look out the viewport at the *Orisson,* now settling into orbit in the distance. "And hurry back," she added. "I get the feeling we're going to need you. Probably sooner than later."

MEMORIES VII

The hyperspace swirl collapsed to star-flares, and the Sty-bla patrol ship *Jandalin* arrived in its target system.

"Destination confirmed, Senior Aide," the pilot reported. "Glastis Three."

Thrass looked at the status displays. *Destination,* in his opinion, was putting it far too generously. Glastis 3 was little more than a flashfly speck in infinite space: a single Defense Force emergency repair blackdock orbiting a marginally habitable planet midway between Csilla and Copero in the south-nadir part of the Ascendancy. The fact that not a single family in the Ascendancy had deemed the system worth developing suggested that *marginally habit-able* was also something of an exaggeration.

Senior Aide Lappincyk gestured to Thrawn, seated to the right of the center section on the curved acceleration couch that stretched across the back of the bridge. "Mid Commander?" he invited.

Thrass leaned forward to look past Lappincyk at Thrawn, noting the single-edged focus on Thrawn's face as his eyes flicked between the viewport and the displays. The center seat of the couch was reserved for the ship's mas-ter, Thrass knew, with the seat on either side normally left empty. Only when the master deemed one of his companions or passengers worthy of special honor were those seats offered.

Thrawn to Lappincyk's right, Thrass to his left. Distantly, Thrass wondered if Thrawn recognized the honor he'd been granted by being offered the right-hand seat. Given that it was Thrawn, probably not.

"Thank you, Senior Aide," Thrawn said. "Sensor officer: Begin a scan of the outer system around us. We're looking for a dead Stybla cargo ship of Vivan configuration."

Thrass felt a fresh heaviness in his heart. *Dead.* He'd been afraid that would be where this would end up. "So you think the hijackers killed them?" he forced himself to ask.

Thrawn sent him a puzzled look. "Of course not," he said. "Didn't you read the files I gave you?"

"Most of them," Thrass said, feeling a bit defensive. Even for someone who dug through official documents for a living, the Clarr legal text was mind-numbingly dry. "I was starting to fall asleep about an hour ago."

"But you *did* get to the part about penalties due to blood who commit crimes against other families, didn't you?"

"Oh, yes," Thrass said, wincing. *Those* sections had been the exception to the dryness, switching from mind numbing to blood chilling. "I assumed there was some hyperbole involved."

"There wasn't," Lappincyk assured him. "A few centuries ago, the Ascendancy had such a problem with Clarr raiders that several of the other families threatened to band together and obliterate the entire family. Those criminal statutes are the result, and the Clarr guarantee that such atrocities will never happen again."

"At least, not for long," Thrawn said. "I'd draw your attention in particular to the punishment for any death that results from a felony crime."

"You mean the death-by-torture clause?"

"Yes," Thrawn said. "What can you infer from that?"

Thrass gave a little snort. His first thought was that such a thing was utterly barbaric. His second was that the Clarr must *really* have needed to reassure their neighbors if they felt the need to enact such laws in the first place.

But it was clear from Thrawn's look of expectation that neither of those was what he was going for. So what *did* he want Thrass to see?

Thrass turned to look out the viewport, scowling. Thrawn had already been disappointed at least twice since their arrival at Patriarch Lamiov's mansion by people's inability to follow his reasoning. The least Thrass should do was give it a try.

All right. Punishment. Death by torture. Clarr raiders. A Defense Force blackdock in an edge-of-nowhere system. A lonely system, out of the way, with virtually zero chance that anyone would happen by.

And then he had it. "The hijackers can't risk any of the Stybla crew dying," he said, turning back to Thrawn. "But they also can't hold them aboard their ship, at least not for long."

"Why not?"

"Because kidnapping from another family carries the same punishment as killing them."

"Exactly," Thrawn said, the anticipation in his face replaced by approval. "So why would they be here at Glastis Three?"

"They can't just park the crew out in space," Thrass said. "If they don't make it back in time after they make their deal, the crew will run out of air or food and the hijackers will face full Clarr law. But they also can't just turn them loose, because then the alarm will be given and they'll have the Defense Force and every family patrol ship in the region looking for them."

He gestured out the viewport. "So they find an empty system to park the cargo ship where nobody's likely to stumble across them. But they also need a system that's not *quite* empty, so that there's someone they can call afterward to come out and rescue the crew when they've finished selling the stolen goods."

"Very good," Thrawn said. "One small addition: The hijackers won't want to risk calling or having any other direct contact with the blackdock."

"So they'll put the cargo ship in an elliptical orbit," Lappincyk spoke up suddenly. "Disable their drive and their comm and put them in a long orbit that will take a few days to get close enough for the blackdock to spot them."

"That would work," Thrass agreed. So simple, really, once it was explained. "Of course, that assumes the hijackers are smart enough to think of it."

"They are, and they will," Lappincyk assured him. "Three hundred years ago, the Clarr defeated a numerically superior Irizi force using this exact maneuver to drift one of their warships in close. It was a Clarr triumph, and a blood will certainly be familiar with it."

"As are you, obviously," Thrass commented. "A three-hundred-year-old battle. You Stybla certainly keep up with things."

"Three hundred twenty, if we want to be precise," Lappincyk said. "As I once told you, we compensate for our lack of influence and successes by keeping track of everyone else's."

"I remember," Thrass said. "So they're out here somewhere. How do we find them?"

"That would indeed be the next question," Thrawn said, pulling out his questis. "There are a mathematical infinity of possible curves to choose from, and depending on how long they planned for the cargo ship to be incommunicado the orbit could extend a considerable distance out into space."

"Any chance the sensors on this ship are good enough to just brute-strength find them?" Thrass asked.

"Unfortunately, no," Lappincyk said. "This is a close-in patrol ship, and not designed for extensive survey work."

"So what's the plan?" Thrass asked, watching Thrawn working at his questis. "Start looking and hope for the best?"

"Fortunately, many of those possible courses can be eliminated," Thrawn said. "If they came from Sposia on the easiest course, they'll have arrived twelve degrees below the ecliptic plane. They also won't have gone very far from their entry point, lest their drive emissions be spotted by the blackdock crew. A Vivan cargo ship carries three weeks' worth of life-support supplies, so they won't have set its course to bring it into the blackdock's view any later than that."

"What if they don't bother with any of this?" Thrass asked, an unpleasant thought suddenly occurring to him. "What if they just dump them in deep space somewhere between stars? Without bodies, the Clarr won't be able to prove there were any killings."

"Not true," Lappincyk said. "Clarr law specifies that if a person is missing for over a year they can be presumed dead. If Patriarch Lamiov can prove to his satisfaction that this gang hijacked the Stybla ship, those missing crew would automatically add the further charge of murder."

"So a three-week drift at the most," Thrawn said. "Probably no more than two." He made one final calculation, then tapped his questis. "They should be within the region marked."

Thrass looked at the overview display, now showing a hazy green region of space around them. "Still a lot of territory to look at."

"Let's see if we can narrow it further," Thrawn said. "Senior Aide Lappincyk, may I have control of the comm?"

"Give me comm control," Lappincyk called to the bridge crew as he unfastened a mike from the bulkhead behind Thrawn's head and handed it to him. "What exactly do you have in mind?"

"The hijackers will of course have destroyed the cargo ship's transmitters," Thrawn said. "But it's possible to convert a ship's electromagnetic sensor into a receiver. Let's see if the crew were clever enough to do so." He keyed the mike. "Stybla cargo ship V-484, this is Stybla patrol ship *Jandalin*, under the command of Patriarch Senior Aide Lappincyk. We're looking for you, but there's a great deal of space to cover. If you can hear me, vent your aft oxygen reserves and aft thruster fuel tanks and ignite the mixture. The resulting plume should help reveal your position."

He repeated the message three times, then keyed off the mike and handed it back to Lappincyk. "While we wait, Senior Aide, you should contact the blackdock and alert them to our presence and the fact they'll be called upon soon to tow in the damaged cargo ship."

"We won't need their help," Lappincyk said. "The *Jandalin* is fully capable of towing a cargo ship."

"Capability is not the issue," Thrawn said. "Once we've spoken to the cargo crew and learned where the hijackers have gone, we'll need to head out immediately if we hope to intercept them."

"You really think they told the cargo crew where they were going?" Thrass asked.

"Oh, I'm certain they didn't," Thrawn said drily. "But perhaps they weren't as clever as they thought. Senior Aide?"

"Yes," Lappincyk said, sounding somewhat less than enthusiastic. "I think perhaps we'll wait to alert the blackdock until we have some solid evidence that the cargo ship—"

"There!" the sensor officer snapped, pointing out the viewport. "Seventy-two degrees to portside."

Thrass felt a sense of relief wash over him. The distant plume of burning thruster fuel was small but clearly visible against the blackness and unwavering starlight behind it. He looked at the sensor display, watching as the patrol ship's computer calculated the crippled ship's course and vector and overlaid them on the visual.

"Helm: Get us over to them," Lappincyk ordered. "Best possible speed and course for an intercept." He sent a wry smile at Thrawn as he keyed his mike. "And now, Mid Commander, I believe you suggested that I call the blackdock?"

"They moved fast," the cargo ship's captain said, his voice low and pained. He looked up at Lappincyk, sitting across from him, then quickly lowered his gaze back to the deck. "Much faster than we guessed they could. Before we even knew what was happening they were on the bridge, and in the engine room, and were pumping gas through the entire ship."

"Probably tava mist," Thrawn commented absently from the side, most of his attention on his questis. "Harmless and relatively easy to obtain."

"I don't know what it was," the captain said, throwing a sideways look at Thrawn. He'd been doing a lot of that during his debriefing, Thrass had noted, even while he was ostensibly talking to and being questioned by Lappincyk. Probably wondering why a Stybla senior official was having him go through such a humiliating failure—and right on his own bridge—in front of a pair of Mitth. "When our minds finally cleared, we were prisoners and the hijackers were transferring our cargo to their own vessel."

"Did they transfer *all* of it?" Lappincyk asked. "Every crate?"

"Every crate," the captain said tiredly. "It took all fifty

hours of our journey here. It was only once they'd left that we discovered they'd disabled our thrusters, hyperdrive, and transmitters."

"How long ago since they left?" Thrawn asked.

The captain sent him another sideways look. *Definitely* resentful at having a couple of non-Stybla present, Thrass decided. "Twenty-seven hours," he said. "We had just barely cobbled together our receiver when you signaled."

Lappincyk looked at Thrass. "Your thoughts, Syndic?"

"I don't know," Thrass said. The cargo ship's captain's dubious expression, he noted, had now been transferred from Thrawn to him. Not just a non-family military officer, but a non-family syndic, as well. There were probably more humiliating combinations for a simple working person, but offhand Thrass couldn't think of any. "They're over a day ahead of us, and we still don't know where they're headed."

"On the contrary," Thrawn said calmly. "I believe I know exactly which planet they're going to." He stopped, raising his eyebrows at Lappincyk.

The other took the cue. "Thank you, Captain," he said, gesturing to the other Stybla. "You may return to your cabin. A Defense Force ship is on its way to tow you to the blackdock and begin repairs."

"I obey, Senior Aide," the captain said, standing up. He bowed deeply to Lappincyk, gave tentative and abbreviated versions of the bow to Thrawn and Thrass, and left the bridge.

The hatch closed behind him, and Lappincyk turned to Thrawn. "Explain," he said.

"The hijackers are going to a planet designated as Pleknok," Thrawn said. "It's about fifty-two hours—"

"No, not just the final answer," Lappincyk interrupted. "I want the full explanation, if you please."

Thrawn shot a look at Thrass, then gave a small shrug.

"The placement and orbit of the cargo ship would have brought it into sensor range of the blackdock approximately seven days from the hijackers' departure," he said. "That means seven days before the alarm goes out. Those same seven days are all the time they have to travel to the trading planet, sell the stolen goods, and return to their base in the Ascendancy. If we assume one day to meet the traders, arrange a deal, and off-load the goods, that leaves six."

"So three days there and three days back?" Thrass suggested.

"More likely two there and four back," Thrawn said. "They'll want a buffer to make sure their ship is on the ground and out of sight before any search begins. But three is definitely the upper limit."

He handed his questis to Lappincyk. "There are several areas of the Chaos beyond Glastis Three that are particularly difficult to traverse. Most travelers avoid them, which makes them ideal for clandestine criminal activity. If we limit our search to three days' travel time from here, the marked section is the only one in range. There are no developed worlds or systems in there, and only one marginally habitable planet."

"If they're doing all their business in orbit, the world below them doesn't have to be habitable," Lappincyk pointed out as he studied the questis.

"Agreed," Thrawn said. "But if it comes to a choice, most people prefer to have somewhere nearby as an emergency retreat. A world with water and an oxygen atmosphere can make a crucial difference if repairs are needed or one is forced to go into hiding."

"We'll have to hope the hijackers and their friends feel that same way," Lappincyk said. "So Pleknok, you say." He frowned. "*Pleknok.* Why does that name sound familiar?"

"You've demonstrated considerable knowledge of ancient battles, Senior Aide," Thrawn said. "Focus your memory on more recent conflicts. Say, nineteen years ago."

For a long moment Lappincyk stared at the questis. Surreptitiously, Thrass slid out his own questis and punched in the relevant date and planet name.

Lappincyk got there first. "Of course," he said. "A Boadil group was in the system studying it for possible development when it was attacked by a pair of Paataatus warships. The survey ship was damaged but was able to escape back to the Ascendancy. The Defense Force sent out a response, found the Paataatus doing their own survey, and beat them soundly enough that they never came back."

"Haven't come back yet," Thrawn corrected. "But treaties, agreements, and even painfully learned lessons only stay with Paataatus for that single generation."

"I didn't know that about the Paataatus," Thrass said, frowning. "Is that new?"

"The theory is at least a hundred years old," Thrawn said, "though most of the Council and Syndicure reject it. But I've studied the record and the pattern, and I personally have no doubts."

"Interesting," Thrass said. "So how long *is* a Paataatus generation?"

"It's usually assumed to be between seventeen and twenty-five years," Thrawn said.

Lappincyk looked up sharply. "That deciding battle was nineteen years ago."

"Indeed," Thrawn said. "Whether today or at some future date, I believe the criminals who've been using Pleknok as a rendezvous point will discover to their dismay that the Paataatus once again consider that world theirs. I suggest, Senior Aide–"

But Lappincyk was no longer listening. Tossing Thrawn's questis back into his lap, he snatched out his comm. "Captain, this is Senior Aide Lappincyk," he snapped, standing up and striding toward the hatch. "I'm invoking emergency protocols. The *Jandalin* is to be ready to fly in five minutes."

"What is it?" Thrass demanded as he and Thrawn also stood. "Senior Aide?"

"Hurry, or be left behind," was all Lappincyk said over his shoulder. Picking up his pace, he slapped the hatch control and disappeared through the opening.

"Thrawn?" Thrass asked as they hurried to catch up.

"I don't know," Thrawn told him. "I knew the situation was bad, but I didn't realize it was *this* bad. Come—let's see what we can find out."

CHAPTER TWELVE

Early on in the *Springhawk*'s mad dash to Sunrise, Samakro had realized that, as far as Sky-walker Che'ri was concerned, there were only three possible outcomes.

The first and best was that Che'ri would succeed. Given the fatigue the girl was still shouldering from their previous and equally mad rush to Rapacc, he didn't hold out much hope for that one. The second possibility was that her brain and body would simply give up somewhere along the way and send her into a deep sleep from which she couldn't be roused until it was too late to intervene in whatever Thrawn and the Paccosh had planned. That one, in Samakro's opinion, was the most likely result.

And then there was the third option: the possibility that Che'ri would push herself so hard that she blew past all normal points of physical shutdown and collapsed into some form of psychotic dysfunction.

That one would be disastrous, and not just for Che'ri. Even though the medics would probably be able to cure her once the *Springhawk* limped back to Naporar, he and Thalias would then be dumped straight into the career-ending scenario he'd warned her about before she and Che'ri agreed to this madness.

Samakro had no way of knowing what the odds were on that one. Frankly, he was afraid to even research it.

Still, as the hours and days crept by, the plan seemed to be working. Che'ri continued to guide the ship through the Chaos on the course Azmordi had worked out for her, taking her breaks when protocol required them, eating meals when she was hungry or when Thalias insisted, and sleeping the four hours per day that Samakro had calculated was the most he could allow her. At every break Samakro checked the *Springhawk*'s progress and confirmed it was on course, and during Che'ri's brief sleep periods Azmordi or one of the other pilots continued the ship's progress via jump-by-jump.

And finally, to Samakro's relief and mild surprise, they were there.

"One more short jump to go, Mid Captain," Azmordi reported, offering his questis to Samakro. "I can handle it if you want to let Skywalker Che'ri get some sleep."

"She definitely needs it," Samakro said, checking the data on the questis and confirming that the *Springhawk* was situated correctly for their arrival at Sunrise. The single jump Azmordi had specified, he noted, would only take about five minutes. "Go set it up," he said, handing back the questis. "I'll tell her she's done."

Che'ri was at the desk in the duty office, just finishing the last couple of bites of the meat-striped fruit squares she'd requested for today's lunch. Thalias was standing over her, ready to take the empty plate and holding a fresh juice box ready. Both of them looked over as Samakro came in. "How are you two doing?" he asked as he walked over to them.

"I think we're okay," Thalias said. "Che'ri?"

"I'm fine," the girl said. "Are we ready to go?"

"*We're* ready to go," Samakro corrected. "*You're* ready to go get some sleep."

"No," Che'ri said, shaking her head. "Not yet. I need to finish it."

"You're as finished as you need to be," Samakro said firmly. "It's a single five-minute hop, then an in-system jump, and we'll be there. Lieutenant Commander Azmordi could handle it with his eyes closed."

"No, Che'ri's right," Thalias said. "She needs to do it. The timing . . . she needs to do it, that's all."

"Does she, now," Samakro said, peering closely at them. Che'ri's eyelids were drooping, and her face looked gaunt and a little pale. But aside from that she seemed bright-eyed and alert. Way too alert, actually, for someone who'd had as little sleep as she had over the past few days.

Bright-eyed.

"Finish your lunch and we'll discuss it," Samakro said. "Caregiver, I'd like a word with you outside, if I may."

"Certainly," Thalias said, handing Che'ri the juice box. "Drink a little more juice, Che'ri. I'll be back in a minute."

A fully crewed bridge wasn't the ideal place for a private conversation. But right now, it was more important that Che'ri be out of this particular conversation. "All right," Samakro said in a low voice as the office hatch slid shut behind them. "Let's hear it."

"Hear what?" Thalias asked.

"You know what," Samakro growled. "Che'ri is way more alert than she ought to be after the run she's just had. Is this the Magys playing more brain games?"

"I don't know," Thalias said tiredly, rubbing her eyes. "Che'ri is . . . she wants to finish the job, Mid Captain, that's all. She *needs* to finish the job."

"Why?" Samakro countered. "We're here. The job's done. What else does the Magys want her to do?"

"I don't know," Thalias said again. "She won't tell me. Maybe she doesn't know herself."

"Not good enough, Caregiver," Samakro said, shaking his head. "I need answers." He eyed her closely. "Or I'll take speculation, if that's all you've got."

"I don't know if I've got anything even *that* solid." Thalias exhaled a long, painful-sounding breath. "As best as I can figure, the Magys can . . . I don't know. See or know things that are going to happen."

Samakro felt a tingle at the back of his neck. The Magys affecting the *Springhawk*'s sky-walker from light-years away was bad enough. But if she was also manipulating the girl toward the future and things that hadn't even happened yet, that would be far worse. "That's absurd," he said.

"Maybe," Thalias admitted. "Probably, even. And no, I don't have any proof that that's what's happening. But think about it. Isn't seeing into the future exactly what sky-walkers do?"

"That's different," Samakro insisted. "Sky-walkers can only see ahead a few seconds, and only events like hyperspace bumps that are governed solely by physics. You're talking—what? Hours? Days? And all of it involving people doing things and making their own decisions. How is that even possible?"

"I don't know," Thalias said. "But I keep thinking about how we got to Rapacc just in time to keep the Kilji warships from attacking and kidnapping the Magys's people. The only reason we got there when we did was because Che'ri was having terrible nightmares."

"It's still not possible," Samakro said.

But what if it was? Because he had to concede that there was a certain logic to it.

The Magys was carrying the burden of responsibility for her refugees, and had a connection to something she called the Beyond. Che'ri was a sky-walker, with the ability to use Third Sight to see a few seconds into the future. The Magys needed to protect her people and her world. Che'ri was close to Thrawn, whom the Magys had now proclaimed to be her people's Guardian. Could the two of them somehow be mixing those emotional connections and combining their individual abilities?

"Fine," he said. "I still don't believe it, but I'm willing to be convinced. Go check with Che'ri. If she still thinks she can handle the approach, have her report to the nav station." He leveled a finger at her. "If you think she's too fatigued—in fact, if there's any doubt at all in your mind—you take her back to the suite right now and put her to bed. Clear?"

"Yes, sir," Thalias said. "Thank you."

She opened the office hatch and disappeared inside. Samakro stood still another moment, then returned to his command chair.

He was checking the *Springhawk*'s combat status when Thalias and Che'ri returned to the bridge and crossed to the nav station. The girl was a little unsteady on her feet, Samakro noted, but otherwise seemed all right.

Azmordi turned and looked at Samakro, his eyebrows raised in silent question. Samakro answered with a nod. Azmordi nodded back and keyed flight control over to the sky-walker's station.

Two minutes later, with Che'ri once again in Third Sight, the *Springhawk* was in hyperspace. Five minutes after that, they arrived in the Sunrise system.

"Sensors: Full scan," Samakro ordered. "Lieutenant Commander Azmordi: Locate the planet."

"Combat range clear," Dalvu reported from the sensor station. "Mid-range, clear. Far range . . . clear."

"Sunrise located, Mid Captain," Azmordi added. "Computing in-system jump."

"No," Thalias said in a quavering voice. "Not yet."

Azmordi turned a frown toward Samakro. "Mid Captain?" he asked.

"A moment, Lieutenant Commander," Samakro said, watching as Thalias bent down and held a whispered conversation with Che'ri. He waited until she straightened and turned to him. "You have an explanation, Caregiver?" he asked.

"She says we can't go closer, Mid Captain," Thalias said. "I mean, we *shouldn't* go closer. It's not time yet."

"Any thoughts on when it *will* be time?"

Again, Thalias leaned over for a couple of seconds, talking to the girl half hidden in the navigator's chair. "We'll know, sir," Thalias said. Her lip twitched. "*She'll* know."

For a moment the bridge was silent. "Very well," Samakro said. "We'll hold here for now. Senior Commander Afpriuh, confirm that all weapons systems and crews are ready."

"Yes, sir."

The normal bridge conversation resumed, though at a more sub-dued level than usual. Samakro checked the status boards, did quick evaluations of his bridge crew, and did all the other things a Chiss commander was supposed to do when preparing for action.

But mostly he watched Thalias, standing rigidly behind Che'ri's seat. If the caregiver even *looked* like she was falling asleep on her feet, he would have both of them summarily hauled back to their suite and tossed into their beds.

In fact, that might be the best thing to do whether they were half asleep or not. Because Thalias clearly hadn't thought this though.

The Magys hadn't had these exaggerated Third Sight abilities when she first came aboard the *Springhawk*. There were too many things back then that had taken her by surprise, too many decisions she would surely have adjusted or revoked if she'd been able to see even an hour into the future. It was only after she'd been in hibernation in the sky-walker suite in Che'ri's proximity for several weeks that this connection had happened. Normal logic might not work here, but Samakro assumed there was a fair chance that connection would likewise fade once the two of them had been apart for a similar length of time.

The Magys had had her first success with the Rapacc intervention. Now, if things worked out the way Che'ri and Thalias clearly expected them to, the alien was about to garner herself a second. Two triumphs in a row should be ample confirmation that she now possessed an awesome and incredibly useful power.

What if she decided she didn't want to give up that power?

The sky-walkers are the key to our entire mission statement, Samakro had once told Thalias. *We need to protect that resource as much as we can.*

And he would. Against any force or manipulation that might come against her.

Whatever the cost.

With one last touch of the Great Presence, Qilori brought the *Aelos* out of hyperspace.

They had arrived at the system Thrawn had designated, the one he called Sunrise, the one the other Pathfinder had arrived in a few hours ago. At least they'd proved that Thrawn's guess as to the *Hammer*'s destination was correct.

The Paccosh were ready. All of them were outfitted in heavy commando fighting suits, encased from the tops of their heads to their splay-toed feet, though their feathery headcrests were curiously left uncovered. Thrawn was similarly dressed for the occasion, wearing an armored version of the usual Chiss military uniform.

And Qilori still had no idea what exactly was going on.

One thing he *did* know, though. In his time as a Pathfinder, he'd seen hundreds of different planets. He'd seen major worlds, minor ones, worlds that held nothing but mining colonies, worlds that were all but uninhabited.

This world was different. This world had been utterly devastated.

The evidence was everywhere he looked. The clouds on the sunlit side were laced with the gray and black of smoke or blast debris. The strips of land visible beneath them were charred, with mere patches of fading green or the muted glitter of contaminated rivers and small lakes. He could see no city or travel lights at all on the night side.

And Thrawn, who'd clearly already seen the catastrophic panorama now stretched out in front of them, had chosen to call the place *Sunrise*?

"Are they there?" Uingali demanded, looming suddenly over Qilori like an angry storm cloud as he gazed out of the bridge viewport. He turned slightly, the massive weapon holstered at his hip coming uncomfortably close to the side of Qilori's head. "Pilot?"

"There!" one of the other Paccosh announced from his station. "Two ships, alien design, in a low synchronized planetary orbit."

Qilori leaned a little forward, trying to see what the alien was pointing to. It was no use—his eyes weren't good enough to even pick up the dot that should be all that was visible at this distance.

"Why are they so far away?" Uingali asked.

"We arrived farther out than planned," the pilot said.

"Is this your doing, Pathfinder?" Uingali demanded, an edge of suspicion coloring his voice.

"It wasn't my choice," Qilori protested, his winglets going flat. "This area of hyperspace is unusually difficult to navigate. I did the best I could to follow your directive."

"Yet you didn't succeed."

"I did the best I could," Qilori repeated.

"It's all right, Uingali foar Marocsaa," Thrawn said from the rear of the bridge. "Navigation is indeed difficult here."

"It is from those united with the Beyond," the alien voice that Qilori had heard once before came from somewhere near Thrawn. "They seek to protect their world from invaders."

"They didn't stop the Kilji who arrived before us," Qilori pointed out.

"The invaders faced their own difficulty," the Magys said. "They succeeded only through the same effort as your Pathfinder."

"That may be as it is," Uingali said. "The plan remains?"

"It remains," Thrawn confirmed.

Uingali made a rumbling noise. "Pilot: Show us the targets."

"Yes, Commander." One of the displays at the station next to Qilori lit up, showing a magnified view of the planetary edge and the two warships.

He felt his cheek winglets twitch. One of the two ships was a Kilji picket cruiser, undoubtedly the *Hammer.* The other was larger, similar in size to the Kilji battle cruiser *Anvil,* the ship Qilori had barely escaped from at Rapacc.

But its appearance was notably different from that of either of the Kiljis. A Grysk warship, maybe?

That could be very bad. Jixtus didn't talk about his own warships much, but from the bits and pieces Qilori had put together it sounded like they were large, well armed, and extremely formidable. On Uingali's side, in contrast, was a single Nikardun blockade frigate and a relative handful of Paccian commandos.

Plus they had Thrawn. Who'd engineered the Nikardun defeat at Primea, and who'd then plucked General Yiv straight off his own flagship. Whatever happened, it would probably be inventive and deadly.

And Qilori, a simple Pathfinder, was stuck squarely in the middle.

"Senior Captain Thrawn?" Uingali invited.

"One is the ship that escaped from Rapacc," Thrawn said. "The other is of the same design as the Battle Dreadnought the Chiss fought here a few weeks ago." He paused. "And which we then destroyed. Qilori of Uandualon: Confirmation, if you please."

"Yes, that's the Kilji picket cruiser *Hammer*," Qilori said. There was clearly no point in lying or trying to confuse the issue. "I have no information on the other ship."

"Is the Pathfinder you were following still aboard the *Hammer*?"

"Yes," Qilori said. "If you want, I can call and ask to speak—"

He broke off as the *Aelos* leapt forward, the compensators responding with just enough delay to give the occupants a brief wave of acceleration. "Emergency!" Uingali shouted from right behind him.

"What is it?" Qilori gasped, cringing in his seat. "What's happening?"

"We are the Nikardun warship *Aelos*, requesting emergency assistance from the Kilji picket cruiser *Hammer*," Uingali continued in the same bellowing voice. "Our weapons and defenses are damaged, and a Chiss warship is in pursuit. We request safe haven and protection until we can make repairs."

He stopped, and for a long moment the bridge was silent. "Again," Thrawn said quietly.

"Emergency!" Uingali roared again. "We are the Nikardun warship—"

"Nikardun, how did you find this place?" a stiff voice spat from the bridge speaker.

"We are in need of assistance—" Uingali began again.

"How did you find this place?" the voice interrupted. "You have no purpose here."

"We rescued the Pathfinder navigator from the *Anvil*," Uingali said. "It was he who guided us here."

"You lie," the voice accused. "Neither Pathfinder was told in advance of this world."

Qilori's winglets stiffened as he looked furtively over his shoulder at Thrawn standing silently beside Uingali. The Pathfinders' ability to sense and follow each other in hyperspace was the Navigators' Guild's deepest and most dangerous secret, one that Thrawn had assured Qilori he would keep to himself. If he and Uingali were about to shred the wall the guild had so carefully built around it, the results could be disastrous.

"The Pathfinder told me that his Kilji captain spoke secrets when he shouldn't have," Uingali said. "A mistake we of the Nikardun would never make."

"You don't think much of our Kilji allies, then?"

Qilori winced. He'd already been thinking that didn't sound like a Kilji voice. But now, with this new layer of arrogance, he realized how much it reminded him instead of Jixtus.

Which strongly implied that was, indeed, a Grysk warship keeping station with the *Hammer*.

He looked again at the magnified image on the nearby display. The only Grysk ship he'd ever seen up close was Jixtus's personal transport, and this vessel didn't look anything like that.

Or at least, it didn't look that way to him. Did Thrawn see it differently? He'd already identified it as akin to the Battle Dreadnought the Chiss had faced and destroyed, but did he realize those ships belonged to the Grysks?

"I think very little of a captain that runs from battle," Uingali said contemptuously, "leaving its fellow ship and an ally to face the murderous Chiss alone. The other Kilji paid with its life; and we will do likewise soon unless the three of us stand together."

"I see no sign of any pursuit," the voice said. "But you may approach so that we can discuss your situation." He paused. "And, perhaps, your true identity."

"I look forward to our meeting," Uingali said. "In the meantime, I urge you to prepare for combat. Whether or not you see pursuit, it is coming."

"If you're lying, you will die slowly, and in great pain," the other said, his voice going cold. "But I greatly hope you are not. The Chiss have taken the lives of many of my people. It's time we balanced that scale."

Thalias was standing behind the nav station chair, drifting in and out of waking dreams and wondering distantly when this would all be over, when Che'ri suddenly gasped.

"What is it?" Thalias asked sharply, snapping fully awake. "Che'ri?"

"They're here," Che'ri said.

"About time," Samakro said briskly. "Azmordi, confirm in-system jump coordinates and prepare to execute."

"No, wait," Che'ri said urgently. "It's not . . . it's changed. It's a different spot."

"What do you mean, a different spot?" Samakro asked. "Where exactly? Do you have the coordinates?"

"I can't . . . it's just a little . . ." Che'ri gave a little whimper. "I don't have . . . I can't . . ."

Samakro muttered something. "Dalvu, give me a complete sweep," he said. "Find them, figure out what's changed and where we need to go."

"That'll require active sensors, Mid Captain," the sensor officer warned.

"I know," Samakro growled. "But it's either that or we do the planned jump and hope Sky-walker Che'ri is wrong."

"What if Che'ri does the jump?" Thalias spoke up.

"What?" Samakro asked, frowning at her.

"I asked what if Che'ri does the jump," Thalias repeated, trying not to let her own surprise show. All she'd been planning to do was ask why active sensors would be a problem.

Only the other question was the one that had popped into her head and then out of her mouth. "She's done in-system jumps before," she told Samakro. "Even if she can't tell Lieutenant Commander Azmordi where he needs to go, maybe she can take us there herself."

Samakro's gaze shifted slightly from her to Che'ri. "Sky-walker?" he asked.

"She learned how to do them when she and Senior Captain Thrawn were exploring the edge of Lesser Space," Thalias added before Che'ri could answer. "She told me—"

"I asked the sky-walker, Caregiver, not you," Samakro cut her off. "Sky-walker?"

"Yes, sir," Che'ri managed, though to Thalias's ears she didn't sound at all confident. "I think so."

"You *think* so?"

"I can do it," Che'ri said, sounding more confident now.

"That's more like it," Samakro said. "Azmordi, transfer control."

"Yes, sir," the pilot said, and the helm section of Che'ri's board once again lit up as it went active.

Che'ri hunched her shoulders and set her hands timidly on the controls. "You can do this, Che'ri," Thalias murmured. "Just take your time."

"I can't," Che'ri murmured back. "There isn't any." She braced herself—her hands twitched—

Abruptly, the view outside changed. Sunrise, which had been too far away to see, now filled nearly a quarter of the starscape. Ahead, Thalias could see the vague shapes of two distant ships near the planet. Between those ships and the *Springhawk* was a third vessel, driving hard away from the Chiss cruiser and toward the planet.

"Combat range: one warship," Dalvu reported. "Identification . . . it's the *Aelos*."

Thalias frowned at the image of the fleeing ship on the sensor display. "How do you know it's not some other Nikardun ship?" she asked.

"Look at the underside," Samakro said, his voice sounding distracted. "The multiple snake design."

"Right—I see it," Thalias said, feeling like a fool. The symbol painted on the blockade frigate's ventral surface was subtle but visible enough from the *Springhawk*'s angle: a nest of small stylized snakes with two larger ones curving up from among them, intertwined as they reached toward the ship's bow. It was the emblem of Uingali foar Marocsaa's subclan, matching the double ring Uingali had once given Thrawn for safekeeping back when the Nikardun were blockading and threatening his world.

So that was Senior Captain Thrawn and the Paccosh, and they were heading straight toward the two unidentified ships. "Are we going to attack?" she asked.

"Sky-walker, do you have further instructions?" Samakro asked, ignoring Thalias's question. "Sky-walker?"

There was no answer. Frowning, Thalias looked down, to find

Che'ri slumped in her chair, her eyes closed, her hands lying limp in her lap, her breathing slow and steady. "She's asleep, Mid Captain," she told him.

"I'm not surprised," Samakro said. "Fine. When in doubt, follow the leader's lead. Give me comm."

"You have comm, Mid Captain."

Samakro cleared his throat. "Unidentified ships, this is Mid Captain Samakro of the Chiss Expansionary Defense Fleet warship *Springhawk*," he called in the Taarja trade language. "You stand near our prey. Move clear of the Nikardun blockade frigate *Aelos* or suffer the humiliation of becoming collateral damage."

Qilori's only warning was a shout from the sensor officer. He looked back and forth among the displays, his winglets stiffening.

There it was, directly aft: A fourth warship had joined the three already in the Sunrise system, its thrusters blazing as it drove straight toward them.

His winglets stiffened against his cheeks as he grabbed for the controls. There was no time for him to get his headset on, but they might still be able to escape into hyperspace before the ambushing ship behind them opened fire. He didn't know if he could reach out to the Great Presence with the distraction of sounds and sights in front of him, but he had to at least try. If he let the *Aelos* get too deep into Sunrise's gravity well, they would be caught between two forces with no way out. He reached for the controls, discovered to his horror that they'd already been disengaged—

"Unidentified ships, this is Mid Captain Samakro of the Chiss Expansionary Defense Fleet warship *Springhawk*," a voice boomed over the bridge speaker. "You stand near our prey. Move clear of the Nikardun blockade frigate *Aelos* or suffer the humiliation of becoming collateral damage."

Qilori's winglets went completely rigid. The *Springhawk* really *had* followed them?

That was bad. Very bad. He'd overheard snippets of the comm discussion between Thrawn and his first officer before they left Rapacc, and while he couldn't understand the Cheunh words it had been clear from the two blueskins' tones that the conversation had been tense. More than that, Thrawn had abandoned his ship, and Qilori knew enough about military cultures to know that such an action was a serious offense. Thrawn had told Uingali he'd sent Samakro and the ship away; apparently, Samakro had ignored the order.

And now he was calling out Thrawn and the Paccosh as his prey?

"Full power to the thrusters," Thrawn said calmly.

The *Aelos* leapt forward, blazing its way toward the Kilji and Grysk warships. Qilori stared out the viewport, wondering what in the Depths Thrawn was planning. Was he perhaps hoping to build up some speed and some distance from the *Springhawk,* force the bigger and heavier Chiss ship to commit to a pursuit vector, then suddenly veer to the side and angle toward the edge of the gravity well, hoping that the *Aelos*'s lower mass and better maneuverability would let them escape?

It was worth a try. And if that *was* the strategy, the ship would need its navigator ready for hyperspace. He picked up his headset, smoothing back his winglets so that they wouldn't be in the way, and got ready to put it on.

"You won't need that."

Qilori turned his head. Thrawn was gazing out the viewport at the distant ships and planet, not even sparing a glance in Qilori's direction. Still, it was clear the words had been directed toward him. "Sir?" Qilori asked.

"You won't need your headset," Thrawn said. "Uingali?"

"Emergency!" Uingali shouted. Again, Qilori twitched with the sudden noise. "The Chiss have arrived, and our weapons are still nonfunctional. We are in desperate need of a safe haven."

"You may approach, Nikardun," the earlier voice said, now almost purring with anticipation. "Draw the Chiss to us, and to their doom."

"You will not regret this," Uingali said. "Even now we work with frantic zeal to repair our weapons. By the time we reach your safe haven, your battle line will have the mighty Nikardun standing as a part of it."

"We will be ever so grateful to add the strength of your mighty weapons to our own," the other said, a thick layer of sarcasm coloring the anticipation in his voice. "You may take up position to portside of the Kilji warship *Hammer*. Make haste, that we may face this threat together." There was a double tone as the comm was shut down.

Qilori took a careful breath. At least now he'd finally figured out the plan. Mid Captain Samakro wasn't genuinely angry with Thrawn, nor was he planning to attack him. Samakro was merely playing a role for the Kiljis' and Grysks' benefit, persuading them that the Nikardun ship was in danger. Once Thrawn and the Paccosh were inside the *Hammer*'s point defenses, they would open fire on it at point-blank range. The hope would be that they could incapacitate it before it could do any damage, while the *Springhawk* similarly attacked the Grysk ship.

It was a bold plan, he had to admit. It was also a huge and dangerous gamble. Qilori had seen enough battles from the bridge of General Yiv's flagship to realize that, while the *Springhawk* was probably only slightly less powerful than the Grysk warship awaiting it, the *Aelos* was far outmatched by the Kilji picket cruiser they were racing toward. Even if Thrawn could get in the first shot—and the second, third, and fourth as well—the Paccosh would probably be overwhelmed.

"Tell me, are you proficient with weapons?" Thrawn asked.

Qilori's winglets rippled. What kind of question was that? Surely he wasn't inviting Qilori to take over the weapons console, was he? "No, not at all," he said. "I'm a navigator, not an armaments expert."

"I know," Thrawn said. "I was asking about hand weaponry, not shipboard."

And with a jolt of stiffened winglets, Qilori finally understood. Thrawn wasn't going to get in close to the Kilji picket cruiser and trade spectrum laser shots.

He and the Paccosh were going to board it.

"I . . . no, I'm not," he managed. No—surely Thrawn wasn't think-ing of dragging him into the middle of their attack. "The Navigators' Guild forbids us from carrying sidearms."

"That also wasn't what I asked," Thrawn said. "But no matter. The Paccosh and I will protect you."

"You can't do this, sir," Qilori begged, the winglets now vibrating at high speed. "If the guild ever found out that I was involved in a military action, I would be instantly expelled."

"I think they're likely to be more charitable toward you than that," Thrawn said. "Certainly once they learn your involvement was solely to help rescue a fellow Pathfinder."

Qilori stared at him. "To *rescue*—?"

"Commander, they have us in a tractor beam," the pilot cut in.

"Maintain course," Uingali said. "Do not attempt to break free. Se-nior Captain Thrawn?"

"They want to control our approach," Thrawn said, stepping to Uingali's side and studying the helm and sensor displays. "Do you have an origination point?"

"The outer edge of the portside shoulder weapons cluster," the pilot told him, pointing to a partial schematic of the *Hammer* that had now appeared on one of the displays.

"Near the midships docking port," Uingali commented.

"I expect their plan is to park us right at the tractor projector," Thrawn said. "That will position us directly beneath the weapons cluster, where we'll be out of position to damage it."

"And put us far enough from the docking port that we won't have easy or immediate access to their ship," Uingali added.

"Indeed," Thrawn said. "I think we can modify their plan some-what."

"I think we may," Uingali agreed with dark amusement. "Weap-ons?"

"The Crippler net is ready for deployment," one of the other Pac-cosh confirmed.

Qilori looked at the weapons display, trying without success to decipher the unfamiliar Paccian script. *Crippler net*—what kind of weapon could *that* be?

He had no idea. But the orange marker that had just begun flickering seemed to be located in or near one of the *Aelos*'s forward missile tubes. Was a Crippler net some kind of Chiss missile he'd never heard about?

"Prepare to launch on my signal," Thrawn said. He looked at Qilori, and it seemed to him that the Chiss almost smiled. "Don't be concerned, Pathfinder. It will be over soon."

The glowing red eyes glittered as he turned back to the viewport and the Kilji ship rushing up at them. "Very soon."

CHAPTER THIRTEEN

Samakro had assumed that both Thalias and Che'ri would have to be carried back to their suite, and had made sure there were enough warriors on hand for transport duty. To his mild surprise, Thalias managed to make it off the bridge under her own power, and was even able to rouse Che'ri enough to stagger along beside her. Samakro made sure the warriors went with them anyway, just in case they collapsed halfway to the suite.

Then they were gone, and the bridge hatch was sealed behind them.

And Samakro could finally get to work.

"Afpriuh: Report," he said, resettling himself in the command chair.

"Barriers at full power, weapons and weapons crews ready," Afpriuh said. "Still no attacks from Bogeys One and Two."

"Bogey Two has a tractor beam on Senior Captain Thrawn," Dalvu added. "Looks like he's being pulled to their portside near the amidships docking port."

Samakro nodded. So far the scenario was playing out exactly the way Thrawn had anticipated, with the Kiljis and their unidentified companion allowing the *Aelos* to race past their point defenses and into their protection.

Though as Thrawn had also predicted, and as Samakro himself now recognized, there was very little altruism involved. With Samakro having loudly proclaimed his intent to capture or destroy the

Nikardun blockade frigate, the enemy commander was playing on that apparent obsession in the hope of drawing the *Springhawk* close enough to launch a withering attack, ideally inside Sunrise's gravity well where there would be no easy escape.

"Azmordi, increase speed to match," he ordered. "I want us slowly gaining on them, but I also want to stay out of the bogeys' laser range until Senior Captain Thrawn makes his move. Can you do that?"

"No problem, sir," Azmordi assured him, hunching over his helm controls.

The *Springhawk* leapt forward. Samakro kept an eye on the tactical, watching as both ships approached the waiting enemies. As always, the timing on this one was going to be critical.

Timing that Samakro had nearly screwed up.

He'd assumed Thalias would come to confront him as soon as the *Springhawk* and *Aelos* left Rapacc to head off in their respective directions. If she had, he could have had the necessary conversation with her then and there, and wouldn't have had to spend the next five hours sending the ship back toward the Ascendancy.

But Thalias had fallen asleep, and the conversation had been delayed, and as a result they'd been far enough out of position that Che'ri had had to really push it in order to get the *Springhawk* here in time.

But Samakro had had no choice but to play this little charade. If Thalias was still acting as a spy for Patriarch Thurfian, letting her see Thrawn disobeying Ba'kif's order to return to Naporar *and* once again trying to dodge the prohibition against preemptive combat would have given Thurfian a double handful of fresh ammunition.

Never mind that Thrawn was completely within his authority as commander on the scene to countermand Ba'kif's order about a swift return. Never mind also that the senior captain was riding with Uingali aboard a Paccian ship where Syndicure prohibitions were meaningless. Thurfian and those members of the Syndicure who were already predisposed to dislike Thrawn would still have found a way to use that against him, and would possibly have dragged in the rest of the *Springhawk*'s officers as well.

But as it now stood, all Thalias could tell her Patriarch sponsor was that Thrawn had accepted a plea for help, and that it was she and Che'ri who had forced Samakro to chase after him. The Council and Syndicure might take issue with parts of it, but at least there wouldn't be any calls for the wholesale slaughter of everyone's careers.

Assuming, of course, that Thrawn was able to pull this off.

"Ten seconds to Crippler net deployment at Bogey Two," Afpriuh said. "Targeting orders, sir?"

Samakro eyed the tactical display. Bogey One, the bigger of the two ships and the one that looked like a smaller version of the Battle Dreadnought the Chiss had tangled with twice over Sunrise, hadn't yet made any aggressive moves toward the *Springhawk*. That, according to strict Syndicure doctrine, meant the *Springhawk* couldn't fire on it.

On the other hand, Bogey Two, the Kilji ship currently tractoring the *Aelos* toward itself, *had* opened fire on them back at Rapacc. That made them fair game.

And even at the *Springhawk*'s distance, a barrage of breacher missiles or plasma spheres would wreak havoc on their ability to fight. It was the obvious move for the *Springhawk* to make.

"No targeting orders," he told the weapons officer.

But then, no one had ever said Thrawn's plans went for the obvious.

"Ten seconds to deployment," Uingali called, his voice echoing across the bridge as it was picked up by his mike and sent to all the ship's speakers. "Crew, prepare; commandos, stand ready. Senior Captain Thrawn: At your order."

Qilori pressed his fingertips against the chest plate of the light armor the Paccosh had strapped onto him only two minutes ago. Until that exact moment he'd hoped Thrawn had been lying about dragging him along on whatever this reckless intrusion was they were planning. But it was now painfully clear that the blueskin had been dead serious.

"Deploy," Thrawn said. Through the viewport, Qilori saw a dark package blast from one of the *Aelos*'s missile tubes and streak toward the *Hammer*'s weapons cluster.

His winglets twitched. No drive emissions, no sleek missile shape. In fact, paradoxically, even as it sped away from him its apparent size didn't seem to be changing. Was it somehow getting bigger? Even as he puzzled over that paradox it seemed to leap ahead, probably caught in the same tractor beam that was still pulling the *Aelos* toward its final position. The object hit the side of the weapons cluster— there was a diffuse flash of light indicating a violent electrical discharge from the Crippler net into the tractor projector—

And the *Aelos* abruptly jerked as the tractor beam was cut off. "Hard to portside," Thrawn ordered.

An instant later Qilori was thrown against his restraints as the ship angled sharply to the left, away from the *Hammer*'s weapons cluster and toward the hull. He barely had time to see that they were making straight for the docking port—

With a final surge from the *Aelos*'s maneuvering thrusters and a muted thud, they were there.

"Commandos!" Uingali bellowed as he charged toward the bridge hatchway. Qilori struggled to get upright in his seat from the sort of tangled slouch that last maneuver had shoved him into—

A hand reached over and popped off his restraints. "Come," Thrawn ordered. The hand shifted to a grip on the front of Qilori's torso armor and hauled him out of the seat.

The entrance hatch on that side of the *Aelos* was two decks down and a quarter of the way back toward the stern. Thrawn and Qilori arrived to find the two ships locked together, the *Aelos*'s hatch open, the *Hammer*'s hatch blasted to smoking fragments by focused charges or shattercord. Four armored commandos were waiting by the hatch, but Uingali and the rest of the Paccosh were gone.

"Remain here on guard," Thrawn said, pointing to two of the commandos. "You are with us," he added to the other two. Without waiting for an answer he drew a Chiss weapon from a holster at his hip, got a firm grip on Qilori's arm with the other hand, and headed through the hatchway.

It was instantly clear that there had been a battle just inside the hatch. Six Kiljis were lying motionless on the deck in the entrance vestibule, looking very dead. From the distant sounds Qilori could now hear, it was also clear that the battle wasn't over.

"You can see they weren't expecting trouble," Thrawn commented as he maneuvered his way through the scattered bodies. "Which way to the bridge?"

"How do you know?" Qilori asked, his winglets quivering as he tried to look away from the bodies but found himself morbidly drawn to the sight.

"The Kiljis weren't set up in a defensive posture," Thrawn said. "Moreover, they came into the vestibule individually instead of in organized fire teams. Which way to the bridge?"

Qilori drew a shuddering breath. "It's probably that way," he said, pointing to the corridor leading out of the vestibule's center.

"*Probably?*" one of the Paccosh asked in an ominous tone.

"I was never aboard this particular ship," Qilori explained hurriedly, wincing back from the big shoulder-slung weapon gripped in the alien's hands. "But this would have been the way on the *Anvil.*"

"That should be sufficient," Thrawn said. "You two take point."

"You need a rearguard, sir," the alien who'd spoken objected.

"I'll guard the rear," Thrawn said. "We need to go."

For a second the alien looked like he was going to object. Probably, Qilori suspected, he'd been ordered to protect the visiting blueskin and took his job seriously. But he merely gave a curt nod and stepped past Qilori, the other alien moving to his side. Weapons at the ready, they hurried off.

"Follow," Thrawn said, nudging Qilori with his weapon. "Don't worry, they've done this before."

"Done what?" Qilori asked, his winglets vibrating like they were on fire. He was going to die here, he knew. He was going to be slashed to charred pieces by laserfire and die right here.

"Entered and captured an enemy vessel," Thrawn said. "Observe their feather crests."

Qilori's winglets slowed as he focused on the delicate tufts rising from the tops of the aliens' heads. He'd seen earlier that that part of their anatomy was unprotected by their combat armor, but he still had no idea why. "What about them?" he asked.

"Note how they sway in the air as the Paccosh move forward," Thrawn said. "They're responding to the small changes in airflow as the Kiljis come toward us—"

Abruptly, the two Paccosh stopped in the middle of the passageway, both of them swinging their weapons toward the right-hand edge of the cross-corridor the group was approaching. Even as Qilori wondered what was going on, three Kiljis leapt out of cover into view, their own weapons tracking toward the invaders.

They never had a chance to use them. Before any of them could get off even a single shot they were cut down by multiple flashes of laser-fire from the Paccian weapons.

"—or even as they speak among themselves," Thrawn continued as if nothing had happened.

One of the Paccosh spun around, his laser tracking somewhere behind Qilori. Thrawn turned in response, raising his own weapon. Qilori twisted his neck to look; and an instant later two more Kiljis appeared from another cross-corridor, again dying instantly and uselessly as the brilliant Paccian laser and the more subtle blast from the Chiss weapon cut them down.

"Commando?" Thrawn prompted.

"Clear," the alien confirmed.

"We continue," Thrawn said, again taking Qilori's arm and turning him back toward the bridge. "Our time is limited." He hefted his weapon. "I trust you won't forget to let us know if we need to change direction to reach the bridge."

Qilori winced back from the weapon, his winglets flattening. "No," he assured the Chiss. "I won't forget."

Thrawn had estimated it would take five minutes, a number Samakro remembered thinking at the time seemed rather low. But Thrawn had also said Samakro would know when the time was right.

It actually took an extra two minutes before the laserfire erupted from Bogey Two toward Bogey One. Nevertheless, Samakro made sure he was standing behind Afpriuh's weapons station at the five-minute mark.

"Mid Captain?" Afpriuh said hesitantly. "It appears that Bogey Two is firing on Bogey One."

"So it does, Senior Commander," Samakro acknowledged. "Ready a full salvo of spheres on Bogey One, followed by four breachers, on my command."

"Ah . . . yes, sir." Afpriuh craned his neck to look up at Samakro. "Can we *do* that, sir?" he asked, dropping the level of his voice to just above a whisper. "They haven't fired on us."

"Trust me, Senior Commander," Samakro said, watching the viewport. Any minute now . . .

And there it was, again as Thrawn had predicted: a volley of laserfire from the big alien warship blasting into the smaller Kilji craft. "They haven't attacked *us,* no," he said, pointing at the distant battle. "But Senior Captain Thrawn is currently aboard the Kilji ship. As Bogey One attacks it, they also attack him, which makes it an attack on the Ascendancy."

"Yes, sir," Afpriuh said, lowering his eyes to his board as he lined up his plasma sphere volley. "I thought that protocol only applied if the officer was flag rank."

"Do you really care, Senior Commander?"

Afpriuh shook his head. "No, sir, not at all," he said evenly. He keyed one final switch, and Samakro felt the deck move beneath his feet as the plasma spheres shot outward. "Volley away," Afpriuh said, his hands once again moving swiftly across his board. "Breacher salvo ready, awaiting your command."

"Stand ready," Samakro said, watching the spheres' track on the tactical. Presumably Bogey One had spotted the incoming Chiss plasma sphere attack.

But so far there was no response. Could they be so focused on the laserfire coming from Bogey Two that they weren't paying attention anywhere else?

Personally, Samakro had never felt himself to be that lucky. But whether or not Bogey One was distracted, it was time. "Breachers: Three, two, *one*."

Again, he felt the small jolt through the deck as the breachers blasted from their tubes. "Stand by, lasers," he said. He would let the spheres and breachers get a little closer to their target, he decided, which would also close the gap a bit and make the spectrum lasers more effective—

"Missiles incoming!" Dalvu snapped. "Repeat, Bogey One has launched missiles. Four . . . eight . . . *ten* missiles on their way, sir."

"Target and destroy," Samakro ordered, throwing an uneasy look at the tactical display. Even at their current distance, ten missiles was a *lot* for the *Springhawk*'s lasers to handle. More than that, sending that many missiles in the very first salvo suggested that Bogey One had plenty more in reserve.

"Lasers firing," Afpriuh said. "Missiles . . . sir, lasers aren't taking them out."

"What?" Samakro demanded, shifting his eyes to the visual. The *Springhawk*'s lasers were firing accurately, and there were flashes where each one connected to its target missile. But the salvo kept coming. "Increase laser power and double-check spectrum tuning," he ordered. "They must have some impressive armor."

"It's not armor, Mid Captain," Dalvu put in, her face pressed against the sensor station's glare-hooded focus monitor. "It's dibbers. They've got a group of dibbers screening each of the missiles."

Samakro took a closer look at the sensor display. Now that he was looking for them, he could see the cluster of tiny anti-fighter nuisances running ahead of each of the larger missiles.

"Must be why the missiles are traveling so slowly," Afpriuh commented. "They don't want to outrun the dibbers."

"Yes," Samakro muttered. Normally, the missiles' lower speed would be a good thing, translating into more time for the *Springhawk*'s lasers to track and destroy them.

But that reduced speed would likely last only until the dibbers had intercepted all of the *Springhawk*'s defensive laserfire they could before they themselves were destroyed. At that point, the missiles could go to full acceleration, effectively starting their attack that much closer to the Chiss warship.

"Target spheres on the missiles," Samakro ordered. If they could shut down the missiles or the screening dibbers—or both—that would buy them more time.

Unless they ran out of plasma sphere fluid before Bogey One ran out of missiles or dibbers. And with the *Springhawk* still closing on the two warships, the timing was becoming ever more crucial.

"Spheres ready," Afpriuh confirmed.

"Fire."

Qilori had to step over two more small clusters of Kilji bodies before he, Thrawn, and their escort reached the *Hammer*'s bridge. Given the carnage outside the broken bridge hatch, he wasn't particularly surprised when they arrived to find two more Paccian commandos standing guard over three more Kilji bodies and one absolutely terrified Pathfinder.

One of the bodies, he noted, was that of the *Hammer*'s commander, Colonel Tildnis. At least, Qilori thought distantly, he wouldn't have to face any awkward questions from the Kilji as to how he'd ended up aboard an enemy warship.

As for the Pathfinder, it was clear that he was way beyond awkward questions. "It's all right," Qilori soothed, walking over to him as he tried to remember the other's name. They'd met only once, back when they were first recruited and before they were taken to their respective ships. It had been quick and perfunctory, and Qilori hadn't bothered listening to the introductions. "We won't hurt you."

"Speak Taarja, please," Thrawn said, crossing to the front of the bridge and peering out the viewport. "I need to know what you're saying to each other. What's your name, Pathfinder?"

"I am Sarsh," the Pathfinder said in a quavering voice, his own winglets shaking.

Qilori nodded to himself. Right. *Sarsh*.

"We'll soon be taking you to safety aboard the *Aelos*," Thrawn told him, leaning toward the viewport to look to starboard in the direction of the Grysk ship. "Before we leave, I need you to pull all the data from the ship's computer. All the records that involve navigation, personnel, communication, and combat."

Sarsh flashed a startled look at Qilori, a spike in his anxiety level Qilori could well understand. If not carrying sidearms was a major rule, not snooping was *the* major rule. "I don't think I can do that," he said.

"I think you can," Thrawn said, turning back to look forward and gesturing behind him at the lines of consoles. "I note that the controls are laid out with the extreme simplicity that I anticipated. The sooner you begin gathering data, the sooner we can get you to safety." He raised his eyebrows. "Assuming you prove you're worth taking along. Qilori, go to the helm."

Qilori's winglets twitched. "I thought you said we would be leaving aboard the *Aelos*."

"We just need a few degrees of rotation," Thrawn said. He took one final look outside, then turned and headed back to the consoles. "I need an easy way to line up the lasers. Which is the weapons station?"

"That one," Qilori said, pointing as he dropped into the pilot's chair. The Kiljis had started bringing the main drive up from standby, but it would be several more minutes before it was fully up to speed. But all he needed for Thrawn's maneuver were the directional thrusters, and those were ready to go. "Are we going to attack the other ship?"

"No," Thrawn said. He sat down at the weapons station, looked briefly over the control board, then began punching keys. "Uingali and his team have that part of the plan covered. Prepare a ten-degree yaw to starboard; I'll tell you when to execute. Commandos, please inform Uingali we'll be yawing ten degrees to starboard momentarily. Warn him he'll need to compensate his aim."

"He acknowledges, and stands ready," one of the Paccosh said.

"Good," Thrawn said. "Pathfinder?"

"Yaw turn is ready," Qilori confirmed.

"Stand ready."

Thrawn looked around the bridge, his eyes settling on the tactical display. Qilori followed his gaze, wincing at the intense laserfire duel taking place off the *Hammer*'s starboard side. He'd already figured out that Uingali and the other Paccosh had commandeered the starboard laser-control station and were firing on the Grysk ship, and from the markers starting to flash red on the status display it was clear the larger ship was starting to dig into the *Hammer*'s own hull and weapons systems. But what Thrawn was planning now was still a mystery.

"There," Thrawn said, pointing toward the viewport. "Do you see them, Qilori?"

"Yes," Qilori said. A set of missile trails had appeared, driving away from the Grysk ship, heading straight out into space. There were four . . . now eight . . . now ten of them. Fortunately, none of them was coming anywhere near the *Hammer*.

His winglets flattened across his cheeks. Flying *away* from the *Hammer,* but flying *toward* the incoming Chiss warship.

"Qilori: Yaw turn on my mark," Thrawn ordered. "Commando?"

"Uingali is ready," the alien confirmed.

Thrawn settled his hands on the weapons controls. "Qilori: *Go.*"

Qilori keyed the controls, watching the starscape outside slowly shift as the ship began making its sluggish turn to starboard. The missile trails were starting to fade into the distance, but a new light show had erupted as the Chiss ship began firing its spectrum lasers in an attempt to neutralize the attack.

Only it wasn't working. The lasers continued to flash, but they didn't seem to be having any effect. Were the Chiss gunners missing their targets? "Why are the missiles still flying?" he asked.

"They're being shielded," Thrawn said. "Clusters of smaller missiles are running ahead of them and deflecting or absorbing the laserfire."

"Ah," Qilori said, his winglets slowly undulating. "I've never seen that technique before."

"I have," Thrawn said, a note of grim satisfaction in his voice. "And it gives final confirmation of our enemy's identity." He reached over his panel and tapped a pair of keys.

Qilori jerked back as a blaze of light flashed out from the *Hammer*'s bow, a full volley of laserfire aimed squarely at the departing missiles. Even as the afterimage of the multiple flashes faded, he saw that all ten of the missile trails were gone.

"They weren't expecting to be targeted from behind," Thrawn said, standing up. "Sarsh? Have you finished collecting those files?"

"I—yes," Sarsh said. "All that I could. Some are encrypted and unreadable—"

"Did you copy those, as well?"

"Yes."

Thrawn crossed the bridge to him and held out a hand. Shying back a little, Sarsh pulled a Kilji data rectangle from its slot and handed it over. Thrawn glanced at it, then slipped it into a pocket. "Commando, inform Uingali that we're finished," he said as he beckoned to Qilori and started toward the hatch. "If he can set the lasers on autofire, he should do so. Whether he can or not, he's to gather his teams and retreat to the *Aelos*."

"He has been so informed," the commando confirmed.

"Good," Thrawn said, throwing a wary glance out the hatch and then stepping aside so that the Paccosh could pass him to their usual vanguard positions. "Qilori, you're in charge of your companion. Keep him quiet, and keep him moving. Paccian commandos: Take us back."

The *Springhawk*'s first salvos of plasma spheres and breachers were intercepted and destroyed by Bogey One's lasers and dibber missiles well short of the warship itself. The second salvo of spheres, the volley targeting Bogey One's incoming missiles and their dibber shields, was somewhat more successful.

But only somewhat. Two of the missiles faltered as enough of the spheres' charge got through the dibbers to paralyze the larger weapons' drive electronics. But the other eight missiles kept coming, though with several of their small protective missiles now fallen away.

Afpriuh was preparing another barrage, and Samakro was double-checking their sphere fluid level, when Bogey Two opened fire.

Its laser shots were harder to see than the much closer flashes from the *Springhawk*'s own attack. But they were far more effective. With no flying shield array set up behind them, the missiles had no defense against the energy pouring through their drive emissions and straight into their reaction chambers.

Most missiles were designed to handle a specific range of heat and stress levels and generally couldn't cope with that much excess energy. Bogey One's missiles, it turned out, weren't an exception to that rule.

"Bogey One missiles destroyed," Dalvu said, sounding both awed and puzzled. "How did—? Oh. Right." She turned a slightly puckered look at Samakro. "Senior Captain Thrawn?"

"You know anyone else who would deliberately let enemy missiles get close enough to his ship to let us gather additional data on them?" Samakro asked her. "And would then destroy them in a sneak attack?"

"Good point, sir."

"One of the reasons the *Springhawk* has the reputation it does," Afpriuh added under his breath.

"True," Samakro agreed, wondering if the comment was meant to be a compliment or a gibe. "We *did* get that data, didn't we?"

"Yes, sir, we did," Dalvu assured him. "On both the missiles and the dibbers. Definitely look like the same ones the Battle Dreadnought used on the *Vigilant* the last time they were here."

Samakro had already concluded that was the case, but it was good to get confirmation. Certainly the Council and Syndicure would appreciate it. "Can't seem to get rid of these aliens for long, can we?" he commented, taking another look at the tactical. They still didn't know who these mysterious opponents were, but at least the Ascendancy was starting to build up a library of their ship types, weapons, and tactics. "No follow-up attack. Interesting. I'd have expected a second barrage by now."

"They may already have thrown everything they could," Dalvu suggested. "The first missiles came from their starboard tubes, and they may be having trouble reloading. And I'm guessing Bogey Two's attack has made their portside tubes nonfunctional."

Samakro nodded. Yet another victory for Thrawn and the Paccosh. "Let's see if we can help that process along," he said. "Prepare breachers, both flanks."

"Bogey One's on the move," Azmordi warned. "Running minimal power, but definitely angling away from the planet . . . there they go," he added as the image on the displays now visibly began pulling away from Sunrise. "Looks like they're making a run for it."

"Breachers and lasers are targeted," Afpriuh said, his fingers hovering over his board.

"They're picking up speed," Azmordi said. "Bogey Two has ceased fire. Bogey One is rolling."

"They're bringing starboard lasers to bear on Bogey Two," Dalvu warned.

A second later, as those starboard weapons came within range, the space between the two alien ships once again blazed with laserfire.

Samakro clenched his teeth. Bogey One, intent on abandoning Sunrise and a losing battle, was nevertheless determined to destroy Bogey Two on its way out.

And the *Springhawk* was in no position to help. Azmordi's projected course for Bogey One had it out of Sunrise's gravity well and escaping into hyperspace before breachers or plasma spheres could reach it, and it was still out of effective range of the Chiss lasers.

Which didn't mean they couldn't try. "Full laser salvo on Bogey One," he ordered. "Target starboard weapons and weapons sensors."

"Yes, sir," Afpriuh said, and the bridge lit up with the fury of the *Springhawk*'s own attack.

Samakro looked at the tactical. Bogey Two wouldn't last long, not against that kind of attack. But if the *Springhawk*'s distraction could give Thrawn even a few extra seconds, that could make the difference.

"Mid Captain, we're picking up a transmission," Brisch announced. He keyed the comm—

"Grysk warship, this is Senior Captain Thrawn of the Chiss Expansionary Defense Fleet warship *Springhawk*," Thrawn's calm voice came from the speaker. "We're permitting you to leave that you may take a message to your leaders."

Samakro smiled tightly. *We're permitting you to leave.* As if the *Springhawk* and *Aelos* were in any position to stop them.

Still, the enemy commander couldn't know that for certain. And given the aliens' last couple of encounters with the Chiss, only a fool would fail to take the comment seriously.

Of more immediate interest was the fact that they finally had a name to go with these aliens. That was a huge leap forward.

"Sunrise belongs to us now," Thrawn continued. "You, your people, and your friends and allies will stay clear of the system or face the full might of the Chiss Ascendancy." He paused. "If your leaders need persuasion, I suggest you remind them we've already driven you from this world three times. I trust a fourth will not be—"

In the distance, Bogey Two exploded.

Someone on the *Springhawk*'s bridge gave a startled curse. Samakro felt his stomach tighten as he watched the shattered fragments of the Kilji ship expanding outward into the vacuum, wrapped in smoke and a churning but dying flame. Bogey One was nearly far enough out from the planet to reach hyperspace—

"I trust a fourth defeat will not be necessary," Thrawn continued, his voice glacially calm. "Take that message to your leaders."

There was no response from Bogey One. Five seconds later, it flickered and was gone.

"Cease fire," Samakro said. "Dalvu, find the senior captain; Brisch, get me a signal to him. Kharill?"

"Sir?" The third officer's voice came from the speaker connecting the bridge to secondary command.

"Check the records for anything on these *Grysks* that Senior Captain Thrawn mentioned."

"Yes, sir."

"Sir, I've got him," Dalvu said, peering at her displays. "Mid-range, level, fifteen degrees starboard."

"Azmordi, get us there," Samakro ordered. "Brisch?"

"On it, Mid Captain," Brisch said briskly. "You have comm, sir."

Samakro reached over Afpriuh's shoulder and tapped for the weapons board's mike. "Senior Captain Thrawn, this is Mid Captain Samakro," he called. "We're on our way."

"Welcome to Sunrise, Mid Captain," Thrawn said. "The timing of your arrival was flawless."

Samakro felt his lip twitch. No argument there . . . except that it had been Che'ri's timing, not his.

But he couldn't say that, not on an open channel, not even if it was only the *Springhawk*'s own bridge crew able to listen in. Anyway, there was a fair chance Thrawn already knew that. "Are you in need of assistance, sir?" he asked.

"We're relatively undamaged, Mid Captain," Thrawn assured him. "Some minor hull damage and two casualties, currently under treatment."

"Sounds like warrior's fortune was with you."

"More decisive were the skill and valor of Uingali foar Marocsaa and his commando force," Thrawn said. "Were you able to listen in on my final message to the enemy warship?"

"Yes, sir," Samakro said. "So they're called Grysks?"

"So I'm informed," Thrawn said. "Are there any references to that name in our files?"

"Senior Commander Kharill?" Samakro prompted.

"There's nothing I can find, sir," Kharill's voice came again. "Whoever or whatever they are, we don't have any records on them here."

"Though Csilla or Naporar might," Thrawn said. "I also have data from the Kilji warship I'll want you to take back with you. Unfortunately, it's in a format the Nikardun ship can't read, so I can't simply transmit it to you. Can you rendezvous with me here to pick it up?"

"We're already on our way, sir," Samakro said, frowning. "I assumed you'd be coming back with us."

"I can't leave yet, Mid Captain," Thrawn said. "Paccian reinforcements are on their way from Rapacc with the rest of the Magys's refugees, and they won't be here for another two to three days. I want to wait for them and then accompany them to the surface for a closer look at the mining area Admiral Ar'alani's low-altitude search located."

"I trust you remember that Senior Warrior Yopring and his shuttle were chased away from there by armed fighters," Samakro warned.

"That shouldn't be a problem," Thrawn assured him. "The Paccian warrior team will include a number of air-support vehicles. I also have the Magys's assurance that her people will stand ready to assist."

"I hope you're right, sir," Samakro said heavily. So instead of just having to tell the Council and Syndicure that the *Springhawk* had violated orders and made a side trip to Sunrise, he'd now have to explain why his ship was returning without its captain. Terrific.

"I know I'm putting you in a difficult position, Mid Captain," Thrawn said. "But there are mysteries here, details and connections that need to be resolved before we can understand why enemies of the Ascendancy want to destroy these people and take over their world."

"I understand, sir," Samakro said. He didn't, entirely, but in these matters Thrawn's instincts generally proved to be correct. "We'll get the data back to Naporar as quickly as possible."

"I'm sure you will." Thrawn paused. "How is Sky-walker Che'ri?"

"Dead to the world," Samakro told him. "She and Caregiver Thalias put in long hours in order to get us here in time. They'll probably sleep another ten hours, maybe more."

"I appreciate their sacrifice more than they'll ever know," Thrawn said. "Please offer them my deepest gratitude when they wake. In the meantime, you'll have to start back via jump-by-jump."

"Lieutenant Commander Azmordi is already working on the calculations," Samakro assured him, gesturing to the pilot. Azmordi gave an acknowledging nod and turned to his board. "Is there anything more we can do for you before we leave?"

"Nothing I can think of, Mid Captain," Thrawn said. "You've done far and away more than could be expected just by being here to help resolve the situation. Now it's in the hands of the Paccosh here, and in the hands of the Council in the Ascendancy."

"I hope both sets of hands will be up to the challenge."

"As do I, Mid Captain," Thrawn said. "I'm told our rendezvous is approximately fifteen minutes away. I'm going to take that time to write up as complete a report as I can for you to take back with the battle record and the Kilji data."

"Yes, sir," Samakro said. "We'll see you shortly."

"Good," Thrawn said. "*Aelos* out."

"Comm signal lost, Mid Captain," Brisch reported.

"Understood," Samakro said. "Lieutenant Commander Azmordi, keep us moving."

"Yes, sir," Azmordi said. "And I'll have that course ready by the time we arrive."

"Good." Samakro leaned on the back of Afpriuh's seat and lowered his voice to a level where only the weapons officer could hear him. "The end of a perfect day. What do you think?"

"I think he's playing with fire, sir," Afpriuh said bluntly. "He has enemies in both the Council and the Syndicure who are just begging for an excuse to drop him down a deep hole. This could be their chance."

"I know," Samakro said. "But if he's right, there may be considerably more at stake than one man's career."

"Or even ours?"

"Or even ours," Samakro said. Though with the way he and Thrawn had set up this whole thing, the rest of the *Springhawk*'s senior officers should be out from under whatever firestorm the Syndicure chose to rain down on them. "Let's just hope that when they drop him down that hole, they don't drop the rest of the Ascendancy down there with him."

"Hopefully, they're smarter than that," Afpriuh said.

"Hopefully." Samakro straightened up. "In the meantime, we have data and a message to deliver." He shifted his eyes to the viewport, and the glittering cloud of debris now marking the spot where the Kilji warship had been. "Let's just hope someone on Csilla has heard of these Grysks."

MEMORIES VIII

Thrawn had suggested that the *Jandalin* approach the Pleknok system from a specific direction. Lappincyk had countered that the hijackers' transport would be coming straight from Glastis 3, and that the best chance of intercepting it would be to follow that same vector.

Six hours before arrival, the two of them had a long, quiet talk beside the navigation console. Thrass couldn't hear what they were saying, but when the conversation was over Lappincyk ordered the pilot to follow Thrawn's course.

Thirty-two hours after leaving Glastis 3, they arrived.

"Scan the area," Lappincyk ordered from his usual seat in the center of the acceleration couch. "Passive sensors only. Focus on low-orbit corridors."

"Hopefully, they haven't already completed their business and left," Thrass muttered, watching the display fill in as sensors began collecting and compiling the data.

"Unlikely," Lappincyk said. "We should be faster than their transport."

"Considerably faster," Thrawn agreed. "Actually, I'm almost certain we've arrived ahead of them."

"What if they're running with an augmented drive?" Thrass asked.

Thrawn shook his head. "The fifty hours required for them to travel from the initial attack at Sposia to where they released the cargo ship at Glastis 3 argues against that theory."

"They *were* lugging a cargo ship with them that whole time," Thrass pointed out, wondering why he was even arguing the point. Apparently, the low-level tension that had been nagging at him since they left Glastis 3 had suddenly blossomed to full strength now that they were actually here. "That would have slowed them down."

"I took that into account."

Thrass ground his teeth. Every single time he tried to debate something with Thrawn, he ended up on the losing side.

"We have movement, Senior Aide," the sensor officer said. "Two ships in low orbit. Configuration . . . difficult to establish with passive sensors, but they appear to be freighter-class vessels of non-Chiss design."

"The thieves' buyers, presumably," Lappincyk said.

"Or other customers," Thrass said.

"Perhaps," Lappincyk agreed. At least with him, Thrass thought sourly, he could occasionally win one. "Keep an eye on them. Now—" He threw a quick look at Thrawn. "—run an active sweep across a thirty-degree cone behind us."

"Sir?" the sensor officer asked, frowning at Lappincyk over his shoulder.

"Thirty-degree sensor cone aft," Lappincyk repeated. "We're looking for—"

"Contact!" the pilot snapped. "Portside zenith, range twenty kilometers. Course running parallel and closing."

"Sensors?" Lappincyk prompted.

"On it, sir," the sensor officer said tensely. "It's . . . sir, it's a Chiss light cruiser. Configuration and markings identify it as Clarr family."

"Senior Aide, they're demanding we identify ourselves," the pilot put in. "Tight beam, low power."

"Respond with the same parameters," Lappincyk ordered. Pulling out his mike, he keyed it on. "This is Stybla'ppin'cykok, senior aide to Patriarch Stybla'mi'ovodo, aboard the patrol ship *Jandalin,*" he said. "And you?"

There was a short pause. "Captain Clarr'os'culry," a voice came back. "Currently in command of the Clarr light cruiser *Orisson*. What the hell are you doing here, *Jandalin?*"

Thrass caught his breath as the name suddenly clicked. *Captain Roscu . . .* only the last time he'd heard that name it had been Mid Captain Roscu of the Expansionary Defense Fleet, and she and Thrawn had been clashing over Chiss non-intervention policy in the middle of a pirate attack on a Garwian trading hub.

And now she was commanding a Clarr family ship?

"We're hunting pirates who hijacked a Stybla cargo ship over Sposia a few days ago," Lappincyk told her. "We believe the pirates were led by someone of Clarr blood, which I presume is the reason you're here."

"Our reasons and activities are our concern," Roscu growled. "How did you find this place?"

"That's *our* concern," Lappincyk said. "So you concede that the hijackers are Clarr blood?"

"I concede nothing," Roscu said. "Nor do I need to justify Clarr actions to a Stybla. I'll say this just once: This is a Clarr family matter, and you will leave this system immediately."

"Excuse me, Captain, but it was *our* ship and cargo that were stolen," Lappincyk reminded her. "We have every right to be here."

"Check your guidelines and protocols, Senior Aide," Roscu said. "As an agent of one of the Nine and a former Expansionary Defense Fleet command officer, I have every right to order you out of a region where imminent military action is expected."

"I don't accept your authority to give that order," Lappincyk said stiffly. "The Stybla family has a vital interest—"

"Senior Aide?" Thrass murmured. "I believe you have a better hand to play." He pointed at Thrawn.

For a second Lappincyk just stared at him in apparent confusion. Then his expression suddenly cleared. "You misunderstand the situation, Captain Roscu," he said.

And to Thrass's surprise, he stood up and gestured Thrawn to the couch's center command position. "The *Jandalin* is currently under the command of someone who is not only also a member of the Nine, but is a *current* military command officer." He handed the mike to Thrawn. "Mid Commander?"

Thrawn hesitated, then inclined his head in acknowledgment. "This is Mid Commander Mitth'raw'nuru, Captain," he said as he sat down. "There's no reason we can't work together—"

"Thrawn?" Roscu cut in. "What in hell's name are you doing on a Stybla ship?"

"As Senior Aide Lappincyk said, I'm working with them to resolve this issue," Thrawn told her. "Congratulations on finding this system, by the way. From the data I was able to locate, I estimated there could be as many as ten other possibilities before I was able to narrow it down to this one. How did you know they were coming to Pleknok?"

"What, you think you're the only clever one in the Ascendancy?" Roscu countered scornfully.

"Ah—I see," Thrawn said. "You *didn't* know, did you? The Clarr simply sent ships to all of them."

"I didn't say that!"

"Yes. I know."

"Senior Aide, we have incoming," the pilot said, sounding a little nervous at having to cut into the middle of a clearly deteriorating conversation. "Obbic transport—probably the hijackers. Moving along the vector Mid Commander Thrawn predicted."

"Understood," Lappincyk said, and Thrass could hear the satisfaction in his voice.

"Wait a moment," Roscu said. "You knew where they were coming from but came out way over here? Why didn't you pick a better spot to intercept them?"

"Because I don't *want* to intercept them, Captain," Thrawn said. "Not yet. Not until we learn which of those two orbiting ships they're meeting."

"I thought you wanted your precious cargo."

"We'll retrieve it soon enough," Thrawn assured her. "Both target ships are too deep in the planet's gravity well for a quick escape. Once we know which ship they're going for, we'll move in and take them both."

"We'll do nothing of the kind," Roscu bit out. "Haven't you learned *anything* about Ascendancy policy since you blatantly interfered in that pirate attack at Stivic? How the *hell* are you still an officer in the fleet?"

"Senior Aide, we have another ship incoming," the pilot reported. "Seventy degrees starboard, twelve zenith, angling in toward the planet. Configuration unknown, but its size is consistent with that of a freighter."

"Sensors, full scan of the newcomer," Thrawn ordered. "Get me a configuration as quickly as you can."

"So much for meeting someone inside the gravity well," Roscu said. "Any other brilliant ideas, Thrawn?"

"We haven't finished with this one yet," Lappincyk put in. "Our projection shows that if both ships keep to their current vectors, they'll still be inside the gravity well when they meet. Plenty of time for us to move in and take them both."

Roscu's snort was clearly audible. "Enough," she said. "If that's how you want to play it."

And to Thrass's disbelief, the glowing orb of a plasma sphere burst out from the *Orisson*'s bow, arrowing straight at the Obbic transport.

"*Captain!*" Lappincyk snapped.

"Too late," Thrawn said. "Pilot: Get us moving toward the transport—full speed."

"Senior Aide?" the pilot asked.

"Obey your commander," Lappincyk told him tartly. "What about the other ship?"

"Captain Roscu, we need you to disable the other incoming ship," Thrawn said into the mike as the *Jandalin* leapt forward.

But not as quickly as the *Orisson*. Even before Thrawn had finished speaking, the Clarr cruiser threw full power to its thrusters, passing the *Jandalin* and charging toward the transport. "Bit busy here," Roscu said. "If you want it disabled, do it yourselves."

"This ship isn't equipped with plasma spheres."

"Too bad," Roscu said. In the distance, the sphere she'd launched intercepted the transport, flashing a momentary glow as it shut down the ship's electronics. "Handy little things, aren't they?"

"Captain, we need that incoming freighter disabled," Lappincyk put in. "In the name of the Stybla, I ask you please to assist us."

"Request denied," Roscu said. "I suppose you'll need to use some of that Thrawn cleverness. Have fun. Don't worry—once we've got the transport, we'll be sure to deliver your cargo back to you on Sposia."

"That cargo is not to be touched," Lappincyk insisted. "We'll take it aboard the *Jandalin*."

"Of course," Roscu said, a note of malicious humor in her voice. "You're welcome to it *if* you can keep up. But it looks like you can't. Too bad the Stybla don't have any *real* warships."

"Captain, that's *our* cargo."

"I *said* you'd get it back," Roscu said. "I swear, you Stybla are always so *nervous.*"

"Perhaps it's time you were, as well," Thrawn said, his voice suddenly grim. "Take another look at the newcomer."

"What about it?"

"It's not running," Thrawn said. "In fact, five seconds after you launched your attack it increased its speed toward the transport. Does that sound like a criminal crew's behavior?"

"It sounds like a criminal crew who anticipates free goodies," Roscu said. "Don't worry, we'll get there before they do."

On one of the side displays, the sensor profile of the freighter appeared. "Perhaps not," Thrawn said. "That's not a freighter. It's a Paataatus light frigate."

For a long moment there was nothing but silence. "Damn," Roscu breathed.

"Agreed," Thrawn said. "Pilot, can you increase speed?"

"We're at full power, sir," the pilot said.

"Go to emergency power," Lappincyk ordered. "Mid Commander, all we've got are three spectrum lasers."

"That should be enough," Thrawn said. "*Orisson*, why are you slowing?"

Thrass felt his throat tighten. The Clarr cruiser, which a minute ago had been blazing toward the disabled transport, had now slowed its mad rush.

"Because Paataatus light frigates don't travel alone," Roscu said darkly. "There are bound to be a few gunboats—"

"Incoming!" the *Jandalin's* pilot interrupted. "Five new ships, coming in along the freighter's—the light frigate's—vector."

"Like I said," Roscu said. "Afraid there's nothing we can do now but destroy the transport. I'll set up a laser barrage—"

"No!" Lappincyk snapped.

"Use your head, Senior Aide," Roscu snapped back. "We can't take on six Paataatus ships by ourselves. Either we destroy the transport, or we let the aliens have it. *And* the cargo."

"We can't do that," Lappincyk said. "We *have* to retrieve the cargo."

"We will," Thrawn said, his calmness in sharp contrast with the anger and frustration in Roscu's voice and the fear and growing panic in Lappincyk's. "We'll retrieve the cargo and drive away the Paataatus. Are the Clarr ready to assist, Captain Roscu?"

"*You* may be casual about violating Ascendancy standing orders, but I'm not," Roscu said. "Nor am I willing to sacrifice my ship and crew in a futile and losing battle."

"In that case, we'll do it ourselves," Thrawn said. "Pilot: Ready the spectrum lasers. Your target will be the outer cowlings of the Obbic's aft thrusters."

"You're shooting at the *transport*?" Lappincyk asked in clear disbelief.

"They've already been disabled," Thrawn reminded him. "I don't think damage to their thrusters will matter that much to them."

"Then why do it?"

"Because the Paataatus will see us do it," Thrawn said. As if, Thrass thought distantly, that actually explained anything. "Captain Roscu? It's not too late to join us."

Thrass looked at the status display. Running now at full emergency power, the *Jandalin* was about three minutes from the spot that indicated spectrum laser range. The Paataatus frigate was five minutes away from possible combat, the five gunboats eight minutes away. The *Orisson*, he noted, could be within intercept range of the frigate in four minutes should Roscu decide not to leave the Stybla patrol ship to face the aliens alone.

And then, even as he watched, the *Orisson* began veering away from the planet. "Thanks for the offer," Roscu said. "But as I said, I take standing orders seriously. It's still not too late for you to let me destroy—"

"Shut her off," Lappincyk growled.

There was a click from the mike. "Thrawn, are you sure about this?"

"How badly do you need to retrieve the cargo?" Thrawn asked.

Lappincyk closed his eyes briefly. "Very."

"Then we retrieve it," Thrawn said. "This is an armed vessel of the Chiss Ascendancy. We'll prevail."

"Against six Paataatus warships?" Thrass retorted. Up to now he'd seen the situation in almost theoretical terms; a power struggle between Thrawn and Roscu that would surely end with the two Chiss joining forces. Now, with Roscu's final refusal and desertion from the field of battle, the full reality had flooded in on him. "One patrol ship armed with nothing but lasers? It can't be done. *It can't be done.*"

"Nothing is impossible, Thrass," Thrawn said calmly. "As Captain Roscu said, we simply need to be clever. Senior Aide, you don't happen to have any mines or other explosives aboard, do you?"

"Nothing useful, I'm afraid," Lappincyk said. "We have some shattercord for burning through sealed hatches, but that would require the target to have already been disabled by one of our Crippler nets, so they won't—"

"You have a *Crippler net*?" Thrawn interrupted.

"We have two," Lappincyk said, frowning at the sudden excitement in his voice. "But they need the target to be mostly unmoving—"

"Where are the launchers?" Thrawn again cut him off. "Portside or starboard?"

"Starboard," Lappincyk said. "One forward, one aft. But—"

"Perfect," Thrawn said, pulling out his questis and working rapidly at it. "Pilot, I'm giving you a new course. You'll follow it precisely until and unless I give you modifications. Understood?"

"Yes, sir," the pilot said.

Thrass looked at Lappincyk. "What's a Crippler net?"

"It's a flexible netting with powerful capacitors attached at various points around its edges," Lappincyk said, his full attention on Thrawn. "Once it's wrapped around a ship, it delivers a massive electrical charge through the hull. Like a plasma sphere, but not as powerful. But because the launcher is gas-propelled, it can't chase down its target like a sphere can."

"So the target ship has to be motionless."

"Or nearly so," Lappincyk said. "In this case . . ." He shook his head.

Thrass looked at the displays. If there was any term that could describe those Paataatus warships, *nearly motionless* wasn't it.

"In this case, fortunately, we won't need to deliver the weapon," Thrawn said. He looked at his questis, nodded in satisfaction, and tapped the data to the helm. "Pilot? Questions?"

Thrass frowned as the course came up on the overview. The path Thrawn had marked out was incredibly twisty, looking rather like a drunkard's staggering path. "No questions, sir," the pilot said.

"Senior Aide?" Thrawn invited, turning to Lappincyk.

"I still don't see the plan," Lappincyk admitted. "But I have nothing better to offer. Do it."

"Thank you," Thrawn said. "May I handle the weapons?"

"Use the monitor station," Lappincyk said, pointing him to an empty bridge chair. "Pilot, transfer weapons control as requested."

"Yes, sir. Weapons control transferred."

Thrawn moved to the seat and strapped himself in. "Thirty seconds," he announced. "Senior Aide, Thrass, make sure you're solidly strapped in." He threw a tight smile over his shoulder at Thrass. "This may be a bit bumpy."

"I'm ready," Thrass said, wishing that were true. In fact, he was quietly terrified.

And then, as he tried to relax his mind and body, his thoughts flicked back to the Taharim report he'd read all those years ago.

The unorthodox tactics Cadet Thrawn had used in the training simulation. The academy director's unwavering disbelief that it was possible. Thrawn's subsequent real-world demonstration in front of not only the director but General Ba'kif himself.

This was just like that, Thrass told himself firmly. This was completely and exactly like that.

Except that Ba'kif wasn't here. And Thrass would give anything to have the general and a full Expansionary Defense Fleet task force with them.

"Prepare," Thrawn said. "Pilot: Three, two, *one*."

CHAPTER FOURTEEN

Ar'alani had never been in this part of the Syndicure complex before. It was deeper than the main office and functional areas, deeper than the staff living areas, deeper than the storage, recycling, and power-generation equipment that serviced the entire region, deeper even than the emergency refuges built for the Aristocra.

And as she walked along the bare corridor, listening to the echoing of her footsteps and those of the four armed warriors walking stolidly at her sides, she decided that she never wanted to be here again.

There was evil down here. Evil that had once brought sudden, violent, or torturous death, sometimes to a few, sometimes to thousands. Evil that for one reason or another the Syndicure or Council had decided needed to be kept alive. She could feel the brooding of the occupants, the angry hopelessness, the utter hatred.

But she'd asked for this, and her request had been granted, and she would see it through.

There were five guarded checkpoints between the elevator that had brought her to this level and the small room that was her destination. When they reached the end of the last corridor, her escort unlocked the door and retreated behind the last checkpoint to wait. Straightening her shoulders, reminding herself firmly that there was nothing to be worried about and anyway that she'd asked for this, she watched as the metal panel slid back over the face of the stone wall and stepped through the doorway into the brightly lit room.

Sitting in a bolted-down chair in a posture of casual arrogance, the tendrils of the fungoid symbionts undulating idly as they hung over his shoulders, was General Yiv the Benevolent.

"Hello, General Yiv," Ar'alani said in Minnisiat as she took another step into the room. Behind her, the door again slid closed. "My name is Ar'alani. I thought we might have a chat."

"Did you?" Yiv asked, his cleft jaw opening slightly like the mouth of a predator deciding whether or not he was hungry enough to pounce on a bit of promising prey. "Did you also consider that you were intruding upon my solitude?"

"I'd have thought you'd have had enough of solitude."

"And that I would thus welcome conversation?" Yiv asked. "With *you*?" The jaw snapped shut, the tendrils on his shoulders giving a slightly magnified twitch. "For someone who has made the arduous trek to my final resting place, you are curiously ignorant of my situation."

"How so?"

"I have had many conversations over these last months," Yiv said. "All have been long. None has been pleasant. Solitude is my companion, not my enemy. Do you think you have found a new topic that would change that balance?"

"Not a new topic, no," Ar'alani said. "But perhaps I have a new angle on an old topic you probably thought you'd grown weary of."

"And what would that topic be?"

"Betrayal."

Yiv gave a booming laugh that seemed to echo oppressively from the stone walls of his private prison. "You are indeed a lost child," he said scornfully. "So many have pressed me in vain to betray my generals or my people. Do you truly think you can succeed where they have failed?"

"Your generals no longer exist," Ar'alani told him. "They squandered the empire you left them in vain attempts to take power. Your conquered nations are once again free, and the remnants of your people are scattered and lost."

"So others have told me," Yiv said calmly. "I believe it no more from you than I did from them. Why else would you keep me alive, save to bargain me to the might of the Nikardun Destiny when it brings you to your knees?"

"We keep you alive because we don't slaughter defeated enemies," Ar'alani said. "And because you may still have useful information."

"I will tell you nothing."

"Though up to now your journals and records have mostly given us everything we need," Ar'alani continued. "Tell me, which of your allies encouraged the construction of listening posts KR20 and KR21?"

"We have no allies," Yiv said scornfully. "We need none. We are mighty conquerors who stand on our own."

"Of course," Ar'alani said, mentally crossing her fingers. If her bluff didn't work, she would have made this trip for nothing. "Still, after all that's happened—including your disappearance—I imagine Jixtus pretends he wasn't *your* ally, either."

The tendrils hanging from Yiv's shoulders gave a subtle twitch, as if they'd detected something bad in the air. "What nonsense are you babbling now?" he demanded.

"Didn't they tell you?" Ar'alani asked, feigning surprise. "Your friend Jixtus has a new set of allies now. Or maybe *tools* would be the better word. Allies, tools—they seem to be the same with him. At any rate, they're busy converting the two listening posts he suggested to you into minor shipyards."

"That *he* suggested to me?" Yiv asked, his tone changing. "What are you talking about?"

"I told you, General," Ar'alani said. "I'm talking about betrayal. Jixtus persuaded you to build those listening posts because he needed a pair of structures in those particular spots and figured he'd let you do all the work. Unfortunately, the plan wouldn't work with their original Nikardun crews, so after they were up and running he made a precise attack on both bases, killed everyone aboard, then set about rebuilding them to his own specifications."

"You lie," Yiv said flatly.

Ar'alani shrugged as she pulled the remote from her pocket and keyed it on. The cell's wall display lit up with one of the vids the *Vigilant* had taken on its last check of the ruined base. "See for yourself," she invited.

Yiv watched in silence until the vid ran to the end. "More," he said.

Ar'alani keyed the next one. Yiv again watched to the end, again without comment. Without waiting for another order, Ar'alani keyed in the next vid, then the next, switching from outside views to the ones her survey team had taken of the base's interior. That one finished and she started to key up the fifth vid—

"No more," Yiv said softly.

"I'm sorry," Ar'alani said, a bit surprised to realize she actually meant it. "It's hard to watch your people being betrayed by an ally."

"How would you know?" Yiv countered acidly. "You Chiss *have* no allies."

"Perhaps not," Ar'alani conceded. So no denials, no complaints, no accusations. Did that mean her guess was correct, that Jixtus really *was* the one behind Yiv's campaign against the Ascendancy? "That doesn't mean we don't have a great deal of experience with betrayal on a personal level."

"For a commander it is always personal, is it not?" Yiv smiled, his symbionts again twitching. "Oh, yes, I know who you are, Admiral Ar'alani of the Expansionary Defense Fleet. Tell me why you are here."

"To show you the evidence of Jixtus's betrayal."

"No," Yiv said. "Gloating is beneath you. Why are you here?"

"For information about Jixtus," Ar'alani said. "We know he's working with the Kilji Illumine"—now for the second bluff—"and the Agbui. Does he have other allies we don't yet know about?"

"The Agbui," Yiv said contemptuously. "Creatures of loud arrogance and silent uselessness, able to persuade a target merely into doing what he already wanted to do."

"They *do* have a high opinion of themselves," Ar'alani agreed, a shiver running up her back. Yiv could be as scornful as he liked, but Agbui uselessness had nearly pushed the Ascendancy into civil war. "Are there others?"

"There are other names."

"Allies?"

"Perhaps," Yiv said. "Perhaps simply names of those Jixtus encountered or had heard of. But even those names may yield useful results under careful analysis."

"Ah," Ar'alani said, eyeing him closely. "And what will these names cost us?"

Yiv regarded her thoughtfully, the tips of his symbiont tendrils tracing out small patterns across his chest. "You want more than simply names or species," he said. "You want times and locations of meetings and conversations. You want bits of information that were too vague or unrelated to Nikardun triumphs for me to bother adding to my records."

The tendrils gave a final twitch, then settled back to their earlier slow undulation. "You want everything there is to know about Jixtus and the Grysks."

Ar'alani felt her back stiffen. *That* was a species name she hadn't heard before. "Jixtus's people are known as the Grysks?"

"Yes." The cleft jaw cracked into a smile. "That name was offered at no cost. The rest will have a price."

"What do you want?"

"I want to be free of this place," Yiv said without hesitation. "I want to see the sun and the stars again. I want to feel the wind in my face and at my back, and to walk for more than twenty paces before encountering a barrier. I want *life* again."

"You know we can't do that, General," Ar'alani murmured, her heart sinking. So close, and yet so far.

"Because you need me in custody to trade to the Nikardun Destiny when it threatens to overwhelm you?" Yiv turned to look at the wall display, where the last frozen image from Ar'alani's vid remained. "The Destiny is no more. I know that."

He looked back at Ar'alani. "I have no fleet, no soldiers, no power. I'm not a threat to the Chiss. There is no reason you can't send me away."

"I'm sorry," Ar'alani said. "Even if we just moved you to a cell on the surface—"

"Do you not hear me?" Yiv demanded. "I do not wish to live any longer among the Chiss. Take me elsewhere, leave me sufficient equipment and provisions to establish my home, and in return I will tell you everything."

Ar'alani frowned. "Do you mean *exile*?"

"Of course," Yiv said. "Is that such a difficult request?"

"No, not at all," Ar'alani assured him.

Though actually it was. It was a *hugely* difficult request. As far as she knew, the Ascendancy had never exiled anyone, certainly not within the scope of modern history. "I can't promise anything, but I'll speak to my superiors and see what they're willing to do," she said.

"Just be certain to warn them that the time to act is limited," Yiv said. "Jixtus is on the move, and the Chiss Ascendancy is his target."

"They're more than aware of that," Ar'alani assured him, stepping back to the door and giving the rap-rap rap rap-rap signal she and her escort had agreed on. "You'll be informed of their decision."

Ba'kif was waiting in the prison command center when she arrived, sitting in front of a bank of displays. "Did everything come through all right?" she asked as she walked toward him.

"Perfectly," Ba'kif said, waving her to the chair beside him. "I thought he might try to keep his voice down so he could talk with you privately. But that didn't happen."

"If anything, he kept his voice deliberately loud," Ar'alani agreed. "I think he wanted all of us—you, me, and everyone else in here—in on the conversation."

"Given the direction the talks went, I'm sure he did," Ba'kif said. "What do you think of his offer?"

"It seemed genuine," Ar'alani said, looking over the monitors. One of them was showing a silent replay of her conversation with Yiv, with overlays tracking the Nikardun's subtle physical changes and extrapolating the parallel flow of mental and emotional states. "You're the ones who've been building up his truth/fiction database. What did *you* see?"

"The same," Ba'kif said grimly. "And that worries me."

Ar'alani frowned. "How so?"

"In the months since Thrawn brought him here, he's never once even hinted at the possibility of a deal," Ba'kif said. "What's the only thing that changed with your visit?"

"He trusts a Chiss admiral more than a Chiss general?" Ar'alani suggested, trying for a bit of levity.

Ba'kif shook his head. "He saw your evidence of his listening posts' destruction."

Ar'alani felt her face warming, silently cursing her attempt at humor. She'd been so focused on the possibility of getting more information out of Yiv that the full implications of his offer hadn't registered. "He said Jixtus was on the move," she murmured. "Yiv expects us to lose."

"He does indeed," Ba'kif said. "And he's trying to find a way off Csilla before that happens."

Ar'alani nodded, her stomach twisted into a hard knot. She'd gone into military service expecting that the Chiss would be attacked on occasion, and that there would be corresponding ups and downs in its power and influence. But never in her life had the thought occurred to her that the Ascendancy might actually be destroyed by one of those enemies.

"Of course, just because he believes it doesn't mean it's going to happen," Ba'kif pointed out. "But the fact that he *does* believe it means we need to take the possibility seriously."

"Especially coming from someone who lost his own fight against us," Ar'alani agreed. "What's the plan?"

"I'll contact the Council at once and get this thing rolling," Ba'kif said. "I have no idea what sort of equipment and provisions Yiv was referring to, but I'm sure he'll be happy to offer suggestions. We'll also get him busy listing all those names and other details he promised."

"I notice you didn't mention the Syndicure," Ar'alani said. "Aren't we going to tell them about this?"

"Not yet," Ba'kif said, his lip twisting. "You know the Aristocra. They'll want to debate it and haul us into hearings, and at the end will probably tell us we can't do it. We don't have time for the process, and we can't afford that decision. We'll let them know when they need to. Not before."

"Yes, sir," Ar'alani said, keeping her tone neutral. That wasn't how these things were supposed to go, and they both knew it. Keeping the Syndicure in the dark that way could bring a galaxy of pain down onto Ba'kif's head.

But it was nothing compared with the pain that the fall of the Ascendancy would bring. "I understand," she added. "I'd also recommend the Council formally call on the Nine to provide warships to strengthen the Defense Force."

Ba'kif huffed out a sigh. "I can suggest it," he said. "But I don't think the Council will follow through."

Ar'alani frowned. "Why not?"

"Because I strongly suspect several of the families will refuse the request," Ba'kif said bluntly. "The Dasklo and Clarr almost certainly, the Irizi and Ufsa probably. The rest . . ." He shook his head. "I don't think the Council will want to aggravate tensions by forcing the Nine to choose between being allied and being loyalist."

"I see," Ar'alani said, hearing an edge of bitterness in her voice. Once again, politics were driving the fleet's agenda. This time, the politics of risking disaster in order to allow someone else to maintain appearances. "Are there any families who have declared themselves allied?"

"Yes, but unofficially," Ba'kif said. "Patriarch Thurfian has told the Council they can call on up to half the Mitth fleet, and is in the process of deploying them to critical systems where they'll be instantly available if and when they're needed. Patriel Lakooni has also offered the frigate *Midsummer,* currently back at Celwis, though she warns us that the Defense Force would have to find officers and warriors to crew it."

"Not much help."

"No," Ba'kif agreed. "But better than nothing." He stood up and gestured toward the door. "Come, I'll escort you back to the main level. I'll also make sure you get a full copy of the interview and our pattern analysis before you leave, in case you want to review it on the trip back to Sposia."

"Thank you, sir."

They walked past the other officers on duty, then out through the command center's armored door. Ba'kif nodded briskly to the armed warriors standing guard outside, gave a small all-clear hand signal, and led the way down the corridor toward the elevators.

"Don't look so glum, Admiral," Ba'kif said as he unlocked the control bar and keyed for the main levels and the less oppressive air far above them. "Just because the families are squabbling now doesn't mean a looming disaster. They'll come together as one when the crisis hits. It's happened many times in the Ascendancy's past, and it'll happen again."

"I know, sir," Ar'alani said.

Only she *didn't* know that. Not for certain.

And she was pretty sure Ba'kif didn't, either.

The long-range comm conversation lasted longer than most of the calls that had taken place between Jixtus and his people during the *Whetstone*'s voyage. The Grysk at the other end did most of the talking, which was also unusual, while Jixtus only made occasional comments.

When it was finished, Jixtus sat quietly for over a minute, thinking or scowling or brooding behind his veil. Nakirre watched him, wondering what the message had been, and whether the news the other Grysk had delivered was good or bad.

Actually, Nakirre didn't have much doubt that it was the latter. Jixtus had never yet withdrawn into himself like this with good news. Always before he had immediately shared it or boasted about it. No, something had gone wrong.

Inevitable, really, though Jixtus still didn't recognize that. Only with true enlightenment did anyone achieve full wisdom and ability, and Jixtus's refusal to even consider the Kilji path meant his plans would always be bumpy and tangled. Perhaps the Grysk would someday learn that lesson. Nakirre rather doubted it.

The big question now was how this news would impact the Kiljis and their attempts to bring enlightenment to the Chiss and the other peoples of the Chaos.

Finally, Jixtus stirred. "Generalirius Nakirre, we are taking a new direction," he said. "Have your servants calculate a course for the Chiss world of Ornfra."

"As you wish," Nakirre said. Jixtus had mentioned that system, but it had figured into one of the later stages of the Grysk plan. "Vassal One: Compute course to Ornfra."

"I obey," Vassal One said, and turned to his board.

"So we're no longer going to Sharb?" Nakirre asked, eyeing Jixtus closely. "You said earlier that you wanted to draw more attention to the Xodlak."

"That was earlier," Jixtus said. "As I said, a new direction. The Xodlak are only minor players, as befits their status as one of the Forty. The Clarr and Dasklo are the focal points, and the key to inciting the Nine to civil war. When their simmering resentments have been forced into full combat, the rest of the Ascendancy will inevitably follow. Vassal, are you ready?"

There was no response. "My vassals take orders only from me," Nakirre said calmly. "Vassal One: Execute course."

"I obey." The stars turned and melted, and the *Whetstone* was again in hyperspace.

"You enjoy being master of your ship and your servants," Jixtus commented. "Perhaps you enjoy it too much."

"I enjoy it purely because it was through my efforts that these vassals became enlightened," Nakirre said. "You said *when* the Chiss have been forced into combat, the Ascendancy would fall. Would not the correct term be *if*?"

Jixtus stirred again, the veiled face shifting a fraction to point directly at Nakirre. "Do you question my words and my skill, Kilji?" he asked. "Or do you mock me? Because you should think long and deep before you step onto that path. You have no concept of the true power of the Grysks. We can crush the Illumine like boulders that can be turned to fine sand, or we can twist your culture, your lives, and your very souls to do our bidding. Do not force me to choose which of those fates would be the more satisfying."

Nakirre's skin again stretched. "No," he said flatly.

Jixtus seemed taken aback. "What do you mean, *no*?"

"I mean you cannot twist us," Nakirre said. "We are the enlightened. No falsehood of yours can lure us away from truth."

"You may believe that if it comforts you," Jixtus said. "Do you then choose for the Kiljis to be crushed to sand?"

"Perhaps even that is no longer within your power," Nakirre said, his skin stretching with daring. The inner turmoil he'd witnessed in Jixtus after the conversation with his fellow Grysks had left him at his lowest point yet. If he was like most species whom the Kiljis had encountered, this was the point where he would be most vulnerable to enlightenment.

But that was not the immediate goal here. Enlightenment would come once the Grysks were comfortable with the Illumine and their emotional defenses had been lowered. Now was the time to start down the road to that ultimate end. "Tell me, what was the news just now that so upset you?"

"I never said I was upset."

"Your silence and subdued attitude said it for you," Nakirre said. "Your problem, Jixtus, is that you see the Kiljis as minor tools to be used at the edges of your ambition. You stated that yourself: We were merely to conquer small nations so as to close them off to Chiss retreat."

"*And* you would then be free to meddle in their culture and bring them enlightenment," Jixtus said. "That was what you wanted, wasn't it?"

"It was and still is," Nakirre agreed. "But it's not *all* we want."

For a moment Jixtus was silent. "Very well," he said. "Tell me of this new ambition."

"You look only to destroy the Chiss," Nakirre said with cautious anticipation. Jixtus was listening to him. For the first time, he was actually *listening* to him. "I look instead to put them alongside us as your allies."

"That attempt has already been made," Jixtus growled. "We selected the most malleable of their leaders and inflamed their desires past the abilities of rational thought. It failed."

"Because you misunderstood them," Nakirre said. "You inflamed their desires, and now you inflame their fears and rivalries. What if, instead of fear, they could be induced to work cooperatively for the glory of the Grysks?"

"Through the enlightenment of the Kiljis?" Jixtus gave a sort of low snorting sound. "You reach now beyond *your* abilities, Generalirius."

"Not at all," Nakirre said. "All beings secretly dream of having someone to give them order and purpose, who will allow them to serve without the need for burdensome thought or uncertain decision. That is the enlightenment we offer."

"No," Jixtus said firmly. "You may have the remnant once we have broken the Ascendancy's back. But its back *will* be broken. Even now, the fuse is lit, and the first explosion of their civil war is set." He gestured toward the viewport. "Would you like to see the beginning of their end?"

Nakirre stretched with deep frustration. Jixtus was listening, but he wasn't hearing. He still didn't understand what the Kilji Illumine offered, or what the Kilji enlightenment could do to a people like the Chiss.

No matter. There were other nations besides the Chiss in the Chaos, nations the Grysks surely hoped to turn into that fine sand Jixtus had threatened him with. And once that was accomplished, there was all of Lesser Space and the beings inhabiting it.

There would be time for Nakirre to show Jixtus the full scope of what the enlightened could do. And if not Jixtus himself, then perhaps his successor. Even Grysks, after all, presumably didn't live forever.

And then the Kiljis' would-be masters would finally accept the Illumine as full partners in their dominion of the galaxy.

"I would like to see that, yes," he told Jixtus. "It is to be at Ornfra?"

"It is," Jixtus said. "We will travel one more hour, then you will return the ship to star-space so that I may make one final call."

"Of course," Nakirre said with sudden doubt. If he'd pressed his petition too hard, that call might be to that terrible Grysk warship. In the shadow of his thoughts, he saw boulders being reduced to dust . . .

"Have no fear, Generalirius," Jixtus said in a voice that was both soothing and mocking. "Truthfully, I was impressed by your passion for joining the Grysks as equals. It's a topic we shall revisit when the Chiss lie dead at our feet." He gestured. "And this call you will be welcome to listen in on. It will be to the Clarr family warship *Orisson*."

Nakirre felt a stretch of annoyance. He should have guessed Jixtus's call would be to his tame Chiss. "I dislike having to tie our travels to this person and her schedule," he said. "When will we be done with her?"

"When she has served her full purpose," Jixtus said. "Tell me, Generalirius Nakirre of the enlightened: When do you think that will be?"

Nakirre considered. "I think it is now," he said. "You speak as if your plan is fully under way. I believe we can now let her go."

"Interesting," Jixtus said. "Perhaps you do indeed have enlightenment."

Nakirre eyed him closely. "What do you mean by that?"

"I mean that as you were there for her beginning with us, so shall you be there for her end," Jixtus said. "I will speak with her one more time, and then we shall travel to Ornfra and witness her death."

"She will *die*?"

"She will." Jixtus paused, and Nakirre could imagine a malicious smile behind that veil. "And with her death will come the end of the Chiss Ascendancy."

Roscu had never liked schedules. They were fine for other people, but not for her. She had the rare combination of professionalism and instinct that allowed her to recognize and take advantage of unexpected opportunities, options that would be stifled by an inflexible schedule.

But in this case, it was a necessary evil. With ships traveling in hyperspace unable to communicate with one another or the universe in general, and with the *Orisson* and *Whetstone* both roaming around the Ascendancy on their individual tasks, the only way she could keep up to date on anything Jixtus learned was for both of them to commit to being in space-normal at certain specific times. It could be annoying and disruptive of her plans, but sometimes it paid off.

This time, it paid off *very* well.

"I apologize for calling at this hour, Your Venerante," Roscu said. "But I had news I needed to pass on to you."

"Not a problem, Captain," Patriarch Rivlex assured her. "I assume you've heard about the battle at Csaus between the Tahmie and Droc?"

"Yes, I picked up the news feed when I stopped to talk to Jixtus," Roscu said, wrinkling her nose a little. Personally, she wouldn't call a few laser shots exchanged between armed freighters a *battle*. Even *skirmish* would be pushing it. "It sounds like the *Bellicose* was able to intervene before things got out of hand."

"Yes, but that's not really the point," Rivlex said. "If even minor families are starting to shoot at each other, we could be on the edge of a disaster."

Roscu rolled her eyes. And then, there were people who went all drama at the slightest provocation. She hated that even worse than she hated schedules. "Has the Council called on the Nine for support?" she asked.

"No, not yet."

"Well, then, they probably aren't all that worried about it."

"Or they know that Patriarch Kloirvursi will refuse to contribute," Rivlex said. "And I can tell you right now that if the Dasklo don't hand over any of their ships, *we* certainly won't."

"Yes, probably a prudent move," Roscu said. Yet more drama.

Still, he might have a point. The Council might have already done some quiet probing, concluded that not enough of the Nine would contribute to overall Ascendancy defense, and decided a call would simply exacerbate the situation. "But that's not why I called," she continued. "While I was picking up the news, I also heard from Jixtus. It seems that while we're focused on the Dasklo, the Mitth are quietly making a move against the whole Ascendancy."

"Wait a moment," Rivlex said. "You said the *Mitth*?"

"Yes," Roscu said. "You'll recall that the Xodlak, Pommrio, and Erighal claimed they went to Hoxim because there was supposedly a largely untapped nyix mine there."

"*Eventually* they claimed that."

"Yes, fine, it took them a while to come clean," Roscu said, fighting down her annoyance. Rivlex had a bad habit of bringing up irrelevant details when he should be listening. "At any rate, Jixtus says that the Mitth have found the actual planet the nyix jewelry came from, a planet that has incredibly rich deposits." She paused for emphasis. "He also says that a group of aliens led by Senior Captain Thrawn are already in the process of capturing it, with a plan to claim it for the Mitth."

"Interesting," Rivlex said, not sounding nearly as troubled by this news as he ought to be. "Does Jixtus have a name and location for this planet?"

"He doesn't know the actual name," Roscu said. "Thrawn has apparently code-named it Sunrise. But I *do* have its location."

"And you believe him?"

Roscu frowned. What kind of question was *that*? "Don't you?"

"I don't know," Rivlex said. "That's why I ask. You're the one who's been in closest contact with this alien. Have you found his previous information reliable?"

"Yes, Your Venerante, I have," Roscu said firmly. "More than that, this is exactly the sort of underhanded move Thrawn would pull."

"Perhaps," Rivlex said, clearly still not convinced. "Tell me about these aliens he's supposedly recruited."

"They're called the Paccosh, from the Rapacc system," Roscu said. "The names are in our datafiles, though there's not much detail. Thrawn first contacted them when he was searching for the origin of the refugees who were trying to get to Dioya when they were attacked and killed."

"Yes, I remember," Rivlex said. "That was the mission that also led to the discovery and identification of General Yiv, was it not?"

"Yes, it was," Roscu confirmed, scowling at the comm. This was urgent and dangerous news. Why was the Patriarch dragging his feet with irrelevant questions? "The point is that while we're all looking and now shooting at one another, the Mitth are poised to reach a level of power that hasn't been seen since the Stybla handed over their rule to the first Three Ruling Families."

"I think you may be overstating the case, Captain," Rivlex said mildly. "Granted, a rich source of nyix would buy the Mitth a great deal of prestige in the Syndicure. But it would hardly translate to the kind of power you're talking about."

"With all due respect, Your Venerante, I think you may be forgetting Mitth history," Roscu said stiffly. "That gravity-well generator they brought back from Thrawn's first encounter with the Vagaari pirates was what finally persuaded the Obbic to ally with them. The enhanced energy shield they found at the edge of Lesser Space bought them a complete pass on Thrawn's blatant violation of standing orders, and also took the Krovi out of the Irizi list of allies and turned them neutral. And let's not forget the Mitth's cozy connection with the Stybla."

"What are you referring to?" Rivlex asked, his tone gone all cautious and guarded.

"You know what I'm referring to, Your Venerante," Roscu said. "The point is that after the Hoxim incident, I'm told Thrawn ignored the order to come to Csilla and instead went directly to Sposia and a meeting with Stybla Patriarch Lamiov. There's no reason for him to have done that unless he was bringing something new to the UAG, and in that case he should have first presented it to the Council. He certainly shouldn't be showing it first to a Patriarch of one of the Forty."

"I can see that, yes," Rivlex agreed, the moment of strange caution disappearing from his tone. "I'll see what I can find out about that. I presume you're still on your way to Ornfra?"

"Yes, to take a look at the Krolling Sen shipyard," Roscu confirmed.

"One more thing. Jixtus also warned that the Mitth have an observation and communications post hidden inside an artificial asteroid shell that may have been deployed into the Ornfra system."

"That sounds like an awful lot of effort to go to," Rivlex said. "Especially when everyone else just uses freighters or transports to keep track of their rivals."

"Freighters and transports are too obvious for someone like Thrawn," Roscu said sourly. "Or did you forget that Jixtus told us the vid of the Dasklo incident was taken in the Ornfra system?"

"Of course I didn't forge—" Rivlex broke off. "Are you suggesting the *Mitth* are the ones who recorded that vid? And then, what, sold it to Jixtus?"

"Why not?" Roscu said. "Clearly, the Dasklo didn't know they were being recorded. A fake asteroid drifting along, watching their war games—who would have suspected something like that?"

"But if the recording came from the Mitth, why didn't Jixtus tell us?"

"He probably doesn't know himself where it came from," Roscu said. "You have to look at the larger pattern of Thrawn's behavior. He's already working with one alien species to grab the Sunrise nyix mines, and we know he also made some kind of private deal with the Paataatus during his latest pirate hunt."

"The Syndicure seemed pleased enough with that last one."

"Who is or is not pleased is irrelevant, Your Venerante," Roscu persisted. "I'm talking about how Thrawn uses aliens for his own purposes. In fact, now that I think about it, he practically started his career that way, manipulating the Garwians and Lioaoi. So why not Jixtus, too? What's one more alien for him to lie to?"

"Well, you know him better than I do," Rivlex said, still sounding like he didn't want to believe it. "Just be careful not to make any public accusations until you have solid evidence."

"Don't worry, Your Venerante," Roscu said as patiently as she could. "I'll let you know what I find at Ornfra."

"Very good, Captain," Rivlex said. "And be careful. Patriarch Rivlex out."

The comm pinged off. "Or should I say, I'll let you know what I catch the Dasklo doing," she added under her breath.

"Orders, Captain?" Commander Raamas asked, stepping to the side of her command chair.

"Back into hyperspace and continue on to Ornfra," Roscu told him. "Best possible speed."

"Yes, ma'am." Raamas gestured across the bridge. "Helm: Reinitiate course to Ornfra."

"Acknowledged, Commander," the pilot said briskly. Outside the viewport, the stars stretched into star-flares, then faded into hyperspace swirl.

"On course for Ornfra, Captain," Raamas said formally. "Any further orders?"

"Not right now," Roscu said. "You're relieved for now, but I'll want you on the bridge when we reach Ornfra."

"Yes, ma'am." Raamas paused. "Captain . . . did you notice something odd in the Patriarch's voice when you mentioned the Mitth and the Stybla?"

"Maybe a little," Roscu said, keeping her voice casual. There was nothing odd about Rivlex's reaction, as far as she was concerned—clearly, he'd been remembering the fiasco with Thrawn and that Stybla senior aide at the alien world Pleknok.

But that incident had been deeply and deliberately buried, and Roscu had no intention of digging it up now. "Maybe he was thinking about the fact that the Mitth routinely hand over any alien artifacts they find to the Stybla."

"I thought everyone did that."

"Mostly," Roscu said. Actually, he was right—everyone *did* hand over alien artifacts to the Stybla. But only in the sense that the Stybla ran the UAG and all such items were examined by that agency before being dispersed elsewhere. "Or maybe he was thinking about the old theory that the two families worked a treasonous deal with the invaders during the Final Assault on Csilla."

Raamas smiled. "I doubt the Patriarch's worrying about thousand-year-old stories academy cadets tell each other when they don't feel like studying," he said. "Especially stories that don't hold air. Can't be much of an alliance when the invaders end up dead and the Mitth and Stybla don't end up dead beside them."

"Or even censured by everyone else," Roscu said. "It was just a thought. Probably he just hadn't had his caccoleaf yet."

"That's probably it," Raamas said. He hesitated. "One more thing, Captain, if I may. Forgive me if I'm out of line, ma'am, but I'm wondering about Admiral Ar'alani."

Roscu felt her stomach tighten. "You mean why she and I don't get along?"

"Yes, ma'am," Raamas said. "I know it's none of my business. But with the ramped-up tensions we're seeing in the Ascendancy—"

"You need to know what might get in the way of cooperation with other Ascendancy forces," Roscu finished for him. "Fair enough. All right. A few years ago Ar'alani was my commander aboard the patrol cruiser *Parala* when we happened on a pirate attack against a Garwian merchant-hub station. The Garwians were losing, when suddenly they switched to new tactics that saved the day. I suspected those tactics were illegally given to them by our fourth officer, Senior Commander Thrawn, and I lodged a complaint against him."

"What happened?"

"Nothing at all," Roscu said, forcing her voice to remain steady. The incident belonged to the distant past, and she'd already dredged up more of its emotional coloring recently than was good for her. "Ar'alani covered for Thrawn, Supreme General Ba'kif covered for Ar'alani, and the whole thing was swept out the door."

"I see," Raamas said. "Is that when you left and joined the Clarr family forces?"

"It was a couple of months later," Roscu said. "But yes. I was ready to leave, the Patriarch offered me a position, and I took it. End of story."

"I see," Raamas said. "Thank you, Captain. I appreciate your honesty."

"You're welcome, Commander," Roscu said. "Senior officers shouldn't have secrets from each other."

"I agree," Raamas said. "Thank you again for your time. I'll see you when we reach Ornfra."

For a minute after he left the bridge Roscu sat quietly in her chair, her eyes doing the methodical sweep of stations and status boards that her years in the fleet had ingrained in her.

No, the captain and first officer shouldn't have secrets between them . . . unless those secrets were dark and shameful.

Such as the true reason Roscu had left the Expansionary Defense Fleet. Not out of some high-minded protest against Thrawn and Ar'alani, but because a month after the Garwian incident Roscu had herself been brought up on charges for a minor protocol infraction. It had been a small lapse, certainly far milder than the crime Thrawn had committed.

Only in her case, no one came to her defense. No one worked tirelessly to clear her name. In the end, all they did was offer her the choice between official discipline and quiet departure.

She'd chosen the latter, and had never regretted it.

And then had come Pleknok.

Roscu glowered at the displays, feeling a trickle of the old emotions seeping through despite her efforts to suppress them. The fact that the Clarr had emerged from that incident more or less intact didn't matter. The fact that no one had died and the family had even managed to save face didn't matter.

What mattered was that the Mitth and the Stybla knew the truth about Pleknok. They knew what her part had been, and they knew how she'd failed, just like she'd failed to hold on to a position in the Expansionary Defense Fleet.

Worst of all, *Thrawn* knew.

There was a score there that needed to be settled between her family and Thrawn's. Maybe today, at Ornfra, Roscu would finally have the chance to do so.

MEMORIES IX

"Prepare," Thrawn said. "Pilot: Three, two, *one*."

With a sudden surge of power, the *Jandalin* twisted off its vector, angling to the right in a tight curve that had Thrass grabbing for his restraints. The starscape outside spun madly as the patrol ship continued its turn, and he could feel the rumbling vibration beneath him as the pilot ran the thrusters back to full power. For a second he could see the approaching Paataatus formation straight ahead of them—there was a sort of soft *chuff*—and then the pilot continued their curve, turning the ship back toward the crippled pirate. There was a muted flash as the *Jandalin*'s spectrum lasers fired again—

Lappincyk muttered something that sounded like a curse. "What?" Thrass asked. He looked among the various displays, trying vainly to figure out what Lappincyk was seeing and wishing he knew better how to read the data. Had Thrawn taken out one of the alien gunboats, or maybe even the frigate?

"He fired at the transport again," Lappincyk said tightly. "What in—?"

He broke off as the ship abruptly reversed the direction of its turn, again briefly facing off against the Paataatus ships—which were significantly closer now, Thrass noted uneasily—before continuing on again out of their path. Another right-hand curve, this one slightly less fierce than the last ones, and then the pilot straightened them out onto a vector that showed nothing but stars ahead. Thrass again looked at the displays, and this time was able to at least see that the pirate ship was behind them and that the *Jandalin* was now running parallel to the squadron of incoming Paataatus ships, only in the opposite direction.

He frowned. Paralleling the Paataatus, moving past them within easy attack range. Yet none of the aliens was making any move against them? "Thrawn?" he called. "What's going on?"

"Exactly what I expected," Thrawn said, a new and subtle note of confidence in his voice. "Something else I deduced from the records of the previous Paataatus battle."

"Which is?" Lappincyk asked impatiently.

Thrawn pointed to the side out the viewport. "Paataatus tactics are based on a swarm mentality," he said. "You see how they're now opening up their cluster as they continue toward the transport?"

Thrass studied the displays. He hadn't noticed the change in formation before, but now that he knew to look for it he could see that Thrawn was right.

"But why the transport?" Lappincyk asked. "We're already in laser range. The transport isn't. Why not attack us?"

"Because part of their pattern is to go after the weakest target first," Thrawn said. "To swarm it, destroy it, then move on to the next target—"

"Wait," Lappincyk cut him off, suddenly horrified. "To *destroy* it? Thrawn, we need that ship intact. You can't—"

He broke off as the *Jandalin* again turned into a tight curve that once again had Thrass grabbing for his safety straps. "*Thrawn!*" Lappincyk shouted over the roar of the thrusters.

Thrawn didn't answer. The curve straightened out, and Thrass once again saw the Paataatus ships directly in front of them.

But unlike the last two times he'd seen the aliens, this time they weren't blazing toward the Chiss patrol ship. This time they were blazing *away* from them. Thrawn's last maneuver had brought the *Jandalin* into position directly behind the attack formation.

And even as Thrass belatedly realized that all the twisting and turning had been about getting the *Jandalin* into precisely this position, the ship's three spectrum lasers opened fire.

The closest of the Paataatus gunboats took the full impact of the barrage, and on the sensor display Thrass saw a warning cone appear as the lasers dug deeply into the alien's main thrusters. Thrass watched closely, wondering if the next salvo would destroy the craft completely, or whether it would take a third or even a fourth attack to achieve that end.

But destruction was apparently not Thrawn's goal for this battle. His second laser blast wasn't directed at the damaged Paataatus ship, but instead focused on the next nearest gunboat. Another triple laser blast, and Thrawn again changed targets, this time to the third nearest. Even as he fired, the *Jandalin* was again in motion, accelerating toward the farther wing of the opening Paataatus formation.

Yet Thrass hadn't heard Thrawn give any additional orders. Did that mean the pilot was still following the original course pattern? If so, had Thrawn really anticipated the battle this far in advance?

Thrass looked at the displays again, concentrating on the one showing the distant transport. It was all well and good to pick off the gunboats one by one from behind while they were focused on a different target. But that strategy had now left the disabled Chiss transport completely exposed to the alien forces arrowing in on it. The frigate was still there, two of the swarming gunboats were still undamaged—

He stiffened. Had that been a flash of laserfire from the frigate?

There was no indication of any fresh damage to the transport. But Thrass was certain he'd seen a flash.

And then, even as he tried to figure it out, the gunboat moving along the frigate's portside flank sparked a small flash of its own. What in the name of Csilla—?

"Pilot: Ahead full power," Thrawn ordered, his voice calm but with an edge of urgency to it. "Get me in optimal laser range of the frigate."

"Yes, sir," the pilot said, his words disappearing into the suddenly enhanced roar of the *Jandalin*'s thrusters.

"As you see, Thrass," Thrawn said, half turning toward Thrass and raising his voice to be heard over the noise, "the target of a Crippler net doesn't have to be motionless if you can drop it in front of him and persuade him to run into it."

"Yes," Thrass murmured. So that was what the twin flashes had been: the frigate and gunboat slamming into the pair of charged nets that Thrawn had earlier dropped in their path, with all the twists and turns designed to hide their release from the Paataatus.

Only in order to make it work, Thrawn had had to not only precisely anticipate the swarming tactic, but also predict with a high degree of accuracy the vectors the individual alien ships would travel on their way to the transport. Just like he'd apparently anticipated the maneuvers that would be needed to get the *Jandalin* behind the attack force.

And all he'd had to go on was the data from a single battle nineteen years ago?

Thrass stared at the back of Thrawn's head, a chill running up his back. What kind of person could do all that?

"Fortunately, Crippler nets are large," Thrawn commented, as if anticipating Thrass's thoughts and concerns. "They're nearly impossible to detect, certainly at warship attack speeds, and they don't have to hit their targets squarely in order to temporarily disrupt their systems."

"Impressive aiming nonetheless," Lappincyk said. "What now?"

"We retrieve the transport and their hijacked cargo and leave," Thrawn told him. "Observe the Paataatus ships."

Thrass again looked at the displays. The gunboats had broken off their attack, the ones Thrawn had fired on limping away from the transport with the clear intent of making their escape into deep space. The single undamaged gunboat had joined with its partially paralyzed comrade and were together nudging the semi-incapacitated frigate off its attack vector toward a similar departure.

"Senior Aide Lappincyk?" the pilot called over his shoulder. "We're coming within laser range of the Paataatus frigate. Do we attack?"

"Mid Commander Thrawn?" Lappincyk asked.

"As Syndic Thrass rightly pointed out earlier, we can hardly hope to stand face-to-face against six warships who've been forced to continue hostilities," Thrawn said. "If the Paataatus have reconsidered their course of action, I see no reason not to let them go."

He pointed toward the left-hand side of the viewport. "Of more concern right now is Captain Roscu."

Thrass felt his throat tighten. The *Orisson*, which had been hanging well back from the field of battle, was again in motion, driving toward the hijackers' transport. With the danger now past, Roscu apparently thought she could just swoop in and pluck the cargo out of the *Jandalin*'s fingers.

"Pilot: Emergency power to the drive," Lappincyk ordered grimly. "Get us to the transport ahead of the Clarr."

"Yes, sir," the pilot said. The roar of the thrusters increased even more, and Thrass felt a brief twitch as the *Jandalin* leapt forward.

"Arriving ahead of the *Orisson* may not gain us anything," Thrawn said over the noise. "Captain Roscu has more than enough weight of weaponry and personnel to force us away."

"Just get us there," Lappincyk growled. "Roscu wouldn't dare block the senior aide to a Patriarch of the Forty by force."

"Under the circumstances, I'm not sure there's anything she wouldn't dare," Thrawn warned. "But perhaps we can persuade her to reconsider."

The *Orisson* was steadily picking up speed as Roscu likewise pushed her cruiser's drive to its limit. But the ship's more powerful thrusters also had to contend with the ship's greater mass, and the computer's projection still showed the *Jandalin* reaching the transport first.

"Pilot, on my mark you will execute emergency braking," Thrawn said.

Thrass frowned. Interrupting the *Jandalin*'s forward momentum would slow them down and possibly give the *Orisson* the advantage necessary to reach the transport first.

"On my second mark, resume course and acceleration," Thrawn continued.

"Thrawn—" Thrass said.

And stopped at a cautionary gesture from Lappincyk. "Let him go," the senior aide said, just loudly enough for Thrass to hear over the thruster noise. "I think he's more than demonstrated he knows what he's doing."

Thrass ground his teeth, but nodded. The *Jandalin* continued on—

"Pilot, first mark: Three, two, *one*," Thrawn said.

Thrass felt the slight surge as the *Jandalin*'s forward thrusters went into full braking mode, killing some of the ship's acceleration. He clenched his hands around his safety straps, wondering what game Thrawn was playing at now.

"Second mark: Three, two, *one*."

Once again, Thrass felt a small twitch of acceleration as the compensators lagged slightly behind the surge of the main thrusters' emergency power. The *Jandalin* again leapt forward, and he looked back at the displays, wondering if Thrawn's baffling maneuver had cost them the race to the transport.

He was still trying to figure it out when the glow of a plasma sphere sizzled past the viewport across the *Jandalin*'s bow.

Thrass jerked, feeling his mouth drop open. "What in the–?"

"Roscu fired on us," Lappincyk said, his voice hovering somewhere between disbelief and fury. "She *fired* on us."

"As I said," Thrawn called back to them. "There's little she wouldn't dare."

"How did you know?" Thrass asked.

"About the plasma sphere?" Thrawn gave a little shrug. "I served with her. I know how she thinks and behaves."

"And you knew she would attack us?"

"I suspected she would try to disable us," Thrawn said. "She probably reasons that once she has the transport and its cargo, there's nothing we can do about it."

Thrass mouthed a curse. Thrawn was right on that one, anyway. The Stybla could file a complaint once the *Jandalin* was back in the Ascendancy, but in the meantime the Clarr would have the transport and the cargo.

The cargo that belonged to the Stybla. The cargo that Lappincyk and Patriarch Lamiov were desperate to retrieve. The cargo Roscu was going to simply walk away with.

He squared his shoulders. Like hell she was.

"Are you saying there's nothing we can do to stop her?" Lappincyk demanded.

"He's not saying that at all," Thrass said before Thrawn could answer. "The comm, if you please?"

Lappincyk sent him a brief, speculative look. Then, without comment, he pulled the comm speaker from its holder and handed it over. "Thank you," Thrass said. "Pilot: Communications, if you please."

"You have comm," the pilot confirmed.

"Thank you." Thrass keyed the mike. "*Orisson*, this is the *Jandalin*," he said. "Captain Roscu, you should be aware that someone under your command has just committed a serious violation of Ascendancy law. As I assume you know, launching an attack on a member of the Syndicure can be considered an act of internecine war. I'm sure your Patriarch would be shocked to hear that someone aboard your ship has been careless enough to put him in that position."

"Don't be ridiculous," Roscu's scornful voice came back. "You already identified yourself as nothing more than a senior aide."

"Attacking a Patriarch's senior aide is also a serious breach of protocol," Thrass said. "But this isn't Senior Aide Lappincyk. You're talking to Syndic Mitth'ras'safis. I suggest you think long and hard before you continue along your current path."

There was a short pause. "You're lying," Roscu accused. "Why would a Mitth Syndic be aboard a Stybla patrol ship?"

"For the same reason Mid Commander Thrawn is aboard," Thrass said, an odd thought suddenly occurring to him. Family relationships were sometimes vague and always complicated, and the perceptions of those relationships were often even more so.

But if properly presented, erroneous perceptions could be useful, providing leverage and manipulation in a way that couldn't later be denounced as outright falsehoods. Thrass, as a Mitth cousin, had some of the same rights and privileges as those enjoyed by blood.

And one of those rights, he knew, was to make personal declarations of—

"My brother and I were asked by our Patriarch to assist Senior Aide Lappincyk in his recovery operation," he continued, dropping the critical word into the conversation with a casual familiarity, as if he'd referred to the relationship a thousand times over the years. The question now was whether Roscu would catch the designation and the significance he hoped she would place on it.

From the length of the silence at the other end of the comm, it appeared that she had. "This operation is a matter for the Clarr," Roscu said at last.

Quietly, Thrass let out the breath he'd been holding. "Retrieval of the cargo is a matter for the Stybla," he countered. As he'd hoped, Roscu had taken the most literal meaning of his comment.

And really, it would have been extraordinary if she hadn't. She didn't know Thrawn's standing with the Mitth—she would assume he was a merit adoptive, as were most of the Nine's military personnel, but would never have been so crass as to ask.

Now that lack of definitive information had turned around to sting her. Syndics were always either blood, cousins, or ranking distants; and Thrass's identification of Thrawn as his brother strongly implied that he, too, was in that lofty peak of the Mitth family pyramid.

Roscu might be willing to kill a Stybla Patriarch's senior aide, especially if she could make it seem like a result of the brief battle with the Paataatus. Killing a high-ranking Mitth, on the other hand, would be far more dangerous.

Killing *two* high-ranking Mitth should be completely out of the question.

Especially if she could be persuaded that she wasn't the only one on her end of the conversation. "One other thing," Thrass said. "Be advised that we're currently copying these transmissions to the transport. Whatever course of action you decide on, your Clarr family hijackers will be witnesses to it."

"Impossible," Roscu insisted. "The plasma sphere we fired earlier will have knocked out their comm."

"I didn't say we were using the comm," Thrass said. "Mid Commander Thrawn has retuned one of the *Jandalin*'s lasers to a comm frequency and is feeding the transmissions through the transport's sensor network."

There was another brief pause. Then Roscu bit out a curse Thrass had never heard in polite society. "I *knew* it," she snarled. "I *knew* he'd meddled in that pirate attack."

"On the contrary," Thrass said. Thrawn had half turned in his seat, Thrass noted, a rather stunned look on his face. Thrass gave him a reassuring smile in return. "Just because he knows how to do something doesn't imply he's ever actually done it."

"Syndic Thrass—"

"At any rate, right now your focus needs to be on your own situation," Thrass cut her off. "As I see it, your only option is to withdraw gracefully."

"You don't understand, Syndic," Roscu said, the anger and frustration in her voice edging toward veiled desperation. "I have orders. I cannot return without the hijackers."

"Then take them," Lappincyk spoke up.

Thrass looked at him in surprise. "Excuse me?"

Lappincyk gestured for the mike. Frowning, Thrass handed it over. "Captain Roscu, this is Senior Aide Lappincyk," Lappincyk said. "If all you want are the hijackers, you're welcome to them. All *we* want is our cargo. Once it's aboard the *Jandalin,* we'll withdraw and you can do as you please with both the transport and the criminals."

Thrass felt his eyes narrow. Was Lappincyk really authorized to make that sort of deal?

Of course he was. Patriarch Lamiov had already said he'd tried to work a deal with Patriarch Rivlex to avoid a crisis between their two families. Bringing a group of Clarr hijackers back to Naporar would force the dangerous confrontation Lamiov had always hoped to avoid.

"Captain?" Lappincyk prompted.

"I suppose that would be acceptable," Roscu growled.

"I would hope so," Lappincyk said, his voice going dark. "Because otherwise you're going to get nothing at all. So. Here's what you'll do. First, you'll break off your rush and take up position three hundred kilometers from the transport. You'll then transmit an order that we can record and play for the hijackers after we've docked, instructing them to leave all weapons on the deck by the air lock and retreat to the engine room. We'll transfer the stolen cargo to the *Jandalin,* then confirm the hijackers didn't accidentally take a piece or two into the engine room with them."

"I hardly think—"

"If they have," Lappincyk continued, "or if they resist us in any way, we'll lock our two ships together and transport the hijackers to Naporar to face the full horror of death by torture as specified in the family accords. I expect you to make the consequences of such foolishness *very* clear in your message to them."

"I will," Roscu said, and Thrass could imagine the words coming out from between clenched teeth.

"Good," Lappincyk said, giving Thrass a tight smile. "We're prepared to record your message. You may begin whenever you're ready."

CHAPTER FIFTEEN

Ornfra was an important economic and political hub of the Ascendancy's northeast-zenith sector. All Nine Ruling Families had strongholds there, as did seventeen of the Forty Great Families. In normal times, it was a thriving and vibrant place, full of life and political intrigue.

Right now, it was a major explosion waiting to happen.

"Have you figured out what you're going to say to her, Senior Captain?" Apros asked.

"I have most of it," Ziinda said.

Which was mostly a lie. She actually didn't have the foggiest idea of how she was going to approach Captain Roscu when the *Orisson* finally arrived. For that matter, given Roscu's attitude during their last encounter, she wasn't even sure the other wouldn't simply order her comm officer to refuse any attempt at conversation.

But a ship's captain was supposed to look competent to her officers and warriors, whether she felt like she was or not.

She scowled out the viewport. The space around Ornfra was buzzing with ships, the transports and merchants skittering around timidly, the patrol craft and warships taking a much more aggressive stand. Most of the general comm conversations the *Grayshrike* was picking up were terse and anxious.

She looked at the tactical, and the prominent icons marking the warships floating watchfully in their various orbits. All of them were from the Dasklo family's private fleet, of course—Ornfra wasn't exactly a private Dasklo province, but it was about as close to one as any planet in the Ascendancy got. The other eight Ruling Families had interests here, of course, but they were relatively small, certainly when compared with the Dasklo holdings. The biggest minority presence was probably the Clarr and their massive farming operations, which had themselves been a source of low-grade political tussling between the two families for decades. But despite that rivalry—or perhaps because of it—the Clarr didn't have any of their own warships here.

The overall System Patrol was a shared force, as it was on all other Chiss worlds. But with the far more powerful Dasklo warships dominating the system it was Patriarch Dasklo'irv'ursimi who was calling the shots, and everyone knew it.

Normally, that somewhat lopsided arrangement seldom rose above the level of minor annoyance. Now, with tensions heightened and accusations and counter-accusations being thrown around, the whole system seemed poised like an air dancer preparing to launch herself off her chosen cliff.

It wasn't just the civilian ships that were acting skittish, either. For all their outward confidence, the Dasklo were feeling the strain, too. The *Grayshrike* had already been challenged twice by Dasklo warships, both family commanders demanding to know what an Expansionary Defense Fleet ship was doing in their system. Ziinda had been able to ease their concerns, but from the continual pings of active sensors it was clear her ship was being watched closely.

What those other warships would do when she accosted an incoming Clarr warship wasn't a question she wanted to think about.

"Basically, I'm just going to explain the situation," she told Apros. "Hopefully, she'll be willing to listen."

"Yes, ma'am." Apros hesitated. "May I ask you a question, Senior Captain?"

"About Captain Roscu?"

"No, ma'am," Apros said. "Not directly, anyway."

Ziinda gestured. "Go ahead."

"I've been looking over the Jixtus vid," Apros said, pulling it up on his questis, "and I was struck by something odd."

He keyed it to play and handed it to her. "Is it my imagination, or is the cam that's taking the vid moving?"

Ziinda studied the image. Unfortunately, five seconds wasn't much time to establish any kind of baseline. "I assume you've run an analysis on it," she said, handing the questis back.

"Yes, ma'am, I have," he said, scowling at the image. "It's too short for the computer to make anything of it. But I could swear the cam is moving past the other ships. And that just seems wrong."

"How so?"

"If you're trying for secrecy, I'd think any movement by the cam would attract attention," Apros said. "So letting it drift seems to be exactly what you wouldn't want."

"Agreed," Ziinda said. "On the other hand, if this is a fraud like we're thinking, maybe Jixtus just has a flair for the dramatic."

"Except that he's trying to sell it as the real thing," Apros pointed out. "Just seems sloppy, somehow."

"I get your point," Ziinda said. "If we can talk the Clarr into giving us a copy of the longer version, maybe we'll be able to find out for sure."

"Maybe." Apros hissed out a breath. "Thank you for your time, Senior Captain."

"No problem," Ziinda said. "And keep at it. If there's one thing I've learned serving with Admiral Ar'alani, it's that small details can turn out to be more important than anyone expects."

"Senior Captain, we've got incoming," Vimsk announced from the sensor station. "Light cruiser, Clarr crest . . . it's the *Orisson*, ma'am."

"Mid Commander Shrent, signal Captain Roscu," Ziinda ordered, settling herself firmly in her chair. And with that, she was out of time to come up with anything fancy or clever. As she'd told Apros, she'd just have to lay it out and hope Roscu listened. "Tell her it's urgent that I speak with her."

"More movement, Senior Captain," Vimsk added. "Two Dasklo destroyers changing orbits. Looks like they're moving to intercept the *Orisson*."

"Senior Captain, I've got Captain Roscu," Shrent said, keying the comm over to Ziinda's chair.

Ziinda hit the mike key. "Captain, this is Senior Captain Ziinda," she said. "We have evidence showing that the vid Jixtus gave you is—"

"Sorry, but I'm a bit busy right now," Roscu's voice came back, sounding gruff and distracted. "I've been told the Mitth have placed a big floating spy platform here, and I intend to find it."

"Captain, this is important," Ziinda tried again. "The vid is a fraud. Do you understand?" Faintly, she could hear the sounds of conversation from the *Orisson*. "The ships are all fakes," she said, raising her volume in the hope of cutting through the verbal clutter. Was Roscu even listening to her? "Captain Roscu—"

"There it is," Roscu said, her attention clearly on whatever her people were doing and saying. "Bigger than I expected. I wonder how many people Thrawn has stuffed inside. Raamas, are we even going to be able to tow it in?" There was an indistinct reply—"That's all right—we'll figure out something. Maybe Senior Captain Ziinda can lend us the *Grayshrike*'s tractors. I have to go now, Senior Captain. We'll talk when we get back."

"Captain Roscu—"

"They've cut off comm, Senior Captain," Shrent said. "I'll try to get them back."

"What was *that* all about?" Apros asked, frowning at Ziinda.

"No idea," Ziinda said, the back of her neck tingling. There was something very wrong here. "Mid Commander Shrent?"

Shrent shook his head. "Sorry, ma'am. They're not responding."

"Those two Dasklo destroyers are still moving toward her," Wikivv said. "Maybe she's talking to them."

"There's no evidence of any comm activity from the *Orisson*," Shrent said.

"Apros, pull up the specs on that ship," Ziinda said. "I want to know its towing limit."

"Yes, ma'am," Apros said, working his questis. "Do you want me to check on Mitth spy platforms, too?"

"Get me the *Orisson*'s towing limit first," Ziinda said. "Wikivv, I'm seeing an aspect change. What are they doing?"

"Looks like a yaw-pitch rotation, ma'am," the pilot reported. "Seem to be lining up on a new outward vector."

"Vimsk, track along the *Orisson*'s likely vector cone," Ziinda ordered. "I want to know what they're aiming for."

"The Dasklo destroyers are picking up speed," Wikivv said. "I'm guessing they've spotted the turn, too."

"Afraid that Roscu is going to cut and run," Apros commented. "Here's the towing data, Senior Captain."

"That's not the plan I was hearing from her," Ziinda said, looking at her chair displays as Apros's numbers appeared. As she'd expected, the *Orisson* could tow pretty much anything up to a medium-large freighter.

So how big was this Mitth spy platform she thought she was seeing? "Vimsk, what have you got?"

"There are no likely systems along that vector cone," Vimsk said. "In-system, none of the planets line up. There are a few asteroids stretching out toward the outer system—"

And with a horrible shock, Ziinda got it. "Shrent—emergency comm system," she snapped. "Get Roscu's attention—I don't care how you do it—"

"There she goes," Wikivv cut in as the Clarr light cruiser disappeared from the viewport and displays. "Looked like an in-system jump."

"Track it," Ziinda ordered. "And go to battle stations."

"Senior Captain?" Apros called tensely over the noise as the battle station alert sounded.

"You heard Vimsk," Ziinda said, cutting off the sound. All across the bridge the officers were hunched over their boards, and on the status displays the patterns of standby lights flicked to green as the *Grayshrike*'s weapons systems came fully to life. "The moving camera that you spotted in the vid. It wasn't just *moving*—it was doing a slow inward orbit, like an asteroid." She pointed at the tactical. "Like one of the asteroids Roscu is chasing down."

"Oh, *hell*," Apros bit out, his eyes going wide. "You mean like the asteroid at Sunrise? But she said it was a Mitth spy platform."

"She was *told* it was a Mitth spy platform," Ziinda retorted, looking at the sensor display. Vimsk had refined her data now that the *Orisson*'s final exit vector was known, but there were still at least five possible targets the Clarr ship might be headed for.

But which one?

Ziinda felt sweat breaking out on her forehead. The *Orisson* was charging straight into a trap, and the *Grayshrike* was the only ship that could react fast enough to save it. But there would only be time for a single in-system jump. If Ziinda guessed wrong, Roscu and her crew were dead.

And the hell of it was that it would *be* a guess. The *Orisson* had made a brief hyperspace jump, arriving almost instantly somewhere else in the system. But its image and drive emissions were all heading back from that spot at the far slower speed of light. Depending on how far Roscu had gone, it could be seconds, minutes, or even hours before the *Grayshrike* or anyone else on Ornfra could physically spot it.

"Senior Captain, I think she missed," Wikivv said.

"What?" Ziinda asked, frowning.

"I think she missed with her jump," Wikivv repeated. "It's been too long. She should have shown up by now at one of the three most likely asteroids."

"She might have jumped to one of the farther ones," Apros pointed out.

"No, she's right," Ziinda said with a renewed bit of hope. "Those others are all too far away. If Jixtus is trying to drive the Clarr and Dasklo into all-out war, he needs all of Ornfra to see the *Orisson* get destroyed."

"Preferably with a couple of Dasklo destroyers nearby that the Clarr can blame it on," Apros said. "And they won't jump to confront Roscu until they can see her."

"So the *Orisson* overshot and has to come back," Ziinda agreed. "That gives us a little breathing space. Vimsk, is there anything about any of those asteroids that makes it stand out?"

"Nothing I can pick up at this distance, ma'am," Vimsk said, her face pressed against her glare-hooded monitor. "But the missile trap at Sunrise didn't give off anything I could get, either, even when we were right up beside it."

Apros muttered something under his breath. "Any ships out there that are just hanging around?" he asked. "It'll probably be something small and unobtrusive."

"Scanning now, sir."

"Apros, what are you thinking?" Ziinda asked.

"They're not going to leave it to automatic sensors and firing systems," he said. "Not something this important. They'll have someone nearby to keep an eye on the asteroid and pick the right moment to fire the missile."

"Good call," Ziinda said. She really should have thought of that herself. "Vimsk?"

"Still scanning," Vimsk said. "But if they're running on standby, I may not be able to pick them up."

"We need to get closer," Apros said. "Wikivv, work us up an in-system jump to someplace midway between the two closest asteroids. Hopefully, that'll put us close enough."

"Put it somewhat closer to the closest one, though," Ziinda added. "I'm still leaning toward that one."

"And after you get that course, start us on one from that point to midway between the second and third," Apros said. "We may not have time for a second jump before the *Orisson* walks into the trap, but we have to try—"

"Got it!" Shrent interrupted, a note of triumph in his voice. "Apologies for the interruption, sir, but I've got the status reports from Patrol Command. They've got a freighter listed as undergoing repairs in that area."

"They didn't tow it in?" Ziinda asked.

"The freighter refused," Shrent said. "Said they could fix it themselves and didn't want to pay bluedock fees."

"Sounds like our controller," Apros said. "Wikivv?"

"Got it," Wikivv confirmed. "How close do you want us, Senior Captain?"

Ziinda looked at the tactical and the new mark where the freighter's position had been added. With Wikivv's skill with in-system jumps, she could put the *Grayshrike* well within combat range of the freighter. A thorough pelting with plasma spheres before it knew what was happening, and no one aboard would be triggering that missile anytime soon.

But the asteroid would have its own backup sensor and firing mechanisms in place, and the *Grayshrike*'s tangle with a similar weapon over Sunrise had shown just how tough the things were to knock out. Taking out the freighter would make the *Orisson*'s destruction less precise, but no less inevitable.

No, Roscu's only chance was for the *Grayshrike* to get close enough to intercept her and wave her off before she got within firing distance of the missile.

"Put us here," she told Wikivv, marking a spot on her questis and sending it across the bridge to the helm station. "That should keep us out of easy shot of the missile but close enough to everything to warn off the *Orisson* when it arrives."

"Understood, ma'am," Wikivv said. "A few more seconds."

Ziinda looked at the weapons status boards, confirming everything showed green. "Ghaloksu, are your crews ready?"

"They are, Senior Captain," the weapons officer confirmed.

"In-system jump ready, ma'am," Wikivv announced.

"Acknowledged," Ziinda said, bracing herself. This was it. "In-system jump: Three, two, *one*."

The view outside flickered, and suddenly the ship traffic was gone. In the near distance, off the *Grayshrike*'s portside bow, was the asteroid Wikivv had brought them to. "Yaw rotation seventy degrees portside, four degrees zenith," Ziinda ordered, searching the starscape for the freighter. There it was, forty degrees further off to portside and about three times the distance currently between the *Grayshrike* and the asteroid. "Apros, pull up the record of our battle with these things at Sunrise. Roscu will probably need some convincing. Shrent, stand ready to signal the *Orisson* the instant it—"

And then, flicking in from the outer system, the *Orisson* was there.

Face to face with the asteroid. Two kilometers away.

In perfect position to be destroyed.

Family fleet officers, Roscu had long since recognized, weren't nearly as adept at tight warship maneuvers as their counterparts in the Expansionary Defense Fleet. Some of that was lack of regular practice, but most of it was simply the fact that such maneuvers normally weren't needed. Most defensive combat took place inside a planet's gravity well or close to the edge of it, where an attacker's maneuverability was restricted, so in-system jumps weren't emphasized in training.

Fortunately, like Roscu herself, the *Orisson*'s pilot had come out of the Ascendancy military, and the Defense Force emphasized such training almost as much as the Expansionary Defense Fleet. His first in-system jump was long and wide, exactly as Roscu had instructed, and his second was equally on the mark.

In fact, it was just a little *too* perfect. The *Orisson* came out of hyperspace barely two kilometers from the asteroid. A little closer, and they would have crashed right into the thing.

But they hadn't hit it, and they had it pinned with no place to go, and the Mitth family was now cooked. She'd give whoever was inside a chance to surrender first, and if they refused she was in perfect position to crack open the hull, haul everyone and everything out, and expose the scheme to the entire Ascendancy.

And if she found enough dirt inside, the fallout might be enough to break Patriarch Thurfian's prestige. Maybe not drop the Mitth from the Ruling Families, but at least damage them enough to alter the flowing web of relationships that existed in the Syndicure. And any such disruption could only work to the Clarr family's advantage.

"Combat range: two ships," the sensor officer warned. "One active warship; one dormant freighter."

Roscu looked at the tactical. So one of the Dasklo destroyers had followed them?

Her lip twisted as the ship's ID came up. No, not one of the destroyers. Just the *Grayshrike* and that insufferably annoying Senior Captain Ziinda.

"Captain, the *Grayshrike* is hailing us," the comm officer added.

"Ignore them," Roscu said. "Set me up a tight-beam signal to the spy platform."

"Captain, the asteroid is rotating," Raamas said, peering over the sensor officer's shoulder.

Roscu eyed the sensor display. It was rotating, all right. Not very fast, but it was definitely on the move.

Turning its main sensors toward the *Orisson* to see who exactly they were dealing with? Or was it perhaps turning their own tight-beam transmitter around so their upcoming conversation would have more privacy? Either was fine with her. "Comm?"

"Tight-beam is ready, Captain."

Roscu nodded and keyed her chair's mike. Jixtus hadn't been completely certain that Thrawn was personally involved in this project. But knowing the man as she did, she personally had no doubts.

And when Patriarch Thurfian fell, she would make absolutely sure that Senior Captain Thrawn fell with him.

"Asteroid is rotating, Senior Captain," Ghaloksu said tensely. "Bringing the missile launcher to bear."

Ziinda nodded, her throat tight. The *Grayshrike* was too far away for Ghaloksu or Vimsk to pick out the hex pattern that would definitively tell them which of the two Chiss warships was the attackers' target.

But she had little doubt as to which one the hidden controllers would choose. The *Grayshrike* was far enough away to have at least a chance of destroying or disabling the missile before it could cover the distance between them. The *Orisson*, on the other hand, was a sitting flashfly.

And it was the Clarr and Dasklo families that Jixtus seemed determined to force into open warfare. A Clarr family ship destroyed in a predominantly Dasklo system might be all it would take. "Shrent?"

"Still ignoring our calls, ma'am."

"Fine," Ziinda bit out. If Roscu wouldn't talk, she'd just have to give the stubborn idiot something she *couldn't* ignore. "Ghaloksu: Sequential laser burst across the *Orisson*'s bow."

"Yes, ma'am," Ghaloksu said, his fingers moving rapidly across his board as he set up the shot.

"Senior Captain?" Apros asked, a note of warning in his voice.

"I'm banking on her being the type to come charging at us to demand an explanation, or at least to tell us why shooting at her was a bad idea," Ziinda said. "If we can get her to move even a little, it'll buy us some time to make her understand what she's walked into. Ghaloksu: *Fire*."

The bridge lit up with reflected light as the lasers cut across the empty space between the *Orisson* and the asteroid. "Fire again," Ziinda said. "Shrent? Keep trying—"

"What the *hell* are you doing?" an outraged voice boomed over the bridge speaker.

Ziinda twitched involuntarily even as she belatedly recognized the fury-distorted voice as Roscu's. "You're in danger, Captain," she called. "That asteroid—"

"This is *my* prize, Irizi," Roscu snarled. "You will back off, and you will back off *now*."

"*Orisson*'s moving, Senior Captain," Vimsk murmured. "But it's not . . ."

Ziinda looked at the display, her heart sinking. The *Orisson* had turned toward the *Grayshrike*, bringing its main weapons to bear on the larger ship.

But it wasn't moving away from the asteroid, as Ziinda had hoped it would. In fact, if anything, it was drifting closer to the floating rock.

And with the *Orisson*'s flank now presented to the hidden missile, it wouldn't have even the slightest chance of surviving an attack.

Ziinda hadn't made the situation any better. She'd just made it worse.

Somehow, she had to find a way to fix that.

"And if you think you can intimidate me, or order me away, you and the whole Irizi family can go straight to—"

Ziinda took a deep breath. This was her only chance. "Shut up, you blithering *ass*!" she bellowed.

It was a word that Ziinda had seldom used, and never to another officer's face. But despite that, or perhaps because of it, the word and the sheer ferocity behind it had the desired effect. For the first time since both ships arrived at Ornfra, the Clarr captain was shocked into silence.

"Now listen carefully," Ziinda said, her voice low and under rigid control. Her own bridge had gone totally quiet, too. "That is not a spy platform. It's an artificial asteroid shell concealing a remote-controlled missile. A big, nasty, hull-shattering missile that can blow open the side of an armored space station. It'll destroy the *Orisson,* and if you had a sister ship beside you it would destroy that, too. Do you understand?"

"I'm listening," Roscu said, her voice under the same rigid control as Ziinda's.

"Ar'alani and I tangled with one of these things over Sunrise," Ziinda said. "My first officer is sending over the record now." Across the bridge, Apros broke out of his stunned paralysis and keyed his questis. "The asteroid is turning to line up the launcher," Ziinda continued. "When it finishes, you and your crew will die. We need to figure out a way to get you clear before that happens."

"Understood," Roscu said, and Ziinda could hear both the dread and the steel now coloring her voice. A quick skim of the relevant parts of the *Grayshrike*'s Sunrise record and she was finally up to speed. "I assume I can't maneuver fast enough to get out of the way. An in-system jump?"

"Can she do it, Wikivv?" Ziinda asked.

"Depends on their sensor capabilities," Wikivv said. "They're close enough that they might be able to detect the hyperdrive spinning up before it's ready—"

"Too late," Vimsk cut in, her voice taut. "The asteroid's stopped turning. The missile's lined up.

"They're going to die."

CHAPTER SIXTEEN

The seconds ticked by, each one stretching toward eternity. Ziinda stared out the viewport at the *Orisson* and the asteroid, poised together like an oblivious whisker cub sitting beside a hungry groundlion, a knot of futility twisting in her stomach. So that was it. She'd tried to save the *Orisson,* and she'd failed. Out of the corner of her eye she saw Vimsk working at her board . . .

"Senior Captain?" the sensor officer spoke up, her voice odd as it broke the taut silence. "I checked back . . . ma'am, the asteroid's been in position for nearly a minute."

Ziinda turned her eyes to the secondary sensor display, watching as Vimsk replayed the record. She was right: The missile had been ready to fly since before the two captains even began talking about an in-system jump.

So why hadn't it?

"Some kind of malfunction?" Roscu asked. "In that case, I'm getting clear—"

"No, no, don't move," Ziinda interrupted, her brain racing. It wasn't a malfunction. Not with these people. No, for some reason they'd deliberately decided not to fire.

But why? Were they waiting for one of the Dasklo destroyers to make an appearance? Having both families present when the *Orisson* was destroyed would give an extra push to their hoped-for war, a bigger slap across the face than if the Clarr warship died out here on its own.

But there was something else. Something Ziinda could sense, but not quite put her finger on.

And then, abruptly, she had it. *Their hoped-for war.*

"It's not a malfunction," she told Roscu. "Remember why they sent the missile into the Ornfra system. They're trying to goad the Ascendancy into war."

"Yes, I got that," Roscu said impatiently. "Why aren't they firing?"

"Because they're hoping they won't have to use it," Ziinda said. "It'll look better if we start fighting on our own, without any more help from them."

"So what do we do?"

"Exactly what they want." Ziinda braced herself. "You're going to open fire on the *Grayshrike*."

"*What?*" The word came simultaneously from Roscu and Apros.

"I fired across your bow," Ziinda said. "They'll have seen that as a challenge, and you need to respond."

"Ziinda, I can't do that," Roscu insisted. "An act of aggression by the Clarr family—"

"There's no time for argument," Ziinda ground out. "They're sitting out there in that freighter with their finger on the firing button. We have to assume that if you try for a jump they'll pick up on it and take you out before you can move. We need to give them a show while we figure out what to do next."

"Very well, *Grayshrike*," Roscu said, her voice gone glacially calm. "Here we go . . ."

And with that, a full volley of laserfire erupted from the *Orisson*'s bow and shoulder weapons and blasted across the *Grayshrike*'s hull.

"Evasive," Ziinda ordered. "Pull us back and to starboard—make it look like we're trying to get away from the *Orisson*. Roscu, keep on us like you don't want us to get away. Not too quick—we don't want them to realize you're also moving away from the missile."

"Acknowledged," Roscu said as a second salvo raked across the *Grayshrike*'s hull. "You going to fire back?"

"One more salvo," Ziinda said. "Right now, I'm trying to talk you down, pointing out that this doesn't help your case against the Dasklo. Ghaloksu?"

"Barrier down thirty percent," Ghaloksu said tightly. "You want to ease up a little, *Orisson*?"

"Belay that," Ziinda said before Roscu could answer. "These people know what a fake fight looks like. This one has to be a hundred percent real."

"One hundred percent it is," Roscu said grimly. "Let's just hope we don't kill each other in the process."

"Yes, let's hope that," Ziinda agreed. "Ghaloksu, get ready to return their laserfire." The *Orisson*'s third salvo slashed into the *Grayshrike*— "*Fire.*"

The *Grayshrike*'s lasers blasted away, the focused energy cutting across the *Orisson*'s hull. "Keep us drifting to starboard," Ziinda ordered. "Roscu, keep your bow turned toward us. I think I've got a plan."

"Understood," Roscu said, a subtle change in her voice. "Yes, I see where you're going with this. You've got a better handle on my position—just let me know."

"Another few seconds should do it," Ziinda said. "Wikivv, keep us moving. Vimsk, what's happening with the asteroid?"

"It's holding position," Vimsk said. "But the *Orisson* is still at its targeting point."

"Understood," Ziinda said, looking at the tactical. Another few seconds, maybe two more exchanged volleys, and the *Orisson* would be in position.

"Incoming!" Apros snapped. "Portside zenith; portside nadir."

Ziinda looked out the viewport, biting out a quiet curse at the two warships that had suddenly appeared.

The two Dasklo destroyers had arrived.

"Shrent, warn them off," she ordered. "Make sure they know who we are, inform them that our mission has the official backing of Supreme General Ba'kif, and tell them we have the situation under control."

"I'm not going to sit by and let them harass me," Roscu said. "Be advised that if they fire on me, I *will* fire back."

"You do that and you'll be walking right along the enemy's path."

"I don't care," Roscu said flatly. "You get them clear, or I will."

Ziinda clenched her teeth. Only Roscu would never get to fulfill that promise, she knew. The aliens watching eagerly from their freighter would let the fight start, maybe even let the *Orisson* inflict some damage on the Dasklo ships, then turn the Clarr ship into scrap and corpses.

"The Dasklo senior captain refuses to acknowledge, ma'am," Shrent said tightly. "They say we have no jurisdiction here."

"Of course they do," Ziinda muttered. Didn't *anyone* in this damn system listen?

Of course they listened. They just didn't listen to anyone except themselves. The families were folding into their own defensive rings, gathering their allies and facing off against their rivals.

The stage was set. Jixtus had made sure of that. Now it would only take a single spark to turn the Ascendancy into its private version of hell.

"Senior Captain?" Apros called, gesturing out the viewport. "Look, ma'am. What do you think?"

Ziinda followed his pointing finger. One of the destroyers was moving across the field of view, clearly planning to circle behind the *Orisson* where the two Dasklo ships would have Roscu in a crossfire. It was a standard tactic, designed to force an opponent away from their chosen position or risk annihilation.

But what Apros had spotted was that the destroyer's path would take it across the *Grayshrike*'s bow . . . and, perhaps more significantly, would briefly pass between it and the distant freighter.

"Do you think they're smart enough?" she asked.

"Don't have to be smart, ma'am," Apros said. "They just have to be quick."

"Then let's hope they're quick," Ziinda said grimly, shifting her attention to the tactical. Perfect—the *Orisson*'s subtle maneuvering during its battle dance with the *Grayshrike* had shifted its bow almost far enough out of line with the missile's launch vector. "Apros, set it up," she confirmed. "Roscu, time to go. Surge forward to get a closer shot at me—that'll get you completely out of the target zone, hopefully long enough for you to fire up the hyperdrive and make your jump before they can counter. Ready?"

"Negative on that, *Grayshrike*," Roscu said. "I'm not leaving."

"Roscu, you need to get the hell out of here."

"Not with a pair of Dasklo punch-cans in my face," Roscu growled.

"You'll leave, or I'll destroy you myself," Ziinda warned.

"And start the war you keep babbling about?" Roscu said scornfully. "You wouldn't."

"It wouldn't start a war," Ziinda said. "Patriarch Rivlex might relish an excuse to take a poke at the Dasklo, but he's not going to go up against the Defense Force."

"Look, *Irizi*—"

"More to the point, I need a distraction if I'm going to pull this off," Ziinda said. "And I need it in ten seconds. So is it going to be pride, or results? Your choice."

Silence. Across the bridge, Apros was talking urgently with Ghaloksu, who was nodding and working the weapons board. Three seconds of silence . . . four . . . "Fine," Roscu said, her voice trembling with anger and frustration. "Surge forward and in-system jump set. Give me a count."

Silently, Ziinda let out the breath she'd been holding. "Acknowledged, *Orisson*," she said, looking out the viewport. The Dasklo destroyer was almost in position. "Stand by: Three, two, *one*."

There was a burst of power from the *Orisson*'s thrusters, shoving it toward the *Grayshrike* just enough to take it out of the hidden missile's line of fire as the Clarr's hyperdrive activated. A telltale surge, and the Clarr warship was gone.

"Ghaloksu, stand by," Ziinda said, watching the Dasklo destroyer. It was still on its original vector, but its acceleration had slowed as the captain saw that its quarry had escaped. It continued on, moved into position—

"Fire spheres," Ziinda ordered.

The plasma spheres shot out of the *Grayshrike*'s bow launchers, arrowing toward a collision with the destroyer. Ziinda watched them disappear into the starscape, again holding her breath. If this didn't work, she was going to be in severe trouble with the Council, the Syndicure, and at least two of the Nine. *Be quick,* she thought urgently toward the destroyer's captain and crew. *Please be quick.*

And then, just when she was starting to think the Dasklo captain was the most oblivious warship commander she'd ever seen, he finally spotted the attack bearing down on him. The sensor display showed his maneuvering thrusters suddenly come to life, his main thrusters desperately kicking up to full power, as he squirmed to get out of the way. The destroyer leapt forward and angled upward, just far enough to let the spheres shoot harmlessly beneath its stern.

The freighter lying dormant in the distance directly behind it, its own view of the *Grayshrike*'s launch having been blocked by the destroyer's bulk as it passed between them, never saw it coming.

"Lasers," Ziinda snapped as the spheres impacted on the freighter, multiple sparks of released ionic energy engulfing the ship and paralyzing its electronics systems. "Take it out before they can—"

She broke off as the freighter disappeared in a violent explosion. She shifted her eyes to the asteroid, feeling a horrible and helpless premonition.

Just in time to see it, too, disintegrate in a shattering of multiple internal blasts.

"Damn," Apros muttered into the sudden silence. "So the freighter *wasn't* there to trigger the missile."

"No," Ziinda agreed soberly. "They were there to keep the missile from launching on its own."

"A dead-man switch," Apros said. "One way or another, that missile was going to do damage."

Ziinda nodded, watching with sudden weariness as the expanding cloud of debris reached the *Grayshrike* and washed over its hull. Tiny pieces, of course, with nothing large enough or threatening enough to kick in the viewport's automatic blast shields. If there was one thing consistent about Jixtus's alien friends, they were very good at making sure they didn't leave anything behind that could give investigators a clue as to their identity, location, or capabilities.

Still, it wouldn't hurt to try. "Mid Commander Shrent, send a message to Supreme General Ba'kif," she said. "Include the record of everything that's happened since we first hailed the *Orisson,* and request that someone be sent to collect as much of this debris as possible and get it to Sposia. Maybe the UAG can dig out something useful."

"Yes, Senior Captain," Shrent said. "Ah—Senior Captain? The Dasklo destroyer is hailing. The captain demands to know what the—ah—what you were doing firing on him."

Ziinda looked at Apros, noting the sour look on her first officer's face. "Put him through," she told Shrent.

She and the *Grayshrike* had thwarted Jixtus's plan to start a war, had opened Captain Roscu's eyes a little to what was really happening in the Ascendancy, and had cost the enemy a powerful and expensive weapon that they'd spent a lot of time drifting into position. Now she was going to have to placate the very angry representative of one of the Ruling Families and try to open *their* eyes a little.

She sighed. This was turning out to be a *very* long day.

Even by Qilori's standards, which were the standards of a Pathfinder who sometimes had to be in the depths of the Great Presence for ten or twelve hours at a stretch, it had been a very long day.

It had also been a chillingly instructive one. The Paccian commandos Uingali and Thrawn had sent to commandeer the *Hammer* had been more competent and far deadlier than Qilori had expected. But even that group paled in comparison with the heavily armed and armored troops who showed up at Sunrise two days after the ship battle. At Thrawn's direction, and under Uingali's command, the soldiers had descended on a small mountain mining region on the surface and quickly and efficiently demolished the Grysk forces that had been running the slave operation.

At least, Qilori assumed they were Grysks. The presence of a Grysk warship in the earlier battle was evidence that the slavers were either Grysks or one of their client species. But he would probably never know for certain. The defenders' armor was equipped with self-destruct systems that could apparently either be triggered by the wearer or activate automatically if he was killed. What little the self-destruct left behind gave no clues as to the appearance of the beings that had been wearing the armor.

It was the logical extreme of Jixtus's own obsession with hiding the details of his face and body. Clearly, the Grysks didn't want their appearance known, and were willing to go to extraordinary lengths to achieve that end.

The downside to their fixation was that in the close quarters inside the mines, where the battle progressed and ultimately ended, some of the Grysk casualties came from the collateral damage of their own comrades' exploding armor. Combined with the deadly skill and precision of the Paccian soldiers and the apparently unexpected resistance of the natives themselves, a battle that might otherwise have taken days or even weeks was over by nightfall.

For Qilori, it was a sobering reminder that, no matter how much knowledge, power, or influence the Grysks might possess, there were still some nasty surprises lurking in the Chaos.

He was sitting alone in a corner of the compound's dining area, watching the red clouds surrounding the sun as it sank toward the horizon and trying to put some of the day's more stomach-turning images out of his mind, when he had a pair of visitors.

"Qilori of Uandualon," Thrawn greeted him, gesturing to the alien standing beside him. "This is the Magys. She wished to speak with you."

"Yes, I remember you from the *Aelos*," Qilori said. "How may I serve?"

For a moment the alien was silent, the dark eyes set deeply into her face over the twin jutting jaws boring into his. Out of the corner of Qilori's eye he could see Thrawn holding perfectly still, his glowing red eyes taking in everything.

The Magys's stare seemed to fade. "No," she said. "He will not suit."

"Yet he, too, is a navigator," Thrawn said. "Does he not therefore touch the Beyond?"

"He touches, but not in a way that is useful," the Magys said.

"What do you mean, not useful?" Qilori asked, a mix of confusion and bruised pride tweaking at his winglets. "I'll place the navigation skills of the Pathfinders in the balance against any other navigators in the Chaos."

"Space is not where I wish to navigate," the Magys said. "You are of no use."

"If he's of no use, then we shall move on," Thrawn said, taking the Magys's upper arm and gently turning her away. "Apologies for the interruption, Pathfinder. You may return to your meal."

"Thank you," Qilori muttered, his winglets undulating slowly with uncertainty as he watched them go. What did she mean, *Space is not where I wish to navigate*? Where else but in space was a navigator supposed to navigate?

He turned back to his meal. But the food, which had already been rather tasteless, had now lost all interest for him. He kept at it just the same, knowing nutrition was important, as he watched Thrawn and the Magys leave the dining area and head across toward the barracks where the miners and their families were having their first evening of peace since the onset of their civil war.

"Good evening, Pathfinder."

Qilori turned his head. Uingali was walking toward him from the other direction, four armored Paccian commandos walking close behind him. "Good evening, Uingali foar Marocsaa," he said. "I thought the Paccosh had eliminated the enemy."

"I ask your pardon?"

Qilori gestured to the commandos. "I was speaking of your bodyguards."

"Ah," Uingali said. "Yes, the enemy is defeated, or so I'm told. But we stand in a wilderness region, surrounded by woods and mountain crevices. Such terrain can conceal predators and other natural dangers. You seem upset."

"I am," Qilori said, thinking fast. The Magys's comment about non-space navigation had been both intriguing and unsettling, but he didn't want it to look like he'd placed any special significance on it. Best not to even bring it up. "I was wondering how much longer Sarsh and I would be staying here before we were returned to our home at Navigator Concourse Four Forty-Seven," he improvised.

"Returned?" Uingali asked, sounding surprised. "The Paccosh didn't hire you, Pathfinder. We're under no obligation to provide you transport to your home base or elsewhere."

Qilori stared at him. That wasn't the answer he'd expected. "You can't be serious," he said carefully. "I navigated you here from Rapacc, and risked my life to assist your attack, all without charge. Surely some obligation on your part attaches to such actions."

"Normally, it would," Uingali agreed. "But in this case, you were part of an attack on Rapacc. As such you are effectively a prisoner of war."

"I was merely the navigator," Qilori protested. "I played no part in the Kilji threat."

"Nevertheless, you brought them to Rapacc and were present during the battle," Uingali said.

"Navigators are always to be held blameless in such things."

"The Paccosh have not made any such agreement," Uingali countered. "Nor have we signed any relevant treaty."

"I understand," Qilori said, trying to calm his winglets. He'd started this conversation as a way to avoid talking about Thrawn and the Magys. Now, suddenly, it had become far more serious. If the Paccosh weren't willing to transport him off this planet, he could be stuck here forever.

Or, more likely, would be stuck here until the next Grysk warship came to destroy the Paccosh and take back their mines. He had no idea what Jixtus's timetable was, but that invasion could theoretically happen at any time. "But you must also understand that it's vital that I be returned to my concourse as soon as possible."

"I doubt it reaches to the level of being *vital*," Uingali said offhandedly. "The Navigators' Guild will simply have to do without you for a few weeks."

Qilori's winglets tensed. A few *weeks*? "No, no—that's impossible," he protested, trying to sound calm. "I can't be here that long."

"I'm sorry, but we cannot spare a ship to take you home," Uingali said firmly. "If you wish a different answer, you must talk to Senior Captain Thrawn."

"I will," Qilori said, standing up. "Thank you for your time and your words."

He found Thrawn outside at the edge of the mining compound, sitting alone on a rock outcropping at the edge of a patch of thick woods. The Chiss was gazing meditatively at the last sliver of sun still visible over the hills to the west, the failing light starting to fill the valley below them with twilight. An evening breeze whispered gently through the woods a few meters to Thrawn's left, stirring the branches and creating little swirling eddies in the dead leaves on the ground all around them. The Magys was nowhere to be seen, having apparently taken her search for a new navigator elsewhere.

Nor were there any bodyguards in attendance. Apparently, Thrawn wasn't as concerned about predators as Uingali was.

"Senior Captain Thrawn," Qilori greeted the Chiss as he walked up behind him. "It's Qilori of Uandualon."

"I know," Thrawn said, not turning. "I heard your footsteps as you approached."

Qilori hadn't realized his steps could even be heard over the breeze and evening noises. "I urgently need to speak with you," he said as he came up beside the Chiss. "If now is inconvenient, please set a time when it will be."

"Now is acceptable," Thrawn said. "Before we speak, I must first apologize for the Magys's needlessly unkind words."

"No apology needed," Qilori assured him, his winglets twitching. The Magys and her strange comments could wait. Finding a way off Sunrise was the more critical issue here. "Uingali foar Marocsaa told me—"

"Because you certainly aren't useless," Thrawn continued. "On that we all agree. You're only useless to her attempts to see through time."

"—that he couldn't get me back to—" Qilori broke off as Thrawn's comment suddenly registered. "Excuse me? You said she wants to see through *time*?"

"Yes," Thrawn said. "You see, she's more than simply a political or social leader, as we first believed. Just as you have a connection to what you name the Great Presence, she has a connection to something she calls the Beyond. She is hoping to use those connections and similar ones to see into the future."

Into the future. So *that* was the not-space she wanted him to navigate. "But how can the future be seen? Is it not created by the combined yet separate decisions of trillions of beings?"

"How can a Pathfinder see into the future to know where a hyperspace path will lead to danger and thus change the ship's course to avoid it?" Thrawn countered.

"That's not how we navigate," Qilori told him. "The Great Presence guides us away from such dangers."

"Then how does the Great Presence know?"

"The Great Presence is—the Great Presence," Qilori finished, wincing at how lame that sounded. "We don't know how it functions. Or even, really, what it is."

"As I don't fully understand the thought behind the Magys's quest." Thrawn gave a little shrug. "Still, though the future is indeed uncertain and ever-changing, it may be that certain events are fixed once those making the proper decisions have committed themselves to those paths."

"It would certainly make navigating easier," Qilori commented. "If we could plot out a course even ten or fifteen minutes in advance, it would make for much easier travel."

"I don't think the Magys is concerned with hyperspace travel," Thrawn said, his voice going darker. "Her goals are more focused on the defense of her world."

Qilori's winglets stiffened. He hadn't even thought about how something like that could be applied to warfare.

But the possibilities were instantly clear. If she knew in advance Jixtus's commitment to destroy the Chiss Ascendancy, or the commitment the Grysks would surely make to take back this world, it would give her a huge strategic advantage. "You're speaking of knowing an enemy's overall plans?" he asked.

"Perhaps even the sequence of a particular battle," Thrawn said.

Qilori's winglets twitched. "That seems terrifying."

"Only if you're the aggressor facing such foreknowledge," Thrawn said. "The Magys would use it solely to defend her people." He paused. "Though others, of course, have been hoping from the start that they could utilize it for conquest."

"Others?" Qilori asked carefully. "What others?"

"Let us follow the history," Thrawn said. "First, General Yiv brought his Nikardun forces against the star nations in this part of the Chaos, seeking to conquer or otherwise subdue them. At some point, while nearly all attention was on him, Sunrise was destroyed by a civil war orchestrated from the outside by creatures called the Agbui."

"I don't think I've ever heard of them," Qilori murmured.

"I believe they and the Nikardun are both client species of your employer Jixtus," Thrawn said. "Having pushed the people here on Sunrise into destroying their civilization, the Agbui tried to do the same to the Chiss Ascendancy. But we were able to see through their intrigues and turn back their influence."

He gestured in the direction of the recently liberated mines. "But the true genius was the successful attempt to make us believe Sunrise's nyix mines were the ultimate goal of their destruction. Certainly the metal is valuable, but the true prize was the Magys and her ability to touch the Beyond."

"The *Magys* was the prize?" Qilori asked, trying to make sense out of the whole thing. "I'm not following you."

"It's not difficult to understand," Thrawn said. "Those who perpetrated the deception hoped that combining the Magys's abilities with those of a navigator might expand the navigator's view of the near future and permit them to thus use the combination in warfare."

"I see," Qilori said, his winglets rippling slowly as the tangled plan slowly started to make sense. "Only they didn't expect the Magys to escape Sunrise's civil war and travel to Rapacc."

"Exactly," Thrawn said, sounding pleased that Qilori was finally up to speed. "Or else they didn't recognize her value until after the refugee ships were already gone. Once they did, they faced a dilemma. The only military forces close enough for a quick reaction were the Nikardun, so they were the ones sent to hunt down the refugees. But Yiv was only a tool, and his masters didn't want him to know the true nature of the person they were seeking. Thus when the Nikardun forces found Rapacc, they merely blockaded the system and awaited further orders instead of invading and capturing her."

"I see," Qilori said again. There was more complexity woven into Jixtus's plan than he'd ever realized. "So after Yiv was defeated, Jixtus sent the Kiljis to Rapacc to get her?"

"Yes," Thrawn said, giving Qilori a small smile. "Only they, like the Nikardun before them, would have failed . . . because from the time of the *Springhawk*'s first visit to Sunrise until the time your Kilji warships arrived at Rapacc a few days ago, the Magys has been with me."

Qilori's winglets went rigid. "With *you*?"

"Indeed," Thrawn said, and there was no mistaking the satisfaction in his voice. "Earlier today the mine workers told the Magys that their enslavers repeatedly conducted large-scale searches of the planet hunting for her." He waved a hand out across the valley. "The true irony is that the search was not only futile but unnecessary."

"What do you mean?"

"The Magys isn't the only one of her people who can touch the Beyond," Thrawn said. "There are others among them who could rise to her same position and ability if necessary."

"Amazing," Qilori said. "So all the Grysks needed to do was look for others with the Magys's ability instead of hunting for her specifically?"

"The Grysks?" Thrawn turned a puzzled look on him. "The Grysks aren't the ones behind this scheme, Qilori. It's being controlled by Generalirius Nakirre and the Kiljis."

Qilori's winglets went rigid. "*What?*"

"Jixtus may *think* he's running the operation," Thrawn said. "He may even be giving the orders. But those orders aren't ultimately coming from him."

"That wasn't what I heard aboard the *Anvil*," Qilori objected, forcing his winglets to slow down. "General Crofyp always said that he was acting under Grysk command."

"Really," Thrawn said sounding amused. "He said this in your presence, did he? Knowing full well your relationship to Jixtus, and that you would report everything to him?"

Qilori looked over his shoulder at the mining compound, his winglets slowing with the sheer strain of trying to follow this zigzag of revelations. Jixtus had always seemed to be in complete control. Had that been a lie? Had Crofyp actually been telling the truth back at Rapacc?

Worse, had it been a lie that Jixtus himself truly believed?

"Why do you think the crew of Kilji ships are called vassals?" Thrawn continued, his voice now gone quiet. "Why do you think the controls are so simple and so well laid out that Paccian commandos could quickly learn how to fire the ship's weapons? The Kiljis aren't concerned about quality or expertise, but only in those whom they can successfully control."

"They call themselves the enlightened," Qilori murmured.

"And they say their vassals are likewise," Thrawn said. "No, Qilori of Uandualon. Jixtus is also of the enlightened. But unlike the Kilji vassals, he doesn't know it."

For a moment the only sounds were those of the forest and breeze. Qilori gazed across the valley, watching the darkness creep across the landscape.

Enlightenment. The Kiljis had talked about that a lot during the time he'd been aboard the *Anvil*. They'd boasted about how superior their path was, and about how one day they would bring that path to everyone in the Chaos.

But surely Jixtus wouldn't have fallen for their schemes or their enlightenment. Would he?

He frowned as something caught his eye. Halfway down the valley, in the center of a cluster of what looked like dull-roofed prefabricated huts, something was glinting in the last ray of sunlight where it peeked through a gap in the western hills. Three somethings, actually, their faint shimmer reaching upward from the cluster.

A worship hall spire? A stray tendril of silk from some horrify-ingly huge local spider?

A three-lobe hyperspace transmitter antenna?

"At any rate, it's time for me to retire for the night," Thrawn said, sliding off the outcropping and giving a small stretch. His right hand brushed the belted weapon at his side, as if reassuring himself it was still there as he sent one final gaze around the area. "I suggest you don't stay out much longer," he added. "As Uingali warned, there may be predators that roam the darkness. I'll speak with you again in the morning."

With a final nod, he walked past Qilori and headed off toward the buildings where the Paccosh had set up their headquarters and their barracks. Qilori watched until he was out of sight, then turned back to the valley. The brief triple glint had vanished, and the twilight was fading rapidly, but it was still light enough for him to see that there was a path leading down from the mining compound in the general direction of the huts.

He stepped to the edge of the trees to try for a better look. If that was in fact a hyperspace transmitter, and if he could get to it, he might be able to send Jixtus a message. Too late tonight, of course, but maybe in the morning. There was a faint crunch of dried leaves from somewhere behind him—

And without warning his arm was caught in a solid, metallic grip. Even as he opened his mouth to shriek a second hand locked itself across his mouth and winglets, stifling the scream into a muffled gasp. A second later he was dragged through a gap in the outer line of trees into the forest.

"Be silent," a voice muttered in his ear. "Be silent, and live."

There was no way to verbally agree to the order with his mouth covered, but Qilori managed a microscopic nod of acceptance. In the failing light a second person moved into view in front of him.

Qilori felt himself wilt with relief. He'd feared his assailants were Paccosh or some kind of local militia. Instead, they were a pair of armored Grysks who had somehow escaped the Paccian slaughter. The one holding him must have felt the loosening of his arm muscles as his panic faded and cautiously released his dual grips. "I am Qilori of Uandualon," Qilori identified himself, keeping his voice low.

"We know who you are," the Grysk in front of him said.

"Good," Qilori said. "Tell me, how did you escape from today's battles?"

"We escaped because we were never in them," the Grysk said. "Our task was to stay away from the mines and the savages working them at all times. We would thus remain uncounted among our forces and free to maintain surveillance if such proved necessary."

"As it now has," the Grysk behind Qilori added. "You must take a message to Jixtus."

"Yes, I would be happy to do so," Qilori assured him. "That group of huts down the valley—did I see a tri-lobe transmitter in their midst?"

"You will *take* a message to Jixtus," the Grysk repeated more harshly. "Not *send. Take.*"

"All right," Qilori said hastily. "What is the message?"

From the direction of the encampment came the sound of approaching footsteps and muttering voices. "You will tell Jixtus that we stand ready," the first Grysk said. "He need only speak the word, and we will sow chaos and reap death among his enemies. We will bring him the one—"

"Who goes?" a Paccian voice demanded.

Instantly, the two Grysks melted back into the trees. "It is I, Qilori of Uandualon," Qilori called carefully.

"Approach."

Qilori stumbled out of his partial concealment to find himself facing three armed Paccosh. "I am here."

"So we see," one of the Paccosh said. "It grows late. You will return to the barracks."

"Of course," Qilori said. Walking gingerly past them, he headed for the encampment.

Qilori had been assigned a bed out of the twenty or so that had been laid out in one of the larger buildings. About half of the other beds were already occupied, he noted as he made his way through the dimness to his cot and began to undress.

Today's combat had been stressful enough. Tomorrow's efforts to come up with a plan of escaping the death trap that was Sunrise would be even more so.

He'd settled down and drifted toward sleep when he was abruptly shaken awake. "Qilori," a whispered voice came. "*Qilori.*"

Qilori opened his eyes. Thrawn was leaning over him, a warning finger to his lips. "What is it?" Qilori whispered back, his winglets vibrating with surprise and tension.

"Get up and get dressed," Thrawn said. "We're leaving."

Qilori's still foggy mind snapped to full alertness. "We're *leaving*? Where are we going?"

"To Csilla," Thrawn said. "*I'm* going to Csilla, at any rate. You'll be dropped off at Schesa, just inside the Ascendancy. Enough freighter traffic passes through the system that you should be able to pick up a job. If not, you can use the triad transmitter there to call back to your concourse and ask your dispatcher to arrange a pickup."

"Yes, that will work," Qilori agreed, wincing a little as he sat up and started pulling on his clothing. "May I ask why this sudden rush?"

"I need to obtain some specialized equipment," Thrawn told him. "We've just located someone who may have the same abilities as the Magys."

Qilori felt his winglets freeze. "You're going to replace her?"

"Ideally, we're going to supplement her," Thrawn said. "But we won't know for certain until we can run some tests."

"I see," Qilori said. And if it worked, then this newcomer and the Magys would be able to see battles before they actually happened?

A shiver ran through his winglets. More than ever now, it was vital that he make contact with Jixtus. Fortunately, Schesa and its triad transmitter would be perfect for that task. "How soon do we leave?" he asked.

"As soon as you're ready," Thrawn said. "I trust that will be acceptable?"

"It will," Qilori assured him. "Very much so."

MEMORIES X

Patriarch Lamiov stood beside the conference room table, gazing down at the crate Lappincyk had set there, shaking his head in a gesture of relief. "Against all odds," he murmured, running his hand gently over the box. "Against all hopes." He looked up and gave Thrass and Thrawn a wry smile. "Against even all my expectations. You did it."

"Hardly alone," Thrass pointed out. "It was Senior Aide Lappincyk who found the key to defusing the situation."

"But you were the ones who led Roscu to the door where that key could be used," Lappincyk reminded him.

"I recognize it was a team effort," Lamiov said. "I also recognize that the Stybla are in debt to the Mitth, as I personally am in debt to you. If there is anything I can ever do for you, you have only to ask."

"There is one thing," Thrawn spoke up. "Tell us what's in that box."

Lamiov smiled again. "I believe I mentioned once that that's a secret."

"I know," Thrass said. "But the question is no longer whether it's a secret. The proper question is whether it should remain one. I'm a warrior, Patriarch. The more I know about the weaponry available to me, the better I can defend the Ascendancy and its people."

"You're letting your imagination run away with you," Lamiov said, still smiling. "Whoever said it was a weapon?"

Thrawn nodded toward Lappincyk. "Senior Aide Lappincyk."

Lamiov looked at his aide, his smile slipping a bit. "Excuse me?"

"Not in words, of course," Thrawn said. "But in actions and responses. The first indication was actually before our departure. Your own comment *he knows* suggested a fear that the Clarr Patriarch knew something he shouldn't. That was followed by Senior Aide Lappincyk's violent reaction when he learned the hijacked transport might be captured and plundered by the Paataatus."

He gestured toward the box. "There's nothing I can think of that would fit inside that crate and cause such fear except a weapon."

"An *alien* weapon," Thrass added, a small fact connecting in the back of his mind. "The Universal Analysis Group center on Sposia. That's under Stybla control, is it not?"

"I believe that's enough speculation for one day," Lamiov said, standing up. "Once again, I thank you for your assistance—"

"No," Lappincyk spoke up softly.

Lamiov looked down at him, his eyes hardening. "Excuse me?"

"It's no use, Your Venerante," Lappincyk said. His tone was respectful, but firm. "They already know too much. If we let them go now, they'll just continue to poke and investigate until they uncover the truth." He looked at the two Mitth. "And in the process, they may shake loose the stones of the wall we've worked so hard to build."

For a long moment the two Stybla stared at each other. Beside Thrass, Thrawn shifted in his seat, clearly preparing to speak. Thrass got there first, touching his arm warningly. Thrawn hesitated, then settled back again in his chair, leaving unspoken whatever he'd been about to say.

There were times for persuasion, Thrass knew. There were times for arguments, promises, and even threats. Here and now, though, was the time for silence.

He counted twenty heartbeats before Lamiov finally stirred and turned reluctantly back to the two Mitth. "You understand," he said, "that what I'm about to tell you is a secret of the highest order. A secret that could bring ruin to the Stybla and Mitth families, perhaps even lead to the destruction of the Chiss Ascendancy. Are you prepared to embrace this secret to your graves and beyond?"

Thrass felt a prickling on his skin. *Embrace this secret to your graves and beyond.* Those were the words of the most stringent and binding oaths in the Mitth repertoire. "I am," he said.

"As am I," Thrawn said.

"Very well." Reluctantly, Thrass thought, Lamiov sat back down. "Five thousand years ago, under the leadership of the Stybla, the Chiss entered a period of exploration, traveling outward into the Chaos and even into Lesser Space. We dealt with many alien races, and obtained a number of unknown artifacts. Those artifacts, as you're aware, have been hidden away in the UAG center for observation and study."

He seemed to brace himself. "Let me tell you about the one called Starflash.

"We no longer remember who obtained the item and brought it back to the Ascendancy. But they brought with it a report of what it did, how it worked, and the terrible consequences of its use. The Stybla built the Bastion, the forerunner to the UAG, and hid it away, never to be used.

"But then, centuries later, came an invasion by a merciless enemy. Our outer worlds were overrun and the Defense Force pushed back, until only Csilla remained unconquered. The enemy gathered all its ships and armies, preparing for what is now known as the Final Assault on Csilla. We knew there was no way we could stand against them, and we knew that if we lost the Chiss faced extinction.

"And then, the Stybla Patriarch remembered Starflash."

He stopped, and for a moment the room was utterly quiet. Lamiov gazed off into the distance, his eyes holding a hint of that long-past horror. Thrass waited in the stillness, keeping watch on Thrawn out of the corner of his eye, ready to make another move if the other began to speak. But this time, at least, Thrawn recognized it was a time for silence.

"We'd never seen Starflash in operation," Lamiov resumed the story. "Indeed, its very design made it a single-use weapon. But we knew how to operate it. The problem was that it would take twenty warriors to activate it . . . and for those twenty it would be a suicide mission." His eyes focused on Thrawn and Thrass. "The Mitth volunteered."

"The Tragic Patriarch," Thrawn murmured with the air of someone finally understanding a long-elusive mystery. "Her four sons, the ones who died in battle. They were part of the Starflash team, weren't they?"

Lamiov nodded. "All four volunteered, insisting that they face the same dangers and sacrifices as the rest of the Mitth."

"What exactly did the weapon do?" Thrass asked.

"Starflash is an energy weapon," Lamiov said, "but something entirely different from spectrum lasers or plasma spheres. It sends a massive burst of tachyonic and lightspeed energy into the surface of the sun, which then triggers a return burst many thousands of times more powerful."

A shiver ran up Thrass's back. "A return burst, as in back at the Starflash itself?"

"Yes," Lamiov said softly. "As I said. A suicide mission."

"So I gather the plan was to load the weapon into a heavily armored ship and send it into the center of the waiting fleet," Thrawn said, his voice almost calm. Small wonder, Thrass thought—for him, this wasn't so much a heartbreaking chapter in Chiss history as it was a military problem. "They waited until the enemy had gathered as closely as possible, then triggered it."

"Yes," Lamiov said. "Afterward, once the Ascendancy had freed the outer worlds from the minor garrisons the enemy had left behind, the Patriarchs unanimously decided to keep the details locked away in secrecy, never to be revealed to the Syndicure or the general public. The truth of the Final Assault was known only to the Patriarchs of the Ruling Families and their senior aides, the latter group tasked with passing the secret on to each successive Patriarch."

He paused, a whisper of fresh pain crossing his face. "What we *hadn't* anticipated, and what the Starflash records hadn't described, was the effect on Csilla's sun. Apparently, the brief disruption of its surface layers extended deeper than expected into its core. Over the next few decades it began to cool, ultimately forcing Csilla's citizens to either move underground or abandon it entirely." He gave Thrass a small, tired smile. "And no, we don't know if it will ever recover. My personal feeling is that it won't."

"At any rate, the Aristocra were impressed by the courage and sacrifice of the Mitth," Lappincyk said. "It was the impetus for bringing them into the ranks of the Ruling Families. It's also the reason your family emblem is that of a blazing sun, though of course the true significance of that has been buried beneath the ice of time."

Thrass winced. "Ironic, given that the sun actually blazed *less* afterward."

"True," Lamiov said heavily. "But of course no one could have anticipated that. Even if they had, the choice was between using Starflash or facing annihilation. I doubt the Patriarchs would have chosen otherwise." He waved a hand as if trying to wipe away the memories. "But you can see why it was also decided that this part of our history should never become public knowledge."

He raised his eyebrows. "Needless to say, as per your oaths, you'll likewise keep it to yourselves."

"To our graves, and beyond," Thrass assured him. "So what exactly is in the box?"

"We salvaged what we could of Starflash after the destruction," Lamiov said. "The Defense Hierarchy Council has occasionally asked to study one or more of the pieces as part of their effort to duplicate or adapt the device to other uses. Efforts that have never borne fruit, I may mention."

"The box contains a section of one of the tachyon flow synchrotron accelerators," Lappincyk added. "The Council thought it might be adapted to a new particle beam weapon they're working on."

"Under the circumstances, I'd have thought you'd have asked them to examine it on Sposia," Thrass said. "There it would at least have still been under UAG security."

"Normally, we would have," Lamiov said with a wry smile. "In this case, the Council balked at taking their prototype out of *their* research security."

"May we see it?" Thrawn asked.

Again, Lamiov and Lappincyk exchanged looks. This time, the silent debate was shorter. "If you wish," Lamiov said. He gestured to Lappincyk, who produced a foldknife and began slicing into the seals. "Though I'll warn you there's nothing much to see."

They sat in silence until Lappincyk had finished opening the box and pulling out the top section of customized molded padding. "Please," he invited, gesturing at the contents.

Thrawn stepped around the table and over to the box.

He craned his neck, peering at the object inside. "Syndic?" Lamiov added to Thrass.

"That's all right," Thrass said, waving away the offer. "I trust that it's what you say."

"Then your trust is misplaced," Thrawn said his voice suddenly dark. He straightened up, his gaze steady on Lamiov. "This isn't a piece of the Starflash weapon."

"What makes you say that?" Lamiov asked evenly.

"The cylinder surface is pitted, and the edges are ragged as if it had been part of something torn apart by violence," Thrawn said. "But the casing connectors show no sign of the degradation that would have occurred had it been hit by a massive particle flux."

"Where would you have seen an instance of such effects?" Lappincyk asked.

"You saw one yourself," Thrawn countered. "The ions in a plasma sphere impact are well known to cause similar degradation."

"And your conclusion?" Lamiov asked, his voice still calm.

For a long moment Thrawn locked eyes with him. Then, abruptly, he stiffened. "The Stybla didn't have just one Starflash weapon," he said. "You had a second."

He threw a hooded look at Thrass, then returned his gaze to Lamiov. "You *have* a second."

"Indeed," Lamiov said, his own voice now as grim as Thrawn's. "And therein lies the true hope and threat to the Ascendancy. You see now why we were so desperate to retrieve the waylaid accelerator section. Not only could the Paataatus conceivably gain an understanding of the underlying technology, but our reserve Starflash would be useless without it."

"Does the Council know about this second weapon?" Thrawn asked.

"The second item," Lamiov corrected. "We refer to it only as *the item*."

"Where did it come from?" Thrass asked. "Did you create it?"

"No," Lamiov said, shaking his head. "The technology remains far beyond our capabilities. Like the first item, it was obtained from somewhere in Lesser Space, though this one has been in our possession for only a few hundred years. The details have been either lost or deliberately suppressed, but it's said the Stybla learned of its existence and sent a team to locate and capture it."

"Who else knows about it?" Thrawn asked.

"Those of us in this room, plus General Ba'kif and Admiral Ja'fosk," Lamiov said. "No one else. Not even the techs studying the device know what it is."

"So there are six of us," Thrass said.

"Yes," Lamiov confirmed. "Six of us, holding together the future of the Ascendancy."

"What will you do with it?" Thrawn asked.

"You mean now?" Lamiov gave a little shrug. "We'll continue as we have. We'll guard it, study it, try to learn from it, and hold it against the desperate day when its horrible devastation may once again be needed." He blinked, and Thrass noticed with surprise that the Patriarch's eyes were wet with tears. "And if that day comes," he said, almost too softly to hear, "perhaps there will then be *two* Chiss Patriarchs who will be known to the future as the Tragic."

"Perhaps," Thrass said, and Thrass saw a muscle in his cheek give a small twitch. "If that's all, Patriarch, the *Springhawk*'s departure has already been delayed longer than the Council is probably comfortable with. If you can call a shuttle, or allow Syndic Thrass to do so—"

"Actually, Mid Commander, I'm afraid the Council and *Springhawk* will have to wait a bit longer," Lamiov said, holding up a warning hand as Thrass started to stand up. "The Stybla Patriels are gathering for a short ceremony that will be taking place in three hours."

Thrawn shot a frown at Thrass. "A ceremony that concerns the *Springhawk*?"

"A ceremony that concerns *you*." Lamiov paused, as if gathering his thoughts or words. "In the two days since Senior Aide Lappincyk sent his message reporting on the success of your mission—and speaking particularly of your pivotal role in retrieving the wayward section of the item—I've had several conversations with the Patriels and other top-ranking Stybla officials. While I obviously couldn't express the full nature of your success, I could and did emphasize to them the incredible importance of your act. As a result of those conversations—"

He paused again, and to Thrass's surprise he seemed to draw himself up a little taller. "I wish to offer you an honor that has seldom been given to Stybla, and even more infrequently to members of other families. Your name, Mitth'raw'nuru, will henceforth carry the additional appellation *odo*. In Tybroic, the original language of our family, it was the word-mark of a guardian or protector who had proved worthy of the most extraordinary respect."

Thrawn darted another quick look at Thrass. "I'm honored, Patriarch Lamiov," he said, a bit uncertainly. Wondering, Thrass suspected, whether this was truly a reward for reclaiming the Starflash, or whether it was to be a perpetual reminder of his commitment to keeping the secret. "I respectfully wonder if the Mitth leadership will be bothered by such a name change."

"You're welcome to ask Patriarch Thooraki about that yourself," Lamiov said, smiling. "He's already arrived to attend the ceremony. Now." He lifted his hands, pointing one finger each at Thrawn and Thrass. "Lappincyk will take you to your rooms so that you may dress and look over your parts of the ceremony. Your clothing is already laid out, and the procedures will be on your questises shortly. If there are no further questions, I'll see you in three hours."

CHAPTER SEVENTEEN

Early on in his career, Samakro had discovered that if the timing was just right a dubious report could sometimes fall between the cracks during either the filing, reading, or official attention stages. That extra time could be useful if the officer in question needed to dig up additional data, precedents, or legal loopholes. If the officer was *extremely* lucky, the whole thing might disappear into the record storage facilities without anyone who cared ever even looking at it.

Here, unfortunately, there wasn't a chance in hell of any of that happening.

"Of course he's angry," Samakro growled as he stood just inside the *Springhawk*'s sky-walker suite, impatience digging at him as he watched Thalias and Che'ri frantically throwing together the travel bags Ba'kif had ordered them to bring. "His neck was already stuck out all the way to the Plikh homestead with the whole Magys thing. Now we come back late, without Senior Captain Thrawn, and with two more battles with alien ships to report? We're lucky he hasn't melted down completely."

"But it's not your fault," Che'ri said, her voice tense and miserable. "I can tell Supreme General Ba'kif that it was me, not you."

"I appreciate that, Che'ri," Samakro said, forcing back some of his own anxieties. Whatever part Che'ri had played in this, she didn't need him throwing more weight on her shoulders. "But I was the commander on the scene, and I gave the orders. That means it's on me. *All* of it is on me," he added, emphasizing the word. "Don't worry—I've been in trouble with the Council before."

"So have we," Thalias said, giving Che'ri what was probably the best smile she was able to pull off right now. "It'll be okay."

"Of course it will," Samakro said, eyeing the tension lines in Thalias's face. She was worried, too, and with a lot more reason than Che'ri. The absolute worst the Council would do to a wayward sky-walker would be to order an early retirement and a transfer to her permanent family. Thalias could be facing anything from loss of family position to full eviction from the Mitth to actual prison time. "I should also point out that making senior officers wait won't exactly endear us to them."

"Ready," Thalias said, snapping her travel bag shut and sealing it. "Let me just grab those last things, Che'ri—we can pack them in during the shuttle ride."

There were three warriors waiting at the shuttle landing site, more than the one that would indicate a simple courtesy guide, but less than the eight that would normally be deployed for an honored Aristocra or a dangerous prisoner. They gave Samakro the restrained and perfunctory greetings typical of warriors who wanted to keep themselves as uninvolved as possible, and the group piled into a twelve-person tube car and were whisked to Defense Force HQ.

Samakro had guessed there would be two other officers besides Ba'kif waiting for them in the hearing room. There were, in fact, four others plus the supreme general.

Not a good sign. But at least no one from the Syndicure had talked their way into the inquiry.

"Thank you for your promptness, Mid Captain," Ba'kif said after the usual introductions and official greetings had been made. "Please take a seat at the table." His eyes shifted to Thalias and Che'ri, standing a little to Samakro's side. "Thank you for coming as well, Sky-walker; Caregiver," he continued. "Please wait in the lounge area where you first entered this corridor until we're ready for you. One of the warriors will show you the way."

"Yes, sir," Thalias said, and out of the corner of his eye Samakro saw her take hold of Che'ri's arm and turn them both toward the door. One of their escort warriors opened it and gestured them through, then followed, closing the door behind him.

"And now, Mid Captain," Ba'kif said as Samakro eased himself into the witness chair, "let's start with Senior Captain Thrawn's decision to put an alien into hibernation aboard the *Springhawk*."

For once, Thalias thought glumly as the second hour ticked over into the third, the waiting itself wasn't the hardest part. Here, it was the uncertainty of what was happening down the hallway and what was going to be done to Mid Captain Samakro that weighed most heavily on her heart and soul.

That, plus the knowledge that whatever happened to him, it was ultimately her fault. Hers, and Che'ri's.

The most frustrating aspect was the knowledge that everything that had happened—everything she, Che'ri, Samakro, and Thrawn had done—had worked. Every bit of it. The Magys's presence aboard the *Springhawk* had helped undercut and then defeat the Agbui's attempts to precipitate a civil war; Rapacc and the Paccosh had been saved from the Kilji attack; and Thrawn and the Paccosh had driven away yet another attempt to enslave or kill more of Sunrise's people. What more could Ba'kif and the Council want?

She let out a silent sigh. They wanted order, of course. Order, and obedience to protocols that had guided the Ascendancy for centuries. They wanted the Chiss to be detached from the Chaos and everyone in it. They wanted to not care if the people out there suffered or died when the Ascendancy could have helped them.

Those people were, after all, just aliens.

Beside her, Che'ri stirred and looked at the door leading to the corridor. Thalias looked, too, tensing.

But it wasn't Samakro who appeared, merely a young officer striding briskly along on some Council business. Out of the corner of her eye Thalias saw Che'ri wilt a little and return to staring at the floor. "You might as well relax," Thalias advised her. "Sometimes Third

Sight just gives you the general knowledge that someone's coming but not the specifics of who it is."

"It used to," Che'ri said, her voice quiet and gloomy. "I used to be able to see everything."

"Yes, I remember," Thalias said, thinking back to her own days as a sky-walker. "But there's a difference between distinguishing a star from a planet or large asteroid."

"That's not what I meant," Che'ri said. "I was talking about when the Magys was . . . you know. The nightmares."

Thalias eyed her closely. Up to now Che'ri had avoided offering any details of those dreams. "What exactly did you see?"

"I saw attacks," the girl said, her voice shaking with remembered pain. "People getting hurt. People getting . . ." She trailed off.

"Getting killed?" Thalias asked gently.

"Yes," Che'ri said. "Or no. It was confusing."

"That's what war is like," Thalias reminded her. "Some people die, others don't."

"No," Che'ri said, shaking her head. "I meant some of the people were getting killed but they weren't dying."

Thalias frowned. "I don't understand."

"I don't, either," Che'ri admitted. "It was like they were there, but not . . . you know?"

"Alive?" Thalias asked. A sudden thought struck her—"Or do you mean they were alive, but not in their bodies?"

"I don't know," Che'ri said. "Maybe."

"I see," Thalias said, a shiver running through her. *So we will therefore die, and touch the Beyond,* the Magys had said when speaking of her willingness to let her fellow refugees die. *And through the Beyond bring healing to our world.*

"Then later it was even . . . I don't know. Clearer," Che'ri said. "I could see the Guardian in danger from those ships, and knew we had to go save him—"

"Wait a minute," Thalias interrupted, frowning again. "I don't understand. The *Springhawk* and Senior Captain Thrawn wouldn't even have been at Sunrise without you taking us to Rapacc. How could he have been in danger?"

"Not Sunrise," Che'ri said. "Before that, like you said. At the Guardian's planet, Rapacc."

"The Guardian's—?" Thalias broke off. "Che'ri, who exactly is the Guardian you and the Magys talk about?"

"I told you already," Che'ri said, sounding puzzled. "Uingali."

"Oh," Thalias managed, feeling both embarrassed and stupid. When Che'ri first talked about the Guardian, she'd naturally assumed it was Thrawn. "No, I don't think you'd mentioned that before. That's okay, I'm with you now. So you saw Uingali in danger, so you drove the *Springhawk* to Rapacc. Did you then also see the ships at Sunrise and know Senior Captain Thrawn would need our help?"

"Yes," Che'ri said, starting to sound a little frustrated. "Well, no, *I* didn't see it. The Magys saw it. Through me. Somehow."

"It's okay," Thalias soothed, patting her knee. "I know some things are really hard to put into words."

"It's not just that," Che'ri said. "It's that . . . I'm scared, Thalias. The Magys wants me to keep doing it, and I'm . . . scared."

"It's okay," Thalias said again. "Don't worry, we won't make you do anything you don't want to."

"But she says I need to," Che'ri said. "She says the only way we can win battles is if we work together to—" She broke off, turning her head again to look at the door. Thalias followed her gaze, expecting another false alarm.

But this time it wasn't. The door opened and Mid Captain Samakro stepped into view, followed by the other two warriors who'd brought them from the shuttle. Samakro spotted her and Che'ri and headed over, the warriors staying close but making no effort to stop him.

Thalias took a deep breath. And now, it was her and Che'ri's turn.

"You two look bored out of your minds," Samakro commented as he arrived, giving them a smile that was probably supposed to look casual.

"Oh, no, it's really quite exciting out here," Thalias assured him, trying for the same casual attitude and missing just as badly.

"Is it over?" Che'ri asked anxiously.

"Not even close," Samakro said. "They still need to interview some of the other officers and review the ship's records. But my part is done, at least for today."

He gestured at Thalias. "So is yours. Supreme General Ba'kif has decided to postpone their conversations with you until after they've talked to everyone else."

"I see," Thalias said, trying to decide whether being at the end of the line was good or bad. "So Che'ri and I can go back to the ship?"

"You can if you want," Samakro said. "Or you could stay here on Csilla. You've already got your bags packed—I'd hate to see all that effort go to waste."

"What would we do?" Che'ri asked.

"Anything you wanted," Samakro said, his smile looking more genuine this time. "There's a lot to see and do on Csilla, you know. The lieutenant at the reception desk will give you a credit chit good at any hotel, restaurant, or entertainment center anywhere on the planet, for as long as you need it."

"Sounds like fun," Che'ri said with a complete lack of enthusiasm. Still worried about Thrawn, Thalias suspected, or about the Magys and the dreams. Unfortunately, there was nothing Thalias could do about that.

Or maybe there was. "Do we have to stay here?" she asked.

"You mean in Csaplar?"

"No, I mean on Csilla," Thalias said. "Could we go somewhere else?"

"Well, *Che'ri* can't," Samakro said. "She has to stay on or near the ship."

"What about me?" Thalias asked. "Could *I* go?"

"You want to go somewhere without me?" Che'ri asked, frowning at her.

"It would only be for a few days," Thalias assured her. "I need to visit someone on Ool."

"I don't think that's allowed," Samakro said. "You're Che'ri's caregiver. You're supposed to stay with her at all times."

"I know," Thalias said. "But—"

"Who do you want to visit?" Che'ri interrupted.

"It's a woman who was mentioned on that data cylinder we got on Naporar," Thalias said, choosing her words carefully. She'd mentioned her brief encounter with Senior Aide Thivik to Thrawn, but only because the warriors waiting at the *Springhawk*'s shuttle had seen him and would probably report it. But she'd kept the existence of Syndic Thrass's data cylinder totally secret. "There are some questions I need to ask her."

"Well, it doesn't matter," Samakro said firmly. "You can't leave Che'ri."

"I don't mind," Che'ri said, her eyes steady on Thalias. "I'm old enough to be alone for a few days."

"And it's not like she would be *alone* anyway," Thalias added, trying to read Che'ri's face. She clearly recognized that this was important, though there was no way she could know its full gravity. But she was also clearly willing to trust Thalias. "She'd have a whole ship full of people around her."

"That's not the point," Samakro insisted.

"She left me alone before once, when she and Senior Captain Thrawn went to the asteroid base at Rapacc," Che'ri reminded him. "I did okay then."

"Yes, but you had Ab'begh and her caregiver to look after you," Samakro countered. "And as I recall, Admiral Ar'alani looked in on you occasionally, too."

"*You* could look in on me," Che'ri said. "And Mid Commander Dalvu said she would play Gribblehex with me whenever I wanted."

"There's plenty of prepared food, and Che'ri knows how to use the cooker," Thalias added. "Or you could maybe bring in a temp caregiver."

"No," Che'ri said flatly. "I don't need one."

"And I don't want one," Samakro agreed. "There are enough strangers running around the *Springhawk* as it is."

"Then just let me stay alone," Che'ri persisted. "I'll be all right." She looked at Thalias. "I'll even promise to do my lessons."

For a minute Samakro looked back and forth between them, his forehead wrinkled in thought. Letting Thalias abandon her sky-walker for more than a few hours at a time was probably a violation of protocol, and he and the *Springhawk* didn't need any more trouble than they already had. But he'd clearly figured out that this wasn't just some whim on Thalias's part.

His shifting gaze steadied on Thalias. "What is this about?" he asked.

"It concerns Che'ri and her recent dreams," Thalias said carefully, mindful of the two warriors standing within earshot.

Samakro's lips compressed briefly. "All right. There are emergency circumstances under which I can circumvent normal protocols. I suppose I can invoke one of them."

"Thank you, Mid Captain," Thalias said. "Che'ri?"

"I'll be fine," Che'ri again assured her. "Besides, I've been wishing I had someone else to play Gribblehex with. No offense, but you're terrible."

"So I've been told," Thalias said drily, feeling a sense of relief. "Just don't go easy on Mid Commander Dalvu."

"Because she certainly won't go easy on *you*," Samakro warned. "She's one of the most competitive gamers I've ever seen. All right. It's a day and a half each way to Ool, and Supreme General Ba'kif wants you available in one week. That gives you four days, maximum."

"That'll be enough," Thalias said, nodding. "Thank you, Mid Captain."

"You're welcome." He leveled a finger at her. "This just better not be a social call."

"It isn't," Thalias promised.

"All right," Samakro said. "Go see the receptionist, and make sure she gives you a chit that's good on Ool, too, and not just on Csilla."

"I will." Reaching over, Thalias gave Che'ri a quick but firm hug. "Thanks for being brave, Che'ri," she murmured. "I'll be back before you know it."

"I know," Che'ri murmured back, her voice muffled by Thalias's shoulder. "Be careful."

"I will." Giving the girl one last squeeze, she let go and stepped back. "Go with Mid Captain Samakro now."

"Okay," Che'ri said. "See you soon."

Samakro nodded a silent farewell to Thalias, then headed down the corridor toward the exit, Che'ri beside him with the two guards trailing a watchful step behind them. Che'ri sent a single lingering look at Thalias, then turned back and started talking inaudibly to Samakro.

Thalias watched them go, a picture flashing through her mind: Che'ri's internal child striving for balance with her internal midager. This time, at least, the midager had won out.

Shaking away the image, she turned and headed toward the receptionist station. Fortunately, ever since she'd first read Syndic Thrass's data cylinder she'd kept it close to her, storing it in her questis's spare cylinder rack.

Just as well. With her about to be away from the ship for several days, it was more important than ever that she not leave it lying around the sky-walker suite where someone might stumble across it. Not until she'd decided exactly what she should do with the information it contained.

The woman on Ool was someone Thalias very much wanted to meet. She could only hope that she would be equally happy to meet Thalias.

"I don't know what you thought you were doing, Captain," Patriarch Rivlex bit out, glaring at Roscu with an intensity she'd rarely seen him use except on rival Patriarchs or minor Aristocra who had annoyed him. "You had exactly two jobs at Ornfra: to catch the Dasklo family in the act of making fake patrol ships at Krolling Sen, and to find and expose the Mitth spy platform. You failed at both."

"It wasn't a spy platform, Your Venerante," Roscu said stiffly. "As my report detailed, it was an enemy weapon."

"Which was conveniently destroyed before it could be examined."

"Which *self-destructed* before it could be examined."

"You're sure that's what happened?" Rivlex asked scornfully. "Were you even there at the time?"

Roscu scowled to herself. No, unfortunately, she hadn't been. The in-system jump Ziinda had sent her on had put her out of the immediate area when all the fireworks took place. By the time she got the *Orisson* turned around and jumped back, the asteroid and freighter had both been reduced to rubble fields. "No, Your Venerante, not personally," she said. "But I have the records that were made of the—"

"Records made by Dasklo warships?" Rivlex asked pointedly.

"*And* by the *Grayshrike*."

Rivlex snorted. "An Expansionary Defense Fleet ship that shouldn't even have *been* at Ornfra, let alone been issuing orders to anyone. More than that, a ship with an Irizi captain and a Csap first officer, neither of whom would be sympathetic to a Clarr problem."

"Family alliances don't matter in the fleet, Your Venerante."

"Family alliances matter *everywhere*," Rivlex shot back. "Just because your protocols say that doesn't mean it's true."

"Deliberately faking a record is grounds for a court-martial," Roscu said stiffly, the memory of Thrawn's own deliberate manipulation poking into her gut like a heated knife. Rivlex was right—just because it was illegal didn't mean it was never done.

And the Csap family *were* allies of the Obbic family, who were in turn allies of the Mitth. Would the *Grayshrike*'s first officer take the risk of falsifying the records to protect the ally of an ally? The way things were going in the Ascendancy right now, it wasn't beyond possibility.

But no. The flaw in Rivlex's theory was that Mid Captain Apros was only the *Grayshrike*'s first officer. His captain, Ziinda, was an Irizi, who were as antagonistic to the Mitth as it was possible to get. Even if family alliances *were* tearing into the Expansionary Defense Fleet, there was no way she would help cover for her family's biggest rivals.

"Unless someone is there to cover it up," Rivlex growled. "With the Mitth, it's Supreme General Ba'kif. With the Clarr, it's no one."

"We don't need anyone to plead our case, Your Venerante," Roscu said with a flicker of family pride. "The Clarr stand on our own."

"Not for long we don't," Rivlex said softly, a faraway look in his eye, a sort of knowing smile twitching at his lips. "Not for long."

Roscu frowned. "Your Venerante?"

"I've made a deal, my dear Captain Roscu," he said, an edge of malice now in his smile. "Let the Dasklo play with their pathetic fraudulent ships. We, the Clarr, now have a family fleet the likes of which the Ascendancy has never known."

"But all within the rules, I assume?" Roscu asked carefully.

"Rules are for children," Rivlex said, making a dismissive slash with his hand. "The Council makes up its own. Why not the Clarr?"

The smile vanished. "But first things first; and first above all is to shame and break the Dasklo. To that end, you and the *Orisson* will go back to Ornfra and get me proof of their deceit."

"Yes, sir," Roscu said, her heart beating harder. The Patriarch's fervor was starting to send chills up her back. "And then?"

"And then, Captain Roscu, the Clarr will take their rightful place in the Ascendancy," Rivlex said softly, "In the Ascendancy, and in the universe."

Raamas was waiting on the bridge when Roscu returned to the *Orisson*. "How did it go, Captain?" he asked, eyeing her closely. "The Patriarch's order sounded . . . rather harsh."

"It was fine," Roscu said, her mind still back on that final scene in Rivlex's office. "You got my order to set course back to Ornfra?"

"Yes, ma'am," Raamas said, pulling out his questis and tapping something. "First, though, this arrived half an hour ago with instructions to pass it on to you."

Roscu frowned at the note that had now appeared on her own questis. There was nothing there but a list of numbers. "Looks like a set of coordinates."

"Yes, they are," Raamas confirmed, tapping his questis again. "It's a spot in the outer system near the Junkyard."

"Is it, now," Roscu said, eyeing the map that had replaced the numbers. "Which part of the Junkyard is this, exactly?"

"It's just spinward of the Gem," Raamas said.

"Mm," Roscu murmured. The so-called Junkyard was a group of metal-rich asteroids in the outer part of the Rhigal system that had been pushed together hundreds of years ago by an Ufsa family mining consortium who thought gathering them closer together would facilitate extraction and refining. Those resources had long since played out, though, and the region had been abandoned.

But rumors still occasionally popped up that new veins had been found by one family or another and that mining was about to begin again. The Gem, once the richest area, now the most mined-out one, usually figured prominently in those rumors. "Where did you get this?"

"That was a little hard to track down," Raamas said. "The transmission was via tight-beam, and the sender clearly wanted to remain anonymous. But from what I've been able to piece together, it looks like it came from someone in the Stybla Patriel's office. Possibly the Patriel himself."

"Really," Roscu said, sifting through the possibilities. The Stybla weren't anyone's allies in particular, but they maintained industrial and transportation operations throughout the Ascendancy. If there was something going on out in the Junkyard, they would be the perfect ones to have tumbled to it.

Which of course then raised the question of why they would pass on such information to the Clarr in general and Roscu in particular. "Well, if the Stybla think it was worth pointing out to us, I suppose the least we can do is take a look," she decided, keying her questis for nav. A direct heading would be simplest, but with the Ascendancy in its current state it might pay to be a little more circumspect. She certainly didn't want anyone else on or orbiting Rhigal to figure out where they'd gone. "Set it up as two in-system jumps," she continued, making a pair of marks on the questis and sending them to the helm.

"First will be out and to the side, more or less in the direction of Orn-fra; the second will take us across and back to the Gem. How does that look, Commander?"

Raamas stepped over to the helm station and leaned over the pilot for a closer look. "It'll put us about fifty kilometers from the Stybla coordinates," he confirmed. "Close enough to see if there's a secret mining operation, far enough to keep from spooking them."

"Good," Roscu agreed. "Might as well also have that Ornfra course ready. A quick look at the Gem, and then we'll be off."

"Yes, Captain," Raamas said, gesturing the order to the pilot as he checked the nav displays. "We're out of the gravity well, ma'am . . . hyperdrive's spinning up . . . ready for the first in-system jump."

"Stand by to jump," Roscu said. "Three, two, *one*."

The planet behind them vanished. Roscu watched as the pilot confirmed their position, made a yaw rotation to bring the *Orisson* into position for the second jump, and calculated the numbers. "Ready with second jump, Captain," Raamas confirmed.

"Stand by," Roscu said. "Full scan as soon as we arrive; passive sensors only. Pilot: Three, two, *one*."

The starscape twitched again, and they were there.

"Combat range clear," the sensor operator reported, leaning a little toward her displays. "Mid-range—" She caught her breath. "*Captain!*"

"I see them," Roscu said, fighting to keep her voice calm as something dark and heavy gripped at her throat. In the distance, sitting right at Raamas's coordinates, were a group of warships.

Large warships. *Alien* warships.

"I'm counting six of them," Raamas confirmed Roscu's own observation, his voice showing the same strain Roscu was feeling. "Could be more—there may be others being blocked from our view."

"Acknowledged," Roscu said as she tore her gaze away from the viewport and looked at the sensor display. Her voice sounded marginally calmer this time. "They look dark."

"Dark *and* cold," Raamas confirmed. "Whatever they're doing here, they've been doing it for at least a couple of days."

"Waiting for someone," Roscu said. "Or some*thing*. Sensors?"

"Rest of mid-range clear, Captain," the sensor officer said. She sounded mostly back on balance, too. "Far range . . . clear. There could be more of them behind some of the other asteroids, though. I can't tell with just passives."

"Well, we're sure as ice not firing up the actives," Roscu told her. "Thoughts, Commander Raamas?"

"We have to call it in, Captain," he said. "This many alien ships, lurking in a Chiss system? And they're definitely warships—that configuration can't be anything else."

"Agreed," Roscu said, her throat tightening a little more as a strange thought occurred to her.

"So do we call it in?" Raamas pressed.

"Not yet," Roscu said. Pulling out her questis, she keyed for the data Ziinda had sent them during their Ornfra confrontation. "Pull up the *Grayshrike*'s records of the asteroid attack at Sunrise. Tell me what you see."

"All right," Raamas said, frowning as he worked his questis. "It's the asteroid . . . it pops open . . . there's the missile . . ."

"No, no, go farther," Roscu said, fast-forwarding through the record. There it was, just as she'd remembered. "Move it to there," she added, keying the mark to him. "The big ship the *Grayshrike* is charging toward. The one that's engaging the *Vigilant*."

"Oh, my—" Raamas broke off, looking up at the sensor display, then down at his questis again. "Captain, it's the same design."

"Yes, it is," Roscu agreed. "They're smaller, but they definitely come from the same shipyards."

"Captain, we *have* to call it in," Raamas insisted. "The homestead—the Patriarch—they're sitting flashflies."

"Are they?" Roscu countered grimly. "I don't think so."

"What do you mean?"

"The Patriarch told me he'd made a deal," Roscu said. "Specifically, he said the Clarr now had a family fleet the likes of which the Ascendancy had never seen." She pointed out the viewport. "I think those are his new ships."

"His new—?" Raamas broke off. "Captain, these are the same sort of ships that attacked the *Vigilant* and *Grayshrike*. Where could the Patriarch have gotten them?"

"From Jixtus, of course," Roscu said. "From the very start, he was offering ships to bolster our own forces."

"But if they're from Jixtus—" Raamas breathed a curse. "Then Senior Captain Ziinda was right. About Jixtus, the asteroid missile—everything."

"So it would appear," Roscu said. "Or maybe it's not that easy. What if there are two factions of the same aliens out there, one led by Jixtus, the other by someone else? What if the someone else attacked Sunrise, while Jixtus is just trying to arm us to fight back against them?"

"That seems a little far-fetched," Raamas said cautiously. "If that's the case, why doesn't he just tell us?"

"I don't know," Roscu conceded. "I assume he has his reasons. But *far-fetched* doesn't mean *impossible*. Until and unless we have evidence to the contrary, we have to obey our Patriarch and assume he has the best interests of the Clarr in mind."

"And assume he knows what he's doing?" Raamas countered.

"Careful, Commander," Roscu admonished. "Comments like that are not only disrespectful but border on the disloyal."

"My apologies, Captain," Raamas said. To Roscu's ears he didn't sound especially apologetic.

"I'll also point out that if those ships came to attack Rhigal, there's no reason for them to still be sitting here," Roscu said. "They could have popped in from hyperspace, blasted the homestead or any other location to slagged rubble, and been gone before anyone could even have sent out an alert. With the Defense Force and Expansionary Defense Fleet ships dispersed all around the Ascendancy, there wouldn't have been a chance of stopping them."

"Yes, ma'am," Raamas said reluctantly. "So we do nothing?"

"Of course we do something," Roscu said. "We slip away and continue on to Ornfra as we've been ordered. Pilot?"

"Yes, ma'am," the pilot said. "Turning onto vector."

The fleet and stars shifted as the *Orisson* made another yaw turn back toward the distant Ornfra system. Raamas hesitated, then stepped away from the helm and crossed the bridge to Roscu's command chair. "There is one other possibility, ma'am," he said, lowering his voice.

"Which is?"

"I'm thinking about the fact that the coordinates for that alien fleet skulking in the Junkyard were given to us by the Stybla Patriarch on Rhigar," Raamas said. "The histories say the Stybla voluntarily handed over their rule to the Three Families. But I've never quite believed that." He gave Roscu a significant look. "And if their power was taken away, they might see the current state of the Ascendancy as their chance to get it back."

"I hope not," Roscu said. "We've got enough trouble with the Dasklo without having to fight the Stybla, too."

"I hope not, too," Raamas said. He nodded toward the viewport, where the alien fleet was just disappearing from sight as the *Orisson* continued its rotation. "But you have to admit that an ambitious member of the Forty that doesn't have a fleet of its own might be tempted by something like that. And if Jixtus offered ships to the Clarr, why not to the Stybla?"

"Good point," Roscu said. "All I can say is what I've already said. We stick with our Patriarch and trust his decisions."

"Captain?" the pilot said. "We're in position, ma'am."

Roscu looked at the nav display. The vector alignment wasn't perfect, but right now neatness was less important than getting out before someone spotted the *Orisson* skulking around. They could return to space-normal and correct the vector anywhere along the way. "Prepare for hyperspace," she said.

"I hope you're right, Captain," Raamas murmured. With a nod, he headed back across the bridge to the helm.

"So do I, Commander," Roscu muttered under her breath as she gazed out at the silent warships. "So do I."

She raised her voice. "Hyperspace: Three, two, *one*."

Generalirius Nakirre had resigned himself to the necessity of having to periodically take the *Whetstone* out of hyperspace so that Jixtus could receive messages and information updates. Accepted it, but never really liked it. The stops slowed their journeys, sometimes for hours on end, and afterward Nakirre often had to endure Jixtus's gleeful cackling as the pieces of his quiet campaign against the Chiss came together.

The delays were even more irritating now that the Kilji Illumine's own fleet, the Kilhorde, had finally received Grysk permission to move against the small nations south and southeast of the Chiss Ascendancy, the ones Jixtus had chosen as being ready for Kilji enlightenment. Some of the influx of messages to the *Whetstone* now came from Nakirre's field commanders, giving details of their victories and mapping out the progress of their campaigns.

And Nakirre, instead of being there to guide and inspire, was stuck traveling the Ascendancy with Jixtus.

It wasn't right. Not for Nakirre, not for his commanders, not for the wretched beings who would soon look up from their battered worlds to the hope that only Kilji enlightenment could provide. Now Nakirre began to eagerly await Jixtus's communication stops, hoping each time to hear that the Ascendancy had exploded into anarchy and that the Grysk fleet was ready to move in as soon as the passions died and the flames of war finally burned themselves out. Then and only then could Nakirre take Jixtus back to his *FateSpinner* flagship and finally be free to join his people in their own march to this glorious new concept of conquest.

The present communication stop, though, wasn't that one.

And Jixtus wasn't doing any cackling.

"You understand, Your Venerante, that this is a potential problem for both of us," Jixtus was saying. "Your fleet must remain secret until the time is right to announce the Clarr family's newly enhanced status among the Nine. If Captain Roscu talks about it to anyone, it could spark resistance among your enemies. Perhaps even panic."

"First of all, I'm as surprised as you are that the *Orisson* was even out in the Junkyard where it could see your ships," Patriel Rivlex's voice came over the *Whetstone*'s bridge speaker. "I accept the word of your commander that it was there, but I can't for the life of me guess why. Captain Roscu's orders didn't include any stops along her way."

"The reason isn't important," Jixtus said. "We just need her not to speak of it until you give her authorization. I presume you can send a message to that effect?"

"Of course," Rivlex said. "Though it may be a couple of days before she gets it. She knows her mission is important, and could easily stay in hyperspace the whole way."

"Clearly, a dedicated officer," Jixtus said. The words were complimentary, but Nakirre could hear the growing frustration in the Grysk's tone. Jixtus had been trying for the entire conversation to get Rivlex to tell him where the *Orisson* was headed, and so far the Patriarch hadn't taken the hint. "Perhaps I could assist in your efforts. As you know, I periodically depart hyperspace to retrieve my own messages. If you care to record something I can broadcast, that would double our chances of contacting her before she arrives at her destination."

"I'm afraid that won't be possible," Rivlex said. "Messages to senior officers and staff are sent via a family code, which I can't allow you to have. Besides, there's no need. I'll simply contact our Patriel on Ornfra with an order for Captain Roscu to contact me when she arrives."

Under the black robe, Jixtus's shoulders visibly relaxed. "That should be sufficient," he said. "Thank you for your time, Your Venerante. I look forward to the day when you announce our new treaty to the Ascendancy."

"As do I," Rivlex said. "Now if you'll excuse me, I'll get that message on its way."

"Of course," Jixtus said. "May your day hold profit and fulfillment."

He motioned to Nakirre. "Cease transmission," Nakirre ordered.

"I obey."

"So," Jixtus said, turning his hidden face to Nakirre. "She returns to Ornfra."

"Yes," Nakirre said. Ornfra, where somehow Roscu and the *Orisson* had evaded the asteroid missile trap. "I trust you'll be able to deal with her before she speaks to anyone?"

"Oh, yes," Jixtus said softly, and once again Nakirre could imagine an evil smile beneath the veil. "She escaped death once at Ornfra. She won't do so again."

CHAPTER EIGHTEEN

Thalias had never been to Ool before. In fact, up until she read Thrass's data cylinder she'd barely even known the planet existed.

During the trip back from Sunrise, though, she'd made it a point to learn as much as she could about the place. Ool had over two billion inhabitants, a rich and diverse agricultural base, several large manufactory groups and thousands of smaller ones, and a fair amount of tourist traffic, especially for its beaches and mountain skiing. It also had extensive mining in some of the mountain spines, including one of the Ascendancy's only three pure nyix mines.

And situated near a small town, wedged between a modest packbull ranch and a spring-fed lake, it had a scholars' retreat that the data cylinder identified as Seekers' Shadehouse.

A place that was totally and ominously absent from all of the guidebooks and location listings she could find.

That part of Ool also turned out to be somewhat difficult for a casual traveler to get to. The nearest interstellar transport landing area was over a thousand kilometers away, the skybus from there to that sector only got her within fifteen kilometers, and the local driver Thalias hired at the depot had never heard of Seekers' Shadehouse. Fortunately, he was willing to fly her to the Ardok Ranch, which was the actual address Thrass had provided.

The ranch house was situated in roughly the center of the fenced land, with the barns, feed storage, and other outbuildings scattered around it. As the skycar made its descent, Thalias caught a glimpse of a small group of buildings nestled alongside a line of trees between the ranch's eastern fence and the lake. That, presumably, was the Shadehouse.

A woman was waiting on the ranch house porch beside the front door as Thalias walked up the steps, the skycar that had brought her already headed back to the bus depot. The rancher was dressed in coveralls, boots, and jacket, with a questis hanging at her side on a shoulder strap. "Afternoon," she said in a cheerful tone. "Welcome to the wilds of Ool. What can I do for you?"

"I think I've come to see you," Thalias said. "My name is Mitth-'ali'astov."

"Nice to meet you," the woman said. Her voice was still friendly, but there was a hint of caution as she looked Thalias up and down. "I'm Cohbo'rik'ardok, co-owner with my husband Bomarmo of the Ardok Ranch. What did you want to see me about?"

"Let me make sure first that I have the right person," Thalias said, aware that she was stalling. She knew perfectly well who Borika was; she was just reluctant to carry the conversation where it had to go. "You're the Cohbo'rik'ardok who used to be Irizi'rik'ardok?"

"Yes," Borika said, her eyes narrowing slightly. "I became part of the Cohbo family when I married Bomarmo." Her lip twitched in a wry smile. "I hope you're not here to help the Mitth make a list of former Irizi. That would be a full-life job."

"Certainly more of my life than I would want to spend on the effort," Thalias assured her. "No, I'm here to talk about a girl I know named Che'ri, and some problems she's been having. Am I also correct that before you were Irizi you were Kivu'rik'ardok?"

Borika's smile faded. "I don't know," she said. "I don't remember much about my early life." She raised her eyebrows slightly. "As I imagine your friend Che'ri doesn't, either."

"No, she doesn't," Thalias said cautiously. "How did you know?"

"Oh, come now," Borika chided gently. "For anyone familiar with the Seekers program, her lack of a family name is a dead giveaway that she's a sky-walker."

"Yes," Thalias murmured. "*Seekers,* you said. As in the Seekers' Shadehouse?"

Borika nodded. "Not its official name, of course. Rather, not the name that's listed on maps and reference tables. But there are a few of us around who know. How do you know Che'ri'?"

"I'm her caregiver," Thalias said. "I understand you do some research with the girls?"

Borika's eyes flicked over Thalias's shoulder, doing a quick sweep of the horizon. "We should probably move this conversation off the porch," she said, opening the door and gesturing Thalias inside.

"Thank you," Thalias said, stepping past her through the opening.

She found herself in a large, homey great room. In one of the near corners a pair of couches faced an entertainment center; in the other, another group of couches and individual chairs were arranged in a circle around an open-air firepit topped by a conical vent hood. At the far end of the room were a dining table and six chairs, with a pass-through to a half-seen kitchen beyond. It was as if the stories of old-time backwoods ease and comfort had come to life. "Very nice," she said.

"Thank you," Borika said as she closed the door behind them. "And now, I think you need to show me some authorization."

Frowning, Thalias turned around.

Borika was no longer just a simple country rancher. Her face was hard and unreadable, her gaze heavy with suspicion as it dug into Thalias's face.

Her hand rock-steady as it held a charric pointed at Thalias.

Once, back on the Rapacc space station, Thalias had wondered if she would be able to shoot someone, even in the heat of battle, even if she knew a failure to do so might cost her her own life. Gazing now at Borika's steady hand, she had no doubt this woman would feel no such hesitation.

With an effort, she raised her eyes from the charric to Borika's face. "I don't have any authorization," she said. "What I have is information on you that was given to me by Senior Aide Mitth'iv'iklo."

"Never heard of him."

"Senior aide to Mitth Patriarch Thurfian," Thalias said. "Formerly senior aide to the late Patriarch Thooraki."

"Don't know them, either," Borika said, lifting the charric a bit. "You aren't supposed to even know about the Seeker program, let alone be crashing one of its training sites."

"Well, the first part's easy enough," Thalias said. "I know about the program because I was in it."

"I don't think so," Borika said. "You just told me you're Che'ri's caregiver."

"And I was also once a sky-walker," Thalias said. "Though I don't think it was called the Seekers program back then."

"No," Borika said flatly. "Nice story, but no. Sky-walkers don't become caregivers. It's just not done."

"I was an accidental exception," Thalias said. "And it *was* done, once upon a time."

"So I've heard," Borika said. "Sorry, but digging up obscure history doesn't buy you anything here. Either you come up with authorization, or I'm afraid you're going to sit for an unpleasant conversation with some unpleasant people."

"My information about you and the Seekers' Shadehouse came from Syndic Mitth'ras'safis," Thalias said, trying one last time. "Does that help?"

Borika's expression changed subtly. "You told me it came from Senior Aide Thivik."

"The data cylinder came from him, yes," Thalias said. "But he told me Syndic Thrass had compiled it."

Borika seemed to measure her. "You have the cylinder with you?"

"Yes." Carefully, keeping her movements slow, Thalias opened the back of her questis and pulled out the data cylinder.

"Set it on the back of that couch, then take two steps back."

Thalias did as ordered. Borika stepped forward, picked up the cylinder, and slipped it into her shoulder-slung questis. She keyed it, then lifted it with her free hand and peered at the display. Thalias waited, listening to the thudding of her heart.

"Yes," Borika murmured, lowering the questis. "The dates match up."

"So you knew him?" Thalias asked.

"He came and talked to me once," Borika said. "Back when I was Irizi." Her lips quirked in a brief smile. "Obviously kept tabs on me afterward or he couldn't have sent you here." She hesitated, then lowered her charric. "Why did you come?"

"Two reasons," Thalias said. "First, I told you that Che'ri's been having trouble stemming from some interactions with an alien who seems—"

"An *alien*?" Borika interrupted. "What alien? Where?"

"She's called the Magys," Thalias said. "We don't know what they call their people or world. She seems able to give an extra boost to Che'ri's Third Sight so that she can see farther into the future than any sky-walker I've ever heard of. I thought that, as one of the program's researchers, you might have some insight as to what's going on."

"Sounds interesting," Borika said thoughtfully. "I wish you'd brought her with you."

"I wanted to, but our first officer wouldn't let her leave the ship," Thalias said. "But I can tell you most of it."

"I guess that'll have to do." Borika waved her to one of the couches around the firepit. "Sit down."

She waited until Thalias was seated, then took the couch across from her, returning the charric to a holster hidden under her jacket. "Go ahead."

"It mostly started with nightmares," Thalias said.

She launched into the story, giving Borika as many details as she could about the changes that had taken place since the Magys was brought aboard the *Springhawk*. As she talked she looked around the room, studying the furniture and layout, listening to the whinnying of the packbulls as they wandered around the fields that surrounded the house. She'd heard that sound before, she knew, but she couldn't figure out where or when.

"Are you remembering the house?" Borika asked.

Thalias broke off, startled. "Sorry," she apologized. "I guess my attention was wandering."

"So I saw," Borika said, gazing thoughtfully at her. "I asked if you remembered being in this house."

"No, not really," Thalias said. "Why, did I do my training here?"

"I don't know," Borika said. "Those records are sealed away *very* deeply. I'm actually rather surprised Thrass was able to dig them out." She waved her arm, her gesture taking in the entire room. "But if you *were* here, you probably spent time in this place. It's been used as an auxiliary to the Shadehouse for decades. Under previous owners, obviously."

"Yes," Thalias murmured, feeling a pang of a loss she hadn't really known that she had. "What is it about the training that takes away all your memories?"

Borika's throat tightened. "It's not the training. You were telling me about the Paccosh?"

Thalias nodded and went back to Che'ri's story. "What do you think?" she asked when she was finished.

"I don't know," Borika conceded. "Some sky-walkers are able to see farther into the future than others, which naturally makes them the most highly valued. Which ship did you say you were on?"

"I didn't," Thalias said. "But it's the *Springhawk*."

"Ah," Borika said. "*Oh*," she said with more feeling, looking sharply at Thalias as the name suddenly seemed to register. "Yes, I've heard of you. You've been through the grinding mill, all right."

"It's not that bad," Thalias said, wincing a little at the note of defensiveness in her voice. "And as for your high-valued sky-walkers, I'd match Che'ri up against any of them."

"I wasn't making any judgments," Borika protested mildly. "I'm just telling you what the fancy folks in the Hierarchy Defense Council think. You and I both know that how far ahead you can see is only part of navigating a ship through the Chaos."

"Absolutely," Thalias growled, still only partially mollified. Some of the ships she'd served on, and some of the officers aboard those ships, were hardly top of the crop, either. "What did you mean, it wasn't part of the training?"

"Sorry, that's classified," Borika said. "I shouldn't even have said that much."

"Oh, come on," Thalias pressed. "Surely we're past that by now."

"No, actually, we're not," Borika said. "Well. I can look into this extended Third Sight thing, but I can't promise anything. Is it still happening?"

"I don't think so," Thalias said, her mind going back to the corridor outside Samakro's hearing room. "Her Third Sight seems to be back down to a few seconds. But she's also a long way from the Magys right now, and they haven't been physically close for over a week. I'm thinking it might come back if that changes."

"It might," Borika agreed. "Or it might not. That's the problem with single-point data sets. Your other option would be to get her an official reassignment here so that the professionals at the Shadehouse can run some tests."

"I doubt they'd agree to that," Thalias said, feeling her stomach tighten. "Not with the whole Ascendancy looking like it's coming apart at the welds."

"It's looked that way before," Borika said with a shrug. "We'll get through this one, too. Once the political mess is over, maybe you'll be able to at least arrange for some leave time for the two of you. Let me talk to the Shadehouse and see what their schedule looks like. If you want to wait until they get back to me, there are a couple of nice inns back in Pomprey near the skybus depot. I'll take you to one of them."

"So that's it?" Thalias asked.

Borika frowned. "What else do you want?"

"I already told you," Thalias said. "I want to know why my childhood memories are gone. If it's not the Seekers program itself, what is it?"

"And I already said I can't tell you," Borika said with a note of finality in her voice. "If that's all, I'll take you back to Pomprey." She stood up and gestured toward the door.

"No, that's not all," Thalias said, making no move to get up. "I said there were two reasons I wanted to see you. I've told you the first. Do you want to hear the second?"

Borika snorted. "If it's to ask for another favor, you've already used up today's quota."

"It's not a favor," Thalias said. "The fact is, I simply wanted to meet you."

Borika's eyes narrowed. "Why?"

"You said earlier that you'd heard about our ship, the *Springhawk*," Thalias said. "Its commander is Senior Captain Thrawn."

"Yes, that sounds right," Borika said. "And?"

Thalias braced herself. This wasn't how she'd planned for this to go, but Borika had pushed her to it. "And I wanted to meet you . . . because you're his sister."

For a moment Borika just stared at her. Then, slowly, she lowered herself back onto the couch. "No," she said, her voice barely above a whisper. "You're lying. You can't possibly know that. Those records are sealed."

"You have Syndic Thrass's data," Thalias reminded her, nodding toward Borika's questis. "Take a look."

Borika held her pose another few heartbeats. Then, slowly, she raised her questis and looked at the display, scrolling through the pages. Thalias waited, not daring to move, watching the play of emotions across the other woman's face.

Finally, reluctantly, Borika raised her eyes again. "That's not supposed to happen," she said. "We're not supposed to . . . they don't want us to know where we came from."

"Why not?" Thalias asked. "Is it like how senior flag officers have to give up their families?"

"No, it's—" Borika broke off, and Thalias could see her fighting a quiet internal battle. "They don't want us to remember our families because too many of us would have quit."

Thalias frowned. "You're joking."

"You think so?" Borika countered. "You're five years old. You've just been taken from your parents and the only world you've ever known. You wouldn't be homesick?"

"Well . . ." Thalias thought back to her first awkward meeting with Che'ri, and how touchy and uncertain the girl had seemed. And *that* was just the girl changing caregivers, not the far bigger trauma of having to say goodbye to her family forever. "All right, I might have been a *little* homesick," she conceded.

"Then you'd have been the exception," Borika said, her face and body sagging with a sudden weariness. "Too many of the girls cried themselves to sleep for weeks at a time. Too many of them were too miserable or frightened or just too distracted to learn how to use their Third Sight. There were never many candidates to begin with, and now the program was losing them like water from a tipped bucket."

She took a breath, exhaled in a long sigh. "So the decision was made to . . . remove . . . that distraction."

A shiver ran up Thalias's back. "They wiped our memories?"

"The term they used was *faded*," Borika said. "But basically, yes."

"But I remember the packbulls whinnying," Thalias protested. "I remember—" She looked around them. "I think maybe I remember this room."

"The fading process wasn't perfect," Borika said. "There were always pieces left. But the family memories, the ones that were getting in the way . . . those were gone."

"Che'ri mentioned a carnival once," Thalias said slowly, thinking back to a long-ago conversation. "I was playing some music, and she said it reminded her of what they'd played there."

"That would have been the Thearterra center," Borika said. "I spent some time there before getting married and settling here. The caregivers used to take the girls to that carnival as a break from their training. I wish they could do that on Ool, but there's nothing close enough."

"But some of those things happened *during* training," Thalias objected. "If they were just trying to take away memories of our homes and families, why did we lose that, too?"

"I don't know," Borika said. "They talk about *fading creep,* but I think that's just their way of saying they don't know, either. All I know is that the system has been in place for the past couple of hundred years. Every time a new Patriarch of the Nine comes to power, it's brought up again for a special confirmation. So far, they've always voted unanimously to keep it in place."

"And then—*oh,*" Thalias interrupted herself as an old puzzle suddenly resolved itself in her head. "And that's why they don't want former sky-walkers acting as caregivers, isn't it? They're afraid we'll compare notes and realize we both have the same memory loss."

"Very good," Borika said with a touch of black humor. "I don't think even the people who are running the program right now realize that's why that particular protocol was originally put in place. You said you got in as a caregiver by accident?"

"More or less," Thalias said. "Patriarch Thurfian—he was just Syndic Thurfian at the time—had a private agenda going. When he found out I wanted aboard the *Springhawk,* he saw me as a way of achieving it and pulled the necessary strings."

"What did he want you to do?"

"Don't worry about it," Thalias soothed her. "I dumped the whole thing off my back a long time ago."

"Does *he* know that?" Borika asked pointedly.

"I'm sure—" Thalias broke off as the comm at her waist signaled. "Just a second," she said, frowning as she pulled it out. Who could possibly be calling her here? "This is Thalias," she said.

"Mid Captain Samakro," Samakro's voice came back. "Are you still on Ool?"

"Yes, sir," Thalias said. "I thought you said I could stay another couple of days."

"Apparently, I was wrong," Samakro said grimly. "I need you back at Csilla right away."

"Of course, sir," Thalias said. "I'll catch the first transport I can get."

"Good," Samakro said. "Send me the flight details, and I'll see if I can have a shuttle waiting along the approach vector to take you off and bring you straight across to the *Springhawk*. No point going all the way down just to turn around and come back up again if you don't have to. Go make your arrangements; I'll see you soon. Samakro out."

The comm went dead. "What is it?" Borika asked.

"The *Springhawk*'s first officer says I'm needed back at Csilla," Thalias said, standing up and punching for flight data with suddenly shaking fingers. What could have happened that Samakro had to do something this drastic? "I'm sorry—I was hoping we could talk a little more." There was the skybus information she needed. The next one leaving for the spaceport . . .

"Never mind the skybus," Borika said, putting away her own comm. Thalias hadn't even noticed her pulling it out. "I'll fly you to Ibbian Spaceport. If we leave now, you can make the late-afternoon transport."

"That's a thousand kilometers away," Thalias protested.

"So I'll take the rest of the day off," Borika said, standing up. "Come on, come on—senior officers don't make calls like that personally unless it's important."

Five minutes later, they were in the air. Five minutes after that, Thalias had finished booking passage for the flight back to Csilla.

"All done?" Borika asked as Thalias put her comm away.

"Yes," Thalias said. "Back to Csilla, and the *Springhawk*."

"And Thrawn."

"Actually, he's not there at the moment," Thalias said. "It's a long story."

"And probably one you can't tell."

"Probably." Thalias eyed her. "Too bad you can't come along."

"Why would I want to do that?" Borika asked.

"To meet him."

"Why?"

"What do you mean, *why*?" Thalias said, frowning at her. "Because he's your *brother*?"

Borika shook her head. "There's no point."

And as Thalias gazed at her profile, she saw to her surprise that the other woman's eyes were welling with tears. "Don't you understand?" Borika said softly. "There's no point.

"I don't remember him."

In some ways, the Stybla honoring ritual reminded Thrass of all the Mitth welcoming ceremonies he'd attended over the years. The clothing was equally formal, the precise and stylized invocations and responses were all too familiar, and the overall air of solemnity could have placed the event at any homestead, stronghold, or Patriel mansion in the Ascendancy.

And yet, despite its closeness and simplicity, this ritual was far deeper than anything he'd ever experienced.

There were only eighteen people present: Thrass, Patriarch Lamiov, Senior Aide Lappincyk, Patriarch Thooraki, the thirteen Stybla Patriels who were able to travel to Naporar for the ceremony, and Thrawn himself. In addition, while Mitth welcoming ceremonies were invariably performed in Cheunh, the core section of this particular rite was carried out in Tybroic, the long-dead ancient language of the Stybla family.

It was a considerably rarer ceremony than any other that Thrass had ever heard of. He'd asked Lappincyk about it earlier, while Thrawn was off practicing his lines, and learned there'd been exactly eight other non-Stybla who'd been granted this honorific over the past five thousand years. When Lamiov had said such events were infrequent, he'd been vastly overstating the case.

It was considerably shorter than the Mitth ceremonies, too. But then, unlike any of those, there was no one here whom anyone was trying to impress.

Thrass was talking to a couple of Stybla Patriels afterward, officials who were trying hard to pretend they cared who he was, when he was thankfully rescued by Patriarch Thooraki. "Good to see you again, Syndic," the Patriarch greeted him, taking Thrass's arm and steering him toward an unoccupied corner of the chamber. The room, too, was smaller than the usual Mitth norm, yet somehow carried a far greater depth of age and significance. "How is your mother? I keep meaning to look in on her, but somehow never get around to it."

"She's fine, Your Venerante," Thrass assured him, feeling a twinge of guilt. It had been over two months since he'd talked to her for more than five minutes himself. "I'll tell her you asked about her."

"Thank you." Thooraki gestured around them. "Impressive place, isn't it? I understand some of the tapestries and carved wood decoratives are from the original Ruling Family assembly hall."

"Really," Thrass said, looking around. "And they put them here on Naporar instead of in their homestead?"

"The Stybla assembly hall was impressively large," Thooraki said drily. "They should have plenty of such mementos to spread around. I presume you're wondering why Lamiov didn't also grant you the *odo* honorific?"

"To be honest, Your Venerante, that didn't even occur to me," Thrass told him truthfully. "I did very little to retrieve the item."

"Because Lamiov and I *did* discuss it," Thooraki continued. "Your modesty notwithstanding, you *did* play a key role."

"But you decided that having a Mitth cousin carrying a Stybla honorific might not be well accepted in the Syndicure?" Thrass hazarded.

Thooraki shrugged. "If a Mitth Patriarch can carry the honorific, I don't think a cousin having it would be a problem." He smiled wryly at Thrass. "Or hadn't you noticed?"

Thrass winced in embarrassment. The Twelfth Patriarch, Mitth'omo'rossodo the Tragic. "No, I hadn't," he admitted. "It never even occurred to me."

"She was the first Mitth to receive the title," Thooraki said, a shadow of sadness creeping into his tone. "Though I doubt even such a rare honor did anything to alleviate the pain of her sons' deaths."

"According to Thrawn, she gave up her art shortly afterward."

"I don't doubt it," Thooraki said. "But no, it wasn't your contribution or your family status that tipped the balance. We decided that it would be best if you and Thrawn weren't *quite* so obviously a team."

Thrass frowned. "What kind of team?"

"The best kind," Thooraki assured him. "The two of you combine impressive political and military skills, which will put the Mitth in position to influence future decisions in both the Syndicure and the Council. The kind of team that can only be achieved by people who know each other, trust each other, and can work fully in sync. A team of kin, of friends—" He gave Thrass a faint smile. "—of brothers."

Thrass stared at him. "How did you know?"

Thooraki waved a hand. "Senior Aide Lappincyk's report was quite thorough."

"So this was a setup from the very beginning?" Thrass asked, the first stirrings of anger starting to weave their way through him. "You pushed Thrawn and me together, forcing us to become"—his tongue tripped over the word— "close friends?"

Thooraki snorted. "*Forcing* you? Please, Syndic. No one *forces* friendship or brotherhood on anyone. I merely noted how well you and Thrawn got along, how your interests meshed, how comfortable he was with you. As you may have noticed, he's not particularly relaxed with many people."

"And the incident with Lappincyk after Thrawn's graduation from Taharim Academy?" Thrass countered. "He wasn't trying to rematch him to the Stybla at all, was he?"

Thooraki looked Thrass straight in the eye. "If you hadn't acknowledged that Thrawn was indeed your friend—and I mean acknowledged it to yourself, because everyone else had already seen it—then yes, he was indeed going to offer Thrawn a position."

Thrass swallowed hard. What could he say to that? "I see," he murmured.

Thooraki held the stern look another moment. Then he smiled, the reproving glare fading into an almost fatherly expression. "Come now, Thrass, don't be sullen. This was at its heart politics, and you know how politics is played."

"Yes, I suppose I do," Thrass conceded. "And you're right. Thrawn was probably my friend long before I realized it."

"And your brother?"

Almost unwillingly, Thrass smiled. "And my brother."

"Good." Thooraki paused, turning to look around the room. "We've been watching the two of you for a long time, Thrass. Thrawn since General Ba'kif was alerted to point him out to your colleague Syndic Thurfian, you from—well, from your birth."

"And what do the Stybla get out of all this?" Thrass asked.

"A quiet and lasting friendship with the Mitth," Thooraki

said. "An alliance that has survived intact for over a thousand years."

"A situation rarer even than the *odo* ceremony itself," Thrass commented.

"Indeed." Thooraki nodded across the room. "And speaking of alliances and friendship, your teammate looks to need rescuing."

Thrass followed his gaze. Thrawn was conversing with two of the Stybla Patriels. From their expressions, it looked like they were politely probing for information. From Thrawn's expression, it was clearly information he wasn't prepared to give them.

"You'd best help him out," Thooraki continued. "I'll be spending a few more days here talking with Lamiov, but I have a shuttle waiting to take Thrawn to the *Springhawk* and you back to Csilla. No rush, just whenever you're ready."

"Thank you, Your Venerante," Thrass said, bowing. "Thank you, too, for your time and your insights." He smiled tightly. "And for guiding me where I needed to be, whether I recognized that need or not."

"You're welcome, Syndic Thrass," Thooraki said, smiling back. "I'll look forward to speaking with you again in the future. *And* to seeing to what new heights you and Thrawn will carry the entire family."

Extricating Thrawn from the Patriels was a relatively easy operation. After that came farewells to Senior Aide Lappincyk and Patriarch Lamiov, the latter accompanied by one final reiteration of Thrawn's gratitude for the honor he'd been granted.

And then, there was nothing left but the long walk down the quiet mansion corridors and out the door toward the landing field where their shuttle was waiting.

They could have taken a car, Thrass knew—he'd seen

several vehicles parked near their exit. But Thrawn seemed distant, even troubled, and Thrass suspected this would be the last time they would have for a private conversation for a while.

"So," he said as they walked down the wide flagstone path through the cool dusk air. "Mitth'raw'nuruodo. Has a nice ring to it."

"Yes," Thrawn murmured. "Though it's going to take some getting used to."

Thrass looked sideways at him. "You seem concerned," he said. "Are you worried about the name?"

"No, not at all," Thrawn said, frowning at him. "Why would I be concerned about such a tremendous honor?"

"So you *do* recognize there was honor involved," Thrass said. "I wasn't sure you would. Are you worried about the item?"

"Even less worried than I am about my new name," Thrawn said. "The fact that I've never heard even rumors about it suggests that the UAG security wall is extremely solid. The fact that it's under the control of the Stybla, the only family who've ever had the wisdom and self-confidence to voluntarily relinquish power, offers the confidence that it won't be misused. Why, are *you* worried?"

"Not really, and for the same reasons," Thrass said. "So why the look of a man planning a major battle campaign?"

Thrawn gave a little snort. "How would you even know what that expression looks like?"

"Don't be snide," Thrass reproved with mock annoyance. "We have battles in the Syndicure, too, you know. We just use speeches and favors instead of lasers and breacher missiles."

"And theatrics."

"Especially theatrics," Thrass agreed. "So if it's not the name or the item, then what *is* bothering you?"

Thrawn hesitated. "I'm confused, Thrass. During our

final confrontation with Captain Roscu—and I recognize the primary purpose was to gain tactical leverage—"

"Wait a second," Thrass interrupted. "Are you talking about me calling you *brother*?"

Thrawn actually winced. "Yes," he said. "I know that as a cousin you can create your own personal family relationships. But for a cousin to name a Trial-born as brother . . . of course, if it was only for that tactical advantage I fully understand."

"It's all right," Thrass soothed. If he hadn't recognized the friendship link between them, he mused, at least he'd been ahead of the curve on the brotherhood aspect. "We were already kin and friends. If I want to name you as a brother, I can do that."

"I know," Thrawn said, still looking pained. "It's just . . ."

Mentally, Thrass shook his head. The unspoken rules of family etiquette. "Would it be easier to think of me as a brother if I was only a ranking distant instead of a cousin?"

"Perhaps," Thrawn said, frowning. "But you *are* a cousin."

Thrass hesitated. He'd never told anyone else this. But then, it wasn't *exactly* a secret. "Tell you what," he proposed. "Let's trade secrets."

"What kind?"

"The kind we've never shared," Thrass said. "The kind that brothers *do* tell each other." He held up a hand, palm outward, before Thrawn could object. "I'll start. While I'm listed in the family ranks as a cousin, I'm technically—sort of—just a ranking distant."

"Really," Thrawn said, frowning. "How exactly did you pull that one off?"

"*I* didn't." Thrass took a deep breath. "Here's the story. My parents were from a very minor family—I don't even remember which one. Just before I was born, my father happened to be at the right place and time to thwart an assassination attempt on Patriarch Thooraki. The Patriarch was saved, but my father was killed."

"Your father must have been a highly honorable man to make such a sacrifice," Thrawn murmured.

"Yes, he was," Thrass agreed. "Even more impressive is that the Patriarch was traveling incognito and my father had no idea whose life he'd saved. He simply saw a desperate need and stepped in."

"I trust the Patriarch was grateful?"

"Very much so," Thrass said. "He invited my mother—who was pregnant with me at the time—to the Csilla homestead and offered to rematch her into the Mitth as a ranking distant, the highest position he could confer on a commoner."

"Honor given for honor received," Thrawn said. "I would expect nothing less from him. How then are *you* a cousin?"

"That's where it gets tricky," Thrass said. "You know how the bloodlines work, with the offspring of ranking distants being born as cousins. Well, I was born just a week after my father's death, so under the rules I would also have been a ranking distant like my mother. *But.*"

He held up a finger for emphasis. "I was still unborn when the assassination attempt took place. So the Patriarch decided to fudge the date of the rematching to after my father's death but before my birth. Since my mother was now officially a ranking distant when I was born . . . ?"

"You were born a cousin," Thrawn said, smiling faintly. "Ingenious. I wonder what the Patriels and syndics thought about it."

"I think they were mostly just glad to have the Patriarch still alive," Thrass said. "Okay—your turn. The day we first met, when we were talking about Patriarch Thomoro the Tragic, you told me that some losses run too deep to ever fully heal. What personal loss were you remembering?"

Thrawn seemed taken aback. "All these years, and you still remember that?"

Thrass shrugged. "It made an impact on me."

"It's really not that important," Thrawn warned.

"You're my brother, and my friend," Thrass countered. "If it's important to you, it's important to me."

Thrawn looked away. "You say we're brothers. I never had any others. But I once had a sister. When I was three and she was five, she simply . . . disappeared."

"I'm sorry," Thrass said quietly. *Disappeared.* An odd way of putting it. "Did she die?"

"I don't think so," Thrawn said, an odd evasiveness suddenly coming into his voice. "At any rate, the day you and I met was her starday, and her loss was weighing particularly heavily on my thoughts at the time. I hadn't meant for you to notice."

He gave Thrass a wry smile. "I *certainly* hadn't meant for you to brood over it all these years."

"It wasn't *brooding,* really," Thrass corrected. "More just thinking or pondering. But there must be records somewhere about what happened to her. I might be able to help you look them up."

"That's all right," Thrawn said, waving away the offer. "I'll find the time myself someday. Besides, you have all that Syndicure combat and theatrics to engage in."

"There's that," Thrass conceded.

Still, just because he had other work to do didn't mean he couldn't find the time to look into this, as well. Or maybe he could suggest Patriarch Thooraki start an official inquiry. It was the least he could do for his brother.

Brother. Yes, he decided: That word had a proper ring to it. And just as Thrawn had never had a brother, neither had he. "Speaking of combat, does the Council really expect you and the *Springhawk* to find any pirates out there?"

"I don't know," Thrawn said. "Commodore Ar'alani's

opinion is that what the Council *expects* is for me to disappear from the Ascendancy for a while so they won't have to look at me." He shrugged. "Still, one never knows about the future."

"No," Thrass agreed. "One doesn't."

But Patriarch Thooraki knew, or at least he thought he did. Were Thrass and Thrawn really destined to do great things for the Mitth? Were they really going to be—?

He smiled to himself at the phrase that popped into his mind. *Brothers-in-arms.*

But really, why not? If Thooraki was right, that was indeed what the two of them had already become. The man born to be a privileged member of the family, teaming up with the promising outsider who'd been welcomed in. In many ways it echoed like an old legend brought to new life.

Thrawn was right. No one knew what the future held. But Thrass was going to give it all he could, for the honor of the Mitth and the glory of the Ascendancy. Or he would die trying.

CHAPTER NINETEEN

Qilori didn't like dealing with Chiss. Not in ones or twos, not in groups, especially not on ships that were crawling with them.

Which made being on a massive orbiting transfer station with a couple of thousand of the cursed creatures something on the order of his own version of hell.

But there was nothing for it. Schesa was a major Chiss world, right at the edge of the Ascendancy, and aliens weren't allowed on the surface without an escort, a sponsor, or official authorization. Thrawn was gone, Qilori didn't know anyone else here, and getting the necessary permissions would take longer than he had.

Luckily, he had neither the desire nor the need to walk among that many blueskins. All he needed was access to Schesa's massive orbiting triad long-range transmitter, and for that the transfer station and the credit chit Thrawn had given him worked just fine.

Besides, there was something delicious about directing the destruction of a Chiss senior captain from one of the Chiss's own stations.

"You're fortunate you caught me," Jixtus's voice came over the comm booth speaker, his tone unnaturally reserved. "I was just about to continue my journey to Ornfra."

"With all respect, sir," Qilori said, "I think you're going to want to go to Csilla instead."

"And why would you think that?"

"Because Thrawn is on his way there right now," Qilori said. "And he's not aboard his usual Chiss warship. He's on a Nikardun blockade frigate that was co-opted by the Paccosh."

"Really," Jixtus said. "And how would you know this, Qilori of Uandualon, given that your job was to guide General Crofyp and the *Anvil* against those same Paccosh?"

Qilori's winglets twitched. In his excitement over delivering this news, he'd almost forgotten that Jixtus had set up the plan that Thrawn had so deftly turned into a fiasco. "The attack didn't go as expected, sir," he said, pulling back some of his enthusiasm. "The Paccosh had the blockade frigate, as I said. And Thrawn arrived at . . . an inopportune moment."

"You're saying two of the Kilji Illumine's mighty warships couldn't handle a Paccian blockade frigate and a Chiss heavy cruiser?"

"No, sir, they couldn't," Qilori said. He'd *really* forgotten how badly this had all gone. "But one of the Kilji ships *did* escape back to Sunrise." He braced himself. "Unfortunately, the Paccosh and the Chiss were able to follow it."

"And yes, to destroy it," Jixtus said. "Did you think I wouldn't have heard of this from the Grysk vessel that escaped that disaster?"

"I . . . wasn't sure how far from Sunrise it would get," Qilori said. "Before it had to stop for repairs, I mean. I thought . . ."

"You thought to deliver me news in a timely fashion," Jixtus said, the veiled threat in his voice disappearing. "That was well done. Certainly you couldn't have changed the course of any of those events. You say Thrawn is on his way to Csilla?"

"Yes, sir," Qilori said, his winglets relaxing, a brief gush of annoyance coloring his relief. This wasn't the first time Jixtus had pretended to be dangerously upset with him, and he hadn't liked it any of those times, either. "He spent a couple of hours using the triad transmitter to send some messages, then said he needed some specialized equipment to test one of the other people at Sunrise." He paused. Jixtus wasn't the only one who could play to the drama, after all. "He thinks that person could be another Magys."

"He *said* that?" Jixtus asked, his voice suddenly heavy with suspicion. "He said those words?"

"I don't remember the specific words," Qilori hedged. "But that was the intent. He said you'd wanted to find the Magys, but that others on Sunrise would do as well."

"He told you that, did he?" Jixtus asked. "Just came out and told you?"

"Yes," Qilori said. "You don't believe him?"

Jixtus gave a snort. "Of course not. He's manipulating you, Pathfinder. Trying to deflect or diffuse my attention away from the Magys."

"I don't know," Qilori said hesitantly. "He sounded sincere."

"Nonsense," Jixtus said. "I've investigated the matter thoroughly. The Magys is the only one. Thrawn is simply trying to make us think otherwise."

"Or perhaps there's only one at a time?" Qilori suggested.

There was a short pause. "An interesting thought," Jixtus conceded, some of his contempt fading. "But if that's even a possibility, why tell you? Why not keep it a secret?"

"Maybe because he doesn't expect it to remain a secret much longer," Qilori said, feeling the pieces starting to come together. "I spoke briefly with two soldiers who'd eluded the Paccian slaughter. They said—"

"What Paccian slaughter?"

"The Paccosh brought in a force to reclaim the mine you'd set your slaves to working," Qilori said, the nervous twitching of his winglets starting up again. "They . . . all the Grysk overseers died in their attack."

"I see," Jixtus said. "Not unexpected, I suppose, under the circumstances. You were speaking of my two outriders?"

"The two soldiers who'd eluded the attack, yes," Qilori said. "They wanted me to tell you that when you spoke the word they would sow chaos and reap death among your enemies. But they also said they would bring you the one."

"The *one*? What one?"

"I don't know," Qilori admitted. "We were interrupted before they could finish. But I wonder if they might have learned about another like the Magys."

"And so Thrawn gives you that same message," Jixtus said thoughtfully. "Suspecting you would pass it on to me, and that I would automatically reject it."

"Which would make you less likely to believe it even if it came from another source," Qilori said.

"Yes. Interesting." Jixtus muttered a word too softly for Qilori to catch. "Or possibly the outriders were referring to someone else entirely. Still, it's worth considering. Did Thrawn say anything else?"

"Nothing of value," Qilori said. If Jixtus was still on the *Whetstone*, it was likely that Generalirius Nakirre was listening in on the conversation. Definitely not the time to bring up Thrawn's theory that the Kiljis were manipulating Jixtus and his entire plan. "But the fact that he wants testing equipment would suggest he has some idea who this other Magys candidate is."

"*If* such truly exists," Jixtus cautioned. "But I agree that the chance is too good to pass up, especially since it can be investigated without a major disruption of other plans. I'd intended to intercept and destroy Captain Roscu at Ornfra; now, I'll hand over that task to the *FateSpinner* and travel to Csilla myself. I assume you'll remain on the Schesa transfer station for the immediate future?"

"Certainly, if you want me to," Qilori said.

"I do," Jixtus said. "Tell me, what became of the other Pathfinder, the one on the *Hammer*?"

"Thrawn and the Paccosh took him with them," Qilori said, his winglets setting up another flutter. "Thrawn wanted to get to Csilla as quickly as possible."

"Before I could intercept him?"

"I don't know, sir," Qilori said. "He may be in a hurry for other reasons."

"He may," Jixtus agreed. "Remain where you are. After I've dealt with Thrawn, I'll arrange for you to be picked up. It won't be long."

"Yes, sir," Qilori said, his winglets calming. Waiting here meant more time spent among the blueskins, but at least there was an end in sight.

"And your other mission?" Jixtus added. "What is its status?"

Qilori's winglets flattened. The mystery of how the Chiss navigated through the Chaos. "I've made some progress," he said, keeping it vague. Fortunately, Jixtus was unlikely to ask for details, not with the Kiljis sitting there listening.

"Good," Jixtus said. "Then I bid you farewell for now, Qilori of Uandualon. The next time we speak, Thrawn will have been eliminated." He paused. "And then you can offer your explanation on how Pathfinder Sarsh survived the destruction of the *Hammer* at Sunrise."

Qilori's winglets twitched. "Of course," was all he could think to say. "I look forward to that conversation."

"Helm, stand by," Roscu ordered, eyeing the nav display and the chrono. "Space-normal: Three, two, *one*."

The hyperspace swirl and star-flares went through their usual transformation, and the *Orisson* was once again in the Ornfra system.

And *this* time, Roscu promised herself, she would absolutely get that close look at the Krolling Sen shipyards that Patriarch Rivlex had ordered. Senior Captain Ziinda could talk all she wanted about Jixtus and alien threats, but that didn't mean the Dasklo weren't also creating a ghost fleet. Because that was exactly what the Dasklo would do in a situation like this.

"Approach vector, Captain?" Raamas asked, turning from where he was standing behind the pilot's station.

"Straight in," Roscu told him. "Full acceleration. The minute they see we're back, they might try to close down and hide the evidence. We want to get there before they can do that."

"Acknowledged," Raamas said, turning back to the viewport and signaling the order to the pilot.

"Captain, we've got something coming up behind us," the sensor officer warned. "No ID, but it's big."

Roscu frowned as the image appeared on the aft sensor display. Her first assumption had been that it was a Dasklo warship, maybe one of the destroyers that had harassed her during the *Orisson*'s last trip here.

But the vessel bearing down on them was way too big for that. It looked to be comparable to a Defense Fleet man-of-war, a Firewolf or maybe even a Groundlion.

She'd never heard of any of the Nine having warships larger than a heavy cruiser. Was this a Defense Force ship, then? But the bow configuration didn't seem right for that. In fact, it wasn't like any ship she'd ever seen.

Her blood froze. No, she was wrong; she *had* seen something like this. Back at Rhigal, floating silently amid the asteroids of the Junkyard.

One of the alien ships had followed them.

"Comms, let's give them a hail—" Raamas was saying.

"Belay that!" Roscu snapped. "Emergency power to the drive—*now!* And go to battle stations."

The alarm was just starting to sound when the alien warship opened fire.

"Evasive, Captain?" Raamas asked, grabbing for a handhold as the *Orisson* leapt forward.

"Negative," Roscu said, looking at the tactical. Clarr family warships were built very tough in the stern in order to handle the extra heat and radiation of their overpowered drives. But the alien's spectrum lasers were already starting to push those boundaries. Worse, any evasive maneuver would expose one of the *Orisson*'s flanks to that same withering fire, with disastrous results. "I need an in-system jump. How soon?"

"Captain, we're just out of hyperspace—" the pilot began in a tight voice.

"How soon?"

"Forty seconds," Raamas said, his head turning back and forth as he looked among the displays. "I'm not sure we can last that long."

Roscu hissed out a curse. He was right—even at emergency power, the *Orisson* was barely holding its own against the onslaught. The only thing that would save them now was a flat-out escape into hyperspace, which didn't require any of the fancy calculations needed for an in-system jump.

The problem was that Roscu's straight-in vector meant the *Orisson* was pointed directly at Ornfra. Jumping into hyperspace would almost instantly slam them into the edge of the planet's gravity well, dropping them back into space-normal right in the middle of a crowded traffic pattern. If they didn't kill themselves, there was a good chance they would kill someone else.

But the alien's laser barrage was beating at the electrostatic barriers, and the aft sensors were starting to flash critical. The *Orisson* would never survive long enough for the pilot to finish the in-system jump calculations.

They had just one chance. "Set for hyperspace," she ordered. "On my command, you'll flutter the main starboard thrusters twice, then shut them down."

"That'll drastically drop our acceleration," Raamas warned.

"And the thrust imbalance will skew us to starboard, opening that flank to attack," Roscu said. "That's why the instant the starboard thrusters shut down, you'll also fire the starboard-bow maneuvering jets—all of them—at full power."

"Skewing us instead to portside," Raamas said, nodding as he understood.

"Exactly," Roscu said. "I'm hoping they'll see the flutters and shift their targeting in anticipation of a clear shot at our starboard flank. Once we're clear of the gravity well edge, jump us to hyperspace."

"Understood," Raamas said. "Helm?"

"We're set, Captain," the pilot confirmed.

"Execute."

Roscu gripped the arms of her chair tightly as the *Orisson* twitched twice with the thruster fluttering, then twitched one final time as the thrusters were shut down. The bow swung to portside, moving off the line leading to the distant planet—

And the stars stretched into star-flares and melded into the swirl.

Roscu huffed out a breath. They'd made it. "Secure from battle stations," she ordered. "Commander, get me a damage report."

"Three of the aft hull plates have warped, but not critically," Raamas said, pulling up the status on his questis as he left the helm and crossed back toward her command chair. "Thruster Four took some damage; we probably shouldn't run it past sixty percent until it's been looked at. Otherwise, we seem to have made it through mostly intact."

"Any damage to the portside hull?"

"Nothing registering," Raamas said. "Looks like your plan caught them off guard exactly as you predicted."

"Sometimes it's good to go up against a competent enemy." Roscu paused, waiting until Raamas had stopped beside her chair. "So," she said, lowering her voice so that only he could hear her. "How exactly did they pull *that* off?"

"If you'll pardon the language, Captain, that's a damn good question," Raamas said grimly. "There's no way one of those ships could have followed us from Rhigal. They were still showing cold when we left."

"Unless there was an active one lurking where we couldn't see it."

"In which case, how did they see our vector and know where we were headed?" Raamas countered. "If we couldn't see them, they shouldn't have been able to see us." He winced. "No, wait. It's actually worse than that, isn't it?"

"Yes, it is," Roscu said, her throat tightening. The *Orisson* hadn't been quite lined up on Ornfra when it left Rhigal, and had required a mid-route stop to correct its course. Even if the aliens had observed the *Orisson*'s departure vector, they'd have had no way of narrowing down the Clarr warship's destination farther than between Ornfra, Sharb, Noris, and Schesa. "They couldn't have been waiting here unless they had ships waiting at all four of our possible destinations."

"Not a pleasant thought," Raamas said. "If they have enough warships skulking around the Ascendancy that they can get four of them to the northeast sector ahead of us, it isn't about Patriarch Rivlex borrowing a fleet anymore."

"I agree," Roscu said. "Unfortunately, the alternative isn't any better. If Jixtus doesn't have a lot of spare warships available—if he only maybe has one, in fact—then there's only one other way this one could have been waiting for us."

Raamas looked out the viewport at the undulating hyperspace sky. "If the Patriarch told them where we were going."

Roscu nodded. "Yes."

For a moment Raamas pondered that in silence. "So what do we do?"

"I wish I knew," Roscu admitted. "We can't alert the Defense Force without telling them about the fleet hidden in the Junkyard. This attack would seem to settle the question of whether the Patriarch is involved, which would mean telling them about him, too."

"But if he's a traitor?"

Roscu winced. She hadn't even wanted to use that word in the secret confines of her own mind. To hear Raamas say it out loud . . . "We don't know that," she said stubbornly. "Maybe he set this up in good faith and Jixtus is just playing him."

"I don't see how that makes it any better."

"It makes it better because it now means we can hold off on alerting Csilla until we've had time to look into this," Roscu told him. "See if we can figure out Jixtus's ultimate plan."

"Stall, in other words."

Another word Roscu hadn't wanted to acknowledge. "We're Clarr, Commander," she said quietly. "We're a family. We don't lightly open up our flaws or mistakes for everyone to see. We don't denigrate or accuse our Patriarch without evidence, and we *absolutely* don't hand him over to others unless that evidence is stone-solid."

"I understand," Raamas said. "I'm just . . . we're standing on an edge here, Captain. I can feel it."

"And you're afraid of heights?" Roscu suggested, trying for a little humor.

He gave her a small, tight smile in acknowledgment. "Terrified of them, ma'am." The smile faded. "Especially when everything and everyone I care about is standing there with me."

Roscu nodded. "I understand. But we'll get through this, Commander. We will."

"Yes, ma'am." Raamas straightened up. "Orders, Captain?"

"We head back to Rhigal," Roscu said. "The Dasklo shipyards can wait. It's time we had a talk with Patriarch Rivlex."

She stared out the viewport. "A long and *very* thorough talk."

"Mid Commander Octrimo, stand by," Ar'alani ordered, eyeing the nav display and the chrono. "Space-normal in sixty seconds."

"Acknowledged, Admiral," the pilot confirmed.

Beside Ar'alani, Wutroow shook her head. "Did I miss the part about the Ascendancy having an expiration date?" she muttered.

"If you did, so did I," Ar'alani said, wincing. A standoff at Sarvchi between a pair of Chaf and Ufsa freighters. A loud argument at Shihon between an Erighal transport and a Boadil-crewed system patrol ship in which other patrol ships had had to intervene. The Tahmie and Droc on the edge of restarting their recent hostilities, only this time at Jamiron instead of Csaus.

And the *Vigilant,* ordered by an increasingly nervous Syndicure to get to Jamiron and deal with it.

"Do we even know what this is about?" Wutroow continued. "I read the orders and data feed twice, and I still can't figure out what the Droc are mad about this time."

"Excuse me, Admiral?" Octrimo spoke up from the helm. "If I may offer a bit of insight into my family's mindset?"

"Go ahead, Mid Commander," Ar'alani said.

"We and the Tahmie have a long history of locking antlers on every topic imaginable," Octrimo said. "All that aside, I don't think our current Patriarch needs any particular reason to be mad, at the Tahmie or anyone else."

"Yes, but going up against one of the Forty?" Wutroow asked. "That requires you to load courage into the bucket where you're supposed to keep good sense."

Octrimo shook his head. "I can describe it, ma'am, but that doesn't mean I can explain it."

"Let's hope this group is at least willing to listen to reason," Ar'alani said. "Here we go. Stand by, helm: Three, two, *one.*"

The star-flares collapsed into stars. "Full scan," Ar'alani ordered. "Let's see if we can find them—"

"Laserfire!" Biclian snapped. "Bearing ten degrees portside, six degrees zenith."

"Octrimo, get us over there," Ar'alani ordered, suppressing a curse. The Syndicure order had mentioned that both sides of the squabble were calling in additional forces, and had strongly encouraged her to get the *Vigilant* to Jamiron before any actual shooting started.

So much for that hope.

The *Vigilant* was too far away for a good read on the situation. But even a casual survey of the number and overall spread of the laser flashes showed that the battle was both intense and wide ranging. Unfortunately, there was no way to know whether the sudden arrival of an Expansionary Defense Fleet warship would cool down the participants or just inflame them more. She checked the *Vigilant*'s weapons status displays, waiting for Octrimo to get his in-system jump set up—

"Ready, Admiral," the pilot said.

"All crews stand ready," Ar'alani called. "In-system jump: Three, two, *one.*"

And with the usual jagged-edged change in position, the *Vigilant* arrived at the battle.

To find it was bigger and messier than Ar'alani had realized. There were no smooth planes of battle here, no coordinated wedges of attack or spheres of defense. Eighteen ships swarmed in and out of the battleground: patrol ships, gunboats, even a couple of armed freighters. They circled or arced around each other, some of them trading laser shots with a chosen opponent, some of them seemingly just shooting at whichever rival ship happened to be closest.

There was no overall strategy Ar'alani could see, nor any sense of individual tactics. The largest ship taking part in the brawl, a Tahmie patrol cruiser, seemed to be trying to organize the rest of the Tahmie forces, but it was clearly not having much luck. Two battered gun-boats drifted at the edges of the battleground, but both still showed minimally functional power levels, and there were no shattered hulks or debris clouds.

"Larsiom, give me full broadcast," Ar'alani ordered.

"Full broadcast, Admiral," the comm officer confirmed.

Ar'alani squared her shoulders. "This is Admiral Ar'alani of the Chiss Expansionary Defense Fleet warship *Vigilant*," she announced in her most intimidating voice. "All Tahmie and Droc ships, you are ordered to cease hostilities."

There was no reply. Moreover, as far as the running battle was concerned, the *Vigilant* might as well have been invisible. "Tahmie and Droc ships, I gave you an order," Ar'alani said, raising her volume. "Stop this nonsense immediately."

"*Vigilant*, you have no jurisdiction here," a voice came over the bridge speaker. "Get clear or we won't be responsible for the consequences."

"Who is this?" Ar'alani asked. "Identify yourself."

"The Expansionary Defense Fleet has no authority inside Ascendancy borders," the other continued. "I again warn you to withdraw."

"Larsiom, where's that signal coming from?" Wutroow asked.

"I'm not sure, Senior Captain," Larsiom said. "I think it's the Tahmie patrol cruiser, but there's too much interference from the other ships' barriers."

"Maybe we should make this more private, Admiral," Wutroow suggested, turning to Ar'alani. "Shall we set up a laser comm?"

So that she could make more pointed threats to the Tahmie and then work out a deal with them, all without anyone else in the area listening in? It was a standard approach, and for a moment Ar'alani was tempted.

But only for a moment. The *Vigilant* had been given a job, and Ar'alani was in no mood to let some pompous patrol cruiser commander tell her she hadn't. "Stay with broadcast," she said. "Tahmie and Droc ships, this is your last warning. You've got ten seconds to cease hostilities, or we *will* take action."

"You attack one of the Forty, and *you'll* be the one regretting it," the voice countered. "The Syndicure won't stand for it."

Wutroow raised her eyebrows at Ar'alani, clearly offering to tell the other captain that it was the Syndicure, in fact, who had sent the *Vigilant* here in the first place. But Ar'alani shook her head, watching the battle and concentrating on her countdown. She reached zero—

"Junior Captain Oeskym: plasma spheres," she ordered the weapons officer. "Prepare to flicker them."

"Target, Admiral?" Oeskym asked.

Ar'alani looked out at the battle. "All of them," she said.

"*All* of them?" Wutroow asked, her eyes going a little wider.

"Every single damn one of them," Ar'alani confirmed. She pointed at the patrol cruiser, which was in the process of firing at two different gunboats. "Starting with that one."

"Yes, *ma'am*," Oeskym said briskly. Clearly, he hadn't liked the *Vigilant* being told to mind its own business, either. "Octrimo, get ready to yaw us in a starboard arc."

"Yaw turn ready," Octrimo confirmed. "Just tell me when."

"Admiral?" Oeskym asked.

Ar'alani settled herself in her command chair. "Have at it, Junior Captain."

It took four plasma spheres to completely silence the patrol cruiser. Most of the smaller combatants required only two or three before their lasers and thrusters fell silent. The tightly localized battleground began to expand as the various ships coasted outward along the vectors they'd been on when the spheres froze their control electronics.

"Probably just as well their comms are out," Wutroow commented from beside Ar'alani as they watched the dispersal. "They're all probably screaming their best obscenities at you right about now."

"Let's hope they kept a few of the tastier ones in reserve," Ar'alani said. "Oeskym, secure spheres and fire up the tractor beams. As long as they're not going anywhere for a while, we're going to haul them away from each other."

"We are?" Wutroow asked, her tone suddenly cautious. "That may not be the most politically astute thing to do."

Ar'alani gazed out the viewport. Wutroow was right, of course. Flickering the Tahmie and Droc combatants with plasma spheres would anger both families, but they would privately concede it was better than blasting the ships with spectrum lasers or breacher missiles. But following up the attack by tractoring them away from each other would be seen as the equivalent of dragging out a bar brawler by the back of his collar.

For families whose lives and interrelationships were permanently wrapped in pride and appearance, that would be a terrible and humiliating insult. The Ascendancy military was theoretically above such political issues, but Ar'alani had always tried to be sensitive to them anyway, if only to avoid unnecessary friction with people she had to deal with every day.

But for once, she didn't especially care.

"I know," she told Wutroow. "But they created a war zone in the middle of a public traffic area, and they need to be sent a clear message that that's unacceptable. *And* that if they insist on having that message beaten into their thick skulls, the Expansionary Defense Fleet is willing and able to do so."

"Understood, Admiral," Wutroow said. She still sounded dubious, but she recognized that her commander had made up her mind. "In that case, may I suggest we also move them into different orbital shells? That way, they'll at least have to work at it if they insist on restarting their fight."

"Good idea," Ar'alani said. "Oeskym, Octrimo: Get to it."

She pointed at the patrol cruiser. "And again, we'll start with that one."

"I'm not sure what your goal was here, Admiral Ar'alani," Supreme Admiral Ja'fosk ground out. "But if it was to infuriate the entire Syndicure, you've succeeded beautifully."

"I'm sorry the Syndicure sees things that way, sir," Ar'alani said, glowering at her cabin's speaker. She'd just turned over the watch to Senior Commander Biclian and was looking forward to a shower and a good meal when Ja'fosk's call came through.

Which all by itself marked the occasion as unusual. Supreme General Ba'kif was the one who normally supervised Expansionary Defense Fleet forces and acted as liaison between them and the Council and Syndicure. The fact that Ja'fosk had felt the need to intervene directly—or, more likely, that someone in one of those bodies had ordered him to do so—shaded this conversation toward the ominous. "Did any of these irate Speakers and syndics happen to notice that some of their own ships were in the vicinity when the Tahmie and Droc started shooting at each other?" she continued. "And that stopping the fight when I did may have saved those lives and those cargoes?"

"They did," Ja'fosk said, his tone marginally less hostile. Having delivered the obligatory rebuke, he perhaps felt he could now tone down the rhetoric a bit. "A couple of them mentioned that, and expressed some appreciation. But even they were adamant that the Expansionary Defense Fleet isn't even supposed to be hanging around Ascendancy worlds, let alone opening fire on anyone."

"Did they have any helpful suggestions as to what I should have done instead?" Ar'alani asked. "Or what you or Supreme General Ba'kif should have done, for that matter?"

"There were plenty of suggestions," Ja'fosk said. "But since you added the word *helpful*, I can spare you the list."

"Yes, sir." Ar'alani hesitated. "They're worried, aren't they?"

"Worried, angry, *and* frightened," Ja'fosk said heavily. "That's a bad combination, Ar'alani. Half of them see Jixtus deliberately provoking the Nine and Forty and trying to goad them into fighting among themselves, while the other half are starting to wonder if the Kilji offer of additional warships might just be the lesser evil."

Ar'alani nodded. That was how she was reading the situation, too. She'd hoped she'd been overly pessimistic. Apparently not. "And we can't just kick him out."

"Not unless and until he actually attacks someone," Ja'fosk agreed. "I'd wonder if any of the Syndics were starting to regret the whole non-intervention policy, except that I also know most of them consider those protocols to have descended from the stars on a sea of fire."

"Can we at least kick him out of our systems?" Ar'alani pressed. "Sending a laser barrage across his bow doesn't count as attacking."

"You've been spending too much time with Senior Captain Thrawn," Ja'fosk said sourly. "Just because he thinks he can get away with it—and because Ba'kif lets him—doesn't mean the Syndicure will put up with it forever."

"Just the same, in this case Thrawn might have a good point."

"I'm not arguing, Admiral," Ja'fosk said. "I'm just stating facts. Are you ready to head back to Sposia?"

"Almost," Ar'alani said. "Senior Captain Wutroow just has to finish her part of Patrol Command's datawork."

"Tell her to make it fast," Ja'fosk warned. "The *Venturous* is en route to Sposia, but it won't arrive for another few hours. Under the circumstances, I don't like leaving the UAG unguarded."

"Understood," Ar'alani said. "Though I'd rather like to see Jixtus try to break into their vault."

"You would?" Ja'fosk grunted. "Frankly, *I* wouldn't. Get back to guard duty and let's try to avoid finding out what would happen."

"Yes, sir," Ar'alani said. "We'll be on our way soon."

"Good. And Ar'alani?"

"Yes?"

"Try not to irritate anyone else today."

"I'll do my best, sir," Ar'alani said. "But I won't make any promises."

"I didn't think you would," Ja'fosk said. "Safe travels, Admiral."

"This is unacceptable," Zistalmu bit out, his face on Thurfian's comm display twisted with anger and passion. "Completely unacceptable. The Tahmie were merely defending their perfectly legitimate claims;

and this Expansionary Defense Fleet admiral thinks she can just move in and humiliate them in front of the entire Jamiron system? Those ships aren't even supposed to *be* inside the Ascendancy, let alone involving themselves in struggles that are none of their official concern."

"I understand your frustration, Syndic Prime," Thurfian said, though he doubted Zistalmu would be nearly as outraged by the *Vigilant*'s action if the Tahmie weren't an on-again, off-again ally of the Irizi. "But with possible enemy warships moving around the Ascendancy, we need all of ours to be close at hand."

"What enemy warships?" Zistalmu scoffed. "Jixtus and that pathetic little Kilji war cruiser? *Really,* Your Venerante. The Defense Force could swat down a dozen ships like that before breakfast. And *they*, at least, know how to properly behave around the Nine and the Forty. I think people like Ar'alani spend so much time outside the Ascendancy that they've lost all sense of understanding and propriety."

"That's possible," Thurfian said evasively, determined not to let himself get verbally pinned down. "I'm not clear on what you want from me."

"I want the Mitth family's support in getting their collective nose out of our business," Zistalmu said. "I already have petitions from three of the Nine demanding the Council pull the Expansionary Defense Fleet ships from any world where one or more of the Ruling Families have major interests and send them back out into the Chaos where they're supposed to be. We have our family fleets; we can protect our own worlds."

"I'm not sure I agree with sending them out of the Ascendancy," Thurfian said. "But I can join in a recommendation that they go off and park in Naporar orbit while we find some compromise to keep them from meddling in family affairs."

"Not exactly what I was looking for."

"I know. But it's the best I can do."

Zistalmu glared a moment, then gave a little shrug. "Very well," he said. "As long as they're not poking their fingers everywhere, I suppose they can sit at Naporar. Easier to ignore there, anyway."

"Agreed," Thurfian said. "I'll have my petition drawn up and sent to you within the hour."

"Thank you." Zistalmu paused. "I presume you've also heard that the *Springhawk* has returned without Senior Captain Thrawn?"

"I heard, yes," Thurfian said, a sour taste in his mouth. "Apparently, he's been working with aliens again."

"*And* fighting battles with them, *and* making deals with them, *and* taking them on as allies," Zistalmu said. "None of which he has the slightest authorization to do."

"What would you like me to do about *that*?" Thurfian asked with strained patience. "As long as he's out in the Chaos, there's not much chance of hauling him back and sitting him down in one of your hearing rooms."

"He has to come back sooner or later," Zistalmu said. "I've already put out an order to the Defense Force to detain him if and when he shows his face."

Thurfian frowned. "*You* put out an order?"

"With the backing of our Speaker, yes," Zistalmu said. "Do you have a problem with that?"

"Yes," Thurfian said. "Because the Syndicure doesn't have jurisdiction over the military."

"Maybe it doesn't, but it should," Zistalmu countered. "We're the Ascendancy's ultimate authority, after all. If Ja'fosk and Ba'kif won't rein him in"—his eyes flashed—"and if you *can't* rein him in, then it's up to us."

"Interesting thought," Thurfian murmured.

Except that it *wasn't* up to them. Not to the Syndicure as a whole, and certainly not to a single Syndic Prime or even a Speaker. The Aristocra of long ago had had solid reasons for insulating the Chiss military from Ruling Family politics, and those reasons hadn't changed.

"As to jurisdiction, I'll point out that the order was issued several hours ago and Supreme Admiral Ja'fosk still hasn't taken issue with it," Zistalmu continued. "It would be helpful if in the future such orders could be issued jointly by the Irizi *and* the Mitth."

"I think that would be a bit awkward," Thurfian pointed out. "The Mitth Patriarch can hardly be seen asking the Defense Force to detain one of its own family members."

"I wasn't talking just about Thrawn," Zistalmu said. "I was talking about other matters that might need to be addressed."

"You're welcome to bring them to my attention when they occur," Thurfian said. "But I can't simply make a blanket offer to support you."

For a moment Zistalmu seemed to study his face. "I remember a time when you and I were willing to ignore, circumvent, or even manipulate the political and military establishments for the good of the Ascendancy," he said. "I warned you that becoming Patriarch would change your attitudes. I see I was right."

"I have new responsibilities now," Thurfian said. "Not to mention heightened visibility. I can't skulk around the March of Silence having clandestine meetings with rival family syndics."

"Would you if you could?"

"I don't know," Thurfian conceded. "It would depend on the topic."

"And if that topic was still what we were going to do about Thrawn?"

"We'll have to see what he says in his defense when he returns."

"And then?" Zistalmu waved a hand in dismissal. "Never mind. I think I already know the answer." He straightened up and gave a curt nod. "Thank you for your time, Your Venerante," he said, his voice gone stiffly formal. "I'll await the delivery of your petition."

"Good day, Syndic Prime," Thurfian said, reaching for his comm control.

Zistalmu got to his first, and the display blanked.

Thurfian sighed. Over the past few weeks, as he settled into his new position, he'd wondered what being Patriarch would do to his friendships. Most of them had thankfully survived, though in somewhat altered form. But it was looking like his relationship with Zistalmu was already dead.

But then, it had probably never been a real friendship in the first place. They'd been rivals united in a cause they believed in, trying to protect the Ascendancy from a threat they thought only they could recognize.

Zistalmu still saw Thrawn as a threat. The question was, did Thurfian?

He snorted under his breath. Of course he did. Thrawn was still a danger to the Ascendancy's stability, and the sudden increase in tension just underscored how fragile that stability was.

But as he'd tried to tell Zistalmu, things weren't as simple as they'd been before. Not only did he have to consider the Mitth family's best interests, but he also had to factor in the other families' perception of him and those interests. And *that,* he was rapidly discovering, was a difficult balance to maintain.

Besides, anything he did right now was probably moot. Thrawn had abandoned his ship, and Zistalmu had forced through the detention order, and that was that. Expansionary Defense Fleet officers could talk all they wanted about camaraderie and protecting one another's backs, but when official decisions had been made and orders issued they *would* be followed. And once Ba'kif had him in custody, that threat, at least would be gone.

Though as a matter of interest, he would still like to hear whatever Thrawn had to say in his defense.

In the meantime, there was Mitth family work that needed to be done.

He keyed his intercom. "Senior Aide Thivik, please come in," he said. "I need you to draw up a petition for me."

CHAPTER TWENTY

Standing just inside Vault Four, far below the surface of Sposia, Patriarch Lamiov listened to the brief report and gave the proper acknowledgment. "His shuttle just landed," he announced as he put away his comm. "He should be here shortly."

Ba'kif nodded. About time. "Do you want me to go back up and meet him halfway?"

"No, that's all right," Lamiov said. "The guards have their orders. And there's no point in drawing more attention to this whole thing than we already have."

"I suppose," Ba'kif said, wincing a little. "I hate to think how many panicked reports have already flooded Csilla and Naporar about an alien warship orbiting Sposia."

"Oh, probably no more than a few hundred," Lamiov said with a wry smile. "Hopefully, all of them will be automatically attached to my assurances that everything is under control before Ja'fosk sends half the Defense Force charging to the rescue."

"Hopefully," Ba'kif said. "Though if he didn't react that way when Jixtus and his Kilji friends showed up, I don't see why he'd do it now."

"Never discount the novelty factor," Lamiov said. "No one on Sposia has ever seen a Nikardun blockade frigate before."

"Certainly not one painted with a Paccian subclan symbol."

"No," Lamiov agreed. "Like him or hate him, Thrawn's always had a knack for bringing fresh problems to the table."

"And the Syndicure does so enjoy fresh problems."

"Indeed." Lamiov looked over at the Vault Four door. "Do you ever regret it, Labaki? The path we started down all those years ago?"

"Do I regret *it*?" Ba'kif asked, feeling a fresh sense of his own age. Once, there'd been ten or twelve friends who'd persisted in calling him by his old Stybla core name when they were in private. Now Lamiov was the only one left. "Or do I regret *him*?"

"Not sure that's a different question," Lamiov said. "But without Thrass . . ." He shook his head. "It wasn't supposed to end this way."

"It hasn't exactly ended yet," Ba'kif reminded him. "And to answer your question, no, I don't regret it. Though I'll admit there've been times when I was defending him in front of some group of syndics that I wished we'd chosen someone else."

"*Was* there anyone else?"

"No," Ba'kif said. "But that's the point, isn't it? There wasn't, there isn't, nor is there likely ever to be one again. Not since Thomoro the Tragic has the Ascendancy produced anyone with Thrawn's unique combination of strategic and tactical skills plus the ability to observe, analyze, and predict."

"If only he also had Patriarch Thomoro's political skills," Lamiov said ruefully.

"Which I doubt he ever will," Ba'kif said. That had, after all, been the whole idea of working with Patriarch Thooraki to team him up with Thrass. The two of them working together . . . "But it's no good dwelling on what might have been."

"I suppose not." Lamiov gave a small, rather pained chuckle. "I heard once that pondering what-ifs and other missed opportunities is a sign of old age. I wonder which one of us it is."

"It's you, of course," Ba'kif assured him. "I gave up aging years ago."

"Ah, yes. I'd forgotten." Lamiov nodded toward the vault door. "You have any idea what he wants?"

"He didn't say," Ba'kif said, a shiver running through him. "But with the turmoil in the Ascendancy, and the sudden and suspicious alien focus on Sunrise . . . I don't really want to guess."

"Neither do I," Lamiov said. "But that hasn't stopped me. You?"

Ba'kif shook his head. "No."

For the next few minutes they waited together in silence. Then, at last, the door was opened from the outside by the guards, and Thrawn stepped into the vault.

Ba'kif watched Thrawn's face closely as he strode up to them, wondering if his own presence here had caught the other off guard. But if Thrawn was surprised to see his superior it didn't show in his expression. "Patriarch Lamiov," Thrawn greeted him, giving each of them a small head bow. "Supreme General Ba'kif. Thank you for seeing me."

"Your request didn't leave much room for argument," Lamiov said.

"Yes, and I'm sorry if my communication was overly brusque," Thrawn said. "But the timing is going to be critical, and I still don't know how much margin for error I have."

"Apology accepted," Lamiov said. "Tell us what you want from us."

"I need an item from Vault Four," Thrawn said. "I know UAG policy is to not allow alien artifacts to leave Stybla control—"

"Tell us what you need," Lamiov said.

"*And* what you need it for," Ba'kif added.

"I believe Jixtus is part of an alien force seeking to conquer this region of the Chaos," Thrawn said. "Or possibly even the entirety of it. I also believe he has a fleet nearby that he intends to bring against the Ascendancy." He seemed to draw himself up. "My intent is to draw him into an ambush before he launches his attack."

"Violating explicit Syndicure protocol," Ba'kif murmured.

"If necessary, yes."

Lamiov twitched his fingers in invitation. "Tell us all."

They listened in silence as Thrawn described his plan . . . and as he spoke, Ba'kif felt a coldness settle over him. It was madness, he told himself over and over, the coldness in his heart deepening with each detail Thrawn revealed.

The recitation ended, and Thrawn stood waiting for comment. Ba'kif gave Lamiov a furtive look out of the corner of his eye, but the other seemed to have attention only for Thrawn. Ba'kif waited, allowing the Patriarch to break the silence first.

Finally, Lamiov stirred. "So," he said, his voice as hollow as Ba'kif's heart was feeling. "Sunrise."

"Sunrise," Thrawn confirmed.

"I assume you know what this could do to the people there."

"I do."

"And you're still willing?"

A shadow of pain crossed Thrawn's face. But his nod was firm. "I believe it to be the Ascendancy's best chance, Your Venerante. Sunrise is the only place Jixtus cares enough about to gather his forces to. If we don't do this—if *I* don't do this—he'll continue to pit family against family until we've battered ourselves so far down that we won't survive his assault."

"But all that prodding will take time," Ba'kif pointed out. "Surely he won't attack until he's sure he can win. That gives us time."

"Does it?" Lamiov countered. "We've had skirmishes at Csaus, Sarvchi, Shihon, and now Jamiron. It seems to me the Ascendancy is doing its very best to tear itself apart. Willingly, even eagerly."

"You approve of this plan?" Ba'kif countered. "Have you considered the implications? *All* the implications?"

"If you mean am I aware of what the cost might be for giving my consent, then the answer is yes," Lamiov said. "And I accept it." He waved Ba'kif toward the door. "If you prefer to choose otherwise, you're welcome to wait in my office."

Ba'kif looked at Thrawn. So many years on this path. Perhaps Lamiov had been right earlier about that path coming to an end.

But if so, it wasn't going to end with Supreme General Ba'kif cowering from consequences in an underground room. "Thank you, Your Venerante," he said. "But no. I've trusted Senior Captain Thrawn in the past, and I've seen him achieve remarkable results. I think I can trust him one more time."

"Thank you," Thrawn said quietly. "Both of you."

"Save your thanks until we've seen the final end," Lamiov warned. "As you said, time is short. Let's get to work."

An hour later, they were finished.

"You know how to use it?" Ba'kif asked as Thrawn made one final check of the straps securing the crate inside the shuttle's cargo bay.

"I do," Thrawn said. "Once again, Supreme General, I thank you—"

"Your thanks can wait," Lamiov cut in, gazing at his comm, a tense expression on his face. "You need to get back to your ship right away. Admiral Dy'lothe and the *Venturous* have just arrived . . . and the admiral's calling on your Paccian friends to surrender.

"Or to be destroyed."

"Three, two, *one*," Ar'alani called, resisting the impulse to rub her eyes. A commander, she reminded herself firmly, needed to look at all times like she was fully in command of herself, her crew, and her ship.

But four hours of sleep *really* wasn't cutting it.

"Home again, home again," Wutroow murmured the old children's sing-song. "Senior Commander Biclian?"

"Combat range clear, ma'am," Biclian reported. "Mid-range—"

"Admiral, we've got company," Larsiom cut in from the comm station. "The *Venturous* is here, currently in low planetary orbit." He half turned toward Ar'alani. "Admiral Dy'lothe reports he has a Nikardun blockade frigate pinned inside the gravity well."

"*What?*" Wutroow demanded.

"Octrimo: in-system jump," Ar'alani ordered. "Get us in as close and as fast as you can. Larsiom, acknowledge and request that Admiral Dy'lothe hold off any action until we arrive."

"Oh, no," Wutroow breathed as the two officers began working their boards, her eyes wide with sudden understanding. "You don't think . . . *Thrawn?*"

"You know anyone else who's got a friend with his own Nikardun warship?" Ar'alani ground out. She'd skimmed Mid Captain Samakro's report of the Rapacc and Sunrise incidents, and had no doubt that the Council and Syndicure were ready to run Thrawn through the shredder.

So naturally, he'd come to Sposia. Of all the times—and all the places—for him to pop randomly back into view.

Or *was* it random?

Thrawn could easily have heard that she and the *Vigilant* had been assigned to protect Sposia. Had he come here expecting to find an ally and a sympathetic ear?

Very likely. Unfortunately, he couldn't have predicted the Tahmie and Droc would decide to pick a fight at Jamiron, and that Ar'alani would be sent to break it up. Now, instead of a sympathetic ear, he had Dy'lothe, admiral of the Chiss Defense Force, who was reputed to have not a single sympathetic bone or ligament in his entire body.

"Jump ready, Admiral," Octrimo called.

"*Venturous* says this is none of our business, ma'am," Larsiom added.

"Do they," Ar'alani said coolly. "Octrimo: Three, two, *one*."

A flicker of stars, and they were there. Ar'alani did a quick scan of the sky through the viewport—

"There," Wutroow said, pointing. "There's the *Venturous*."

"I see it," Ar'alani said. The Groundlion man-of-war was at a mid-orbit altitude, but using its thrusters to maintain a geosynchronous position instead of circling the planet. Ten kilometers farther inward was the Nikardun blockade frigate, facing the *Venturous* and also using thrusters to hold position.

And both ships were sitting directly over the UAG complex.

Ja'fosk had been right, Ar'alani thought distantly. Someone *had* gotten into the UAG vaults. The supreme admiral had simply been wrong about who that person would be.

"Get me a tight-beam to the *Venturous*," she ordered Larsiom. "Biclian, is that a shuttle loading into the blockade frigate?"

"Yes, ma'am, it is," Biclian confirmed. "Not a familiar configuration—must be one of theirs."

"A Paccian one, yes," Ar'alani said. "Larsiom?"

"*Venturous* says Admiral Dy'lothe is busy, ma'am," Larsiom reported.

"Tell him that Nikardun ship is commanded by a Chiss officer," Ar'alani said. "Oeskym, prepare a laser salvo, aimed through the open space between the *Venturous* and the blockade frigate."

"And make sure the backtrail is clear of patrol ships or civilians,"

Wutroow added, leaving Ar'alani's side and crossing to stand behind the weapons station.

"Larsiom?" Ar'alani asked.

"They say they already know that, ma'am," Larsiom said. "They say Admiral Dy'lothe contacted Csilla and was told the Syndicure has ordered that Senior Captain Thrawn be detained."

Ar'alani scowled. This just got better and better. "I need to talk to him."

"I'm sorry, ma'am, but he's refusing your call."

"Sounds like he needs a tap on the shoulder," Wutroow said darkly.

"Apparently so," Ar'alani agreed. "Oeskym?"

"Ready, Admiral."

"Fire."

The *Vigilant*'s spectrum lasers spat out, cutting through the gap between the other two ships. "I'm guessing a four-count," Wutroow said. "One, two—"

"Ar'alani, what the *hell* are you doing?" a voice bellowed from the speaker.

"Just getting your attention, Admiral Dy'lothe," Ar'alani said. "I'm told you have an order to detain Senior Captain Thrawn?"

"Yes, I do," Dy'lothe growled. "Would you care to see it?"

"All I need to know is if it's from Supreme Admiral Ja'fosk, Supreme General Ba'kif, or someone on the Council."

"You need a comm officer with cleaner ears," Dy'lothe said. "Mine already told him the order came from the Syndicure."

"And since when does the Syndicure have direct authority over the Defense Force?"

"It doesn't matter who gave the order," Dy'lothe countered. "The Syndicure wants Thrawn, I have him, and I'm going to deliver him. You can assist or stand down—your choice."

"Did you ask Senior Captain Thrawn why he's here?" Ar'alani asked.

"I don't care why he's here."

"Maybe you should," Ar'alani said, some impatience creeping into her voice. "You need to look past your orders to the bigger picture."

"My eyesight is just fine, thank you."

"Maybe, maybe not," Ar'alani said. "I know Thrawn, and he has a good reason for everything he does. Whatever his reason for being on Sposia, it's important."

"Maybe to your Expansionary Defense Fleet it is," Dy'lothe said disdainfully. "All you do is look out at the Chaos. The Defense Force sees things rather more on that larger scale you just mentioned."

"How about the survival of the Ascendancy?" Ar'alani countered. "Is that a large enough scale for you?"

Dy'lothe chuckled, a dry, humorless sound. "You always *did* tend toward the overly dramatic. Well. It's been nice chatting with you, but I have work to do. The warship's captain requested that I hold off any action until Thrawn's shuttle was aboard, and now it is. If you'll excuse me, I have a tractor beam operation to direct."

Ar'alani stared out the viewport, trying to sort through the possibilities. Was the request to allow the shuttle back aboard the frigate before being taken into custody nothing more than stalling? Or did Thrawn already have a plan for getting out from under the *Venturous*'s thumb?

In other words, should Ar'alani sit back and watch, or should she intervene?

More risk. More consequences. But down deep, she knew she couldn't leave this to chance, or even to Thrawn's tactical skill. Whatever he was doing, it was important, and it was part of her job as an Expansionary Defense Fleet officer to do what she could to help him succeed.

"I'm sorry, Admiral," she said. "But I can't let you do that."

"Excuse me?" Dy'lothe said, his voice gone dark. "*You* can't let *me* carry out my orders?"

"Your *illegal* orders," Ar'alani countered, looking at the tactical. The *Vigilant* was in combat range now, which meant she could fully engage the *Venturous* if she chose. If she picked her target carefully enough . . .

"And who are you to decide which orders I should obey and which I should ignore?" Dy'lothe retorted. "I swear, Ar'alani. One more word out of *you*—"

And in that instant, Thrawn made his move.

The blockade frigate leapt forward, charging straight at the *Venturous*. Ar'alani caught her breath, waiting for the man-of-war's lasers to open fire and blast the Nikardun warship into bits of broken metal and ceramic. But before Dy'lothe's weapons crews could react, the frigate did a pitch-and-roll, turning away from the *Venturous* and blazing off at an angle across the edge of Sposia's atmosphere.

"Electrical discharge from the *Venturous*," Biclian snapped. "Looks like a massive short circuit around the bow laser and tractor emplacements."

"Run it back," Ar'alani ordered, turning to the secondary sensor display. With her full attention focused on Thrawn's maneuver, she hadn't even noticed whatever it was Biclian was talking about. The sensor image of the *Venturous* flowed backward as Biclian reversed the recording . . . there was the flash . . . was that something that had been launched from the blockade frigate . . . ?

"That's not a short," Wutroow said suddenly. "That was a Crippler net." She looked at Ar'alani, her expression seemingly caught amid surprise, outrage, and admiration. "Thrawn threw a *Crippler net* at him."

"And there he goes," Octrimo said.

Ar'alani looked back at the viewport. Thrawn's blockade frigate was tearing at full speed across the starscape, weaving slightly as it bounced across Sposia's upper atmosphere, heading for the planetary rim and the edge of the gravity well beyond. The *Venturous* was also under way, running up its drive and charging off in pursuit.

But the man-of-war was far bigger than the blockade frigate, with correspondingly more mass and inertia, and it was quickly clear that with Thrawn's head start there was no way the *Venturous* would catch him before he escaped to hyperspace. Dy'lothe's only other option was to open fire and try to bring him down.

Ar'alani looked at the sensor display. Only he couldn't, she saw. His bow weapons cluster had been paralyzed by the Crippler net's massive electrical jolt, and he hadn't bothered to activate the *Venturous*'s shoulder weapons during the two ships' brief confrontation. By the time those lasers could be brought to sufficient power, Thrawn would be out of range.

Wutroow crossed back to Ar'alani's command chair. "Another thirty seconds and he'll be clear," she said quietly. "Until then, a breacher or sphere can still reach him."

"He won't fire," Ar'alani said. "He just saw how fast and maneuverable that blockade frigate is. He'll realize that Thrawn will be able to dodge either weapon."

"He might do it out of spite," Wutroow warned.

"No." Ar'alani cocked an eyebrow up at her. "You didn't *really* think he wanted to follow the Syndicure's orders, did you?"

Wutroow frowned. "Excuse me?"

"All that *legal order* blather was purely for the official record," Ar'alani explained. "Now, if *Ja'fosk* had given him the order, Thrawn would be in the *Venturous*'s brig right now. But Dy'lothe has spent way too many years in the Defense Force to be impressed by any group of Aristocra."

"Interesting," Wutroow murmured. "He certainly had *me* fooled."

"As I said, that was the idea," Ar'alani said. "But there were signs."

"Such as?"

"Such as leaving his shoulder lasers powered down so Thrawn only had to disable the bow cluster," Ar'alani said. "Such as chatting with me instead of simply tractoring in the frigate as soon as the shuttle was secured." She gave Wutroow a small smile. "Such as trying to goad me into taking a shot at him so that he could pretend I'd distracted him long enough for Thrawn to slip out of his pin."

"Thereby shifting some of the blame onto you?" Wutroow gave a gentle snort. "Nice of him."

"I would have been willing to share it with him," Ar'alani said. "And just for your private amusement, I was getting ready to fire on him anyway."

"Admiral, the *Venturous* is pulling back from its pursuit," Octrimo reported. "Looks like they've given up."

"Acknowledged," Ar'alani said. "Larsiom, signal to Admiral Dy'lothe."

"Yes, ma'am," Larsiom said. "You have comm, Admiral."

"Ar'alani here, Admiral," Ar'alani called. "My sensor officer tells me he's observed some problem with your bow weapons cluster. Do you need any assistance?"

"Thank you, no," Dy'lothe said. His tone was frosty, but Ar'alani thought she could hear some private relief beneath it. "Your boy Thrawn is certainly a clever one. I hope you're happy."

"I'll be happy when the Ascendancy is back to normal," Ar'alani said. "Until then, we of the military have to trust each other and watch each other's backs. There's a lot of darkness out there that we're being called on to stand against."

"As I said before, overly dramatic," Dy'lothe growled. "Now if you'll excuse me, I have a cargo of debris to deliver to the UAG."

Ar'alani frowned. "Debris?"

"Yes," Dy'lothe said. "Don't worry, it wasn't one of ours. Seems some missile tucked away inside a fake asteroid blew itself up in the Ornfra system."

Ar'alani looked up, exchanging startled looks with Wutroow. "Was anyone hurt?"

"As I already told you, it wasn't our debris," Dy'lothe said. "I'll send you the records of the incident. Dy'lothe out."

"*Venturous* has ended comm," Larsiom said.

"Hell," Wutroow muttered. "They're bringing the damn things into the Ascendancy now?"

"Sounds like it," Ar'alani said grimly. "At least the Defense Force should now know what to look for."

"They'd have already known that if they bothered to read our reports," Wutroow grumbled.

"I'm sure *some* of them read them."

"Admiral, we have a tight-beam from the surface," Larsiom said, sounding puzzled. "It's Supreme General Ba'kif."

"Ba'kif?" Wutroow repeated, frowning. "What's he doing—? Oh. Right. Thrawn."

"Probably," Ar'alani said. "Send it over here, Junior Commander."

"Yes, ma'am."

Ar'alani keyed her chair's speaker, making sure it was at the private volume setting. "Ar'alani."

"Ba'kif, Admiral," Ba'kif's voice came back. "That was quite a show you put on up there."

"We were mostly spectators," Ar'alani said.

"So I saw," Ba'kif said. "Still, it's fortunate that you arrived when you did. Senior Captain Thrawn recorded a message for you before he left Sposia. Are you secure?"

"Yes, sir," Ar'alani said. Beside her, Wutroow made a questioning rumble in her throat. Ar'alani shook her head and gestured for her to stay by the chair. "Ready to receive."

"Here it comes."

Ar'alani listened in silence as the message played out. "Measured by sheer boldness," she commented when it was finished, "I think Thrawn has finally outdone himself. I take it this isn't an official order?"

"You know it's not," Ba'kif said heavily. "Nor can it ever be. No, for the myriad political reasons I'm sure you've already thought of, this has to be completely on Thrawn's shoulders."

"Understood," Ar'alani said. So even if it worked, Thrawn was going to face some serious consequences from the Syndicure. If it failed . . .

Her stomach knotted. If it failed, nothing mattered anyway. The Ascendancy would be doomed.

"If we're going to do this, we'll need to leave within the next few hours," she told Ba'kif. "Can you get us taken off Sposia protection duty?"

"Admiral?" Larsiom called from the comm station. "Admiral, a message marked *urgent* has just come through."

"I'll look at it in a minute, Junior Commander," Ar'alani called back.

"No, I think you'd better look at it now," Ba'kif said, sounding distracted. "I just got one, too. You're being recalled to Naporar."

"We're *what*?" Ar'alani said, pulling up the message.

From: Supreme Admiral Ja'fosk, Csilla

To: All Expansionary Defense Fleet Ships

Effective immediately, all ships are relieved of planetary guard duty and ordered to return to Naporar.

"Okay, *that's* different," Wutroow muttered, leaning over Ar'alani's shoulder to read the message.

"If by *different* you mean *utterly nonsensical,* I'd have to agree," Ar'alani said, frowning at the message. "General, does this make any sense to you?"

"My version has a bit more detail," Ba'kif growled. "Apparently, the Syndicure is furious with you over your stunt at Jamiron a few hours ago. Toss that on top of the skirmish between the *Grayshrike* and *Orisson* at Ornfra, and some of the families have had enough. Irizi Syndic Zistalmu led the charge, pushing through an order for the Expansionary Defense Fleet to withdraw all its ships from worlds where any of the Nine have interests."

"Which is all of them," Wutroow put in.

"Basically, yes," Ba'kif said. "Ja'fosk is appealing for calm—and common sense—but while he tries to work something out he's pulling everyone back to Naporar."

"He'll need to make an exception for the *Vigilant*," Ar'alani reminded him. "Thrawn wants me at Schesa."

"Yes, but the location may not be critical," Ba'kif said. "Thrawn didn't know about this order when he recorded his message, after all. Why would it matter where you and the other ships rendezvous?"

"I don't know," Ar'alani said. "But I've worked with Thrawn enough to know that details are usually important."

"Point," Ba'kif conceded. "Let me call Ja'fosk and get you an exemption."

"Or maybe you can suggest he leave it a little vague as to where we're supposed to gather," Ar'alani suggested. "As long as Naporar is at the top of the list, most ships will go there."

"But you and whatever other captains you're able to persuade won't be officially violating the order," Ba'kif said. "And if he words it properly, Syndic Zistalmu probably won't even notice there's a loophole. Good enough. I'll get on that right away."

"Thank you, sir," Ar'alani said. "We'll head out immediately."

"Good luck," Ba'kif said. "Any idea who else you're going to ask into this madness?"

"I have some ideas," Ar'alani said. "I'll start with Thrawn's friends."

Ba'kif grunted. "I'm guessing that's a short list."

Ar'alani nodded heavily. "Yes. It is."

"You realize that there's nothing at all official about this," Ar'alani's voice came from Ziinda's chair speaker.

An urgent voice. A worried voice. A determined voice.

"If we do this, we do it without orders or sanction," the admiral continued. "We do it because we see a terrible threat looming over the Ascendancy, and we believe this to be our best and possibly only hope of defeating it."

"I understand," Ziinda said, looking up at Apros. Her first officer's stance was unnaturally stiff as he stood beside her chair, his face troubled. "Mid Captain Apros? You have a comment?"

"Yes, Senior Captain," Apros said. "First of all is the plan itself. Even if this device works the way Senior Captain Thrawn says it will—and I'm personally a bit uncomfortable with staking our hopes on a piece of alien tech—there's still a horrible potential for death. Actually, if it works it'll probably mean *more* death."

"That's the idea, Mid Captain," Ar'alani said. "If we can isolate the Grysk fleet—"

"Excuse me, Admiral," Ziinda said. There was a look in Apros's eye that she knew all too well. "I'd like a brief consultation with my first officer."

"Of course," Ar'alani said. "Take as long as you need."

"Thank you." Ziinda touched her chair's mute key. "Okay, Mid Captain. From your expression, I'm guessing it's your family?"

"It's all right, ma'am," he assured her. "I'm all right. You need to finish your consultation with Admiral Ar'alani."

"I need to make sure my first officer is fully aboard before I commit to anything this crazy," Ziinda said.

"I'm aboard, Senior Captain," Apros assured her. "This doesn't have anything to do with the mission. I'll be happy to talk about it later, but not right now."

"All right," Ziinda said, giving him one more hard look before keying her mike again. "Admiral Ar'alani?"

"I'm here, Senior Captain."

"We're good to go, ma'am," Ziinda said. "What do you want us to do?"

"Thrawn wants us to rendezvous at Schesa in three days," Ar'alani said. "Pass the word if you can. But only to those you can trust. If the Syndicure gets even a whisper of this, it'll be over before it even starts."

"Understood," Ziinda said. "Is the invitation limited to Expansionary Defense Fleet ships?"

"Not necessarily," Ar'alani said. "You have someone else in mind?"

"Maybe," Ziinda said. "I'll let you know."

"Do that. Ar'alani out."

"Comm ended, Senior Captain," Shrent confirmed from across the bridge.

"Acknowledged," Ziinda said. She raised her eyebrows at Apros. "All right, Mid Captain. Talk to me."

"Yes, ma'am." Apros winced. "But it's going to sound stupid."

"I've done more than my fair share of stupid," Ziinda said. "Unless you're thinking about starting a war with two other families over a non-existent nyix mine, I'm already way ahead of you on that one. So spit it out."

"Yes, ma'am." Apros hesitated. "The thing is . . . the Csap don't get much respect in the Syndicure. We're mostly ignored or used as bargaining levers. And we're the butt of a lot of jokes. You'll remember Captain Roscu's comment at Jamiron about the Csap not being a step up."

"You're still one of the Ruling Families," Ziinda reminded him.

"Yes, and we're justly proud of that," Apros said. "It's just . . . if this works it'll be you, Thrawn, and Ar'alani who'll be remembered."

"*And* probably brought up on charges."

"But you'll be *remembered*," Apros repeated. "I'm willing to die for the Ascendancy, Senior Captain, and I hope that if that happens it'll be because I've made a difference. But . . . I know it's petty, but I don't want that sacrifice to be forgotten."

"I understand," Ziinda said. "First of all. The important part of your statement is that, yes, you'll be making a difference. That's the whole point of this."

"Yes, ma'am, I know."

"As for being remembered . . ." Ziinda shook her head. "History isn't ours to write, Apros. None of us know how we'll be remembered by scholars a hundred years from now. But be assured that those who know you, who have worked with you, and who respect you will hold your memory close. Everyone else—" She gave him a small shrug. "Does it really matter?"

Apros pursed his lips. "No. No, I suppose not."

"And look at the bright side," Ziinda continued. "If things work out right, you might just end up being the hero your family has been waiting for all these years. The one who will finally put an end to all the Csap jokes."

"With all due respect, Senior Captain, I think that might be pushing it," Apros said, giving her a tentative smile. "All right, ma'am. Self-pity moment over."

"Good," Ziinda said. "Have Wikivv plot a course for Schesa. We'll head out after I've made a couple of calls."

"To others who might be willing to risk their lives on this ridiculous plan?"

"To others who are ready to make a difference," Ziinda corrected. "And to be remembered by their friends." She motioned toward the helm. "Get to work on that course, Mid Captain. We've got a long path ahead of us."

MEMORIES XII

He would give it all he could, Thrass remembered promising himself as he and Thrawn left the Stybla honoring ceremony. He would do it for the honor of the Mitth and the glory of the Ascendancy. Or he would die trying.

Even now, careening inexorably toward his death, he could nevertheless appreciate the irony.

A massive alien spaceship, snatched out from under the noses of a Chaf task force determined to gain sole possession of it. He and a single human female from Lesser Space, attempting to take the ship to an uninhabited refuge world from which they could offer the treasure trove of Republic technology to the full Hierarchy Defense Council.

Only it hadn't worked out that way. The ship was too damaged to reach the world they'd hoped to bring it to. Worse, there was a whole group of survivors aboard that no one had known about when Thrass first agreed to this mission.

And the reality of their chosen crash site dictated that either he and his human pilot companion could survive, or the other innocent humans could. But not both.

"You can't handle the landing alone," the pilot said, her voice grim but resolute. "But I could do that while you go."

She was right, of course. Thrass *could* escape. There

was a ship aboard that he should be able to fly back to the Ascendancy. He could yet survive to do all the great things Patriarch Thooraki expected of him and Thrawn.

But no. "And who would keep the remaining systems from self-destruction while you cleared a path through the pylon for me?" he countered.

She had no answer for that, because there wasn't one. If Thrass left, everyone aboard would die.

He thought about his father, and how he'd given his life for a man he didn't even know. How could Thrass turn his back on these people, save himself, and condemn all of them to certain death?

The answer was simple. He couldn't.

There would be no honor in this for the Mitth. Nor would there be glory for the Ascendancy. It was likely no one would ever even know what happened here today. They almost certainly would never find whatever remained of the ship.

Perhaps that was for the best. He'd seen the Ruling Families battling together, striving to turn small advantages into political gains. A ship bristling with alien technology could spark a frenzy that might have huge and lasting effects on the always precarious balance of power.

If Thrass couldn't bring glory, at least he could perhaps succeed in not bringing destruction.

"Your people will come here someday," the woman said quietly. "Until then, the survivors have enough food and supplies to last for generations. They'll survive. I know they will."

Thrass looked at the displays, at the image of the stone-filled valley rushing up toward them. He hoped she was right. But like the ship itself, it was probably something no one would ever know.

The survivors might eventually figure out what had happened. But even if they did, they wouldn't remember

Thrass. Perhaps they would remember the woman who had worked to save them, but not the Chiss who'd died at her side.

But that wasn't important. He would know, and the woman would know.

Are you prepared to embrace this secret to your graves and beyond? The old Mitth oath whispered through his mind. Was that promise heavy with responsibility but empty of reality? Or did its words truly hint at something beyond death?

He didn't know. But he was about to find out.

"I hope someday humans and Chiss will be able to work side by side in peace," he told the woman.

"As do I, Syndic Mitth'ras'safis of the Eighth Ruling Family," she said, taking his hand.

"Then let us bring this part of history to a close," he said, trying to put some confidence into his voice. "May warrior's fortune smile on our efforts."

And if not on theirs, he added silently, perhaps warrior's fortune would smile on Thrawn.

The man who was, and who had truly always been, his brother.

CHAPTER TWENTY-ONE

The stars reappeared, and the *Orisson* was finally back home.

And the time had come, Roscu thought with a certain dread, for that conversation with Patriarch Rivlex.

But not quite yet. The *Orisson* had made the last half of the voyage in a single leg, and even in the relatively smooth space between Chiss worlds prudence dictated that a pilot build a hefty margin of error into the course calculations. As a result, the *Orisson* had emerged from hyperspace a long way from the planet itself, far enough in fact that Rhigar's sun was barely distinguishable from the background stars.

"Helm, get me an in-system jump," Roscu ordered.

"To the planet?" Raamas asked.

"Where else?" Roscu asked, frowning.

"I thought you might want to take a look at the Junkyard first," Raamas said. "See if that alien fleet is still there."

"And see if we can get one of them to chase us again?" Roscu countered. "No, I think we'll give that a pass. At least until after we've talked to the Patriarch."

"Yes, ma'am." Raamas nodded to the pilot. "In-system jump to Rhigal."

"Acknowledged."

And as the pilot started the necessary calculations, Roscu thought about her last contact with the outside universe. That strange conversation with Senior Captain Ziinda.

Her proposal had been sheer insanity, of course. Heading off to an alien world to try to trap and destroy an enemy fleet wasn't something a responsible captain did, certainly not on a whim, and absolutely not without orders. Roscu's primary responsibility was to the Clarr family, her second was to her ship and crew, and neither obligation permitted that kind of adventurism. She and Raamas had discussed it briefly after Ziinda's call, and both had been in agreement.

Which didn't mean they were ignoring the situation's potential for disaster. The *Orisson* had already tangled briefly with one of these alien warships, and if Jixtus was indeed the imminent threat Ziinda claimed he was then he and his forces definitely needed to be dealt with. But not in some haphazard way, and not in the midst of family distrust and heightened antagonism.

And *definitely* not if it meant blindly following Senior Captain Thrawn. She wasn't ready to take a step like that.

"Ready, Captain," Raamas said.

"Take us in."

There was the usual flicker, and they had arrived. "Contact System Patrol and get us a low equatorial orbit," she told the pilot. "Commander Raamas, have a shuttle prepared. Comm, get me Lieutenant Rupiov at the homestead defense center."

"Captain, we have a signal already coming through," the comm officer said. "Patriarch Rivlex is calling you."

"Send it here," Roscu said, keying her chair's speaker. The things she had to say to the Patriarch weren't for the rest of the bridge crew to hear.

"Yes, ma'am." The officer keyed for reception.

"Captain Roscu, this is Patriarch Rivlex," the Patriarch's voice boomed, the words stiff with anger.

Boomed across from the bridge speaker. Roscu looked sharply at the comm officer, got a helpless look in return and a gesture at the comm board. Apparently, Rivlex's ground-based comm center had overridden her choice of speakers, forcing the conversation to go public.

And that, Roscu realized with a sinking heart, was not good.

"Captain Roscu here, Your Venerante," she said.

"Finally," Rivlex bit out. "I've been trying to reach you for the past day. Jixtus said you'd been attacked, and that he hadn't been able to contact you."

"We've been in hyperspace, Your Venerante," Roscu said. "We wanted to get back to Rhigal—"

"You wanted to get *back*?" Rivlex interrupted harshly. "Did I or did I not send you to Ornfra to find evidence of Dasklo duplicity?"

"Yes, Your Venerante, you did," Roscu said. "But as Jixtus said, we were attacked and decided—"

"You don't look damaged, Captain," Rivlex said, again cutting her off. "You made it all the way here without putting in at a bluedock for repairs. I'll ask again: Were your orders to go to Ornfra?"

Roscu ground her teeth. It was a pattern she'd seen before: The Patriarch picking someone who'd displeased him and grinding that person into the dirt in front of friends, colleagues, and other officials. A double helping of shame and humiliation, usually topped off with a withdrawal of position, status, or sometimes even family affiliation. "My orders were to go to Ornfra," she said.

"And did you achieve the goal that was set before you?"

"No, Your Venerante, I did not."

"That was all I needed to know. Commander Raamas?"

"Yes, Your Venerante?" Raamas called.

"You're hereby promoted to captain and reinstated as commander of the *Orisson*," Rivlex said. "You will prepare a shuttle and send former Captain Roscu to the homestead. Then you will go to Ornfra and get me the proof I need to take down the Dasklo."

"Understood, Your Venerante," Raamas said briskly. "Do I report back to you on my findings, or do I communicate directly with Jixtus and your new fleet?"

"Ah, yes—my new fleet," Rivlex echoed, his voice going even darker. "I'd almost forgotten that Roscu deliberately intruded on a secret military assemblage that she had no business pressing her nose into. Did she tell anyone else about it?"

"No, Your Venerante, she didn't," Raamas assured him. "I assumed it was to be kept within the family, and have therefore kept close watch on her communications."

"Excellent, Captain," Rivlex said, some of the anger easing from his voice. "Excellent indeed. See that Roscu is put into wrist restraints before she's returned to me. There may be charges of treason added to the list."

"Yes, Your Venerante," Raamas said. "We'll communicate our findings directly to you. May I ask if we may take a day or two of leave before traveling to Ornfra? My crew's been in space for a long time."

"Are you hard of hearing, Captain?" Rivlex growled, the anger back in full force. "No, you may not take leave. I want that evidence now. Do you hear me? Right *now*."

"Of course, Your Venerante," Raamas said. He looked at Roscu, a small smile touching the corners of his lips.

Roscu felt a bitter taste rise into her mouth. So here it was, the final hammer on the end of her career. Only now did she remember how casually Raamas had accepted his demotion when Roscu first talked the Patriarch into letting her take command of the *Orisson*. Looking back, she could see now that he'd simply hidden his resentment until he could stab her in the back.

And by her own actions, Roscu had set herself up for destruction.

"Then prepare your ship, Captain," Rivlex said. "As for you, Roscu, I'll see you very soon."

The comm chimed, and he was gone.

"Orders, Captain?" the pilot asked in an uncertain voice.

"Prepare the *Orisson* for hyperspace," Raamas said.

"Yes, sir. And the shuttle?"

Raamas looked at Roscu. "What shuttle?"

Roscu frowned, noting peripherally that none of the rest of the bridge crew was reacting in the slightest to his strange comment.

"Yes, *sir*," the pilot said, all brisk and businesslike again. "Course?"

"Wait a minute, Commander—Captain," Roscu corrected herself. "The Patriarch ordered you to send me to the homestead."

"I was also ordered to head out as soon as possible," Raamas reminded her.

"But—"

"I believe Senior Captain Ziinda specified Schesa as the rendez-vous point," he continued. "Set our course there."

"Captain, what are you doing?" Roscu asked in a low voice. Raamas was about to make the worst mistake of his career, and she couldn't just sit by and watch him do it. "You can't simply ignore the Patriarch that way."

"You mean the Patriarch who ordered an alien ship to track us down and shoot us out of the sky?" Raamas countered, his voice suddenly cold. "The Patriarch who's made a deal with the owner of that alien ship? The Patriarch who relieved you of command because you were more worried about the Ascendancy than his vendetta against the Dasklo?"

"None of that makes a difference," Roscu said.

"I believe it makes all the difference," Raamas said. "I told you before that I thought we were standing on an edge. I'm even more convinced of that now."

"But you also said you didn't like Ar'alani's plan," Roscu pointed out.

"Because *you* didn't like it," Raamas said. "And that was mostly because Senior Captain Thrawn was going to be in charge, and it was clear you didn't want to submit your ship to his authority." He smiled tightly. "But it's not your ship anymore, is it?"

Roscu felt her throat tighten. It wasn't that easy, she knew. Given her history with Thrawn, turning over her command was only part of it.

But Raamas was right. The Ascendancy was in trouble, and it was the suspicions and passions of people like Patriarch Rivlex that were driving that rush to destruction. Someone had to step out of the tangle, rise above the family politics, and do something.

She and Raamas were Clarr. But they were Chiss first.

"Your ship, Captain Raamas," she said, standing up and stepping to the side of the command chair. "Your orders."

"Thank you," Raamas said, stepping over to the chair and sitting down. "Helm, you have your orders. Schesa, if you please. Best possible time."

"Yes, sir."

"And once we're under way," he added, looking up at Roscu, "Captain Roscu and I will explain exactly what it is we've gotten the rest of you into."

Mid Captain Samakro had told Thalias he would try to arrange for a shuttle to take her off her transport from Ool. Unfortunately, when she arrived at Csilla a message was waiting that the transport company had refused to disrupt their schedule that way. A follow-up message from Samakro had informed her that he would have someone meet her at the ground terminal when she arrived.

Given the urgency of the recall, and Samakro's no doubt busy schedule aboard ship, Thalias expected some lower-level officer to be waiting when she walked out of the arrival terminal. To her surprise, Samakro himself was there, standing stiff and tall and in full dress honor chains.

"Thalias," he greeted her tersely as she came up to him. "I'll take that," he added, plucking the travel bag from her hands. "The shuttle's this way."

Without waiting for a response, he turned and headed through the crowd of pedestrians toward one of the other corridors. "I'm sorry about the transport," Thalias said, hurrying to catch up. "Should I have talked to the captain myself?"

"Wouldn't have done any good," Samakro said as she settled in at his side. "I'm Ufsa and the transport company's owned by the Droc family. They were already disinclined to do me any favors." He huffed out a breath. "And of course, Jamiron didn't exactly help the Expansionary Defense Fleet's image any."

"What happened at Jamiron?" Thalias asked, frowning.

"Oh, right—you've been in hyperspace," Samakro said. "The Tahmie and Droc picked Jamiron to hold an impromptu punching match. The *Vigilant* was sent to break it up, but by the time it got there they were already shooting at each other. With noncombatant civilian ships at risk, Admiral Ar'alani decided to flicker the whole lot of them and then tractor the various ships to different orbital shells."

"Oh," Thalias said.

"*Oh* is right," Samakro said. "Needless to say, that didn't exactly endear us to any of the Nine or Forty." He nodded sideways. "As you can see."

Thalias looked around, focusing for the first time on the people they were passing. Most of them simply ignored him, while some glanced at the uniform and then looked away with complete indifference.

But there were a few, invariably in Aristocra garb, who stared at him with narrowed or openly hostile eyes. "I'm sorry," she said.

"Don't worry about it," he said. "We don't do this because we want to be loved. We do this because it needs to be done. Come on—I'll put you on the shuttle so you can get to the ship and settle in. We'll be leaving as soon as I'm back."

"You're not coming with me?"

"I need to talk to someone important first," Samakro said. "Don't worry, it shouldn't take long."

"Who is this important person?"

"I don't know yet," Samakro said. "Hopefully a Speaker, though I may have to settle for a Syndic Prime if I can't find one. Basically, I'll talk to whoever will listen."

"Is there anyone in particular you're looking for?" Thalias persisted.

"Well, I won't be approaching the Tahmie or Droc, that's for sure," Samakro said, frowning at her. "It's something Senior Captain Thrawn needs that only someone at the Syndicure level can provide."

Thalias braced herself. "Would a Patriarch do?"

Samakro stopped dead in his tracks, his eyes suddenly hard and suspicious. "Interesting question," he said softly. "Why do you ask?"

Thalias forced herself to meet his gaze. There it was at last, the end of the path she'd been walking since she first boarded the *Springhawk*. Probably the end of her career, as well. "Enough games, Mid Captain," she said softly. "We need to talk."

"Fine." His eyes flicked around the corridor, settled on an unoccupied vender alcove. "Over there."

A minute later they were in the alcove. "I'm listening," Samakro
said.

"I know that you've never liked me," Thalias said. "You also think
I came aboard the *Springhawk* to spy on Senior Captain Thrawn."

"Correct on both counts," Samakro said evenly. "I'll note that the
one comment feeds directly into the other."

So apparently he didn't dislike her just for herself? That was something, anyway. "And you were partially right," she said. "Syndic Thurfian's price for getting me aboard as Che'ri's caregiver was a promise
that I'd report Thrawn's activities to him, especially anything that
seemed illegal or improper."

"Why?"

"Why did he make me promise?" Thalias asked. "Or why did he
want to know about the senior captain?"

"Let's go with the latter," Samakro said. "The reason for making
you promise is pretty obvious."

"He wanted a reason to get Senior Captain Thrawn off the *Springhawk*," Thalias said. "Possibly out of the Expansionary Defense Fleet
entirely. He thought—probably still thinks—that he's a danger to the
Mitth and to the Ascendancy as a whole." She winced at the memory
of that painful conversation she and Thurfian had had just before she
went to the Mitth homestead to take the Trials. "The point is that I
never gave him anything."

"What about your promise?"

"I told him I never saw Senior Captain Thrawn do anything questionable, illegal, or unethical, and never anything against the Mitth."

"He accepted that?"

"Not really," Thalias conceded. "He threatened to have me rematched out of the Mitth completely if I didn't cooperate. But I got
around that."

"How?"

"I took the Trials and passed them," Thalias said. "That meant he
couldn't just casually get me thrown out of the family without going

through official procedures that might attract attention he didn't want. More important—to me, at least—while I was at the homestead I met Patriarch Thooraki, who asked me to keep an eye on Senior Captain Thrawn and keep him out of—what's funny?" she interrupted herself as Samakro's lip suddenly curved into a smile.

"Nothing," Samakro said, the smile fading. "I'm just thinking of you as Senior Captain Thrawn's big, strong protector."

"Smile all you want," Thalias growled. "Physical threats aren't the ones he needs protecting from."

"Point taken," Samakro conceded. "So where does that leave us?"

"It leaves us with you able to trust me," Thalias said quietly. "I interpreted Patriarch Thooraki's support as meaning Thurfian no longer had any hold on me. Here and now, it leaves us with you needing a favor, and me having a lever I can use against him."

"What lever?" Samakro scoffed. "Blackmail? He's the Patriarch now. Who are you going to take those charges to?"

"It's not blackmail, and the lever's just for him," Thalias said. "I can't explain further. Just—" She felt her throat tighten. "Just trust me."

"Tell me about this lever."

"I can't," Thalias said. "Not now. Maybe not ever. But it'll work. I know it will. Just tell me what you need Thurfian to do."

For a moment Samakro looked at her. "I'm still not convinced," he warned. "But I'm not having much luck finding someone myself. I suppose you can't fail any worse than I have already. Fine. Here's what Thrawn needs."

He laid it out for her, everything Thrawn needed Thurfian to do. "Any questions?" he asked when he'd finished.

"No," Thalias said, feeling her head spinning. Talk about climbing a tall hill.

But then, she'd climbed a tall hill back in the Mitth homestead, a literal one, during the Trials. She'd survived that ascent, and had come back better and stronger and more focused than she'd ever been in her life. She could climb this hill, too.

"I'll call the homestead and see if I can get permission to come talk to him," she went on. "Are you going to wait, or go back to the ship and send another shuttle for me?"

"I'll wait," Samakro said. "I get a feeling it might not go as smoothly as you seem to think."

"All right," Thalias said. "I'll call when I'm back from the homestead."

She was within sight of the tube car terminal, her comm pressed to her ear as she wove her way through the pedestrian traffic, before she finally got through to Senior Aide Thivik. "Senior Aide, this is Mitth'ali'astov," she said. "It's urgent that I speak with Patriarch Thurfian as soon as possible. Can you help me?"

And as they talked, Thalias found herself understanding like she never had before how warriors like Samakro felt. She was doing this because it needed to be done.

And she absolutely wasn't going to be loved for it.

"I apologize for passing on incorrect information," Qilori's voice came tensely over the *Whetstone*'s bridge speakers. "But he *told* me he was going to Csilla, and I had no reason to suspect he was lying."

"Except that he's Thrawn, and you are a fool," Jixtus growled.

Nakirre stretched with disdain for both of them. Conflict, fear, anger—all were marks of the unenlightened. They would never know order or discipline until they and all around them had been taken down that path. By persuasion if possible; by the new tool of conquest if not.

The Kilji Illumine couldn't hope to conquer the Grysks, of course. One look at Jixtus's terrifying warship had convinced him of that. Their enlightenment would have to be done from the inside, as partners to the Grysks' shadowy leadership. Jixtus had already hinted that such cooperation might be possible when the Chiss Ascendancy finally lay broken and vanquished at their feet.

Qilori and the Pathfinders, though, were a different story. Nakirre didn't know how many of them there were, or where they were centered, or even whether they were a species, a cult, or something else.

But the Illumine would find them and conquer them, and they would be led to enlightenment, just like those nations the Kilhorde was even now battering into submission.

Or so he assumed. The glowing reports of victory he'd been receiving had ceased a full day ago, and all of Nakirre's efforts to resume communication had failed. He hoped his generals hadn't been so foolishly ambitious as to stretch their attack to the southeast-nadir Ascendancy world of Colonial Station Chaf. The long-range triad transmitter there was his only link to those forces, and disrupting its operation would leave them entirely on their own.

His generals were enlightened, certainly. But they needed the firm hand of their generalirius to truly find the proper path.

"Perhaps I am," Qilori said stiffly. "But Thrawn's whereabouts may not be the most urgent issue at the moment. I've been watching the arrival listings, and two major Expansionary Defense Fleet ships have now shown up at Schesa: the *Grayshrike* and the *Vigilant*."

"Well, well," Jixtus said. His voice was soft, but there was something there that sent a ripple of dread through Nakirre's skin. "I've been hoping I'd run across those two ships again."

"You know them?" Nakirre asked.

"Oh, yes," Jixtus said in the same unnerving tone. "Our encounters have cost me dearly. I wonder why they're all the way out there instead of guarding some of the more major planets."

"I have no idea," Qilori said, sounding suddenly even more nervous.

"I know that," Jixtus said. "Stay there and collect as much information as you can. I'll gather my fleet, then come to Schesa and pick you up."

"Yes, sir," Qilori said.

"End transmission," Jixtus ordered. "Open another one for Rhigal and Patriarch Rivlex."

There was a moment of silence. "End transmission," Nakirre ordered. "Open contact for Patriarch Rivlex."

"I obey," Vassal Four said.

Jixtus turned his veiled face toward Nakirre, probably annoyed yet again that the Kilji vassals obeyed only their generalirius. "You're going to have Rivlex send his fleet to Schesa?" Nakirre asked before Jixtus could complain.

"I don't need him to send *my* fleet anywhere," Jixtus countered. "Is my transmission ready?"

"Vassal Four?" Nakirre prompted.

"Transmission open," Vassal Four confirmed. "Wait. No. The transmission is being redirected."

"Redirected where?" Jixtus asked.

"To a ship," Vassal Four said, clearly confused. "But I set the transmission to go to Rhigal."

"Obviously, the Patriarch is traveling somewhere," Jixtus said. "Accept the redirection and follow it."

"But if the message is not direct, Patriarch Rivlex may not know to answer," Vassal Four protested.

"It's his same private contact," Jixtus said impatiently. "Just accept the redirection."

"Accept the redirection," Nakirre confirmed.

"I obey."

For a moment there was silence. Then the comm pinged with the signal of a connection. "This is Patriarch Rivlex," Rivlex's voice came. "Is that you, Jixtus?"

"It is, Your Venerante," Jixtus confirmed.

"What are you calling about?" the Patriarch asked, sounding distracted. "And make it fast—my shuttle leaves for the Syndicure landing area in fifteen minutes."

Nakirre felt a stretch of sudden concern. Rivlex had gone to *Csilla*? Had the Chiss figured out what Jixtus was doing?

"This won't take long, Your Venerante," Jixtus promised. "I merely wanted to ask you what was happening at Schesa."

"Schesa? As far as I know, not a thing. Why?"

"A group of warships has gathered there," Jixtus said. "I wondered if there was a mission being planned for the Chaos."

"Were these Expansionary Defense Fleet warships?" Rivlex asked. "If so, it's probably nothing. The Syndicure has ordered them removed from guard duty and to assemble at Naporar or other out-of-the-way systems while the Aristocra decide what to do with them."

"Oh?" Jixtus asked. "Are there thoughts of dismantling that part of the fleet?"

"I don't know," Rivlex said with strained patience. "I imagine that'll be one of the items the Circle will discuss."

"The Circle?"

"The Circle of Unity," Rivlex said. "It's a gathering of all nine of the Ruling Families' Patriarchs. It's going to convene soon, and I have no intention of being the last one there."

"My apologies, Your Venerante," Jixtus said. "We'll speak again later."

He gestured to Vassal Four. But Rivlex had already closed the communication. "So *all* the Chiss leaders will be in one place?" Nakirre asked with cautious excitement. The opportunity such a convocation presented . . .

"No," Jixtus said firmly. "I know what you're thinking, but no. Even if we could get through Csilla's defenses, killing the Ruling Families' Patriarchs would accomplish nothing."

"I never said we would kill them," Nakirre said, skin stretching with frustration. Were death and destruction the only things Grysks could imagine? "If they could be captured and brought to enlightenment, we could subdue the Ascendancy without firing a single laser."

Jixtus gave a contemptuous snort. "You're a fool, Generalirius. The Chiss won't accept your path. Certainly not willingly. Weren't you listening to Thrawn at Zyzek, when he said the Chiss have their own ancient paths? They won't be interested in yours."

"Our path is superior," Nakirre insisted.

"No," Jixtus said flatly. "Your path is simplistic, self-contradictory, and self-defeating. The only ones who accept it are those the Kiljis are able to force it upon."

"You lie," Nakirre bit out, suddenly furious. How *dare* he denigrate the enlightenment that way?

"No, for once I'm telling the truth." Jixtus waved a gloved hand at the bridge consoles. "Look at your own servants. Did you choose them for skill, initiative, or even enthusiasm? Of course not. You chose them because they were willing to trade their last scraps of freedom to you in the hope that you would take care of them for the remainder of their lives."

"The path of enlightenment provides all their needs."

"*You* provide all their needs," Jixtus said. "You run every facet of their lives for them, and in turn they happily repeat the words of your so-called enlightenment back at you."

"You claim they lack skill and enthusiasm," Nakirre said stiffly. "How then do you explain the Kilhorde's battle victories against their foes?"

"Why do you think I chose those particular nations for the Kilhorde to face?" Jixtus countered. "They're poor worlds and desperate, unable to resist your attack but also willing to accept your enlightenment in return for peace and comfort."

Nakirre stared at him. "Then the Kilji Illumine has meant nothing to you?"

"It has meant exactly what it was always intended to mean," Jixtus said. "Your Kilhorde has blocked any surviving Chiss refugees from fleeing to those worlds and regrouping. You have provided me with a transport that the Ascendancy's military can examine at length, assuring itself that the Kiljis are not a threat, while the reality of their true enemy remains hidden. *Those* are the services that the Kiljis have provided."

"Nothing more?"

The black hood moved side-to-side as Jixtus slowly and deliberately shook his head. "Nothing more."

Nakirre's skin stretched in humiliation and powerless anger. To reach out to Jixtus, to reach past that veil and into that hood to the Grysk's neck and wrap his hands around it. To listen to Jixtus's gasps and whimpers as Nakirre choked the life out of him . . .

But he couldn't. Not with the Grysk fleet lurking nearby. Not with them surely knowing where the Kilhorde was and, worse, where the Kilji homeland lay.

He could kill Jixtus. He could do that. But the aftermath would be that the Illumine and the Kilji species would face an even more horrible death.

And no one would ever again be enlightened.

"You're angry," Jixtus said. "Don't be. Rather, be thankful that you were of even that much use to the Grysks. Otherwise, the Kilji Illumine would by now surely have joined so many others beneath our feet in the cold ashes of history."

He turned and gestured to Vassal Four. "Now order him to contact my fleet. Whatever the Chiss are planning at Schesa, they're in for a bitter surprise."

CHAPTER TWENTY-TWO

"**D**oes the summons always come this quickly?" Thurfian asked, skimming over the Circle of Unity protocols with one eye and keeping the other on two of his servants as they packed a travel bag with his official robes of office and a couple of spare sets of informal clothing.

"I really don't know, Your Venerante," Thivik said. Unlike Thurfian, he had both eyes and his full attention on the servants and their packing. "There hasn't been one called since well before my time."

Which also meant well before the late Patriarch Thooraki's time. Apparently, this kind of official meeting was as rare as was suggested by the slightly archaic language of the protocols. "Is the tube car ready?"

"Yes, Your Venerante," Thivik said, checking his chrono. "Don't worry, we still have time."

"I know," Thurfian said. "But I don't want to be the last one there."

"You won't." Thivik cleared his throat. "There's one other matter. There's a young woman on her way here to see you. Mitth'ali'astov—you may remember her?"

Thurfian looked up sharply, the Circle of Unity protocols suddenly forgotten. "Thalias is coming *here*? Who authorized that?"

"I did," Thivik said calmly. "She said it was vitally important."

Thurfian grunted as he looked back at his questis. "Unless it has something to do with Jamiron or our missing Senior Captain Thrawn, it can wait."

"She didn't say what the matter concerned."

"Of course not," Thurfian said. Which probably meant it *was* about Thrawn, only she didn't want to say so.

No surprise there. Ever since Thurfian made that deal with Thalias to get her aboard the *Springhawk,* she'd completely ignored her side of the bargain. She'd outmaneuvered him first by taking the Trials and moving up the family ranks, then by somehow gaining Patriarch Thooraki's favor. Those two ploys together had made her essentially untouchable.

But Thooraki wasn't here to protect her anymore. Thurfian was Patriarch now, with all the power of the Mitth family at his fingertips. Maybe it was finally time to collect on her unpaid debt. "When is she due?" he asked.

"She could arrive at any time." Thivik pulled out his comm. "In fact, her tube car's just pulling in. Shall I escort her to your office?"

"No time for that," Thurfian said. "She can ride to Csaplar with us, or she can wait until I'm back. Her choice."

"Yes, Your Venerante," Thivik said, heading for the door. "I'll ask her."

Thurfian and the servants arrived a few minutes later to find Thivik and Thalias seated in the center seat cluster of the Patriarch's private tube car, the four guards who would be accompanying him to the capital spread watchfully around them. The driver was also ready, seated in the top bubble and running a last check on the car's equipment. "Your Venerante," Thalias said solemnly to Thurfian as he stepped inside. "Thank you for seeing me on such short notice."

"I presume Senior Aide Thivik has already informed you I'm heading to Csaplar for an important meeting," Thurfian said as he seated himself across from her. Outside, the servants finished stowing the luggage in the external compartments, and the car glided smoothly away from the mansion and toward the exit from the vast underground homestead chamber.

"He did," Thalias said. "He also said you still have some additional work to do before we arrived."

"Then we're both on the same page," Thurfian said. "Whatever you came to say, say it and then go sit in the back of the car."

"Could we have a bit more privacy?" Thalias asked, pointing to the seats at the front of the car. "What I have to say is confidential."

Thurfian suppressed a grimace. The Patriarch's tube car was longer than the standard versions, and as a result had a tendency to bob and sway somewhat more. Most of the homestead's staff didn't have a problem with that, but Thurfian had found it a bit disconcerting, especially when he was trying to read.

But he wouldn't be reading while he was talking to Thalias, and if moving up there got her part of this trip finished off faster, it would be worth it. "Go ahead," he said.

She stood and headed toward the front group of seats. Thurfian followed, waving back the two guards who started to follow. Thalias sat down in the right-hand seat, and Thurfian took the one facing it. "All right," he said. "I'm listening."

Thalias braced herself. This was it. Samakro, Che'ri, Thrawn—they were all counting on her. "I have a request from Senior Captain Thrawn," she said. "He needs you to—"

"Is he back in the Ascendancy?" Thurfian interrupted.

Thalias broke off, her already tentative conversational momentum skidding to a sudden stop. "What?"

"I asked if Senior Captain Thrawn was back in the Ascendancy," Thurfian repeated. "Is he ready to surrender himself and to face charges?"

"What charges?" Thalias asked, hearing the bewilderment in her voice.

"Abandoning his command," Thurfian said. "Making unsanctioned alliances with aliens. Violating the protocols against preemptive strikes and unilateral aggression against those not at war with the Ascendancy. Shall I go on?"

"No, he hasn't returned," Thalias said. She took a careful breath, trying to gather together the broken thread of her presentation. "He needs you to help him—"

"No," Thurfian said, standing up again. "Until he surrenders himself to the Council and the Syndicure to answer for his crimes, neither he nor his surrogates are entitled to a hearing. Not from me." He gestured to the seat she was still occupying. "You're welcome to stay up here for the remainder of the trip." He turned back toward the car's center—

"Wait a minute," Thalias protested. She snaked her hand toward him, managing more by luck than by design to catch hold of his sleeve. "That's it? You don't even want to hear it?"

"I believe I just said that," Thurfian said. He tried to pull away; Thalias tightened her grip in response. "Whatever he's gotten himself into this time, he can just get himself out. We have plenty of trouble right here in the Ascendancy."

"It's not just him," Thalias persisted, again fighting his attempts to break her hold. "And the trouble in the Ascendancy is why he needs your help."

"Then let him come back and ask for it himself," Thurfian said. With a final wrench he pulled his arm free. "He manipulated us into attacking General Yiv, then did something at Hoxim we still haven't fully sorted out. But no more." He took a step toward the center seats, again waving back his guards.

Thalias clenched her teeth. She had hoped she wouldn't have to play this card. "It also concerns *your* personal survival," she called after him.

Thurfian snorted as he continued walking. "Please. Has the great Senior Captain Thrawn been reduced to threats?"

"This isn't from him, but from me," Thalias said. "I know the truth about the Seeker program. *And* I know your part in it."

Thurfian's feet came to a stop. "Excuse me?" he asked, still facing away from her.

"I know about the Seekers," Thalias said. Thurfian knew she knew about the sky-walkers, of course—she'd *been* one of them, after all. But from the way Borika had talked, Thalias had gotten the impression that the term *Seeker* was considerably less widespread. "Are you ready to hear me out?"

Thurfian hesitated another second. Then, deliberately, he turned back to face her. "All right, I'll play along," he said. He retraced his steps to his seat and sat down. "Tell me about this truth you think I should be worried about."

"I know what the Syndicure and Council are doing to those girls," Thalias said, lowering her voice. Whatever attention the others at the far end of the tube car might be paying to this conversation, her words were for Thurfian's ears alone. "I know about the fading process you use to wipe the memories of everything that happened in their lives before they came into the Seeker program. I know that the reason you forbid former sky-walkers from becoming caregivers is so that they don't spend time together, realize they have the same suspicious memory loss, and start putting the pieces together." She ran out of words and stopped.

"And?" Thurfian prompted.

She stared at him. Did he really not see the consequences she was laying out in front of him? "What do you mean, *and*? You talk about Thrawn manipulating people, but at least those are adults. *You're* manipulating little girls—taking away their families and their childhood, enslaving them in all but name. Do you have any idea what would happen if the general public knew about this?"

"Of course," Thurfian said calmly. "Some of the people running the program would lose their jobs. Those of us who knew about it but had no actual hand in the day-to-day activities would be vilified and complained to."

"You also directly and personally confirmed its authorization," Thalias shot back. "You wouldn't just be vilified, you'd be thrown out of office and brought up on charges."

"As you just said about Thrawn, what charges?" Thurfian countered. "I'm afraid you overestimate the public's capacity and stamina for outrage. Especially now, with the Nine and Forty at each other's throats, they have far more urgent matters vying for their attention. Certainly there would be some anger, but it would quickly pass."

Thalias could feel her throat working, her mind hunting desperately for something she could say that would refute his scenario.

But he was right. She'd seen it time and time again. Something would catch the public's attention, sparking joy or surprise or out-rage; and then barely a week or two later, it would have been completely displaced by the next item of interest.

"After that, though, we'd get to the long-term problems," Thurfian continued into her frustrated silence. "Assuming the Ascendancy survives our current crisis—and I personally have no doubt we will—some of the parents who now bring their children in for special abilities testing would keep them away from the centers. That would not only cut back drastically on the number of available sky-walkers, but would also hurt the fine arts and sciences programs and the promising children who would no longer be identified early and provided with specialized training and instruction."

"That kind of talent will always come through," Thalias murmured.

"Sometimes," Thurfian said. "Not always." He raised his eyebrows. "And even longer-term, that same lack of sky-walkers would weaken the Expansionary Defense Fleet, drastically slowing their warships' passage through the Chaos and as a result limiting their reconnaissance of the regions outside the Ascendancy. Limit it enough, and the next General Yiv could be on our threshold before we even knew of his existence. Is that what you want for the Chiss people, Caregiver Thalias?"

"I—no, of course not," she managed, a swirl of disbelief and horror running through her. "But—"

"But what?" Thurfian pressed. "Let me give you a bit of historical reference you're probably too young to know about. The gambit you just tried to use was once called the volcano option. That's where one side threatens mutual destruction if they don't get what they want."

Thalias winced. "I've heard of it."

"Good," Thurfian said. "Then you know that the problem is that word *mutual*. The only way it works is if the side doing the threatening genuinely believes they have nothing to lose."

"But there *is* nothing to lose," Thalias said, hearing the pleading in her voice. She had no more points of logic; no facts or reasonings or warnings. All she had left was pleading. "If Senior Captain Thrawn isn't able to stop Jixtus and his fleet, the Ascendancy will be gone."

"I don't believe that," Thurfian said. "No, Thalias, it's over. You had your chance to work with me for the betterment of the Ascendancy, and instead you aligned yourself with Thrawn. I don't owe you anything." He cocked his head. "Are there any other cards you'd like to play? If not, I have work to do."

Thalias swallowed hard. Yes, she did have one final card. One desperate, desperate card. "Yes, I do," she told him, her heart thudding in her chest. "As you said: the volcano option. Only this time, it's more personal." She put her hand into her side jacket pocket and wrapped her fingers around the hard, cold metal concealed there. "Your death, and mine.

"Right here. Right now."

"Oh, *really*," Thurfian scoffed, more amused than annoyed. "The essence of a good bluff—"

He broke off, his throat going tight. Her hand had partially emerged from her pocket . . . and held tightly in it was a compact charric.

"No sound," Thalias said. Her voice was shaking and barely above a whisper, but the weapon in her hand was rock-steady. "No movements, no gestures. I know your guards can kill me." She swallowed visibly. "*Will* kill me. But they aren't holding their weapons. That means I'll be able to kill you first."

"What in hell's name are you doing, Thalias?" Thurfian demanded, keeping his own voice low. "Do you *want* to die?"

"Of course not," Thalias said. "But if the Ascendancy falls, we all fall with it. If I die a few days early, what does it matter?" She tried a tentative smile that failed miserably. "As you said. Nothing to lose."

"I see," Thurfian murmured. He lowered his eyes to the charric, wondering how she'd been able to sneak a weapon past the guards who would have met her tube car.

Only now he saw that she'd done nothing of the kind. Because the weapon she was holding was Thivik's.

Thurfian's own senior aide had given her his charric to use against his Patriarch.

Casually, keeping his movements small, Thurfian looked back at the rear of the car. Thivik was seated beside one of the guards, furtively watching him. The senior aide's expression was strained, but he was making no move to alert the others to the confrontation taking place a few meters away.

Thurfian looked back at Thalias, his mind spinning. Thivik, his senior aide. Once senior aide to Patriarch Thooraki, friend of Thalias, supporter and protector of Thrawn.

Was that what this was about? Thivik carrying on his late Patriarch's legacy, even if it meant threatening the life of his current Patriarch? Was Thivik so full of anger or resentment toward Thurfian, or perhaps wallowing in nostalgia for days now gone?

Or did he really, truly believe Thalias needed to be listened to?

He looked back at Thivik. No, there was no anger or resentment in his face, Thurfian saw now. Just fear and pleading.

And, perhaps, a hint of desperate hope.

Thurfian turned again to Thalias. "What do you want?"

"I want you to hear me out," she said. "I want you to listen to Thrawn's assessment of the situation, and his plan to deal with it and save the Ascendancy."

"I won't make any promises."

"I'm not asking you to." She swallowed. "I know you don't like Thrawn, Your Venerante. But I believe you care deeply for the Mitth family and the entire Ascendancy. I'm counting on you to make the right decision. But either way—" She braced herself. "Once you've heard me out, I'll give you the charric."

Mentally, Thurfian shook his head. Such simple, childlike trust. Didn't she realize that promises or statements made under duress weren't legally binding? "All right," he said, forcing himself to settle a bit deeper into the seat cushions. If Thivik was wrong about the people he was willing to put his trust in—if Thurfian was going to die today at the hand of a fanatic—he might as well be comfortable while it happened. "I'm listening."

———

Qilori hadn't particularly enjoyed his time aboard the *Anvil*, what with having to endure Kilji arrogance and their continual talk about enlightenment. His time aboard the *Whetstone*, he suspected, wouldn't be a lot better, especially given that he'd also have to deal with Jixtus and *his* brand of arrogance.

But it beat the chaff off his time of being surrounded by blueskins.

"Where are the warships?" Jixtus asked as a couple of Kilji vassals escorted Qilori onto the *Whetstone*'s bridge. "Didn't you tell me there were warships?"

"Yes, sir, there were," Qilori said, wondering if his relief at being back under Jixtus's unseen gaze was perhaps a bit premature. "They left two days ago."

"And you didn't think it necessary to inform me?" Jixtus asked, his voice darkening.

"I tried to send a message," Qilori said, his winglets starting to quiver. "But you were in hyperspace, and I'd run to the end of my credit chit so I couldn't set it to repeat."

"Unfortunate," Jixtus said, his voice back to its usual calm. "I would have preferred to deal with the *Vigilant* and *Grayshrike* here at Schesa, within sight of their fellow Chiss. More satisfying in many ways. Still, whatever they and Thrawn have planned, a few days' head start will do them no good. Certainly they'll be just as dead there as they would be here. You've done well, Qilori of Uandualon."

"Thank you," Qilori said, his winglets slowly settling down. Just more of Jixtus having fun twisting someone's fears.

"There is, of course, the other matter," Jixtus continued.

Qilori's winglets abruptly went into about-face. "Yes," he managed. "I—there unfortunately isn't very much I can say about that."

"Certainly not here," Jixtus agreed, turning his veiled face pointedly around the bridge. "Perhaps later in the voyage we'll find an opportunity to discuss it."

"Yes," Qilori said. "Ah . . . I assume you'll want me to navigate this ship?"

"When the time comes," Jixtus said. "But as I said, there's no rush. The Grysk fleet is not yet entirely assembled." He paused, and Qilori had the sense of a sly smile. "There may also yet be additional news of our enemy."

"Yes, sir," Qilori said, wondering where he was expecting to get this additional news from.

"The Kiljis will take you to your cabin now," Jixtus continued. "Rest well. And rest quickly. The end is fast approaching.

"And when it comes, there will be no rest. For anyone."

According to the protocols Thurfian had read, each Patriarch at the Circle of Unity was permitted a single aide, who would sit behind him or her during the meeting and could offer quiet advice or information as their Patriarch requested. Thivik was already seated behind Thurfian at the Mitth section of the ancient round table, and as the others settled in Thurfian saw that most had brought either their senior aide or their family's Syndicure Speaker.

Patriarch Irizi'fife'rencpok, to Thurfian's surprise, had brought Zistalmu.

From Thurfian's position, the Irizi Syndic Prime was only partially visible, the view blocked both by Zistalmu's own Patriarch and the Chaf Patriarch seated beside him. But he could see enough of his former collaborator's face to recognize the other was still holding on to the bitterness of their last conversation.

And he would be the one advising Patriarch Zififerenc on how he should deal with the Mitth and everyone else.

Thurfian sighed. This was going to be a long day.

The Circle of Unity began.

Each Patriarch was permitted an opening statement. Most of them used their time to list their grievances, though to their credit most spoke calmly and also offered ideas as to how they could compromise with their rivals. Patriarch Rivlex gave the most heated of the presentations, accusing the Dasklo family of planning violence against the Clarr, though Thurfian noted that he presented no proof to support his allegations. The Dasklo's response was far more measured, which only seemed to add additional heat to Rivlex's simmer.

And then it was Thurfian's turn.

"I appreciate Your Venerantes' willingness to come here today," he said when he'd finished going through the prescribed greetings. "I also welcome the opportunity to air our grievances and look to each other for solutions. But instead of adding to that list, I'd like to speak of a hitherto unknown threat to the Ascendancy. A threat that has just been made known to me; a threat posed by Expansionary Defense Fleet Senior Captain Mitth'raw'nuruodo."

A small ripple ran around the table. They all knew that name, all right. "Ah, yes—the Syndicure's favorite ungimbaled laser," the Ufsa Patriarch said, a hint of snide amusement in her face and voice. "What's he done now?"

"You may have heard that he abandoned his ship, the *Springhawk,* in favor of joining an alien expedition to a world known to us as Sunrise," Thurfian went on, ignoring the interruption. "What you may *not* have heard is that he's persuaded some of his colleagues to join him in laying siege to that world and ultimately conquering it."

"*What?*" the Ufsa demanded, her amusement vanishing.

"We don't conquer inhabited worlds," the Plikh put in, sounding more puzzled than outraged. "What does Thrawn think he's doing?"

"It appears there's a colony of aliens on that world who can see . . . well, it's a bit vague," Thurfian conceded. "But these particular aliens are sometimes able to touch something they call the Beyond, which Thrawn believes may be connected to the same force that gives our sky-walkers the ability to see into the future the few seconds necessary to guide our ships in hyperspace. Because of this connection, the aliens seem able to sometimes work with a sky-walker to allow both to see more deeply into the future than either can do alone."

"How far in the future are we talking about?" Rivlex asked, his eyes narrowed. "Days? Weeks? Months?"

"That, too, is a bit unclear," Thurfian said. "What we know for certain is that one of the aliens, known as the Magys, interacted twice with the *Springhawk*'s sky-walker and was able to see several hours ahead. The key seems to be that the sky-walker and alien together can only see future events that are completely outside their control."

"So it wouldn't be useful for investments or organizing a construction job," the Boadil said thoughtfully. "But it might help in planting crops, where weather is a major factor."

"Or in warfare," the Dasklo said darkly, his eyes on the Clarr. Behind Zififerenc, Thurfian noted, Zistalmu had leaned forward and was whispering into his Patriarch's ear. "It might allow a defender to anticipate the enemies' moves."

"Indeed it might," Thurfian agreed. "And therein lies its greatest value, as well as its greatest threat."

"Why are you telling us all this?" Zififerenc asked as Zistalmu leaned back in his chair again. "A resource like this would greatly benefit the Mitth. If Thrawn is the one identifying and collecting these aliens, why aren't you keeping it to yourself?"

"Because he doesn't plan to give the Sunrise aliens to us," Thurfian said. "He plans to give them to another group of aliens called the Paccosh."

There was a moment of stunned silence. "That's outrageous," the Ufsa said.

"It's not just outrageous," the Plikh countered, his face rigid. "It's *treason*."

"How do you know all this?" Zififerenc asked.

"One of his companions came to me with a request," Thurfian said. "She was concerned that—"

"What companion?" Zififerenc interrupted. "What's her name?"

"Mitth'ali'astov," Thurfian supplied. "She's the caregiver aboard the *Springhawk*."

"What was her request?" Zififerenc asked.

"Basically, that we give him more time," Thurfian said. "She was concerned that the Syndicure might send a force to Sunrise to bring him back before he'd finished collecting all the prescient aliens. She wanted me to persuade them to wait until he was finished. If I did that, she said he'd be willing to bring some of the prescient aliens back to the Ascendancy with him."

"*Some* of them?" the Ufsa bit out. "Not *all* of them?"

"Completely unacceptable," the Dasklo said firmly.

"I can only tell you what she said," Thurfian told him. "He would collect some of the aliens, leave the rest and the planet to the Paccosh, and return to the Ascendancy."

"I presume you refused?" the Ufsa bit out.

"On the contrary, I thought it was an excellent idea," Thurfian said, giving her a thin smile. "Not the part about giving him extra time, of course, or accepting only part of what's due to us. But I agreed with the part about sending a force to haul him and the aliens—*all* of them—back to Csilla. Which is why I placed an immediate call to Supreme General Ba'kif." He tapped his questis. "Here's the result."

He watched, trying to look calm and nonchalant as they began reading through the document he and Ba'kif had come up with. If he couldn't get them to agree to this . . .

"I'm counting fourteen ships here," the Plikh said. "What percentage is that of the entire Expansionary Defense Fleet?"

"A bit under a third," Thurfian said. "Six of them are the smaller patrol cruisers, the rest light and heavy cruisers. You'll also note that Ba'kif is keeping the Firewolf man-of-war *Bellicose* here in the Ascendancy."

"You said Thrawn persuaded some of his colleagues to join him," Rivlex said. "Which ones?"

"Ba'kif thinks the *Springhawk* and *Grayshrike* may be with him," Thurfian said. "Both ships are commanded by friends of his, and neither has responded to communication requests for over a day."

"They could just be in hyperspace," the Ufsa said.

"Going where?" the Chaf countered.

"Any number of places," the Ufsa said. "Even a warship can take a couple of days to cross the Ascendancy."

"What about the *Vigilant*?" Zififerenc put in. "It's the Expansionary Defense Fleet's largest ship, and its commander is also one of Thrawn's friends. Where is it right now?"

"Supreme General Ba'kif said he sent Admiral Ar'alani to guard the triad transmitter at Schesa," Thurfian said. "There was apparently some alien activity in the region that concerned him."

The Chaf grunted. "So Ba'kif wants to send a third of his ships to Sunrise to bring back this upstart. Where does that leave the Ascendancy's own internal security needs?"

"Relatively unaffected," Thurfian assured him. "The supreme general told me the Syndicure has already ordered him to pull his ships back to Naporar while their proper role within the Ascendancy is discussed and defined. And the trip to Sunrise would be only a few days each way."

"And once Thrawn is back?" Rivlex asked. "What happens to the aliens?"

"That would be up to the Circle or the Syndicure," Thurfian told him. "My recommendation would be to send them to one of the Shadehouses, or else create a new one especially for them, where we can learn how their ability interacts with our sky-walkers."

"And if Thrawn refuses to come back?"

"Refusal wouldn't be an option," Thurfian said flatly. "That's why Ba'kif wants to send an overwhelming number of ships. Even Thrawn would hesitate to take on that many opponents."

"Especially when they're members of his own fleet," the Obbic murmured.

"Yes," Thurfian said.

"Question," the Dasklo said, his eyes narrowed with suspicion. "I received a report that Thrawn had been seen on Sposia, having possibly visited the UAG vaults. Did you happen to ask your source what he was doing there?"

"I did," Thurfian said. "She told me he'd borrowed an alien device he recently brought back from Hoxim, a system for anticipating the arrival of a ship just before it emerges from hyperspace."

"I thought these Sunrise aliens were supposed to do that for him," Zififerenc pointed out.

"Thalias said he was going to use the device as a baseline to calibrate their abilities," Thurfian said. "He hoped he could learn how much better—or how much worse—the aliens' own prescience was."

"I don't know," the Boadil said pensively as he worked his questis. "It looks like the ships would be gone at least a week, maybe longer.

I'm not sure I like having that many warships out of contact that long. Especially when there's so much turmoil going on here."

"Those particular ships would normally be out of the Ascendancy anyway," the Plikh reminded him.

"Personally, I'd be just as happy to have them out of the way where they aren't going to ruffle any more feathers," the Chaf added. "I suspect other families would agree on that."

"I think we would also agree that an officer openly defying the Ascendancy and threatening to give away potentially vital resources is unacceptable," Thurfian said. "And though this may be an overly cynical way of looking at things, sometimes it takes a crisis of this magnitude to draw our families together and remind us that we're all Chiss."

"If we approve this document, how fast can Ba'kif get things in motion?" the Obbic asked.

"He told me he could issue the orders within the hour," Thurfian said. "Most of the ships are already at Naporar, as I said, which would save them having to rendezvous for the trip. They would just have to prep, refuel, rearm if necessary, and go."

"And their instructions would be to bring Thrawn back?" Zififerenc asked.

"Yes," Thurfian said. "As I said already."

"Yes, you did," Zififerenc said, eyeing Thurfian closely. "I just wanted to confirm it."

"All right, then," the Obbic said briskly. "I'm in." He touched his questis, keying in his approval.

"So am I," the Boadil added.

In the end, though with varying degrees of enthusiasm or reluctance, all nine Patriarchs gave their approval. "Thank you," Thurfian said, keying to send the result to Ba'kif and the Council. He'd hoped that moving this strongly against Thrawn might appease Zistalmu, at least a little. But what he could see of the Syndic Prime's face, half hidden behind his Patriarch, was still hard and cold.

And there was nothing Thurfian could do about it. Not now; maybe not ever. All he could do was keep going along this path, and hope it ultimately worked out.

"I thank you for hearing me out," he continued. "I also apologize for using up more than my fair share of the time allotted for opening statements. With your permission, I'll now yield the table to initial discussion."

The hurried conversation ended, and the *Whetstone*'s comm went silent. Qilori sat unmoving, his winglets fluttering gently, watching Jixtus. "So," the Grysk said at last, turning his veiled face toward Qilori. "These prescient aliens are indeed Thrawn's goal." He cocked his head. "Yet you told me there was just *one* other alien besides the Magys who had that ability. How do you account for this discrepancy?"

"I don't know," Qilori said, his winglets starting to quiver a little harder. "Maybe Thrawn thought there was only one when he spoke to me."

"No," Jixtus said flatly. "The fact is that he lied." He cocked his head slightly. "Why do you think he did that?"

"I don't know," Qilori said cautiously.

"The reason is obvious," Jixtus said. "He lied to you because he knew you would pass that lie to me. He used you to feed me false information. That would seem to make you useless to me." He paused. "Do you know what I do with tools that are no longer useful, Qilori of Uandualon?"

"But I'm not useless," Qilori insisted, his voice shaking now in rhythm with his winglets. "I can still serve you."

"How?" Jixtus countered. "As a navigator? I can return to the *FateSpinner* and use my own. As an information source? You just saw how much better Patriarch Rivlex serves in that capacity."

Qilori looked around the bridge, trying to think, noting the utter stillness of Generalirius Nakirre and his vassals. Jixtus was probably still just playing with him, he told himself firmly. This was the Grysk's petty little game of driving fear into Qilori's soul.

But what if it wasn't? What if Jixtus's increasing frustration had finally pushed him over the edge? What if he was descending into rage and really, really wanted to kill someone?

What if he'd already decided he didn't need his tame Pathfinder?

"Patriarch Rivlex may have more knowledge," he said. "But I know Thrawn better. I've talked with him. I know how he thinks, and what's important to him." He paused, trying to wrap his thoughts around the germ of an idea that had just occurred to him. "In fact, I think I know why he told me there was only one other alien besides the Magys."

"Do you?" Jixtus said. "Very well. Tell me."

"I think he expects you to come to Sunrise," Qilori said. "I think he plans to allow you to put him in a losing stance, then offer you the Magys and one other alien in exchange for pulling back and leaving him and his people alive. You would then leave, thinking you had all the prescients, while he left with the rest of them."

"Interesting theory," Jixtus said thoughtfully. "And what of the Chiss force the Patriarchs are now sending to bring him home? What if they take him from Sunrise before my forces can arrive?"

"They won't," Qilori said. "He'll try to persuade them to wait until he's finished with his collection before they leave Sunrise. Even with the device Rivlex said he brought from Sposia, that procedure will certainly take enough time for you to confront him."

"To confront him *and* fourteen or more Chiss ships," Jixtus said, still thoughtful. "At the very least, he surely has the *Springhawk* and *Grayshrike*. And Rivlex's assurances notwithstanding, I presume the *Vigilant* is also with them. Still, my fleet will be more than sufficient to deal with them."

Across the bridge, Generalirius Nakirre stirred. "If you wish, I could summon some ships from the Kilhorde to assist," he offered.

"Hardly necessary," Jixtus said. "You really think Thrawn would willingly sacrifice a pair of aliens?"

"To keep all the others?" Qilori said. "Yes, sir, I do. Actually, I believe he would give you all of Sunrise if you insisted on that as part of the deal."

"He would hand me an entire world in exchange for a few aliens who might or might not prove useful?"

"If he wants them, you can be sure they'll be useful." Qilori's winglets twitched as he thought back to that quiet moment aboard the *Aelos*. "He told me once that the sole reason for his existence was to defend the Chiss Ascendancy and protect his people. He said he would do whatever was necessary to achieve that goal, and that nothing and no one would be allowed to stand in his way."

"And you believed him?"

A shiver ran through Qilori's winglets. "Yes. If you'd heard him . . . yes, I did."

"An interesting analysis," Jixtus said. "I will consider it. Tell me, what price will you pay if you're wrong?"

Qilori's winglets twitched. "Sir?"

"If I plan my actions at Sunrise according to your analysis, and if you prove to be wrong, what price are you willing to pay?"

"I . . . can't answer that question," Qilori stammered.

"Then I will answer it for you," Jixtus said. "If you are wrong, you will die."

The word hung in the air like a poisoned mist. Nakirre and his vassals, Qilori noted distantly, had again gone quiet.

"Just so we understand each other, even as you claim to understand Thrawn," Jixtus continued into the silence. "Go and rest, now, Pathfinder. In a few hours we'll reach the edge of the Ascendancy and enter into the Chaos, and your navigation skills will be required."

"Yes, sir," Qilori managed.

"And who knows?" Jixtus added, the hidden eyes nevertheless somehow seeming to bore into Qilori's face. "If you're wrong about Thrawn, perhaps you will join the aliens of Sunrise in learning what it means to touch the Beyond."

CHAPTER TWENTY-THREE

A couple of days in hyperspace, and the *Springhawk* reached the Sunrise system. A quick in-system jump later, they'd arrived at the planet itself.

"Full scan," Samakro ordered, looking between the sensor display and the starscape outside the viewport. There shouldn't be much to see out there, he knew: a couple of Chiss warships, a couple of Paccian ones, maybe a transport or two if the Paccosh had managed to bring in additional forces. Jixtus and his Grysk fleet, at least, should still be well behind them.

"Signal coming in, Mid Captain," Brisch called from the comm station. "It's the *Vigilant*."

"Thank you," Samakro said, keying the comm as the *Vigilant*'s location came up on the display. The Nightdragon man-of-war was in low orbit directly ahead of the *Springhawk,* just about to disappear around the planetary rim. "This is Mid Captain Samakro aboard the Chiss Expansionary Defense Fleet warship *Springhawk,*" he said formally.

"This is Admiral Ar'alani," Ar'alani's voice came back. "Welcome to Senior Captain Thrawn's last stand."

Samakro grunted. "Not really funny, Admiral."

"Sorry," Ar'alani apologized. "How did your mission go?"

Samakro focused on Thalias, standing stiffly beside the navigator's seat. She hadn't said much about her meeting with Patriarch Thurfian since her hurried return from the Mitth homestead and her insistent request that Samakro get the *Springhawk* into hyperspace as quickly as possible. "I'm told the contact went fine."

"You're *told*? I thought you were the one handling that."

"Thalias convinced me that she had a better chance of persuading one of the Aristocra to deliver our message to the Syndicure than I did."

"And did she?" Ar'alani persisted.

"Thalias?" Samakro invited.

Thalias stirred. "I think so," she said.

Which was about as much as Samakro had gotten out of her already. Apparently, she still wasn't going to offer more detail. "We'll know soon enough," he said. "Where's everyone else?"

"Thrawn and Uingali are out at that asteroid cluster you passed on your way in," Ar'alani said. "With all that clutter it's fairly hard to see into, which would make it a perfect sniper nest. Thrawn thinks he has a better plan for it."

"I'm not surprised," Samakro said drily. "What does Uingali think?"

"They're keeping this one very close to the table," Ar'alani said. "If they come back with Uingali convinced, that'll be your answer. Thrawn also has a group towing some of the asteroids of various sizes closer in toward the planet. The Paccian troop transport is still on the ground with the Magys, clearing out one last pocket of Grysk slavers."

"We ever get confirmation that's who they are?"

"Not really," Ar'alani said. "We're just assuming Qilori's name for them was accurate. The *Grayshrike*'s on the other side of the planet from you, along with nine Paccian gunboats that arrived yesterday. Senior Captain Ziinda is having a conference with all the commanders, and she left an invitation for you to join them if you got in before they finished."

"We're on our way," Samakro said, motioning the order to Azmordi. "How many of your old subordinates were you able to contact before you left the Ascendancy?"

"More than I expected, frankly," Ar'alani said. "I talked to the patrol cruisers *Parala* and *Bokrea* and the light cruisers *Whisperbird* and *Stingfly.*"

"How did they sound?" Samakro asked.

"Receptive," Ar'alani said. "I'm guessing the Syndicure's order kicking us off planetary defense duty was part of it. None of us joined the Expansionary Defense Fleet to sit on our hands in orbit while some Aristocra explains what ungimbaled lasers we all are."

"And Senior Captain Thrawn *does* have something of a reputation," Samakro pointed out.

"As a commander or an ungimbaled laser?" Ar'alani said. "Never mind—he probably has both. Speaking of reputations, we also have a surprise guest: Captain Raamas and the Clarr family warship *Orisson* caught up with us just as we were getting ready to leave Schesa and asked to come along."

"Really," Samakro said, frowning. *Orisson*—why did that name sound familiar? "Unnaturally generous of the Clarr family, I must say."

"I don't think family kindness had anything to do with it," Ar'alani said. "That's the ship that nearly got taken out by the asteroid missile at Ornfra."

"Oh—right," Samakro said as the name finally clicked. He'd read that report, but his attention had been focused on the weapon itself, plus the part the *Grayshrike* had played in neutralizing it. "I thought the captain's name was Roscu."

"It was," Ar'alani said. "Raamas isn't saying much about it, but it sounds like their Patriarch kicked Roscu out of the command chair when she questioned his role in the current situation."

"What role would that be?"

"That's another topic Raamas isn't talking much about. But I get the feeling that with the Clarr Patriarch comfortably out of sight and earshot he's unofficially returned command to Roscu. Her stint in the Expansionary Defense Fleet gave her a lot more combat experience than he has, and Raamas is smart enough to know that."

"Right," Samakro said, making a face. Once again, family politics running into military realities. "Well, I'm sure we're happy to have them aboard."

"Ziinda seems to think so," Ar'alani said. "I need to go out to the asteroid cluster for a quick consultation with Thrawn, but I've told Ziinda that you're on your way. She'll give you all the current thinking for our preliminary setup."

"Sounds good," Samakro said. "I'll see you later."

"Will do. Ar'alani out."

The comm went silent, and Samakro shifted his attention to the nav display. Azmordi had put the *Springhawk* on a vector that would skim them across the upper atmosphere behind the *Vigilant* and bring them around to where they could rendezvous with the *Grayshrike* and the other assembled ships. The estimated ETA, he noted, was twenty minutes. "Lieutenant Commander Azmordi, any way you can speed us up a bit?"

"I can dig us a little lower into the atmosphere if you'd like," the pilot offered. "That would shave off a couple of minutes."

"Do it," Samakro said. "I've always hated being late to parties."

"Yes, sir," Azmordi said, throwing a quick grin over his shoulder at Samakro as he worked his board. "Eighteen minutes to rendezvous."

Samakro nodded. "Thank you," he said. "Thalias, you and Che'ri might as well head back to the suite. Excellent job, Che'ri, on getting us here."

"Thank you," Che'ri said.

Samakro frowned. There'd been something odd in her voice. "You all right?" he asked, standing up and crossing the bridge toward her.

He was halfway there when the girl let out a scream.

Samakro covered the rest of the distance in three long strides. "Che'ri?" he demanded, braking to a halt. Thalias had crouched down beside the chair and was staring up at the girl's face, her expression rigid, her hands stiff where she gripped Che'ri's arms. Taking another half step forward, Samakro leaned past her for a closer look of his own.

One glance was all it took. Che'ri's face was twisted almost beyond recognition, her neck strained, her eyes wide and bulging as she stared at something light-years beyond the *Springhawk*'s viewport. "Medic to the bridge," he snapped.

"No," Che'ri said, her voice as unrecognizable as her face. "Don't take her away."

Samakro felt his blood turn to ice. He looked down at Thalias, saw the tension in the caregiver's face turn to horror. "Che'ri?" he asked. "*Che'ri!*"

"Don't take her," the girl said in that same voice.

"Who are you?" Thalias asked. She shot a look up at Samakro— "Are you the Magys?"

"I need her," Che'ri said. "We all need her. An enemy is coming."

"We know that," Samakro said. "We'll be ready."

"You will not," Che'ri said. "The way is uncertain. Our futures are uncertain. Only together can we see the path."

"Magys, you're hurting her," Thalias said, clearly fighting to keep her voice even. "Whatever you're doing to Che'ri, it's hurting her."

"I will not harm her," Che'ri said. "She and I will see the path. Only she and I together can see the path."

"You're already hurting her," Samakro said. A part of his mind was still refusing to accept what he was seeing and hearing.

But it was real. It was horribly real. Che'ri might be here in body, but she was speaking someone else's words with someone else's voice. Already he could see her twisting into something he'd never seen before. "The nightmares—remember the nightmares you gave her? Those could have killed her."

"But they did not," Che'ri said. "Nor will this kill her."

"Mid Captain Samakro is right," Thalias said. "Even if it doesn't kill her, it'll hurt her. It'll hurt and change her. She may never be whole again."

Che'ri shook her head, a brief and disjointed turn to the right and another to the left. "She will not mind. She will accept being us."

"I don't believe you," Thalias bit out. "If she's really willing, release her and let her say that for herself."

"Release her?" Che'ri's lips curled in an almost smile, her mouth opening as if she wanted to laugh but couldn't quite remember how. "Do you think I alone hold her? All those who now touch the Beyond are gathered together for the protection of our world. All are in agreement. All will help us to find the path."

Samakro felt his lips curl back from his teeth in a snarl. So not only was the Magys invading Che'ri's mind, but a whole damn planet's worth of dead people thought they should get in on this, too?

"They will not approach her," Che'ri said.

Samakro frowned. "What are you talking about?"

"They will not approach her."

Samakro looked at Thalias, got the same puzzled look in response—

Behind him, the hatch opened. Samakro turned his head, saw two medics hurry onto the bridge.

"They will not approach her," Che'ri repeated more sharply.

Samakro waved the medics back, cursing to himself. Even without the Magys's meddling, Che'ri's Third Sight could see that far into the future. What would it be like when she'd fully taken control of the girl?

"You can't do this to her, Magys," Thalias said. "You owe us, remember? We saved your life and freed your planet from its conquerors."

"Triumphs that will turn to dust if all is ultimately lost," Che'ri countered. "Only if we can see the path can any remnant be saved."

Samakro looked down again at Thalias, his stomach tightening. How much of Thrawn's plan had the Magys already seen? Any of it? *All* of it? Was she even now glimpsing the scene of mass destruction Samakro knew was coming?

"All right," Thalias said suddenly. Her face was pale, but her voice was firm. "We'll see the path together. But it won't be you and Che'ri. You'll take me instead."

"You cannot see the path," Che'ri scoffed.

"No, actually, I can," Thalias said. "I told you once before that I also had Third Sight."

"You had it once," Che'ri said. "But you long ago lost it."

"Not all of it," Thalias said doggedly. "I felt the presence of those in the Beyond as we approached the system. I knew of the existence of the Guardian before Che'ri told me of him." She looked up at Sa-makro. "And I know the Guardian would be displeased with you if you tore the life from a young girl."

For a moment Che'ri didn't answer. "Your Third Sight is gone," she said.

"It's not gone, merely dormant," Thalias said. "You and those in the Beyond will just have to push a little harder to get it to work."

"Thalias, you can't do this," Samakro murmured. "You can't let her take you."

"If I don't, she'll take Che'ri," Thalias said. "She already has her. This is the only way to persuade her to let go."

"But she's right," Samakro said. "Your Third Sight is long gone. It'll be like running a fire hose through you to get this to work."

"I don't care," Thalias said.

"Maybe I do."

"Well, you shouldn't," Thalias shot back. "You and the *Springhawk* can't do without Che'ri. You *can* do without me."

"No," Samakro said firmly. "I'm not sacrificing your future, either."

Thalias shook her head. "I don't have a future anymore, Mid Captain," she said quietly. "I pulled a charric on Patriarch Thurfian."

Samakro felt his eyes widen. "You *what*?"

"I had to," Thalias said. "He let me leave Csilla, but I know he won't forget." She shifted her eyes again to Che'ri's face. "Argument over. Magys, I'm ready. Let her go and take me."

Samakro looked into Thalias's eyes . . . and with that, he finally knew the truth.

She was no spy, no matter what Thurfian had forced her to say. Her loyalty was to Thrawn, to Che'ri, and to the *Springhawk*. She would die before she would betray any of them.

Which left him only one option.

"Just a minute, Magys," he called. "There's one more point you need to consider."

"What point is that?" Che'ri asked.

"You speak about the future," Samakro said. "The question you need to ask is whether or not you yourself have one."

"You speak a riddle."

"Then let me make it clear," Samakro said. "Mid Commander Dalvu, are we within view of the Sunrise nyix mine area?"

"Yes, Mid Captain."

"Good," Samakro said. "Senior Commander Afpriuh, prepare a spread of laserfire for that region."

"Mid Captain, what are you *doing*?" Thalias asked, her eyes going wide.

"And prepare two breacher missiles as follow-up," Samakro added. "Are you listening, Magys?"

"I am," Che'ri said.

"Here are your choices," Samakro said. "You release Che'ri—right now—and you leave her and Thalias strictly and completely alone. Otherwise, in sixty seconds you and every one of the people within ten kilometers of you dies."

The bridge, Samakro noted, had taken on a brittle silence. "Magys, did you hear me?"

"I heard," Che'ri said uncertainly. "You would never do such a thing. Your commander would never do such a thing."

"Senior Captain Thrawn isn't here. I *am*."

"He cares about non-Chiss lives."

"Yes, he does," Samakro agreed. "You threaten his people, and see how fast that changes. Forty-five seconds."

"Mid Captain, you can't do this," Thalias pleaded.

"I can, and I will," Samakro said coldly. "She's threatened you and she's attacked Che'ri. As far as I'm concerned, that's an automatic death sentence. Thirty-five seconds."

"Without me, you will die," Che'ri said, a strange sense of pleading in her voice. "Without seeing the path of battle, we will all die."

"You underestimate Senior Captain Thrawn," Samakro said. "He understands his enemies. He knows their patterns and their weaknesses, and what it'll take to defeat them. In fact, I'd wager he sees a battle's future even more clearly than you do. Twenty seconds."

He counted out five more seconds. Then, abruptly, Che'ri stiffened and collapsed in her seat, her breath coming in quick, shallow bursts.

Silently, Samakro exhaled out his tension. "Secure lasers and breachers," he ordered. "If you're still listening, Magys, you've made the right decision. Senior Captain Thrawn and I *will* continue to protect your world and your people to the best of our ability." He lifted a finger. "Just remember that if you're tempted to change your mind, I haven't changed mine. And my order can always be reinstated."

He stood up, wincing at the sudden twinges in his knees. "Caregiver, do you need help getting her back to the suite?"

"No," Thalias said, her face unnaturally pale as she also stood up, her hands still gripping Che'ri's arms. "I can manage. Che'ri?"

"I'm okay," Che'ri said. Her breathing had slowed, but she was unsteady as Thalias helped her to her feet. "I . . . could I get something to eat?"

"Of course," Thalias assured her as she guided the girl around the chair and started maneuvering them toward the hatch. The two medics were still standing there; at a gesture from Samakro, they hurried forward to assist. "You can rest while I fix you something."

The medics reached them, taking Che'ri's arms and continuing her path across the bridge. Thalias started to follow, hesitated, and turned back to Samakro. "Thank you, sir," she said.

He shrugged. "Just protecting the *Springhawk*'s assets."

"I thought we were real, live, socially valuable people," she said, giving him a small, tired smile.

"There's always some middle ground."

"Yes." Her smiled faded. "Would you really have fired those lasers?" she asked, her voice almost too soft to hear.

He looked her straight in the eye. "Would you really have fired that charric?"

A muscle in her cheek twitched. "I need to see to Che'ri."

"Yes," he said. "Keep me advised about her condition."

She nodded and hurried after Che'ri and the medics. The group disappeared through the hatch, and Samakro returned to his command chair. "We still on course for the *Grayshrike*?" he asked.

"Yes, sir," Azmordi said. "That was . . . intense, sir."

"Indeed it was," Samakro agreed. "Let's hope the Magys took the lesson to heart."

"Mid Captain, we have incoming," Dalvu said tightly. "Multiple warships coming out of hyperspace."

"Acknowledged, Mid Commander," Samakro said, eyeing the tactical, watching as the ship count slowly increased. "Lieutenant Commander Brisch, signal Senior Captain Thrawn. Tell him our guests have arrived."

CHAPTER TWENTY-FOUR

Sunrise.

Qilori found himself running the name through his mind back and forth, over and over, as the Great Presence guided him along the final leg of the long journey. It was the name Thrawn had coined for the planet, he'd been told, and Jixtus had accepted it for convenience of discussion. But surely the world's inhabitants had originally called it by another name.

Had that name been something bright and glorious, reflecting a satisfying past and an optimistic future? Did those who still remained call it by a different name now that it had been shattered by war? Would they rename it yet again after witnessing the battle about to take place in the sky above their heads?

Or would there even be anyone left there to remember or rename? Qilori had seen the horrific damage, the aftermath of a brutal civil war. According to Thrawn, that war had been instigated and encouraged by Jixtus and his Agbui agents. Once the Grysks had taken all they wanted from the world, would Jixtus then finish the job, destroying whatever was left?

After all, the galaxy had a long history of ruthless destroyers who preferred not to leave witnesses behind. Would the people of Sunrise fall into that category?

More important, would Qilori?

Something in the distance ahead touched his mind: another Pathfinder, deep within the Great Presence, approaching the world ahead.

Probably Sarsh, he decided, the navigator whom he'd helped rescue from the *Hammer* only to then be forced into the service of Thrawn and the Paccosh. Unfortunate, probably even unfair, but at least his presence showed that Thrawn was definitely still at Sunrise.

Or was he?

Qilori's winglets twitched beneath his sensory-deprivation headset. Sarsh was near Sunrise, but it almost seemed as if he was coming toward the *Whetstone*. Was Thrawn leaving the system, then?

He hoped not. Jixtus would be furious if the Chiss had finished his search ahead of schedule and was returning to the Ascendancy with his cargo of prescient aliens.

Or was Thrawn instead somewhere beyond the planet and now returning to it? Qilori couldn't tell. The Great Presence could provide the location of another Pathfinder and a certain degree of identification, but distances and directions of movement were always tricky to estimate.

And then, Sarsh vanished from Qilori's awareness.

The surprise of it nearly jolted him out of his trance. But a second later the other Pathfinder suddenly reappeared. Only now he seemed to be going the opposite direction, traveling back toward Sunrise. For another few seconds he continued on; then, once again, he disappeared.

Had he dropped back out of hyperspace? That was the usual reason a Pathfinder's presence vanished. But if Thrawn was out in the vast nothingness between the stars, why would he suddenly choose to drop back into space-normal?

There was no time to figure it out now. Jixtus had ordered the fleet to rendezvous at the far edge of the Sunrise system, beyond any chance of being detected from the inner system, and the *Whetstone* was fast approaching its destination. Qilori made one final microscopic adjustment to the ship's direction, awaiting the guidance of the Great Presence.

And then they were there. He keyed the controls, and the Great Presence faded as the *Whetstone* once again returned to space-normal.

Qilori reached up and slipped off his headset, blinking in the subdued bridge lights as he checked the nav displays. They were in the outer Sunrise system, just as he'd been ordered.

His winglets smoothed with relief. Whatever else happened, at least Jixtus couldn't add a navigational mistake to Qilori's list of failings. He looked at the sensor display, mentally counting down the seconds.

And then, suddenly, there they were, bursting into view all around him: the *FateSpinner*, the three WarMasters, and the eleven Battle-Chiefs. All fifteen arrived in perfect formation as their silent Attendant navigators brought them back to space-normal in rapid-fire succession. Qilori had seen the Attendants' exquisite coordination before, and he still didn't know whether they could sense one another in hyperspace the way Pathfinders could or whether they simply had an incredible sense of position and timing.

Jixtus was already on the comm, speaking with the other Grysk commanders in their own language. Off to one side, Generalirius Nakirre's skin was shifting around even more than usual in that unpleasant alien way of theirs. Anticipation or dread, Qilori didn't know which.

Or perhaps it was frustration. Qilori hadn't had very much interaction with the Kiljis, but even so he'd gotten the impression that Generalirius Nakirre had expected to be a major part of Jixtus's grand scheme. Instead, his role had apparently been merely to ferry Jixtus around the Ascendancy, looking innocent, while Jixtus stirred up discord until he was ready to reveal the true invasion fleet.

Apparently, the suggestion that the Kiljis were in fact Jixtus's masters had just been another of Thrawn's lies.

Qilori had spent a lifetime of navigating aliens through the Chaos, most of whom had treated him like the hired servant that he was. He'd seen Nakirre's level of self-importance in many others, the most recent being General Yiv's Nikardun and Haplif's Agbui. Both species had challenged the power of the Chiss Ascendancy and both had broken against it.

Maybe this time it would be the Chiss who would find themselves breaking before a greater force.

Jixtus finished his conversation. "The fleet stands ready," he said, switching back to Minnisiat. "You, Pathfinder, will take us on an in-system jump to the planet."

Generalirius Nakirre stirred in his seat. "Vassal One can do that."

"The Pathfinder will do it," Jixtus said, his tone making it clear that there would be no further argument. His veiled face turned briefly to the Kilji leader, then back to Qilori. "Pathfinder?"

"Yes, sir," Qilori said. "Shall I send the jump coordinates to your other ships?"

"The fleet will follow in its own time," Jixtus said. "I will first speak alone with the Chiss. I'm curious to see if Thrawn will offer me two alien lives as you predicted."

Qilori's winglets stiffened. He'd hoped Jixtus had forgotten about that conversation, or at least had put aside the threat he'd appended to Qilori's fumbling theories about Thrawn's strategy. "Yes, sir," he managed. "In-system jump is ready."

"Execute," Jixtus ordered.

Bracing himself, Qilori keyed the helm. A flicker of stars, and the planet Sunrise loomed dark and all but dead.

A fitting backdrop, Qilori thought as he stared in stunned disbelief at the utter devastation that had now appeared in front of them.

Qilori had expected to find Thrawn and his allies ringed by the force the Ascendancy had sent to detain him. The number of vessels was the first surprise, with nearly thirty warships visible, ranging in size from gunboats to the Nightdragon he'd warned Jixtus about.

But they weren't in any battle array. Nor were they even standing defiantly against Thrawn. They were dead.

All of them.

CHAPTER TWENTY-FIVE

Qilori let his gaze sweep slowly across the scene, winglets undulating in horror and revulsion. The warships were everywhere, some drifting in more or less stable orbits, others in the more extreme hyperbolic paths that would in hours or days end their existence in fiery crashes on the planet's surface. None of them was showing any signs of internal activity. The *Whetstone*'s sensors indicated that most of their reactors were still providing power, but that power was minimal and slowly fading. Battle debris was scattered everywhere, with some of the larger ships trailing thin tendrils of smoke. One of the gunboats off to the side was slowly turning, the light from the distant sun glinting off torn hull plates, its own trail of smoke long and thick and twisting in a bizarre expanding corkscrew shape that surrounded it. The smoke glistened in the distant sunlight as if it was more of a drifting metal slurry than simple vaporized debris, and he wondered briefly what kind of weapon could have generated such a cloud. A couple of ships showed spots of flickering flame where broken oxygen lines fed into laser damage. Whatever had happened here, the *Whetstone* must have just missed it.

"Move us," Jixtus ordered. "I wish to see it all."

"Move closer," Nakirre repeated. As if, Qilori thought, the Kilji's orders or presence aboard his ship truly mattered anymore.

The thrusters activated, sending the *Whetstone* past the edge into Sunrise's gravity well. All the ships must have likewise been deep in the well, Qilori noted with a quiet ache, with no hope of escaping into hyperspace. No wonder all of them had died where they stood.

"The ships still exude the heat of life," the vassal at the sensor station said. "The bodies aboard continue to cool."

"A few hours at the most, then," Qilori said. Did that explain what he'd seen while nestled within the Great Presence? Had Pathfinder Sarsh been trying to escape the carnage of battle in a ship whose hyperdrive had first sputtered and then failed completely?

"So Thrawn refused the order to surrender," Jixtus said, a mix of satisfaction and disappointment in his voice. "I thought he might."

"Why would he do such a thing?" Qilori murmured.

"He's always considered himself unbeatable," Jixtus said. "Now, here, his luck finally drained away." He gave a sound that was half snort, half chuckle. "And as the Ascendancy spirals toward its doom, so these Chiss have engaged and destroyed themselves and each other. Sunrise and its people are ours."

"So it would seem," Qilori said, his eyes still fixed on the wreckage. Jixtus could invoke comparisons all he wanted, but to Qilori the whole disaster was still inexplicable. How could such a thing have happened?

A glint caught his eye: A small asteroid in the near distance, drifting just outside the field of wreckage, had reflected a ray of sunlight. There were probably a dozen of the rocky objects out there, he saw now, their sizes ranging from that of gunboats all the way down to that of single-person escape pods. Probably strays from the asteroid cluster the sensors showed in the near distance behind them. As if nature itself had observed the battle and sent representatives for a closer look.

He frowned, throwing a longer look at the cluster. A tight-knit group of rocks like that, within sensor and comm range of the planet and close enough for a quick in-system jump, would offer perfect cover for an observation post.

And in fact, now that he was focusing on it he thought he could see some faint glints of reflected light.

But the *Whetstone*'s sensors showed no sign of movement or energy readings out there. If someone had indeed set up such a post, the battle had apparently ranged far enough to take it out as well, leaving only dead ships or scrap behind.

Or else the glints were coming from metal deposits in the asteroids, and all the rest was Qilori's own nervous imagination.

"There," Jixtus said, jabbing a finger toward the viewport. "Those two ships close in to the planet. Did I just see laserfire between them?"

Qilori shifted his attention from the asteroids and the wrecked ships and peered in the direction Jixtus was pointing. Beyond the corkscrewing smoke trail were two ships drifting along together, neither of them under power. Both were ships he recognized: the Chiss Nightdragon *Vigilant* and Uingali Foar Marocsaa's stolen Nikardun blockade frigate *Aelos*.

And as Qilori watched, feeling an odd sadness, a small, useless flicker of laserfire did indeed flash between the two derelicts.

"Take us over to them, vassal," Jixtus ordered, shifting the jabbing finger to the Kilji at the helm. "And you, vassal"—he pointed at the comm station—"send a broadcast signal calling for survivors."

"Do as he orders," Nakirre muttered.

"A signal is already coming in," the comm vassal said, keying his board.

"Is that you, Generalirius Nakirre?" a voice came tentatively from the speaker, the words half buried in the crackle of a damaged transmitter.

"It is," Nakirre confirmed. "Is that you, Senior Captain Thrawn?"

"It is I," the other said, and this time Qilori was able to recognize his voice.

But it was no longer the voice of calm confidence and borderline arrogance that had always been the mark of this particular blueskin. Thrawn's voice was wounded, dismayed, lost. His schemes, his plans, his self-assurance—all had come to nothing.

Earlier, Qilori had wondered if Thrawn and the Chiss would break against the Grysk fleet. Instead, they'd broken against each other.

"I'm afraid you've arrived too late to bring the enlightenment you

once promised me," Thrawn said. "Perhaps you will have more success elsewhere. Does Jixtus of the Grysks still travel with you?"

"I do," Jixtus spoke up. "Tell me, Thrawn of the Chiss: Did you find
those prescient cousins of the Magys you came here to seek?"

"I found him, yes," Thrawn said.

Jixtus turned toward Qilori, and Qilori could imagine a knowing
smile behind the black veil. "*Him,*" Jixtus repeated. "So there was
just the one?"

"There are never more than two," Thrawn said. "The Magys and
the Magysine, they're called."

"Ah," Jixtus said. "And do you have both of them with you aboard
the *Aelos*?"

There was just the barest hesitation. "No," Thrawn said. "They're
on the surface, traveling to a place of safety."

"I see," Jixtus said. There was a dull thunk somewhere beneath
them as the *Whetstone* bumped against a small piece of floating debris. "Safety from me? Or safety from you?"

"Why would they need safety from me?"

"Of course," Jixtus said. "Let me tell you what *I* think. I think you
lied to Qilori of Uandualon and somehow managed to pass that same
lie to the Grysk observers left behind on Sunrise. I think there are
more than one of these Magysines. I think you've already found all
of them. I think they're currently huddled together with you aboard
your wrecked ship."

"My ship is hardly wrecked," Thrawn said. "Our repairs are already
under way."

"Efforts that will soon come to naught," Jixtus said calmly. "You
have no electrostatic barrier, no lasers to speak of, and insufficient
power to activate either to any real effect. A single laser salvo, a single
missile, and you will be just more battle debris. I notice our sensors
suggest there may yet be a great many survivors aboard the *Vigilant*."

"Your quarrel is with me, Jixtus of the Grysks," Thrawn said, a bit
of life coming back into his voice. "Leave the dead and dying alone."

"If they are truly dying, would it not be merciful to ease their suffering?" Jixtus asked. "But you're right. *You* are the one I came to

Sunrise to destroy. I have only pity and contempt for those who unwisely chose to fall at your side. I therefore offer a trade: their lives for the alien Magysines aboard your ship."

There was another pause, a longer one this time. "I can't give them to you," Thrawn said. "They're too young, too delicate. Their lives are too precious."

"I would treat them well," Jixtus assured him. "They would be as honored guests among the Grysks."

"And guests is all they would ever be," Thrawn said bluntly. "I doubt you would be willing to invest the time and patience necessary to properly train them."

Jixtus gave a contemptuous snort. "Time and patience, you say? Truly, you underestimate me. I've put a great deal of time and patience into you and your Ascendancy already. A little more invested to obtain such a prize would hardly be a loss."

"*What* time?" Thrawn scoffed. His voice was a little stronger, as if he'd realized the end was near and had decided to face his final enemy with dignity. "You've just barely arrived in this region of space. I tell you that years of patience would be required to train the Magysines."

"I am hardly new to this war, Thrawn of the Chiss," Jixtus retorted stiffly. "Years of patience, you say? That is indeed what was required to train and nurture General Yiv the Benevolent and his Nikardun. Guiding him and pointing him toward his conquests took even more patience."

"I fail to see what patience was necessary," Thrawn said. "Yiv simply lashed out at everyone in his path. That hardly required guidance."

"If you believe that, you're less perceptive than I realized," Jixtus said. "The order and locations of his conquests and alliances needed to be carefully mapped out if we were to create the necessary encirclement of your Chiss Ascendancy."

"By conquests, you refer to the Vak Combine and Garwian Unity?"

"There was no need for Yiv to conquer the Garwians," Jixtus said. "All that was needed to keep them quiet and cowering was to create a treaty between Yiv and their Lioaoin enemies."

"So you conquered some and intimidated others," Thrawn said. "What of the nations you drained of their resources and then crushed underfoot?"

"What of them?" Jixtus asked, his black robe shifting as he gave a small shrug. "They were of no value except as practice for Yiv's soldiers. A few others, like the world currently below us, had certain specific resources, but weren't worth the effort of conquering."

"So those were the ones the Agbui were sent to destroy from within?"

"Some of them were," Jixtus said. "The Agbui are quite good at such things. The one named Haplif, in particular, was one of the best. The Chiss will pay dearly for depriving me of his future services."

"His service against whom?" Thrawn countered. "You've already destroyed everything in the region."

"Not everything," Jixtus said. "Perhaps I'll send the Agbui against your Paccian friends. Or against the Vaks and Garwians."

"Trying to make their worlds like Sunrise would be a mistake," Thrawn warned.

"Possibly," Jixtus said. "True, Sunrise was an entertaining exercise in subjugation and destruction, but as you can see it was quite costly. Perhaps I'll simply enslave the Garwians and Vaks, lest I discover too late their worlds also have hidden resources. Agbui persuasion isn't limited to destruction, after all."

"Indeed," Thrawn said. "It was quite clever, using the nyix the Agbui confiscated from Sunrise to corrupt your targeted Chiss officials. Fortunately, we were able to thwart that ploy."

"Only temporarily," Jixtus said. "Our latest effort will soon bear the same bitter fruit you see below you."

"Perhaps," Thrawn said. "Still, you made a serious error when you sent Yiv against the Paataatus."

"Why do you say that?"

"So you claim that after years of working destruction from the shadows you've finally stepped into the light," Thrawn said, ignoring Jixtus's question. "You've traveled among the Ruling Families, offering proof of treachery with one hand and the assistance of Grysk warships with the other. Only it was all lies. There was no deceit among the families, and your warships were never going to be given to any Chiss family. They would always remain under your sole control."

"Would *you* hand over warships to beings already marked for destruction?" Jixtus countered. "If you had any warships left to hand over, that is."

"Point taken," Thrawn said heavily. "But surely you couldn't have known this would be the view you would face upon your arrival. Did you truly think it would be safe for you to come alone, without your fleet to support you?"

"Of course not," Jixtus said, an edge of malicious satisfaction in his voice. "If you can still see, look outward, and witness the arrival of your final doom."

And then, sweeping into view directly behind the *Whetstone*, the fifteen massive ships of Jixtus's fleet arrived. "Do you see them, Thrawn?" Jixtus asked. "Do you see them?"

"I see them," Thrawn confirmed. "An impressive array. I believe introductions are in order?"

"You wish to know the names of the warships that will slaughter you and finish the destruction of your pitiful force?" Jixtus asked. "Why?"

"Why not?" Thrawn replied. "Are you so desirous of personal glory that you would deny your force captains their share of it?"

Jixtus snorted. "Do you think to drive a wedge between my captains and me? You are indeed foolish. But no matter. The largest ship, the one now coming up along the starboard side of this pathetic little Kilji war cruiser, is my flagship, the *FateSpinner*."

"Impressive," Thrawn said. He was hiding his apprehension well, Qilori thought, but the sight of the massive Grysk warship had to be digging a claw into his heart.

"It is indeed," Jixtus agreed. "It's a *Shatter*-class WarMaster, the greatest class of warship in the Grysk armada. Flanking it on portside, starboard, and dorsal are my three *StoneCrusher*-class WarMasters *Emery*, *Armageddon*, and *SkySweep*. Screening the core ships are my eleven *Prism*-class BattleChiefs. I'd offer their names, but there's no point in overburdening you with details when your time is so short."

"Fifteen vessels in all," Thrawn said. "I note that there are more here than you offered the Clarr Patriarch."

"Of course," Jixtus said. "A moment, if you please."

He rattled off a few sentences in the Grysk language, and Qilori saw the battle formation slowly break apart as the warships headed toward different sections of the battleground.

"I'm sending them off to search for the ships most likely to hold survivors," he said, switching back to Minnisiat. "You'll recall I offered to trade Chiss lives for the Magysines?"

"You spoke only of the *Vigilant*."

"I'm adding further inducements," Jixtus said. "And you're correct about the numbers. Patriarch Rivlex wasn't the only arrogant fool who accepted my warships. The Chaf and Ufsa Patriarchs were also eager to add Grysk power to their fleets. I, for my part, was happy to have safe harbors where my ships would have easy access to supplies and fuel."

"Yet you've now brought all of them here," Thrawn said. "What if the Patriarchs notice their departure? Will they not wonder whether your promise of control was a lie?"

"Is that where your final hope rests?" Jixtus asked. "That the Patriarchs will see their folly and reconsider their agreements with me?"

He gave a contemptuous snort. "No, Thrawn. As you once thought to utilize the Magys and her people to see your battles laid out before you, so too is this final expectation also in vain. My warships will return to their nests once we finish here, long before the Patriarchs can become concerned, probably before they even notice their absence."

"It would have been wiser to leave one or two behind to calm any concerns," Thrawn suggested.

"As I see now, I could have," Jixtus agreed. "But I came to Sunrise expecting to fight a major battle. I didn't expect to find that you'd done my job for me."

"So this *is* your entire fleet?"

Qilori's winglets twitched. That was an odd question.

Jixtus apparently thought so, too. "Why do you ask?"

"I offer a trade," Thrawn said. "Answer my question, and I'll tell you why it was a mistake to send the Nikardun against the Paataatus."

Qilori looked sideways at Jixtus. The Grysk was sitting motionless, his veiled face turned toward the viewport and the two damaged ships the *Whetstone* was making its way toward. "Very well, I'll play your game," he said. "I really don't care about Yiv or his failures, certainly not now that he's gone. But I'll admit to some curiosity. Yes, this is my entire fleet. Not the entirety of Grysk forces, certainly—our armada would fill the Csilla sky. These are merely what I deemed necessary for the destruction of the Chiss Ascendancy."

"Minus the warship we've already taken from you."

Jixtus made a rumbling sound in the back of his throat. "The *HopeBreaker*. Yes. The *FateSpinner*'s sister ship. Like Haplif's death, be assured that the loss of that ship will be held for full payment against you."

"I apologize for bringing up a painful subject," Thrawn said. "I merely mention it because the record of its destruction will provide detailed instruction to the Chiss Defense Force as to how to face your warships and destroy them. You might wish to ponder that before you consider another move against the Ascendancy."

"Pondered, and dismissed," Jixtus said contemptuously. "By the time I bring my warships openly into your war, there won't be enough left of your Defense Force to worry about. Especially not with well over half of the Expansionary Defense Fleet already lying waste here. Explain to me Yiv's mistake."

"The mistake was that the Paataatus were quite unhappy at his attempt to conquer them," Thrawn said. "That anger was matched with an equal degree of gratitude for my assistance in breaking the last Nikardun stranglehold on them."

"And so . . . ?"

"And so they were happy to do me a favor," Thrawn said. "Are you still there, Generalirius Nakirre?"

"I am," Nakirre spoke up.

"You sent your Kilhorde against several of the small nations to the south and southeast of the Ascendancy," Thrawn said. "Unfortunately for them, that also put them to the north and northwest of the Paataatus Hiveborn. Having a large military force operating that close to their borders was deemed unacceptable."

"What are you saying?" Nakirre demanded.

"I'm saying that your Kilhorde is gone," Thrawn said. "A multipronged Paataatus attack fleet engaged and destroyed it. *All* of it. The worlds and peoples on whom you hoped to force your enlightenment have been set free."

"No," Nakirre insisted. "You lie. The Illumine Kilhorde is mighty and unshakable."

"Unfortunately, it also had several weaknesses, both in design and in combat doctrine," Thrawn said. "Flaws that were easily gleaned from the battle data we retrieved from your picket cruiser *Hammer.* That information was of course shared with the Paataatus prior to their attack."

Qilori looked sideways at Nakirre, cringing as the Kilji's skin roiled across his body like waves on an agitated sea. Jixtus, in contrast, was utterly unmoving, his face turned toward the generalirius.

And then, abruptly, Nakirre leapt to his feet. "*You* did this!" he snarled, jabbing a finger at Jixtus. "Your arrogance—your refusal to accept the Kilji Illumine as true allies—your failure to provide adequate support for our conquests of enlightenment—"

Without a word, Jixtus pulled a small hand weapon from inside his cloak and fired a single shot.

Qilori's winglets spasmed with shock as Nakirre jerked and collapsed to the deck, his skin finally and forever going still. "Sir—!" Qilori gasped.

"Calm yourself, Pathfinder," Jixtus said. "If the Kilhorde is gone, the generalirius is of no further use to me." He looked around the bridge, his covered face turning to each of the Kiljis in turn. Then, apparently satisfied that there would be no further resistance, he returned the weapon to its hidden holster. "And now, Thrawn of the Chiss. Are you ready to give me the Magysines?"

"One final comment before I answer," Thrawn said. "I wish to remind you that the data from the *Hammer*'s recent confrontation here at Sunrise, along with our observations during our own battles with your warships, have likewise highlighted several weaknesses in Grysk combat abilities and tactics. You would be wise to take that into account before you answer my question."

"And what question would that be?" Jixtus asked.

"The most critical one of all," Thrawn said. "Are you ready to surrender?"

"Are you ready to surrender?"

For a few seconds the comm was silent. Ar'alani's eyes flicked around the *Vigilant*'s bridge, looking at the dark displays and the lines of red status lights, wondering if Jixtus's mouth was hanging open in surprise at the sheer brashness of Thrawn's question. Wondering, too, what Grysks looked like so she'd know if an open-mouthed stare was even physically possible for them.

She gazed out the viewport, her brief contemplation of Grysk physiology disappearing into more pressing issues. The Grysk warships currently spreading out among the drifting debris field were big and ugly, bringing back unpleasant memories of the one the *Vigilant* had tangled with over this same planet.

True, only the *FateSpinner* was as big as the warship she and Ziinda had eventually taken down. But at the time of its final defeat, the *HopeBreaker* had already taken serious damage from its earlier encounter with Ziinda and Thrawn. The *FateSpinner*, in contrast, looked to be in pristine condition.

As for the other ships of Jixtus's fleet, the *SkySweep*, *Armageddon*, and *Emery* were at least somewhat smaller than the *Vigilant*. Unfortunately, they were still larger than the *Springhawk* and *Grayshrike*. The eleven BattleChiefs were only a little smaller than the Chiss heavy cruisers, and larger than the light cruisers and patrol cruisers that the Council and Ba'kif had sent. No matter how this worked out, it was likely to be bloody.

And in the end, the whole battle plan rested on the alien device hidden in the Paccian gunboat currently twisting out its corkscrew of black metallic smoke. A device that might or might not perform the way Thrawn claimed it would.

But these were the cards they were holding. Ar'alani's job was to play them as cleanly and as cunningly as possible.

"Are you ready to surrender?"

Someone across the *Grayshrike*'s bridge let out a small half chuckle. Ziinda's first impulse was to warn against unprofessional outbursts; her second was to recognize that releasing a little tension before battle was not just understandable but beneficial.

She shifted her attention from the blank tactical display she'd been contemplating to the viewport. In the distance, she could see the spiraling smoke that marked the Paccian gunboat where the alien device was being held in readiness.

And she wondered distantly if Mid Captain Apros, standing watch over that device, was chuckling away any of his own tension.

She hadn't wanted him to take that duty. In fact, she'd fought strenuously against it, arguing that her first officer's place was aboard his own ship. But Thrawn and Ar'alani had insisted in turn that the device couldn't be simply left in Paccian hands and that a core group of Chiss needed to be aboard to operate it. Apros had volunteered to command the contingent, Thrawn had accepted, and the discussion had been over.

It had been a bold and honorable offer, Ziinda knew, given that if Apros hadn't volunteered someone else would have had to take his place. It demonstrated the kind of courage and commitment that was supposed to be the hallmark of the Expansionary Defense Fleet.

But lurking in the back of her mind was the quiet conversation the two of them had had on the *Grayshrike*'s bridge, their discussion of family pride and personal recognition.

Had Apros asked to be caretaker of the alien device out of a desire to be remembered by his family and the Ascendancy?

Ziinda hoped not. That wasn't how decisions were supposed to be made.

But there was no going back now. All she could do was fight the enemy to the best of her strength and ability, and leave the rest to the universe and warrior's fortune.

And she would also make sure that, whatever happened, Mid Captain Csap'ro'strob *would* be remembered.

"Are you ready to surrender?"

For a long moment Jixtus didn't speak. Qilori sent a furtive look at him, wondering what was going on behind the veil, whether the Grysk was surprised, amused, or outraged.

Was Thrawn *trying* to get himself summarily killed?

Qilori's winglets flattened. Of course he was. The Magys and the Magysines were aboard the *Aelos* with him, and a quick, violent death at Jixtus's hand would rob the Grysk of his prizes.

But Jixtus wouldn't fall for it. He would hold back his anger until he was able to board the *Aelos* and either confirm the Magysines' existence or establish that they weren't there. Only when that task had been completed would Jixtus allow himself the pleasure of watching Thrawn die.

And then, as Jixtus presumably was still choosing his response, the *Whetstone*'s bridge speaker gave a clear, bright tone as a general broadcast from the *Aelos* came over the comm. Qilori twitched, his winglets twitching along with him. An alarm? A warning?

A signal?

And as he gazed out the viewport in horror, the dead Chiss fleet came back to life.

The drifting ships seemed to gather themselves together, their running lights reappearing, their slow, random rotations ceasing as they stabilized and rotated their weapons clusters toward the Grysk ships. Those surrounded by battle debris shook themselves free of the floating clouds, the tendrils of smoke or liquid ceasing their flow, the lingering fires vanishing. On the *Whetstone*'s displays Qilori saw the reactor power readings of the nearest ships surge smoothly upward. Laser capacitors ran to full charge; electrostatic barriers winked into existence along nyix-alloy hulls.

Barely fifteen seconds after the tone sounded, the Chiss fleet was ready.

And with the Grysk warships having split up their battle formation, each now found itself in the center of a group of enemies.

"Well, Jixtus?" Thrawn asked, his voice no longer tentative and broken. "I offer you one final chance."

There was no response. Qilori tore his eyes away from the awakening enemy and looked at the command chair.

It was empty.

"Jixtus?" Qilori looked around frantically, turning his head to the starboard side of the bridge just in time to see the escape pod hatch on that side slam shut. "Jixtus!"

Too late. There was the muffled sound of the ejection thrusters, and Jixtus was gone.

Qilori looked around, his winglets quivering. When Nakirre had died, the vassals had all hunched over in their seats, remembering or mourning or perhaps gone catatonic. They were all still in that posture, apparently oblivious to both Jixtus's exit and the threat rapidly forming in front of them. Their enlightened master was dead, and they had given up hope.

And Qilori was trapped in here with them.

"Everyone stay sharp," Samakro warned, watching with grim satisfaction as the *Springhawk* came to full battle readiness. He and the others had practiced this crash ramp-up twice a day since the arrival of the rest of the Expansionary Defense Fleet ships, supposedly at Sunrise to arrest Thrawn, actually under Ba'kif's private order to join his forces and place themselves under his command.

There'd been some grumbling about the whole mutual-destruction scenario Thrawn had proposed, Samakro knew. But even those who'd disagreed with him could see now that a field of supposedly wrecked warships had been the perfect way to split Jixtus's warships apart and draw them into close-combat range.

Though if any of the captains had known the size of the Grysk ships, they might have voiced even stronger reservations.

But for the moment, at least, the Chiss and their Paccian allies had the initiative.

"*Springhawk;* Paccian Four," Thrawn's voice came over the bridge speaker.

"Acknowledged," Samakro said briskly. "Afpriuh: *Go.* Paccian Four, *go.*"

And as the *Springhawk* opened up with a withering laser barrage on the *Armageddon,* the nearest of Jixtus's three StoneCrushers, in the near distance off the Grysk's portside bow one of the Paccian gunboats also leapt to the attack, its lasers spitting fire. A true whisker-cub-to-groundlion matchup, and Samakro had no doubt that the aliens aboard the *Armageddon* knew exactly how such a lopsided duel would end.

Only for once, they would be wrong. The *Armageddon* swiveled ponderously toward the *Springhawk,* its launchers erupting with missiles, while it also sent a salvo of small dibber missiles to deal with the Paccian gunboat. It was a quick and standard response, no doubt, one requiring little concern or control, an idle swat against an annoyance while it dealt with the more challenging Chiss heavy cruiser now engaging it. The dibblers arrowed toward the Paccosh, forming a tight cluster designed to strike and bore through the gunboat's bow, accelerating as they flew.

An instant later the lead dibber slammed into the plasma sphere that Afpriuh had sent, unseen amid the glare of the *Springhawk*'s laserfire, into the dibbers' path.

The Grysks had only used dibbers against Chiss warships in a single previous battle, utilizing the small missiles mainly to disrupt plasma spheres or take out incoming breacher missiles. In those cases, the dibbers had most often been fired singly or in pairs. Against a gunboat, though, the *Armageddon*'s commander had opted for a more focused, clustered approach.

Which meant that when the *Springhawk*'s plasma sphere hit and paralyzed the lead dibbers, the others still accelerating behind them had no choice but to slam squarely into them.

The last row of dibbers were still plowing into the pileup when the whole group violently exploded.

The Paccian gunboat was still far enough away that the explosion didn't damage its hull. The *Armageddon*'s hull, too, was far too tough to be harmed.

Unfortunately for the Grysk, that same durability didn't extend to the embedded targeting sensors.

And as the *Springhawk*'s lasers tracked and destroyed the Grysk missiles hurling toward it, and the Chiss electrostatic barriers fended off the enemy's lasers, the Paccian gunboat flew straight through the expanding cloud of missile debris and shrapnel and delivered a devastating laser attack to the *Armageddon*'s blinded flank. The gunboat veered off just in time, dodging belated laserfire from the Grysk's unaffected dorsal weapons, then curved sharply around for a second pass.

"Well done," Thrawn said. "Secondaries: Engage the enemy and keep them occupied. Primaries: Begin your attack.

"It's time to end this threat."

CHAPTER TWENTY-SIX

Fifteen Grysk warships.

Roscu again ran the analysis through her head as she gazed at the images starting to swarm around one another on the tactical. All of them larger than her own light cruiser; three of them considerably larger; one of them ridiculously larger.

And so naturally Thrawn was sending her against the *SkySweep*, one of the midsized StoneCrushers.

At least he wasn't sending her against it alone. Two other light cruisers from Ba'kif's reinforcement group were hitting the *Sky-Sweep* from two other sides, trading laserfire and fending off its missiles while simultaneously trying to slip in plasma spheres and breachers. So far only a couple of each weapon had made it through the *SkySweep*'s point defenses, but those had successfully hit the vulnerable areas Thrawn and Ar'alani had identified and marked.

If the Chiss were going to prevail, Roscu knew, that targeting data was going to be the key. So far, despite the Grysk warship's lopsided size advantage, the skirmish was playing out better than would normally be expected. Certainly it was going better than the records Roscu had seen of the last time Chiss warships had gone up against one of these things.

And of course, Thrawn's numerical advantage meant none of his forces had to deal one-on-one with any of the enemy. Even though most of the Chiss warships were smaller than any of their opponents, attacking at two or three to one allowed them to keep the Grysks off balance and unfocused.

In the distance off the *Orisson*'s starboard flank, Roscu could see Paccian gunboats and a pair of Chiss light cruisers buzzing around two of the smaller BattleChiefs, keeping up the laserfire and plasma sphere attacks while at the same time maneuvering to keep the two warships blocking each other's fire and otherwise hampering their movements. Beyond them, the *Parala* and *Bokrea* had taken on another BattleChief, and while both patrol cruisers were taking serious fire they were still operational.

But that could change at any moment. Roscu had spotted the escape pod that left the Kilji warship and was immediately tractored across to the *FateSpinner*, presumably with Jixtus aboard. Once he was on the bridge of his flagship and directing his side of the battle, the Grysk superiority in ship size and firepower could quickly make itself felt. Roscu could only hope that Thrawn was on top of things on the Chiss side.

In the meantime, the *Orisson* had a Grysk warship to destroy.

"Continue laserfire," she ordered, checking the tactical one last time, then focusing her attention on the viewport. "Prepare three breachers; launch on my command."

"Brace yourselves," Ziinda warned as the *Grayshrike* shot straight toward the bow of the BattleChief trading fire with the *Parala* and *Bokrea*. She checked that her electrostatic barriers were at full power, then threw a last-second look out the viewport to make sure nothing had wandered into their path. "Thrawn?"

"I'm on it," Thrawn's calm voice assured her from the bridge speaker. "*Parala, Bokrea,* stand ready to break off . . . three, two, *one.*"

In perfect unison the two patrol cruisers ceased fire and veered hard ventral and dorsal, shooting off in opposite directions.

And with the BattleChief's commander presumably watching to see if the twin maneuver was a feint, if they were going to loop back around for a second pass, the *Grayshrike* drove straight through its forward point-defense laserfire and skimmed along its portside flank, raking it with laserfire and dropping plasma spheres and breacher missiles into its hull as fast as the launchers could fire them. A final barrage at the portside shoulder weapons mounts, and the *Grayshrike* was past, heading toward deep space.

The encounter had lasted barely five seconds. But it was enough. Even as Wikivv threw extra power to the thrusters, Ziinda could see on the sensor display that the full length of the BattleChief's portside flank was stained with blackened spots where the breachers' acid was digging into the nyix-alloy hull, its lasers and missile tubes torn apart by laserfire, its sensors frozen by the spheres' ionic blasts.

"Damage?" she called, checking the nav display to confirm Wikivv had them on the correct exit vector.

"Not good," Ghaloksu warned from the weapons station. "Portside lasers mostly gone, sphere tubes inoperable, breacher tubes empty or warped. Portside aft thrusters also took a hit from the shoulder cluster and are down to forty percent. "

"Acknowledged," Ziinda said. So in those same five seconds the *Grayshrike* had gone from a fearsome nighthunter to a wounded growzer pup. The question was, had the Grysks noticed?

They had. Even as the *Parala* and *Bokrea* circled back and resumed their attack on the half-crippled BattleChief, the StoneCrusher *Emery* had shaken off its own patrol cruiser and gunboat harassment and was charging after the *Grayshrike,* clearly intent on teaching a lethal lesson to the audacious heavy cruiser that had so severely damaged one of its smaller compatriots.

And with the damage to Ziinda's portside thrusters eating into her acceleration, the Grysk knew it would have no trouble running them down.

Fortunately, Thrawn had anticipated this result of the *Grayshrike*'s attack.

In fact, he'd counted on it.

———

Across the battleground, the Chiss warship blasted away from Sunrise, clearly trying to get to the edge of the planet's gravity well and escape into hyperspace. Behind it, the *Emery*, one of Jixtus's three *StoneCrusher*-class WarMasters, was charging in pursuit, clearly intent on bringing an end to it.

It was going to catch it, too, Qilori saw. Even if the Chiss got to the edge of the well in time, the *Emery* was close enough to jump right behind it. And with the eerie skills of the Attendant navigators, the *Emery*'s commander might well be able to stay right on the Chiss's tail all the way to its final destination.

Shifting in his seat, surrounded by the *Whetstone*'s all-but-catatonic crew, Qilori settled back to watch the Chiss ship die.

"Stand ready." Thrawn's voice came over the *Grayshrike*'s speaker. "*Grayshrike* jump on three; activate field on one. Five, four, three—"

There was the usual flicker of stars, and as Ziinda looked in the aft displays she saw Sunrise now in the distance behind them.

But not too far in the distance. Thrawn had specified a very short in-system jump, one that would leave the *Grayshrike* visible to the *Emery* and encourage it to continue its attack.

"One-eighty yaw turn," Ziinda ordered. The visual display showed the *Emery* was still back there and still coming toward them.

But it was also still in space-normal. And as Ziinda looked at the sensor display, she could see faint and irregular tachyon pulses as the Grysk warship's hyperdrive tried and failed to activate.

"Now, *that's* something you don't see every day," Vimsk commented.

"You do today," Ziinda said, trying to put aside her lingering concerns. It had been only a few days since Thrawn first introduced them to the gravity-well generator he'd taken from the Vagaari pirates after his first clash with them, and which he'd now somehow managed to borrow or steal from the UAG vaults. At the time, and during all their practice runs, he'd continually assured them that the generator would continue to function properly through the entirety of the upcoming battle.

Despite his assurances, Ziinda wasn't entirely happy about trusting her life to this device. But unless and until it failed, she and the rest of the Chiss battle force might as well make the most of it. "Vimsk, you have the edge of the field marked?"

"Yes, Senior Captain," Vimsk confirmed. "Tagging it now."

"Wikivv?"

"Got it, Senior Captain," the pilot confirmed. "And I must say, it's nice to get an easy jump calculation for a change."

"You're welcome," Ziinda said. "Just don't get used to it. Ghaloksu?"

"Weapons ready," Ghaloksu confirmed. "May I remind the senior captain that our portside is still a mess?"

"Noted. Wikivv?"

"Also noted," Wikivv assured him. "I didn't see any serious damage on the *Emery* before we jumped, so I thought we'd work on its starboard side. We'll come out starboard-to-starboard, but I can roll us to bring in the dorsals or ventrals anytime you want. Just let me know."

"I will," Ghaloksu said. "The starboards should last long enough, but it's good to have options."

"Stand ready," Ziinda said, shifting her gaze to the tactical. The *Emery* was still coming toward them, still trying to get its inexplicably balky hyperdrive to function. A little farther, right to the edge of the Vagaari gravity field . . . "Here we go," she said. "Wikivv: Three, two, *one*."

Qilori was still gazing out at the distant drama, wondering why in the Depths the *Emery* hadn't jumped—and really, with the Chiss warship having come out of hyperspace so close that even the *Whetstone*'s sensors could still see it, the Grysk should have charged in right on top of it—when, without warning, the Chiss was suddenly back.

But it didn't arrive like a normal in-system jump, with the small and fleeting flicker that Pathfinders were able to see that marked the positioning uncertainty that even the most precise jumps never completely eliminated. Here, instead, the Chiss popped in with a precision that Qilori had never seen except on those rare occasions when a ship miscalculated and ran into the critical edge of a planetary gravity well.

But the parameters of Sunrise's gravity well had been automatically calculated and marked as soon as the *Whetstone* entered the system. Those limits were routinely laid out on a ship's nav display, and a single glance was all it took to confirm that neither the *Emery* nor the Chiss ship were anywhere near it. How could even the most gifted pilot have pulled that off?

And then, as the Chiss warship sped along the *Emery*'s flank, firing and tearing into its hull exactly the way it had done to the smaller BattleChief a few minutes ago, he suddenly understood.

The Chiss had a gravity-well generator.

Qilori felt his winglets freeze like ice with the sheer impossibility of it. There were stories about such things, secondhand reports from distant regions that had only rarely been visited in person by anyone in the Navigators' Guild. But none of those stories connected the technology to the Chiss, let alone suggested that the Ascendancy actually had one in their possession.

But the *Emery*'s pursuit had been stalled where it shouldn't, the Chiss warship's return had held a precision it shouldn't, and the lasers and other weapons tearing into the *Emery*'s hull were proof that what Qilori had seen wasn't just an illusion. The Chiss warship reached the *Emery*'s stern and did a hard yaw swivel, turning its lasers and breachers into a concerted assault on the StoneCrusher's main thrusters.

And then, as if to underline the impossibility of what had just happened, the *Emery* exploded.

Qilori felt his breath catch in his throat, his frozen winglets drooping as stunned shock gave way to stunned disbelief. A Chiss heavy cruiser, singlehandedly taking out a Grysk StoneCrusher? Like the presence of the gravity-well generator itself, it was impossible.

But it had happened.

And for the first time since Jixtus had dragged Qilori into the Grysk war effort, it was no longer a given that the Chiss would lose.

"I believe Jixtus has fully assumed command." Thrawn's voice came over the *Vigilant*'s bridge speaker.

"So it would seem," Ar'alani agreed, looking out the *Vigilant*'s viewport. Up to now the giant warship *FateSpinner* had floated motionless above the planetary surface, staying aloof from the melee and letting the other ships' commanders handle their individual battles without any attempt at coordination. She and Thrawn had speculated earlier that the warship's extended idleness was probably due to the time it was taking for the *Whetstone*'s escape pod to be pulled into a docking bay, Jixtus himself to be extricated from it, and however long it then took him to get to the *FateSpinner*'s bridge.

Chiss warships' passageways were relatively easy to get through, making for quick transits between different areas. Aliens concerned with slowing down potential boarders, though, might deliberately make such internal travel more difficult.

But now, finally, the *FateSpinner* was on the move, turning toward the *Vigilant* and *Aelos* where they nestled together at the edge of the battleground. "You still want to play it as planned?" she asked.

"I think it's our best option," Thrawn said. "The *FateSpinner* is the most dangerous of the enemy ships. Jixtus has to be hurt sufficiently that he continues to hold back, but not so badly that he'll feel threatened enough to take his forces and run."

Ar'alani felt her throat tighten. Unfortunately, he was right. Without knowing where in the Chaos the Grysks were located, if Jixtus escaped there would be no chance of tracking him down.

And if that happened, the next time he challenged the Chiss he wouldn't allow himself to be lured to some out-of-the-way place like Sunrise for their battle. The next time, he would hit directly into the center of the Ascendancy.

He had to be stopped: right here, right now. "Understood," Ar'alani said. "*Stingfly*, we need you."

"Acknowledged, *Vigilant*," *Stingfly*'s commander said briskly. "Moving into position."

"Stand by."

The *FateSpinner* had fully turned toward the *Vigilant* now, lining up its bow and shoulder weapons clusters on the Nightdragon, and was nearly within combat range. Ar'alani looked past the Grysk's dorsal surface, searching the starscape for the nearest of the small asteroids Thrawn had moved close to Sunrise two days ago in preparation for this particular part of his battle plan. There it was, right where it was supposed to be. "Lock tractors on asteroid," she ordered Oeskym. "Full power."

"Tractors locked," the weapons officer said. "*Aelos*?"

"Tractors locked," Thrawn confirmed. "Admiral, your sight angle is better than mine. You give the orders."

"Acknowledged," Ar'alani said. The *FateSpinner*'s distance and speed . . . "Tractor beams: Activate," she ordered. "*Stingfly*: Stand ready."

"Tractors locked," Oeskym confirmed. "Asteroid's on the move."

"*Stingfly*, your estimate is three seconds after the *FateSpinner* opens fire," she reminded the other commander. "Oeskym, stand by lasers and spheres. We've got about twenty seconds before things get nasty."

"Weapons and weapons crews standing ready," Oeskym said. "Barriers at full strength."

Ar'alani made a quick visual check of the battle swirling in the distance behind the *FateSpinner*, then paused for a longer look at her tactical display. So far things seemed to be following Thrawn's anticipated schedule.

But hanging over everything she could feel a vague sense of foreboding. The *Vigilant*'s sky-walker, Ab'begh, had reported a strange resistance during the last leg of their approach to Sunrise, and Samakro had told her and Thrawn how the Magys had tried to take over Che'ri, purportedly to help the Chiss win against the Grysks. Samakro's counterthreat had gotten Che'ri and Thalias out of that situation, and since then the Magys seemed to be staying out of it.

The question now was what she might do if, having refused her help, the Chiss lost the battle. Would she seek vengeance against them as punishment when the Grysks reestablished their control of her world?

Or what if Jixtus was able to capture her? Would he be able to force her to see into the roiling futures of his next battles, giving him a preview of his opponent's moves in time to counter them? Would that make him and the Grysks truly and permanently invincible?

But that was if Jixtus won. What would happen if Ar'alani and Thrawn prevailed today? The Magys had already made a bid for Che'ri, and had even considered taking Thalias. Would she want Che'ri *and* Ab'begh and maybe even the *Grayshrike*'s sky-walker Bet'nih?

Ar'alani had no feel for how the Magys's mind worked, or what motivated her, or what limited her abilities to touch the Beyond. But through Che'ri she'd apparently experienced a level of foresight power she'd never before tasted.

And if there was one thing Ar'alani had learned about power, it was that for far too many people a small and fleeting taste wasn't nearly enough.

The *FateSpinner* was nearly to combat range. "Stand by spheres; stand by lasers," she called. The range indicator ran to the designated mark—"Fire spheres; fire lasers."

The plasma spheres erupted from their tubes as the *Vigilant*'s lasers simultaneously lanced out. The *FateSpinner* replied with its own lasers, the barrage accompanied by a salvo of dibber missiles targeting the *Vigilant*'s spheres. "Continuous laserfire," Ar'alani ordered. From the *Vigilant*'s starboard side, the *Aelos* opened up with its own lasers, Thrawn concentrating his attack on the dibbers. "Fire spheres; breacher salvo behind them," Ar'alani added.

Six more plasma spheres erupted from their launchers, with six breacher missiles running close behind. Again, the *FateSpinner* responded with more dibbers. Ar'alani kept one eye on the duel, the other on the asteroid steadily picking up speed toward the *FateSpin-*

ner's stern. If Jixtus was too distracted by the battle in front of his ship to notice the threat to its rear . . .

And then the Grysks finally seemed to spot the danger hurtling in behind them. The *FateSpinner*'s aft batteries came to life, the spectrum lasers blasting away huge chunks of rock and metal ore as they tore the asteroid apart. Ar'alani watched as it was whittled down; and then with one final, massive salvo, the remnant disintegrated into a shower of gravel. The final bits dispersed across the starry sky.

Revealing the *Stingfly*'s breacher missiles that had up to now been traveling in the asteroid's visual shadow.

The *FateSpinner*'s lasers instantly shifted to the new targets. But the breachers were too close, and going too fast, and the entire group slammed unimpeded into the Grysk's stern, their acid loads splashing against the hull and chewing into thrusters, weapons, sensors, and electrostatic barrier nodes.

And charging in right behind the breachers was the *Stingfly,* lasers blazing, clearly intent on making its first kill of the day a memorable one.

Thrawn had anticipated that delivering a severe blow to Jixtus's flagship would force him to retreat from the battle while he made running repairs of the damage. But Ar'alani hadn't expected that retreat to take quite so extreme a form. Even as the *Stingfly* blazed its way in from the rear and the *Vigilant* and *Aelos* continued their barrage from the front, the *FateSpinner* swiveled ninety degrees, turning its flanks to both attackers and launching a full salvo of missiles at each. Then, as the three Chiss warships shifted from attack to missile defense, the Grysk gave a blast from its main thrusters that sent it diving straight toward the planet below.

"Get those missiles clear!" Ar'alani snapped, watching the *FateSpinner* plummet into Sunrise's upper atmosphere. If Jixtus didn't pull out soon, he would be out of the battle permanently.

But it was quickly clear that Jixtus hadn't panicked, and moreover that he knew precisely his flagship's limits and capabilities. The *Vigilant*'s sensors were picking up the first atmospheric tendrils from the

FateSpinner's edges when the warship swiveled up again, pulling out of its dive and curving into a low orbit parallel to the planet's surface. One final pitch, and the *FateSpinner* was racing along its new path in a sideways position, its thrusters pointed at the ground, its bow and shoulder weapons pointed straight up. "Thrawn?" Ar'alani called.

"Nicely done," Thrawn said with the cool admiration Ar'alani had heard from him when remarking on cleverness and skill from an enemy he nonetheless still fully intended to destroy. "Pursuing him would mean having to deal with the uncertainty of atmospheric effects, plus his current posture makes it nearly impossible to come up on his damaged stern. A relatively secure position which also permits him to monitor and direct his forces."

"Unless we jam his comms," Ar'alani pointed out. "Might be something to consider."

"It might," Thrawn agreed. "Once we've eliminated enough of the enemy that we can spare a ship for that duty, perhaps we can do that. Until then, I think we need all the firepower we can bring to bear."

"Good point," Ar'alani said. "*Orisson*? How are you doing?"

"Qilori!" Jixtus's voice bellowed from the *Whetstone*'s bridge speaker.

Qilori twitched, his winglets going rigid. The *FateSpinner* had disappeared out of his line of sight, diving toward the planet, and he'd wondered if the massive Grysk warship had been destroyed.

Clearly, it hadn't.

"Qilori, answer me!"

The vassal at the comm station was still bowed over his panel, clearly oblivious to the rest of the universe. Qilori hurried to the vacant command chair instead and fumbled for the comm control. "I'm here, sir," he said. "Are you all right?"

"No, I'm *not* all right," Jixtus snarled. "The Chiss have some impossible wizardry going on, some way of disabling our hyperdrives while not affecting their own. Tell me how they're doing it."

"I—how should I know?" Qilori asked, his winglets fluttering.

"Tell me how they're doing it," Jixtus repeated, "or you will die. I still have more than enough firepower in hand to destroy the Chiss and their allies. Tell me Thrawn's secret, or you will die alongside them."

Qilori looked at the tactical, then out the viewport, then at the tactical again. Was Jixtus right about still having the upper hand?

He was, Qilori realized with a sinking heart. Or at least he could be. Several of the Grysk ships had taken damage, and one of them—the *Emery*—had been completely destroyed. But at least eight of the Chiss ships were no longer under power, drifting through space, clearly out of the fight. The only reason they and their crews were still alive was that the Grysks were smart enough to focus on disabling the more immediate threats instead of wasting time delivering complete destruction to the wounded.

And when the battle ended, and Jixtus set about destroying his weakened enemies, he might well put the *Whetstone* in that category. "I don't know for sure," he told Jixtus, cursing his trembling voice. "But I've heard tales of a device called a gravity-well generator that supposedly creates a field that simulates a planetary mass. Not like *real* mass, of course, but something that fools a hyperdrive into thinking it is."

He stopped, bracing himself. If Jixtus dismissed the idea as ridiculous, Qilori had nothing else to offer.

But there was no outburst of disbelief, no scornful insult, no repeated or intensified threat. Jixtus was silent.

Qilori peered out at the battle, waiting, his eyes darting to the side as one of the BattleChiefs exploded. Two Grysk ships gone, but the *FateSpinner* and two of the StoneCrushers were still functional, along with most of the BattleChiefs.

"And you think the Chiss might have created such a device?" Jixtus asked at last.

"I don't know if they could create one," Qilori said, pulling his thoughts away from ship counts and back to the topic at hand. "But they could have found or stolen one. I'm just saying that it fits what I've seen so far."

"That it does," Jixtus agreed. "Where is it?"

Qilori's winglets twitched. "I have no idea."

"Where is it?"

Qilori looked at the tactical, feeling panic rising in him again. How could he possibly know that? He didn't know how big it was, or what it looked like—

"Never mind," Jixtus said. "I see it."

Qilori frowned. "Where?"

"The gunboat that's not moving," Jixtus said. "The one still making that spiral plume of smoke."

"Yes, I see it," Qilori said. Odd he hadn't noticed how that particular gunboat hadn't moved even when the rest of the Chiss force went charging to the attack. "What are you going to do?"

"What do you think?" Jixtus bit out. "I'm going to destroy it."

"I'm a bit busy at the moment, Vigilant," Roscu said tartly, wincing as another shot from the *SkySweep* burned through the *Orisson's* electrostatic barrier and took out one of its starboard lasers. She and the other Chiss light cruisers were slowly whittling the enemy down, but they were taking a lot of battering in return. "What do you need?"

"The *Springhawk's* ready to play bait," Ar'alani said. "I need you and the *Grayshrike* to play hunter."

"Understood," Roscu said. So Thrawn was ready to initiate that part of his plan? Good. She and Ziinda had practiced this one extensively in the past two days, and she was looking forward to seeing how it worked in actual combat. "I'll be there—wait a second," she said. One of the Chiss light cruisers had gotten a breacher through to the *SkySweep's* aft ventral flank, and the Grysk commander had responded by twisting out of line to keep the Chiss from following up with a laser barrage.

Unfortunately for him, the maneuver had merely sent the vulnerable spot rolling across the *Orisson's* own line of sight. "There!" she snapped, pointing. "Hit it—*now!*"

Raamas, at the weapons board, was on it. Even before Roscu finished her order the *Orisson's* lasers were blazing at full intensity toward the pitted section of the *SkySweep's* hull. There was a glint of muted interior light as the lasers sliced through to the compartments beyond—

And that entire section of the ship exploded violently.

"*Got* it," Roscu snarled. "Okay, *Vigilant,* the others can finish it off on their own. You have my vector?"

"Sending it now," Ar'alani said. "Good work, all of you. Now get in position, *Orisson,* and let's see if this actually works."

The *Springhawk*'s final salvo of breachers thundered toward the *Armageddon,* the last remaining Grysk midsized StoneCrusher warship.

Unfortunately, between the enemy's lasers and dibbers, the salvo ended up being as ineffective as all of Samakro's previous attempts. Whoever was commanding this particular warship was damn good at his job. "I'm out of breachers," he reported. "You have my new target?"

"Location and vector sent," Thrawn said.

"You heard the senior captain, Azmordi," Samakro said. "Get us out of here."

"Acknowledged," Azmordi said, and the battle and starscape twisted crazily as he put the *Springhawk* into a tight turn and accelerated away from the *Armageddon* with all the speed he could manage.

Which was considerably below the *Springhawk*'s normal capabilities, Samakro noted uneasily. Like all the rest of the Chiss warships, he'd taken his share of damage from the battle, and reduced speed and maneuverability were a big part of that bundle. If the *Armageddon* decided to chase down its latest opponent and finish it off, the *Springhawk* would seem to be in serious trouble.

If the *Armageddon* didn't see it that way, this whole careful setup would be for nothing.

The *Springhawk* settled onto the vector Thrawn had sent, and Samakro smiled tightly. No, the *Armageddon* would come after him, all right. Thrawn was sending him directly toward a pair of injured BattleChiefs fighting a group of patrol cruisers and Paccian gunboats. The *Springhawk*'s sudden insertion into that melee would seriously tip the odds in the Chiss's favor, and he doubted Jixtus would let that happen without at least making an effort to stop it. Especially since saving the BattleChiefs would have the bonus of giving the *Armageddon* the chance to eliminate the *Springhawk* and deprive Thrawn of one of his heavy cruisers.

"*Springhawk,* slow four percent," Thrawn called. "The *Grayshrike*'s in position, but the *Orisson*'s still on its way."

"Acknowledged," Samakro said, watching the tactical as Oeskym obediently slowed the *Springhawk*'s acceleration. The *Armageddon* was still maintaining its own acceleration, he noted, possibly even picking up the pace a bit. "Come on, Roscu," he muttered under his breath.

"I'm here," Roscu's voice came over the speaker. "You can pick it up again, *Springhawk.*"

"In fact, increase your acceleration by ten percent," Thrawn put in. "We want to make sure he can't evade."

"Acknowledged," Samakro said. "Oeskym, ten percent increase."

And as the *Springhawk* once again leapt forward Samakro took a quick look out the sides of the bridge viewports. Thrawn had said that the *Grayshrike* and *Orisson* were in position.

Samakro hoped he was right. Because he sure as hell couldn't see either of them.

The *Grayshrike* was in position. Directly in front of it, five kilometers away, the *Orisson* faced it bow-to-bow like some distant mirror image. In the distance off to the *Grayshrike*'s portside, Ziinda could see the *Springhawk* racing along a line bisecting the one between her and the *Orisson.* The Grysk StoneCrusher warship *Armageddon* was racing along behind it in hot pursuit.

Not just in pursuit, but closing rapidly. "Do we have a count?" she called toward the mike.

"We do," Thrawn's calm voice came back. "*Grayshrike, Orisson:* Lock breachers."

"Breachers locked," Ghaloksu confirmed.

"Breachers locked," Raamas echoed from the *Orisson.*

"Stand ready," Thrawn said. "Three, two, *one.*"

The *Grayshrike* twitched, and the two breacher missiles Ghaloksu had set up blasted away, heading directly toward the *Orisson*.

Ziinda watched the tactical, distantly aware that she was holding her breath. She'd already noted that the Grysk warships gave small, random tweaks to their speeds and accelerations, presumably as a way of thwarting any attempt by the Chiss to hit them with side-approach breachers or spheres.

The critical question now was whether the *Armageddon*'s commander would spot these two pairs of missiles, reflexively and incorrectly assume they were aimed at him, and take evasive action. Hopefully, he would instead wait for the numbers, realize the missiles were going to pass harmlessly well ahead of him, and continue on with his goal of chasing down and destroying the *Springhawk*.

"Track confirmed," Ghaloksu said softly, as if afraid talking too loudly would disturb the missiles' paths. "*Orisson* track confirmed." Ahead, the *Springhawk* flashed across the intersect line ahead of the missiles, still running from the *Armageddon* for all it was worth.

A fraction of a second later the breachers from the *Grayshrike* and those from the *Orisson* slammed together nose-to-nose, their exactly equal and exactly opposite vectors canceling out to bring all four missiles to an instantaneous halt. An instant after that the metal-crushing impact shattered them, sending a thick acid cloud bursting outward directly in the *Armageddon*'s path.

And with less than half a second's warning, and no chance to do anything else, the Grysk warship drove straight through the cloud.

"Got it!" Raamas shouted triumphantly. "*Springhawk,* you're clear."

"I see it," Samakro's voice came back. "Azmordi, yaw one-eighty. Let's take it down."

"*Orisson,* move to assist," Thrawn ordered.

"We can help, too," Ziinda put in, a flicker of old reflexive suspicion running through her. Surely Thrawn wasn't trying to squeeze her out of her share of the glory *again,* was he?

"You're needed elsewhere, *Grayshrike,*" Thrawn said. "Get over to Apros's gunboat as quickly as you can.

"Jixtus has figured it out."

CHAPTER TWENTY-SEVEN

"Uh-oh," Ar'alani said. Two of the Grysk BattleChiefs had abruptly broken off from the Chiss forces and were on the move.

Heading straight for the Paccian gunship that held the Vagaari gravity-well generator. "Thrawn?" she called.

"I see it," he said. "Mid Captain Apros, I think you've been identified. Get ready to run."

"Understood, Senior Captain," Apros's voice came tightly over the *Vigilant*'s speaker. "Am I still on the primary vector?"

"Yes," Thrawn said. "Turn onto it now, but hold position until your attackers have delivered their first volley. Then turn off the field and run at full acceleration."

Ar'alani felt her stomach tighten. The gravity-well generator ate up a lot of the power that could otherwise be utilized by the drive and the enhanced electrostatic barrier Uingali had added to the gunboat while the *Springhawk*'s techs were busy getting the generator installed. On an immediate tactical level, it made sense for Apros to do his running with the generator off.

But on a slightly longer strategic level . . .

"I'll tell you when to turn it back on," Thrawn continued. "At that time you'll also dump the rest of your load of smoke."

"Understood, sir," Apros said. "Standing ready."

Ar'alani keyed the comm back from general to Thrawn's private frequency. "You sure you want the Grysks to have a clear shot?" she asked.

"We need them to," Thrawn said. "Their first shot will be from a distance, and we need them to think that the gunboat has extra protection—"

"Which it does."

"Yes, though not the kind they'll assume," Thrawn said. "I want them thinking they need to get closer, possibly to point-blank range, before they fire again."

"You realize how risky that is, don't you?" Ar'alani warned. "We could lose it all."

"Not all," Thrawn assured her. "But I agree it would make the rest of the battle far more costly."

Ar'alani nodded, acutely aware that the rest of the *Vigilant*'s bridge was listening in on this conversation. She was the senior officer on the scene, which meant that she should be the one making these victory-or-defeat decisions. Handing them off to Thrawn or anyone else still made the end result her responsibility. "I could go to his assistance," she offered.

"You can't get there any faster than the *Grayshrike*," Thrawn pointed out. "Besides, right now the *Vigilant* is the only thing keeping the *FateSpinner* pinned down and out of the battle. I need you right where you are."

"Understood." Ar'alani keyed back to the general frequency. Unfortunately, he was right on both counts. "Everyone stay sharp," she called. "Apros . . . good luck."

Ziinda had hoped she would be able to cut off one of the Grysk BattleChiefs, which would at least have left Apros with only one enemy warship on his immediate tail. But the breacher ambush had put the *Grayshrike* too far away and had taken her momentum too far down. Even with the best speed Wikivv could coax out of the drive, it was clear both BattleChiefs would get to Apros first.

Ziinda was still racing across the battleground when the enemy opened fire.

The laser blasts were simultaneous, twin stabs of energy blazing across the sky into the spiraling black smoke that still twisted slowly out of Apros's gunboat. Ziinda braced herself, leaning forward in her seat . . .

And then, like a flashfly escaping its cocoon, the gunboat blasted out of the encircling smoke and took off, headed away from the planet.

Ziinda felt a small surge of relief. So the metal-infused slurry that the Paccian techs had created really had diffused the Grysk lasers the way Uingali had promised it would.

And now, with the smoke and presumably surprised Grysks behind him, Apros opened up the gunboat's thrusters at full power.

"Whoa," Vimsk commented from the sensor station as the gunboat leapt forward like a scalded stingfly. "Who lit a fire under *him*?"

"Mid Captain Apros said the Paccosh did some upgrades on the thrusters," Wikivv said. "I didn't realize how upgraded they were."

"Easy, Apros," Thrawn's voice came over the *Grayshrike*'s speaker. "Don't get so far ahead that they give up the chase."

But also don't let them get close enough to kill you, Ziinda wanted to add. But Thrawn and Ar'alani were in command here, and Ziinda knew better than to throw conflicting orders into the mix.

Once again, her only hope was that Thrawn knew what he was doing.

A laser flashed across the sky, glancing off the *Grayshrike*'s bow. "Evasive," Ziinda ordered.

Wikivv pitched the *Grayshrike* upward out of the laser's focus as Ghaloksu fired back at the BattleChief that had taken that shot at them.

But with that attack, and that single twitch off its path, there was no longer any chance the *Grayshrike* could get to Apros's pursuers before they settled into chase positions behind him. It was all up to Apros and Thrawn now.

And to the surprise Thrawn had only half promised he could deliver.

Once again, a drama was about to play out at the far side of the battle-ground. Once again, Thrawn was rolling the dice and making an out-rageous bet.

Only this time, Qilori knew, it would be the Chiss side that was going to lose.

At least it would be quick. Even as the gunboat raced for its life, the two Grysk BattleChiefs were steadily closing the gap between them. The gunboat was well outside Sunrise's gravity well now, which sug-gested that the only reason it hadn't jumped to the safety of hyper-space was that it couldn't.

But of course it couldn't. Not with a gravity-well generator blast-ing away right on top of its hyperdrive.

Qilori's winglets twitched. Odd. Earlier, it had looked like the commander could turn the generator on and off. Why wasn't he doing so now? Had Qilori simply been mistaken about that?

No, he'd read that scene correctly. All he could think of was that having a generator operating that close to the hyperdrive had some-how caused some damage. The stories about such tech didn't say any-thing about any side effects, but such stories were seldom fully reliable.

Either way, the gunboat's commander had apparently been left with the lone option of running as fast as his ship could manage and hoping his pursuers would lose interest or be called back to the main battle. He couldn't even turn away to try to find refuge near one of the bigger Chiss ships—his pursuers were far too close for that. All he could do was run.

And in the end, he would still die.

That end would come soon enough, Qilori knew. The *Whetstone's* tactical display marked a sudden faltering of the gunboat's drive, a warning twitch that the thrusters were about to fail. A distant puff of black appeared, the commander perhaps making a last futile bid to throw off his pursuers by disappearing into a smoke screen. There was a flash of laserfire as one of the BattleChiefs took a shot into the cloud—

Abruptly, a dozen new ships appeared, spread out in loose battle array in the space directly in front of the gunboat. Qilori felt his winglets flatten against his cheeks in shock.

And as the fleeing gunboat sped harmlessly through the center of their formation, all twelve ships opened fire on the Grysks.

From the comm, Jixtus snarled something in the Grysk language, the words sounding both furious and disbelieving. "Qilori!" he bit out. "Who are those? *What* are those?"

"I don't know," Qilori said. "All I know is—"

He broke off as, in the distance, the two BattleChiefs at the center of the firestorm disintegrated in a pair of violent explosions.

"All I know," Qilori said weakly, "is the Chiss seem to have found some new allies."

"I greet you, Senior Captain Thrawn." The Minnisiat words came over the *Vigilant*'s speaker, spoken by a familiar voice. "Your timing and positioning were exactly as you promised. I trust our timing was equally so?"

"It was indeed, Senior Security Chief Frangelic," Thrawn assured him. "We are in the Garwian Unity's debt."

"No more than the Ruleri are in yours," Frangelic said, his voice going grim. "Long have we wondered if there was a power behind General Yiv and his threats against the Unity and the Garwian people. Long have we wondered if there would be more such threats. The Ruleri thank you for answering both questions, and for giving us this chance to settle the balance."

"As does the Vak Combine," another voice joined into the conversation, this one in Sy Bisti. Ar'alani didn't recognize this particular speaker, but the ship identification that had already come up on the *Vigilant*'s sensor display was again exactly as Thrawn had promised. "We now owe the Chiss Ascendancy a second debt."

"The Combine has already repaid both," Thrawn assured him. "As has the Unity. The Ascendancy thanks you for your assistance."

"The Unity's assistance is hardly at an end," Frangelic said. "Not when there are still others who need to feel our vengeance."

"The Combine agrees," the Vak commander said.

"Vengeance is yours for the taking," Thrawn said. "If you wish to coordinate with our forces, you may do so through Admiral Ar'alani. If not, I request only that you avoid damaging our warships."

"Admiral—behind you!" Apros cut in.

Ar'alani's eyes shifted to the rear display. The only ship that should be back there was the *FateSpinner*, floating along in its low orbit.

Only Jixtus was no longer sitting in defensive posture. The massive warship was on the move, skating along the upper atmosphere as it drove away from the *Vigilant* along the underside of the battle, apparently intent on getting to the far end of the battleground.

Or of finding an open path among the brawling ships through which it could escape.

"Octrimo: Full-power intercept course," she snapped, cursing to herself as she looked at the tactical. The sensors showed that the *FateSpinner* still had some thruster damage from the *Stingfly*'s breacher attack, but Jixtus had clearly been able to make sufficient repairs to get his warship under way. It was moving along at a good clip, faster than Ar'alani would have expected it capable of.

It was her fault, and it was going to cost her. Distracted by the battle and her own relief at the arrival of the Garwians and Vaks from the asteroid cluster where they'd hidden while they decided whether or not to join the battle, she'd forgotten to keep an eye on the *Fate-Spinner*. Now, with the *Vigilant* starting from essentially a dead stop, there was no way she could build up enough speed to intercept the Grysk warship before it cleared the battle and escaped Sunrise's gravity well.

She looked at the tactical. If the *Vigilant* couldn't stop Jixtus, maybe someone else could. Every ship of Thrawn's fleet had taken damage, but the *Orisson* and *Springhawk* should still have enough firepower to stand a fair chance against the *FateSpinner*.

But the *Orisson* was already deeply embroiled in a skirmish with one of the remaining BattleChiefs, and even if Roscu broke free right now she was at the same speed disadvantage as the *Vigilant*. The *Springhawk* had just helped finish off one of the other BattleChiefs and was therefore theoretically free for a new mission, but its thrusters had taken a lot of damage and it wasn't really in position for an intercept.

But Ar'alani had to try. "*Springhawk*, the *FateSpinner*'s on the move," she called. "Can you get to it?"

"I'll try, *Vigilant*," Samakro said. "Coming around now. Azmordi?"

"I don't think so, Mid Captain," Azmordi's voice came faintly from the *Vigilant*'s speakers. "Thrusters are down to fifteen percent. Unless Jixtus makes a mistake, I don't think we can reach him before he's clear."

"That's all right, *Springhawk*," Apros's voice cut in. "I've got it."

Ar'alani frowned. With her contingency plans focused on the *FateSpinner* and the heavier battle-line Chiss warships, she'd almost forgotten Apros and his gunboat.

But there he was, blazing at full power at an angle across the battleground, oblivious to the flashing lasers and driving missiles all around him, heading with his gravity-well generator to intercept Jixtus and block his escape.

Or rather, to block it until he reached combat range and died in a flurry of Grysk laserfire.

Thrawn had clearly run the same thought process. "Apros, break off," he ordered. "You're too vulnerable. We'll find another way to stop him."

"With respect, Senior Captain, I don't think so," Apros said. "I've got the same tactical data you do, and you can't reach him in time. But I can hold him long enough for the *Vigilant* or *Springhawk* to get there."

"You can't go in alone," Ar'alani insisted.

"He's not alone," Ziinda put in. "Apros, shift to the vector I just sent you."

Ar'alani looked at the tactical, focusing on the *Grayshrike*'s current combat condition. It wasn't any better than the *Springhawk*'s.

"*Grayshrike,* you've got nothing left but lasers," she reminded Ziinda. "You're not in any shape to take on the *FateSpinner.*"

"I'm not going to take it on," Ziinda said. "Apros and I are going to run in parallel, with the *Grayshrike* staying between him and the *FateSpinner.* It'll take Jixtus a lot of time and a *lot* of firepower to turn us into scrap, and as long as there's enough of the *Grayshrike* left to shield the gunboat we'll still have him pinned. Apros?"

"I agree, Senior Captain," Apros said, his voice tight but firm. "Let's do it. And whatever happens, it's been an honor to serve with you."

"And I with you, Mid Captain," Ziinda said. "Move in close to my starboard, and let's show Jixtus what it means to take on the Chiss Ascendancy."

The *FateSpinner* was on the move, slipping away right out from under the noses of the Chiss who were supposed to be watching him. The big *Shatter*-class WarMaster was skittering across Sunrise's upper atmosphere, searching for a gap in the battleground where it could safely drive up out of the gravity well and make its escape.

Against all odds, Jixtus had pulled victory from defeat.

Qilori looked at the tactical, his winglets waving slowly. Though if this was a victory, it was a vanishingly small one.

Jixtus had brought fifteen massive warships to Sunrise. Of that number eight had already been destroyed or disabled, including all three of his StoneCrushers. The six remaining BattleChiefs were still fighting, but he doubted they would survive much longer. And while they were tearing viciously into the Chiss forces swarming around them, it was abundantly clear who was going to win the day.

And the victor hadn't been Jixtus.

Or had it?

Because there were certain advantages to being the only survivor of a battle like this. If Jixtus escaped while the other Grysk forces died, it would be he and he alone who would tell the story of what happened today. His fifteen ships had gone up against nineteen Chiss warships plus twenty-one Paccosh, Garwians, and Vaks; but who knew if that was what the Grysk leadership would hear? Perhaps it would hear that fifteen Grysks had fought to the death against a hundred Chiss, or two hundred, or three.

Perhaps such a story would persuade the Grysks to avoid this part of the Chaos in the future. More likely, it would simply ensure they would send an entire armada the next time. In that case, not only would the Chiss be doomed, but so would everyone else in the region.

And if the Grysks continued to employ the strange alien Attendants as their navigators, that doom might not stop at Concourse 447 or all the rest of the Pathfinder bases. Or at the Pathfinders themselves.

Qilori's winglets suddenly stiffened. Yes, Jixtus's story would be the only one told . . . but only as long as there were no other witnesses to the Grysk debacle. Witnesses such as the remaining Kiljis.

Witnesses such as Qilori.

The *FateSpinner* was moving up behind and beneath the *Whetstone,* and from the sudden slowing of its acceleration Qilori could tell that Jixtus had spotted the opening he was looking for. If he turned in the next thirty or forty seconds, he could angle up, slip through the gap before anyone could move to stop him, and be gone.

And on the way to that gap, he would pass directly in front of the *Whetstone.*

Qilori looked at the Kilji vassals, still hunched over their consoles. "Generalirius Nakirre called you his vassals," he reminded them. "Jixtus called the *Whetstone* a pathetic little war cruiser. Do you agree with either of them?"

The Kilji at the helm raised his head a little. "We *are* as he says," he said in a low voice. "We can make no move, nor create any thought, without our master."

Qilori looked desperately at the tactical. There had to be something he could do to revive these brain-deadened aliens.

Maybe the answer was right there in front of him. "Without *your* master?" he asked. "Or without *a* master?"

This time, all the heads came up a little. "What do you say?" the pilot asked.

"I say that *I* am your new master," Qilori replied with all the confidence and bravado he could manage. "*I* will lead you until you can return to your people."

And suddenly, the Kiljis all sat upright, their hands once again poised over their control boards. "What do you order?" the pilot asked.

"How quickly can the peace-sealing be removed from the *Whetstone*'s lasers and missile tubes?" Qilori asked.

"Very quickly."

"Do it."

One of the Kiljis keyed a series of controls, and Qilori felt a sputtering shudder through the deck as a series of explosive bolts detonated. "Weapons are clear," the Kilji confirmed.

"Good," Qilori said, wondering distantly if he was really doing this. The Navigators' Guild forbade its members from engaging in any military activity . . . "The *FateSpinner* is about to pass in front of us. When it does, we're going to show Jixtus what a Kilji war cruiser can do."

"Which weapons do you wish us to use?" the Kilji at the weapons station asked.

Qilori looked again at the tactical. "All of them," he said. "At point-blank range, as accurately as you can."

"I obey."

"Tell me when you're ready."

Another pair of ships had appeared now on the tactical: the Paccian gunship carrying the gravity-well generator and one of the two Chiss heavy cruisers. They were angling on an intercept vector, clearly hoping to get to the *FateSpinner* before it cleared the battleground and keep it from escaping.

Qilori's winglets flattened. He would show *them* what a Kilji war cruiser could do, too.

"Weapons ready." The Kilji's hands stretched out over the board as he keyed the various switches.

And suddenly, for no apparent reason, Qilori's mind flashed back to Thrawn's warship as they chased the *Hammer* from the Rapacc system. Qilori sitting at the nav station, wondering why the chair was set so far forward.

He stared at the Kiljis' arms and hands. Kilji arms stretched over their boards; Chiss arms presumably stretched the same way over theirs. Only the two spans were different, with the Chiss one markedly smaller—

And then, it hit him. The truth—the strange, inexplicable truth, slammed squarely into his head.

The Chiss navigators were children!

The revelation vanished into the mists of Qilori's mind as the reality of the moment rushed back over him. The *FateSpinner* was coming into range, angling up right where Qilori had expected it to, trying to get through the gap before the shifting forces moving across the battleground sealed it closed. The warship would cross in front of the *Whetstone* barely three hundred meters away . . .

"Fire," Qilori said.

And as the viewport erupted in a blazing firestorm of laserfire and missile explosions, the *FateSpinner*'s entire starboard aft flank disintegrated.

For a long moment an awed, disbelieving silence filled the *Grayshrike*'s bridge. "Well," Vimsk managed at last. "*That's* something you don't see every day, either."

"No, it's not," Ziinda agreed. "Mid Captain Apros?"

"Yes, ma'am?"

"You can throttle back a little," she told him. "I don't think there's any rush now. Admiral Ar'alani?"

"Yes, ease off, Apros," Ar'alani confirmed. "In fact, both of you head toward the *Aelos*—I'll rendezvous with you along the way and escort you back.

"I think the battle is just about over."

But it wasn't. Not completely.

"Jixtus?" Thrawn called, his voice sounding oddly subdued as it came from the *Vigilant*'s bridge speaker. "Are you still there?"

"For the moment," Jixtus's voice came back. There was pain there,

Ar'alani could tell, and a quiet anger. But mostly what she could hear was resignation. "Are you calling to gloat?"

"No," Thrawn said. "I wanted to state our terms of surrender and offer medical aid for your people."

"You know I can't accept," Jixtus said. "Neither you nor any other Chiss is ever to see our faces or know our forms. Not until we sit on the thrones of the ancient kings on Csilla."

Ar'alani tensed. The last time they'd wrecked a Grysk warship— "All ships: Move immediately away from the Grysks," she ordered urgently. "Even the wrecks. Move away *now*."

"Actually, there are no such thrones or ancient kings," Thrawn corrected mildly. "But I understand your meaning. I'll look forward to our next encounter with your people."

An instant later, all across the battleground, the Grysk warships exploded.

All of them except the *FateSpinner*.

"A question, if I may," Jixtus continued calmly, as if he hadn't just ordered the final destruction of his fleet and his warriors. "Just to satisfy my curiosity. There are no Magysines, are there? Not aboard your ship, nor on Sunrise."

"No, there are none that I know of," Thrawn confirmed. "The Magys has told me that she is the only one. Still, even an imaginary bargaining point can be of use."

"Provided the enemy strongly wishes to believe in it," Jixtus said, a hint of bitterness coloring his tone. "I wish you luck in dealing with her in the future. Perhaps you will find yourself regretting that you allowed her and her people to live."

"There may indeed be challenges," Thrawn said. "But I'm sure we'll find solutions."

Ar'alani looked at the tactical, running her eyes over the status reports from the various ships, noting to her relief that the Grysk ship explosions hadn't inflicted any additional damage. Again, just as with the last Grysk warship's self-destruction, each of these explosions had shattered everything to tiny, harmless bits in order to prevent any useful analysis of the debris.

"You and your allies?" Jixtus countered, his voice now mocking. "You and the Paccosh, Garwians, and Vaks? Don't fool yourself, Thrawn of the Chiss. You are no different from we of the Grysks. Neither of us has allies, but only enemies and servants."

"You're wrong," Thrawn said. "Allies of convenience are still allies. Consider the irony that it was your own statements that finally convinced them to fight alongside us."

"But they hate you," Jixtus insisted. "All of them. They hate and fear the Chiss. Why would they work with their enemies?"

"We aren't their enemies," Thrawn said. "I doubt most of them actually hate us, though I'll concede that they fear the Ascendancy, or at the very least distrust it."

"Then why would they ally with you?"

"Because," Thrawn said, and Ar'alani thought she could hear a note of sadness in his voice, "at this one time, and in this one place, we were the lesser evil."

"I see," Jixtus said. "Then enjoy your victory, Thrawn of the Chiss. It will be your last."

"How so?"

"Your career is over," Jixtus said. "Possibly your life, as well. Certainly your leaders will demand you pay a crushing price for your treason this day, especially given their shortsighted overindulgence in the pursuit of personal power and family honor."

Ar'alani looked across the bridge, saw the quietly pained expression on Wutroow's face. Yes, the Syndicure would demand Thrawn pay, all right. It would likely make *all* of them pay, in fact.

"The Grysks will be back," Jixtus continued, his voice cold and dark and malevolent. "But you will not be here to stand against them. I wish you and your allies the pleasure of this final memory as you watch your worlds burn."

And as Ar'alani looked out the viewport, the *FateSpinner* followed its fellow Grysk ships into annihilation.

"All ships, secure from battle stations," Thrawn called, sounding as tired as Ar'alani suddenly felt. "Report damage and injuries to the

Vigilant." There was a tone as he keyed to a wider comm broadcast. "Qilori of Uandualon, this is Senior Captain Thrawn. Are you there?"

"Yes, I'm here, Senior Captain," a tentative alien voice came.

"Thank you for your assistance," Thrawn said. "What is your current status?"

"Generalirius Nakirre is dead," Qilori said. "Murdered by Jixtus before he left the *Whetstone.* I'm . . . the crew have accepted me as their commander, at least for now."

"Can you return them to their home?"

"I—don't know," Qilori said, sounding surprised. "I assumed you'd want to take possession of the ship."

"Not really," Thrawn said. "Though we'll of course examine and disarm it before you'll be allowed to depart."

There was a brief pause. Ar'alani focused on the distant Kilji warship, wondering if Qilori was thinking about making a break for it before the Chiss could do anything to stop him. "Apros, cease acceleration and yaw one-eighty," she ordered. "In case the *Whetstone* decides to leave early. *Grayshrike,* stay with him."

"On it, Admiral," Apros confirmed.

"Acknowledged, Admiral," Ziinda said.

"Of course, Senior Captain," Qilori said with a highly unconvincing enthusiasm. "That won't be a problem. I'll await your convenience."

"After you leave, you'll also need to make a detour to return Pathfinder Sarsh to Concourse Four Forty-Seven," Thrawn continued. "I trust that won't be a problem."

"It would be my pleasure," Qilori said, sounding puzzled. "But I thought . . . Sarsh isn't lost between stars?"

"Not at all," Thrawn assured him "He's currently waiting in the outer system aboard a Paccian troop transport. He was going in and out of hyperspace so that we would know when you and Jixtus were coming."

"Oh," Qilori said. "Yes. Of course. I'll—do you have an orbit you'd like us to wait in?"

"Admiral Ar'alani will instruct you," Thrawn said. "We'll speak later." He keyed off, and Ar'alani heard him shift back to the private Chiss broadcast. "Admiral, have you received the damage reports yet?"

"They're coming in now," Ar'alani said. "It's not as bad as I was afraid it would be. Certainly not as bad as it could have been. Do you want me to talk to the Garwians and Vaks? Thank them again for their help; that sort of thing?"

"I can do that," Thrawn said. "And Uingali, too, of course, for his assistance in convincing them to wait and observe. If you'll take over damage coordination, I'll set up that conversation."

"Admiral, we have incoming," Biclian snapped from the sensor station.

Ar'alani spun around to the viewport. Floating ahead of the *Vigilant* in the near distance—

"This is Admiral Dy'lothe aboard the Chiss Defense Force warship *Venturous*," Dy'lothe's resonant voice boomed from the speaker. "I've been sent by the Chiss Syndicure to assess the situation."

Ar'alani let out her breath in a relieved huff. "This is Admiral Ar'alani," she said. "Welcome to Sunrise."

"Thank you, Admiral." Dy'lothe paused, perhaps taking a longer look at the battleground. "So . . . what exactly did I miss?"

CHAPTER TWENTY-EIGHT

"I'm told the Syndicure has begun an investigation into our family over your dealings with Jixtus," Roscu said, gazing unblinkingly at the man across the desk. "An inquiry running in parallel with those into the Chaf and Ufsa families."

"So I hear," Patriarch Rivlex said, staring back just as unblinkingly. "Once again, the Syndicure oversteps its bounds and authority."

"I'm told the Chaf and Ufsa Patriarchs have already agreed to step down," Roscu said. "And that the Clarr Patriels have asked you to do the same."

"The Patriels likewise overstep *their* authority," Rivlex said. "Why exactly are you here, Roscu?"

Roscu. Not *Captain Roscu,* but just *Roscu.* Rivlex's entire senior officer corps had petitioned Rivlex to reinstate her rank in the Clarr family fleet, but the Patriarch wasn't going to back down over even that small gesture. He'd dug in his heels, defined his enemies, and was in for the long term.

Unfortunately, at the moment his enemies list seemed to include everyone in the Ascendancy who wasn't him.

"This is merely a courtesy call, Your Venerante," Roscu said. "I've been offered reinstatement in the Expansionary Defense Fleet."

"Congratulations," Rivlex said sourly. "I trust you'll be happy scouring the Chaos for new threats."

"I've also," Roscu continued, "been offered a commission in the Defense Force."

And *that* one finally sparked a reaction. Rivlex's eyes narrowed slightly, and he seemed to draw back a little. "The Defense Force?"

"Yes," Roscu said. "Specifically, the position of Admiral Dy'lothe's second officer aboard the *Venturous*." She paused. "The Groundlion man-of-war currently in orbit over Rhigar."

"I know where the *Venturous* is," Rivlex said. His voice was still carefully controlled, but Roscu could tell he understood the full implications of such an assignment.

The Syndicure had tried to cover up the whole Sunrise incident, and for a while they'd succeeded. But now, after five weeks of silence, the details had begun to leak out to the general public. Rather to Roscu's surprise, her name was being batted around nearly as often and as prominently as Ar'alani's, Ziinda's, and Thrawn's.

Which meant that putting Roscu into an honored and powerful post aboard the *Venturous* wouldn't just be a show of gratitude. It would also be a deliberate and pointed message that any sanctions Dy'lothe was ordered to enforce weren't directed at the Clarr family as a whole, but solely at the intractable Patriarch who refused to accept responsibility for his actions.

"That's all," Roscu said, standing up. "I understand you'll be meeting with the Patriels in half an hour. I imagine you'll want some time to prepare." She nodded. "Good day, Your Venerante."

Rhigar Patriel Clarr'etu'vilimt was waiting in the corridor as Roscu left the office and headed toward the homestead defense center. "Well?" he asked, falling into step beside her.

"I don't know," Roscu admitted. "He wasn't happy about me being aboard the *Venturous,* but I don't know if that was enough to change his mind about resigning."

"Let's hope it was," Retuvili said grimly. "Turning him over to the Syndicure for interrogation and censure would be a horrible precedent to set. But keeping a possible traitor as the family's Patriarch would be even worse." He looked sideways at Roscu. "Are you going to take the *Venturous* post?"

"Depends on if Patriarch Rivlex decides to see reason," Roscu said.

"I'd rather stay with the family fleet, but our honor and position are more important than my personal wishes."

"Well, whatever happens, rest assured you'll always have a place here," Retuvili said. "Commander of the homestead defense force, captain of the *Orisson*—whatever you want, it's yours."

"I appreciate the offer, and I'll certainly consider it," Roscu said. "As regards the *Orisson,* though, I'd say it already has an excellent commander in Captain Raamas."

"I agree," Retuvili said, a small smile playing at his lips. "Though prestige-wise, he's hardly on a level with The One They Could Not Kill."

Roscu frowned. "The *what*?"

"Hadn't you heard?" Retuvili asked, all innocence behind his smile. "That's what they're calling you these days on Rhigar. The One They—"

"Yes, I got it the first time," Roscu interrupted. "How do they figure *that*?"

"There was the asteroid missile attack at Ornfra," Retuvili said, ticking off fingers. "The sneak attack by the Grysk ship later in that same system. Then finally the Sunrise battle. You survived them all."

"So did Raamas and the rest of the *Orisson* crew," Roscu growled. "So why are they hanging the name on *me*?"

"Because the Clarr family needs heroes right now," Retuvili said quietly, his smile fading. "For better or worse, you're the one they've latched onto."

Roscu sighed. "Fine," she said. "But as soon as Rivlex is gone, the hero thing ends. All right?"

"I'll do what I can," Retuvili promised. "But that isn't exactly how the hero thing works."

"Then figure out how to *make* it work that way," Roscu said firmly. *The One They Could Not Kill.* It was silly, it was embarrassing, and it was inaccurate.

But she had to admit it *did* have kind of a nice ring to it.

"This," Ziinda said flatly, "is ridiculous. How is it that I'm getting a commendation and Mid Captain Apros isn't?"

"You already know the answer to that," Ba'kif said patiently, looking and sounding like a man who'd already faced enough trouble for one day and didn't really want to take on any more.

Ziinda sympathized. She also didn't care. Ba'kif was her only contact with the Defense Hierarchy Council, and the only way to get a message to the Council was through him.

And she'd had a *lot* of experience lately going through things that didn't want to be gone through.

"I know the official answer," Ziinda said. "The Irizi co-sponsored a commendation for me, so I got one. The Csap declined to co-sponsor one for him, so he didn't. And you and I both know that's nonsense. A commendation is military, and the military is supposed to stand outside family politics."

"Rank, promotions, and assignments are military," Ba'kif corrected her. "Commendations are prestige. Since families always get a share of that glory, they also have to be part of the process."

"And you think that's *fair*?"

"I never said anything about fairness," Ba'kif said, still far too calm for Ziinda's taste. At least he could be a little indignant about this travesty. "But you have to look at the situation from the Csap point of view. Apros had in his possession at Sunrise an alien artifact that by all rights should never have left the UAG vaults on Sposia."

"An artifact that *Thrawn* walked off with, not Apros."

"The point is that the records show Apros was the one credited with operating it," Ba'kif continued. "The Csap Patriarch evidently decided he didn't want to open that particular can of trouble by calling extra attention to it."

Ziinda ground her teeth. Time to try a different approach. "Fine," she said. "If a commendation is out of the question, how about a promotion to senior captain?"

Ba'kif's eyebrows went up a bit. "You think Sunrise is enough to justify that?"

"Absolutely," Ziinda said firmly.

Because it wasn't *just* Sunrise. Apros had also commanded the *Grayshrike* at Hoxim, after Ziinda let herself be duped into joining Councilor Lakuviv's disastrous attempt to claim that useless world for the Xodlak. As her first officer he'd handled the ship with calm efficiency, worked with her and Thrawn to pull off the deception that had prevented the Ascendancy from possibly collapsing into anarchy right then and there, and never breathed a word of the secret to anyone. For that alone he deserved every bit of gratitude the Council could scrape together.

"Interesting," Ba'kif murmured. "That might be possible. I suppose you're going to insist he be given his own ship, as well?"

"That would be only fitting," Ziinda agreed. "A patrol cruiser would be a good place to start. Maybe the *Parala* or *Bokrea*—"

"What about the *Grayshrike*?"

Ziinda twitched, feeling like she'd just been slapped in the face. "What do you mean?" she asked carefully.

"The Expansionary Defense Fleet only has so many ships to go around, you know," Ba'kif reminded her. "I'm simply asking if you want Apros to have a ship badly enough to offer him yours."

"I—" Ziinda broke off, the rest of her reflexive refusal sticking in her throat. She'd worked long and hard to be worthy of commanding a heavy cruiser. It was a testament to her ability and determination, and she'd handled the position with skill and integrity.

Except when she'd deserted her ship and crew for the Hoxim madness. Something Apros had never done, nor would ever do.

And she had the audacity to complain about family politics in the military?

She took a deep breath and looked Ba'kif straight in the eye. "Yes," she said. "If the *Grayshrike* is the only ship available . . . yes, he deserves it."

"That's good to hear," Ba'kif said. "Still, a heavy cruiser might be a bit much for a freshly minted senior captain." He frowned, as if suddenly remembering something, and picked up his questis. "By the way, I received a message from him about an hour ago," he said, scrolling briefly down the display and peering at it. "He said if you came in demanding he receive a commendation—" He looked up, his eyes steady on Ziinda. "—that I was to tell you not to worry about it. That he was content to be remembered by those who know him, who work with him, and who respect him." He set the questis aside. "I assume you know what that means."

"Yes," Ziinda said, feeling like a prizewinning fool. "You might have started with that, sir."

"I might have," Ba'kif agreed calmly, his eyes still on her. "But the most important part of my job is the people who serve under me. Whenever I get the chance to find out how those people feel about each other—" He shrugged, and for the first time since Ziinda came in his face creased in a satisfied smile. "I take it."

"So the *Grayshrike* is still mine?" Ziinda asked.

"Of course," Ba'kif assured her. "And now that I know that one of my finest commanders strongly feels one of her subordinates is ready for his own command, I'm ready to set those wheels in motion. Especially since the *Parala*'s commander has already informed the Council of his intent to retire." He cocked his head. "Did you know that the *Parala* was Admiral Ar'alani's first command?"

"No, sir, I didn't," Ziinda said. "I think Mid Commander Apros would consider it an honor to follow in her footsteps."

"I'm sure he will," Ba'kif said. "And now, you'd best go." He gave her another smile, this one with a hint of mischievousness to it. "I suggested he meet you in the Markenday Bar in half an hour. In case you and the senior captain wanted to celebrate his promotion."

"I'm glad I'm finally getting to meet you, Che'ri," Borika commented as she set a mug of caccoleaf on the table in front of Thalias and a cup of grillig juice in front of Che'ri. "I just didn't expect it to be quite this soon."

"Neither did we," Thalias said, looking around the ranch house's great room. Some of the chairs were different, and a cracked stone around the firepit had been replaced, but otherwise it looked the same as the last time she'd been here. "I assume you've been given the whole story?"

"I have," Borika said, taking a sip from her mug. "Sunrise and the Magys. Nightmares and strange visions." She peered at Che'ri across the top of her mug. "Possibly being taken over by an alien mind?"

Thalias felt her stomach knot up. Che'ri, gazing into her grillig juice, didn't even flinch.

"And yes, I've been asked to look into it," Borika continued. "But it'll take time and insight and resources."

"All of which you have?" Thalias asked hopefully.

"We have the time, certainly," Borika said, reaching over and touching Che'ri's hand. "We'll have to figure out the insight and resources as we go."

"So I'm going to stay here now?" Che'ri asked in a small voice.

"For at least a while," Borika told her. "Sky-walkers are rare enough as it is, and you now hold the record as the most unique of us all."

"But the nightmares are gone," Che'ri said, looking up with pleading in her eyes. "No one's ever going to go back to Sunrise—Supreme General Ba'kif said so. Why can't I fly some more with Senior Captain Thrawn and the *Springhawk*?"

"Oh, come on," Thalias said, mock-severely. "We just got off five weeks with him, searching the edge of Lesser Space for any sign of the Grysks. That's five weeks more than any of us expected."

"And we didn't find them, did we?" Che'ri shot back. "The Council's going to send him back—they *have* to send him back. Why can't we go with him?"

"Because you need to tell Borika and the others everything about the Magys while it's still fresh in your mind," Thalias said, catching Borika's eye and giving her a small warning shake of her head. She didn't know if Borika had been told, but Che'ri hadn't, and this wasn't the time to remedy that omission.

"*Fresh,*" Che'ri muttered. "It's not exactly *fresh* anymore."

"You know what she means," Borika soothed. "It'll be all right. And just think. What you help us learn could mean important things for every sky-walker who comes after you."

"Maybe starting with how caregivers can do better at their job," Thalias added pointedly. Important research or not, as long as she was being pulled into the middle of the Seeker program anyway she was going to make sure the sloppiness that had pervaded the system for the past century got a complete overhaul. "And don't worry. I'll be here with you the whole way."

"But then you won't get to fly, either," Che'ri said.

"That's all right," Thalias assured her. "I really only wanted to go aboard the *Springhawk* so I could meet Senior Captain Thrawn again. Now that I have—" She gave Che'ri a lopsided smile. "—I think maybe I could use a little peace and quiet."

"As I'm sure you could, too," Borika added.

"But what if it takes a long time?" Che'ri asked, her face screwing up. "What if . . . you can't stay here forever."

"I said I'd be with you the whole way," Thalias reminded her as she took the girl's hand. "And I will."

"Even if it takes forever?"

"Yes," Thalias promised quietly, a chill running up her back. "Even if it takes forever."

It had been a long time, Patriarch Thurfian thought, since he'd been in the March of Silence. Not since his rise to the leadership of the Mitth family; not since he and Syndic Zistalmu last met to discuss more of their private agreement to bring down Thrawn.

A lifetime ago.

He stood beside his chosen section of wall, watching the syndics and Speakers as they gathered in their own little groups: holding their private meetings, having their private conversations, most of them probably wondering what a Patriarch of the Nine Ruling Families was doing here.

Let them wonder.

He was just about to give up when he spotted Syndic Prime Zistalmu arrive at the far entrance. Thurfian watched as he slowly made his way through the March.

And then, finally, his onetime friend was in earshot. "Good day, Syndic Prime," Thurfian greeted him. "Thank you for coming."

"I almost didn't, Your Venerante," Zistalmu said, his voice studiously neutral. "I assumed that if you genuinely wanted to talk, you'd simply summon me to the Mitth homestead."

"I wanted to meet in private," Thurfian said, marveling at how many subtle insults had been laced through that single sentence, and ignoring all of them. "This seemed a good place to do that."

"If you were hoping for anonymity, you seriously miscalculated," Zistalmu said. "Even without your official robes, everyone here knows who you are."

"Good," Thurfian said. "Let them see a Patriarch choose to meet a rival Aristocra on that rival's ground. A little wonderment is good for the soul. Almost as good as a little humility."

"Mm," Zistalmu said noncommittally. "And which one of us is being humble today?"

"There was another Circle of Unity two hours ago," Thurfian said. "We've decided what to do with Thrawn."

Zistalmu gave a little snort. "If it involves putting another medal on his honor chains, I don't want to hear about it."

"No medal, no honor chains," Thurfian said. "Exile."

The word clearly caught Zistalmu by surprise. "*Exile?*"

"A habitable world has been chosen near the boundary between the Chaos and Lesser Space," Thurfian said. "He'll be given some supplies, plus the means to hunt, fish, and farm. What he makes of his life there will be by his own choice."

"For how long?" Zistalmu asked. "Until some new crisis arises and you, the Council, or the Syndicure insist that he be brought back?"

"I will never so insist," Thurfian said. "Nor, I believe, will the Council." He shrugged. "Keeping the Syndicure out of that particular flavor of madness will be *your* job."

Zistalmu had clearly been trying to keep his expression polite but strictly professional. But that comment managed to induce at least the hint of a smile. "I think you overestimate the strength of my authority."

"Maybe at the moment," Thurfian conceded. "But that will change. The Irizi are poised to rise in the estimation of the Nine, particularly with heroes like Senior Captain Ziinda on your side. The Mitth, on the other hand, will inevitably suffer with people like Thrawn on ours."

He raised his eyebrows. "Which, if you'll recall, was the end that we both ultimately expected."

"Yes." For a moment Zistalmu studied Thurfian's face. "He's really being exiled?"

"He is," Thurfian said. "Thrawn's story is at an end. My question today is what of ours?"

"Ours?"

"I don't claim we were ever friends," Thurfian continued. "But we had a relationship once, one that enabled us to bypass family rules and rivalries and work together for the betterment of the Ascendancy. Do you think such a relationship could ever again be possible?"

"I don't know," Zistalmu said. "I'll have to think about it."

"Take all the time you need," Thurfian told him. "I'll be ready to speak again whenever you make a decision."

"I will." Zistalmu paused, and another reluctant smile tweaked the corners of his mouth. "But next time, let's make it your homestead. As you said once, the seats and food there are far superior."

"Indeed they are," Thurfian said. "I must go now. Farewell, Syndic Prime. And once again, thank you."

Zistalmu would definitely think about it, Thurfian knew as he made his way toward the nearest exit. Unfortunately, he would no longer be thinking in terms of taking down a single ungimbaled laser like Thrawn, but in terms of how he could exploit his relationship with Thurfian to benefit the Irizi family.

But that was all right. The Syndicure's balance of power had always been precarious, and Jixtus's plot had violently underscored that danger. Whatever Thurfian could do to reduce tensions between the Mitth and the Irizi would be a step in the right direction.

And if Zistalmu chose to use their relationship to try to destroy both Thurfian and the Mitth?

It was a risk, Thurfian knew. His family relied on him now, and he had a duty to protect it. But the risk was worth taking . . . because while Thurfian was a Mitth, he was first and foremost a Chiss.

He could only hope that, no matter what Zistalmu's original plans and goals, he, too, would eventually reach a similar conclusion.

"We thank you for coming this afternoon, Mid Captain Samakro," Supreme Admiral Ja'fosk said as the board seated itself at their table.

"I'm honored to be here," Samakro replied, feeling a twinge of uneasiness as he eyed the five men and women and their full dress honor chains. He'd never been at an inquiry hearing where there were more than three flag-rank officers. Now he was facing five of them, all admirals to boot, and one of them Supreme Admiral Ja'fosk himself.

Whatever they wanted this time, they were clearly very serious about it.

And that worried him. Thrawn had already gone through this particular shredder, disciplined by the Syndicure with a casual cruelty that Samakro wouldn't have thought them capable of. They'd thrown a bunch of crimes and infractions at him, but the most serious charges had been defying standing non-preemptive protocols by going to Sunrise and forcing Jixtus into combat.

The problem was that Samakro, Ziinda, Ar'alani, and all the rest of Thrawn's group had done the exact same thing. Did that mean they were all on the line for the Syndicure's wrath?

At least the follow-up force, the warships Patriarch Thurfian's fast-step presentation had persuaded the Circle to authorize so that Supreme General Ba'kif could send them out in Thrawn's support, had been given the laminate-thin cover of official sanction. Their commanders and officers should be in the clear.

Samakro and Thrawn's primary force, not so much.

"First, we wanted to again congratulate you on your performance at Sunrise," Ja'fosk said.

Samakro gave a small nod: recognition, acceptance, and appreciation all rolled into a single gesture. Given the size and power of those Grysk warships, Ja'fosk and the Council should damn well be pleased that the Chiss forces had pulled it off.

As for the deals Thrawn had made with the Paccosh, Vaks, and Garwians, the diplomatic corps was still sifting through those, with the Aristocra looking nervously over their shoulders. Foreign alliances had never worked out well for the Ascendancy, and the Syndicure seemed disinclined to give them another try.

Though in this case, they might wind up not having a choice. They'd declared Sunrise to be off limits to Chiss ships and personnel, which was probably a good idea, and which might work in the short term. But there were still unanswered questions and unexplained resources there, not to mention the incredible wealth of the nyix mines . . . and with the Magys having named Uingali as their Guardian, the Paccosh were now the only path available for the Council and Syndicure to explore those resources.

It was going to be an interesting tangle for the diplomats and Aristocra to sort through. Samakro was glad all he had to deal with was a single Expansionary Defense Fleet warship.

Assuming that wasn't about to be pulled out from under him.

"Second," Ja'fosk continued, "we want to officially confirm your upcoming promotion to senior captain, and your assignment as commander of the *Springhawk*."

"Thank you, Supreme Admiral," Samakro said, noting the irony of it all. Back when General Ba'kif had first taken the *Springhawk* away from him and handed it over to Thrawn, Samakro had resented the move like hell itself. He'd cooperated with the new commander, as his position as Thrawn's first officer required, and had ordered his officers and warriors to do likewise. But it had been strictly a matter of duty, and he'd firmly promised himself that he would never truly like the new arrangement.

He'd been right. He never had. But the Expansionary Defense Fleet wasn't about what anyone liked or didn't like. Rather to his surprise, Samakro had slowly learned to respect Thrawn. Even more important, he'd learned to trust him.

And trust was what made a warship function. Trust between the commander and his officers, trust among the officers themselves. Knowing one another's strengths, knowing one another's commitments, was what let them charge confidently into battle. It was what let them face off against a fleet of giant alien ships without hesitation or qualm.

It was especially what enabled them to win.

Samakro had never liked Thrawn, not the way he liked some of the *Springhawk*'s other officers, and he probably never would. But that didn't mean Thrawn should have had the *Springhawk* ripped away from him. Not even if his loss was Samakro's gain.

Back when he lost his ship, Samakro had wondered if there was truly any justice in the universe. Now, to his mild surprise, he was wondering that same thing again.

"And now, to point three," Ja'fosk said, his expression going a little odd. "During Lieutenant Commander Azmordi's testimony, he told us that at one point you told Caregiver Thalias that you and Senior Captain Thrawn suspected the Nikardun remnant had gathered in the Sunrise system for their final stand. Do you remember that conversation?"

"I do," Samakro managed, fighting to keep his voice even. In the heat of everything else that had happened, he'd completely forgotten about that story.

A story that had been completely made up. A story he'd pitched to Thalias so that, when Patriarch Thurfian demanded to know how Thrawn had come up with such a ridiculous idea, Samakro would finally have proof that Thalias was passing confidential information to him.

Only now it was Samakro who found himself trapped. Senior officers weren't supposed to spread disinformation, especially disinformation that could influence important tactical decisions. If he confessed what he'd done, he might well find the *Springhawk* again taken away from him.

But there *was* an alternative. Thrawn was already disgraced in the Council's eyes. If Samakro pushed the blame for the story onto him, the whole issue would probably simply fade away, leaving Samakro completely untouched.

It would be quick and easy. It would also be wrong.

He squared his shoulders. His lie. His responsibility. His consequences.

"Granted that it was the Grysks and not the Nikardun who were assembling there," Ja'fosk continued, "the Council was still impressed by the accuracy of the information."

He leaned forward a little in his chair. "Tell us, Senior Captain: How did you and Thrawn *know*?"

For a moment Samakro just sat there, feeling the universe gently turn sideways around him. Not only were they not angry, but they were actually *pleased*?

The universe might not have much justice to it, he decided. But it *did* appear to have something of a sense of humor.

He cleared his throat. "I wish I could tell you, Supreme Admiral," he said, putting some regret into his voice. "But you know as well as I do that Senior Captain Thrawn . . . well, sometimes he just pulls these things out of thin air."

"Yes, he does," Ja'fosk murmured, leaning back again. "That's a talent we're going to miss."

Samakro nodded, suppressing a sigh. So the rumors were correct. The Council was going to demote Thrawn, possibly even below command rank. Hardly unexpected, but certainly ungracious and petty.

Still, it wasn't as if that was the end. Sooner or later, the political storm would pass, and Thrawn would be quietly reinstated. The Council might sometimes have to bow to the Syndicure's anger, but it wasn't stupid. "Yes, sir," he said. "As shall we all."

————

Ba'kif had been seated in the hearing room for about five minutes when the observers were finally allowed in.

He watched as they filed through the doorway, studying their faces and listening to the low murmur of conversation. For the most part they seemed at ease, their expressions solemn but calm, their low voices holding that unique combination of seriousness and comradeship that marked those who'd faced death together in battle. Samakro and Thalias came in together, talking quietly with Wutroow; Ziinda and Roscu, a few people back, seemed to be having a slightly more animated conversation.

There were a fair number of faces Ba'kif didn't recognize, junior officers and warriors from the *Springhawk* here to support their captain. They, too, had the same nonchalance as their more senior colleagues, the sense that they were here to watch Thrawn and his victory be once again recognized and—perhaps reluctantly—rewarded by the Council.

Only Ar'alani seemed to recognize the darker sense floating through the hearing room air. Her gaze turned to Ba'kif as she entered, her eyes narrowing with sudden suspicion and doubt, clearly wondering why he was in the observers' gallery instead of one of the tribunal members who would be entering shortly to pronounce judgment.

She was right, of course. As head of the Expansionary Defense Fleet, Ba'kif *should* have been on the tribunal. But Thurfian had urged the Syndicure to order him to step aside, and as Thurfian was Thrawn's Patriarch the other Aristocra had deferred to his wishes. So, reluctantly, had the Council.

The observers were all seated, and the conversation had quieted, when the five admirals of the board entered through the side door.

Supreme Admiral Ja'fosk was there. So were Admirals Dy'lothe of the *Venturous* and Ers'ikaro of the *Bellicose* and two others from the Defense Force that Ba'kif only knew in passing. All five were wearing the same rigid, solemn expressions. As they seated themselves at the table, Patriarch Thurfian appeared behind them and walked over to a chair a little way from the end of the table.

And the solemnity in *his* expression, Ba'kif noted, carried more than a hint of grim satisfaction.

Ja'fosk turned back and forth to the other admirals seated to his right and left, making quiet comments to each in turn and getting equally inaudible responses. He threw a glance at Thurfian and another, almost surreptitious one at Ba'kif. Then he turned to face forward and touched the stone on the table in front of him with his fingertips.

"He will enter," he intoned.

There was a moment of silence. Then the rear door was opened, and Thrawn stepped into the chamber.

He was in full-dress regalia, the gold epaulets on his shoulders gleaming in the light, the honor chains and their medals clinking softly against his chest as he walked through the gallery toward the table. The four warriors accompanying him broke off to the sides as they passed the front edge of the gallery, standing rigidly as he continued on. Ba'kif looked around the gallery, seeing concern starting to register in some of the observers' faces as they began to realize something was wrong. Thrawn reached the patterned circle centered in front of the table, and as he came to a halt the five admirals rose to their feet.

Ba'kif looked across the observers again, noting that the concern in their faces had turned to stunned disbelief. Now, finally, they realized that what was coming wasn't a commendation, but judgment.

Only they still had no idea of the depth that judgment would take.

"Senior Captain Mitth'raw'nuruodo, you have been found guilty of deliberate and knowing violations of Defense Hierarchy Council protocols and Chiss Ascendancy law," Ja'fosk continued in the same heavy tone. "Have you anything further to say in your defense before sentence is passed?"

"No, Supreme Admiral," Thrawn said. His voice was even, almost calm.

But Ba'kif could hear the pain there, the frustration and weariness. He'd fought so long and so hard in the Ascendancy's defense, only to have his dedication turned against him.

"Very well," Ja'fosk said. "It is the will of the Syndicure, and the obligation of the Council, that the following sentence be passed."

He paused, and Ba'kif could see the conflict in his eyes. Ja'fosk had accepted the inevitability of this moment, and he understood the reasons for it. But that didn't mean he or any of the other officers on the tribunal liked it.

"You will be stripped of your rank and all privileges and responsibilities pertaining to the Expansionary Defense Fleet. You will also be—" Ja'fosk flashed another look at Thurfian. "—removed from your status as a merit adoptive of the Mitth family. You will at present remain a member of that family, but without rank."

Ba'kif focused on Thurfian, noting the slight twist to his lip. He'd been all for rematching Thrawn back to his original Kivu family, but Ja'fosk and Thurfian's own senior aide had apparently talked him out of such a drastic and irrevocable step.

"The Syndicure has further decreed—"

Ja'fosk paused, and Ba'kif could sense the sudden rise in the level of tension in the chamber.

"—that in two days' time, you will be taken from Csilla to an uninhabited but life-supporting world, where you will remain for the remainder of your days."

A sudden, disbelieving stir rippled through the room. Someone gasped, and Ba'kif heard the sound of someone preparing to speak. Ja'fosk shifted his gaze to the gallery, the full weight of his rank and experience focused like spectrum lasers through his eyes, and the sounds and movements subsided. "You will have those two days to set your affairs in order," the supreme admiral went on, his voice emotionless. "At the appointed time, you will report to the *Parala* for transport to your place of exile."

He turned to Dy'lothe and nodded. Dy'lothe nodded back and walked around the end of the table, coming to a stop in front of Thrawn.

And as the admirals watched with stoicism, Patriarch Thurfian watched with satisfaction, and the observers watched with dismay or disbelief or anger, Dy'lothe proceeded to remove the honor chains from across Thrawn's chest.

Another uncomfortable rustle rippled through the gallery. Again, the stirring faded away under Ja'fosk's stern gaze.

Ba'kif watched in silence, feeling a lump come to his throat. Patriarch Thurfian hadn't wanted him on the tribunal, but he *had* wanted him to perform this part of the ritual. *That* request Ba'kif had flatly refused.

Dy'lothe finished and took a step back, the honor chains draped over his left palm. He hesitated a moment; and then, to Ba'kif's surprise, he gave Thrawn a small but respectful nod.

Ba'kif shifted his attention to Thurfian, wondering if the Mitth Patriarch had caught Dy'lothe's gesture. From the sudden stiffness of his expression, it was clear that he had.

"Sentence has been passed," Ja'fosk said as Dy'lothe made his way around the table and stood with the other admirals. "In two days, sentence will be executed."

He reached over the table and again tapped the polished stone. "This tribunal is now ended."

The admirals filed back out the door, Dy'lothe stepping into his proper place in line, Thrawn's honor chains still draped carefully across his hand. Patriarch Thurfian waited until they had disappeared out the door, then rose from his chair. For a moment he locked eyes with Thrawn; and then he, too, left the room. Thrawn turned back toward the rear door, and as the four warriors returned to escort formation he strode back through the gallery, his face set, his eyes focused straight ahead of him. The door opened, and he was gone.

For a few seconds Ba'kif stayed where he was, bracing himself for the inevitable rush of confrontation and outrage. But the room remained silent and still. Apparently, everyone was still too stunned by the verdict to organize their thoughts or their voices.

But that would come, Ba'kif knew. In time, it would come.

Quietly, he stood up and made his way through the gallery to the door, feeling disbelieving and hostile eyes on him the whole way.

And wondered how much angrier they would all be if they knew the judgment, and the exile, had been Ba'kif's idea.

CHAPTER TWENTY-NINE

It was seldom, Ar'alani thought to herself, that she'd seen a single word that could be packed with so much hostility, hopelessness, and sheer injustice. But this one managed all that, and more.

Exile.

She looked up at the two men sitting across from her. Supreme General Ba'kif, seated behind his desk, was wearing his usual neutral face, with nothing there for her to read. Thrawn's face, as he sat silently at the desk's other front corner, was mostly unreadable, with a hint of pleading in his eyes.

Pleading for understanding, perhaps? Pleading for sympathy?

He'd better not be pleading for forgiveness, Ar'alani thought darkly. She wasn't in the mood to forgive someone who hadn't done anything wrong.

She focused on Ba'kif. "This is wrong, sir," she said. "Completely and totally wrong. Senior Captain Thrawn deserves a promotion, a new honor chain, and the gratitude of every single one of the Nine and the Forty."

"So what exactly does that make this sentence of exile?" Ba'kif asked mildly. "What do you see in it?"

"Resentment," Ar'alani told him. "Embarrassment." She looked at Thrawn. "Revenge."

"Good," Ba'kif said. "Because that's exactly what the Syndicure intended when they approved it." He paused. "And that's exactly what we want them continuing to believe."

Ar'alani frowned, focusing a little harder on Thrawn. She'd been right the first time: The pleading was indeed for understanding.

But not understanding for his situation. Understanding for something else entirely.

"Well, that clears *that* up," she said. "Would you like to scrape a little more dirt off the viewport for me?"

"There was no other way," Ba'kif said, his voice quiet. "The Syndicure was looking for a scapegoat, someone to blame for what happened at Sunrise."

"What happened at Sunrise was the salvation of the Ascendancy," Ar'alani said bluntly. "You know that as well as I do."

"The temporary salvation, at least," Ba'kif agreed. "And I know that many in the Syndicure share that view. But agreeing with it and accepting it are two different things. The Ascendancy's unity had been fractured, with serious tensions lingering within the Nine and the Forty. Blaming everything on Thrawn was the only way to offer closure, and to allow all the aggrieved parties to save face and regain their honor. The only way to put the Ascendancy back together."

"They should have found another way," Ar'alani growled. "If they wanted a scapegoat, they could have picked any one of us."

"They did," Thrawn said quietly.

Ar'alani frowned at him. "What?"

"He means they *did* pick," Ba'kif said. "Only they picked *all* of you."

Ar'alani looked back at the supreme general. "I don't understand."

Ba'kif sighed. "There was a sizable percentage of the Aristocra who wanted to bring charges against every commander and every senior officer in Thrawn's core group," he said. "You, Wutroow, Samakro, Ziinda, Roscu—" He snorted. "There were even some who wanted to charge Thalias and Che'ri. The point is that by putting Thrawn at the focus of their anger and embarrassment, we could persuade them to leave the rest of you alone."

"Think of it as a game of Tactica," Thrawn suggested. "Supreme General Ba'kif has sacrificed his nightdragon in order to protect his groundlion and whisperbirds—"

"Wait a minute." Ar'alani fixed Ba'kif with a hard stare as one more part of this insanity suddenly became clear. "This was *your* idea?"

"It was," Ba'kif said, holding her glare calmly. "The Grysk threat isn't over, Admiral. You know that. We need you and the others—the people who've seen Thrawn in action and learned from him—to continue in your positions of authority if the Ascendancy is to be protected."

"And so you sacrifice him to the Aristocra?" Ar'alani demanded. "You send the Ascendancy's best protector to uselessly waste the rest of his life on some lost planet?"

"Well . . . not exactly." Ba'kif gestured to Thrawn. "Senior Captain? This part was your idea."

"As I'm sure you know," Thrawn said, "after the Sunrise confrontation the Council sent the *Springhawk* to the edge of Lesser Space to see if we could gather any clues as to the Grysks' location."

"And to look into those other names you got from General Yiv," Ba'kif added.

Ar'alani nodded. To search for Grysks and other threats, and probably also to get Thrawn out of sight while they figured out what to do with him. Again. "Did you find anything?" she asked.

"Not about the Grysks or Yiv's other names, no," Thrawn said. "But we *did* learn one bit of potentially disturbing news."

"I know you read Senior Captain Thrawn's earlier report after his encounter with General Anakin Skywalker of the Galactic Republic," Ba'kif said. "At the time, the Republic was embroiled in a war with a faction calling themselves the Separatists. According to a group of refugees the *Springhawk* encountered—aliens calling themselves Neimoidians—that war has ended."

"Congratulations to them all," Ar'alani said. "Which side won?"

"To hear the Neimoidians tell it, neither," Thrawn said. "The Separatist forces were apparently crushed, or perhaps simply collapsed when their leadership was destroyed. But the Republic also disappeared, with a new government rising in its place that calls itself the Galactic Empire."

"Congratulations on that, too, I suppose," Ar'alani said. "What does that mean for us?"

"It was clear from my conversations with General Skywalker that the Republic was weak and fragmented," Thrawn said. "Its leadership included many different factions and alien viewpoints, and it was continually being pulled in different directions. The Empire, in contrast, is unified under a single man and a single vision."

"Sounds like General Yiv and the Nikardun," Ar'alani said with a shiver. "Are we thinking the Empire could be a problem down the road?"

"It could," Ba'kif said. "But it could also be a solution." He waved a hand toward the sky. "The Grysks are out there somewhere, Admiral, and they're an enemy like none we've ever faced before. Warships and weapons we can deal with, but alien races who can subtly strike at the Ascendancy's very heart and turn us against one another are something new. We've turned back this assault, but we know there will be more to follow."

"And so Senior Captain Thrawn pretends to go into exile," Ar'alani said, finally seeing the whole picture. "But instead, he travels to this Empire to consult with its leader?"

"That's our hope," Thrawn said. "Though it naturally can't be *quite* so obvious. The Syndicure would never permit direct contact with an alien government." He smiled faintly. "Certainly not from a diplomatically useless agent such as myself."

"You saw how violently they reacted to a simple onetime battleground alliance with the Paccosh, Vaks, and Garwians," Ba'kif reminded her. "This would send them into a hyperbolic trajectory."

"Yes," Ar'alani murmured. That part, at least, didn't require additional explanation. "So what's the plan? Thrawn sits around on some deserted planet until this Empire bumps into him?"

"Basically, yes," Ba'kif said.

"Really?" Ar'alani asked, frowning. That had mostly been a joke. "Out of all the systems and habitable planets out there, you're just going to pick one and hope for the best?"

"It won't be *quite* that random," Thrawn assured her with a smile.

"We were able to find and map out a few trade routes and communications networks that have given us insight as to the most likely places."

"And we'll have someone watching from a discreet distance," Ba'kif said. "If no one appears within a few weeks, we'll pack him up, pick another planet, and try again."

"Sounds a bit iffy to me," Ar'alani said. "And if the Empire *does* find you? What then?"

"If General Skywalker survived the war, I'm quite sure he'll remember me," Thrawn said. "If not, surely someone will recall him fondly enough to grant me a hearing."

"And then?"

"I'll gather whatever information I can about the Empire, then return and discuss my findings—quietly, of course—with Supreme General Ba'kif and the Council," Thrawn said. "Between all of it, I don't expect to be gone from the Ascendancy more than a few months. A year, perhaps, at the most."

"I hope it works," Ar'alani said. "Regardless, I appreciate you both letting me know what's really going on."

"You're welcome," Ba'kif said. "But don't fool yourself into thinking it was entirely altruistic. You're one of the most prominent and celebrated members of the Expansionary Defense Fleet right now. We couldn't have you running around making noise and demanding that Thrawn be brought back from exile."

Ar'alani gave him an innocent look. "Would *I* do something like that?"

"Absolutely," Ba'kif assured her. "And now, Thrawn and I need a few minutes to finalize the last details. He'll be traveling aboard the *Parala*; I'll let you know his departure time in case you wish to see him off."

"Thank you. I would." Ar'alani looked at Thrawn as she stood up. "I'll say my goodbyes then, Thrawn. Don't you *dare* leave before I get that chance."

"I won't," Thrawn promised. "That's not what friends do."

———

And so at the end, as it had been at the beginning, it was just the two of them. Ba'kif and Thrawn: contemplating the past, looking to an uncertain future.

Ba'kif watched silently as Thrawn scrolled through the Council's final equipment checklist, nodding in satisfaction at each item. It was just as well, Ba'kif thought distantly, that Ar'alani's deal for General Yiv's own exile had given them some experience in codifying the resources a castaway needed to survive.

Unlike Yiv, of course, Thrawn wouldn't be gone forever. But it had to look to any prying Aristocra eyes that he was.

Finally, Thrawn looked up. "This will do nicely," he said, handing back the questis. "Thank you."

"I think the thanks should all be going in your direction," Ba'kif said.

Thrawn shrugged. "I did what was necessary. As do we all."

"Yes," Ba'kif murmured. "An odd thought. When you first contacted Patriarch Lamiov about taking an item from Vault Four, we both assumed you meant *the* item. You can imagine my relief when it turned out to be the gravity-well generator and not the Starflash."

"Though it might have been," Thrawn said evenly. "If I'd thought Starflash was necessary to destroy Jixtus and the Grysk threat, I would have used it without a second thought."

"Even if it meant the destruction of Sunrise?"

Thrawn's eyes seemed to focus on something in the distance behind Ba'kif. "My job is to protect the Ascendancy and the Chiss people, sir," he said quietly. "Whatever it costs to achieve that goal, I will pay it."

A chill ran up Ba'kif's back. *Whatever it costs.*

Something had happened at Hoxim, something Thrawn had been involved with that had never been revealed to him, the Council, or the Syndicure. Something evidently important or explosive or damning.

Senior Captain Samakro knew what it was, as did the rest of the *Springhawk*'s bridge crew. So did Thalias and Che'ri. Senior Captain Ziinda apparently also knew, and if the reports of a long conversation between her and Ar'alani were true it was likely that the admiral also knew the truth.

But none of them were talking about it, and none of them were likely to do so. Whatever the costs might be to their own careers.

Did Thrawn even recognize the depth of loyalty he inspired in those who worked with him? Knowing Thrawn, probably not.

"I understand," Ba'kif said as he put away his questis. "I suppose you're ready, then. I have to admit, though, that I'd always looked forward to seeing how you looked in admiral white. I suppose I'll never get the chance now."

"You were never likely to in the first place," Thrawn said drily. "No one here would ever make *me* an admiral."

"I suppose not," Ba'kif said. "One other thing. Two, actually." He opened the desk drawer beside him and lifted out the four-point pin-wheel medal that had been given to Thrawn so long ago at the Stybla honoring ceremony. "Supreme Admiral Ja'fosk recovered this before your other medals and honor chains were put into storage," he said, handing it across the desk. "We thought you might like to take it with you."

Thrawn took the medal, cupping it in his palm, and for a moment gazed at it in silence and remembrance. Then he looked up and handed it back. "Thank you," he said. "I'd prefer you keep it safe for me, if you don't mind. The path I'm on may turn out to be rockier than expected, and I'd hate to lose it."

"As you wish," Ba'kif said, taking the medal and returning it to the drawer. "And no, I don't mind at all, but would consider it an honor. This next item, though, I think you should consider taking with you." He paused, recognizing even in that moment that he was being overly dramatic, then pulled out a distinctive double ring. "Caregiver Thalias asked me to give this to you," he said, again handing it across the desk. "Uingali foar Marocsaa wanted you to have it as a token of gratitude from himself, his subclan, and the Paccian people."

For another moment Thrawn stood motionless, a series of emotions playing across his face. Then, with the same reverence he'd shown the Stybla medal, he took the ring. "I shouldn't accept this," he said, his voice oddly hesitant. "Uingali and the Paccosh did far more in their own defense and the defense of Sunrise than I did." He took a deep breath and carefully slipped the ring onto the two middle fingers of his right hand. "But in the spirit that it was given, I must with humble gratitude accept it."

"Indeed," Ba'kif said, feeling a small flicker of relief. He'd *not* been looking forward to having to tell Uingali that Thrawn had rejected his people's honor. Not to mention having to face Thalias while delivering the same message. "Then I believe we're finished here," he continued, checking his chrono. "We have time for one final meal together, if you wish."

"If you don't mind, I'd like to eat alone," Thrawn said. "There's a bistro where Thrass and I used to meet. I'd like to spend my last evening on Csilla remembering him."

He gave Ba'kif a small, melancholy-edged smile. "He explained to me once that theatrics could be used either as a diversion or as a way of focusing an opponent's attention elsewhere. I thought about that when you first presented your exile plan to Supreme Admiral Ja'fosk and me, and noted how it combined both of those aspects. My brother would have been proud."

"I believe he would have," Ba'kif said, inclining his head. "That is a high compliment indeed. Thank you."

"You're welcome," Thrawn said, rising to his feet. "I'll be back soon."

"Take all the time you want," Ba'kif said. "We'll be ready when you are."

"Thank you." With a final nod of his head, he was gone.

For a moment, Ba'kif gazed at the closed door, Thrawn's words echoing through his mind. *Whatever it costs to achieve that goal, I will pay it.*

Ba'kif could only hope that, whatever that final cost was, it wouldn't be impossibly high.

EPILOGUE

All beings begin their lives with hopes and aspirations. Among these aspirations is the desire that there will be a straight path to those goals.

It is seldom so. Perhaps never.

Sometimes the turns are of one's own volition, as one's thoughts and goals change over time. But more often the turns are mandated by outside forces.

It was so with me. The memory is vivid, unsullied by age: the five admirals rising from their chairs as I am escorted into the chamber. The decision of the Ascendancy has been made, and they are here to deliver it.

None of them is happy with the decision. I can read that in their faces. But they are officers and servants of the Chiss, and they will carry out their orders. Protocol alone demands that.

The word is as I expected.

Exile.

The planet has already been chosen. The admirals will assemble the equipment necessary to ensure that solitude does not quickly become death from predators or the elements.

I am led away. Once again, my path has turned.

Where it will lead, I cannot say.

ABOUT THE AUTHOR

TIMOTHY ZAHN is the author of more than sixty novels, more than one hundred short stories and novelettes, and five short-fiction collections. In 1984, he won the Hugo Award for Best Novella. Zahn is best known for his *Star Wars* novels (*Thrawn, Thrawn: Alliances, Thrawn: Treason, Thrawn Ascendancy: Chaos Rising, Thrawn Ascendancy: Greater Good, Heir to the Empire, Dark Force Rising, The Last Command, Specter of the Past, Vision of the Future, Survivor's Quest, Outbound Flight, Allegiance, Choices of One,* and *Scoundrels*), with more than eight million copies of his books in print. Other books include *StarCraft: Evolution,* the Cobra series, the Quadrail series, and the young adult Dragonback series. Zahn has a BS in physics from Michigan State University and an MS from the University of Illinois. He lives with his family on the Oregon coast.

Facebook.com/TimothyZahn

ABOUT THE TYPE

This book was set in Minion, a 1990 Adobe Originals typeface by Robert Slimbach (b. 1956). Minion is inspired by classical, old-style typefaces of the late Renaissance, a period of elegant, beautiful, and highly readable type designs. Created primarily for text setting, Minion combines the aesthetic and functional qualities that make text type highly readable with the versatility of digital technology.